Dark Legacy Vol. 1
The Bearer of Secrets

By Kyle Belote

I0615795

Copyright Page

Initial Edit by: J.C. Wing: https://www.wingfamilyediting.com

Book Cover by: Ivan Zann: https://www.bookcoversart.com

Author's Substack: https://www.outpostdire.com

Dedication

For two great men that were a part of my life and shaped me—in no small way—into the person I am today. Had it not been for their love, cherished moments, or uniqueness, perhaps this novel would have turned out differently or not at all. So, with utmost appreciation, love, and humility, I dedicate this to my grandfather Lt. Col. Lem Yeates Belote (Ret.) and my uncle, Harold Krueger. You both are loved and missed.

Acknowledgements

I originally dedicated this book to the authors who shaped my imagination. It's still dedicated to them, and a few new names deserve a place among them: Trudi Canavan, Timothy Zahn, J. K. Rowling, Troy Denning, R. A. Salvatore, Mercedes Lackey and James Mallory, Michael Crichton, George R. R. Martin, Joe Abercrombie, Jim Butcher, Patrick Rothfuss, and Nicholas Eames.

I also dedicated this to the people who pushed me to publish—my first War Council: Sarah Bickel, Carlos Carrasco, Christina Fulwider, Dwayne Demastus, David Williamson, and Josh Essary. I remain grateful.

To the members of House Eti: you've been an incredible writing group to have in my corner.

To the Organization of Military Community Writers (OMCW): you were a catalyst and a damn good place to start.

And to my Ko-dons, the Founder-tier supporters on Substack—Ioleta and S.Hould. Thanks for believing.

Oblus ina'ti Sepan Eti!

Terms

Current Date: 185th year of the Second Revolution, of the second season.

Fortnight—Two weeks
Moon turn—One month
Season—Three months
Tour—Two years (for military and government term)
Score—Twenty years
Epoch—100 years
Era—500 years
Age—1,000 years
Legend—10,000 years
Fathom—100,000 years
Revolution—Ten Fathoms.

Titles:

Arysto—a title for someone of noble birth, a male, with an undisclosed name or House, the same as saying Sir to a knight or lord to nobility.

Arysta—a title for someone of noble birth, a female, with an undisclosed name or House.

Mage—another common title like wizard, except while everyone can be technically called a wizard, a mage is someone of magical skill that pursues a career in magic beyond school level.

Madam—proper title of a lady, regardless of birth.

Sire—proper title of a man, regardless of birth, the head of his house.

Lady—woman of noble or minor noble birth.

Lord—man of noble or minor noble birth.

Sorcerer—an evil Rumigul user, a person who can do magic without incantations.

Warlock—a Rumigul user, a person that can do magic without incantations, but is not evil.

Wizard—general term used for all people with magical abilities.

Witchen—an evil magical user but not a Sorcerer, Witchens must use incantations and generally use Derengi magic.

Dramatis Personae

Main Cast:
Julie—Female, Unknown
Judas Lakayre—Male, wizardkind, Rallocan, Warlock/Exile
Meristal Raviils—Female, wizardkind, Advocate of Law

Krey:
Daniel—Male, wizardkind, The Heir of Valin
Xenomene—Female, wizardkind
Raven—Male, wizardkind
Bitcher—Male, wizardkind, Forgotten Islander

Antagonist:
Xilor—Male, Sorcerer/Dark Lord
The Betrayer—Male, wizardkind

Kothlere Council Members:
Daylynn Reese—Female, wizardkind
Sedrus—Male, centaur

Supporting:
Lily—Female, wizardkind, Rallocan
Kam—Male, wizardkind, Forgotten Islander
Ava—Female, fairy
Rusem—Male, spirit
Fife Doole—Male, Warlock/ gnomling
Harold the Hermit—Male, Unknown

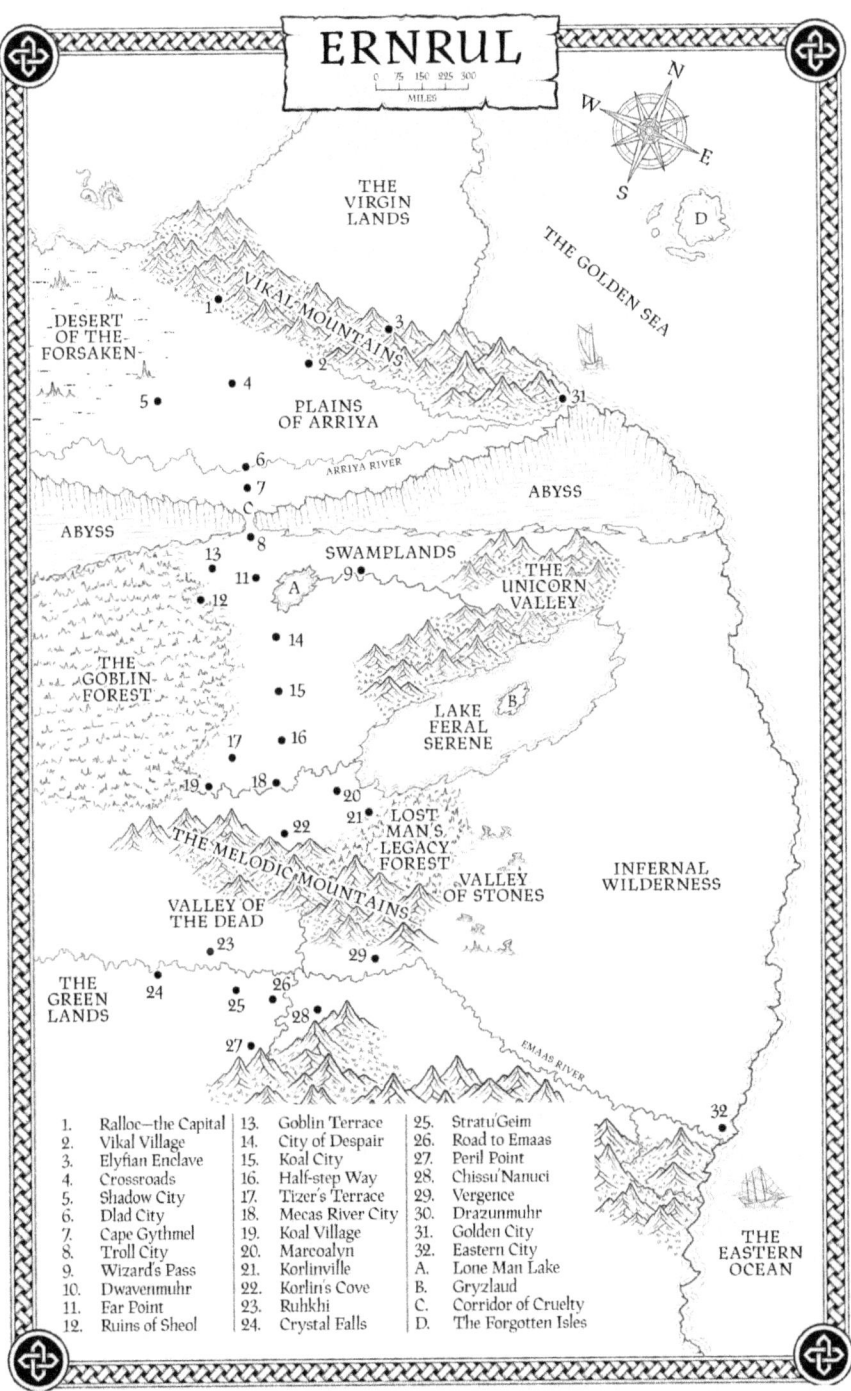

ERNRUL

0 75 150 225 300
MILES

THE VIRGIN LANDS

THE GOLDEN SEA

D

N
W   E
S

DESERT OF THE FORSAKEN

VIKAL MOUNTAINS

PLAINS OF ARRIYA

ARRIYA RIVER

ABYSS

ABYSS

SWAMPLANDS

THE UNICORN VALLEY

THE GOBLIN FOREST

LAKE FERAL SERENE

B

LOST MAN'S LEGACY FOREST

THE MELODIC MOUNTAINS

VALLEY OF STONES

INFERNAL WILDERNESS

VALLEY OF THE DEAD

THE GREEN LANDS

EMAAS RIVER

THE EASTERN OCEAN

1.	Ralloc—the Capital	13.	Goblin Terrace	25. Stratu'Geim
2.	Vikal Village	14.	City of Despair	26. Road to Emaas
3.	Elyfian Enclave	15.	Koal City	27. Peril Point
4.	Crossroads	16.	Half-step Way	28. Chissu'Nanuci
5.	Shadow City	17.	Tizer's Terrace	29. Vergence
6.	Dlad City	18.	Mecas River City	30. Drazunmuhr
7.	Cape Gythmel	19.	Koal Village	31. Golden City
8.	Troll City	20.	Marcoalyn	32. Eastern City
9.	Wizard's Pass	21.	Korlinville	A. Lone Man Lake
10.	Dwavenmuhr	22.	Korlin's Cove	B. Gryzlaud
11.	Far Point	23.	Ruhkhi	C. Corridor of Cruelty
12.	Ruins of Sheol	24.	Crystal Falls	D. The Forgotten Isles

Epigraph

Sometimes the things we aspire to be are the things that cause us to fail.

Prologue

A cacophony thrummed in her ears, the thunderclap resonating in her chest. Pain pelted her skin, sharp and stabbing. Fire belched out and engulfed her; the heat blistered her back.

Julie arched away as shrapnel burrowed into her limbs.

Confusion clutched her mind in an opaque fog; chaos rocked the world around her.

What the hell's going on?

The repugnant stench of burnt hair hung in the dust-filled air.

Oh my God, the old man! Where is he?

Julie rose, adrenaline coursing through her. He stood alone against the storm, no more than a few feet away, protecting her from the unseen. Another violent detonation flung them to the ground, and she screamed in pain.

She tried to rise, to run, but the old man's hand latched around her arm, and he held her down.

He's stronger than he looks!

He never faltered, not even when he pulled her behind him, protecting her.

Teetering on her feet, she settled her eyes on the blonde woman who accompanied them. Before all this…she'd been hostile, but now, fear etched her face.

Another detonation cleaved the air, and she found herself on the ground, the wind knocked from her lungs. The man fell on top of her, sheltering her from the fragmented rock.

A shriek ripped through the air, and Julie clamped her hands over her ears. She still couldn't see who was attacking, and nothing made sense.

The old man helped her stand.

Shadows danced beneath her feet.

Glancing up, she saw the sky swirl in a dark smog. Ominous clouds obscured the last rays of a dying sun. A tenebrous ring descended like a sudden hush. Streetlights flickered as the darkness deepened.

Movement above drew her attention.

Gargoyle statues stirred, the stone encasing falling away. Cement eyes crumbled to reveal blood-red orbs. The masonry shattered as one turned its head, sensing prey. Screams sheared the air between razor-sharp teeth.

Massive, leathery wings unfolded, casting off the last of the crumbling stone.

It leaped for her.

Out of the corner of her eye, she glimpsed the man and woman raise their hands, small wooden sticks pointing at the oncoming beast.

Her heart fluttered like the rumble of thunder. Whatever they were going to do, it was too late. She turned away, ducking behind them.

She waited for the end.

Chapter 1: The Return

Judas Lakayre stepped back into his world, passing through the Mirror of Imaesion, a gateway between the two planets.

The cool dungeon air greeted him. His robes still smoldered from his encounter, a fight for their lives; rips and tears peppered his ruined clothing.

I need to change.

But that didn't matter now—surviving did.

His knee gave out and struck the stone floor. For once in his life, he wished the dungeon had the same lush, phthalo-blue carpet as the castle above.

Daylynn Reese, with her honey-colored hair, blue eyes, and long legs, tumbled to the floor after him. She appeared even more disheveled.

She's lucky I saved her.

Atz and Lurx, the guardians of the Mirror of Imaesion, came in on her heels, the nimblest out of the original quartet.

But the fifth member, a young, anemic woman with golden brown hair—like Daylynn's—and delicate features, lay unconscious in Judas's arms, lifeless and unwieldy.

Judas rearranged her for a better grip. She wore different clothing than them: a shirt that clung to her body, and blue farmer trousers.

Never seen that color in trousers before.

"I told you not to bring her back!" Daylynn snapped, sitting upright. "You shouldn't defy the will of the council!"

"That's your opinion, mine's of a different nature," Judas retorted.

When he made up his mind, no force in the Underworld could change him.

"You expect me to leave her to die? Would you want me to leave you to die?"

"The council will make you return her."

Her proclamation lacked conviction. His poignant remark about leaving her to die hit home, and there was something like fear there.

He, as a warlock and exile, had saved her life.

"They will try and fail. She'd perish if I did. She's not a book borrowed from the library; you can't return her."

"She'll die if she stays! No one survives. You've doomed the girl, you damn fool."

Judas glanced at the two dwaven, then back to her.

"So, she was meant to die either way. At least here, she has a chance."

"Why hasn't she woken?"

The warlock touched the girl's face, pausing.

"She's under my spell. She won't wake."

His eyes trained back to the tall, long-legged woman.

"Go make your report."

"What's that supposed to mean?"

Dark indignation sparkled in her eyes.

He shrugged.

"Go make your report."

"Tell me what the hell you meant by that."

"You know the meaning, Daylynn, as does everyone else. I'm not as foolish as you think I am. Do you need me to say it aloud? He'll be expecting you … I'll be back to do mine later."

"When?"

"When I have time!" he snapped, his voice echoing off the cold, damp gray stone.

He grimaced and pushed his shoulder-length hair out of his face.

"Forgive me. That was rude. I don't know. I need to find out how they tracked us, and more importantly, what happened to the Kothlus Trilogy. Get Kayis, and inform the council."

"It's too late. No one's up."

Judas cocked an eyebrow at that.

"As I said, the consul will be waiting for you, and when you tell him what I did, he'll call for a special session."

"Your absence? What do I say about that?"

Judas looked down to the young woman in his arms.

"Tell them the truth: 'Exiled warlock defies council, and is on the run, Consul Kayis Dathyr livid.' Should make for gripping headlines for the New Suns Times. I'm sure Toddison Wynters will like that story."

She nodded, gathered her robes, and retreated down the corridor to the spiraling stone stairs.

Judas watched her disappear before turning to the two remaining individuals.

Both dwaven, shorter cousins of the dwandur, donned magic-imbued armor. Atz's armor gave a muffled creak as he stirred, shifting on his feet. In daylight, his plate held a vermillion hue with highlights of scarlet. Black runes were etched throughout his chest plate, pauldrons, shield, and the top side of his helm.

Lurx, his partner, appeared identical except a shade of light cobalt blue with arctic blue trim.

The warlock spoke to Atz first.

"Find Meristal. I need her. She'll know how to find me."

The dwaven faded on the spot, carrying out his orders.

Judas turned to Lurx.

"Stay behind and warn me if anyone comes or goes through the mirror."

"Even if it's the council?"

"Especially if it's the council."

"The Wcic?" Lurx inquired, nodding to the young woman in Judas's arms.

"She'll come with me."

"To your manor? Is that wise?"

The warlock shook his head.

"Not at all, that's why we're going on the run until I find out who or what is chasing us."

Without another word, Judas and the young woman disappeared, teleporting away.

The swirling blue mist faded, and his feet touched a hard, stained oak floor. He paused, holding his breath, making sure he was alone. Though the hour was late and most in the city slept, one could never be sure.

Satisfied, he carried the young woman deeper into the room, weaving between tables and chairs, slipping between towering bookshelves. Once out of view of the windows, he knelt, and with gentle ease, laid the girl on the floor, then pulled off his traveler's cloak and tucked it around her small form.

A light touch of his hand to her forehead assured him that she still slept, but his magic trembled a warning.

Somewhere beneath the abyss of magical currents he'd placed, she became aware. Whether conscious of him or that she was sleeping, he couldn't say. Her mind became sharp, focused, and her push against his will was akin to pressure against his skin.

Her rally came like a sudden storm—a raw and unrefined energy, like an unsure novice.

His hand withdrew from her forehead; his robes swished in the silence.

Her concentration snapped at the sound, and she pushed again, much harder this time. The assault startled him, the exertion strong.

He paused, wondering how it could be ….

Her potential, to say the least, was breathtaking, and she could very well rival him with training. Her aptitude came like a frosty gust compared to the stale wizards of the capital—Ralloc—filled with wizards holding prestigious ranks and honors, a shadow of the men and women who came before.

Her simple thrust told him that she'd surpass them. In time, who knew where her limits were?

He smiled to himself.

If there ever was a worthy heir …

He let the thought die.

With half of the night spent, he'd wait until dawn to move her.

Judas peered out into the darkness, the large room's interior glowing with magelight, small spheres of white, heatless luminance. It cast long shadows through the large, expansive room. In the stillness, Judas stood, listening, watching, waiting.

His thoughts turned to Daylynn. She'd go to the consul and tell him everything, well, everything that stained his reputation, and never the redeeming parts, like saving her life.

Some things never changed.

When Kayis Dathyr found out, he'd send others to track him down.

For a moment, he worried, not for their abilities, but for the casualties that tried to apprehend him. No one had the jurisdiction to stop him, not anymore, and Kayis was like a dog with jaws clamped around the throat of his prey; he'd never let it go.

Judas sighed.

The night settled around him. He wondered what made him think of this place.

Well, I was here this morning.

Ironically, this would be the last place they'd search. It bought him a few hours at the very least.

His azure gaze swept the small library, flickering to the familiar table he sat at earlier that morning, writing, waiting for his court proceedings.

A memory of the young librarian waltzed before his eyes like a phantom.

The librarian rounded the small table and sat across from him.

"Excuse me, sire," the boy whispered.

Judas stopped scratching; his cool blue eyes fell on Sam's face. The boy shivered, rattled by his scrutiny. "There's an Essence Transference you could—"

"Yes, I know," he whispered back. He tried to keep his voice warm and kind, pleasant. He returned to his work.

"If you know about the Transference, why don't you use it?"

"Just because it can be done easier doesn't mean it should be."

"Yes, but you've been here all morning. If you know—"

Judas laid down his quill, his movement slow.

"The Essence Transference won't work on this particular volume."

"Why?"

Judas sighed.

"This book is old. Perhaps ten ages, maybe more. The Essence Transference was only discovered in the last age or so, and it works on a different thread of physics. The applications for it are nearly limitless. It could revolutionize the way we learn. In theory, you could transfer a book to your mind, learning everything within minutes. While excessive, it would be necessary for education and legal matters—but it won't hone sword skills. The only way to learn to fight is to practice, like the Krey in Outpost Dire. They train day in and day out no matter the weather, politics, or season. There are also limitations to it, such as the old volume."

"How so?"

Judas patted the tome.

"If I were to do the Transfer to this very old volume full of knowledge and history, we'd lose it forever. Different laws of magic govern the Transference. In short, I'd destroy it trying to implement it."

Judas paused, letting the words settle.

"Would you still like me to try?"

Sam shook his head.

A flutter of magic tore Judas from the recollection. He reached for his wand, pooled his essence tight around him, shrouding himself, dampening his presence.

Whoever came into the library wouldn't know what hit them until too late.

A delicate whistling sound rose as the creature moved closer. Judas paused, making certain before lowering his wand. He hurried down the aisle and turned the corner, coming face to face with an effulgent ball of light.

"Fiosana? What brings an elder fairy here?"

The fairy smiled.

"Warlock Lakayre. I came to see her, the mage you brought back."

A stab of suspicion lanced him.

"How did you find out?"

Fiosana gave him an admonishing look.

"Don't be coy, young Judas. We fairies have our ways. It's not a secret."

The word 'secret' triggered his memories, stirring the words of his master's last command: the Bearer of Secrets wasn't a foe, but he'd spend his whole life searching for that person. That had been three ages ago, over three thousand years.

Another lifetime.

He resisted fixating on that distant memory, but it reminded him of his duty.

I need to get his book and take it with me, but it's at home. Damn!

The fairy's words ensnared his attention.

"I've come to witness, and you wouldn't let her out of your sight. Where is she?"

Judas warred with himself, between being polite and complying, or standing his ground, expecting more. He decided to stand.

"What do you want with her?"

"That's my business."

"Mine as well. I brought her back, I'm responsible for her well-being."

"Do you think I'd harm an innocent child? She's defenseless."

"Child? She's well over the Age of Maturity and has me to protect her."

The fairy paused, her head tilting to the side.

"You're acquainted as to why I'm here."

Judas snorted in derision.

"The fairy prophecy? Prophecies aren't real. Superstitious words by addled minds of wise men and women from long ago."

"To you, perhaps. While I agree with your sentiments, this particular one is ours. Do you know the words?"

Judas shook his head.

"It wouldn't matter even if I did."

"Would it not? How old do you think our prophecy is?"

"Very."

"It came to pass because of you, Judas Lakayre."

His eyes widened.

"You don't know? Your lack of awareness only further proves the truth. The first line of the prophecy dictated your actions legends before your birth."

She chuckled at him.

"'Beyond the pall that rend the realms, one of balance shall supervene.' Don't you understand? We predicted the separation of the realms."

He wanted to argue the semantics of the words, but chose not to. Realms and worlds were two different things.

Judas gestured over his shoulder.

"She's not the first to cross over, to come back."

Fiosana smiled, nodding.

"You're correct, but she'll be the first one to live. I'll make sure."

A dark glimmer crossed the warlock's face.

"You mean you had the ability to save all the others that came back, and you did nothing?"

The fairy fluttered closer.

"No, just this one. I sensed her all the way from home. Her arrival called to me."

Judas's initial suspicion flared to life again.

"Called to you? Did you tell anyone you were coming here? Does anyone else know?"

"Other than you?"

She shrugged.

Judas's eyes narrowed.

"How do you propose to save her?"

"A way that only fairies can. Let me gaze upon her, please."

Judas sighed and stepped aside, allowing her to float past him. He followed in her wake.

The fairy landed on the floor, the light fading enough for Judas to glimpse her wings, crystalline with faint, gilded veins running throughout. Head to foot, she managed to reach nine inches tall.

Fiosana reached out, her hand touching the girl's forehead.

"What's her name?"

"Julie."

"Peculiar name."

"She could say the same of us."

"She would, if she remembered."

The fairy gazed up at Judas before surveying the room.

"All this knowledge wasted until someone comes searching. A shame."

Judas's eyes narrowed, but he took in the room.

"What?"

"You're a clever man, even if you're a warlock."

She gave him a mischievous grin.

"She'll be like the rest, without awareness of the past. You'll be lucky if she can even talk. Use the Essence Transference on her mind."

Judas's face fell. He sputtered.

"There are things in here she shouldn't be acquainted with, not yet."

"I agree; you must be selective."

"It could damage her."

"And yet, she'd die without my intervention."

Judas noted how tart her words were.

"It's a gamble."

"A gamble you started when you brought her here."

"That—" he started, but fell silent.

"—is entirely accurate," she finished.

Her eyes came to rest on his, and she spoke measured words.

"She'll fulfill the prophecy. Use the Essence Transference, but keep out certain aspects, volumes of knowledge. Remove anything about magic, the Wizard's War. Let her learn from you, protect her, and present all things in an unbiased manner. You're good at that. There'll be a time when we come to her. She'll be bonded to us."

"Bonded?"

His brows rose, a flicker of uncertainty on his face.

"Use my wing in the core of her wand. The bond will serve for all time. Keep my other wing safe; my people will return for it so I can be one of them again."

"No, you can't! You'll die."

She held up a hand, stopping him.

"Some chose to forget, others turned their backs, but a few of us still believe. It's my honor, and it's my dying wish. If she's not the one, another will take my place. Use my wing in the core of her wand, and the bond will serve for all time, even if destroyed."

Judas's lips parted to speak but the fairy flared, her head tilting to the sky, eyes closed. Serenity settled over her face, the last image Judas glimpsed before the light extinguished.

Fiosana's two wings fell to the floor, spinning as if caught in an unseen current, but the fairy had vanished, perished.

Judas sighed and closed his eyes as the sting of something acrid burned in his nose.

Kneeling, he plucked up her only remaining elements, the delicate wings from the floor. His gaze focused on the small, crystalline objects while his mind replayed the last few moments.

The elder fairy bonded to the girl, and now she'd have to accept her gift. But the fairy did impart wisdom before she faded. He'd attempt the Transference to a living person.

To his knowledge, no one had tried before. Judas held reservations regarding the daunting task, the moral dilemma.

And when Meristal found out, she'd call him reckless, a trait better left behind in his youth.

Desperate times and all that ...

He needed answers.

The bitterness between Judas and Daylynn notwithstanding, she witnessed their attack firsthand, and he hoped it'd be enough for her to cast aside their differences. Hopefully, she'd listen to reason and sway the council to help.

Even though he had every right to carry their animosity to the grave.

What in the Shades of the Underworld is keeping her?

He should have heard something by now ... anything.

He cast the thoughts aside and pulled his wand out. Commanding his essence, he started the Transference.

Chapter 2: Daylynn

Her breath came in ragged gasps. Sweat gleamed across her body, slickening the polished mahogany. Her robes lay on the floor, her back against the desktop.

She bit her lower lip while Kayis pleased her with his tongue. Her long legs wrapped around his head. A moan escaped her soft, parted lips.

This part of the castle, his office, was vacant. No guards, no politicians, no staff. This deep in the night, everyone went home.

And Kayis had been waiting for Daylynn when she came back through the mirror, just as Judas had said.

She came to give her report in person, as she always did with her assignments, but it was a pretense to drop her robes.

The first dozen times she reported, she blamed her lust for the promiscuous encounters. Daylynn could never keep away from men with power, an arousal for her. She'd claimed the honor of being with many prominent men, and while most formed a mutually beneficial give and take, the consul turned her into his personal whore.

Two problems arose: one, she received no pay for her services, and two, she liked sex. Kayis's attractiveness played a factor, but she'd entertained far better-looking men in the past. To her, sex was not sacred but a tool, as well as entertainment, always enjoyed. Her un-Rallocan view was the way the world was meant to be.

His skills aside, she relished the thought of climaxing on the desk of the most powerful person in Ralloc—if not in magical power, then in title—and she only let him take her there.

He'd tried to maneuver her to the private bed or a chair, but she preferred the desk. Anytime he sat at it, he'd remember.

He used her, and she used him, too. The way of politics.

And Daylynn never passed up an opportunity for pleasure.

Kayis's tongue trailed up her stomach as he stood, slipping inside her as their faces came together.

"What happened?" Kayis asked as he thrust.

"He brought a girl back," she confessed, a moan escaping her.

He stopped.

"What?"

"He brought a girl back with us."

A frown flickered across her face, wanting him to continue. She pulled him closer, trying to reengage.

"What the fuck's he thinking?"

He pulled back, but not out of her. She hid her displeasure, lowering her face.

"Who cares? You can tell him to send her back. And if he refuses…"

His eyes widened with glee as if an intriguing notion struck him.

"I can kill him on the grounds of disobeying the leaders of the realm."

A smile spread across his face; the warlock's actions worked out in his favor.

"Come on," Daylynn urged him. "He'll be back soon. You'll need to recall the council."

She leaned forward, pulling him close by the neck.

"And you owe me a good time before that happens."

She kissed him.

He interrupted the embrace with a thrust, causing her to gasp. Her moans would fill his office, echoing like weaponized secrets, but as pleasure and politics collided in the dark, one universal truth remained.

Kayis might be the consul, but she held power over him, the only kind that mattered.

Chapter 3: The Kothlere Council

"So good of you to join us," Poplu whispered into the consul's ear.

Kayis Dathyr shut the door behind him, a hallway connecting the Council Chambers to his personal office, and he eyed his fellow council member.

Tapestries of the Houses lined the walls, their rods made of precious metals and gems. The Dathyr tapestry adorned the wall beside the door he exited, another gentle reminder of who was in charge.

The fine cloth kicked up at his sudden arrival. His hands fixed his outer robe sash.

Poplu smiled at him.

"I take it her briefing was good?"

Kayis's brow furrowed, his lips tightening.

"How long have you known?"

"Please," Poplu admonished. "The only woman on the council, gorgeous, ambitious."

He shrugged.

"Pity it isn't me."

"How many others know?"

Vamor snorted.

"Everyone."

Poplu moved away and took his customary seat.

Kayis regarded the retreating figure. Normally, he'd be resentful, but he found a staunch supporter in Vamor Poplu. The House of Dathyr and Poplu allied in regard to the exiled warlock. Kayis's other supporter on the council, Capraro, was usually enough to rule the council on most decisions, but even the three of them didn't have enough sway to kill Warlock Judas Lakayre outright.

He could never count on Daylynn. Her vote swung whichever way tickled her cunt. Maybe after her report, the council would vote to hunt Judas Lakayre down.

Kayis eased deeper into the chamber, now conscious that everyone knew what transpired behind closed doors. The charade he and Daylynn played, arriving separately and through different doors, was asinine.

His cheeks flushed before he smothered the embarrassment.

Taking his central seat, flanked by the races, both male and female, Kayis signaled they were ready to begin. No elyfian graced their presence, the reclusive race withdrawing from wizardkind's world of political machinations. The elyves viewed wizardkind as a pretentious and barbarous society.

The double doors at the top of the chamber opened, and Daylynn wandered through, her clothes still ripped and tattered, a testament to the battle that transpired less than an hour ago. And Kayis might've had a hand in that, too.

She walked down the deep phthalo-blue carpet between cypress benches with a glossy black finish. Gossamer curtains decorated the windows while scenic tapestries hung between them. Black walnut paneled the ceiling above in a shallow cone. Diamonds studded the public benches, aligned to the council's dais.

Lanterns and silver sconces lined the walls. A silver ceremonial gong imbued with enchantments sat on the council's podium, its matching hammer with a ruby head nearby. If the treasury went bankrupt, the government could sell everything in this room and keep the domain running for half a score of years—perhaps a full score, if frugal.

Daylynn's movements were stiff, halting as if aware everyone scrutinized her. She climbed on the dais where the council table sat and stood behind her seat.

Once everyone settled, Kayis rang the gong.

The sound carried and echoed, the chambers devoid of all attendants, scribes, and aides which normally muted the noise. Tonight's meeting was closed to the public.

Kayis spoke, "This session's called to order. Forgive the hour, but Madam Reese just returned from the *Other Side*. Given her preliminary report, I thought it warranted a special session. Madam Reese? Your report, please?"

Daylynn cleared her throat, her hands smoothing her garments.

"Earlier this morning, we requested Warlock Lakayre's help regarding the Mirror of Imaesion. Once through the gateway, we followed the source of an otherworldly presence. It was not, however, the Kothlus Trilogy as we originally speculated. Well, it was, but there were two sources."

"The Kothlus Trilogy?" Kayis interrupted. "I don't remember that being part of this morning's meeting."

"That's because you stormed out of here in one of your tantrums," said Kellis, one of the two goblins present.

Kayis glowered in silence.

Capraro turned his head.

"How'd you know it was the Kothlus Trilogy?"

"All magical objects created carry the essence of their maker. Judas Lakayre made the Kothlus Trilogy, so he can sense when it's near. It gives off a unique signature."

"But that's what he said, right?" Poplu asked. "He could be lying."

Daylynn nodded.

"True, except I felt it, too."

"What do you mean you felt it, too?" Sedrus queried.

Kayis eyed the centaur. Sedrus was a neutral force when it came to votes, if not a touch reserved and xenophobic.

"The power was strong, vile, and clung to my insides, making me nauseous."

Kayis cleared his throat.

"How sure are you of what you sensed?"

21

Daylynn's eyes narrowed.

"I know vileness when I feel it."

His lips pressed into a line. He had to tread carefully. If she felt spurned, she might lash out in a way he didn't intend.

He leaned forward.

"Warlock Lakayre created the Kothlus Trilogy, right? If what you're saying is true, the malevolence you sensed was part of him."

Right on cue, Poplu played his part.

"Are you sure Warlock Lakayre didn't influence you by using his magic on you?"

"Warlock Lakayre's a self-righteous ass," Daylynn retorted, "but that doesn't make him evil."

"You wouldn't know if he influenced you, would you?" Kayis prompted.

"What are you saying? I'm incompetent?"

"Not at all," Kayis said hastily. "I'm trying to ascertain the possibility of influence."

Daylynn bristled, and her eyes narrowed.

"I'd notice, if he tried."

"Please, continue," Lagelm, the other goblin, said.

"Warlock Lakayre traced the essence to a small book shop. The young woman said the editions had already sold. A carrier picked them up before our arrival."

She paused. Kayis saw her eyes track to him before she spoke again.

"The girl noticed my robes."

"What?" Capraro asked.

"The girl saw through our magical projection and commented on my robes. The strength she'd need to break through the shroud Warlock Lakayre placed on us is unthinkable."

"What happened next?" Kayis pressed, herding her into the direction he wanted.

"We were attacked. The windows blew in, the shop was destroyed. The girl was unconscious until Judas revived her. We retreated, taking the girl with us. As we neared the gateway, a sheol attacked us."

The quiet in the chamber turned icy and brittle.

The sheol were wraith-like entities, an embodied mist—half incorporeal.

"Judas killed it, but not before he questioned it, tortured information out of it. It died during…"

The goblin, Kellis, leaned forward, interlocking his fingers.

"How did he kill the sheol?"

"With light."

"Did the sheol give up any information?" Sedrus questioned.

"Just that the dark lord will rise again, that he was never truly gone, and the books were already gone."

"Did he say how he managed to get there?" Lagelm asked.

Daylynn locked eyes with him, and Kayis saw her shiver. The consul knew that gaze well, glossy black eyes, bottomless wells of malevolence and ice.

"Xilor's apprentice," she whispered.

Conversation broke between the members, and Kayis let the murmurs carry on for a few moments. Interrogations, or reports, were vital with information, but so was the silence in building tension.

"What happened next?" he prompted.

"Warlock Lakayre picked the girl up and brought her back through the gateway with us."

The consul allowed himself a small smile. Daylynn had played her part well. He peered to his right, in the direction of his supporters, Poplu and Capraro, knowing they would side with him. This was his chance to rid his family of the man who disgraced them.

"Well, you have her report. Madam Reese, please take your seat. The exiled warlock broke our laws, flaunting us with open defiance, and he must be punished."

"I agree," Poplu said. "We tried to be respectful for his efforts in the Wizard's War, but it's obvious he's a danger."

Kayis nodded.

"We should hunt him down and return the girl, for her benefit, of course. If he comes peacefully, we can talk options."

"Consul?" Kellis broke in, his long finger held aloft. "What law did Warlock Lakayre break?"

Kayis ground his teeth. The goblin continued.

"If you're referring to our statutes about finding anyone with magical gifts on the *Other Side*, it states they should be brought forward. In essence, none were broken."

"Yes," Capraro countered, "but we abandoned that practice years ago because everyone who came back died."

"Practice isn't legislation," Lagelm clarified. "We won't be hunting down the warlock today."

"We are the law!" Kayis snapped, whirling to face the goblin.

He fought for control, but his hatred fragmented his composure. When he spoke again, his voice was strained, caged.

"The warlock is anarchy in our midst. He needs to be hunted down and stopped, and the girl will be returned because she's a descendant of Xilor's followers. She doesn't belong in Ermaeyth. We'll clear her memory, and she'll be returned tonight."

Kayis stared at the smaller creature.

"He defied our wishes and isn't here now. His absence is an admission of guilt."

"That depends on your view," Sedrus said. "Perhaps he knows you'll try to imprison him or worse."

Kayis saw the shifting tides. Killing the warlock was so close, and it was starting to slip through his fingers.

"Believe me," the centaur continued, "I have no love for him, but even I'm

23

not so blind to acknowledge that."

Kayis clenched a fist under the table and counted to five.

"Madam Reese, can you clarify what happened to the sheol?"

"He tortured and killed it."

"So ... murdered."

Half the council erupted in conversation.

"Murdered a sheol? Are you mad?"

"What was the creature doing on the *Other Side*? They're forbidden to move from their Ruins."

"How did it even get there?"

"A sheol smuggled into the castle? Preposterous!"

"Warlock Lakayre's transgression is forgivable next to the sheol's violation."

"Enough!" Kayis barked. "For too long we've been lenient on the warlock. He's an exile!"

"And therefore," Sedrus said in a slow voice, "not bound to our republic's constitution. A decision of the council's after the Wizard's War."

"I believe you helped craft the sentencing, Consul?" Lagelm prodded.

"I call for a vote," Kayis said.

Kellis agreed with a nod.

"To clarify, no laws have been broken. He's an exile, and the council requested his help to investigate the Mirror of Imaesion, a device of his making. So, what are we adjudicating?"

"Warlock Lakayre's a menace and must be stopped. An exile beyond our control with more power than most alive."

"More power than *any* man alive," Daylynn said.

When Kayis glared at her, a haunted expression came to her face.

What the hell happened to make her so soft now?

"Those for hunting down the warlock?" Kayis queried.

Poplu and Capraro raised their hands along with Kayis.

Their eyes turned to Daylynn whose lips thinned, but her hand remained motionless.

"Those against?" Kayis prompted.

The goblins, Kellis and Lagelm, raised their hands. Sedrus did as well.

Again, all eyes turned to Daylynn.

"Your vote, Madam Reese?"

She glanced at Kayis and beyond him, to Capraro and Poplu. She turned her head to the other members, those not wizardkind.

She straightened and swallowed.

"I abstain. He didn't break any laws, but I agree he can be a menace. Judas saved my life twice while on the *Other Side*. I wouldn't be here to vote if not for him."

Kayis's lips thinned, but he choked off any scathing remarks. A disquiet crept through the seven council members as they waited for one bold enough to speak first.

"Warlock Lakayre's of the impression we were followed," Daylynn added.

Kayis's eyes narrowed.

"What? Impossible! What a ludicrous thought."

"Made sense at the time," she countered. "It all seems to be a strange set of coincidences."

Poplu spoke behind Kayis, further down the table.

"The sheol can't leave their Ruins without council permission."

Kayis watched Daylynn, her body language, trying to decipher anything. Her eyes narrowed.

"What if they don't give a shit about our permission?"

Kayis crossed his arms and leaned back.

"Explain."

"They'd no longer fear us if they had no reason to."

"Protection? From us?" Capraro asked. "Who'd be so stupid as to stand against us?"

"Not stupid, powerful."

Kayis shook his head.

"No one can defy us."

The words felt right, like sacred scripture with the power of the gods behind them.

"Except an exiled warlock," Lagelm added.

Why you little bastard.

"And a dark lord once thought vanquished," Daylynn finished.

Kayis leaned forward again, giving her a long look. He couldn't believe what he was hearing.

Damn woman has lost her nerve, but she still has her uses, just not in this chamber.

"Don't tell me you believe in the warlock's paranoid nonsense. You don't really believe the sheol's claims, do you?"

Daylynn took a deep breath and held it.

She glanced at him, and the silence built until she broke it.

"So, you acknowledge there was a sheol there…"

Damn it. Can't believe I missed that.

Daylynn shifted in her seat.

"But I believe, after everything I've seen, anything's possible."

Chapter 4: Essence Transference

Multiple books, caressed by a wispy green cloud, floated in silence. Some were thick tomes, and others were slender, frail volumes. The leather-bound texts hovered, rising and falling as if caught in an ocean's gentle wave. The green mist coiled in a serpentine fashion from them to the young woman on the floor.

Mesmerized, Judas didn't notice Atz's sudden arrival, the dwaven with red armor. He blinked into existence behind him.

"I've found her," the dwaven said. "She's coming."

"Good. Tell the others we meet tonight."

"Anyone in particular?"

"The usual."

"Where?"

"Desert of the Forsaken."

Atz nodded and faded again, leaving the elder alone.

He didn't know how long the Transference would take, or to what degree it'd work. When she awoke, would she be educated, or would it take time to untangle the learned material?

Only time would tell.

He carefully selected particular volumes. The warlock wanted her to know the generalities of Ermaeyth and the domain she'd reside in. There were too many texts covering numerous subjects to cram into her mind, so he used great care. Propriety, customs, and culture; their language and grammar; and a brief overview of history and geography—these were subjects of immediacy. Tales and histories of religion, people, and peculiar places such as the Temple of the Ghost Mists, the Abyss, the Void-Knights, the Kran Empire, and the witchen were unnecessary.

They'd leave more questions than answers.

She could do that on her own time.

There was the chance, of course, that he'd destroy her mind in the process —a slim one, but still a burden he felt keenly. Judas didn't like the gamble, but what was the alternative? With each passing moment, he wondered if the notion bothered him—or the fact it had originated with the elder fairy.

He glanced down at the girl. Her consciousness brushed his, a sign of awareness. He thought about the events leading up to this point, wondering if he had made any wrong choices.

Was Daylynn right? Should he have left her on the *Other Side*? He wished someone could tell him which direction to take. Judas never believed in people who claimed they saw the future, and he figured those who could wouldn't go around saying so, but right now, divine insight would prove helpful.

He doubted himself, always. He used meticulous care in his book selection, restricting some knowledge. Those subjects were better explained by him than absorbed through another's bias. She needed to make her own decisions, and he intended her to be a blank slate, free of prejudice. His omission about the Wizard's War might come back to haunt him, but he'd rather teach it himself than let her inherit someone else's fear.

He cast the uncertainty aside, whether he walked the right path or not. The right choice was hard to decipher in the moment, yet simple in retrospect. If necessary, he'd trace the forks of his decisions to repair any damage he might've done.

In the corner he and Julie occupied, he'd littered the place with vast volumes. While they drifted above her, he sensed the swell of her essence, her magical ability. Her power radiated, raw and unrefined. Careful tutelage would craft her into a prosperous wizard, a Grand Master Wizard or higher.

He examined her again, but this time, in a different, more painful light. She reminded him of *her*, his daughter, the one slaughtered before his eyes. He tried to block such thoughts, to forget the pain forged in his younger heart, but failed. That ancient despair filled him again, returning like an old, volatile lover, torn between eternal bliss and the heart-rending sadness.

Julie's about the same age she *would've been.*

He buried the thought, the memories, the grief, though it dug into him like a festering wound, refusing a quiet death. He knelt and gently touched her forehead, her subconsciousness swirling beneath the spell-induced sleep.

Another essence called to him, one not present, familiar yet absent.

A smile crept over his face.

He stood, his head turning to the direction from which the conjury called. He crossed the room to the window and gazed out over Ralloc. From this high up in the mountain, and in the castle spire, shops and other buildings looked like small brown lumps far below.

He answered the essence, gently, not giving himself away to everyone. He focused his thoughts on the woman who called, a discreet answer.

Judas sent his response, then closed off his essence again. She knew where he was, and she did the same.

A tremor of presage rippled through him before she appeared.

All magic gave off tell-tale signs, little vibrations of anticipation. If someone was powerful enough, they could sense the event before it happened —almost like a precognitive ability. Few possessed such insight, and even Judas, when tired, could be caught unawares.

Whenever the conjuring came, the more alien the essence, the more noticeable it was.

She manifested in the deep shadows between bookshelves, hidden by the swaddling black velvet. Madam Meristal Raviils strode forward, her crimson robes with gold embroidery flapping softly with her movement. A petite woman with flaming red hair, violet eyes, and porcelain skin stepped into the light.

If there were a perfect woman, Judas gazed upon her now. To him, she was the epitome of beauty and elegance; how many other men thought the same?

He smiled.

27

"Meristal."

They met in the middle, he bending to kiss her hand.

"Always a pleasure and delight to keep your company. I've been without it for quite some time."

"Of course, it's a pleasure to keep my company," Meristal said.

He noted the fondness in her voice.

They forged their friendship in the Wizard's War, and she had a way of subtle teasing, something he came to expect.

With the formality out of the way, he embraced her fully; a kiss planted on her cheek, her hair tickling his nose as he hugged her. She returned the tight embrace, both holding on longer than friends would.

She let go but held his arms.

"We haven't spoken in forever, thanks to my tour in Mecas River City. It's finally over."

He nodded.

"Welcome home, at least until they send you away again."

She shook her head.

"No, I'm retiring if they do."

"You missed the hearing this morning."

She dipped her head.

"I know, and I'm sorry. I'd wager Consul Dathyr was behind my delay—a sudden arrival of paperwork in the eleventh hour."

"Probably."

"I hear they denied your citizenship again."

"Yes, right before they asked for my help."

"Where is she?"

Judas's jovial manner faded, his smile faltering.

"How do you know about her arrival?"

Meristal answered with cryptic silence.

He sighed, then ushered her between the bookshelves towards Julie. Meristal gazed down at the girl wrapped up in Judas's traveling cloak.

"She seems fragile," Meristal commented. "Unable to withstand the grind of everyday life in the realm."

Judas surveyed the young woman. At first appearance, the girl seemed at peace, in a deep sleep. As they neared, the girl's brow knitted.

Her teeth clenched.

Meristal's head tilted up, surveying the books above them, the green, coiling mist.

"She's aware of our presence," Judas whispered. "She's fighting to wake up."

"Are we disturbing her?"

"Perhaps," he conceded. "She's powerful, trying to fight me."

"What are you doing with these books?"

"Essence Transference."

"Are you crazy?" Meristal hissed in a harsh whisper. "You can't do that!

You'll destroy her mind. The Essence hasn't even been medically proven, let alone tested. You're going to kill her!"

He turned to Meristal.

"Two people told me tonight I'd condemned her to die by bringing her here. At this point, does it matter?"

He didn't wait for her answer.

"If this works, she'll awaken with knowledge enough to survive. She'll understand the realm, its laws, its people. Maybe she'll even forgive me for the method."

He knelt beside the girl and glanced back up to his friend.

Meristal gazed down at him, then after some hesitation, acquiesced to his point with a silent nod.

"When will you let her wake?" Meristal asked.

"Around dawn."

"They'll make you send her back. You know that, don't you?"

"They'll try and fail. I won't do anything I don't want to. They can't order an exile. I'm outside their jurisdiction, a call they made. Considering everything, I've allowed them to keep the Mirror of Imaesion, and they should be grateful. Without it, there's no portal to the *Other Side*. Between destroying the mirror and sending her back, guess which one I'd pick?"

He heard Meristal's lips part, but he sensed the hesitation, too.

"Wouldn't destroying the mirror cause the realms to collapse? You made those magical laws, and now you're an exile. Aren't they void?"

"Maybe," he conceded, "to answer both of your questions. But between their laws and my conscience, I'll risk collapse."

Meristal's lips thinned.

"The big question is: would it reverse what you did to Xilor or his followers?"

Judas turned to her, the movement slow, his eyes tightening around the corners.

"Possibly."

Meristal subsided, content for the moment. Her lips pressed into a line, changing the subject.

"I noticed you called for a meeting tonight. Was it about her?"

"No, something else. I think it's best we arrive separately."

"Okay, I'll wait five minutes after you leave."

Judas looked down to the girl and back to Meristal.

He trusted her with his life, and by extension, the girl's. Meristal fought at his side during the Wizard's War. He nodded, taking a small step back.

He gathered his essence about him with a silent command and vanished.

Chapter 5: Desert Of The Forsaken

The Desert of the Forsaken: a desolate place, hot and unforgiving. During the day, Apor, the larger, pale cerulean sun, and Praema, the smaller, brilliant amaranth globe, bathed the barren wilderness in merciless heat. But darkness had descended, ushering in a welcome reprieve.

The wind rustled as the temperature plummeted to near-freezing. The cracked, dried surface crumbled beneath the shifting weight of two figures standing next to each other, cloaks drawn tight as they hunkered over their fire.

Judas gazed at the two smaller beings, wary of a potential trap. He reached out with his essence and identified them almost at once: Atz and Lurx.

The most reliable to follow orders.

Both still wore their armor and remained oblivious to Judas's arrival. The warlock suppressed a smile, glad he still possessed some undiminished abilities as he aged.

He moved closer and cleared his throat.

Startled, the two turned, drawing swords, but stopped. The two smaller, muscular forms bowed in greeting.

"Don't bow to me; I'm not a king," the warlock admonished.

Monarchies are more trouble than they're worth.

Once, he befriended a wealthy king, but those with riches and power often had a way of making everyone else's life miserable. Since then, the idea of monarchy repulsed Judas.

"No, not a king," muttered Atz, "but you're a supreme wizard. Don't your exploits of casting the dark lord into the eternal abyss grant you some respect?"

Lurx, the second dwaven, nodded.

"Master Guardians, that's very kind of you, but a life without fear is only half a life. Besides, nothing is eternal—not the Abyss, not even death."

"You speak of the myth," Lurx said, breathing deep.

Am I?

If he was, he didn't do so consciously.

"From the fairies," Lurx said.

Judas arched an eyebrow.

"The one about a mage coming forth from beyond the touch of mysticism?"

The two dwaven nodded.

While he'd never read their prophecy in its entirety, he knew elements of it, the way he preferred it. Prophecies weren't real.

He sighed.

"Yes, I remember something about that. The mage will be the restorer of life—in more ways than one."

Equal as scales—life with death, love against hate—the legend said such balance came at a terrible cost. Fulfillment would demand loss; life would thrive only through death.

The two dwaven gave a slight shudder, and Judas caught the movement.

He grimaced.

He'd forgotten about the dwaven's taboo regarding death. They shunned the subject with obscured references, and only the Keeper of the Dead spoke about the deceased.

Some called them superstitious, or worse, xenophobic.

Their dark history had driven them to seal themselves within the mountains, estranged from the surface and mistrusted by Wizardkind in turn. Most never questioned why the Dwaven withdrew, or what wound they were hiding—only that they did.

How did everyone become so short sighted?

But Judas enjoyed their company and cherished them as much as the other races, except maybe the dragons.

Atz combed his stubby, thick fingers through his long waist-length beard.

"Could that mage be you?"

Judas chuckled, and he nipped that thought short.

"No."

"How can you be sure?" Lurx asked. "You could be. You did defeat the dark lord."

The warlock's smile faded.

"I'll admit to the similarities between the myth and my life, but I don't come from beyond the touch of mysticism. That's for those who came from the *Other Side.*"

Lurx nodded, but Atz glanced around, frowning.

"Where is everyone?" the dwaven asked.

Judas relented to the blatant change of the subject.

"The journey's long, and not everyone can slip away from watchful eyes. So, we shall wait."

"Why are we meeting here instead of Ralloc, or your manor?" Lurx inquired.

"I've grown suspicious of Ralloc. Who hasn't? Enemy eyes scrutinize it, and this is the only place where we can be protected by Soma and other benevolent spirits."

He smiled down at the dwaven. Hearing the name of their goddess helped calm them, but he didn't believe in such notions himself, at least, not the dwaven's version.

Now, the other creature who calls herself Soma, that's a different story.

Atz spoke at last, "What makes you think Ralloc's watched?"

"Everyone looks to Ralloc, from all over Ermaeyth, and always will. There are whispers, if you listen."

"We can always trust your judgment, Judas," a woman's voice came from behind them.

All three turned, spying Madam Meristal Raviils as she strode forward.

"Is this a full meeting? Who else are we waiting on?"

31

"Down to business fast—you appreciate what I like," Judas commented.

He held his arms wide to embrace her again, propriety discarded, but the charade intact.

They released each other, quicker this time, and he spoke to all present.

"We're waiting on—"

As soon as he started speaking, more figures appeared and approached the fire together. One was clearly Staell, the unicorn. And among the group, a fairy, an elyfian, and a centaur. They represented the scattered races bound by uneasy alliance: unicorns, fairies, centaurs, and elyves—the remnants of an older order when they were young, held together by necessity rather than by trust.

Sedrus, the centaur and council member, called out a greeting. To the warlock's disappointment, he didn't spy the goblin council members, the newest among them, but he could be patient.

Sedrus stared down as he neared the fire, and upon seeing the two dwaven, turned his head in disgust.

"What are these vermin doing here?"

"They're here on my request," Judas said. "We require their help, and we'll respect them as equals. Their abilities can shield us from prying eyes and sensitive ears."

Sedrus gave them a contemptuous sneer and turned his head away, moving to the far side of the circle.

"I didn't foresee Lagelm's and Kellis's absence," he said.

He waved his hand in a dismissive gesture.

"We'll begin without them. This morning, the Mirror of Imaesion reacted erratically. On the *Other Side* of the gateway, I sensed the Kothlus Trilogy. It seems it's emerged once again despite going missing long ago."

"What's that again?" Sedrus asked.

Judas glanced around the circle, seeing the vast majority of those gathered with blank expressions. Only Meristal seemed to know.

"The Kothlus books are written in Xilor's blood, one of the ways I bound him. If his minions acquire them, he'll be one step closer to resurrection—a bad starting point."

"To what, Judas?" Zmora asked.

Before he could answer, Meristal jumped in, her voice hard.

"I think you know as well as the rest of us, Zmora. It could only be one thing. How many times must he prove himself? By the time you all start believing, it'll be too late."

Mella, the elyfian interrupted, her brows furrowed.

"The dark lord can return to power? I didn't think it possible."

"Not for certain," Judas admitted, "but with one barrier down, he'll be closer. Xilor's in the process as we speak."

He sighed.

"Either way, the books were on the *Other Side*, and someone went to retrieve them. I'm still looking into how they managed to get past Atz and Lurx. But the bigger implication is what worries me."

We have a betrayer in our midst, Staell, the unicorn, stated.

He gleamed, effulgent, his inner light shining through his translucent skin.

A slight shiver went through everyone in the group.

Unicorns spoke with telepathy; each time they spoke, it was like an invasion of privacy unless you became accustomed to it.

Judas glanced up at the majestic creature.

"No," Sedrus said. "There's no way he could come back. You killed him! You told us you killed him!"

"Indeed, I did. Even though I killed him, he still lives."

"What?" Zmora, the fairy, asked.

Sedrus chuckled, a scornful sound.

"The infallible Lakayre lied? You wizardkind are so unsurprising."

I'm sure— Staell began.

Sedrus waved his arm, cutting off the unicorn.

"Your treachery knows no bounds. Perhaps the Kothlere Order's right to cast you out, to hunt you down! If he isn't dead, where is Xilor?"

"Enough!" shouted a voice.

All eyes turned to Atz.

The dwaven kept their silence in the meetings, only present for protection.

"Master Lakayre stopped him. That's all that matters! If he hadn't, you'd all be kneeling at Xilor's feet, or perhaps even ... deceased!"

"We all want to understand," Lurx said. "Even I confess curiosity. How did you stop him Master Lakayre?"

Judas went silent, glancing at the figures around the fire. All eyes were on him, hopeful, expectant.

He shook his head.

"I destroyed his body, but he lived on as a wraith."

He swallowed.

"I tore his soul away, trapped his mind in a mirror, even cast him into the Abyss—yet he endured."

Judas sighed.

"When his voice still spoke from the glass, I knew he couldn't die."

His head quirked to the side as he remembered what else he had to do.

"So, I drained his blood, buried his body where none could reach it, and made his return as hard as possible."

"Where?" Sedrus asked.

Judas shook his head.

"You don't need to know, not unless you plan on reviving him."

This does not help us, Staell interrupted.

The unicorn scanned the others.

Is your curiosity satisfied? Now we need to work on preventing him from returning. You heard Judas yourself, it's a matter of time, not if. We must work to prolong this inevitable conclusion. We must find the betrayer among us.

"It's the bloody vampires," Sedrus murmured, his tone acidic.

His gaze swept over to Atz and Lurx.

"Or these two dwaven."

"Yes," Judas confirmed, his voice sharp, "betrayed by our kind."

"Another betrayer? In Ralloc…?" Meristal asked.

"The same kind?" Sedrus growled. "We're not the same!"

Judas caught the glint of hate in his eyes.

"Your blood may not be the same, but magic connects you. We are all connected."

"Correct me if I'm wrong," Meristal said, "but we never caught the first betrayer, did we?"

"No, we didn't," Judas confirmed, and he couldn't hide the regret in his voice.

"Are you sure it's not the same one?" Mella, the elyfian, asked.

Her raven hair rustled with the caress of a gentle breeze.

Meristal saved him from having to speak.

"It was during the climax of the Wizard's War. We're sure the first one's inactive, either passed on or removed from a position of power. To be honest, we weren't certain at all."

But certainty was a lost luxury from the Wizard's War. Too many turncoats, too many lies, and in the end, a lot of people died, even those closest to him.

"Another one rises?" Zmora asked.

Judas nodded.

"Yes, and it's up to us to find out who did it before too much damage is done. Now, back to what I was saying, the three books were located on the *Other Side*—"

Master Judas? Staell interrupted. *You've spoken in the past tense more than once. Is there something you haven't told us?*

"Ever alert, Staell. Yes, past tense because they were on the *Other Side*. They aren't anymore. I went myself, along with the two guardians, Atz and Lurx … and Daylynn Reese."

"You what?" Meristal asked, her voice sharp, like a stinging slap to the face.

Judas winced.

Meristal hated Daylynn Reese, a bitterness that went all the way back to the war.

He held up placating hands.

"The council's decision, not mine. You're always my first choice, but you were still in Mecas River City. We didn't realize what caused the disturbance at the time, so we had to act."

"Yes of course, you're right."

Even though Meristal relented, he knew the conversation wasn't over. Judas stifled a smile, and he knew that Meristal, just like him, longed for the old days, when it was him and her against the world.

Perhaps I'm not the only one who can't escape the days of the war.

During those darkest days, they both meant the world to each other, and their fierce friendship was forged through warfare.

"That still doesn't explain the past tense expression," Mella spoke up.

"They're in our possession now, are they not?"

"No," Judas said.

"How did this happen?" Zmora inquired.

"It matters not," Mella said, cutting her off. "I'm sure Warlock Lakayre did everything in his power. If someone slipped by him, could any of you do better?"

Judas caught Meristal mumbling a maybe.

His lips pursed before he spoke.

"I want each Head of Creatures to report and keep tabs on their designated species. Be mindful of more signs of Xilor, like the sheol on the *Other Side*."

"I heard about that," Meristal grunted.

"Sedrus, following this meeting, check on the other centaurs; Mella, take the goblins, trolls, and elyves. Zmora, of course, you have the fairies and vampires; Staell, the unicorns are yours, along with the dragons; Meristal, take the saricrocians—you're the only one those damn things listen to."

Judas pointed to Atz and Lurx.

"The dwaven are yours."

An angry voice burst into the silence.

"What will you be doing, Lakayre?" Sedrus demanded.

He stamped his hoof, his muscle rippling beneath his chestnut brown coat.

Judas turned back, seeing the eyes of everyone darting around the group, an uncomfortable silence with Sedrus's blatant disregard for titles or propriety.

"Well," Judas said, "I'll be talking to the sheol, unless, of course, you want to trade, Sedrus?"

A shudder swept through the camp, the fiends of death slipping their minds.

"Well?" Judas prompted.

"I think you know what would be best, Master Wizard."

Judas nodded, pulling the lower hairs of his goatee with his thumb and forefinger.

"We'll meet again, and soon. I'll contact you when we can."

"There's something else," Sedrus interjected.

Everyone stopped, eyeing the centaur.

"Daylynn gave her report to the council. The consul moved for a motion to hunt you down and kill you. We blocked the motion. You'll be surprised, but Daylynn sided with Lagelm, Kellis, and I. She said you saved her life."

"I did," Judas confirmed with a nod. "Twice."

Meristal let out a disgusted hiss of air between her teeth.

"I believe," Sedrus continued, "it's because of your actions, she voted against hunting you down. The consul's livid and still wants to extradite the Wcic. For the moment, you're not officially hunted, at least not by Ralloc."

"Good. Now I need to figure out who *is* hunting me."

Sedrus turned to leave when Staell called out through his mental projection.

I have something to add.

Judas suppressed a sigh. Why couldn't everyone say what they needed in the meeting instead of making it drag on?

My people tasked me to deliver a warning to the council. Since a member is present, I'll do it now. The sheol congregate and are poised to strike. Who is uncertain, but the threat is real. They stirred in the shadows of their ruins. Also, the lower castes of vampires move outside Shadow City. The portents are real. Something sinister twists. War is coming.

The centaur swallowed hard, knowing what a message from the unicorns would imply and the weight of their words.

"I'll deliver the message."

Also, if war does come, our allegiance lies with Warlock Lakayre.

Sedrus nodded and moved off, and others followed him. Judas saw the foreboding on the centaur's face. He didn't relish the thought of delivering the message in its entirety.

Staell moved closer to the warlock.

I wish to bestow a gift to the Wcic.

Judas's eyes narrowed.

"I can arrange a short visit around dawn, my manor. I didn't plan to return there because the council would look there first. Also, being hunted further solidified my choice, but I left something valuable and must fetch it. You can do it, then."

Where will you go afterward?

"Eventually to Wizard's Pass. I have an old acquaintance there. Few are familiar with him, and we should be relatively safe as it's out of the way."

A sound plan. I'll await you at your manor at dawn.

Staell retreated, leaving Judas with Meristal, Atz, and Lurx.

Judas motioned to the dwaven.

"You may leave. Thank you for your service."

The two dwaven bowed and faded to carry out the task Judas gave them.

Judas withdrew his wand from the folds of his inner robe and pointed at the flickering fire. The earth churned, dousing the fire with sand, giving the appearance as if no one had ever come.

Meristal gazed at Judas and raised an eyebrow.

"There's someone among us who's feeding information to the enemy," he confirmed. "I haven't been able to discover who yet, even after all these years, so I must take precautionary actions. Spells can only be so good if someone's trying to listen in. If they track down our location, I don't want to give anything away."

"Any ideas of who?"

"Well, I can rule you out," he mused with a bittersweet smile and mocking tone.

"Oh? Why's that?"

"During the time of your absence to Mecas River City," Judas explained, "things happened only people in the Kothlere Council would be aware of, and it couldn't have been you."

"So, you've narrowed it down to the council?"

"Yes, and no."

"Anything to do with this group?"

"I don't believe so. I cast a powerful charm that will notify us of treacherous thoughts in our midst. We'd know."

"And there's no way to trick you?"

"Sure."

He shrugged his shoulders.

"Anything's possible. I'm not infallible. They'd need to be powerful, intelligent, or privy to some form of ancient wizardry I'm not."

"So, other than suspicions, you can't narrow down the exact perpetrator?"

"No. Too many people are coming and going in the castle for absolutes, but I'm getting closer. I just need more time. Why are you so interested all of a sudden?"

"Well, if the dark lord's coming back—or is back—then time's something we may not have."

"Too true."

"Where are you going? After your manor, I mean?"

He was quiet for a moment, gazing out at the dark, sandy landscape.

"Dlad City. It'll give me time to prepare Julie for her journey."

"Can I see you before you leave? I just got here."

He smiled.

"We don't have the best timing, do we?"

He hugged her again.

"Let me know when you're coming. Okay?"

She pulled away, nodded, and teleported away, leaving Judas alone.

He still had his task to complete.

Gathering his power, he too, vanished.

His teleport carried him to the opening of the Corridor of Cruelty, once a monumental feat to all who crossed its cursed threshold, now a lingering moment of discomfort for the warlock.

Long ago, Judas entered the Corridor, and for three months he suffered all the cruelties it offered. The months seemed like years. But he mastered the Corridor, and now he only experienced the briefest of irritations as he walked through.

No one, nothing, not even him, could teleport through, an anomaly unto itself.

Once across the five-mile gap, he teleported again to his destination.

On the other side, death and decay greeted him. The grass crumbled to ash beneath his feet. Even in the dark, Judas knew the dirt went from a rich brown to a charcoal black.

Stone monoliths littered the way in front of him, each an epitaph of an identified member of some long-forgotten royal family. This place where the sheol stayed—The Ruins of Sheol—was the final resting place of countless millions, both from the Wizard's War and another war from long ago, forgotten by society, a rarity in educated circles of historians.

Ignorance of the place, though common, was due to the meticulous erasure from most texts circulating in the general populace. Who did it remained a mystery, and the Ruins were hard to track down, but slivers of history from the once epic war could be traced back, almost to the beginning of magic.

But the clues were still there, if one knew where to look.

Judas withdrew his wand, and a light glowed from the tip, casting long shadows on the tombstones in front of him.

The sheol, like moths, were attracted to luminance in small amounts, but too much, and they died. Judas peered into the darkness before him, his eyes searching for any signs of movement.

They're here, they're always here.

A skittering noise like fingernails scraped over a chalkboard manifested in front of him. The faint sound of wind sucking in followed. The breath of a sheol, an echoing effect, impossible to determine which was the first and which was an echo.

"What comes?" a deep, rattling called.

"Your Head of Creatures," Judas responded, mustering a tone of command he didn't feel.

The sheol, like the City of Despair, compelled a strange effect on the living. It was said that the City of Despair was once a great splendor, rivaling Ralloc in size, and the Golden City in beauty. Towers and buildings made of crystal and marble, lush green gardens and clear waters.

Now ... just a dead spot on the face of the Ermaeyth. Anyone who entered unprepared never came out again.

"We have no Head of Creatures. We have no want," the sheol responded.

Judas waited for the sheol to come out in the open.

Slowly, the decaying wraith slithered forward like a serpent floating in the air, a wisp of smoke, coiling and recoiling. The wraith stopped meters short of Judas and hovered like a black cloud of toxic gas.

"What is it?" the sheol hissed.

"Let's begin by talking about your master."

Chapter 6: Gryzlaud Palace

Xilor drew into himself, centering his essence. In Gryzlaud Palace, across the sea of rolling plains, rivers, and forests, past the Abyss, Xilor awaited the arrival of the Kothlus Trilogy.

So close, after so many years.

Gryzlaud stood as both monument and tomb—a castle of towering spires and buried halls, its walls fed by centuries of sorcery, a residue that seeped into the stone. In the quiet, he could almost hear the screams of the deceased.

Many hunted his lair, including the warlock, but those without allegiance never set foot inside. Xilor took this bastion from the previous dark lord, Hadius Lacove.

The castle now fell under his rule.

His goblin-slave, Derms, muttered as he polished a silver bowl.

Xilor sensed beyond his prison—a silver-looking glass—and one of his apprentices approached. But it was something else, a new element in Ermaeyth, that upset the balance. He noticed the ripple effect from here, becoming hyper-sensitive in captivity.

In a way, Judas helped him, albeit unwittingly—just as Hagen once helped all beings, drawing ever closer to the madness that consumed him.

Xilor's eyes moved in the mirror, taking in the castle as he awaited.

Rumors circulated that Hagen, the Father of Magic, built Gryzlaud in the ancient past. He introduced magic to all living things, but the fable turned dark, and Hagen succumbed to his madness, becoming the first-ever dark lord.

The irony.

His legacy spawned the line of dark lords, each worse than the last. Vlad Vikal came next, alchemist and tyrant, and the first vampire. The mountains far to the north, which Ralloc nestled against, were named after his family: the Vikal Mountains. The Krey and the elyves resided there now.

His name still stained the northern mountains like the blood he'd spilled.

Because Vlad created the vampires, he tolerated the species's floundering. Vlad's tinkering with alchemy and enchantments led Xilor down a similar path with his creation of the xcix. But Xilor did what Vlad couldn't: cheat death. Even now, in this mirror, in his refuge, he persisted.

And now, centuries later, Xilor ruled their ruins.

Gryzlaud endured as a monument to the past masters, a mausoleum filled with artifacts, trinkets, amulets, rings, and the like. Rulers would envy his expansive throne room; the towers rivaled Ralloc, and the defenses? Bolstered by eons of dark energy.

The door creaked, a hushed stirring of air, and the near-silent footfalls drew Xilor's attention.

His servant, an apprentice, strolled forward, carrying three giant leather-bound volumes ravaged by time. Sidjuous set the tomes on a long table filled with scales, herbs, and brewing cauldrons.

The apprentice smiled, triumphant, his face tilting toward the giant mirror.

"Is it time?" Xilor asked, his voice raspy, like glass shards grinding together.

"It is, my master."

Xilor regarded his smug apprentice.

Pride makes him overconfident.

Sidjuous needed to be reminded the price of arrogance.

Though one of many apprentices, the highest pinnacle eluded him, and the honor belonged to another. But he was powerful enough to snuff out the lives of the few who meddled. Sidjuous was the most trusted apprentice, and that was because he was a coward. Thoughts of betrayal never entered his mind, and that made him the weakest and most unworthy.

But vanity played its part, too.

Sidjuous was tall, framed with long, flowing blond hair. A broad chin and delicate features gave him the visage of imagined noble pedigree.

He understands so little of royalty.

Xilor's attention turned back to the trilogy, the leather-bound volumes that held his blood.

Something close to a sigh of relief slipped out of him.

"At last."

Sidjuous laid a hand upon the ripped bindings, his finger tracing the frayed spine.

A warm glow swelled within Xilor, basking in the moment.

A victory, small next to the grand conclusion.

Sidjuous moved further down the table, towards the mirror and the instruments he'd use for the next step. His gaze went to the bent and twisted goblin.

"Slave, bring me the books," Sidjuous commanded.

Xilor took note of yet another corrective measure that was needed. His apprentices responded differently to each; some needed overt control, others subtle nudges. With his Betrayer running amok, he took a ruthless approach. He had to.

But he couldn't with Sidjuous. Not yet.

"I'll bring them, if my master commands," the goblin croaked. "I don't take orders from his sycophants."

Somewhere within him, Xilor smiled at Derms's spirit.

Sidjuous pulled his wand and barked a curse, throwing the dwarfed goblin against the wall.

Derms slumped and held his arm, rocking back and forth, muttering.

Xilor cut through the distraction.

"Whose blood will we mix with mine? It must be suitable."

Sidjuous turned and regarded the mirror. Beyond him, Derms made it to his feet, grabbed the books, and set them closer to the end of the table.

"We'll use the blood of Judas's nieces."

The two young women flashed in Xilor's mind.

"Miza."

Despite her living conditions, her upbringing, she kept a pure spirit. Her sister, Olga, on the other hand … she could be powerful. She'd already shown signs of his shaping, molded into a weaponized vassal.

Sidjuous nodded.

"And Olga."

A movement from Derms drew Xilor's attention.

"My faithful servant, you have served well. You may retire this evening."

Derms bowed low with reverence, his eyes downward.

"Be gone."

The goblin hurried from the room.

Once the door closed, Xilor shifted his attention to the remaining apprentice, then to the books.

So many years wasted.

The books bore his scrutiny. The thought of being whole once more was so tantalizingly close. Judas Lakayre put him here, turned on him, destroyed him. Xilor's hatred for him ran deep, but so did his respect, misguided fool he may be.

Xilor couldn't blame Judas; the warlock didn't know who hid beneath the cowl. Though unaware of the connection, their paths had crossed. If he'd been aware, it wouldn't have changed anything. Judas's rigidity with his morality couldn't be swayed. It was an unchangeable constant, like death.

And only one controlled that power.

Was that why he hated Judas most? Because he still envied him, or because Judas belonged to something Xilor could never have?

"Bring the vessel."

Sidjuous bowed and moved, using magic to summon the kettle, maneuvering it near the coffin-like vessel. Once set, Xilor continued with his instruction.

"Now the tomes, hover them over the bowl and burn them. Make sure to collect all the ash."

Step by step, Xilor led him through the precarious instructions, blending the fourth branch of magic—Derengi—and alchemy together. The pace was ponderous, the instructions tedious, but his apprentice followed his edicts like an expert.

"Begin the siphon."

On his word, the apprentice cast another spell, the ashes spinning in a cyclone. He laid on another weave of conjury, drawing out the essence of Xilor's blood, weaving it across the air and into two water-filled casks.

The air thickened, metallic and warm, the smell of scorched parchment mixing with blood. Even the mirror trembled under it.

The liquid turned red.

"Now, into the vessel."

The form-fitted coffin was far from ordinary, molded for Xilor's abnormal height. Some people whispered Xilor was half-giant, a ludicrous notion. His towering frame had more to do with his dark ambitions, magical machinations, and twisting his power to alter himself, like the elyfian of old.

A history most forget.

The creature he became was the dark lord everyone knew now.

The crimson liquid sloshed as it settled.

"Soon, my soul will arrive from the Abyss, but I need what remains of my bones. Dispatch the Inium clan to send a squad of trolls to the City of Despair. Retrieve what is mine."

Sidjuous bowed and hurried away.

The apprentice did have his uses, even if he was weak and unworthy. But his ambition and cunning balanced it out. And, Sidjuous was one of the select few who discovered him in a weakened state. Krurik, Xilor's successor, would've killed him without a second thought.

With the trolls to do his menial labor, there were others to bring into the fold.

The vampires, and the Betrayer.

Xilor projected his will into magical existence. An eerie green glow came from the mirror and illuminated the room.

Yes, it was time to talk to the Betrayer in Shadow City, and to remind him what was at stake.

Chapter 7: The Betrayer

Death, and the accompanying cold chill, was an old acquaintance, but not a friend to the Betrayer. Darkness, shadows, silence—this place held the whispers of madness.

The Betrayer's composure slipped in the ringing silence. The porous stone walls of black and red flecked granite were ice cold. The inhabitants of Shadow City, the vampires, were silent as corpses.

Unless it was feeding time.

A smattering of light, the only tidbit granted to him, deepened the shadows and failed to keep the claustrophobia at bay. The lack of fresh air didn't help, either. If he didn't leave soon, he'd lose his mind.

Or become the next meal.

What he'd give to see the suns, hear the chirp of a single bird.

Over a month ago, the dark lord sent him as an emissary to the vampires of Shadow City. His duty was to voice Xilor's displeasure at their lack of commitment. At first, his presence was taken as a joke, but when the sheol encroached upon them, the vampires stirred from their languid slumber.

The sheol herald Xilor's return.

The Betrayer paced his small and windowless room. A cot nestled against the far wall beside a table with a washbasin. A nondescript and unflattering mirror was the only other decoration. One candle burned, striving in vain to hold the darkness at bay.

The mirror swirled in a yellow-green fog, an expected transmission. Then, the eyes appeared, familiar, cold, peculiar. The Betrayer prostrated himself on the floor.

"My lord, this is a pleasant surprise. Is stage one complete?"

"Yes. Your switching of the books in the non-magical realm turned out to be your best accomplishment yet, including your memory charm on the girl. The flawless plan worked; even the great Lakayre was caught unaware. But by now they must know another Betrayer is among them. Instead of you, they'll hunt my apprentice. I can't permit this."

"Have they caught him, then?"

If Xilor's chosen successor was caught inside the walls of Ralloc, that would effectively retire the Betrayer from his vile service, but that might also eliminate Xilor's need of him.

"No, they haven't. But you should heed my words and watch your back, for they'll catch on and come for you. If they capture you, I'll have no need to keep *them* alive."

Dear Spirits, not Olga and Miza. Anything but them.

"Your blood has been returned to you, and the risk was worth it, my lord."

"Yes."

Xilor's eyes moved in the mirror, as if trying to see further into the room.

"What of the vampires? Have they allied themselves yet?"

"Yes, my lord. The clan king will set out tonight to meet you. He'll arrive in a few days."

"And the sheol? Have they been brought to heel? Did they sense my presence growing?"

"They're ready for war, but I'm not certain they'll fight. They know that without them, all's lost."

"Not lost, no, but I might have to remind them the price of desertion."

"Doesn't the attack on Lakayre seal their fate with us?"

"The staged attack? That was my apprentice taking an opportunity to eliminate you and Judas on the *Other Side*. His foolishness tipped our hand early. I didn't command him to do so."

The dark lord paused.

"But the act might favor us, urging the sheol to side against Ralloc. You'd think my creatures would be amenable, but their agendas are their own."

"Perhaps they're waiting to finish off the weakened victor?" the Betrayer mused out loud.

"Careful, turncoat. If I didn't know any better, I would've figured that was your idea all along!"

Shades of the Underworld. Does he really think—?

The Betrayer lowered his head.

"No, my lord, I'd never turn against you."

"How do I know? You betrayed your kind, your own blood."

"My lord, why would I turn against you? Conservation of power in the face of opposition is foolishness. To have power, you must demonstrate it with full might, as you have done."

The eyes narrowed, scrutinizing him, like Xilor's peered into his mind, all secret thoughts bared to him.

"Hatred burns within you, but for whom? Me?"

If you only knew the truth.

"Hatred fuels my power, and I hate mentioning his name."

Xilor's voice came out like a serpent's hiss.

"Judas Lakayre."

"Yes, my lord."

"Good, then you'll have no problem killing him when the time comes."

"My lord?"

Do I really want to kill Judas?

Puzzled, the Betrayer hesitated, trying to find the right words.

"My lord, wouldn't you want the pleasure?"

"Nothing would please me more than to kill him; however, nothing would show me more loyalty than if you took Judas's life."

The Betrayer bowed low to hide the lump in his throat, to give him time to compose his face into a mask.

I can't kill him. I'm no murderer.

He looked up.

"I'm honored. Do you know where he is?"

"Yes, my apprentice saw him in Ralloc earlier today. Two betrayers are better than one, don't you think?"

When the Betrayer opened his mouth to speak, Xilor cut him off.

"How's the clan king getting here?"

"Teleport with a journey stone to the Corridor of Cruelty, fly through during the cover of night, then portal the rest of the way."

"Very well. For your next assignment, go sway the trolls. Incite an uprising in the Ruins, and have them attack Wizard's Pass. There'll be a small window of time. It's a test of loyalty."

The Betrayer's brow furrowed, his lips thinning into a line.

"But the Ruins of Sheol are through the Corridor of Cruelty, in another realm—"

"Don't question my edicts, cur."

The Betrayer swallowed, casting his eyes down.

"Forgive me, I was foolish to think—"

"You are foolish! You think you're even close to understanding my reasons?"

The eyes narrowed to slits.

"I may not be in physical form, but my power is vast. I can reach out and crush you at any time, for the slightest inclination of treachery."

And that's the only sway you have over me.

"And those girls you cling to won't be safe either."

And that ... He's insane.

"Forgive me, I didn't mean—"

"—But you did, otherwise, you would've said nothing. I'll give you five days to carry out my will, or you won't be around to witness my return, and neither will those girls."

Before the Betrayer uttered another word, the eyes in the mirror vanished, the communication severed.

The Betrayer sagged with relief. All those years ago ... he almost wished he'd said no to Xilor.

But how could he?

The lives of two innocent children lay in the balance had he not complied. He threatened their death to make him comply, reminding the Betrayer where he belonged.

What was he to do? Betray everyone and everything, even himself, or let Xilor murder those children? Both choices were horrible, and those babies had turned into young women now.

But he'd rather betray his heart than suffer their deaths.

And if the opportunity to escape ever availed itself ...

He'd need to utilize every bit of guile and ingenuity he could muster. He just hoped he could come away unscathed.

"Five days ..." he muttered to himself.

A near-impossible feat.

And now, he needed to find a journeyman and purchase more porting stones.

The candle of time burned quickly. Five days to prove his usefulness, loyalty, and reliability.

Chapter 8: Lakayre Manor

His feet touched the familiar wood floor in the library. The phthalo-blue carpet lay dark beneath the distant tables. Julie still lay on the floor, his traveling cloak about her. Glancing over his shoulder, he caught a warm orange and purple glow on the distant horizon to the north.

Dawn.

While kneeling beside her, he caught a small tremor of magic.

He spun, pulling his wand, shooting in a sudden, aimless burst. The blast ripped free, crashing through shelves, splintering wood, ripping books, and sending paper flying.

The attacker grunted, but Judas couldn't see through the ensuing confusion.

He stood to his full height, wary of others. He darted down the aisle, dipping around a corner, and saw the feet of his attacker buried under shelves and tomes.

Another tremor came from behind, mere moments before he heard the incantation. Whirling around, he batted the spell away without a word, throwing up his mage-shield. What he didn't reflect, the shield absorbed.

The second attacker stayed in the shadows, cowering in darkness, hoping to lure him away from Julie.

Are they here for me or her?

He assumed for him.

He hurried between the bookshelves, toward Julie. If they beat him, she was as good as dead. Moments later, he knelt beside her. Once in his arms, his mage-shield enveloped them both. Another bolt of energy ripped through the room, breaking and destroying more priceless artifacts. His heart hurt at the sight, the scripts beyond saving.

He called his power, the essence answering his summons.

As he started his teleport, a figure materialized at the other end of the aisle, skidding to a stop. A black-shrouded figure raised a wand, light and force shooting forward, a flash so bright, Judas had to blink several times to regain his sight. When he did, his manor stood before him.

For a brief moment, he pitied Sam, the librarian, who'd come to work this morning to find the place destroyed.

How did they track me?

He adjusted the girl in his arms. A black iron gate guarded the front of his manor and stood fifteen feet high, the brick wall the color of burning coals encompassed the entire grounds. The gate opened at his thought, moving in silence, admitting him inside.

The house was an enormity for one person. Giant, stark-white pillars greeted all guests, as did the double doors of marble and glass, both outlined in silver.

The house boasted four stories.

To the left, as a visitor would face the entrance, sat a huge barn painted deep, dark green. Horses nickering inside floated through the morning air. To the right stood a small cottage, his study.

No one entered, not even Meristal. If he had secrets, he kept them locked up here, but most, especially the darkest ones that weighed on his heart, were tucked away in his head.

He ambled up the front path, carrying Julie like a bride. His feet climbed familiar wooden steps. Without incantation, the door opened, and he carried her through.

Once inside, he kicked off their leather sandals, pushing them aside with his foot so he wouldn't track in dirt. A light stained oak covered the floor, gleaming with its polished finish.

He debated, his eyes tracking from the sitting room to a bedroom, then up through the open ceiling, allowing an unimpeded view of all four stories.

He chose a bed.

The winding oak stairs hugged the wide walls, a daunting task for his age. The marble base supported the silver handrails. On the walls, artistic paintings of people, places, and things adorned his manse. Most depicted rare, beautiful places, tribes of people long gone, and mythical races.

At the second landing, Judas turned left and entered the first door on the right. The house tallied twenty guest rooms, four studies, a small kitchen on each floor, and a master kitchen on the first floor.

With gentle ease, he laid her on the bed. He could've thrown her, and she wouldn't have woken from her magically-induced coma. Judas detected her subconscious underneath the pall of magic, blissful yet unaware of anything. She truly dreamed now: a meadow, a large oak tree, birds …

He smiled at the peaceful dream and hurried to his master bedroom and disrobed in haste, throwing his tattered clothing at the foot of his bed and pulling out a fresh set of formal yet plain robes. He dressed at an alacritous pace, an under robe of white linen, the inner robe of deep tangelo, and a dark indigo outer robe with silver needlework along the cuffs and neck.

A knock at the front door drew his attention, and he frowned.

Staell wouldn't knock…

He hurried to the front door.

Had his enemies come to his house? Wand in hand, he walked to the door. Old habits from the Wizard's War sprang to life, as did the old paranoia. His gut clenched, his breath held.

The door snapped open on his silent command, his wand thrust forward, the tip glowing, magic ready to spill.

The young man dropped his belongings, holding up his hands.

"Please, don't!" he cried out.

Judas lowered his wand, his eyes going round.

"Toddison? What in the Underworld are you doing here? I almost blasted you to hell and back!"

How did he find my house?

"I know, I know, I'm sorry. You told me to come last night, but you weren't here when I arrived. I waited until midnight."

"I did?"

The young man with dark hair bent to collect his things.

"And please, just call me Todd. I hate the name Toddison."

Judas thought back to yesterday, and Todd spoke the truth. He'd run into him—literally—right after they revoked his citizenship in court and before the council summoned him. He had Todd on one side, bumbling and gushing, and a messenger behind Judas, whispering in conspiratorial tones; one asking for an interview, the other saying the council summoned him.

And once the messenger said those coveted words—"It's the Mirror of Imaesion"—that ended any pretense of entertaining the young reporter begging for an interview.

"Hey, but what about me?" Todd asked as Judas moved away.

"Sorry, the High Council calls."

"But when can I interview you? The people need to hear the true story! The people want to know!"

"If you can find my house, come by tonight and you can conduct your interview ..."

"Sorry, Todd," Judas said, retreating from his recollections. "I totally forgot."

"I figured as much," Todd said, scooping up the last of his things. "Or you ducked me again. Why are you so afraid?"

The last question gave Judas pause, like a slap in the face.

"Afraid? Is that what you think?"

The boy shrugged.

"What else? Worried people will hear your story and be inspired?"

Todd finished collecting his belongings off the porch and stood. Judas waited for the young man to make eye contact, and when he spoke, he didn't try to hide his agitation.

"Most people wouldn't understand half of what I endured, and that's why I don't indulge in idle curiosities. The citizens are kind enough to keep their distance, but knowing the truth wouldn't endear me to them. I killed more than I'd want to count, for a cause I once considered holy, but it turned out to be misguided ideals."

"Like what?" Todd asked, his tone breathy.

Judas's gaze darted away. He'd already said too much, but it was best to trudge on and get it over with.

"Believing in our government, a body as corrupt as the enemy we faced. I've seen soldiers die for the notion of freedom, not knowing it was all for a lie. And learning that horrible truth while in the heart of war was almost enough to break me. There's nothing inspiring about that, and that's also why I'm not afraid."

Todd swallowed, opened his mouth to say something, but Judas waved him off.

"Don't. I'm sorry. I'm in the wrong. I apologize. I'll make it up to you.

Meet me in Dlad City for lunch, and we can talk about the interview, okay?"

Todd's eyes narrowed, suspicious.

"I swear, Todd. Just not right now. I'm expecting company, and then I'm leaving. I'll meet you."

"Alright. Dlad City. Any place in particular?"

"A small inn called Traveler's Respite. You know the place?"

Todd nodded, then left, and he wasn't happy about it.

A movement caught Judas's eye, and he spied Staell inside his barn, the unicorn waiting for Todd to leave. As the unicorn crossed the lawn, he called to Judas.

Is she awake yet?

"No, I was interrupted. Since unicorns don't knock ... "

What's her name?

"Julie."

Staell grew silent, thoughtful. When he spoke again, his words were measured.

I plan on visiting the Hive.

"The Hive?"

Judas's throat tightened. Outpost Dire. The Krey. He could still see them in the bloodlust—soldiers raised from childhood, driven mad by it, unleashed only when the war was at its worst. Monsters, unless an A'uri chained them together. Ruthless zealots for death.

"Why in the gods' names would you do that?"

To set them in motion for when the war starts. By the time the council wakes up, it'll be too late. Xilor will be at their walls before reality sets in. Thus, enter the Krey.

Judas nodded. It made sense, but bile rose in his throat, vividly recalling the carnage they wrought.

"Isn't there another way?"

Yes, of course, if more death is acceptable. Do you want that on your conscience?

Judas shook his head.

You know what war's like, what it does to people. How many people will be forced to flee their homes?

Judas sighed. He couldn't let personal feelings impede what was right, even if lawfully wrong.

"You do realize what you're asking them to do is treason. They'll hunt them down."

Staell didn't say anything, but he could've sworn he felt the equivalent of a shrug from the unicorn.

"I'll wake her," Judas said. "Better wait till I call you."

Staell dipped his head in acknowledgment. Judas closed the door, climbed the stairs to the second landing, and slipped into her room.

Soft sunlight filtered through the window as her subconsciousness brushed against his. He'd planned to wake her in the library in the Kothlere Castle. The moral quandary flared within him once more. He played with her future like a god. Best intentions or not, Xilor probably thought the same thing in his quest.

Mastering himself, he walked forward, ready to wake her.

And her eyes snapped open.

For a brief instant, Judas faltered, startled. She awakened, impossible as it seemed; he hadn't lifted the spell. She'd shattered his barrier with sheer force of will.

She lay quite still, eyes blinking, adjusting as she slowly sat up.

Judas suppressed his giddiness at her aptitude. Would she truly be his equal? For a moment, he envisioned her future, someone the youth idolized, a hero for a new generation. But with great power came the seductive pull to do as one wished.

He pushed the thought aside.

"Good morning," Judas said, finding his voice at last.

Her amber eyes snapped to him, and she went still.

"I imagine you have a lot of questions, yes?"

He stifled a smile, noting the similarities between the question he posed and those of his old master, Fife Doole, who always spoke in a similar fashion.

Judas noted the fear on her face. He understood. She glimpsed a stranger and woke in a strange place.

"Do you understand me? You must still be in shock from the whole ordeal."

Now, her eyes darted around the room, frantic and quick, but always returning to him.

The fight-or-flight mode.

Her breathing quickened. He backed away, holding his hands up; he didn't want to seem like a threat.

I don't need someone else thinking of me that way.

Her lips parted, and a croaking voice came out.

"Water."

Judas withdrew his wand, summoned a mug and poured water from the tip. When he handed the mug to her, he was impressed she didn't react to his abilities.

Perhaps she hadn't noticed? Maybe shock? Or maybe his gamble paid off.

"Where am I?" she asked.

"You're in my home: the Lakayre Manor near Ralloc."

"Ral-lock? The capital of Sonkol?"

His eyes sparkled.

So, it worked!

"Yes, my dear, you're correct. Good!"

He pointed to the wardrobe with his wand, calling upon his essence, and pulling out a set of clothing for her. They draped over the chair in the corner of her room.

"Here are some clothes for you. Please, dress. I'll be downstairs. When you're ready, come down. A visitor came to see you. I'm sure you have many, many questions, and I'll answer what I can. The timing's a bit sensitive, but we'll take it in stride."

And he knew he'd said too much, but she also didn't seem too coherent. Maybe she wouldn't hear his blunderings?

With that, he let himself out of the room, closing the door behind him.

Chapter 9: The Betrayer

The Betrayer traveled as light-footed as possible, heading south with all haste, facing away from the two rising suns: Apor and Praema. The power to teleport long distances eluded him—as it did most people—but he managed over short distances. These little hops took hours, if not days, off his traveling. But he needed a journeyman and their porting stones.

Not too far ahead, just north of the Corridor of Cruelty, was Cape Gythmel. He could acquire one there and rest up before continuing. Everyone who traveled this way was grateful for the small town, regardless of the Corridor's proximity.

The deadline pressed down on him; a proverbial lynch tightening around his throat, Xilor holding the rope. Deadlines were a common occurrence. But unreasonable? Illogical. Perhaps now that he was closer to coming back, urgency played a role.

Impatience.

The Betrayer never followed Xilor willingly. The cloying assurance of power almost made the choice worth it, reveling in Xilor's shadow, and the hope of one day learning the dark lord's secrets.

Study the enemy from within.

But as an unwilling follower, he'd betrayed everyone, turning his back on his former life. Now, regret turned his thoughts to that fateful night, Xilor standing before him, a towering wraith, a dark blemish in the night. If he had to make the choice again, he'd make the same, but he turned contrite, realizing his position of weakness. Good reasons or not, he couldn't let the blood of the innocent stain his hands.

He did what he needed, even if unforgivable.

Tutelage at the dark lord's feet had been both horrifying and eye-opening. The magics he performed traumatized him, things other great wizards never did, not even Judas Lakayre.

Judas.

He swallowed. He hated Judas almost as much as himself.

No, that's not true. Not anymore.

That hatred abandoned him long ago. Once the dark lord's facade of power dropped, the Betrayer turned his hate towards Xilor, a creature that transformed him from a man of power into a sniveling lackey, searching for scraps, holding his breath.

But he never prayed for death. What kind of life did he give up for this one?

One that allows you to look at your reflection every morning.

Service to Xilor wasn't an equal trade. It was one-sided, Xilor's side. Even death wouldn't be a reprieve. On that stormy night of choices, with the rain pouring outside, the dark lord granted him one boon: he wouldn't kill for Xilor.

And those children … without them, Xilor held no power over him, and he would've never joined.

Death would be his choice.

He knew why he sided with Xilor, and it pained him. For the longest time, he blamed Judas Lakayre and the Kothlere Order, but the real reason, to his shame, was cowardice.

But the children still lived, and that's what truly mattered. That, and his current duty.

He trudged on, 'til late into the day, and at an inn at the Cape, he fell with weariness. Only then could he escape the consequences of his actions until the suns rose again.

Chapter 10: Julie

The elderly man exited her room, leaving her alone.

The first question that tumbled in her head was wondering where she was.

"You're in my home: the Lakayre Manor near Ralloc."

He must be Lord Lakayre, then.

The proper etiquette came to mind, remembering she shouldn't call him by his birth name unless he gave permission. Perhaps she should use a title, but which was the most proper: lord or arysto?

I don't remember learning this.

The knowledge was present, but not the memories.

She stared at the door for a handful of heartbeats, then surveyed her surroundings. The room, though spacious, was humble in adornments. Stained mahogany covered the floor. A cream-colored rug spread beneath the bed, and the windowsill matched in hue. A peaceful room, comfortable, and the situation could have been much, much worse.

It's not the first time I woke up and couldn't remember how I got there.

Or was it?

An odd sentiment somehow rang with truth.

A red comforter adorned her bed, and the lamp beside her bed was wickless. After searching, she touched the lamp and light surged in a ball of magic. The higher she touched the stand, the brighter the illumination. The converse was also true.

Climbing out of bed, she crept through the room, opening drawers and cabinets before spying the sprawling countryside through the window.

A potted plant—an ivy or something similar—sat on a handcrafted wood table, which looked as though it dated back several hundreds of years. The beautiful plant caught her eye again, lush and verdant. The bark's hue mirrored the floor.

She padded around the room, pausing to admire the peculiar art hanging on the wall. A shudder ran down her spine. The painting was dark and swirling, sinister-like with a diminished source of backlighting. It reminded her of what happened before—before she came here, wherever here was.

Her first memory.

She remembered a creeping chill and shuddered again.

The black shadow morphed in and out of the fog, feeding on her terror, sucking the life out of her, like stolen breath from her lungs.

Dark clouds swirled above, stone crumbled, statues came to life, swooping creatures, gaping maws, and razor-sharp claws. … Its gurgling voice and the sinister, hypnotic laugh filled her head even as it died.

A panic came over her, and her breath quickened with short, ragged gasps. Her forehead prickled with sweat, and she closed her eyes and clenched her fists, fighting for control.

She spied the clothes the elderly man had left for her, and she decided it was best not to remain alone, unless she wanted nightmares for company. With haste, she dressed in the robes and hurried downstairs.

At the first landing, the man beckoned to her.

"Come in."

He stood, his hands clasped behind his back, waiting.

"Good morning, sire."

He smiled at that, but it was more than genuine warmth. Perhaps pride? Uncertainty smothered her.

"Forgive me, sire, but I don't know who you are, not really."

"I know, my dear. I'm Judas Lakayre, and this is my manor. But we'll get to that in a moment. What else can you tell me?"

He seemed excited, but he tried to hide it.

The thought of the dark clouds and hooded menace flashed through her mind, the razor-sharp claws, jagged teeth for tearing, but she didn't want to remember.

"I can't remember anything for certain, vague images, feelings, flashes that don't make any sense. Can you explain it to me, sire?"

His smile put her at ease.

"Understandable. First, I want you to know I'll answer to the best of my abilities. Second, as I said before, timing's a bit of an issue. A precarious situation has arisen, and people need my help."

He leaned forward, putting the back of his hand beside his mouth, whispering conspiratorially.

"Nothing's worse than trying to save people who don't wish to be saved."

He straightened.

"Anyway, the situation warrants most of my attention, but I won't abandon you."

He waved his hand to the door.

"But first, your guest awaits. Staell, you may come in."

Julie peered over his shoulder, training her eyes on the front doors. As they opened, a white stallion—if it could even be called that due to its enormous size—walked in. It ducked low, clearing the entrance, its head near parallel to the floor. A single horn shot out of his forehead, a crystalline spire, something worthy of celestial beings.

Julie stood transfixed.

It's mammoth!

She noted its emerald eyes as he came to a stop.

With reverence, she neared him, scrutinizing the majestic creature, drinking in every detail.

The horn didn't come from within the skull, but rather like an exterior hardening on the unicorn's crown. The structure and the horn itself gleamed, a diamond formation. He glowed brighter the closer she drew, and she squinted as she circled the creature, hand extended, her touch tentative and soft.

The unicorn's translucent skin responded, radiating light in plumes like gentle, crackling energy absent of sound. Several times, she lowered her gaze to give her eyes a reprieve from the harsh luminance. She could peer through the unicorn's epidermis, his skin like a jellyfish, but she couldn't see all the way through. His white core grew opaque.

She circled back to his face.

The unicorn bowed his head.

Greetings, Madam Julie. I'm Staell. I trust I meet your satisfaction?

"Oh … my … Shades of the Underworld, he talks?"

She glanced back at Judas with earnestness, wondering if it was some trick.

"Well, sort of …"

Judas nodded.

"He speaks like all intelligent races of this realm. Staell's here to give you a gift."

"A gift?"

Yes, Madam Julie. A tress of my hair for your wand. I foresee you to have an affinity to heal. Should I ever need, I hope you bring your skill to my aid.

Staell nodded, and Judas proceeded.

Judas lifted a handful of his tail, cut a section with his knife, and held it up for Staell's inspection. Julie marveled when the hair grew back, near-instantaneous.

Staell dipped his head.

I must be going now—pressing matters with the Heir of the Krey. Madam Julie, it was a pleasant opportunity to meet you. May the Spirit of Fortune smile upon you.

On his way to the door, he turned back to face her again.

We have a word similar to your name in Ucoric. Ironic, isn't it?

She shook her head, not sure how to respond.

Perhaps someday I'll share it, when you're ready.

As he exited, Judas closed the doors with a wave of his wand.

She glanced at him, wariness slithering through her.

"You're a Rumigul user, aren't you? A sorcerer?"

"Warlock."

"What's the difference?"

He chuckled.

"Not much. Just the title."

She glanced at the hair in his hand.

"What do we do with his hair?"

"Now, my dear, we'll weave your wand."

Judas's gaze returned to the door where Staell departed. Julie sensed something happened between them, before her arrival, but the warlock kept the matter to himself.

"Weave?" she prodded, bringing his attention back to her. "Isn't wood used for wands?"

He blinked a few times, then turned back to her.

"Wands are made of wood, most of them, at least. Xilor fashioned his out of metal. Some wizards transformed their old ones into New Era wands. Let's begin, shall we?"

He pulled a small box from inside his robes and removed what appeared to her to be a tiny, silk wing with fine lines of diamond running throughout. Holding it up to the light as if to inspect it, he connected the hairs of Staell's tress to its tip.

"What's that?"

She shifted closer for a better view.

"This," he held the wing closer, "is the wing of a fairy. While you slept, I had a visit from her. Rumors of your arrival reached her ears, and she died believing you'll fulfill their prophecy."

"Died? Prophecy?"

"The fairies believe an ancient foretelling of a powerful mage coming from beyond the realm of magic, a perfect balance of light and dark. It was spoken into existence long ago, before I made the gateway."

He continued working, twining the fine hairs on the fragile wing with the aid of wizardry, but his lips twisted after he spoke of the gateway.

"What does that have to do with me?"

"Perhaps everything, perhaps nothing. The second part is that an elder fairy will give a wing to the mage. If the mage is the one, this will forever link the two races together, a greater power beyond death."

"Greater power?"

"They never say what this greater power meant, and no one agrees. It's a broad, vague term, like love in ours. There are many kinds of love, but none are the same."

He swallowed.

"Another curious thing about the prophecy is the term mage, neither male nor female. Does that mean it's open to interpretation?"

He smiled at her.

"How does this relate to me?"

Julie searched his face, watching his expressions while she tuned her ears to his words.

"The elder fairy believed you to be this mage. You're not the first to return. You're the thirteenth. I gave it a name years ago when the first one crossed back. Wcic."

"What was that? Whiz-sick?"

He gave a grim smile.

"Close enough. Wizardkind caught in crossover, a name to keep track, not to make it sound grand. The initialization stuck and became a word."

His eyes darted to her, and he continued speaking.

"Every time someone comes back, a fairy chooses to give up a wing for their wand. The one who died last night gave this one to you. You're fortunate, my dear."

He paused, a shrouded visage crossed his face, hesitating.

"What? Say it."

He sighed.

"By giving this wing, the fairy's forcing the prophecy into fruition and

58

potentially condemning you to certain death."

It took a moment for her to find her voice.

"What makes you think I'll die?"

"I don't, to be honest."

He shrugged.

"Who am I to make such a call?"

"Why would you say such a thing?"

A storm rumbled in her stomach, making her nauseous.

How can he be so calm while sentencing me to death? He's cold and lacks a soul! Where's his remorse?

As if he read her thoughts, he spoke, "I don't mean to be … indelicate, my dear. Only two other would-be wizards lived long enough to form bonds with the fairies, but they did not last long. One went mad with sudden abilities, all raw and unrefined. All twelve … passed."

"Died?"

He gave a single nod. He didn't make eye contact, and his fingers still worked the wing and hair.

She searched for the right words. A cascade of fear and panic washed over her.

"What if I don't accept the wing? I wouldn't die, right?"

Judas shook his head, a slow, sad movement.

"No."

He paused, turning his full attention to her.

"There are bonds even the oldest grimoires can't explain. The first is born of sacrifice. When someone gives their life for yours, the act forges a tether. If broken, the bond lashes back with ruin. Their death shields you—sometimes fatally for the one who threatens you.

"The second is harsher. Refuse the gift, deny the bond, and it turns inward. Life is the greatest price in magic, and wasting it carries a penalty that devours the unworthy.

"And the third … the rarest. It, too, is bound to sacrifice, but not of another's life. It's the rending of your own—an object, a person, an ideal, something carved from the self."

His lips thinned as he frowned.

"There's only one account of the third, and he went mad. We can't truly know the outcome."

He drew a long, steady breath through the nose.

"You must understand, even I can't fully grasp this. It's an ancient, powerful magic. I may be called the strongest warlock alive, but I'm insignificant to those who once wielded those ancient enchantments. Legend says Hagen was the only one who enabled the third sacrifice."

He chuckled to himself, his eyes bright with mirth.

"That reminds me. When I was a young man, I used to joke about an ancient curse on the Lakayre bloodline. Perhaps I shouldn't make light of what I don't understand."

Her brows twitched downward, trying to understand the implications.

"So, I must accept the wing?"

He dipped his head once.

"Did you know she'd do this?"

Julie rubbed an itch away from the tip of her nose.

His lips pursed as he moved his head side to side.

"Yes and no. As of late, the elder fairies vowed to shun the divination, thus nullifying it. I assumed all believed the same, but I misjudged one."

She must've made a face, because he continued on.

"There are those among the fairies who don't believe in the ancient soothsaying, but she staked her life on the belief that you were the mage."

"What will it do?"

"It'll become the core of your wand. I've never heard of a wand possessing a dual core of unicorn hair and a fairy wing. Should be interesting, especially as their Head of Creatures."

Her eyes narrowed, trying to decipher what he meant.

"Their Head of Creatures? What's that? Like a queen?"

He chortled at her remark, shaking his head.

"No, it's a sacred duty and a privilege. This wing, her sacrifice, your wand —they bind you in a way others will never know. They've aided you, and you must return that, in your own way."

He glanced down at the wing and hair.

"There we are. Ready to begin?"

Reaching into his robes, he withdrew his wand. With a flick of his wrist, the potted plant from her room popped into existence. He reached out and attached the wing and hairs to the bottom of the plant.

"It's customary for the one who wishes to create the wand to do this, but exceptions must be made."

The plant floated in the air; the hairs dangled with a lazy list. Judas tapped both the left and right sides, and the greenery fell away, leaving just the wood. He stretched his left hand out, palm up, beneath the ivy. It gave a slight shudder, immobilized.

With the tip of his wand, he pointed to the top of the plant. He tapped once. The ensemble began to twist, the ivy and hair moving in opposite directions.

Pulling his right hand away, he left his hand beneath, the twisting plant hovering above. Soon, the ivy, wing, and hairs, spun too fast for Julie to perceive other than a blur. A pale white light flickered into existence at the tip and grew brighter, working down the length.

Abruptly, the spinning stopped; a plain piece of wood floated before her eyes, carrying the same dark color as the potted plant. The faintest undertones of white like Staell adorned the tip.

Otherwise, it seemed unremarkable.

Julie felt crestfallen at the lack of magnificence. She expected something more. Her wary glance prompted a nod from the warlock.

She reached out, cautious; her fingers brushed the newly formed wood. At her touch, the same white glow reappeared but faded when she snatched her hand away. Again she reached out, but this time, she grasped the base with her fingertips.

The wand glowed again, changing at her touch, her essence imprinting, binding them together.

At the base, a crisp midnight blue materialized with pinpricks of startling white and silver, reminding her of a cloudless night sky and twinkling stars. The deep blue faded up the length, changing to cobalt, sky blue, cyan, and the tip crowned in the purest of whites, like fresh snow.

The glow faded, the binding ritual complete, and she couldn't help but smile.

Breathtaking!

"This, my dear, is your wand!"

She noted the pride in his voice.

"It's stunning. Thank you..."

"Congratulations. Now, we must be off. We've lingered too long."

"Isn't this your home?"

"Yes, but a tale for another time. Suffice to say, we're here so I could retrieve a book."

Her right eyebrow shot up.

"A book?"

He smiled faintly.

"A good one, too."

"What book?"

His head tilted to the side.

"I'm rather secretive about this one. I'll tell you later, I promise. For now, we must hurry. Return to the room and pack a bag. There are robes in the drawers."

Julie eyed him for a moment, knowing he refrained from telling her everything.

She didn't appreciate his omissions. Her heart fluttered, and her breathing thundered in her ears. What was she missing?

She swallowed and nodded, turning to the stairs, taking them two at a time. She yearned to trust him; he seemed nice, but he held back.

Why?

And what was the big deal about telling her about the book? What did she really know about him?

Nothing.

Was she just supposed to take everything on blind faith? That'd be ludicrous.

She glanced at her wand while she entered the bedroom.

For a moment, it didn't quite matter. She could figure it out later. Right now, she had a beautiful wand, met a unicorn, and a fairy made a sacrifice for her.

Hell of a way to wake up—again.
With alacrity, she started to pack.

Chapter 11: Dlad City

Judas eyed his surroundings, and like all teleports, it took a heartbeat to reacclimatize to the new location.

Dlad City stood as a stark contrast from Ralloc. Though smaller, he marveled at the growth and development each time he returned. Ralloc wallowed in its rigid ways—which Judas found comfort in his lack of conformity during changing times—whereas Dlad City adapted to change.

This growing town had no shame in its aspirations, like a public tryst in broad daylight, whereas Ralloc preferred the propriety of curtains.

He started off and Julie walked beside him, her eyes round, her head swiveling, taking in the sights. This was the first metropolitan area she'd visited, and she kept ogling at the size.

He smiled. If she only knew the size of Ralloc.

People moved from the capital to the flourishing urban areas, but for every family leaving Ralloc, ten more arrived, hoping to lay claim to a more prosperous life.

The pair walked down the main road, and compared to the opulent, northern metropolis, the foot traffic was scant.

Wide buildings of white stone and wood hedged the main thoroughfare, something unfound in Ralloc. Lack of space required architects to build up, not out.

Light, merry music trembled through the early morning air. Clumped dirt churned in their wake, sticking to their boots. A few robes from his home fit Julie's small frame, and though she wasn't as small as Meristal, he'd need to buy her a few more before the journey.

While Julie took in the sights, he kept an eye out for something else entirely. On the Other Side, he'd been attacked, and who knew if they'd try again, whoever they were. But the question remained: was he the target, or her?

To keep them both safe, they set to the road.

Off to the east side of town, Judas spied newer buildings in the distance. The progress created many jobs for younger men of the city.

The air was warmer than Ralloc's—a city which snuggled against the Vikal Mountains, swathed in a constant, cool breeze coming down from snow-capped mountaintops.

Judas's stomach grumbled, and the scent of eggs, bacon, bread, and various fruits caused Julie's stomach to echo his.

"We'll break our fast once we reach our destination," he promised.

"I can wait. I wish I could see Ralloc."

"It may be some time before that happens."

"Tell me about it."

His eyes remained forward. A few dozen people milled about through the street, ghosts for all it mattered. Judas, used to traveling through the packed streets of Ralloc, weaved through with ease.

"There's a long, sloping street leading to the front doors of the castle, home of the Kothlere Council. Though a straight line from the furthest gate to the castle, the gates can be closed between the walled tiers. The entire city lies in a valley and against the Vikal Mountains. They've constructed as high up as they can on the mountain, and now, they expand into the valley. Every few legends, they construct a new exterior wall."

He peeked over his shoulder. Julie walked behind him, her eyes on him, her expression a mix of interest and waiting. He turned to the front and continued.

"In the first two tiers of the city, those closest to the castle, is where the noble and minor noble houses reside. About five percent of the population live there. Relative to the castle, the outer limits expand in a massive two hundred and seventy-degree arc. It's a sight to behold.

"Sounds like a plague."

Judas chuckled at her dark sarcasm.

An interesting perspective laced with a tinge of truth.

"How wide is Ralloc?"

His brow furrowed as he thought.

"At the widest? Twenty kilometers."

The warlock heard the titters of women and glanced in that direction, aware that Julie mirrored him.

Prostitutes waved at a younger gentleman walking in the street; he dipped his head, waved, and promised to frequent their establishment later. The ladies blew him kisses.

The elder faced forward, a frown forming. Try as he might, he couldn't help holding his nose up at the wenches. He never understood how women could stoop so low, but as the adage went: prostitution was the first profession.

Judas continued with his recounting.

"It's an injustice to call Ralloc beautiful; it's majestic. Steeple roofs and spires reach for the sky. Each spring, the few, daring men climb atop and paint the clay shingles after the long, hard winters. And you won't find finer manicured lawns; the hired help turn gardening into artistry.

"Two ages ago, stained glass swept through Ralloc like wild fire, and the color brought the buildings to life. But the greatest, in my opinion, is the Ralloc Library. It's massive; a monolith seemingly chiseled out of one piece of marble."

They passed storefronts hugging the broad street to the left and right. Hammers clanked in the distance, pinging off armor or weapons. Shops of cloth, groceries, and bakeries.

Judas peeked back at Julie as they headed for the north end of town.

The muffled tap-tap, tap-tap of horses' hooves pattered on the hard packed roads. Men dressed in the finest robes meandered down the road, and merchants stood on porches hugging their emporiums, awaiting patronage, hoping for coin.

"Pedestrians in Ralloc are of every race; far more common in larger communities than here in Dlad City. I'm sure a few other races are here, though. When we make it to Ralloc, prepare to get jostled a bit, or if brave enough, you can take to the skywalks between buildings."

"Sounds a bit too busy for me."

Judas understood the sentiment, exhaustion a constant companion in Ralloc.

"How many people live in the capital?"

"Last census was about an epoch ago—a hundred years. The city holds two million, but we broke five million for the entire domain, from Ralloc to the Corridor of Cruelty and all the way to the Golden City. Oh, and children under the Age of Maturity weren't counted."

"Please, please," a call came from in front and to the right.

Judas caught Julie's shocked expression as a goblin came hurrying toward her.

"Look at my wares!" the goblin said. "I like, you buy!"

He held a vase up to her for inspection. Judas kept walking, but Julie's steps faltered, a mistake Judas made in his youth. Once you slow down, you will be lucky to leave alive.

"No, thank you," he heard her say.

"So cheapest; I like, you buy. Best wares anywhere, you ask satisfied customer!"

"Sorry."

He glanced back in time to see the creature trying to grab her robe sleeve, but she brushed him off, and the goblin stumbled, almost dropping his vase.

The goblin shouted in his language, and Julie hurried to catch up.

They reached Traveler's Respite moments after Julie caught up with him, the door opening at their approach, a young boy inside.

"Oh, thank you," Julie said.

Judas took note of the front desk of hickory and brass, the latter shined from the ample candlelight. A fire crackled in the room to the left; chairs and tables crowded the chamber, and two dozen patrons ate their meal. A dark carpet of cobalt with narrow, crisscrossing crimson lines throughout covered the floor.

With the front counter lacking staff, Judas rang the small brass bell. He regarded Julie.

"Best if we don't use my real name. I'm Willem Fossard, and you'll be my daughter. Willem and Cynthia Fossard."

"Why not use your real name?"

"I'd rather be safe."

A plump, short woman with curly orange hair and light, golden freckles came from the back room.

"Greetings this morning, good sire. Welcome to the Traveler's Respite. The two of ya'? No missus?"

Judas shook his head.

"The two of us, no Mrs. We'd like two rooms, please."

"Very kind of you, sire, allowing your daughter her privacy."

She opened a ledger and dipped the quill in ink.

"Your names?"

"Willem and Cynthia Fossard."

"Oh!" the lady squeaked. "Minor noble, how lucky we are! I hope you enjoy your stay with us. It'll be two bits a night and comes with two meals a day, breakfast and dinner. How many nights, Lord Fossard?"

"For now, let's do two."

"Warlock Lakayre?" a voice called out.

Judas froze, his shoulders tense. He sought out the voice.

Todd, the writer, stood with his mouth gaping open.

"I didn't expect you until closer to midday."

With a tight jaw, Judas greeted him.

"Morning, Todd."

The warlock glanced back to the woman at the counter, her mouth agape. He gave her a sheepish smile.

"Sorry, I didn't want to concern you. If it's any consolation, I'm still minor noble."

She paled and nodded.

Reaching between the outer and inner robe, procuring his coin purse, he pulled it free. He pushed eight copper bits forward.

"For the rooms."

And he pushed five silver chips forward.

"For discretion."

Her eyes flickered from him to the coins and back half a dozen times before she smiled and scooped up the money.

"Lord Fossard, your rooms are on the second floor, first one on the right and last one on the left. Sorry, these two rooms are the closest together."

She passed two keys across the wood surface, careful not to make contact with him. The warlock ignored this, used to it by now.

Judas flourished a smile.

"Those will do fine, my dear."

He turned and discovered Julie's fallen expression, and he followed her glowering gaze to the dining room and the patrons within. Their gazes were placid, neither friendly nor scowling ... at first. Once the shock abated, suspicion and wariness greeted them.

The looks of disgust were meant for him.

A flush came over Julie's face, and he sensed her resentment. A titter of half-hidden laughter came from a cluster of young women. Others whispered. Long ago, Judas learned to let go of the anger.

If only closed minds came with closed mouths.

Then again, he had no room to talk.

Julie took a step in the direction of the dining room, but he held out a hand, snatching her by the arm.

"Pay no heed, my dear. Their laughs and whispers are for me, not you."

"Why would they do that?"

66

"Because they're young, rich, and foolish."

He winked at her.

"And because they can."

"I don't understand! There's nothing wrong with you! They're afraid."

"Fools often are. Only a fool can choose to abandon his folly, and a wise man would waste his breath trying to show them a path they aren't ready to walk. Forget about them."

He waved them off.

"It's about me, the war, and you're guilty by association."

"And that's why," Todd said from beside them, "this interview is more important than ever."

Judas regarded the young man, then made introductions.

"Todd, this is my apprentice, Julie. Julie, this young man is Todd, a columnist for the New Suns Times. He's been hounding me for an interview for nigh a year. Apparently persistence is key."

Todd smiled. His eyes darted between the two for a moment, then he gave Julie his full attention. They locked eyes, and her polite smile made Todd melt.

Judas felt the ripple of allurement between them, the faint, unseen stirring within his youthful associates.

The *magelust*.

The longer his apprentice and the scribe stared at each other, the stronger the pull. What passed off as infatuation would turn to full-blown lust for both of them, and quicker than they realized.

Judas spotted the glittering in Todd's eyes. He needed to look out for her best interests. She wasn't ready to face this burden, nor have indelicate moments with a stranger in view of everyone.

Knowing this would be a good time to break the two up, he stepped close to Julie, his back to Todd, blocking their eye contact, and pulled out a gold coin.

He handed it to her.

"A bright eye?"

Her eyes went wide. They narrowed just as quick, concern on her face.

"What's this for?"

"We passed, at least, four tailoring shops on the way here. Have your measurements taken and two sets of robes made. Todd and I will need some time. We'll have more made when we reach our destination."

He addressed the young man.

"In installments, okay?"

Todd shrugged, his blue eyes sparkling, happy the moment was coming to pass. Julie beamed and thanked Judas. He gave her a key to her room, the one closest to the stairs while he took the one at the end of the hall.

Both men watched her go.

"I think I'm in love," Todd whispered.

"No, probably not. Magelust, that's all. If you're not careful, she might inadvertently destroy your mind and make you think you're a pretty little girl with pink bows in your hair. Come on; let's get this over."

Judas climbed the stairs to the second floor with Todd in tow. He pushed open the door and entered the snug room holding a modest bed. He tossed his pack on the thin turquoise quilt with gold stitching. Two pillows stuffed with feathers sat at the head. A low flame flickered above a feeble bed of coals. The would-be fire lacked a comforting warmth.

Todd pushed past the threshold, taking a seat in one of the brown chairs, then opened his small satchel and pulled out his supplies.

Why did I agree with this?

The warlock's eyes flickered to the mantle and the crystal filled with a light brown, almost golden liquid. Though still the hour for breakfast, it was a good time for a drink. He hoped a strong, stiff brew lay within. Pouring himself a cup, he sniffed.

A small smile pulled at the corners of his mouth, recognizing the vanilla and peach scent. A favorite! It was as expensive as it smelled. Even the name, Parlaquay, exuded a cultivated allusion.

If today didn't go well, he'd be reimbursing the hotel for a devoured bottle.

Parlaquay came from the south of Ralloc's control. The domains of Ralloc and Marcoalyn fell under the Kothlere Council's sway, but the influence ended at the Melodic Mountains in the south. On the other side was the Geim domain, where Parlaquay was made.

Judas eyed Todd.

The kid grated his nerves, dredging up memories best left buried deep. But Todd wanted to breathe life back into a haunted past. Todd scratched the parchment with his quill.

Too late to back out now.

Judas reached down, his shoulder-length hair falling like a curtain past his azure eyes, pulled out two logs from their sleeve, and set them on the bed of coals. Todd shifted in the seat behind him, the chair creaking.

Judas stood facing the hearth, absentmindedly pulling on his long, thick goatee. The war never gave him a choice, but he wished to spare Julie a similar fate.

Judas was a cursed man, a fact he was well aware—even if he once joked about it. Ghosts from failures and past mistakes haunted his footsteps.

He lifted his crystal glass to his lips and took a long, smooth pull. Sweet—too sweet unless mixed or sipped.

"Want one?" Judas offered, lifting his tumbler so his visitor could catch a glimpse.

He never took his eyes off the fire. When no response came, he took another swig. His guest made no noise other than the constant scratching.

"I'm surprised you found my manor last night."

"Sounds like you didn't expect me to."

Ignoring the comment too close to authenticity, Judas posed a question instead.

"How long did you wait again?"

"Until midnight."

"That's dedication."

Judas faced the young writer. Most couldn't muster the courage to talk to a warlock, but Todd's audacity made him believe and hope.

She *would be a little older than Todd.*

His mind turned to Julie and the world she came from, where time vanishes, lives pass infinitely quick compared to Ermaeyth. On the *Other Side*, lives lasted a tenth of what they do in the magical world.

Judas swallowed, pushing thoughts of his apprentice and his long-dead daughter away.

Hurt helped bury the subject. From the moment he held her, he'd fallen into a deeper love than he'd never known. The memory was all he had.

Xilor's followers were responsible for ripping her away. He made them pay, either in death or exile. In the aftermath of his daughter's demise, rage consumed him. Those were dark moments in his history.

Only Meristal pulled him back from the precarious ledge.

"Where do you want to begin?" Todd asked, glancing up.

His eyes were pale blue under black hair.

"Your family name. You're always hounding me but withheld your House name."

But Judas knew the truth. He used it as a stalling tactic.

"I tell you every time in Ralloc, but you never listen."

"I only hear you flapping your gums," Judas teased.

"Oh, you hear me, but you don't listen."

The younger man sighed and slouched forward.

Brass, kid, real solid.

"House Wynters, and before you say anything else, I work for the New Suns Times, but you already know that. Any more stalling tactics? You may not like my job, but my passion is in inspiring stories, like yours, Master Lakayre."

"You've come to the wrong wizard for an inspirational story, Arysto Wynters."

"Why do you say that? You fought a war and came out unscathed."

"Unscathed? Ever pick up a history book in school?"

"There were gaps left out."

Judas snorted.

"True enough. I'll give you what you asked for, but I don't want it spun in a web of half-truths, making a whole city hate or fear me; I want to be ..."

"Normal?" Todd interjected. "Alone?"

"I'm already alone."

"Why do I have a feeling I'm going to need a stiff drink for this?"

"'Cause you are a smart boy."

Judas gave him a knowing grin. He sat his glass on the hearth and pulled another, setting it by his and filled both, giving himself a more generous serving. With the conversation about to turn ugly, a walk through the Underworld, a little more alcohol couldn't hurt.

Glasses in hand, he stepped close and handed one to the young man.

Todd breathed deep and took a cautious sip. His eyes widened in surprise.

"That's amazing! I never tasted anything like it! What is it? Where do you find something this good?"

"One of the privileges of traveling Ermaeyth, you experience all types of foods and drinks. It's called Parlaquay and hails from the Geim domain."

The elder smiled and patted his shoulder, then took a seat opposite of him.

"There's a lot to tell. Do you remember how to cast the spell so your quill will do all the work while you sit and listen?"

"I think so," Todd replied.

After a few unsuccessful attempts, Judas removed his wand and did the deed.

Judas held up a finger.

"If you misquote me in your editing process, or lie about anything I say, it'll be bad for you."

"Don't worry about me! Worry about the publisher. When they read something they don't like, they want to adjust it, which alters the accuracy and reality of what's said."

Judas leaned forward.

"If your publisher won't let you publish as is, and you can't find an honest one, I'll fund your work myself."

"Really? I always got the impression you didn't like me."

"Quite right."

Judas would never tell him that he enjoyed the spitfire attitude, and he found it refreshing.

"Where do you want me to begin my story?"

"Anywhere is fine. I could ask questions or you could just talk."

"Whichever you prefer."

The investigative writer fired off at ballistic speed.

"Alright, we'll start with me asking questions and go from there. What's the year of your birth? What did your parents do for a living? Any family people don't know? What did you want to be when in your youth? How did the war affect your personal life? Ever been married? Are you seeing someone now? Tell me about your friends!"

"Whoa! Slow down! You're going to stroke out! Cork the enthusiasm. Remember, you're a journalist now, a code of conduct is expected. Breathe. Compose yourself, and try again."

Todd caught his breath and sat back in his chair.

"Do you have any friends?"

"No. Let me rephrase: Yes, one, sort of. It's complicated. She hasn't been around for a tour of years, but she returned last night. I'm looking forward to spending time with her."

"Who is she? Do I know her?"

"Yes. I believe you would know her from being one of the best Advocates of Law in Ralloc. She never fancied to be a politician or a lawyer, you know?

But after the atrocities of the Wizard's War, she told me the only frontier for new adventures belonged in the political arena. Those in roles of authority found her views too drastic for the comfort, so she turned to law."

"What's her name?"

"Meristal Raviils."

"I know her! She's on assignment, a tour down south, right?"

The journalist paused before moving on.

"Is it true she's an appariel?"

"Yes, she can change her appearance to whatever she likes. Isn't this interview supposed to be about me?"

"Any other friends?" Todd asked as he reclined, trying to mimic his interviewee.

"No."

"Why not? What did you do to drive people away? Why don't you have many friends, Master Wizard?"

"Because you didn't use my official title. You should say warlock. If we went by an official title, I'd be Grand Maghai."

"Boast much?"

"Boasting implies there isn't much truth to the statement."

The writer leaned forward, his interest piqued.

"Why are you a warlock? Why is being one bad? What makes someone a warlock?"

Judas's lips twitched.

"People are born warlocks, and I was one since birth. It's just a title, nothing more. The choices we make determine how we're labeled. But the gospel leaked, so to speak. No one cared until they found the link between me and Xilor."

"What link?"

"We do magic the same. No incantations. We think and it happens. But he's a sorcerer, a warlock that dabbles in questionable conjury for malevolent purposes. So, after I had destroyed him, they exiled me."

"That's it?"

Judas gave a single nod.

"Yes. I can do things with magic others can't, that's it. No incantations, songs, dances, or scrolls. Nothing more, and just the same as Hagen."

"Who's Hagen?"

"Damn!" Judas leaned forward, nearly coming out of his seat, dumbfounded by the lack of education in the young generation. "Don't they teach you anything in school anymore? I pity the ignorance of youth."

"Sure, but I don't remember anyone named Hagen."

"Don't worry about it; he's only the Father of Magic. It's not relevant. Next."

"Your family. What are your feelings about your mom and dad and your late brother?"

"I don't want to talk about my brother."

Judas took a breath, trying not to turn maudlin.

"Some things are better left buried in the past."

"If you're not willing to talk about anything, what are we doing here besides wasting our time?"

Brass, and a point to boot.

Judas sighed.

"He was my older twin. Born on separate days, but we appear somewhat similar. That's all the commonality we had. He was an extrovert, well-liked, the first born ... Adoration was all he cared about. I'm the opposite. I discovered books, hoping that one day I'd outshine him."

"Why does being first born matter?"

"Our father was a man of outdated traditions."

Judas twisted his goatee.

"Did you?" Todd asked.

"Did I what?"

"Outshine your brother?"

Judas paused a moment, hoping his words didn't come out full of regret.

"In more ways than I care to admit. Wizard's War aside, I was a man not so different from everyone else, but my brother's ambitions ... he sold me out trying to achieve the coveted consul office. No one cared about my abilities until they found out Xilor was a sorcerer—then everyone drew an unjust connection."

"This is great stuff!"

Todd watched the quill dance under invisible influence. Judas made sure the boy found his scowl when he made eye contact again. Todd's smile faltered.

"You don't realize how many people are going to want to read about you, about your life. They're going to know they don't need to be afraid of you."

"One can only hope."

His eyes drifted toward the window, pushing out with his essence, reaching for Julie. He found her with ease, her potency radiant. He'd need to teach her how to dampen it. Obscuring her aura would make her harder to detect.

Don't forget blocking the magelust.

His mind groaned.

The magelust responded differently to everyone and blocking it required self-discovery; though unteachable, instruction on dampening her aura would give her the foundation of where to start. It was a subconscious response, and it affected the few who couldn't block it.

"What's your next question, Todd?"

"How'd your brother die?"

"In combat. Xilor took him."

"I thought you said your brother was a politician? If so, how did he get on the field of battle?"

"Image meant everything to Josiah, something he learned in our youth. The same can be said of his political career."

"How do you mean?"

"Every once in a while, my brother came to the battlefields. He boosted low morale with appearances, shaking hands, and sometimes engaging in a small skirmish. The oddest part? He was on the battlefield the day before. I didn't expect him for at least another moon turn."

"Why did he come?"

Judas leaned forward. Todd mirrored him.

"I always wondered myself. To make matters more interesting, Xilor teleported into our midst, winked into existence, and sent a blast of energy that knocked down all those around him. I threw up a mage shield in time. For a second, a blink of an eye, my sight fell away from Xilor. When I faced him, I saw him kill my brother, dissolved into nothing."

Judas snapped his fingers.

"Within my grasp."

He snapped again.

"My brother died."

He snapped a third time.

"And just like that, both gone."

He leaned back in his chair, and the young man did the same.

"But we learned a lot from Xilor."

"You're kidding, right?"

"Not at all, Todd; Xilor had ingenuity. I never imagined such abilities, to move between time and space near-instantaneously. I learned to teleport from him, and in many ways, Xilor led me to the answers of how to stop him. Most people lack the power to teleport, but that doesn't stop Ralloc from capitalizing on such a discovery. Though originally Xilor's ability, we incorporated the ability in journey-stones and portals."

Judas rubbed his mustache with his left hand.

"Another invention of Xilor's is the Psimond spell. Instant communication across vast distances on a flat surface. Who would've thought? You can thank him for that, too. Imagine what we could learn from someone as ingenious as him, albeit without the devastation."

Todd looked away, and Judas knew he'd made the boy uncomfortable.

The writer's eyes flickered back to him.

"If the dark lord held the power to teleport into your midst, why didn't he before? Why didn't he kill you? You're the much bigger threat."

Judas's brow arched.

"I've wondered the same. Perhaps Xilor didn't think much of me as a threat, or he mistook me, or did it to demoralize me. He proved himself superior that day, right in front of everyone. Destruction of morale. The vulgar display worked in his favor. The ordeal shook me to the core, and I've never seen magic like that before or since."

"If he killed you, the outcome would have been very different."

Judas nodded, his mind formulating a way to break the interview, using his apprentice as the reason. He needed to secure her safety. Maybe the council was behind it, maybe not. Sedrus claimed they weren't.

"Something wrong?" Todd asked.

"Hmm…?" Judas blinked, reining in his thoughts. "No, of course, not. Can't a warlock act a little suspicious? Adds to the mysterious aura."

His infectious smile made the correspondent smile, too.

"Listen, Todd, can we convene at some other time? I haven't eaten breakfast, and I'd be remiss not to give the majority of my attention to my apprentice."

"Oh, sure," Todd grumbled with evident disappointment.

"Don't worry. I'm not dodging your questions, but I get cranky if I don't eat."

"I understand."

Todd's tone showed he didn't.

"I promise I won't take on another scribe until we complete your interview and you publish. Sound agreeable?"

Todd hesitated, but seeing that he wouldn't get anything else, he nodded.

"Alright."

Judas bid his farewells, the young man retreating down the stairs. He closed the door behind him and let out a sigh of relief.

I don't want to suffer that again.

The window caught his eye, and he found Julie again. The urgent need to train her festered. If he could feel her presence, others could, too. They might even use her to track him.

Soon enough, they'd slip through the Corridor of Cruelty, and no one could follow them through. They'd be safe until they exited.

His stomach grumbled, reminding him that he and Julie needed to eat, and set off to find her.

Chapter 12: Outpost Dire—The Hive

Staell crested the last rise, his eyes falling upon House Eti, the school for the inhabitants. Nestled behind towering trees and the treacherous crags, high in the Vikal Mountains, lay Outpost Dire. Snow drifted heavily in the winter—torrents of ice and snow flurries—but the summers remained pleasant, light rains and cool breezes.

Few dared to venture close; even fewer came willingly. The mysteries surrounding this place were as sharp as the jagged spires. All the rumors rang with one note, the nickname: the Hive.

The school rose four stories high, built against the mountain to thwart an attack from behind. The giant, circular building lacked beauty, built to house and train warriors. Every aspect was meticulously efficient, nothing for vanity's sake, and used as a last line of defense.

A small town—the actual outpost—encroached the keep.

Steep, narrow stairs led up ten meters to the front doors. The optimal width served to choke an invading army. If an enemy took the stairs, the width would whittle their numbers.

A mock battleground in front, dubbed the 'killing field,' stretched twice as long as House Eti and supplied numerous obstacles: uneven ground, trenches, steps, chokepoints, and multidimensional platforms. Now, like every day, swords, hammers, axes, and pikes rang out come rain, sleet, snow, ice, or sunshine.

The clanging died abruptly when Staell came into view. No walls surrounded the place. The warriors gawked. Most had never seen one of his kind, a natural reaction.

One man came forward and dropped to a knee in reverence.

"Welcome to Outpost Dire, may you rest easy among your friends in the Hive. What's your bidding, master?"

Oblus Eti, Staell greeted him, the start of their infamous saying.

The shock in the soldier's eyes was unmistakable.

"Oblus Eti."

I've come to speak with the Heir of Valin.

"And so you shall. Please, follow me."

The warrior led Staell through the heart of the 'killing field' and up the steps to the keep's massive iron doors. Inside, in the center of the room, was a training ring referred to as 'The Pit.' Onlookers and fighters lined the ring while they watched fighters in the slight depression in the floor.

Alcoves lined the outer walls, most used for housing weapons and armor, others for small study areas. Two massive staircases lined the curved walls and led to the second floor and beyond. Many smaller staircases spiraled along the walls in strategic intervals. Adolescents carrying laundry baskets, food, armor, and cleaning products slinked through the doors leading away. A waft of fire-charred meat, boiled vegetables, and a tinge of citrus fruit drifted through the chamber every time a novice used the doors.

Heads turned toward Staell as the guide took him to the second floor. Even the fighting in The Pit stopped. His guide ushered him into an office on the second floor that overlooked The Pit below.

Again the guide knelt.

"Is there anything I can get for you, food or water? The journey must have been long and difficult."

A trickle of humor wormed its way through Staell. No one knew much about the unicorns.

I don't require anything.

He moved to the balcony, sticking his head out to watch the fighters below.

"I'll let the heir know you have called."

The man left.

Staell caught the movement of a robed figure below, and she ducked through a door.

Ah, an A'uri.

Ralloc boasted three castes of battlemages, the Aegis for defense, the Barrage for offense, and the Pharmacon for healing. The Hive battlemages were of a different breed. Ralloc used specific wizards for each caste, the Hive's A'uri could perform all three simultaneously. None were masters of specific crafts, but they formed meticulous pupils and formidable foes. To be fair, most gravitated to one or the other discipline.

But even A'uri would pause before taking on a Krey, the blood-lusting berserkers fighting in The Pit below. Their trance protected them against pain and fatal wounds within reason. Enchanted armor enhanced their defenses against magic.

Unique abilities turned all here into societal outcasts. The Krey for their bloodlust malady, who learned the finer points of slaughtering their enemies. The A'uri for their mind meld, gaining control over the voices in their head.

That same woman A'uri slipped back into the main room, and Staell tracked her movements as she moved across the room to a staircase.

Hello, A'uri.

She paused on the stairs, locking eyes with him, and she smiled, dipping her head in greeting, then hurried off.

The A'uri, when their powers manifested, cried out and acted possessed. An A'uri would come, block the voices, and abscond the victim to the Hive. The ability's other side, entering other people's minds and controlling them, made them perfect for battle with blood-frenzied Krey. For battle cohesion, they'd meld multiple minds into a fighting unit, thus giving them an uncanny hive-like mind.

Staell sensed a presence coming towards the office, but it wasn't magic that allowed him to perceive the approach. Instead, it was a gift innate in all unicorns.

A graying heir entered the office. When it came to stature of the wizardkind, he was on the low end. Staell gazed down at the man. He was a round, meaty man with a pointy mustache and a matching wispy patch on his chin.

Oblus ina'ti Sepan Eti, Heir.

"Oi! A formal greeting! Not many people know our words. Oblus ina'ti Sepan Eti."

He waded deeper into the office, eyeing Staell as he did.

"Do you know what our words mean?"

Staell dipped his head.

Live and die by the sword.

The man grinned and gave a nod.

"And House Eti?"

House of the Sword.

The heir chuckled, waved toward the balcony and front doors.

"What do you think of our humble home?"

Staell narrowed his eyes.

It's suitable for your number of five thousand. A self-sustaining town with every person holding a second profession as craftsmen or blacksmiths. And out here in the mountains, you're far away from the council. That's always a plus. Have you been drinking?

The heir gave a single nod.

"Damn right."

But it's not even mid-morning.

The heir shrugged.

"Could be dead tomorrow, so why abstain?"

Staell took that morsel and held onto it. While the unicorns didn't have many dealings with the outside world, he knew as much about Krey as they did of him.

So, it's true; you live like you'll fall in battle.

"By the Underworld, we do!"

The heir strolled behind his desk and reached for the cupboard.

"They expect us to jump in first. To die. Why live with reservations?"

Grabbing a goblet and a flagon of wine, he filled his cup, turned to face Staell, and raised it in a toast.

"Today's my birthday; here's to another year."

He gulped it down and refilled his cup.

"Here's to all that commotion down in the Pit and the headache it's going to give me."

He slammed the cup back and went to refill his glass again. Once filled, he raised it again to Staell.

"Here's to seeing a unicorn, a rare sight in these parts!"

He drank in the same manner and refilled his cup and settled himself behind his desk.

That's probably not healthy, even for a Krey.

"Neither is not having my cock sucked, but here we are. Know what else ain't healthy? Being impaled by a sword."

Staell cocked his head.

There haven't been any battles in a long time, Heir.

To that, the man grunted. His eyes flickered to the balcony where the cacophony of fighting rose up.

"So, what brings you to my humble shit hole—I mean—outpost?"

He had to nearly shout to be heard.

War's coming, Heir.

"I've heard that before."

He sighed.

"Gods, just the thought of a good fight gets me hard."

A loud clanging of swords drowned out the heir as he rolled his eyes. He walked to the balcony, leaning against the rail.

"Stop that racket!" he bellowed. "I can't hear the unicorn talk!"

Technically, I don't—

The heir whirled around.

"Don't start!"

He returned to his desk, grabbing his goblet, sloshing some wine onto the desk. He glanced at it, then his cup, then leaned forward and slurped at it. When he finished, he leaned back and wiped his mouth with the back of his hand.

"As I've said, I've heard that before, about war. There's none to be had. It ended with the death of Xilor."

He's returning, Heir.

"Ha! Not likely, though I'd almost wish for it, just to grease the cogs. It'd be like an orgasm after a decade of celibacy."

We've foreseen it.

"What's this we shit? Don't tell me you're talking about that cracked warlock, are you? The Shades can fuck him in the ass for all I care. Granted, he killed plenty in his day, but the man's lost it."

Yes, he's aware. But I'm referring to the maghai of unicorns, myself included. I've already done my duty to the council as emissary for my people.

The color drained from the heir's face, and he reached for the bottle, bypassing the cup entirely, and gulped generously.

"Of gods and demons."

The maghai were a council of five unicorns answering to the grand maghai. Wizardkind adopted the formal titles, abbreviating it to mage. All magical professions fell under a maghai, a council of them answering to the grand maghai.

"When was this? How long ago did you have your premonition?"

Ten days past, and the 'cracked warlock' feels the stirrings of the old enemy. His power is growing. Death is coming.

"And what did the Kothlere Council say to your message?"

It was ignored.

"So, they'll do nothing?"

To this, Staell remained mute.

The heir reached for the goblet on his desk and gulped down the red wine.

78

When he reached for the bottle, he found it empty. He swiveled in his chair to the liquor table, refilled it to overflowing and began to chug.

"Why tell me this?"

Because Ralloc will need your help, and so will Warlock Lakayre. If you don't aid them, Ralloc will burn, Judas will die, Xilor will merge the two worlds again, and the fallen angel will join him.

"The fallen who?"

That part doesn't concern you, but that's the full disclosure. If you don't act now, all will be lost. Even you and the Hive won't survive.

The heir shook his head.

"I can't ..."

Weren't you wanting a fight just five minutes ago.

A pleading look entered the heir's eyes. He looked away, shaking his head in disgust.

Staell was quiet for a moment, letting the silence do the work.

There's no wine in death.

The man glared at him.

Or as you put it, someone to suck your cock.

"What you're asking..."

I've asked you to do nothing.

"But you just said..."

That Judas and Ralloc will need your help.

"What you're proposing could be considered treason."

I've proposed nothing. However, I think some of your men have grown tired of House Eti and could benefit from training outside the Hive, don't you agree?

"Training exercise?"

The heir looked at Staell before he took a few more mouthfuls of the bitter, red wine. Then, a mischievous glint glimmered in his eyes.

"I like the sound of that. Show our presence, our strength again, lest the realm forget!"

He slammed his fist down on the desk and stood abruptly, excited by the idea.

"The Black Tide will march once more!"

Calm yourself greatly, Heir. Your movements must be strategic. There must be some meaning as to why you have mobilized without orders, lest Ralloc turn its might against you.

"What would you have me do?"

I'd have you do nothing.

"What would you ... muse about at this conjecture of current and future paths and fates?"

You should just keep to plain talk; you're terrible at being subtle.

"The Black Tide was never about being subtle! You think a sword through the neck, or a deep thrust between a woman's legs is subtle?"

Touché. Then ... I'd muse that you'd need to convene with the army jyneruls of the War Council. Talk war games, what-if scenarios—whatever officers talk about. In the meantime, I think the defenses of Cape Gythmel are in sore need of attention; perhaps you could send a small party there to provide a better assessment?

"Shades of the Underworld! That maggot hole isn't worth two shits of a prostitute! Cape Gythmel holds no strategic value to the Grand Royal Army, and they abandoned that cesspit of a settlement. What the hell am I going to do with that miniscule settlement of farmers?"

When Xilor comes through the Corridor of Cruelty, and he will, that's where we need to choke him. There's no stopping him south of it. There are no strategic points where we could slow his war machine once it starts. He could bypass every town where we set up defenses. But not right outside the Corridor. It's much like your stairs. A small party there to assess the defenses could hit him hard. Your most veteran squad, perhaps? Conducting war scenarios?

"Aye, I can do that. Not many Krey from the last war are still in fighting condition. Most are ko-dons. But the youngest recruits from the Wizards' War, they can still fight."

They must do all they can before Judas reaches there. Once he arrives, the war will be imminent.

The heir scratched his jaw with the back of his thumb.

"Not much twelve can do against a lack of defense fortifications."

I've heard the same said of battle.

The heir smiled.

"Touché."

He stood and walked back over to the railing, gazing down into the Pit. Staell could see much below due to his height. The level had all but cleared out, and now the floors were being scrubbed by neophytes.

"Oi! Wash boy!"

The shout caused another boy across the room to drop the handful of swords and maces he was carrying. Once the clattering died, the heir turned back to the wash boy.

"Heir!" he acknowledged, leaping to his feet and standing at attention.

"Bring me the ko-dons and the do-don of Void-Walker squad. And make it snappy!"

And this is where I leave you, Heir.

"What? Not staying for the battle plans?"

What battle plans?

"You know, for Cape Gythmel … for my little visit to Ralloc?"

Honestly, Heir, I have no idea what you are talking about.

The heir chuckled a hearty, buzzed laugh.

"I like you, horsey."

You're not bad yourself, for a dwaven.

"Hey! I'm only part dwaven!"

Fine! I like you, too, little fat man.

The heir's chuckles echoed through the floors and walls as Staell took his leave.

Chapter 13: The Heir

The ko-dons and the do-don of Void-Walker squad filed into the office.

Daniel, the heir, eyed each as they entered. Since the room lacked a fourth wall, every meeting went without privacy but turned advantageous for listening to someone have their ass thrashed—a mirthful event unless you became the target.

The overseers talked, their voices rising, filling the semicircle of chairs around the heir's desk. Ko-dons Bear and Stallion were the oldest; Craiboar was the youngest at over five ages old. Panther lived up to his name as the quietest, while Adder—whose numerical affinity didn't fit any normal definition—rounded out the council. The only thing Adder could be counted on for was his numbers and a topsy-turvy vote.

Daniel's eyes flickered over to Raven, the do-don of the Void-Walker squad, the last to arrive.

Way to show your ass by being late.

The heir called for attention twice before shouting.

"Oi! Gag your holes!"

Silence ensued.

He tapped on his desk with a meaty finger.

"I think it's time for rigorous training—get those old Krey moving and break in the newer members."

Daniel addressed Raven.

"How many veterans from the Wizard's War?"

"Three."

"That's it? Three old souls and a bunch of bloodless virgins?"

"Not entirely bloodless, Heir."

"Virgins to war, you piss-pot. Am I to understand you're one of the three veterans? Who's the next in line after you three?"

"Debatable."

Raven smoothed back his black hair, sweeping it from his eyes.

"Patch's a veteran, but Xenomene's better with the blade. If my decision, I'd return to the old ways, the best with the sword would lead."

"So, Xenomene?"

Raven nodded.

Daniel's eyes went distant as he tried to recall the young woman.

"The pretty redhead vixen? Scar on her face, right? Sarcastic bitch?"

"That'd be the one."

The heir grunted.

"She isn't a virgin, is she? If so, somebody bed the poor girl. I don't want her to die having not lived at all!"

Bear with his crinkling face and gray hair leaned forward.

"I'd do the honors, Heir, but I'm a married man."

"And old," someone blurted.

"Didn't stop you before," someone else japed.

Stallion barked a laugh.

"Age ain't the problem; your limp sword on the other hand…"

Craiboar's lips twisted.

"There's better looking."

Daniel gave a dramatic sigh.

"Bane of the gods! Send her to me. I'll split her open for her own good."

Raven cleared his throat.

"I don't think you're her type, sir."

"And you are?"

"None in this room are … sir."

"Really? I'd like to see that."

A low chuckle from the group filled the room.

The women matched the men in perversion. All Krey were vile and cutthroat—to enemies and to one another. The bloodlust malady didn't make you a Krey; the way of life did.

"Enough fuckery," Daniel said. "Take her under your wing. Make her your second. If you should die in a violent death, which I hope you do, she'll take over. At least, until I find a suitable replacement."

Ko-don Chimera frowned.

"Know something we don't, Daniel?"

Craiboar leaned forward, eyes narrowed. Daniel suppressed an internal groan, wondering what shit-idea was about to spill from the youngest ko-don's mouth. To call him young was asinine; half his life was already gone. But Craiboar was a unique blend of supplicant stupidity, rebelliousness, and short-sighted fervor, though he'd never brave the course alone, only follow.

"Never mind," Daniel said, cutting him off before he started. "How good's her blade work?"

"Best in my squad, probably best in House Eti."

"Horse shit," Craiboar muttered.

Raven glared at the man.

"She disarmed me and the other two veterans on numerous occasions."

"Doesn't mean she's great."

"If memory serves, she's undefeated in the Pit."

"Good." Daniel nodded. "Undefeated?"

Raven dipped his head.

"Well, there's something else I'd like to see."

"What's wrong, Heir?" Chimera pressed.

Daniel paused to reflect on what he should reveal. Not all words belonged to them, like the truth of the Heir's title. An old, bloodied history—meant only for the true successors.

Valin's son became the first Heir of Valin, but need drove future decisions for the highest-ranking official, descendant or not.

A fickle history ignored the obscured origins of the incident that shaped the Krey's lives. A Mother Centaur, Shadowed Trees, dwaven, and a war party promised riches for rescue. Alone, Valin of Lor entered his first bloodlust and slaughtered the centaurs, beheading the Mother Centaur and placing her head on a spike.

Upon seeing the slaughter, the dwaven of Valin's group plundered the riches, and Valin, haunted by his deeds he couldn't fully remember, walked Ermaeyth alone until he founded Outpost Dire with Hagen, the Father of Magic.

Daniel sighed, leaning back in his chair, his calloused fingers dragging across his chin.

"I was given a warning today."

Craiboar, always first to shit or show his ass, spoke up first.

"What warning?"

"By whom?" Adder asked.

"A reliable source…" Daniel started.

"You mean the unicorn?" Raven blurted.

Daniel's lips thinned into a line, his teeth gritted together.

"By the Lord of the Underworld, I hope Xenomene's got better brains than you."

"A unicorn here?" Adder asked.

"Hard to miss with all the light," Stallion chided.

"I want to see a unicorn!" proclaimed Panther.

The heir lurched to his feet.

"Fucking Shades of the Underworld, you call yourself Krey? You cackle like whores searching for coin and cock. Who gives two shits of a prostitute about whether you wanted to see a unicorn!"

Daniel's head hurt at the end of his rant, but that might not be his irritation. Rather, it might have been that he drank too much earlier in the day. After Staell gave his news, he'd sobered fast.

A silence smothered the office. Only breathing filled the absence.

"Two shits of a prostitute?" Adder echoed, his voice deadpan.

The Krey burst into fits of laughter.

Damn it.

Daniel shook his head.

"It's an older saying."

"Yeah, vintage!" Stallion said.

"Keep the classics fresh," Bear wiped a tear from his face. "Been a while since I heard it."

Once the laughter faded, it was Panther who steered them back on course.

"Heir, what do you know?"

"War's coming."

Daniel glanced around the semicircle of chairs, to his Krey jyneruls.

"And the Black Tide is needed."

He saw the look in each of their eyes, knew what it meant, what they'd be willing to do.

"And we might have to break a few laws to help them."

War: a singular word every Krey hoped for and dreaded. Battle was their purpose, born to die, saviors never thanked.

"What would you have us do, Heir?" Raven asked.

"You'll conduct training via a scenic route. Take your squad and march."

"Where are we going?"

Daniel glanced at his highest officers; while he didn't doubt their loyalty to the Krey people, some might not be as loyal to him. Being put in the highest position came with detractors, especially if they didn't like you to begin with.

"Clear the room," Daniel said.

They stood, glancing between their leader and Raven. Though not unheard of, scarcely did Daniel keep secrets from his ko-dons. If he did, the reason ensured plausible deniability. Once the room cleared, Daniel appraised Raven.

"You'll be going to Cape Gythmel for training."

"That shit-hole excuse of a settlement?" Raven scoffed.

Daniel nodded.

"I would rather eat a pig's ass."

"My exact sentiments."

"An awful long way. Could take two months on foot."

"I know."

Daniel sat behind his desk. Raven pulled up a chair opposite him.

"You can't visit a portal master anywhere without raising suspicion, not without orders to mobilize from the War Council. If the Black Tide shows up anywhere, they'd come here, and not for a polite visit. No, this must be done under their noses."

Raven's lips pursed, and then he said what Daniel knew he would.

"You speak treason, Heir."

"No, I speak of a training exercise."

"What training that we couldn't do here?"

"A real-life scenario of defeating an overwhelming force, creating defenses against imminent siege, and crafting fortifications using whatever the town can provide. The Krey get training and exercise, and we foster goodwill. In the process, a defenseless town receives fortifications, and the squad can share their knowledge with the rest of the Krey. Once we debrief, we can hone the skills for more efficient ways."

"Twelve isn't enough for fortifications."

"The same is said of battle."

I wonder what Staell would think about me stealing his line.

"A squad will have to be enough. In the meantime, I'll head to Ralloc, convening with the War Council. Protocols are in effect while I am away: majority vote amongst the ko-dons. Any questions?"

"Provisions and gear?"

"I'll give you the short run down, and you won't like the restrictions. You'll be marching in full gear, and you should not expect resupply or reinforcements."

Daniel and Raven discussed deep into the night, going over the excursion's finer points. The heir inspected the dragon plate armor and weapons, deciding to wake every essential member: the blacksmiths, rune and sigil grand wizard, and the draycons.

The rune and sigil grand wizards were the first to wake, tasked with charging all the weapons and armor. Following, the grand wizard charged rune stones so the deploying A'uri could revitalize the Krey's armor in the field.

The heir roused the blacksmiths and their aides, and they attended the weapons, sharpened edges on the whetstone, and fresh leather grips. Other than fighting, weapon and armor maintenance was a Krey's highest priority; the task came before eating, drinking, sleep, and even sex. After scrubbing the hybrid armor, they passed it off to the draycons.

The draycon was an obscured profession, and only five remained in the entire realm. They dreamed, breathed, and studied dragons, scrutinized every magical aspect of the creatures. Their familiarity enabled them to manipulate the nearly-indestructible scales, melding them with rune-etched plate to amplify protection against magical attacks. The scales bolstered the durability of the metal armor, and the Krey forged a new type of armor: dragon-plate.

The apothecary crackled to life, packing small bundles of herbs and medicines to cover mild illnesses. A'uri could heal themselves and the Krey, but their gifts were geared towards life-threatening injuries, no annoyances. Fevers and colds were too acute. The apothecary profession was the only non-magical specialty overseen by a high wizard, a rank one-step above the general population.

Neophytes roused early to pack supplies, each bag stuffed with food, apothecary supplies, bandages, sleeping gear, spare clothes, boots, waterskins, weapon and armor oil, and rags. With nonnegotiable and mission essential supplies loaded, the top quarter of the pack remained free so each Krey could take what they wished.

An hour before dawn, the Void-Walker squad assembled in the Pit. Dressed for battle, they moved with fluid grace, lacking the encumbering weight of traditional armor. Each Krey donned a bastard sword, dagger, bow, and a quiver of arrows—though most didn't use the latter, finding it distasteful to touch a coward's weapon. Their helmets crowned the top of their sleeping rolls which jutted over their left or right shoulder, able to snatch it up at a moment's notice.

The heir walked among them, inspecting each Krey—nine total with three A'uri accompanying. He stopped in front of the petite redhead. Standing this close, he inspected the obvious scar on the right side of her face.

A thin line traced from the right corner of her mouth to mid-cheek—a faint, straight graze from a sharp blade.

A nick, nothing more.

For a moment, he wondered why she didn't demand magic to remove the scar. It marred her comely face. His eyes found her intense emerald eyes. Faint gold flecks graced her face with freckles.

Ah, so this is Xenomene.

"Aren't you a pretty one?"

"It's your imagination, Heir. I'm a sarcastic bitch. No, wait, a pretty redhead vixen. My apologies, Heir, you're correct."

Should've figured they'd be listening in.

"You've got a sharp mouth."

"That's what your wife said last night. Too bad you weren't around to see."

Daniel chuckled, a rumble in his belly. He didn't have a wife.

"I like this one," he announced to everyone, pointing at her. "You be sure to come back in one piece."

"I'll come back, dead or alive."

The heir waded through the ranks, inspecting each in turn. Once they left, they'd be on their own.

The only plate they wore was for the helms, shoulder protection, shin guards, and the upper chest, which stopped at the sternum. Dragon scale covered the upper arms, neck, thighs, abdomen, and back, allowing for flexibility of movement in the heat of battle. Boiled leather weaved underneath and held both together.

Satisfied, the heir left the Pit and returned to the open balcony in this office. Raven gave a salute, a hand placed over his heart.

"Permission to depart, Heir?"

The moment arrived, the precipice of sending them or backing out. The heir stared down, seeing their eyes locked on him, almost tangible anticipation filled House Eti. The hardest part of his job was the orders, sending them to their deaths. Those born with the bloodlust malady were considered expendable; all warriors understood that truth.

A lone squad of the rage-induced Krey could carve a swath through an opposing force ten times its size. Member for member, his irreplaceable warriors held a merit and worth the Grand Royal Army would never achieve.

But if his people had to die, they'd die like all Krey should, a sword in their hand and a scream ripping from their throats.

His eyes roamed to the flat black armor. By intentional design, his eyes drew uncontrollably to the darkness, just as the enemy's eyes would.

He gazed at the faces of the virgins, the ones yet to enter true battle. Most probably would die. Then, he glanced to Xenomene, memorizing her face, in the event she didn't come back. He'd considered fucking her before she left—but preparation came first.

And there's no guarantee that she would've said yes.

His eyes found the veterans. They'd die, too. Age granted wisdom while stealing speed and strength. He'd prepare individuals to augment their depleted number once the war kicked off—perhaps more virgins. Who would survive, and who would fall?

Pride and heartache lanced through him, a moment any parent who sent their child off to war would know well.

Damned if I do … fucked if I don't.

"Permission granted."

Sympathy and respect crept into his voice, and he touched his fist to his heart.

"Oblus ina'ti Sepan Eti."

Live and die by the sword, you fucks. Give them hell.

The Krey below slammed their fist into their chest.

"Oblus ina'ti Sepan Eti!"

Chapter 14: Judas

Judas found Julie at a tailoring shop not far from the inn. From the shop's sidewalk, he could still see their quarters, and Julie was finishing up as he arrived.

Madam Rose handed her a receipt and told her not to lose it.

"Pick 'em up around early evening. Mind ya', we close before Apor sets."

The apprentice handed the receipt to Judas, and he pocketed the slip after eyeing the bold letters *Stitched in Time* at the top.

The duo returned to the inn and snagged the last moments of breakfast, dining on eggs, bacon, oranges, fried bread with mashed beans, and goat's milk.

But even now, they both received stares from lingering patrons. He'd come to accept, even expect, them, but Julie couldn't focus on her plate. Despite her periodic glances, she finished in silence, and they left, his reassuring hand on her shoulder, guiding her past the gawkers and to his room.

She plopped down in the chair Todd once sat in, her arms across her chest, her brow furrowing.

"Don't let them get to you," Judas said with a gentle voice.

"I don't understand!"

He sighed.

"You're still new here, but I'll let you in on a little secret: not everyone you meet is intelligent, and some are fools. There are the open minded and the closed. Those people below? They're making judgements on emotions rather than logic, and you can't reason with someone who speaks a different language."

Her eyes darted to his; her brow softened, and she abandoned her scowl.

"Are you closed-minded?"

The question took him by surprise. He expected her to fixate on the patrons. Instead, she turned analytical, a testament to how her mind worked.

Judas took the seat opposite her.

"More often than not," he admitted.

"Why?"

"Probably for the comfort of order and conduct. I value my morals above the words of laws, yet I follow the law to maintain order. It's an appealing structure of symmetry. Magic's about structure, harmony, but people often distort it, turn it chaotic for personal ends."

"You're a warlock, an exile. You're above the law."

"No; never above, outside."

He waved the comment away.

"Let's focus on your training. We won't have much time until we reach our destination, but the hardest part is the first step. I can't tell you what to search for, any more than I can explain what it's like to breathe. That must come from within. Once you sense your magic, the rest will come."

"You trained others, right?"

He hesitated.

"Yes."

"But?"

"I've never trained someone from the beginning. In the past, by the time most came to me, they'd finished their tutelage at school. Some even apprenticed under another master prior to seeking me out."

He stood, his head searching the room for something to help start the process. Spying a candle, he snatched it up and handed it to her. Next, he positioned the small night stand between them before settling the candle in the middle.

"You know how to do magic," Julie said, "why not move the things you want?"

"Just because something can be done easier doesn't mean it should be. There's a certain pleasure in doing things the mundane way."

His eye twitched; a flame flared at the wick's tip.

"I'll be learning as much as you, having never trained someone from the basics."

He reached for her wrists and held her hands up on either side of the candle.

"I want you to influence the flame, and if you can, snuff it out. Reach within, touch the magic coursing through your body. Realize you have the ability to call on magic, command it, and influence the candle. Appreciate the heat, the energy. Absorb it, bask in the warmth, and then—" the wick went out.

A thin, wispy coil of smoke filled the air. He smiled, and the wick ignited again.

"Think you can do it?"

"So, that's it? Just influence the candle?"

"Yes."

She blew the flame out.

"Done."

Judas chortled and relit the wick.

"With magic, my dear, not ingenuity. The task is as much about influencing the flame as sensing your essence, where your ability to call upon magic comes from."

He slouched back in his chair, his gaze never wavering while Julie moved her hands up to the sides of the candle. He hoped it wouldn't take long, but he expected her to fail many times before connecting with her essence.

Even as he waited, Judas realized this menial task might be too much. Those born in Ermaeyth grew up with magic. Everyone influenced their essence to an extent, and those better adapted to magic pursued lucrative careers. By the time children went to school at age five, they performed small magics themselves, but she had no idea what to look for.

To her credit, she didn't whine or falter as the minutes trickled by without success. The wax melted as did the hours. Lunch came and went; another candle was acquired. The only time she moved from her post was to use the privy. She always returned to her seat to study the flickering flame.

By the time dinner came, her stomach growled loud enough that Judas couldn't overlook it, and he insisted she eat.

They dined on a thick stew of potatoes, carrots, pork, and mushrooms over a bed of dense, fried bread, the latter so thick it required a knife. Julie tore into her plate with enthusiasm, devouring her portion moments after receiving it. While she waited for her second helping, she gazed around the dining room.

Some of the faces had changed, some hadn't. The remaining ones still wore scowls of discomfort and suspicion. The new faces were oblivious to who sat in their midst.

"Why don't they recognize you?"

Judas finished chewing his food and shrugged.

"I'm recognizable in Ralloc, but outside? Only by a few. Anywhere else and none would be the wiser. But the whispers will soon follow. Otherwise, it's almost like a myth. It's quite nice to be left alone."

Julie kept her eyes moving, dancing between patrons, memorizing those who showed disdain. She shuddered and rubbed her arms as if cold.

"What is it?"

"I don't know. I get the sense no matter what I see, hear, do … it seems so strange."

"That's to be expected. You have amnesia."

"I don't remember this place, any of it, but the knowledge is there."

She tapped her temple.

He raised an eyebrow.

"I believe that's the point of amnesia, my dear."

"It feels so strange, like I don't belong, or the knowledge doesn't belong."

"Ostracism."

"What?"

"Feeling out of place? Exclusion? Not quite welcomed?"

"Yes! That's it!"

Judas nodded.

What she felt was his fault, and her being with him only intensified it. With reluctance, he told her why she couldn't remember everything, though he was careful to leave certain elements out. He spoke of her origin, why he brought her back, and she took the tale far better than he thought.

"I would've died if you left me?"

He nodded, taking another bite.

"Because someone's chasing you, or me, or both of us?"

He swallowed.

"I believe whoever acquired the books from your shop intended not to leave any trace, including eliminating you. I killed the sheol, but more were coming. I could sense them."

She was quiet for a few moments.

"You made the right decision, especially under the circumstances, and I would've made the same choice."

He smiled, relieved, but doubt crept in. They'd eventually broach the subject again. When they did, her view might not be the same. He'd face that obstacle when the time came.

Her second helping arrived, and they finished their meal. Judas saw Julie off to her room. Leaving the inn, he picked up her robes from Stitched in Time before going to his own.

The next morning, he brought her clothes to her room and found her sitting in a chair, the candle burning, her eyes intent on the flame. He regarded her progress for over an hour before he left her to her devices, unsure how long it would take. He could help, but she might grow dependent on him. The first time was always best on your own, but if she didn't sense her essence by the time they left for the Corridor, he'd help.

Retreating to his room, he had to warn his friend, T'son, of their imminent arrival, planning to stay at his inn at Wizard's Pass.

T'son was a long-time friend, but Judas hadn't spoken to him in many seasons, and failed to visit in many years. Now, he'd be lucky to call him an acquaintance. Some friendships were born out of want or need, some formed in youth, but those forged in war stuck forever.

Like Meristal.

Crossing the room, he closed the cyan curtains, making it easier to see T'son without so much light. Once darkened, he approached the large, oval mirror hanging on the wall to the right of the fireplace. His fingers rippled, and the surface swirled in a fog of green.

"Who's thur?" the thick accent came from the other side.

Instead of seeing his reflection, the image of Judas's friend appeared. The shorter, stockier man filled the mirror. His gleaming pate sparkled with a sheen of oil. What little hair remained grew long and shaggy. His round face was covered with a long, coarse beard of dark brown and gray and hid his cleft chin. His nose hairs rivaled his bushy eyebrows.

"T'son," Judas greeted.

"Judas? That ya? What ya doin' callin' s'late?"

T'son rubbed his eyes.

"Late? It's mid-morning, unless I'm interrupting a nap. What are you going on about?"

"Well, hooey, snooty. Ya run a pub all night an' see ho' ya fare."

"Ah, I always forget."

Long ago, Judas had learned it was best not to ask directly for what he desired. Politicians taught him that, his first teacher, his brother, even that crazy old guy in his youth from the Kran Empire, Peronious something. He didn't want to invite himself to T'son's place, but he had no recourse, at least, not yet.

"Listen, would you like to take some time off and go with me to Marcoalyn? I could use a vacation away from Ralloc's arrogance. What do you say? It'll be like old times."

"Ah, Judas," T'son said, rubbing the back of his neck, "I'd like tha', sure I would; but I can't take off like tha', not anymore. I go' dut'es here now."

"So, let someone else run the bar for you for a few days."

"Nah, they'd drain all m'liquor, and I'd be broke. Besides, the crazy coots 'ere gone an' made me gov'nor. Why the hell they'd tha' no one knows."

"Governor? You didn't write to tell me the good news? Did you forget about us up here in the mountains?"

"Hardly, snooty! Ya' pompous arses up 'n Ralloc can't stan' the stench down here, so ya' forget 'bout the likes of us is mo' like it. Jus' come 'ere."

Judas suppressed the relief in his eyes, but he smiled.

T'son's accent and lack of proper articulation made him high entertainment at balls and political banquets. Whenever Judas could, he always invited his friend along, if for nothing else than to see people squirm while T'son spoke.

A large crash and the sound of shattering glass made Judas look away.

Julie!

He'd been careless to get entrenched with his old friend.

T'son heard it, too.

"Wha' the devils of the Abyss wa' tha'?"

"I've got to go. I'll call back soon, I promise."

"So, in 'bou' a fortnigh'?" T'son asked. "Fo'get vacation, jus' come 'ere ta Wizard's Pass."

"Sooner, I promise, and sure, I'll stop by!"

Judas ended the transmission, the green fog swirling away, and the mirror clearing.

More shattering glass, this time, accompanied by a curse. A chuckle escaped him as he went to rescue her from herself.

He entered her room and found her in the same position as he left her. She turned at his entry, a puzzled expression on her face.

"I thought—"

He glanced at her.

"Didn't you just—"

His eyes went around the room.

"Did you break something?"

Julie shook her head in silence and another glass shattered in the distance, a room across the hall. He wiped his forehead with the sleeve of his robes.

"Thank the gods. I thought you hurt yourself."

"Nope."

Judas pushed further into the room and sat opposite of her, noting the turmoil on her face. The flame burned calm, static, serene. Her eyes glittered with angst. She'd progressed beyond the desire to learn and into resentment. The warlock scrutinized the flame, hoping for a shift, a flutter, anything.

"To the Underworld with this!" she said, lurching to her feet. Her arms swung with her words. "I sit, and I wait, and nothing happens! I feel nothing except anger and embarrassment!"

"Julie?"

"I wasted my time and your time. A day and a half! That's all it's been, but a long time to sit through, to wait for something to happen!"

"Julie?"

"Maybe I'm not meant to be a mage. The fairies are wrong, or they're right, and I'm what's wrong. I feel so …."

"Julie?"

"I feel like I'm missing things, pieces of myself."

She stopped, locking eyes with him.

"I know you aren't telling me everything. You didn't tell me everything when you told me why you brought me here. What are you hiding?"

"Julie!" Judas said in a loud voice.

His eyes tracked from her face to the candle, and she followed his gaze.

The flame danced before their eyes, not the flickering of flame in the wind, but with a mind of its own.

Julie's mind.

It bent and rolled, curling on itself, responding to her emotional state.

He glanced up at her, but her gaze hardened. She ground her teeth and clenched her fist in frustration, the candle burst, as if crushed by an invisible force.

Judas sat as the shower of wax settled, impressed, but troubled by her anger. Though a natural attitude, she overreacted. Her jump to the emotional spectrum unsettled him, but he wouldn't shadow her accomplishment by casting criticism. Julie's raw power was hindered by her lack of affinity with magic. He had faith she'd succeed with time.

"Congratulations, my dear! Wonderful."

"I did it?"

She blinked, casting an apprehensive glance his way.

"Sorry."

"An impressive display, if I may say so."

Pulling his wand from his robes, he flicked his wrist, the wax disappeared, and the small mess cleared away.

"Quite alright. Magic can fix almost everything, or at least, clear away a mess. Now, let's try something else."

He shifted to the window and motioned her to join him. In the distance, a copse of trees formed the edge of a forested area.

"Magic's more than bending a weak flame to your will; it's a complex, binding entity of itself. Each of the five branches of magic has their rules. Magic can aid you, restore your health, help the infirm, educate and restore knowledge … limitless applications. But fun … that's another aspect."

He pointed his finger out the window to the distant tree line.

"Would you like to see them closer?"

"Teleport?" Julie asked, and he noted the excitement in her voice.

"No, not teleport. I'm talking about enhanced vision."

An eyebrow arched in silent question.

She nodded.

"You're still a student, and you'll need your wand for this."

He waited until she extracted it from her robes. Her clothing was a set made the day prior, a midnight blue outer robe with silver collar and lapels, and small white stars on the cuffs that matched her inner robe. With the wand in her hand, Judas instructed her on the finer points of how to hold the wand, and the incantation.

Julie spoke the spell, focusing on her words and intent, but nothing happened. She sighed, dejected, her eyes narrowing.

"No, no. You're trying too hard to make something happen. Let it flow. Be natural. It's there, within, like a quiet whisper in your ear, or a spider crawling across your skin. You don't notice it until you do."

Julie set her teeth and tried again.

This time, as she spoke the words, the trees jumped, and her vision magnified.

Judas cried out; the pain was sudden and unexpected. He saw through her eyes, his magic seeping into her as she used his essence to accomplish the incantation.

Both of their visions swam, focusing on towering trees, twisting trails, thick underbrush, and tumbling waterfalls of fine, white mist.

"Beautiful," she said, and he almost missed it.

Judas grunted with pain.

The longer she siphoned from him, the worse it'd be. In moments, she'd feel it, too. The dull agony crashed in waves through his skull, akin to a blacksmith using his head as an anvil. A sharp point needled his temple, and in the distance, he heard Julie cry out.

He concentrated on his essence, his mage sight watching the cascade between them, and he pulled, reining back in. Once he wrestled control from Julie, the anguish receded.

The warlock reached within, calling on his magic, and rejuvenated his body. The familiar sensation flashed through him, like waking from a week-long slumber. A wave of unfathomable energy permeated his body. Hunger and weariness leeched away. Even at his advanced age, he felt ready to trek up a mountain.

He turned to Julie, who slumped over, holding her head, rocking back and forth. He reached out and touched her, sending his magic through her. She stopped moving almost at once.

Her eyes looked up, blinked a few times in disbelief.

"That was incredible, whatever you did!"

"A rejuvenating spell. Comes in handy."

A grin crept over his face.

"Before you ask, we both caused the pain. In an attempt to control your elusive aura, your mind snatched mine. You siphoned, pulled my essence without acquiescence. The pain's a natural fail-safe. Your essence will fight off the invasion, similar to a fever and an infection."

She shuddered.

"I'll try not to let that happen again."

"Me either. Painful for both of us, and I'll be more mindful in the future."

He moved away, returning to his seat.

She followed.

"Is that common?"

"Pulling someone's essence?"

He shook his head.

"Why not?"

"First, the one siphoning must be strong, which you are. Though powerful enough to snatch it, the pain will make most let go. Second, there are two types, inadvertent and blatant. The latter is when someone rips your essence away from your control. They must possess the strength and endurance to fight off the pain while channeling. The stronger the victim, the stronger the agony."

She grew pensive, almost ready to ask another question.

"Enough practice for the moment, I think."

Her lips thinned.

"Where are the elyfian? I've seen wizardkind and goblins, why not them?"

He swallowed, wondering how deep he should go on the subject.

"The elyfian, or elyves, that reside in the Vikal Mountains are a portion of the entire population. They're scattered throughout Ermaeyth. I can give you a brief summary, but I could never replace a book, but the short: they're the gods of mortality."

"What do you mean?"

"The elyves are considered the wisest, the greatest artisans of crafting, art, and war. Even the Krey couldn't stand against a true Jaikari. They're masters due to their long lives, but they're not immortal."

"War?"

His brows rose as his lips formed into a thin line.

"Yes. They refuse to make weapons except when war's declared, and they destroy all after it's over."

"Why don't they destroy their enemies by magic?"

He paused a moment, considering her word choice. It could've just been the first that came to mind, or it could signal something deeper. If she possessed the power to destroy her enemies, would she hesitate?

That's always the risk when training someone. Look what happened to Xilor.

The thought bothered him.

"Why would anyone wish that transgression upon any sentient race?" he chided.

He shifted in his seat.

"The elyfian turned their gifts inward rather than outward, like us."

He shrugged.

"Who knows what they do up in the Vikal Mountains. They prefer solitude over mingling."

"Why?"

"Same reason why some fear me. The unknown, the different. Why should

I become involved with someone's life when they fear me? Same for the elyfian. To them, wizardkind is nosy and fretting. Who are we to tell people how to run their affairs? Wizardkind, more often than not, is prejudiced as a general rule, but I suppose all races are. Why subject yourself to that? Fear will drive people to do shameful things."

"Ever consider the reason they dislike elyves is because they are so distant?"

"That argument has arisen on numerous occasions."

"So, why are they so distant, other than what you said?"

His gaze flitted out the window, then back to her. He thought about stopping the conversation, as it served no immediate purpose to her training or their moving to a new location, but he had to reward her for curiosity. Not every student was.

"Long ago, elyves and wizards were kin. Archangels took druids—the first race of Ermaeyth—and from their blood came the nephiliam. From them, two branches: wizardkind, who bent magic into knowledge and craft; and elyves, who bent themselves—body and spirit—toward beauty, enlightenment, and strength.

"The elyves delved into the higher mysteries of the arcane, learning enough to augment what they sought. From our perspective, they seemed like vain creatures, obsessed with beauty and elegance. For all their perceived conceitedness, they became easy prey, so they took up war as an art, crafting weapons and armor of the finest caliber. This with their augmented strength, speed, and agility negated wizardkind's magical prowess. Until the Wizard's War, we never witnessed firsthand the beauty and ruthlessness of their prowess in combat."

He swallowed.

"I saw their ruthless strength in the second Wizard's War."

"Can you tell me about that?" she asked, jumping on his words.

He noted the eagerness, but for what exactly?

Wizard's War is closer to magical lessons than the elyves.

"There are many theories, but I recommend a good book. What we call the second Wizard's War was a chain of events that stretched out over time, drawing everyone into confrontation. They call it our war, but we just ended it."

She leaned forward in her chair.

"The actual war started before my birth with the elyves and the goblins. Why the goblins and elyves went to war is still a mystery."

"You have a theory, don't you?"

"Always, but now isn't the time to speculate."

"The goblins struck first, didn't they?"

He gave a slow nod, watching her.

"So, the elyves hunted them down."

He noted the sound of her voice—bordering on resentment, or maybe it was conviction.

96

"That's what history tells us."

The low fire danced lazily in the hearth. He scrutinized the turmoil rolling across her face, thinking about atrocities ending before her time. Judas pondered his new pupil.

And he hated to admit it, but there was a ruthlessness to her.

And if he was honest with himself, very little differentiated between Xilor's hardline approach and Julie's, except the former was inherently evil, and the latter was reactionary.

Without forethought, he started talking about Xilor and the war, but maybe it'd help her see the connection between herself and the fallen lord.

"Sixty-three hundred years ago, the war started. Around twenty-nine hundred years later, Xilor announced himself to Ermaeyth. Most consider this the beginning of the war. He rained destruction, chaos, and death for a long time."

"What was your role in the war?"

"Various. I did fight on the front lines though. My first foray came near Far Point, on the other side of the Corridor of Cruelty."

"What's that?"

He let out a deep breath through his nose.

"The Corridor's in the mind of the perceiver. When I went through, the journey took me ten years. At least, in my head."

"In your head?"

"When we pass through the Corridor, you'll understand."

Julie's eyes narrowed.

"What do you mean 'when' we pass through? Don't you mean if?"

"No, when."

She swallowed, then changed the subject.

"You defeated the dark lord, right? I seem to recall that."

"I stopped him, yes."

"Why didn't you track down his family, hold them hostage or something? That would solve the problem, right?"

Though she was logical, it lacked his fine taste of morality. Perhaps that was his problem and not hers. Part of training her would be instilling her with morals, too.

"Julie, it's much more complicated. Only a select few know of the dark lord's true existence, who he is. His family, if he even has one, may be innocent."

"Do you know who he is?"

He gave a single shake of the head.

"That information eludes me."

"Why?"

"I had suspicions, but found no trace of evidence. In reversed roles, I'd erase such information, and he may have done that. Many things about him seemed familiar, but the possibility bordered on unlikely and improbable, and I disgraced and dishonored someone's memory for even thinking it."

"Who did you think he was?"

"Someone from my past."

"Who?"

"A good friend, and he's gone."

Our conversation turned dark. What does she hope to glean?

"So, your ten year absence. What happened? Did everyone think you died?"

Judas chuckled, waving his hand.

"No, my dear. That's how I perceived my time in the Corridor. I was only gone for a season."

"Three months? How do you get ten years out of a season?"

"Like I said, the Corridor of Cruelty's all in the mind. The curse of fear is similar, but you don't fear the Corridor—you fear what it can do."

"So, what happened during those three months?"

"Dark time, for me, at least. You'll pass through soon, and it'll test your strengths and weaknesses, your fears and hopes."

"So, you told me nothing."

"I can only teach you so much before experience must take over."

Something hot touched his skin, and he bolted to his feet. He fumbled, digging into his robe, pulling out a pouch, and dumping a small mirror into his hand.

A swirl of green fog obscured the surface before a face materialized.

"Judas Lakayre, report to Ralloc on the morrow. The consul has an assignment for you. Bring the Wcic."

The face faded in the green swirling fog.

"What was that?"

"A summon from the Kothlere Council. They're bigger fools than I thought."

"About?"

"Going there with you? Ha! Not until I find out who's hunting us. We're on the run, hence why we're not at my manor. They'll go looking there first."

"If they don't know where you are, how did they manage contact with you?"

He smiled.

"An astute observation. I linked my essence to this mirror instead of a fixed position like my residence. They can contact me, talk to me, thinking I'm at home. You've got to be one step ahead always."

He sighed, returning the mirror to the small pouch. Spying another candle on the mantle above the fireplace, he retrieved it. Rubbing his fingers near the wick, a flame appeared.

He placed the candle in front of her.

"Let's try again, but this time, with your essence."

Chapter 15: The Betrayer

A bead of sweat gleamed on the Betrayer's brow. He'd teleported recently, leeching his magical strength. He regretted making the journey without a horse.

The suns scorched him from high above. A dull ache festered in his feet. Without companionship distracting him, he obsessed over his ailments. His feet weren't his only hurt.

His pride, too.

Cowardice was a caustic venom for the soul, and despite the years, it renewed each day. Choices from long ago wouldn't bring him peace, nor would the fear that still consumed him.

Others couldn't live this life.

But self-pity was a contagion, and passing blame just enabled his weakness.

The tenacity for conflict fled him—if it had existed at all. Youthful memories brought back nostalgia and a tinge of bitterness. In retrospect, he'd been an arrogant sycophant, basking in his personal gratification, and shunning anyone who rightfully deserved attention. If they grasped his insecurities, his image would crumble away, abandoning him as hastily as his followers. False bravado hoarded many friends, and charisma won the competition, but in truth, he didn't measure up in the competition of life.

He winced, feeling his soft flesh form new blisters, sweat clinging between his toes. His socks drowned in perspiration. The grass, thin and withered, became a perfect analogy for the malnourishment of his soul.

In school, Judas had been one of his classmates, and he couldn't stand the brat. Was it just misguided youth and jealousy that spurred him then? Perhaps he'd been wrong.

Beneath the unforgiving dual suns of Apor and Praema, even his tunic did little to cool him, the sweat evaporating fast. His tongue swelled, sticking to the roof of his mouth. In silence, he wished for the ability to port a horse with him, but he didn't have the magical strength. Few possessed the ability for such a feat.

The Betrayer shrugged his pack higher on his back and cinched the straps tighter.

His frown deepened.

As an indentured servant, and with the livelihood he left behind, it all accumulated from a series of failures. Pondering such circumstances made his stomach clench. The gods granted one reprieve in the gloom. In Gryzlaud, sealed away from the rest of the world, two young women resided. Born a little under twenty-three hundred years ago, during the second Wizard's War, Xilor held their lives in his hands, used them to threaten continued coercion.

In the few moments the Betrayer found his spine, Xilor reminded him the cost of disobedience. Without those two girls, Xilor held no sway over him. Death wasn't an option for him in the interim. If he died, by his volition or otherwise, they'd follow him to the Underworld.

Xilor would make sure of it.

A faint, gentle breeze floated towards the weary traveler, and he reveled in the simple pleasure while it lasted. The cooling wind was a balm against his sweaty face.

He raised the girls, Miza and Olga, since their infancy, taking pride and joy in their presence. When they neared the Age of Maturity, the girls' personalities shifted, growing apart in their contrasting individualities.

Olga, prickly by nature, blithe and scathing, hungered for power and glory, willing to do anything to achieve it. Miza was the antithesis, soft, sweet, and naively innocent. She yearned for knowledge, marking her as an outcast at Gryzlaud Palace.

Even innocence can be found in the lair of evil.

So long as Xilor didn't snuff it out.

Perhaps because of this, the Betrayer found Miza to be more fascinating, charming, and engaging. Unconsciously, he devoted most of his attention to her, but it was treacherous footing on a steep incline. If Xilor ever became aware of his attachment to her...

Olga roiled with disdain, jealousy, and spiteful vindictiveness. Her heart hardened against him, and it was his fault. Once he realized what his actions wrought, he tried to turn the young girl away from her path, but that only drove her further away.

When Olga reached the Age of Maturity, she banished the Betrayer from her sight. Even though they wandered the same halls, he hadn't seen her in many years. He still loved the little girl he remembered, but she'd changed long ago, and his heart wrenched every time he acknowledged it.

Miza, however, understood the good in him, the sacrifice he made, and his unbridled shame. He denied it for a long time, the good that clung to some deep, dark corner of his heart. Where he proclaimed failure and weakness, she spoke of his courage and strength. Miza knew the story of how she and her sister came to be in Gryzlaud Palace, how his actions spared her from the Underworld as an infant, and what he gave up.

Most importantly, she was grateful.

The Betrayer had nothing to live for except her—his redeeming grace.

He felt the slight pull of magic, a familiar sensation warning him of the approaching summon. He stopped and drew the small shard of mirror from his pocket, grateful for the reprieve in his journey, but the face wasn't one he expected.

Krurik, the dark lord's chosen successor, glowered on the other end.

"Tell the dark lord Judas has been summoned to Ralloc and instructed to bring the Wcic," Krurik whispered. "The council wishes to see her. I'll arrange her stay overnight. After he leaves the city, she'll be slain. No one will suspect my involvement."

Krurik cast a glance over his shoulder toward the door he'd secreted himself behind. He hid in plain sight, at the heart of Ralloc.

"And if he doesn't heed the summon?" the Betrayer asked.

"I know where he is. I'll personally oversee her death."

"Makes my job easier. I need to give our master the good news."

Relief washed over the Betrayer at the chance to get back into Xilor's good graces.

"Only an incompetent fool like you would. I despise they call you the Betrayer, unsuited for a cur like you. You're nothing. My betrayal is real, visceral, and daily. It is my fruits that bring my master pride, not you."

"Don't you mean *our* master?"

"No. You're not an apprentice but a slave, a dog brought to heel."

The Betrayer moved to cut the communication between them when Xilor's apprentice spoke.

"When I rise to take my master's place, you'll be the first to go, along with those cunts you love so much. I'll destroy all you hold dear, make you watch, and after you suffer, I'll kill you, too."

The green fog swirled, and the image faded before the chastened Betrayer could come up with a retort.

Chapter 16: Julie

The flame fluttered, responding to Julie's pull. A smile spread across her face.

Perhaps Judas is right, and magic comes with time.

Ever since she experienced her essence, the conjury came more easily. However, the incantations he provided failed to manifest, so she started over, calling her essence.

He wrote down two simple spells, but the magic wouldn't heed her beckoning.

She released her influence on the flame before reaching out again. The fire churned, glowing brighter, elongating before curling, bending, looping back on itself.

Julie threw her arms up in silent celebration. In this late hour, she doubted many were awake, and her screaming wouldn't have endeared her to anyone.

Judas retired to his room hours ago, and her grin faltered when she thought of her master.

Master? Such an odd word.

The world had changed for her, a rapid transition over the last few days, and she was still trying to catch up.

Earlier that day, Julie took the warlock's advice and opened a book from the small shelf in her room. She alternated between influencing the flame and reading. A cover-to-cover plodding wasn't a sought-out indulgence, so she skimmed through the short excerpts. Only when a passage grabbed her attention did she read the section.

The thin book, printed in the last year, covered various subjects. A small portion was written in remembrance of the Wizard's War and lacked the detailed events. The tidbits she found, she already knew, either from Judas's Transference or his ramblings. But even as he talked, he withheld information.

Julie was certain some information he hoarded for personal reasons, but he withheld general details, too. Every time she asked, she sensed the weight of his gaze and noted ponderous thinking behind his azure eyes.

A trust issue.

He didn't trust her, and the path worked both ways.

The edge of truth cut deepest, her reality hinged on what Judas relayed. But how could she discern the truth from uncorroborated testimony? Trusting blindly didn't bode well, and the less he trusted her, the more misgivings she had.

Judas said someone hunted them, but she couldn't make sense of why they holed up in an inn when they should be moving. Their journey's end eluded her, but from the little hints she gathered, the place sounded secluded, which implied a small location.

She sighed, and her insides gurgled. Her hands went to her stomach.

She pined to see Ralloc. From the way Judas talked, it sounded majestic. A massive hive of buildings and races intermingling throughout.

An adventure!

One she wouldn't have, not anytime soon.

A spark of resentment flared within her, her magic washing out of her like a wave. The candle burned brighter, reaching higher than before. She reined in her emotions, and the light dimmed, shrinking to its normal size.

She recalled meeting Staell and the brooding mood Judas adopted in the wake of the unicorn's departure. Something bothered the warlock. His sullen mood made her yearn to know what happened. What she'd give to read his thoughts, or what secrets he kept.

Perhaps magic can help you?

An intriguing thought.

When she grew more controlled, perhaps more opportunities would arise? Was that even a possibility, to read people's minds? To possess such a gift would be an invasion of privacy, but she'd be aware when Judas lied to her, siphoning his secrets, knowing whether he warranted her trust.

He would, after all, shape her near-future.

Julie hated being so reliant on him. By wizardkind standards, she was well over the Age of Maturity, an adult, but he treated her like a child. Perhaps she was, and that thought turned bitter in her mouth. She needed guidance, but he did so reticently.

Judas had never trained a novice, and he bumbled through. Perhaps such elementary tasks were too menial for him? That'd explain a lot. Simplicities escaped him, and she gathered that much from the small book she skimmed through.

She found two tiny passages regarding him within the slender confines. One detailed the legality of his banishment and branding him a warlock. Last year alone, he repealed his case three times to reinstate his citizenship.

All were denied.

The second obscure passage focused on the war, notable battles like Far Point and his delayed arrival. The author summed up his greatest accomplishment in a few short sentences:

Judas Lakayre survived his twin brother, Josiah, and went on to defeat the Xilor. Details surrounding his ultimate victory are guarded secrets, and it's unclear who all is privy to such information. Regardless of his legal status or what title he was bestowed with, he single-handedly brought an end to the Great Wizard's War. We should not forget the deeds of our heroes, no matter how far they fall, or the lost lives that granted us a future without oppression.

And that was it.

Nothing more on his exploits, no details on magical prowess, just a few lines summarizing what everyone already knew. A waste of paper as far as Julie was concerned.

Both pieces mentioned nothing about the kind of person he was, his views, philosophy, religion, or political leanings.

The writers knew him as a distant figure, nothing more.

Her stomach grumbled again.

Sighing, she stood, abandoning the comfortable chair and tossed the book on her bed. She tried sleeping earlier, but the elusive comfort abandoned her. Her mind churned with the future, where they were going, what magical abilities she may yet discover.

One bonus of not remembering was the aspect of newness. Each passing moment was a learning experience, discovering the world for the first time. And each day, she found out that it was a bad thing, too.

Julie opened the door to her room, peering out into the darkened hallway. A floorboard creaked in the distance. Her head snapped in that direction, towards Judas's room, a tingling racing through her body.

The hall remained empty and dark.

Her scalp prickled, but she shook the impression away.

It's an old building, probably just sighing.

A funny notion, thinking of buildings with living traits.

Descending the stairs, she eyed the empty lobby and dining room. A fire crackled in the latter, and the lobby's candles burned brightly. Someone was awake at this hour to help late arrivals or wandering guests such as herself.

"Hello?" she called into the quiet.

Noise stirred from behind the counter, through a door to a back room. A young man—older than her but not by much—came through, smoothing his clothes. His dark brown hair contrasted nicely with his pale gray eyes. He was tall, too, enough so that Julie had to look up at him.

His sleepy expression vanished when he saw her. He was attractive, even if he'd just woken up.

"Good evening, Lady…?"

"Uh, Fossard," she stammered, remembering the alias she and Judas used.

"Lady Fossard. How may I assist you?"

A caress so subtle that she never realized its gentle arrival curled through her. A soft stirring within. Warmth crawled, languid and salacious, across her flushing cheeks, the familiar prickling in her tightening chest. Her scalp tingled as if breaking out in a sweat.

What can he assist me with? What am I doing here again?

Her stomach clenched, and the hunger pangs reminded her why she'd come down.

"I know it's late," she said, breath catching in her throat. "Is there anything in the kitchens? A piece of bread or some fruit?"

He revealed a dazzling display of his teeth. The corners of his mouth curled up, a teasing, coy grin.

Heat flushed in her cheeks.

"Sure, I can snatch you something, but you have to do something for me."

She swallowed.

"What—What's that?"

"Tell me your name, Lady Fossard."

She tried to make sense of his asking.

"Why do you want to know my name?"

He gave a lopsided grin.

Oh! Why'd he have to do that?

She tore her eyes away from him, and that seemed almost an impossible task.

"You're beautiful, and not many minor nobles come here. I've never even talked to one. How could I resist?"

She didn't know why, but his words made her smile. Was it the compliment, the mistaken identity for nobility, or something else? Through the haze of her mind, she remembered Judas's warning.

"Cynthia."

He came around the counter, held out his hand, palm up. She placed her hand in his, and he brushed his warm, full lips against her skin, a delicate touch.

"The pleasure is mine, Cynthia."

Heat crept up her throat and into her face, her mind swam. He stood so tall over her—taller than Judas. His hands were rough, calloused, strong. She found Todd attractive, but even the journalist didn't measure up.

She knew she should be doing something—manners, pleasantries.

What in the Underworld is wrong with me?

"What's your name?"

"Does it matter to a woman of your stature?" he said, his voice delicate.

She focused on his robes, the fog in her mind growing thicker and more opaque by the moment.

Swathed in cyan vestments matching the inn, they were linen with a simple gold threading embroidered on the cuffs, a design reminiscent of a vine.

Her eyes found his neck and upper chest, revealed by the plunging line of his robes. She fixated, his flesh calling to her, beckoning her, and she almost missed his soft words.

"I'll check the kitchens for some food, Cynthia."

He walked to the dining room, and she swallowed. Her heart raced as disappointment flooded her that he'd left.

What's happening to me?

Her body thrummed with a new hunger, one not ravenous for food. She turned scarlet, could feel it on her skin.

Her vision blurred again, but weaker this time. She shook her head, but that only made it worse. She took a step toward the stairs, and she could breathe easier. Another step, and the invisible pressure lessened. Another …

I've got to get out of here!

Julie turned her back and climbed the stairs, careful not to make too much noise. She didn't want to disturb the other patrons or worse, awaken Judas.

A fine time for him to show up!

But maybe that's what she needed right, then.

She reached her room, the first door on the left of the second floor, and fumbled the key before making entry. Shutting the door behind her, she sagged against the wood, a refuge as she let out a deep, shaky breath. Tiny prickles beaded her forehead, and she wiped them away on the cuff of her sleeve.

What's happening to me?

A quiet rap on her door, two quick knocks, made her jump. Pride rippled through her for not gasping aloud. She opened the door, a small sliver, spying the man's face. The heady sensation returned as strong as before. Her vision swam, and the opaque fog returned.

Is this magic?

"Your food, Cynthia," he whispered.

Her body thrummed when he called her Cynthia, like silk drawn across the skin.

The door opened wider, his frame filled the doorway, a striking figure. His hands held the plate: a slice of bread dripping with honey and an apple adorned the dish. To control the trembling of her hands, she clenched her fists at her sides before reaching up, taking the plate, and put it on the dresser beside the door.

The food was far from her mind, almost forgotten.

"Anything else I can do for you, Cynthia?"

Before she realized it, she nodded. Her body quivered when she heard his voice, the way he said her name.

"Call me Cynthia again."

"Cynthia," his voice rumbled in his throat, soft.

The moment carried her along swift currents. She reached out for him, kissing him—his warm lips pressed against hers. Her mouth opened, inviting; his tongue slipping through.

He pinned her against the door, one hand at the back of her neck, the other groping her ass. Gods, she loved his strong grip.

Something magical crawled through her, growing stronger as each trickling second lasted a lifetime. His squeezing hand pulled her against his body while he pressed into her, trapping her between him and the door.

The scent of earth and musk filled her nostrils. His hardness pressed against her body. It felt unforgiving and weighty. Her flesh tightened, quivered, her pulse pounding in her neck. His hand reached for her groin, fingers opening her garments.

A cough interrupted them, and the spell broke like a thunderclap. The heat rushed away, and fear and embarrassment slapped her across the face.

"Wait," she said, gasping, pushing him away.

Gods, please don't let it be Judas.

She looked down the hall, but no one was there. She put her hands to her face. What was happening to her?

"I can't," she said.

"But you want to."

She took a few deep breaths, her mind scrambling for reason, for clarity.

Judas filled her mind, and the pull that called to her faded. A reason crystallized in her mind.

"Yes, but my father's just down the hall."

"Are you worried?"

"Yes. You don't know him."

The haze cleared more, and she stepped back. The distance between them aided in her recovery.

He smiled, something less of humor and more deprecating, knowing his hopes of conquest had failed.

"Aren't you glad I never told you my name? Just another boy on the street."

He took a step backward, exiting the room, closing the door behind him. The wistful twist of his mouth was the last thing she saw. Julie went to the door and pressed her ear against the wood, listening to his retreating footsteps, half-sorry she stopped herself.

Gods, I was ready to break my bed with him. Why? I don't even know him!

When the soft footfalls faded, she reached down and locked the door, not trusting herself ... or him. The heady sensation faded as the seconds trickled by.

I wonder who coughed?

Whoever it was, she had them to thank; otherwise she'd have been moments away from being bent over and fucked like a tavern whore. Would she have let him do it, or demanded it?

She turned, putting her back to the door, her knees weak. The slender volume she'd thumbed through earlier fell into her view.

This whole thing ...

With two deft strides, she snatched up the small publishing. Pages turned until she spied the short article titled *Woes of Magelust.*

Ever feel drunk even though you've never had a drink? Found yourself staring across the room at someone you never met? Chances are the magelust ensnared you. Another year has gone by with leaps of progress for the apothecaries, pharmacon mages, and midwives, but nothing for the magelust. Speaking for those few who have difficulty managing the menial task of blocking out other people's aura or dampening their own, I'd like to see some progress made on this front.

Two percent of our population can't block out auras, even though the majority of citizens can dampen theirs. It helps, but not enough. Even people who never sought a higher education in magical practice can turn the magelust on for those more sensitive to its pull. When will the lust become a social issue and be addressed? The Krey's bloodlust is considered a malady, why can't the magelust?

To date, the magelust affects far more people than the bloodlust. The Krey are a tenth of a tenth of our population. The government should be looking out for the welfare of all citizens. While pain, fright, or certain bonds can break through the lust, chances are, nothing is available on hand to those, unless you're a Lord out with your Lady, and she slaps you for kissing the servant. For myself, and two percent of the population, it'll be another year of promiscuous encounters and strange entanglements.

Julie inhaled a deep draw and blew it out noisily through her nose.

The magelust.

Gods, is that what I have? I felt something with Todd, but not near as strong with ...

the man downstairs.

According to Judas, she had a strong aura and had yet to learn how to block out others or dampen her own. Was she part of the two percent? It was another question she needed to ask him, but would he tell her the truth or become elusive?

Her belly growled again, and she closed the book, dropping it to her bed.

A glow outside her window caught her eye. Perplexed, Julie moved towards the glass panes. The illumination hadn't been there earlier.

She pulled the thin curtain aside with the back of her hand and peered out. Flames crackled with life; an entire building engulfed in a towering inferno. For a moment, she hesitated, stricken by panic. The first notion that jarred her was trying to reach out and influence the flames, but this task wasn't a candle.

A muffled scream ripped through the night, muted by distance and the glass. The cry for help was like a slap to the face.

Judas, he can help!

She turned for the door when a vibration, followed by a deafening crackle like distant thunder, echoed through the slumbering hour. Before the brontide abated, her window shattered, the fractured glass lacerating her back, knocking her to the floor.

Her face smacked the floorboards, causing a wave of bright light and pain. Distantly, she heard more screams, louder, closer. The floor rumbled, a vibration she felt through the side of her face, footsteps thundering down the hallway. She was sure Judas was one of them.

She tried to find her feet. A chill crept along her back, but as she stirred, hot, sharp agony peppered her skin, the glass burrowing deeper. She gasped, her vision dimming, shifting out of focus.

Were these the people hunting them?

The door creaked open.

Her head swiveled that way, causing her vision to blur and making her sway.

A large, shadowed figure appeared at the threshold, the edges blurred, the face distorted in magic and shadow.

It entered her room.

She opened her mouth to scream, but pain in her throat—the constriction —cut it off. She doubled over, coughing. Panic poured through her body like fire.

She fell forward, her hand catching her from falling, and she coughed.

The face of the creature loomed near, a mirage shifting before her eyes. Shadow and creature, feline, demonic, twisted, something out of nightmares.

Then something cold plunged deep in her, a fire radiated from it.

She gasped, or attempted to.

The hands released her, and the blurred image fled. She sucked in a breath and coughed, her body tightening around the pain still radiating from her.

She collapsed to her side, looking down her body. Her shaking palms traced to the agony, and she found it. Tilting her head, she caught a glimpse of something protruding from her abdomen.

Warmth pooled about her fingers as she grasped the object and pulled it free.

They got me.

Her eyes rolled as she caught the glinting blade coated in her blood.

They were hunting me all along.

The knife slipped free of her fingers and clattered to the floor.

She was going to die like the thirteen before her.

Her vision swirled, blackness lingered on the edges.

Her lungs burned, and she took one last deep breath.

Chapter 17: Judas

A distant rumble snapped Judas awake.

Between the haze of sleep, fading dreams, and old memories, the Wizard's War came roaring back to life. He jerked to the side, rolling out of his bed like a soldier. His feet thudded against the wood floor, and his knees popped in protest. It'd been years since he moved like that.

He extended a hand toward the window, his essence sensing the rush of energy, and he enveloped the glass with a shield. The window held but vibrated.

Shouts from the hallway, opening doors, panicked voices called to him. *Civilians.*

Having slept in his inner robe, he yanked on his outer robe and donned his sandals. Striding to the door, he opened it, and almost forgetting his wand, he stretched his fingers toward the nightstand. The wand leapt into his outstretched hand without an incantation, and he slipped through the door.

People filled the dark hallway; most rushed toward the stairs. Judas wove through the entangled bodies. At the base of the stairs, most patrons lined the dining room, looking sleepy, shocked, or irate.

Judas paid them no heed as he slipped through the front doors.

The black night reminded him that dawn was still hours away. A wave of heat greeted him; bright orange flames ruined his night vision. An almost silent sound overhead drew his attention, and he tracked it. Whatever cut a swath through the night vanished before he snatched a glimpse, but few creatures could fly.

It wasn't hard to narrow down the list.

Dragons and their lava blasts, more liquid than flame, and vampires.

Another building flared in the distance.

Dragon's breath caused indiscriminate damage, and half the town would be ablaze now, more from molten flow than flame. But this ... this was a calculated, precise attack. Damage, terror, but no lasting effects.

A scream reached his ears, and Judas hurried in that direction. In no time, his lungs were burning, and his legs were on fire. He wasn't as young as he used to be.

Another creature from above landed in the path in front of Judas, and in the firelight, he caught snatches of details. Animalistic features, elongated mouth, razor teeth, giant, leathery wings, elongated ears similar to the elyves—all signs he wasn't part of the elite caste.

Judas raised his wand.

"You're a long way from Shadow City. Return to your masters before all becomes unforgivable."

"We serve another. By his will, we follow."

Another explosion drew Judas's attention, his eyes darting there and back.

"You're declaring war against Ralloc?"

"Inevitable."

The beast shrieked and launched at him. Before his feet left the ground, flames cocooned the beast, and his charred ashes blew away on the wind.

Another casualty of a war that never stops.

A distant scream urged Judas on.

As he ran, he took note of the carnage; Dlad City burned, mirroring a war-torn city. Countless battles from long ago resurfaced, the bodies that fell, the blood salting the earth, the souls snatched away.

Smoke watered his eyes, limited his sight. He glanced down, jumping over something lying in the street. A tiny goblin lay twisted, head at an odd angle. A goblin here meant that it resided with a family, secured by work ethic and loyalty.

The little creature reminded him of the one that spoke to Julie.

Shades, I hope she's okay.

He dodged a wizard bleeding from a laceration in the scalp.

The shrieks were louder now, more desperate, and the fires burned brighter and hotter as he drew near to the epicenter. He hurtled past a blazing building, hoping no one was within. Thick, black smoke curled into the sky, a dark and dense pillar. Flecks of ash fell like gray snow.

A woman flung herself on him as he came close.

"Help me, help me, please!" she screamed.

"What? What do you need?"

"My friend, a goblin ... attacked by a wizard."

She sobbed, pointing southwest.

"What does he look like?"

"Dark hair and eyes, a pointed goatee!"

An all-too-familiar description. Fury kindled in the pit of his stomach.

Slipping free of the woman, he set off in a sprint, caution forgotten. He drew on his essence to sustain him, to fortify his aging body, and he needed it.

Swooping sounds slithered through the air above. More vampires. More proof of Xilor's imminent return, and it was moving away, toward Shadow City, a refuge of dark spires and convoluted tunnels smothered in a habitual obscurity.

Judas rounded the corner of the next building, and he found the man who matched the woman's description. Vamor Poplu, a council member. The man's wand was pointed at a goblin, and the latter screamed in torment.

What's he doing here?

"Let him go!" Judas shouted. Rage consumed him, but he couldn't act, not yet. That'd make him no different than the people he despised.

The command startled Poplu, breaking the younger man's concentration. The goblin slumped in a heap, but he still tried to crawl away, his arms shaking.

Poplu's twisted face turned into an oily smile.

"The renegade warlock? Here? Had I known, I would've hunted you first. Come to visit justice upon me?"

Judas slowed his approach, but he closed the distance between them. If it came to a duel, it'd be less time for Vamor to react, but he'd have all the time he needed.

"Don't test me, boy. You stand no chance against me. Concede defeat now, and spare your pride some dignity."

Even to Judas, his offer sounded hollow and flat. Poplu wouldn't take it, and he'd push Judas's morals to the brink.

"Who are you to offer me anything?"

Poplu snatched the goblin by the arm, dragging him up from the ground.

"I witnessed this goblin engaging in cannibalistic activities with the enemy. There's still blood on his mouth, his teeth, his claws! Can you not see?"

Judas's eyes went to the goblin in question, and it did appear to be true from the evidence presented, but that didn't mean it actually happened.

An idea struck Judas.

"What enemy? I just see you and all this destruction."

Poplu sneered.

"Nice try, Judas, but you know as well as I do that vampires are here. It's their doing!"

Well, at least he admitted it. Now, if I can just get him to say the same thing to the council...

Poplu tugged on the goblin's arm again, as if he was going to drag him away.

"This isn't the way," Judas said.

"When the enemy refuses to talk, you must force them to confess! You blather about justice, fairness, and equality among all races, but look at him!"

Poplu curled his fingers through the creature's hair, jerking his head upright.

"He's an animal, a monstrosity! You've lulled us into thinking we're equal."

Judas swallowed. This would drag on as the city burned down around them, and he needed to be free to help others and check on Julie.

"Step away, Vamor, or I'll remove you."

Poplu rolled his eyes.

"Against me? Your kind? A council member? You disgust me, Lakayre! You'd have us lay with them and breed, wouldn't you?"

I wouldn't go that far ...

Judas raised his wand.

"Last chance."

He had to wait until Poplu wasn't so close to the goblin. The moment wasn't life or death, not yet. Poplu needed to be coaxed away.

Judas hated resorting to low-brow tactics, and he hadn't cursed in ages, but he knew a few from long ago—a different life.

"Don't be arrogant. You really want me to hand you your ass in front of the town? Only a little bastard would try."

Bitterness filled his mouth at the words. Such a mild word would've been common tongue in Judas's youth.

He sighed as Poplu's face hardened.

"But I guess bastards don't learn lessons the easy way, do they, Vamor?"

Poplu's jaw tightened, and he shoved the goblin's head away. The small body fell limp to the ground.

"Of course, I'd hide my bastard birth, too, if I found out my mother was known as Ralloc's communal pony."

Poplu's lips thinned, peeled back, his teeth set against each other.

"Everyone gets to saddle her for at least one ride."

Poplu's arm blurred, wand raised with blinding speed, his essence rushing up, charging forth.

Judas sensed the spell, the shape of it, the taste of the makeup—a blast meant to decapitate.

And Judas was ready for him.

He closed his eyes, sensing that unfathomable energy within him, and he called it forth. As he'd done to defeat Xilor, he tapped into that *other* power he commanded. The spell, which had been closing the distance between them, slowed to a crawl.

Judas opened his eyes; the curse was still moving toward him, but it crept forward like the speed of a snail. His eyes flitted over to the burning buildings, and even the flames bent to his will. They twisted in languid movements. Shattering debris crashing to the ground seemingly hovered in the air. Each indistinct sound now became a river of indistinguishable noise, a thrumming resonance.

He stepped around the oncoming curse, flanking Poplu, bringing his wand to bear on the councilman.

With deft flicks of his wrist, he negated Poplu's incantation, then turned the wand on Vamor, sending out a blast that'd render him unconscious. Poplu would see him disappear—as if he'd teleported away—right before oblivion took him.

Judas relinquished his grasp on time. He couldn't hold indefinitely, nor could he truly stop the progression of time, but he could slow it.

The drift of normalcy soared back into full swing.

Poplu gasped as his curse dissolved. His eyes widened just a fraction before Judas's blast took him in the chest, knocking him to the ground. The councilman lay in a silent heap on the ground, and the impact with the ground was harder than Judas expected.

Serves him right.

Judas let out a deep breath.

Exhaustion overwhelmed him; fatigue riddled his body, limbs shaking. He was too old for this sort of thing. He bent at the waist, hands planted on his knees. The sensation would pass, it always did when he reached out to slow time. As he got older, the ability slipped away, becoming harder to grasp, but when he did, the hefty toll exacted its price.

It'd been at least an age since the last time he called for it.

His lungs heaved, sweat broke out on his forehead. He wiped it away and stood to his full height. His knees trembled, hidden beneath his garments, and he cast a rejuvenation spell on himself.

The ability to slow time called upon a different power than that of his essence. The two were like water and oil, both liquid but immiscible.

The weariness passed, his strength returning. He walked over to the fallen man. He stared down at Vamor. House Poplu, a proud and ancient lineage owed allegiance to none, but they often fell in league with other nobility such as House Dathyr—the current consul.

Judas grabbed hold of Vamor's collar and teleported back to Ralloc.

They appeared in the council chambers; in the midst of the council and their late-night staffers.

Or maybe it's so late that it's early morning?

Consul Kayis Dathyr saw him immediately.

"Lakayre? What in the Underworld? We summoned you!"

His eyes flickered to the disheveled council member.

"What happened to him?"

"I happened to him, Kayis!"

"What did you do to him?"

Judas hauled on Poplu by the neck of his robes, pushing him forward until his head smacked against the council's bench.

"I caught him torturing a goblin. There should be no place for him on the council!"

"Calm down, Lakayre," Dathyr admonished.

Judas didn't like his tone, dismissive, yet trying to maintain control. He glanced around at the staffers. The ensemble observed, and by tomorrow, it'd be a whispered debacle. Peasants would know nothing of what transpired, but the upper tier of society would gossip for fortnights.

Judas noted the wary eyes, the visages of mild rebuke, but who were they for? Him or the consul? Perhaps Poplu? Warlock he may be, but people knew him to be honest. If he said Poplu tortured a goblin, everyone would take it as truth.

Though an outcast, people still listened to him—renowned for being law-abiding when he didn't have to, not as a warlock. Too many nobles were privy to what he did in the war. His words would stick to Poplu as feathers to tar.

"Cruelty?" the consul asked. "What do you think you showed him? You're no better than he, Sorcerer."

Ah, so that's how he'll frame it. Remind everyone that I'm like Xilor with magic.

"I'm consul, Judas, not you. It's not your place to say who should sit on the council."

"Sidestepping allegations again? Deferring to the method of waiting and forgetting?"

Dathyr waved an exasperated hand.

"You witnessed him torturing a goblin?"

"As I told you before."

"How did you know it was taking place?"

"A woman told me."

"A woman came crying to you?"

"I just said so."

"Did you bring back these two? The alleged victim and the witnesses?"

So, that's how you are going to do it!

Judas waved his arm out to the side.

"Your eyes don't deceive you."

"Your word against his? How convenient."

The room thrummed with silence, absorbing the acrid words between them.

"My word against his, yes."

Dathyr shrugged.

"No choice but to throw this case to the Abyss. No witness, no testimony, no conviction."

He sneered.

"As far as we know, it never happened."

Anger boiled within Judas, but he should've expected something like this. He scraped together his composure.

Dathyr waved a dismissive hand.

"Don't bother making a report about the alleged incident. As we all witnessed, it'll be quite biased. We couldn't trust your word after the events of tonight."

Twit!

Kayis cleared his throat.

"But you're a wanted man, and we can't let you just go gallivanting around the country assaulting council members. That's a crime, one you must pay for. You also failed to heed our summon and bring the Wcic. You'll be remanded in custody."

Judas chuckled.

"Not likely."

In a blink, the warlock teleported away from the chambers and emerged in a night filled with falling ash, the curling stench of smoke, and wet embers.

He and Julie needed to move again … tonight. It's not safe here, and it wouldn't take long for the consul to deduce where they stayed. He didn't want to battle men who were just following orders. Any casualty would only further fuel the resentment.

Julie's probably in hysterics by now.

Judas reentered the inn. A throng of people with tousled hair and sleep-deprived eyes glanced in his direction, but none gave him much attention. He slipped upstairs while idle conversation rejoined between the milling guests.

He reached the second landing, and his heart stopped.

Julie's door stood ajar. He rushed forward, pulling his wand, entering the open door.

Julie lay in a pool of blood on the floor. He rushed forward, sliding to his knees beside her.

Shades of the Underworld, how did this happen? Who did this?

A quick touch confirmed what he knew at a glance. Blood loss cooled her skin, but a faint, struggling heartbeat still stirred within. He summoned his essence, harnessing the infinite energy, and channeled it through her.

Splitting his mind, he found a mirror on the wall, and called it to him. The silver surface swirled green. A sleepy face squinted at him.

"Meristal! Help me!"

"What happened?"

"It's Julie. Come quickly. Dlad City, Traveler's Respite, second floor."

She rolled away from the mirror, and he returned the mirror to the wall.

Judas's eyes roamed over the young woman, the panic rising. He could heal himself and others, but had limited knowledge in the healing arts. He needed a pharmacon mage, and most resided in Ralloc.

Meristal had a better understanding of anatomy, often doubling as a healer in the war. All he had to do was keep the magic channeling until she arrived.

His hands shifted over the blood-soaked cloth. A golden glow cascaded from his hands and into her, the energy seeping through clothing, blood, and skin. He closed his eyes to concentrate, feeling the wound. The laceration began to heal, but it was so slow. She'd be dead before he could finish.

Meristal arrived a few minutes later. Even at this time of night, she was still beautiful, despite her disheveled appearance.

"What happened?" she asked, kneeling beside him.

"I don't know, but the trauma is consistent with a puncture. Perhaps a blade, but where's the blade?"

"We need to put her on her back."

They rolled her over, but Julie didn't lay flat. Meristal reached behind her and pulled an object from underneath the girl, a knife materializing in her hands.

"There's your blade. Did you even bother to search?"

Once Julie was flat, Meristal situated herself opposite of Judas. Her hands placed, she closed her eyes for a moment, assessing the damage.

"If you didn't get here when you did, she'd be dead."

"Can you heal her?"

Meristal nodded.

"Then, do it!"

"Does anyone else know you are here?"

Judas frowned at the question.

"What does that have to do with anything?"

"Judas!" Meristal snapped. "This will take time, and then she'll need to recuperate. Judging by the carnage outside, something happened, and knowing you, you went out there to stop it. So, I'll ask again, does anyone know you are here?"

The warlock swallowed.

"The council."

She swore, sharp and scathing.

"We need to move her, now—take her to your house."

"We're hunted, and I'm sure the council will send someone there after tonight's events."

Meristal nodded.

"Okay, but we can't stay here. Keep channeling energy into her and close the wound but do it slowly. I hope to be back before you get too far along. If you mess up, the less I have to reopen, the better."

"Meristal, where are you going?"

"Cape Gythmel. I'll rent a room, then come back for you both."

Judas nodded, and Meristal vanished.

He turned his eyes to Julie. Remorse filled him. He'd failed her, failed to protect her. Now, she was dying. He should've left the fighting to others, left the city as soon as the attacks started. Even as he thought it, he knew he couldn't.

Yes, Julie was his charge and under his protection, but he couldn't let others suffer and possibly die while he did nothing. It went against the grain of his nature. Battle piqued his blood and quickened his heart, but helping others called to him.

He wronged his student when he helped others tonight. No amount of self-loathing would change what happened. He chastised himself until Meristal reappeared.

Kneeling beside Julie, she touched her for a moment before nodding.

"I'll teleport us. We'll go straight to the room, but you've got to carry her."

Judas scooped Julie's small frame up in his arms.

It seemed like an hour ago he carried her through the Mirror of Imaesion the same way. He stood to his full height.

"Meristal?"

She gave him a quizzical look.

"Thank you."

She smiled.

"You don't need to thank me, Judas. I'd do anything for you, but you already know that."

Meristal placed a gentle hand on his arm, and he felt her essence surge, the room disappearing and a new room materializing around them.

"Set her by the fire," Meristal said.

Judas did.

Meristal placed a pillow under Julie's head, then she set to work. He felt Meristal's power thrum, searching the extent of the wound. After a few moments, she gave a thoughtful noise.

"What?"

Meristal's violet eyes looked up.

"The blade was also laced with poison."

"Who would go through so much trouble for a girl?"

Meristal's eyes narrowed.

"You want to try that one again? I don't think you meant it the way it came out."

Judas rolled his eyes.

"She, Julie, the girl, a Wcic. Why would anyone try so hard to kill her? What's she worth? Who profits from her death?"

"I don't think they were after her."

"What?"

"I think it's a pretense to catch you off guard. You're the target; you have been all along, but now, you'll do anything to protect her, thinking she's the real target. It'll leave you vulnerable."

Judas shook his head.

"That's absurd!"

"Is it? If you were my enemy, this is what I'd do: something to lower your defenses so I can kill you."

He snorted.

"Given it much thought, have you?"

"Yes." She swallowed. "I always had what-if scenarios in case you went rogue."

Judas wanted to laugh at the absurdity of her comments, but her voice and visage gave him pause.

By the stars and spirits, she's serious. I'd never go bad!

Meristal focused on a pale and sweaty Julie.

"I need to remove her clothes. When I draw the poison out, the liquid will pool. If it soaks into her robes, it could get back into any of her wounds. And I need to pull the glass out of her back."

"Glass?"

"Shades, Judas! Do you even pay attention? She's got dozens of shards in her back. Probably from the window. Help me!"

Meristal reached for the sash that held her robes closed.

Judas shook his head and backed away.

"I can't."

"You've seen a woman naked before."

He just shook his head.

"Some help you are. You don't have to, but don't leave the room. I may need you later."

Judas turned away just as Meristal exposed Julie.

He took a chair on the opposite side of the room, his back to them, the most privacy he could give them under the circumstances. Meristal didn't understand. Julie was more than an apprentice; she was a bastion for old wounds, buried memories, and a daily reminder of the daughter taken from him. Had Meristal never arrived, he'd abandon all propriety to save her, but now? A boundary rallied within him, one he wasn't willing to cross.

The thought of someone hunting her made little sense. He was the greater threat.

Unless Xilor's aware of her presence.

Judas realized their possessions remained in Dlad City. He asked Meristal for leave to gather their belongings.

"Just hurry back," she growled.

Judas complied, returning moments after he left with his and Julie's possessions in tow. A flash of flesh was enough to avert his eyes, hiding his vision behind a curtain of long hair.

He returned to the vacated chair, facing away. Not long after, Meristal requested his aid, and he lent it. A steady trickle of energy poured into her, bolstering her waning essence.

All magic came with a cost; healing consumed at twice the normal rate. The energy required ...

While Meristal worked, he pulled the leather-bound book from his traveling pack. His master's work lay still in his lap. Judas never understood the language, the strange archaic scrawling throughout the pages, no matter how many times he looked at it.

But it was important to his master, Fife, and therefore to him. He'd go to his grave trying to fulfill his master's dying wish. It was all he had left of him: his last words and an old volume.

"You shall never glimpse the pages, but can you understand the Bearer of Secrets is not a foe? You are entrusted with a special task—my greatest pupil—will you search out the Bearer for the rest of your life? You will do this. My faith is placed correctly, yes?"

Judas smiled, remembering the gnomling.

"I'm done," Meristal declared some time later, her voice careworn.

Judas stood, closing the book and glancing between his charge and his friend. Meristal was covered in blood, her hair tousled, and she looked bone weary.

"Thank you, Meristal."

She nodded and held up a bloodstained hand. He crossed to her and helped her up.

"You look tired. Please," he offered, hand pointed to the bed, "catch some sleep."

Meristal shook her head in a languid movement.

"Nice try. I got two rooms. I'll go to mine as I'm not fit to teleport back home tonight."

"As you wish."

"You might want to put her in the bed, though."

"It'll be done."

She opened the door and stepped through, and once almost shut, Meristal stuck her head back in.

"Judas?"

"Hmm?"

"You owe me."

"Put it on my tab."

"I'll be coming to collect. You've got years' worth of debt."

The door shut behind her, soft and light.

His apprentice loomed into his drooping sight. Sleepiness tugged and called to him as well. Reaching out for his essence, he lifted Julie to the bed. He

took the chair beside the bed, resuming his vigil.
Moments later, he too, drifted off to sleep.

Chapter 18: Julie

A warm blackness comforted her. A hazy sensation buzzed through her head. Harsh brightness greeted her waking eyes, and she squinted against the early morning glare. Strangest of all, the curtains were ivory.

I thought they were cyan?

Her eyes found a figure beside her bed. Judas stared intently at a book in his lap. In the delirium from having just woken up, she could've sworn the glyphs moved, a slow waltz. When she blinked, they weren't.

A fire crackled, but she couldn't see it, and birds chirped in the distance.

The warlock's azure eyes flickered to her, then he did a double take. He snapped the book shut, lurching forward in his seat.

"Good morning, Julie. You gave us quite the scare last night."

A woman spoke up in the distance, and worry saturated her voice.

"She's awake?"

Judas didn't turn away, but he spoke over his shoulder.

"Yes, she is."

Julie stirred, trying to sit up.

"This isn't my room."

"No. We moved during the night. Welcome to Cape Gythmel."

"Why?"

"What can you tell me about last night, my dear?"

"I went downstairs," she stated, the memories crawling back. "I was hungry."

In a flash, she remembered the handsome young man and the desires calling to her. Her will crumbling, his hand on her ass, a passionate embrace. She kept those parts to herself.

"I got some food and returned to my room. I remember a building on fire and went to get you."

"Anything else?" Judas asked.

"The building shook, my window broke, and something came to my room."

"What did this *person* look like?"

Julie's face bunched up as she tried to remember.

"Large. Shadowed, the edges blurred, distorted. It grabbed me by the throat. Its face kept changing. One face I saw clearly was feline, like a cat, but bigger."

She shook her head, then her eyes went wide, rushing to her abdomen.

"My clothes! Where are my clothes?"

Judas reclined in the chair, and a woman came to stand beside him. She had vibrant, shoulder-length hair, a dark orange—almost red, amethyst eyes, and pale, porcelain skin. She was short, probably the same height as Julie, but it was hard to tell from the bed, and she had an enviable petite figure.

"I took the liberties," the lady said.

Judas cleared his throat.

"Julie, this is my dearest friend, Madam Meristal Raviils. She helped me last night."

"Helped?"

"They stabbed you, child," Meristal said.

"Right where you thought they did," Judas finished, pointing at Julie's stomach.

Julie glanced, but she found no trace of the wound.

"Meristal healed you, Julie."

Julie didn't know how she felt about that.

"Not that I'm ungrateful …" Julie met Judas's eyes. "…But why didn't you?"

"Oh," Meristal said, something close to mirth, "you were right, she's a quick one."

Judas grinned.

"Healing's an art, much like painting. Meristal's better for such external things. My gifts lie in a different direction."

Julie absorbed this for a moment, her faint understanding of magic coming a little clearer.

"Why was I attacked? What about the fire?"

Judas's mouth moved, and Meristal shifted her feet. They looked at each other before speaking, but it was Judas who took the lead.

"We're of different minds on this."

Meristal snorted.

"Understatement of the century. I think your assassination attempt was a distraction. Judas is the target, but he wasn't in his room. He went to investigate the fires. Vampires, goblins, wizards … it was a siege."

"An attack?"

Judas waved a dismissive hand.

"A small group. More of a skirmish. But yes, I wasn't in my room."

"When they couldn't find him," Meristal said, "I think they came after you."

Judas's lips moved.

"I have no doubt they're a part of the people hunting us."

"Any ideas on who?"

Judas's head bobbed from side to side.

"A few. Xilor's minions or an unknown apprentice. A small chance the council's behind it, though there was a member present last night. After I disarmed him, I went to Ralloc and sort of … embarrassed the consul. So, possibly them as well."

"You went to Ralloc? I thought you said the capital wasn't safe!"

"I couldn't sit idly by while a member tortured a goblin."

He sighed.

"Anyway, I returned, found you on the floor, called Meristal, and she came."

Meristal smiled, her right brow arching high.

"You forget that I changed her clothes."

Meristal glanced at Julie.

"Judas wouldn't have anything to do with that."

Gratitude enveloped Julie, and she sent the woman a small smile. A thought crossed her mind, and she turned her attention back to Judas.

"The thing that attacked me, what about the shifting faces and the cat-like aspects?"

The warlock took a deep breath.

"I have a theory. Whoever it was used a curse from the Derengi branch, which brings out your worst fear; few know the branch, fewer would stoop low enough to use that pestilence. The only known counter to Derengi, oddly enough, is my own affinity, Rumigul."

He took a deep breath.

"Since afflicted with amnesia, your worst fears are not yet realized, hence the changing face. Maybe once you were afraid of cats?"

"Cats?" Meristal chided Judas.

"Big cats," Judas clarified, waving his hands for emphasis.

"So, I was attacked by a hallucination?"

Meristal shook her head.

"The person was real but came as a hallucination. Derengi's an afflicting magic, capable of spreading maladies of the body, mind, and soul."

Judas cleared his throat.

"The curse in question makes the receiver visualize something they fear, masking the attacker's true presence. I returned the weapon in case they could trace it through magic. Good thing they used a blade."

"Good? I nearly died, and you say good?"

"Of course good! Unbeknownst to your attacker, you now possess an affinity to heal."

Julie squinted at him, unsure if she heard him right, or if he hit his head.

"I can't heal."

"You're forgetting about the unicorn hair in your wand. Staell's people are the greatest healers. Even unconsciously, you will heal at a faster rate, and that's what saved you."

"And me," Meristal added.

She absorbed that little tidbit, glancing between the two.

"I don't follow, about me being a healer. I can barely call my essence."

Judas swept his long hair out of his face.

"Your wand was made with the wing of a fairy and a tress of hair from a unicorn. Of all in Ermaeyth, those two races bear the highest affinity for healing and energy. You and the fairies share a bond; they'll lend you life and aid so long as even one lives. Even if only one remained, you'd survive, barring decapitation or worse."

Meristal shifted on her feet.

"The fairies kept you alive; the hair of Staell augmented that."

Julie studied the woman for a moment. Meristal held herself with a tranquility Julie would never attain. And despite being a stranger, there was something about her that put Julie at ease.

"Once you learn to harness your essence properly," Meristal continued, "you can direct your healing energies to others, healing them with the slightest touch. If what Judas says about your aura is true, perhaps you'll heal without touching them."

Julie turned her eyes back to Judas.

"Who can cast Derengi spells?"

"Quite the investigator. Theoretically? Anyone with enough potential. Some creatures use it like saricrocians—an innate gift born to them. Wizardkind can mimic the effects with difficulty. What's natural for creatures becomes sinister in the hands of a mage. Again, I believe it's an agent of Xilor."

"Like?"

"Well, we can rule out a few races due to their nonviolent nature or xenophobia. It's not the fairies; you're bonded to them. Sheol would've been spotted and the alarm raised. And the actual creatures who naturally use abilities are far too large."

"So, a creature? Can we track them down?"

Judas shook his head.

"I inspected the weapon; it's centaur in origin, but they couldn't have orchestrated the attempt."

"Why not?"

"Because their magical skills are far too feeble. And … other … obvious reasons. Perhaps it was a team, a goblin to formulate the affliction, and a wizard to carry out the deed. Never rule anything out."

"So, how do we figure it out?"

"By finding out who'd profit the most from your death. You being an anomaly isn't justification to want your death."

Judas inhaled, ready to launch into it further, and Meristal placed a hand on his shoulder.

"That can wait, Judas. We need to get you two on the road. Don't fill her head with conspiracy theories."

"Con—?"

She gave him a stern look, and Judas seemed to deflate.

"Yes, perhaps you're right, now's not the time."

"I only have one question," Meristal said. "Who all knew you were in Dlad City?"

"Staell," Judas said with a shrug. "A few dozen people at the inn."

He grew quiet a moment, his eyes distant, and Julie watched as the answer came to him, almost the same time it did her. An expression crossed his face, and to Julie, it almost looked like a preemptive sulk.

But when he didn't speak, Julie did.

"Todd," she said.

Meristal's brows shot up, then she smirked.

"You let that buffoon know you were in Dlad City? He could be the one who assailed Julie!"

Judas rolled his eyes, and Julie shrank into her pillow, sensing an impending argument.

"The buffoon, as you said, uses journey stones to travel."

Meristal shrugged.

"So?"

"If he can't teleport, he doesn't possess the ability to use Derengi. Besides, he's a kid. Where would he receive such training? It'd take years to master— ages."

Meristal shook her head.

"Fine, Judas, fine! You're far too trusting. It'll be your downfall."

"Are you saying you don't want me to trust you?"

Meristal rolled her eyes.

"I think you know me better than that, and I know you far better than any journalist would ever dream of uncovering."

Her voice dropped lower, softer.

"You'd doubt me after how many times I was by your side? Burying loved ones, surviving friends, in battle, in—"

She stopped suddenly, looking away, and Julie realized how close the woman came to striking a nerve and revealing the hurt to all of them.

Meristal's amethyst gaze caught Julie watching them. A flush heated Julie's face.

"Are you two married?"

Meristal burst into a bright, bubbling laughter, covering her mouth with her hand.

Judas looked away in silence, that sulking look returning, but Julie caught the same haunted expression in his eyes now.

There's definitely something here between them. And ... they didn't answer my question.

Julie let go of the thought for the moment.

"How are we reaching our destination?" she asked. "Journey stones?"

Judas snorted, standing.

"Walking and teleporting. Since we're in the Cape, the Corridor is near. Afterward, we'll teleport on the other side."

"You'll teach me to teleport?"

Julie pushed the quilt away, swinging her legs over the side of the bed.

"You have the potential, but your control needs mastering. Teleportation's the simplest way to get around, but not everyone can do it, and it's fatal if done incorrectly."

"That doesn't sound easy."

"He said 'simplest,' not 'easiest,'" Meristal reminded her.

Meristal moved away, reclaiming her chair on the other side of the room. Julie glanced at how the woman sat, and even then, she seemed so in control.

Poised elegance.

"You might not be able to teleport," Judas said, drawing Julie's gaze back to him. "There's also a visible element to it. If powerful enough, which I believe you are, you can perceive the aura of someone teleporting. But there are two other types of movement: winking and blinking."

"What's that?"

"Blinking's a precursor to winking. Blinking moves you a very short distance between two points near-instantaneously. Winking is like you're materializing from nothing. Only the most powerful can wink in and out of places."

"So ..." Julie frowned, "they're pretty much the same?"

"Well—" Judas started.

Meristal cut in from her chair.

"—Yes, in concept."

Meristal shook her head at Judas.

"You're going to bore the poor girl with technicalities; not everything needs to be so long-winded."

Judas's lips moved, but when he spoke, it was still to Julie.

"To answer your question, Julie, we'll utilize the teleport to cover great distances. I'll teach you what I can, or the theory, but it's far too dangerous for you to attempt. Promise me you won't be foolish."

She gave a single nod of the head.

"If we're separated by some chance, you can visit any city and ask a journeyman to port you to Wizard's Pass."

"And how will I afford it?"

"I'll give you some money before we set off."

"Journeymen are the guys with the stones, right?"

"Correct. They charge stones to teleport someone one-way. The energy depletes and must be charged again. Quite expensive the further you go. Portal Masters, however, take groups. Now, we need food for the journey, so I'll inquire with the innkeeper. Excuse me."

Judas left, and Julie immediately felt Meristal appraising her. Just to break the awkward silence, Julie scrambled for anything to say.

"Thanks for changing my clothes."

Meristal winked at her.

"Well, Judas wouldn't. He's far too prudish."

Meristal took a big, noisy breath through the nose.

"But I sensed something when I addressed your wounds. The remnants of lust? Did you copulate before the incident? Did that person attack you?"

"No!" Julie said. Her eyes went wide at being asked such a question. "I mean, almost, but no."

"I wouldn't shame you, if you did. I'd be more amazed you had the fortitude to fight off the magelust. The fact you did implies the longing lacked strength, but if you ever feel it for real, well ... you won't be so lucky a second time. Perhaps the fault lay with the man. Was it a man?"

Julie nodded. The thought of magelust with a woman had never crossed her mind.

"One day, you may fail to pull yourself free."

"Any advice?"

Meristal's lips poised, hesitating to speak.

"Enjoy the moment, regret afterward, move on. It's the only thing you can do, I'm afraid."

"Have you ever been affected by it?"

Meristal nodded, a slow movement.

"Yes."

"Did you regret the moment of indecision?"

This time she shook her head, and a small smile spread across her face.

"Don't tell Judas. It'd tarnish the image he built up around me."

The book Julie read came to mind, and since Meristal was a woman …

"Am I like all the others who can't filter out the lust, or will I master the technique in time?"

Meristal shrugged.

"Let me tell you something you won't get from most books. Rallocans are pretentious, prudish, and closed-minded, and you can probably blame the long history of nobility. Speaking as a foreigner, don't be too quick to dismiss or shut down everything. At times, Judas is fairly progressive, but in matters such as this, I'd advise against broaching the subject. He can get cagey about such … delicate subjects."

Meristal laughed, and it brought a smile to Julie's face. The other woman waved her hand.

"Look, if you need someone to talk to, talk to me. Having entered the magelust myself, it's not as bad as most people make it out to be. Everyday people have sex; wives with husbands, lords with mistresses, arystos with brothel harlots. But … I'd suggest you be a proper lady and keep your private life veiled in secrecy. There's no power in letting everyone know who's been graced with your … charms."

Julie nodded, then swallowed as another thought came to her.

"Is there anyone I won't go into the magelust with?"

Meristal shrugged again.

"Sure. Natural attraction plays a part, but if you view someone as old and infirm, or as a family member, the magelust won't work. Most who enter the lust are around attractive strangers, and they have to be rather potent in their essence."

"Well, that explains why Judas never triggered lust within me."

Meristal's smile widened.

"Very true. He does seem too old or fatherly. He was also warding himself and dampening his aura."

Meristal glanced at the door and back to Julie.

"Better get dressed while he's gone."

Julie went to her pack, heeding Meristal's advice, and dressed quickly. She shrugged into her robes of forest green and tan, the outer and inner robes, respectively. Dressed, she sat beside Meristal on the long chair.

"How long have you known Judas?"

"Since the war. A long time."

"He's trained a lot of apprentices?"

Meristal arched an eyebrow.

"Having trouble?"

Julie winced.

"Yes, but I think it's more to do with me than him."

Meristal chuckled, something warm in the back of her throat.

"I think it's safe to say it's a matter of both you and him. Judas has great abilities, a splendid teacher, but he's reserved, and likes to hold things close to his chest."

"Secrets?"

"Perhaps."

"Secrets involving me?"

Meristal's eyes narrowed.

"Probably, but he keeps secrets from me. You either learn to live with it, or it drives you away. I get a distinct feeling it'll do the latter to you. Address this with him. He's not unreasonable, just set in his ways."

Meristal smiled, and even though she turned her head, she glanced at Julie out of the corner of her eyes.

"He ever mention me?"

Julie tried to think back and shook her head.

"Typical."

Meristal gestured with her hand.

"Well, I'm sure he'll get around to it. But I will explain something now so you're not lost. I'm an Appariel."

Confusion flickered across Julie's face.

"What's that? Some kind of seamstress?"

Meristal laughed, covering her mouth with her hand.

"Gods, no. I can change my features."

"Really? Can you show me?"

Meristal stilled, and her eyes shifted from her amethyst color to Julie's own amber hue, then back to purple.

"By the gods! Are there others like you?"

Meristal's face faltered like an emotion stung her deep within.

"Yes, there are others, but I only know of one: Daylynn Reese, a Kothlere Council member."

Meristal's lips drew into a quick flat line.

"I don't have anything polite to say about the woman, so it's best not to say anything."

Meristal leaned back, changing the subject.

"Has Judas told you about the archangels?"

Julie shook her head.

Meristal sighed, shaking her head.

"Gods, that man! He's failing! Archangels are steeped with majestic power. You can feel it roiling off of them, almost taste it. Their wings are large, white —almost transparent like a unicorn."

Meristal grew quiet for a moment, as if reliving some ancient memory.

"How many times have you been around them?" Julie asked.

Meristal's eyes came back into focus.

"More than anyone else, as far as I know."

"Enough to be old hat?"

"Old and worn and patched together again."

"So, who's your student?"

"I don't have one."

"Can you teach me something?"

Meristal shook her head.

"Why not?"

"It's not considered polite."

"Oh, come on. It won't be that bad, will it?"

Meristal sighed.

"Alright, fine. Best not tell Judas. We skirt a taboo, teaching another's apprentice without expressed permission. Alright, what has Judas taught you so far?"

Julie discerned the uneasiness of her voice. They didn't have much to cover, and Julie finished a few seconds later. Meristal suggested a simple levitation spell, but as with Judas and the other incantations, it didn't work.

Next, Meristal drew out her wand and closed the curtains, performing an illumination spell. She said the incantation multiple times, ensuring the apprentice had the right enunciation. When Julie finally tried, she nearly dropped her wand when it worked on the first try. The white tip spewed a tiny, bright light.

Julie waved the wand, seeing the speck illuminate objects around the room.

Meristal was about to say something but stopped, her ear turning towards the door. She muttered under her breath, and the curtains flung themselves back open.

Light flooded the room, revealing Judas.

"Teaching again, are we?" he said to Meristal.

"Better than you, apparently."

Judas turned to Julie.

"Could you give us a minute? Grab your bag and wait outside for us, please."

Julie left, but her spine stiffened as she walked between the two friends. She considered hovering outside the door to listen, but they'd both know she remained there. Besides, she figured she'd be the center of discussion behind the closed door.

She retreated down the stairs. The new inn was much smaller than the last. An old man with wispy gray hair sat behind the counter, and he eyed her as she went outside.

Warm air greeted her—the morning air much hotter than Dlad City had been. From Judas's Transference, she had a rudimentary idea of where Cape Gythmel was on a map: south by southeast of Dlad City, snuggled up to the Corridor of Cruelty.

She turned south, knowing it lay just a league beyond. Once through the isthmus, they'd be in the Marcoalyn domain.

A bird twittered, and Julie's head turned in that direction, hoping to catch sight of the winged creature. She saw a streak of blue and a flutter of wings and it was gone.

Few pedestrians walked around the small town which boasted a dozen buildings at most. It wasn't even an eighth the size of Dlad City.

She glanced to the north, catching the rising blue sun.

Apor. I wonder if Praema will rise today as well?

A galloping horse drew her attention back towards town, and she watched a man drive his steed hard through the main street, his leather reins hitting the backside of his mount.

"Hyah!" the rider said with each smack.

He thundered past without a backward glance.

The inn's door opened, and Judas and Meristal exited. Julie tried to read their body language but didn't glean much. Their expressions were neutral.

Not for the first time, it struck her there might be more to the Judas–Meristal relationship. How did two friends who survived the Wizard's War together never become romantically involved? She wanted to ask, but the timing wasn't right. She could ask Judas later and judge his reactions. Would he hold back or lie outright?

She let the question fade away.

Today she'd start through the Corridor of Cruelty. Apprehension snaked its way through her, and even though she didn't fully trust Judas, she didn't worry about her safety.

He'll be there to protect me.

With that thought, she waited for Judas and Meristal to join her.

Chapter 19: The Corridor Of Cruelty

Julie slung her pack over her shoulder as Judas joined her. She sensed him inspecting her and the turmoil beneath.

"It's time," he advised.

Julie waved to Meristal, but the woman's solemn expression didn't waver. What had transpired behind the closed door? Julie eyed Judas, and she didn't see any lingering emotions on his face.

"Thank you," Julie called to Meristal. She hoped the woman understood the double meaning—the healing and the talk.

Meristal nodded.

"Judas?" Meristal called from the porch. "You'd better teach her more than a few spells if she's going to survive."

Judas nodded.

"See you when the war begins."

Meristal gave a final wave before she disappeared.

The warlock promised her travel by teleport, and this would be the first time she'd try to pay attention. The last time she'd been away, the sudden disappearance and reappearance of surroundings had shocked her. With a slight ability to perceive the essence within her, she hoped to catch something this go-around.

"Clear your mind," Judas instructed. "Don't let it wander, or you'll be ripped away, and I'll have to search for you. Keep your eyes open, though."

"Okay."

"Right. Here we go."

For a brief moment, nothing happened. Then, the air rippled, a stone dropped into a smooth lake. Blue mist shimmered, shrouding the world, and the heat from the sun was swallowed by shade.

But the location remained.

He placed a hand on her shoulder.

"Take one step forward."

She did, and he stepped right behind her, his hand guiding.

The ambiance changed, elongated, stretched. The environment rippled, blurred out of existence, and swirled. They were traveling faster than anything possible—perhaps thousands of miles per hour, but her feet didn't move.

Glancing back up, in the far distance, she could see their destination, a frozen painting rapidly approaching.

As abruptly as the effects started, the swirling stopped. The blue faded as color returned to normal. She let out a gasp, her foot taking a small lurch forward, and she scanned her surroundings.

The scenery had changed.

Up ahead, two tall cliff faces hedged a strip of land, briefly touching at the entrance, forming an archway. Julie tried to peer past, but the deep obscurity made it impossible.

She turned.

Behind them lay the small village.

"That must be Cape Gythmel," she said.

Judas gave a single nod.

Men worked the farm fields on the outskirts, and deeper within, women hung laundry. The scent of bread lingered on the wind.

Little houses with smoking chimneys sprinkled the area, and rich, brown dirt filled the fields. Thatched roofs covered the off-white homes, and no fence marked off properties. Everyone appeared to discern where the boundaries lay.

She glanced back to Judas.

"How long did the journey take?"

"About five seconds total."

"And how far did we travel?"

"A few kilometers. Our presence went relatively undetected, and I want to keep our visit that way. Strolling through town runs the risk of being recognized, and I want to keep Ralloc guessing."

Judas nodded behind her.

"That opening's the Corridor of Cruelty, and our destination lies on the other side."

Julie turned, and trepidation filled her.

"That thing?"

"Yes, my dear."

He started in that direction.

Julie adjusted her bag and hurried to catch up.

"So, Cape Gythmel? Not much there."

"Very true. It's the last outpost and the first defense of war. Since there's no more war, it became a settlement for retired soldiers and scabs."

Looks rather pathetic for the first line of defense.

"Scabs?"

"Conscripted men for the Grand Royal Army, nothing short of indentured servitude."

"That place won't stop much."

Julie glanced back at the settlement.

"Anyone else there besides old veterans?"

"Wizards; why?"

"Just curious, because Troll City isn't for trolls, so …"

His head snapped around to her, and a smile broke on his face.

"So, you remembered from the Transference?"

He nodded ahead of them.

"Nervous?"

"A little, yeah."

"Once inside, that might change to downright horrified."

"What's in there?"

Judas grew silent for a moment. He seemed deeply focused.

"Anything that'd tax your mind, body, and soul—remember, it's all in your mind, what you control. This place can only influence it."

Julie considered his answer.

"Is there anything in there that I can't defeat?"

"You mean anything that would destroy you?"

He grew thoughtful again.

"No, it can't destroy your body; but if you let the Corridor get in here…" he said, tapping his temple. "You'll shatter like glass. Magic is in the power of the mind, which is crafted with incantations for most. Some theorize the mind is where magic comes from."

He shrugged.

"The Corridor reacts to the wielder. You're in the infancy of your learning, and it should respond accordingly."

Vague answers again.

She couldn't shake the impression that he kept something from her. As they walked, she pondered his oblique answers. She scrutinized him and vowed to keep her guard up. She dissected his words, noting the omissions, and none of it fostered trust.

The seeds of resentment took root.

What's so difficult about getting a straight answer? Why's everything so ambiguous?

Meristal had been upfront with her about the lust, why couldn't Judas with magic? Julie had no qualms talking with Meristal, but Judas's secrets put a divide between them—Meristal had said as much.

She was right.

A rupture formed between them, and it continued to grow, though he seemed oblivious of the schism.

Can an apprentice leave their master? How would I even do such a thing? Would Meristal be willing to teach me?

"I'm worried," she admitted.

"You should be. Most folks don't venture through, only the most powerful. Most people living in the southern domains never see Ralloc, not unless they take the long way by boat to the Golden City."

"There's another way?"

Hope flared in her chest.

He gave a single nod.

"If you want to take a few months getting to where you're going, and that's just one way. It's expensive and treacherous. But what about coming back?"

"What way is that?"

"Follow the south edge of the Vikal Mountains until you reach the Golden City. By boat, you travel south until you reach the northern tip of the Infernal Wilderness, and then you travel dead west until you reach the Unicorn Valley."

She frowned.

"Why doesn't someone teleport away from the Corridor to get elsewhere?"

Judas shook his head, lost in thought.

"It doesn't matter where you are, if you try to teleport across the Abyss, bypassing the Corridor, it drags you here regardless. It's a funnel; like gravity, it draws everyone in, and the only way across is on foot."

Julie digested his words.

"Going through," Judas continued, "will help mold your mind into hardened armor. With that to aid you, everything else will come easy."

In theory, he means.

In silence, the maw loomed larger.

"So, Meristal taught you something? What?"

Julie glanced at him, then returned her eyes to the Corridor.

"Yeah, she uh … showed me a light charm."

"She's right, but you'll need more than a light trick."

"Well, what else is there to know?"

He barked a short laugh.

"More than what even a hundred years' worth of studying will get you. Theory aside, there's a species inside that looks like a flying furry rodent. The true name of the creature is Rafelene. They'd be nothing more than a harassment save one thing: they produce screams that shatter your eardrums and cause you to go deaf. If they keep screaming, they'll kill you."

"How long before you go deaf?"

"Seconds, depending on whether it's an adult or juvenile. But I'll teach you the incantation to stop the scream, or to make whatever's causing the noise to stop. The spell's useful for other things, like walking on rocks. Use it on your feet. Some ancient assassins have employed such conjury."

Judas stopped rambling about the subject and went straight into the incantation. Julie repeated it in her head, articulating each syllable. Perhaps with this new ability, she could go through undetected.

He instructed in measured tones, and Julie listened to each incantation and description. Her first major spell was the mageshield, which responded to her call with ease, far easier than influencing the candle, which she found odd. While she could call the shield almost at will, the protective barrier lacked strength, and her stamina waned fast.

"Mageshields are powerful, but they deplete your essence. With time, your endurance will grow, like using a muscle over and over."

The opening grew darker the closer they ventured.

A shiver ran down her spine.

Judas taught her levitation but the ability was beyond her. She tried lifting rocks along the way, but they refused to wobble. She ground her teeth in frustration, and she returned to calling her mageshield. Each time, a spark of satisfaction kindled within her.

Once she called her mageshield half a dozen times, she induced the quiet spell on her feet with mild success. The sounds muffled, but she could still hear each footfall. She practiced the few spells she could muster in her head, running them together in combination. Mageshield, blind with light, silent footfalls.

She hoped they'd be good enough.

The temperature plummeted as they passed from sunlight and into the looming archway.

"Here we go," Judas said. "The most important advice I can give you is to believe what your soul tells you about this place, not your eyes. Remember: the mind controls perception, but it can be influenced with other realities and lies."

They took a few more steps, and Julie *knew* she was inside the Corridor.

A wall of humidity washed over her. Every move weighed her down as if lethargic. Her body tried to rebel. A wave of drowsiness crashed over her body; her eyes drooped, but she fought to remain conscious.

A creeping sensation of being observed pressed upon her—thousands of eyes gazing upon her every move. The eyes watched and waited.

Heat rippled off her hands, running up her arms, but when she rolled up her sleeves, she shivered with cold. The air dried out her eyes and itched, then watered and stung. Pain needled her nostrils, and when she rubbed it, the leathery skin threatened to bleed.

With each movement, her joints stiffened, as if full of water, making each slow and weighted.

An itch clung just beneath her skin. She willed herself not to scratch the phantom irritations. Her gums felt raw, like she was rubbing them together behind her back teeth.

When they entered, the sounds, what few they were, became muted. An unseen entity pressed upon her head, like the clogging of water flooding her ears. The place even affected her balance.

Torture—that's what this place is.

She hadn't been here long, or had she? She swore she just entered, but the more she pondered the possibility, the farther away it seemed.

Time stilled, or perhaps ran backward.

Is such a thing even possible? I guess anything's possible here.

Julie made a note to ask Judas later.

Noise stirred behind her, like someone trampling twigs.

She spun around, a whimper escaping her mouth. Her eyes darted in that direction, searching. Did something lurk in the shadows?

Her heart hammered in her chest.

"Easy, dear, there's nothing to be afraid of."

Judas's voice soothed her, calming the rising anxiety. She turned to him, her eyes and mind latching onto him, remembering she wasn't alone in this cruel place.

His sympathetic gaze made her feel a rush of affection, his voice chasing away the weariness. In that refuge, she could almost forget his secrecy.

Almost.

Judas became her rock. Since setting foot in here, a tapestry of anguish slowly suffused her until he spoke. He saved her from drowning in the encroaching madness.

Julie glanced back to where she heard the noise.

"What is it?"

She turned back, regarding him.

He shook his head.

"Whatever you want it to be, or whatever you don't."

He turned and moved deeper inside, and reluctantly, she followed, her footsteps tepid in his shadow. He stopped suddenly and Julie, who paid attention to her unsure footfalls, ran into his back, and her agitation flared.

"Sorry," she muttered, though she didn't truly feel it.

She stepped around her frozen mentor.

Why am I so tense? Is it me or this place?

She saw why he stopped.

Before them, a small makeshift sign obviously built in haste, or at least, appeared to be, halted their progression. Made of old, weathered wood, the placard's letters were burned into its surface.

It read: *Three paths ahead; one will be your last, another will surpass. The only one left lies right in front of you.*

The riddle riled her; that earlier irritation boiled into something more sinister, festering inside her until it came out.

The longer she stared at the sign, the more tumultuous she became. That pressing weight returned. Her knees quivered with exhaustion.

How long have we been in here? I shouldn't be this tired.

"It's the Corridor," Judas said, as if he sensed her turmoil. "The Corridor does it and not you."

Every time he spoke, his soothing timbres brought her back from the brink, a lifeline reeling her back in.

"Try not to focus on your feelings. Look past them. If emotions control you, here or in life, they'll destroy you. Emotions can embolden your magic, but they'll leave you vulnerable. Try to concentrate, my dear."

She listened to his words, watching him. As he spoke, he made eye contact with her, but now, his eyes roamed behind her. She glanced back to the dark and gloomy scenery. Perhaps it was a leisure glance, or he was searching for signs of that earlier stirring. His gaze returned to her.

"Who around here likes to speak in rhymes?" Julie asked.

"No one. It's part of the Corridor, confusing and antagonizing. This place reads you and forms tasks. We can go into the theory later."

He motioned with his thumb to the sign.

"What do you think?"

"That we're fucked."

Judas made a face at her words, but he said nothing.

Julie read again for any hint into its mysteries. She almost laughed then, a rush of manic lunacy greeting her like an old friend. Madness pressed against her buckling mind. A buzz grew behind her eyes, filling her ears, a building strain.

Judas cleared his throat.

"Why don't you choose one?"

"Me! Are you crazy?"

She ground her teeth, her gums itching.

"I hate it here!"

Judas's full scrutiny fell on her. His face said what his words didn't.

"Hate means nothing here. I remember when I first entered the Corridor —"

"Please," she snapped, cutting him off. "I don't care about when you came through. How does that help me now?"

She groaned aloud.

"I'm so ... agitated!"

"One can learn from the mistakes of the past," Judas remarked. "The task is at hand. Even if you were to go out the way you came, you'd still face an obstacle. Doing nothing goes nowhere, do something and be somewhere."

Julie debated making a snide remark, then dismissed it, just to skip the long conversation that'd follow. She read the words over and over until they tumbled in her mind, filling her, drowning out the buzzing sensation.

Three paths ahead; one will be your last, another will surpass, the only one left lies right in front of you. The only one left. Right in front of you. Does that mean the middle or the only path is to the left? Or does it mean the right path will lead me to the front?

"Clear your mind."

She fumbled her wand, sweat coating her palms. She imagined the candle in her room, remembering how her essence felt. She called it now, certain it'd show the correct way.

Closing her eyes, she pushed out from herself, searching for the answer. A quiet settling came over her, and she turned her head in that direction. Her eyes opened and a second vision danced over her sight, a magesight, and it illuminated the trail to the left.

The vision retreated like it had never come.

"We go to the left."

"Very well, you may lead, my dear."

"Why me?"

"How will you learn if you don't lead? I can only guide you; I can't do it for you."

"What if I die?"

The oppressive, manipulating force returned, and her ire flared like an exposed nerve.

How can he do this to me?

Another thought crossed her mind.

"What if you die?"

"Nothing will happen while I'm here."

Julie walked past him, muttering under her breath. The anger swelled with each step, her legs snapping out, her heel striking hard against the ground more out of spite.

"Hope you die," she whispered darkly to herself, but regretted the words the moment they left her mouth.

I hate this fucking place!

This hardly seemed the best place to bring her, especially as a novice undeserving of such a lowly title.

Blowing a stray hair out of her face, she took the rut to the left. The route, narrow and rocky, twisted up along the cliffside. The climb was short and taxed her more than she imagined.

A boulder blocked her way.

Julie almost asked Judas to help, but she knew he wouldn't. It was her task, all 'part of her training.'

First, she tried pushing it, but the heavy stone failed to twitch from her efforts.

Next, she tried summoning magic, but it failed to heed her call.

Finally, to skirt past the obstruction, she precariously inched by on the lip of the path. Her heels dangled off the side, her toes had mere inches to find purchase. A quick look over her shoulder was a mistake, realizing the hundred-foot plunge to the ground below.

With grunts and a few fearful tears, she made her way past, and the incline leveled off, dumping into a small plateau enclosed by a rock wall. The trail caught her eye at the same time a movement drew her attention.

A pair of large eyes floated towards her, and she took an involuntary step back. This monster didn't match any of the beasts that crawled through her head. There was no way to mistake it for a saricrocian.

The enormous beast was a hybrid—the serpent head with jagged horns, a feline body, and a scorpion tail. The hideous head extended high above her, and the eyes almost made it impossible to move.

Julie lost her voice and nearly stumbled as she backed away. She turned, and Judas was nowhere in sight. For a few precious seconds, she frantically searched in vain.

It was a few precious seconds she couldn't spare.

Run, stay alive—live so you can hunt down that bastard. Where is he?

Rage gushed forth at his betrayal, driving her trembling legs, keeping her alive a few moments longer. The magic responded to her fury.

A small hope sparked within her.

She heard the screeching roar of the beast, and she did an about-face, wand held steady as she cried out the first words that popped into her head.

The moment she said the incantation, the words retreated to the deep recesses in her mind. The incantation wasn't something Judas or Meristal taught her.

A splash of energy hit the creature's front left leg, washing it in blue light, and the monster slowed.

Now, there was a second chance to escape.

She ran back down the passageway she ascended, the drumming beat of the creature's legs coming close behind her, a quick sequence of clack, clack, clack, clack.

The boulder loomed before her, the trail impossible to navigate. Pointing her wand, she shouted with all the strength she could muster, a flinging motion over her shoulder. She dove for the ground as the boulder flew past her shoulder. The creature roared in pain, and she didn't dare look back.

Fatigue enveloped her, her essence drained. She rose to her feet and crashed into the cliff, her shoulder exploding with pain. With her back to the stone, she saw the leviathan rearing up on hind legs.

She dived to the right, down the trail. A shower of rock peppered her body, exploding where her head had been. The creature's stinger struck almost too fast to perceive. She rolled up on her feet, her legs and gravity rushing her to the bottom of the path.

Spying a hedge of boulders, she changed course and leapt, and—for the briefest of moments—she could've sworn she floated.

The moment passed. She came down hard and rolled again, taking the shock off her feet, and scrambled for the shelter of rocks. She curled up behind them, keeping low.

Luck was on her side.

Behind the boulders, the rocky ground dropped away a meter lower than where the creature now stood. She peered between V-shaped wedges in the rocks below her.

Her body trembled with fear, breath coming in pants. Hot pins of sweat prickled her forehead, and several beads rushed down the sides of her face. The robes clung to her back, sticking from the sweat.

Screeches curled the air as it searched for her. When it turned in her direction, it bounded toward her hiding place with incredible speed. The snake-like head reared to strike when Julie thrust her wand up and yelled the spell Meristal had taught her.

The brightest light Julie had ever seen—rivaling even the light emanating from Staell—burst out of the wand's tip, eclipsing the muted sunlight. The brilliant light flashed like lightning against a backdrop of velvet night, momentarily blinding.

She blinked away the spots floating in her vision.

If I'm blind, so is the creature.

She ran before the monster recovered, but she wasn't fast enough. She dove underneath the legs, her movement quick, but it was faster. A long fang piercing her flesh. She staggered from the impact, then from the paralyzing venom.

She continued on until her legs refused to respond.

Glancing behind her, the monster swung its huge paw, sending her crashing to the ground with a bone-shattering crunch. Dust kicked up in the air, half-obscuring her. The ground rumbled beneath her body as the horrid animal neared. Its claws punctured her flesh, pinning her against the ground. Indelicately, its talons cut into her flesh, tearing her clothes, and rolling her to her back.

Terror gripped her as she gazed up at the horror.

Not like this. Not betrayed and then killed by a beast—not after surviving a murder attempt.

Shadows seduced her.

Like when she leaped over the rocks, time seemed to stand still once again.

The tail rose higher, then twitched, moving, plunging downward. It struck her at incredible speed, plunging into her chest.

Darkness closed in.

She didn't know which claimed her first: the venom, the darkness, or the stinger.

Chapter 20: Gryzlaud

"The hour grows near, and soon I'll be one again," Xilor's voice slithered out.

A crawling sensation twisted down Sidjuous's flesh.

"None in Ermaeyth will be able to contend with my hate once I'm released."

Sidjuous did as expected and bowed, but when his master couldn't see, he rolled his eyes. Xilor had said this all before, for ages, yet nothing came of it. Sometimes, Sidjuous questioned his continued allegiance, and only the threat of his return kept him and others in his thrall.

"Yes, Master."

Sometimes it feels like I'm placating a child.

Sidjuous would accept Xilor's rule, but until he returned, the fallen lord stood little chance without him.

Krurik wouldn't help him.

Krurik, Xilor's favored apprentice, lacked Xilor's vision, relying on subterfuge, while Xilor trusted his overwhelming strength. Sidjuous believed in his master's cause, but was he the best one to lead them?

Xilor's grand vision was akin to the Krey of the Grand Royal Army. The dark lord wanted to cull the weakness out of civilization, but the reasons hadn't been made known.

I'm just a pawn, and a replaceable one at that.

If anyone knew the master's scheme, it was Krurik.

"This *hell* I've been trapped in has taught me more than anyone can fathom," Xilor said.

His eyes rolled around the edges of the mirror's frame to make his meaning clear.

"But it has been useful."

"What do you mean, Master?"

"To enter minds, to influence others, to see what you could never imagine. Had I not been caged, I would've never slowed to learn such arts."

Sidjuous shuddered, cold dripping down his spine, pooling at the base.

If Xilor possessed what he claimed, what kept him from entering Sidjuous's mind and controlling him?

What if it's an idle boast?

Would just the threat keep servants from abandoning him? Other than Krurik, Sidjuous was the only one that remained in his presence. Perhaps the threat was meant for him?

"Then, my lord, why not enter the body of a creature or wizard and come back to us?" Sidjuous asked.

It was a challenge, a subtle way of testing if his master lived in the falsehoods of his mind, or if it was true.

"Fool, I can't stay indefinitely. They'd die. Only my body can hold such

141

power."

"How do you know?"

"Would you like me to demonstrate my capabilities, neophyte?" Xilor whispered.

The implied threat glided over Sidjuous. A touch of panic flushed across his skin, an automatic response from years of servitude, but he had to distinguish fact from an idle boast.

Sidjuous bowed again.

"An excellent idea, Master, I'd be honored for a demonstration."

And then, he reached for his throat and couldn't breathe. His lungs seized. Fire raced through his body. Black spots peppered his vision, mingled with plumes of red, gold, and green, as he longed for a single breath of precious air.

He fell to his knees, but he didn't hear it, didn't feel it. The deep pounding of his heart hammered his ribs and throbbed in his ears. His lungs blazed as if he'd swallowed fiery coals.

The hold released, and he gasped.

Sweet breath rushed in, soothing his simmering lungs and making him gag.

"Master, I ... know ... you ... can ... do that."

"That wasn't a demonstration but a reminder. You're not beyond my reach. Don't ever mock me again."

"Yes, Master."

Sidjuous remained on his knees, his head bowed, hiding the hate in his eyes.

"This is my demonstration."

Sidjuous's mind exploded with pain and light, blinding, lightning arcing out from his frontal lobe on a darkened night. The intensity was like staring into the suns, blinding him forever. He reached for his face, pressing against the anguish flooding through him. He pitched forward, a hand keeping him from toppling to the stone floor. His bones vibrated, threatening to shatter.

Then, it did.

His forearm snapped, a mild annoyance in comparison to his mind.

Another fresh wave washed over him, smothering him, and he toppled. A scream ripped from his throat, but he didn't hear it as he writhed on the floor. It felt as if someone pressed a dull axe into his skull, then drove it home with a hammer. His head threatened to rip inside out, his eyes pressing into the back of the skull and down his spine.

When the light made him turn oblivious to all else, a suffocating darkness enclosed him, a chilling pressure crushing him from every side. The constriction tightened him like a serpent, crushing him to death. He could feel it coiling around his head, ripping his left ear free. It built until his jaw shattered into a thousand pieces.

And then, the pain was gone as if it never happened.

He gasped, blinked in the sudden brightness of the candle-lit room. Unable to believe, shaking hands ran down his body, finding him whole, his arm unbroken, ear still in place, his jaw fine.

At some point during the demonstration, Sidjuous lost control of his body and lay in a puddle of his own secretions and vomit.

He struggled to rise, his energy drained. His throat was hot and angry, raw from screaming. Staggering to his knees, he rested on his heels, his head spinning.

"That's why I can't take over someone else's body. They can't contain my power."

Sidjuous could only gasp, catching his breath.

"That was just a brief touch of my essence to yours. Had I stayed longer, you'd be driven mad."

The eyes narrowed, scrutinizing him.

"Call for Derms to clean up your mess. Remove yourself from my presence and make yourself presentable."

Shaken to the core, cowed by his power, Sidjuous left the chambers. Xilor's impatience was palpable; he'd punished Sidjuous for his insolence, and it'd been only a taste. He'd need to make better use of himself.

He vowed to find a way back into his master's graces.

The trolls hadn't returned with Xilor's body, which meant they'd failed in the City of Despair. He'd have to do it himself, *needed* to do it himself.

Only success would assure his continued existence once his master returned, and he vowed to make sure that happened.

Chapter 21: Meristal

From Judas's porch, Meristal watched Sedrus, the centaur, climb the winding path to the home.

"This had better be important," Sedrus said when he neared.

His hooves stopped just shy of the Lakayre Manor's front porch.

Meristal shifted, then came down the steps. She thought about sidestepping the comment, but she wasn't Judas, and she didn't care to coddle.

"Well, of course, it is," she said. "Do you think I'd waste my time, or want to be dealing with you?"

Sedrus crossed his arms.

"Your tongue's sharp this morning."

"Judas may put up with your insolence, but I won't."

Sedrus glanced up at the four-story mansion, then around the grounds. A red wall surrounded the home, and Judas's cottage, the one he never let Meristal enter, sat unattended.

Gods, what I'd give for five minutes in there.

But she couldn't do that to him, violate his trust, even if he wasn't here. She'd know, and that'd be bad enough, but somehow, Judas would probably know, too.

"Why are we meeting at the warlock's house?" Sedrus asked.

"Do you know of any place in Ralloc where we can meet without being overheard?" she countered.

The centaur bit back a retort, and Meristal turned her eyes to the others gathered.

"Now then, let's get this started. Judas and his pupil will remain out of contact until the war starts. There was an attempt on her life, but she's all right."

"When was this?" Mella asked.

"It happened the night of an attack on Dlad City."

Meristal noted their blank faces.

"Which apparently you weren't aware of. It was the vampires, and there are more rumors of sheol movement the council's keeping quiet."

She glanced at the centaur.

"Right?"

His lips twisted, and he nodded.

"When will Judas return?" Mella, the elyfian, asked.

"As I said, at the start of the war, which won't happen until Xilor's forces push north of the Corridor and into the Ralloc domain. That is, of course, if you don't count Dlad City."

"What can we expect," Sedrus asked, "before the war starts?"

"According to Judas? Small skirmishes, if anything. The real war won't start until they breach the Corridor and move into the Ralloc domain."

"What strategic value is in small skirmishes?" Mella asked.

Meristal eyed the newcomer beside her, an elyfian, and Meristal recognized him. He was the Supreme War Commander of the Elyfian Enclave in the Vikal Mountains.

"I don't question Judas's judgment or Xilor's logic. But Xilor's absence will make some followers leery, and skirmishes will bolster morale and establish who's still loyal."

Sedrus rubbed his chin.

"Do you believe it'll come to another Wizard's War?"

Meristal nodded.

"I do, and it'll be here faster than we realize."

Zmora, the fairy, hovered at the back of the group, little more than sound and light.

"What do you need from us?" the fairy asked.

"Information, updates, pledges of aid."

She glanced at Sedrus.

"I know the council won't act until the dead start piling up."

Her eyes went to the others.

"But if we're not waiting for him once he marches, a lot of people are going to die."

She saw them nodding, thinking.

Scodd Yullus, the Supreme War Commander, shook his head.

"The elyves don't get involved, but we'll take the vampires of Shadow City should they arise again."

He eyed the group, as if daring them to claim the intended target.

"Years don't erase the innocent blood spilled from the first war."

A bleakness settled over the group as they remembered the atrocities.

"We fairies will do what we can," Zmora said, "but our Head of Creatures must authorize us to do so."

Meristal frowned.

If Julie even knows.

"And the Mother Centaur," Sedrus said, "has decreed we will stay out of the war."

"That figures," Meristal muttered. "You centaurs were never too brave."

Sedrus reared up, stamping his hooves, trying his best to glower and appear intimidating.

"What's that supposed to mean, Witchen?"

"It's quite clear what I meant!"

His audacity was a short-lived bravery punctuated by Judas's absence. Sedrus insulted her, calling her an evil magical user, like calling Judas a sorcerer.

Meristal lifted her chin to him.

"Your kind sulks when everyone needs you, but the moment you stumble into trouble, you squeal for help. Pacifists my ass, you're cowards."

Scodd Yullus nodded in agreement, and his brontide voice broke the mounting tension.

"Cowards."

Sedrus glared at him, then swung his attention back to Meristal.

"I'm done. Do you hear me? I'm out. I'll keep your secrets because I know the warlock will come after me if I don't, but don't expect anything else from me."

A smirk crossed Meristal's lips.

"Not like we expected much to begin with."

The centaur turned, galloping for the manor's front gate.

Meristal shouted after him.

"When we're all gone, no one will come to your aid."

"Let him go," Mella advised.

"We don't need him," Zmora said.

Scodd nodded.

"We're acquainted with their position. The past repeats itself."

"I didn't realize the elyves craved revenge," Zmora said, floating closer to the group.

Scodd nodded, his lips pressing together.

"The clan may not be out for revenge, but I am, and I require a lot of blood before I'm satisfied."

Meristal's eyes shifted between the gathered.

"The most crucial battle will be the first—at the Corridor. If we lose there, they'll sweep across the domain without opposition until they're at Ralloc's walls."

"If we lose Cape Gythmel," Scodd said, "we'll exact a heavy toll. I can't make promises for the king beyond our pledge for dealing with the vampires."

Beside him, Mella nodded, then glancing around the group, she spoke.

"Where's the warlock?"

"Inside the Corridor, or so I guess. His apprentice might have difficulty along the way."

Meristal squatted and unfurled a map of the realm. She laid it on the ground by their feet.

"The elyves will march from the Vikal Mountains, through Crossroads in the southwest and into Shadow City. After you defeat the vampires, contact us. We could use you to augment our forces, but that's for your king and our War Council to decide."

She stood.

"Meristal, do we know Ralloc's plan?" Zmora asked.

"You mean besides burying their heads in the sand and pretending it doesn't exist?"

She shrugged.

"They're still in denial about the whole thing."

"So, they won't fortify Troll City?"

Meristal shook her head.

"I doubt it. The council will deny everything until a stream of refugees and mounds of bodies snap them out of apathy."

Scodd crossed his arms, frowning.

"That doesn't bode well for the victims. Your government is terrible."

"Agreed … on both counts."

With a thoughtful look on her face, Mella broke in.

"What if Xilor beats us to Cape Gythmel? Is all lost?"

"No, but it won't be easy."

Meristal addressed the group.

"I'll join Judas in the Marcoalyn Domain and watch for any sign. Cape Gythmel isn't fortified, so whoever can spare the time or resources, that's where we're needed. Build defenses, or evacuate the people. Agreed?"

Sensing their resolve, she moved away from the group. They said their goodbyes and departed.

Meristal turned to the cottage, the lone building taunting her. She shook her head, pushing the thought away. When she turned, the house came into view, and she marveled at it. It was a beautiful home, and she'd spent a lot of time here with him, just not as much as she would've liked.

She swallowed.

This meeting might be the last time she saw some of these people. They all knew the risks of war; she'd seen her fair share of horror and close calls.

A gentle breeze tickled Meristal's hair. As she hooked it behind her ear, she felt a stirring, a power she hadn't felt in a long time. It wasn't the same as Julie or Judas, but of another … entity.

"Meristal?" a woman's voice whispered.

She turned, looking for who called to her, but she found the area devoid of life.

"We can't interfere …" the voice said, "… but that doesn't mean we're just watching."

A small grin tugged on Meristal's lips, and she turned again, facing the wall's gate. Now, the energy she detected turned familiar.

A being materialized. Large white wings folded delicately behind her, full of light and energy. Her face was angular, sharp, prominent cheekbones and a high-ridged nose, and her skin glowed a blue-gray. The creature was bright, but it didn't hurt her eyes.

"Adoreria," Meristal said.

The archangel dipped her head, touching the fingers of her right hand to her forehead.

Meristal waved the gesture away.

"I don't warrant such a greeting, not anymore."

"Perhaps not officially."

"Did—?"

"No," Adoreria interrupted. "No one sent me. My visit is free and clear of ulterior motives. Is it so wrong to come visit an old friend?"

Meristal smiled and sat on the steps, inviting Adoreria to do the same.

The archangel stepped closer.

"Though we're forbidden from direct intervention, that doesn't mean someone's not moving in the shadows. I'm sure difficulties and setbacks are bound to arise…"

Meristal smiled at that. There was so much in that statement, but she didn't begin to know the depth the archangel left out.

Meristal shook her head, looking out over Judas's yard.

"I believe we have some catching up to do, Adoreria."

The archangel sat, facing her.

"Indeed, we do."

Chapter 22: The Corridor Of Cruelty

The world spun: the first sensation she remembered. Her eyes fluttered open. Humidity suffocated her like a thick blanket in summer. Sweat beaded on her brow and ran down her temple.

Sounds, much like the rushing wind on a breezy autumn day, came and went.

Her eyes closed again, but a voice snapped her out of it.

"Wake up. Time to move on to your next task."

Her eyes snapped open, seeing Judas standing over her.

His familiar face churned revulsion in her. She despised him. Bitterness and a shade of hate washed over her.

She bolted upright.

"You left me! You left me to die!"

"Yes and no."

Judas cocked his head.

"Did you ever think I had to leave you? Have you considered I wanted to see what you could do?"

"I had to fend for myself against that … that thing!"

"And were you successful?"

"No! And you know it!"

"Did you succeed the first time you called upon your essence? Did you bend the flame?"

He waited for her response, but she wouldn't answer.

He nodded to himself.

"No, you didn't. I have to let go so you can learn. Right?"

"Yes."

Damn it! I hate that he has a point.

"Why did you have to leave me?"

"The Corridor works in different ways for everyone. My path lies in a different direction. I can't interfere. Well, I shouldn't interfere."

"You could've warned me!"

Her irritation faded with his words, and she resented both.

"Why? Did anyone tell you they were letting go of you while you were swimming? Probably not. If they had, what would've happened?"

"I'd panic."

He gave a single nod.

"There was no reason to make you panic, especially not on top of the panic you already faced when you encountered that D'viquis."

"Is that what the thing is called?"

"Yes. One of the more dangerous creatures, and only found here."

Judas backed away from her and sat a few paces away, giving her room to rise.

"If I died, why am I not dead?"

"You didn't die. This place, the damage, it isn't real. It's like that curse I told you about. It's ... for lack of a better word, a hallucination. This place works the same way, and the damage isn't real. Every time you die, you just fall asleep, only to wake up and face a new horror."

"Do I have to fight a D'viquis again?"

"Maybe, but probably not today."

He rubbed his goatee.

"I'll admit, you did great. You survived longer than I expected. These tests will strengthen your mind or shatter it."

"Great."

Judas's eyes twinkled.

"I'm sensing sarcasm."

"How could you tell?"

He smiled.

"I'll teach while we move."

He shook his head.

"Still, I find it troubling you faced such a creature on your first outing. Your aura doesn't match your knowledge."

"Aura?"

He made a noise in the back of his throat.

"Yes. Your potential ability to draw on magic is phenomenal, but your control is lacking. I'm hesitant to continue. I find it troubling that your first test was rather hard."

I should be powerful.

A sudden yearning ached within her at the thought.

In short order, they broke camp and took off. Judas led the way up the winding trail.

The long ascending trudge sapped their strength for idle conversation. The path twisted around and doubled back, and at times, Julie suspected they weren't making any progress. When her legs started to cramp, they stopped for a break.

Judas instructed her about little oddities of the realm, brief and unimportant histories to take her mind off what lay ahead. He also furthered her education by touching back on the levitation spell he supplied. When they moved again, the pebbles still refused her edicts. They only moved when she kicked them in frustration.

The footpath finally leveled off and wound back downhill. Julie sighed in relief, grateful for the change; going down seemed easier.

Probably because of my short legs.

The decline provided its own unique difficulties. Julie found it hard to slow herself when she picked up speed.

In the distance, birds chirped and wildlife teemed. The more she listened, the less the sounds seemed real. The resonance was off. The chirps seemed flat, and the crickets muted and negligible.

Even the wind rang hollow.

The sky above darkened noticeably; despite the arduous journey, they hadn't traveled all the day's light away. The omen set her on edge. The silent downhill trek was only punctuated by their thundering breath.

After what felt like many hours and several stops, Judas finally spoke.

"Your second task lies ahead."

Still panting, sweat matting her hair to her head, she couldn't believe what she was hearing.

"What? Now?"

Judas pointed above.

"You'll notice the sky has darkened. This won't be a test of skill but of wits. However, my destiny lies along another route. I'll greet you on the other side."

Judas stopped, and Julie stepped around him.

A sign stood in the middle of the trail, tacked together, weathered, and hardly standing. A lantern hung from the post beneath, and the sign read:

This is to light as wet is to rain. Do this to the sign and you can remain.

"Remain?"

She frowned.

"What does that mean?"

"Remain in the Corridor. It'll spit you out if you get this wrong. Take your time."

Julie pondered the riddle before her. She reread the first line, searching for deeper meaning. Could it be trying to trick her? Or was it as easy as it first seemed?

Tension nettled her shoulders.

She frowned, almost acted, hesitated, then, with certainty, said what she thought.

"Fire's the answer. We light it on fire."

Are you sure?

The voice wasn't from someone else; it came from within her mind.

Chills raced down her arms. It wasn't hers or Judas's voice. Could the Corridor enter her mind?

"Yes," she whispered.

The voice grew silent, a sense of waiting settled over her, but for what, she couldn't identify.

She read again.

This is to light as wet is to rain. Do this to the sign and you can remain.

Her eyes flickered to the lantern hanging by a nail. The soft light glowed feebly in the closing, dim gloom. She realized how much of a fool she had been. The answer lay before her the entire time.

Sighing, she reached out with her essence. Fueled either by her growing command or her internal turmoil, the flame flickered and responded to her call with ease. With precise control, she pulled the flame out of the glassless lantern and directed the spark upward. The sign burst into brilliant flames, a luminous homing beacon in the deepening twilight.

"What now?"

When Judas didn't answer, she looked behind her to find him gone.

"Typical."

He left you again. He always will. Your next task awaits.

She squinted at the sign.

"I thought this was my test?"

Realizing she was talking to herself, she shook her head.

That's the first sign of insanity, but as long as it's more truthful than Judas…

But a knot of worry coalesced in her stomach. Was she under someone else's influence?

She doubted it came from a ghost or spirit, and the voice did originate in her head. Was it privy to her thoughts, too? She didn't feel a presence around her other than the Corridor. Since entering, she felt eyes watching her, waiting, observing.

Thousands of them.

Ermaeyth isn't the world where you once lived, child.

Julie rolled her eyes and sighed through her nose.

Brace yourself.

The voice, dark and gleeful, sounded like her own, had she not sensed the malice in it.

"What does that mean?"

A rustle of wind drew her attention skyward. Those watchful eyes fell upon her. The Corridor drew a deep breath and waited.

A large humanoid creature with grotesque features swooped down, landing almost faster than she could register. She jerked back, though he was a good distance away.

The tall creature towered above her. The animalistic form morphed into a man as elongated fangs retracted, pointed cheeks smoothed, and the deep recesses around his eyes filled in. Though she noted the change, the close resemblance to the beast still prevailed. Nothing beautiful or graceful endured through either visage.

Shit, it's a vampire.

His eyes burned with hunger, and she, a succulent morsel to devour. His sallow skin and gaunt face gave him a flair of arrogance, and those eyes leered at her. His limbs were long and spindly with a paralyzing countenance.

Graceful and harrowing.

Her heart fluttered as a vague recollection of vampire vulnerabilities came to mind. The thought of becoming diseased from the sallow wight murmured its disquiet, her chest tightening. She wished the voice would speak, help her, but it waited with clutching breath.

A wispy strain of honeyed hair unfurled, dropping between her eyes, and she shoved it out of the way.

His gaze slid over her body like silk, like oil, and when he smiled, she could hear the saliva move with his parting lips. He stood too still, too cold, like a statue or a predator of the unnatural. His burning eyes lanced her, looking past her robes to her flesh beneath.

She couldn't discern whether he wished sexual vulgarities or to feast on her flesh.

Both would be bad, but which is worse?

"Another upstart waltzing through," he said, his voice raspy, like rough tree bark rubbed together. "Why should I grant you passage?"

Goosebumps sent shivers down her arms and legs.

"I wish you no harm."

"How quaint. Charm, is that it? It's weakness. Shall I stand aside simply because you smile, or exact a heavier toll?"

His head rolled back with laughter, a deep and menacing sound, similar to a dog's growl to a stranger trespassing.

"Give yourself to me, and I'll consider it."

She swallowed.

"Please, don't. I—"

His chuckle drowned her out.

"Let me taste your flesh, my sweet, and I'll let you pass."

She swallowed, processing all the implications of what his words meant, seeing if there was a flaw within.

Then he smiled, and his face transformed, the monster bursting forth.

"Let me devour your ripest meat!"

Jaws agape, drool fell from his mouth. Long, spindly fangs glistened, saliva stretching like a delicate web between the tips.

Fear kept her from speaking. She took an involuntary step backward.

"The more you shiver, the sweeter you'll be."

A long tongue lashed out against his teeth.

"You don't have a choice, do you?"

He edged closer.

She pulled her wand; her knuckles turning white.

"Gonna tickle me with that thing?"

He chuckled.

His elongated tongue slipped free of his mouth, dangling well past his chin.

Fear stabbed her, anger burned within her, and panic smothered her.

And they were powerful tools. Judas had once said emotions could aid her.

"How about I just do to you what I will?"

He hunched like a crouching cat, and she knew there was no escape.

Desperation pounded through her. Panic sparked an ember of rage.

She wanted to cower, to cry, to think it was all a bad dream, but she couldn't—wouldn't—be beaten into submission.

He leapt.

Wrath and fear burst out of her and through the wand.

A vast light poured out, the luminance so pure she turned away to shield her eyes.

And when the radiance faded, nothing remained of her foe.

Did I kill it, or did I pass the test?

She glanced around, just to be sure, even looking up. Seeing nothing, she spun to check behind her.

Judas stood there, his fingers interlaced, a solemn expression about his face.

"What happened?" he asked, almost in a whisper.

"I don't know. I was afraid, but my rage fueled my magic."

He nodded. His head quirked to the side when he spoke.

"You must be careful doing that. You did well, and it saved you now, but against something that can fight back, you leave yourself vulnerable."

She nodded, crestfallen that he didn't have more praise than a cautionary tale.

"What lesson do you take away from this?"

To that, she didn't have an answer. What lesson could come from almost dying, or getting fucked to death by a monster?

She decided it was best not to say that aloud to Judas. Besides, he wasn't there to help her, and she …

"Stand up for yourself," she said, "because no one else will."

A grim smile crossed his face, but it was a smile all the same.

"That's a heavy lesson, but a worthy one."

But a true one, the voice said to her.

A dark look of concern flashed across his face, and it vanished before it could solidify.

"Let's travel a bit further and then we can rest."

With a slow turn, he retreated down the path. Julie noticed his face right after the voice spoke to her, but he didn't say anything.

Did he hear it? Does he know?

A soft chuckle filled her mind.

It's our little secret.

Chapter 23: Judas

Night fell, soothing the humidity to a tolerable level.

Judas sat across from Julie, a small fire separating them. He slouched against a fallen log, his knees high, feet planted on the ground. He used his legs as a makeshift podium, a book lying against his legs. A bead of sweat trickled slowly down his left temple, unnoticed. Lost in his thoughts, the book lay forgotten.

Why's the Corridor testing her with such rigors? Is it basing itself on her power or latching onto mine? It shouldn't, otherwise we'd be tasked together.

He'd watch for signs that the passageway couldn't distinguish between the two of them. If it became too difficult …

Interfering may do more harm than good, but if the erratic behavior continued, he'd be left with no choice. The thought chafed him as it was a dilemma he'd never faced before.

But was it the right answer?

His eyes flitted to her and back to the book.

Julie's magical control bothered him, too. At times, she snatched her essence with ease, and in the next few moments, it evaded her like it never existed.

Granted, she lacked the luxury of growing up in a magical world, and what she grasped came in spurts.

I need to unlock whatever's blocking her abilities.

Her troubles started at the first attempt.

Or maybe the fault lay with him? He'd failed to connect with her, and the blame lay at his feet. Meristal seemed to have no trouble. The staggering majority of magic-wielding civilization derived from the Plotus branch. Her inability might stem from her focal point: her wand. He might need to see if she's destined for the Owlen branch and its orb, or a Mussari user befitting a staff.

If she didn't make significant progress by the time they reached Wizard's Pass, he'd reevaluate her.

I don't understand. A child should be able to go through here.

The mental bombardment should strengthen her, and he hoped the rigors would enhance her abilities.

If she's truly the one in the prophecy and to have a steadfast chance against Xilor, this unfortunate place is a necessity.

Without this abhorrent site, the dark lord would tear her mind apart on a mere whim. Judas still didn't believe in prophecy, but he wouldn't deny the possibility either. It was a reality he hated to admit.

He closed the book propped against his legs. He was no closer to understanding the secrets of the book, the Corridor of Cruelty, or Julie's inabilities.

False night life filled the background with noise, punctuating the stretching silence between master and apprentice. Frogs croaked several octaves too deep; an owl's hoot coming too fast; and then there was everything they couldn't hear —the things that crawled or slithered. The faint sounds were both irritating and a welcome relief against nothing.

Judas sensed Julie's disappointment and frustration. It didn't take a mind reader. Unable to think of something to talk about, he ventured back on the last meaningful conversation they had.

"Have you given any more thought to your lesson, about standing up for yourself?"

"No."

Well, at least she's honest.

"Why not?"

"Because I've been thinking that these tests, these tasks, are more suited for someone like you. You should be handling them. They're beyond my skills."

She shook her head, and her lips opened like she wasn't done.

"But I can't expect things to be handed to me."

His brow arched.

That's an interesting take.

He remained silent, waiting for her to continue.

"Some people want things given to them, and I never thought I'd be one of them. The idea of not earning my keep ..."

Her eyes narrowed, and she glanced up to the treetops, a look of concentration on her face.

"I remember something about a conflict between goblins and elyves. It's jumbled, but ... if anyone has a right to ask for anything, it'd be the elyves, and the goblins should pay retribution for their war crimes. But the elyves did nothing, which reflects greatly on their society."

Her eyes came back down and found him.

"I wouldn't be a good fit there, would I?"

He gave her a small smile.

"None of us would be, but you make good points. There are many like you who want to earn their keep, and there are those who expect the coffers to open for them. I don't condone people starving, and I think they should be helped to a degree; but if a man doesn't work, then he shouldn't eat at the expense of another man's ingot. Injustices of the past, real or not, hold no merit in the present. Tell me, should we let you be the queen of Ralloc because we exiled your ancestors so long ago?"

She scoffed and rolled her eyes. A quick dart of her hand pulled back a loose tress of honeyed hair behind her left ear.

"Of course not! The exiles committed crimes, and the punishment is theirs alone, not mine. The same can be said of me taking advantage of someone else's labor. So, no, I wouldn't rule as queen. Y'all seem to be doing just fine before I came along."

He smiled, reaching for a stick poking out of the fire, snatching it up and poking the ash bed.

"And there you have one of the greatest arguments in history. Traditionalists prefer pain now for greatness later; the open-minded prefer greatness now and the hardship later. Both gravitate to a desired end, but disagree who pays the cost and when. To achieve such admirable results, you need both."

"Why are we talking about this?" Julie asked.

In the darkness, the firelight made her face glow orange, and he saw her nettled brow.

"Well, you turned an introspective question to a larger narrative of society, thinking of others instead of yourself."

He paused to give her a long, measured look. He held up the stick, catching her attention.

"Let me ask you a question: if you received a million ingots and were told to spend it how you see fit but for the good of the people, how would you carry out such a task?"

She went quiet, and he returned to boring small tunnels in the ash.

"I don't know," she admitted. "Build another *Divinity Enigumas*, but closer to Ralloc."

Divinity Enigumas? I don't remember telling her about the school.

A cold suspicion settled over him. Had he missed a book in the Essence Transference? What other subjects managed to find their way into her mind because of his carelessness?

He cleared his throat.

"So, in other words, you'd build a school for higher learning and education, where people could go to learn more in-depth on particular subjects? Sound about right?"

She nodded.

"How would the school make money? Remember, we aren't giving you money to run it each year, so how would you sustain the school without funds?"

She held up her hands in askance.

"Pay-as-you-learn? That's the only thing I can think of. Why?"

"To better understand you. You didn't force anyone to attend or make it free with strings—you offered a path people could choose to better themselves and the domain."

Her brows drew down.

"What does it matter what I'd do with the ingots?"

He tucked his legs underneath him, sitting straighter.

Regardless of capital politics, he genuinely hoped for the people of the realm. He wanted to help, inspire, and make society a better place—to embody the change he wanted to see in the world—but was terrified of his eventual failure. If he fostered this same passion in her …

"To see if you think long term or short term. Not everyone has the patience for a distant future, and most turn to the immediacy of now."

Julie nodded. Her eyes shifted out of focus, but when they found him again, a troubled look washed over her face.

"What happened between you and the Kothlere Council?"

The surprise at the question caught him off guard, and he knew his eyes betrayed as much. He dropped the stick.

"Well, the council hasn't always been—"

She held up a hand to stop him.

"Please, not a detailed recounting of ancient history. The quick version."

His lips pursed and nodded.

"In short, skipping all the important but ancient history, the council's purpose was for troops and borders with neighboring races. Then came the Wizard's War and Xilor."

At the mention of Xilor's name, Julie shivered. She only knew the summed up history of him, a vile monster, a mass murderer, a shadowy figure lurking under the bed. He restricted knowledge on him.

"We were so uncoordinated in the beginning. Xilor had speed, numbers, magical strength, and communication on his side. We had none of that."

"Communication?" She frowned. "How'd you deal with that?"

"By spying—we stole the method from them. Xilor came up with the Psimond spell. We sent in a few goblins, and they caught his followers making contact with their then-unknown master. Xilor didn't reveal himself until near the very end—very cloak-and-dagger. When our goblins returned, we extracted the memories. No matter what, people refused to listen, so I left."

"Where'd you go?"

"I left in search of another master."

"During the middle of a war?"

"The war isn't what everyone thinks; it was sporadic—a skirmish there, a battle here, no declarations. Each incident seemed isolated, nothing but border disputes. Xilor used them to weaken us and reduce our ability to counterattack. He destroyed crops and towns, vampires devoured herds, the damage was endless, and we never suspected anything!"

The price we pay for being fools.

"So, what happened?" she prodded. "Between you and the council?"

"When the war finally ended, the council reformed. There were supposed to be seven members in all—wizardkind, elyfian, goblin, dwaven, troll, centaur, and the consul from any race—but politics, fear, and spite began hollowing that design from the start. Each race argued about what it should be named, its seat, who should be allowed to reside, and so on.

"The point was for one representative per race instead of one representative from each kingdom or empire; in a sense, forcing all rulers to work together and influence the one or two members available to them, regardless of their race.

"Eventually, a few of my friends and I persuaded them to name it Kothlere and seat it in Ralloc, in the house of Kothlus. The dwaven refused their seat outright. The elyves declined their seat after deliberations. Wizardkind wouldn't stand for trolls being on the council, and the goblins refused if we permitted trolls. So, the paper pushers moved legislation, and before anyone knew it, the trolls were classified as animals."

He held up a finger.

"But there was a catch, a clever clause: if a goblin were named consul, one goblin seat would be vacated—ensuring consuls stayed wizardkind ever since. So, wizards found a way to keep power even when they lost it."

Julie yawned, covering her mouth.

"It's late," he said. "You should get some sleep."

"I will, as soon as you tell me why there's bad blood between you and the council."

He shook his head.

"I was a different man in my youth: brash, arrogant, cavalier. They branded me warlock because I made them fear me. The magical storm I unleashed in their midst when I heard what they did to the trolls ..."

He shook his head again and sighed.

"Tales turned into legend, and I fear that the retelling of my story grows with each new whisper. So, that's why there's bad blood. I put the fear of the gods in them, or rather, the fear of Xilor reincarnate."

He eyed her for a moment, then shifted his head in the direction of her bedroll.

"Get some sleep. You've got a big day tomorrow. I sense we're nearing the end of our journey, and hopefully soon, we'll be on our way."

Her head quirked to the side.

"Nearing the end? Already?"

He nodded once.

"Get some rest."

Chapter 24: Here Madness Dwells

Though Julie lay under her blanket, her back facing away from Judas, it was many minutes before she caught his rhythmic breathing. The sound helped drown out the eeriness around her. His soft snores were pleasant, a deep rumble within the hollowness around them.

She curled up on her side, listening to his cadence. Now that she thought about it, this was the first time he'd fallen asleep. The alien nightlight droned about her, peppering her with auditory unease, almost a low, persistent hum. Crickets chirped, a deadening sound, ending moments too early, almost impossible to distinguish, but she could, and it made the fist in her gut tighten.

It was almost like the place was watching her, waiting for her guard to slip, and then it'd come in with a knife—like her killer.

The grass whispered in disquieting sighs as animals slithered or padded. Even the rattle of dead leaves sounded like the approach of a giant spider.

She focused on his snores, hoping to wash away her anxiety. Her skin tightened, her flesh prickling. Her mind spun, worrying about what she couldn't see, and she needed a distraction. While listening to him, she thought back over their conversation. He'd said some things she agreed with, and at one point, she even felt a rush of affection for him, even after leaving her to battle this place alone.

But then, she remembered what it felt like to be abandoned, the terror, and the realization she was all alone.

Gods, what had it been like for his children? How did they manage to live up to a father who was both hero and scapegoat, veteran and warlock?

But there were small moments where she peered past the armor he built up around him, the facade of a mentor, teacher, and she saw the man beneath, his soul naked and bare. In those moments, she almost wished she had someone like him to call family.

She had a father and mother, or so she assumed, but she couldn't remember them. And who knew what they were going through, not knowing what happened to her, where she'd gone, if she was even alive. She made a mental note to ask Judas later.

Tilting her head, she regarded him, smiling as he dozed.

At times, he seemed like he would've been a great father to have, but a part of her couldn't reconcile with the sentiment, having been his apprentice and on the receiving end of his ... faults. She probably glimpsed a side of him his children never did.

Sighing, she let those speculations slip away, and she returned her focus to the conversation they had.

It was nice to hear him talk about long-term plans and ideas. By everything he'd said and showed her, he genuinely cared for the people of the realm, and she supposed, by extension, her, too.

But the council was filled with a bunch of idiots. The people's prosperity was foremost on his mind. His affection meant a lot, showing he had—or would—put a lot of thought into her future and help her achieve her highest potential.

And for the span of a few breaths, all her anger and resentment she had been building towards him since they entered the Corridor seemed trivial. She was ready to let it go, to forgive and try again. Wouldn't that be what she wanted from others?

But even as she thought it, she felt a sneering presence within her mind, that voice that talked about keeping secrets.

Don't ever forget what he is like.

Was that a warning to never forget his sidestepping, or an edict regarding his abandonment? Perhaps her worst fears awoke to remind her? At this point, she wondered what her worst fear would be. She couldn't know, at least according to him. That creature was indistinct.

But perhaps she feared to fail so utterly that Judas would abandon her. Should Xilor rise again, how could she ever help Judas fight him? What look of shame and disgust would he give her?

A stray thought entered her head, the nameless young man in Dlad City. Before she could help herself, she remembered his hand on her ass, the way his lips felt, his fingers curling inside her undergarments.

Her face flushed red at the thought, not for what she'd almost done, but that she had those thoughts here and now.

A soft snore reminded her that she wasn't alone. Her eyes flickered over to Judas.

What if he'd found her with him, pressed up against the door, the boy's tongue in her mouth? What if Judas had seen them in the act—naked, sweaty, grinding helplessly against each other?

Mortification lanced her. Her chest burned with embarrassment, and the perceived humiliation only distressed her further. But beneath her initial reaction, a defense flared to life.

What does it matter what I choose to do with my body and with whom? It's none of his business!

She pushed those embarrassing reflections aside, focusing solely on the young man in Dlad City. Much to her chagrin, she couldn't recall his face, which only escalated the sense of shame—a victim of the seducing lust with the inability to recall her intended.

It's not my fault!

But then why was she being so defensive? And wasn't it her fault since she couldn't block out auras? Was it like that for everyone who succumbed to the lust? How many people suffered that? How many people pretended like they did just to blame it on something else?

Both Meristal and the book's passage told her the fault didn't lay entirely with her, but it still felt that way.

It's not every day you learn you're defective.

Another thought crossed her mind.

What if the defect spilled over into my inability to use magic?

She chased those wayward thoughts until late in the night and discovered another truth. When she had asked Judas what happened between him and the council, what caused the animosity, he answered with a long-winded explanation about the origin of the council and the Wizard's War.

Damn it! He tried to distract me again.

But did he tell her the full truth? Somehow, she doubted it. He still held his secrets close, and perhaps he had the right considering everything that happened to him, but that didn't help them now, their budding dichotomy. The truth, or lack thereof, disillusioned her, marring their relationship without structure, rendering it hollow.

Still, she found comfort listening to his measured breathing. Only when she stilled her mind and returned to listening to his rhythmic breathing did she surrender to sleep.

Julie woke up unexpectedly to the quiet echoes of the Corridor's early morning life. The sounds bathed her with a creepy impression. There was a strangeness in the muted light, more forced than usual, making the uncanniness of the moment prickle her neck.

She listened more intently. There—right there! The chirping cricket didn't seem the same, but at first, she couldn't think why or how. The flat tone and odd timing pulsed out toward her.

In the pause between drawn out chirps, an owl hooted in the distance, and that, too, sounded different, hollow. It didn't carry the same resonance it customarily did—which was odd to begin with.

Peering out into the expanse, she failed to spot the animal in question, but in the murky atmosphere, she didn't see anything past a few feet. Only in the distance did she see a faint ribbon of crimson, heralding the coming dawn.

"Good morning!" Judas said in a cheerful voice. "You're finally awake."

She turned her head, looking over her shoulder, seeing him squat near the fire.

The steady beat of forced sound throbbed in her ears, setting her nerves on fire. Her teeth even ached at the sensation. Today ... was different.

"Breakfast?" he offered, smiling.

Damn, a morning person. Just perfect!

She couldn't stand being bombarded in the early morning.

"Sure."

She rubbed the sleep from her eyes—eyes that were still fighting to remain closed for a few hours more. She wished she hadn't stayed up so late. Her fingers dug into the corners of her eyes, and the sleep she rubbed away felt like sandpaper against her skin, another irritant to start the day.

Rolling out of her sleeping pallet, she hobbled to his small fire where he squatted, stirring something lumpy and flecked in a black pot.

Her face bunched up, her lips twisting.

"What is it?"

She almost heard a chuckle from him.

"Probably best if you don't know. Just eat; it won't kill you."

He handed her a cup, and the steam rose from the dark liquid.

"I made a drink for you, too."

She took a sip and found the drink bitter, and that helped wake her up all the more. Wincing at the taste, she set it to the side.

Seeing as they didn't have bowls, they both ate from the community pot. Julie tried her best to choke down the mysterious creamy substance he'd prepared, and eating would take her mind off the madness around them.

She was grateful until her first spoonful, finding the texture akin to snot dripping down the back of her throat. Something squishy caught in her teeth, like gristle, and she set her spoon down to take a sip of the drink instead.

The hot, bitter substance slid down her throat, triggering a vague familiarity about it, but that didn't make it any easier to swallow. Between the dark drink or the lumpy sludge, it was hard to determine which was more appalling.

But the aroma warmed her, inviting repressed memories to return. She didn't bother to inquire about the liquid, a far better alternative than the mystery slop. Besides, the drink kept the morning chill at bay and helped her wake up, so she kept with the safer of the two options.

As she sat, the noises seemed to grow louder until it was almost screaming at her. She cast a glance at Judas, but he didn't seem affected by it. Either that, or it didn't affect him the same way.

"Why's the Corridor what it is?" she asked, holding the warm mug in her hands.

Just as she spoke, the noise around her lowered to a tolerable level.

"What do you mean?"

"What makes it do things the way it does?"

"Ah, I think I know what you're getting at. You want an explanation as to why the Corridor is here; why it works?"

Julie nodded, remaining mute. Hopefully this time when he spoke, he'd give her some actual insight instead of circling the subject.

He shook his head.

"No one truly knows how it operates, why it's here, the way it influences the people who enter. There is, of course, lots of theories, but nothing certain as unequivocal truth. You could say they're just theories. So, anything I tell you is based on speculation by the best minds and through my personal experiences."

Wow, he just told me a lot of nothing.

She almost prompted him again with another, more pointed question when he continued speaking.

"It was, in theory, created during the time of Hagen, the Father of Magic —an interesting notion that lacks empirical evidence. People speculate that this strip of land is a result of all the sudden infusion of energy during his time and formed from a cesspool of excess—two opposites surviving at the same time, creating and destroying in the same moment, surviving in a constant state of

163

flux."

She frowned at his words, and she glanced around them. Nothing seemed to be destroying and recreating around them, but perhaps it was beyond her ability to see.

"It's both stable and unstable," he continued, "but can never be one or the other. Do you understand?"

He paused, taking a bite of food, and glancing her way. Julie let her face fall into a blank expression. He continued after swallowing.

"Some people say Hagen himself created this place. I don't think so. It'd give him too much credit where none is due. Yes, he's the Father of Magic, and he did introduce a lot into the world, but he wasn't a god."

He paused then, and an expression crossed the warlock's face, and whatever he thought didn't sit well with him. When he spoke, it almost came out as bile on his tongue.

"I've bested Xilor, the strongest known magical wielder of our time, and even I couldn't create the Corridor—or anything similar. I wouldn't know how. Xilor couldn't create this either. So, hopefully that gives you a little perspective."

He sighed, taking another bite.

Julie took a sip of her drink.

"Then, what do you think this place is?"

His brow quirked up at that, and he answered after his swallow.

"I think its creation came about through the Lord of the Underworld."

She frowned at that.

"What does that mean?"

He cocked his head to the side, and a crooked grin came to his lips.

"Have you ever heard of the Shades?"

Before she could respond, he shook his head, answering for her.

"No, of course, you haven't. What was I thinking? A Shade is a side of us, a part of what makes us wizardkind. You have an emotional, physical, and mental presence. Those three things—emotionality, physicality, and mentality —make up the Shades; one Shade per essence, if you will. I think the Corridor is formed through Shades or at least, operating through them with an ... energy I don't understand."

He fell silent and began eating again. After a few bites, he washed it down with the hot, dark, bitter liquid. He shifted as if he was about to rise, and Julie interrupted his departure.

"Well? Go on."

He settled back into place, frowning.

"What are you talking about? That's my theory."

His spoon darted back into the pot, and he shoveled more food into his mouth.

"What is a Shade? What does it mean to me?"

"I just told you. Its meaning is inconsequential, fundamentally unchangeable. If I were to sit and explain every detail of a Shade or the essence of the Underworld, it'd only worry you."

She swallowed, realizing that her questioning was wrong. No, that wasn't right. How she was phrasing the question was wrong, so she'd try a different method. She softened her voice as she altered the approach.

"Still, I'd like to know, for personal knowledge, what the Shades are."

Judas gave a loud sigh and put his spoon in his mouth, pulling out a cleaner utensil after a few moments.

"The Shades are a myth. No, not a myth, a poor choice of words."

He moved his spoon around like a wand, pointing at words only he could see.

"The Shades have never been proven to exist, much like no one god of any creature or race has been proven to exist. It's not that we can't see them, as we put the onus on the gods to prove their existence. That's not faith, that's a demand for evidence. When people talk about the gods, whether it's Jupin, the One, the Creator, Father, Mother, and Child, or any other dozen or so out there, people come at it with three paths, the believers, the nonbelievers, and the analytical."

Julie narrowed her eyes as he took a breath, wondering what this had to do with the Shades.

"It's not always faith that makes people believe. It's not always atheism that makes people disbelieve. And the middle crowd? Those folks look at the world around us, seeing how magic behaves, seeing the miracles in everyday life and think, 'how can the gods not exist?' Those people look around and say the world is proof enough."

"Yeah, but what does that have to do with the Shades?"

He sighed, giving her a lopsided grin.

"I was getting to that. People, like those who look at the world and say, 'how can the gods not exist,' believe Shades are like ghosts or fiends that are neither part of this world nor part of the next. Some judge they're spirits while others swear they're either servants of a god or the ghouls of the Underworld. Perhaps their entities unto themselves."

He held up a finger.

"Or perhaps they're something we made up to explain what we can't understand. There's no way to tell, but the most interesting thing about the idea of Shades existing is this: the Corridor works exactly like the theory of Shades, which tests you emotionally, physically, and mentally. There's nothing else to it than that, and that—in and of itself—is the key."

"I think," Julie said slowly, watching him take another bite of food, "you didn't tell me anything just now."

Judas was silent for a moment as he thought about her statement.

He smiled.

"Indeed."

Agitation flared in her chest as he stood and stretched, rubbing his belly.

He did it again. Why can't I get a straight damn answer out of him?

The warlock set about cleaning the pot and dowsing the fire, tidying up the site with the aid of wizardry. He shouldered his pack not long after, like a young sailor about to make his maiden voyage, but Julie barely managed to scrape herself up from the ground, pick up her bedroll, and shut her pack.

Even though she'd woken up not long ago, and her stomach was still rather empty despite all the drink she consumed, her eyes were heavy with exhaustion as they set out.

They wound their way along the trail for more than an hour until they came upon their first sign. Judas, without pause, continued to the right of the sign. Julie stopped to read and then looked after her master, and the puzzlement she felt made its way to her face.

"Where are you going?" she called.

He turned back to her, and she pointed to the sign.

"It says we need to go left."

There was something in his eyes then, a weariness, or fear, or ... something undefinable.

"No, it says you must go left. I go right."

He gave her a casual wave as he departed for what seemed like the hundredth time since they'd entered. With a weary sigh, she continued along the left trail.

The rickety rut eventually led her to a narrow path along a cliff face. A tree up to her left grew out of the cliffside with its roots winding down in the rock. One root as thick as a branch jutted out over the trail, curving overhead to form what looked like a threshold.

It wouldn't have been so unusual, except that beyond the root—through the threshold—was but a shadow. Her eyes couldn't penetrate the darkness beyond.

Apprehension gnawed at her insides, the tenebrous destination kindled trepidation within her. She took a step forward when something above her caught her eyes. In the root, scratched with a knife and a shaky hand were three words.

Here madness dwells.

What trick is the Corridor trying now?

She took a moment to glance around her, and that's when she noticed that she didn't hear the usual sounds, nor did she feel the presence around her, or the eyes watching her. Even the voice warning her off or laughing at her predicament fell away. It was almost as if the Corridor was holding its breath, waiting on her with anticipation.

It almost made her want to retrace her steps and find Judas, but she had to go forward to get out, so she might as well get this over with.

She eyed the letters overhead again. The trials here had been difficult, but not impossible, and she wondered how such a place, as hellacious as it was, made someone lose their mind.

The scratched letters did little to quell her qualms.

How could someone lose their mind and still have enough sanity to carve the warning?

The uneasy feeling subsided when she analyzed it all, the conclusion

inevitably a paradox, a trick on her mind, like all the rest.
Assured, she entered the doorway.

Chapter 25: Mr. Pleasure

"Wake up!" a coarse voice boomed.

She jerked at the sound. The bellow was deafening and made her wince.

Her eyes snapped open as a massive, meaty hand smashed into the side of her face. Her head snapped to the side, and she saw a little of her surroundings.

The chair rocked back and nearly tipped over. The fall would've hurt even more than the slap. Her skull would've cracked on the stone floor.

The chair stopped its wobble. That's when she realized the metal clamps around her wrists, securing her arms to the armrests; ropes bound her forearms near the crook of her elbows.

She blinked back the stars and the tears in her eyes.

What the hell?

She glanced up in front of her, trying to focus on the man standing there, but every time she did, her eyes grew heavy. Her head lolled, and her eyes rolled back and forth, trying to make sense of what she saw.

And nothing did—none of it made sense.

Last I remember was the tree root...

A large fireplace off to the side illuminated every dirty crevice in the small, brick-lined room. And the place was filthy.

Where am I? Is this a dungeon? This isn't like the other trials I face.

It didn't make sense, nothing made sense, but the contrary evidence was irrefutable.

Around the small, cluttered room, suits of armor stood, some shiny and fresh, others corroded with grime and rust, their design archaic. Weapons of every kind littered the floor, piled up in corners, or crowded what few small tables stood: swords, maces, axes, knives, arrows. Various clothing lay heaped in piles, torn and blood-splattered, discarded by people who no longer needed them.

Was that going to happen to her?

Her eyes moved back to in front of her, and now, everything came into focus. Her gaze latched onto the man, and he turned her blood to ice. She'd never laid eyes on him before, but the way he watched her, that predatory gleam in his eye ... it reminded her of the sensations of the Corridor watching her.

The word huge did him an injustice. His staggering height was rivaled by his rotundness. Beneath the profound fat on his arms, Julie noted the signs of hidden muscle. His immense belly swelled out toward her, and she doubted he could reach her.

Being tied to a chair, not to mention the stinging throb in her face, was a hard argument to sidestep.

His lower jaw jutted out, a profound underbite that revealed chipped teeth, cracked and nicked while he ground them in his slumber. But the worst part?

His stench reached her nostrils, a mixture of sweat, mildew, dirt, and the sweet-rot of shit or a corpse. A faint undertone of copper or something metallic hid subtly as a backdrop.

Her eyes darted around the room, searching for an escape, but there were no windows, not even a door she could see, unless there was one behind her.

A sharp stab of worry pierced her, and her breath came erratically.

"What the fuck?"

He moved closer, taking two lumbering steps; his shaved head glistened with perspiration. A milky-white scar stretched from his left eye down to his jaw, a jagged line like a contour map.

He turned on his heel and walked to a table by the back wall. She kept her attention on him, but she also glanced around, finding anything to help her.

She didn't find anything, and her spirits plummeted.

Moving her arms, she tested the bindings, but they held her fast. She couldn't move at all.

Her eyes darted to the monstrous hearth, the length twice her height. The crackling flames filled the room with stifling heat. This place was almost as insufferable as the Corridor.

But I'm still in the Corridor, aren't I?

Her surroundings told a different story.

With his back to her, he rubbed the sudor from his head, flinging his hand to the side. Flecks of sweat splattered the stone floor. She could almost hear them sizzling for how hot it was.

The bald man faced her with hands wrapped in cloth; a sinister leer split his face.

"My name is Mr. Pleasure," he said, his voice soft, almost a whisper. "You shall call me by no other name than Mr. Pleasure. Call me anything but my name, I'll cut out your tongue."

Julie didn't say anything. Perhaps it was shock or fear that kept her from speaking. Besides, what could she say to that?

"You'll find that pain and torture can be a pleasure—for me, at least; you'll learn to love it, for it's the only thing that makes you know you're alive. Pain connects everything. If you survive, you'll appreciate the pain of other things —the things of the world—and they're *nothing* compared to what I'm going to do to you. In that, you may find comfort, for your life will be painless compared to this."

He pulled out a long thin rod from the cloth, the tip pointed and sharp, and rolled it in his fingers. Admiring the tool, his eyes flickered to hers, making sure she watched, terrified. He lumbered forward, his movement slow, methodical, inevitable as gravity.

"Let's begin, shall we?"

He leaned over her right hand, his hand clamping down on hers.

"This is going to hurt."

He grinned, and a breathy, dark laugh slithered out of his mouth.

He shoved the sharp, thin shaft slowly into the tip of her right index finger. She bit down; her throat constricted, her body twitched, spasmed, tried to jerk away but couldn't move. The bindings held her fast, and the pressure of the man's hand kept her still.

The agony was impossible to fathom.

Julie attempted to kick out while she screamed, bucking against the restraints. She pulled at them, wished them to yield.

A smile spread across the fat man's face.

Curses flew from her mouth as he stood, appreciating his work. Her eyes darted down to her right hand; the iron burrowed deep beneath her flesh, nestling against the bone. Rising panic washed through her, breath coming in pants, her chest heaving.

He cackled. Reaching down to the rod, he just twisted it. The nerve in her fingers erupted. She screamed, her throat throbbing, going raw. Veins bulged in her neck as if they'd burst. He stepped back a pace before turning and retrieving another shaft from the table.

"For some reason," he said, "when I insert sharp objects into the hand, specifically the ends of the fingers, the torment's almost unfathomable. I wonder why that is?"

Julie's eyes flitted up to him, and the look on his face made it clear he didn't care as long as he could inflict suffering. Rage bottled up inside her. Gods, she wanted to kill him. Between worrying about her finger, and looking up, he seemed to grow in size, like her screams allowed him to gorge himself.

With a delicate finger, something obscene for such a corpulent man, he tapped the rod once.

She whimpered, tears flowing down her face. The room tilted around her, or maybe she was just sliding out of the chair.

"See?" he said, bending over and placing his hands on his knees, bringing his face level with hers. "Pain lets you know you're alive. You're not dead. You should be grateful."

She shook her head, trying to make sense of his words.

"What?"

He straightened, his chuckle jiggling his belly. Bringing his hand up, he showed her the next metal pin. As she whimpered, he leaned over her, his drool sloshing from his mouth and over her face.

She wanted to vomit.

His finger caressed her cheek.

"There's nothing more beautiful than someone in pain."

She cringed at his vile touch.

"I'll give you a choice, sweetie. Shall we revisit the right hand?"

He pointed with the rod.

"Or would you prefer we move over to your left? What'll it be?"

She pressed her lips into a thin white line; her body trembled, but her eyes glared at him, promising him a long and painful death. Other than the escaped and trembling whimpers, she held her silence.

He sighed, a deep heave making his belly move perceptibly, and he strained as he stood straighter.

Don't talk, you'll only anger him further.

"You know, if you don't talk, there can't be clear communication."

His hand slammed down on her right hand, clenching it, crushing it beneath his weight, constricting the bones in her hand, hindering her efforts to squirm.

Fighting against his strength was an impossible feat. She was but a morsel in the jaws of a large predator. For such a large slob, he moved far more adroitly than she thought possible.

He drove home the second rod into the middle finger of her right hand, the movement quick and violent, her flesh ripping as he burrowed deep. The first had been slow and gentle by comparison.

The room flashed red, darkening with the color of blood and hate, and it was the first time she thought anything in this place could be beautiful.

But then it was gone, and she was only left with her misery.

She screamed and bucked against the pain, the chair wobbling, even with his added weight. Her head rocked back, bashing into the chair. Her arms twisted and squirmed, skin tearing, rubbing raw from the rope. Blood poured from her fingertips, a steady drip pattering to the filthy floor.

Her lungs burned with each erratic breath. Her chest rose and fell at a frantic pace. Her eyes glazed over, a cold sweat prickled her forehead.

"Oh, no you don't!"

Cold water drenched her to the bone. She gasped, her eyes snapping open, choking as he dropped the metal bucket to the floor with a loud clank.

Where the hell did he get that from?

The water ignited her skin like a thousand tiny needles piercing her. The chill snapped her awake, her eyes opening wide, the sting in her fingers sharper.

A hoarse laugh peeled loose, a deep resonance.

"Kill me!" she shouted.

His laughter boomed louder, his mass seemingly growing with her pleas.

"Yes, yes!"

"Kill me!"

Gods, she just wanted it to end. He'd only started, and it was going to get so much worse.

"Kill me, you fat son of a bitch!"

His laugh ceased, his lips falling into a snarl. A low, throaty growl emanated from him as he stormed to the back wall. He spun around deftly, a large pair of pliers in his hand.

"I warned you!"

He crossed the room in two quick strides and struck her face with the cold, hard iron. Her nose broke in a sickening crunch. Pain washed through her face, and her mouth sat at an awkward angle. The agony masked her fingers but for a moment. She blinked back stars as blood poured from her nose. Something almost choked her, so she spat it out.

Teeth clattered to the floor, and her lip movement while spitting set her face on fire.

By the gods, he broke my jaw!

Strong, gnarled fingers pried her lips apart, causing her more pain. They dug in, searching, the pliers rammed into her mouth, snatching up her tongue. He pulled hard. Julie's head came forward with his jerk.

She could see the soft, pink flesh clamped between the metal. A gurgling whimper turned into a moan as panic engulfed her. Mr. Pleasure drew a large knife—almost short-sword length—from his belt and leaned down.

"This will teach you, bitch."

He slid the sharp blade through her tender flesh, severing her tongue.

Intense cold followed by blinding heat filled her mouth as blood flooded in. In her shock, she inhaled rather than spit. She choked as he lifted her tongue so she could see it, nestled between the unforgiving teeth of the pliers.

"Something ain't connected anymore."

It's all in your mind, a voice said, but it wasn't hers.

The reality of what had happened sank in. Julie leaned forward and vomited, covering the floor with the remains of her stomach and blood. She tried to curse him again but couldn't.

But he seemed to understand anyway.

He snarled, hate in his eyes, then he laughed as he swung the heavy pliers down across her head, rendering her unconscious.

Chapter 26: Mr. Pleasure

"Wake up!"

A strong blow made her face tingle. Her head rocked back, slamming against the back of the chair. Her eyes snapped open as bright floating spots flared in her vision.

She blinked several times, shaking her head, and the world around her still appeared blurry, like water filled her eyes. Focusing proved difficult, but once it did, she was dismayed to see the obese man standing in front of her.

His glistening head shone with sweat, the jagged, milky-white scar highlighting the side of his face. His scowl turned to a leer when she met his eyes.

"My name is Mr. Pleasure," he said, as if they had never met.

But she distinctly recalled meeting him.

"You shall call me by no other name than Mr. Pleasure."

Am I dreaming, or does he not remember me?

"Call me anything but my name"—his eyes darted around the room—"I'll char your flesh over the fire."

He jerked his thumb over his shoulder at the hearth.

"Do you understand?"

This man is mad!

Julie stared up at him for a long moment, taking in his sheer size. Had he gained weight since the last time she had seen him? How long ago was that?

And then, all the horrific moments came back to her: the broken jaw, her missing teeth, the rods in her fingers, the pliers, and her severed tongue.

The man slammed his hands on her bound arms, leaning forward, his face looming close.

"Do you understand?" he roared.

His breath smelled like decay, fetid and malodorous.

"Yes," she whimpered, turning her head away, trying not to breathe in his stench. But even that seemed impossible, her breath coming in short spurts, sweat prickling her body, her chest flushed with fear.

He terrified her, and she couldn't forget what he'd done, what he still might do. He'd waved her tongue in front of her face, seeing it held in the pliers.

He withdrew, standing straight, and turning away as he retreated to his instruments of torture.

Her eyes took in the room. It was the same, full of grime and bricks and hopelessness. She didn't see any windows, no doors, but there still could be one behind her. She twisted as far as she could, trying to see behind her, and while she caught *something*, she couldn't be sure it was a door.

Facing front, she wet her lips, and that's when she noticed the lack of pain. She rolled her tongue inside her mouth. Her tongue and all her teeth were still there. Had she imagined the torture, the brutality?

How did he heal me?

But the only plausible answer was magic. The notion rocked her, that a brute was capable of doing something inverse of the methods he employed.

"Good."

His voice broke into her thoughts, and he turned to face her.

"Then, let us begin, shall we?"

His echoing words sent shivers down her spine.

He picked up a long, thin knife from the table and walked toward her.

"This," he said, holding it up for her to see, "is a flaying knife. This beauty skins beasts. Lucky for you—today—the thing getting skinned is you."

The glee on his lips, the slight peek of his stained teeth, his quivering jowls, told her how much he looked forward to inflicting pain on her.

She swallowed and bucked against the bindings on her arms, hoping against all possibility that they'd free her. But when they didn't budge and bit deep into her skin, fear crawled out of her like a corpse from the earth. With each lumbering step closer, the man seemed to feed on her terror. She tried her damnedest to clamp down on it, the revulsion of her predicament, the realization that she made him more powerful, but it was of little use.

He seemed so large as he towered over her, or maybe it was because she shrank away, trying to be so small, her ass trying to become a part of the wood behind her.

His meaty left hand clamped around her wrist, pressing her arm against the wood, as if she had any hope of squirming away.

He set the knife's sharp edge against her skin.

"This is going to hurt," he promised, echoing his words from before.

And then, he cut.

It was a slow, methodical incision, the kind where the blood only welled up rather than weeped. The steel slipped through the skin on her left arm, shaving off the flesh like a fine wood shaver. She tried not to respond, but she might as well have tried to stop time or destroy the world with a thought.

Convulsions shot through her, her throat hot, eyes burning, tears streaming. She shook hard, desperate to get away from him, from the pain, from this nightmare she couldn't wake from.

And then she screamed, couldn't bottle it in anymore. The dam broke, no longer holding anything at bay, and something inside her broke, too.

In the fog of suffering, one simple thought burned bright and clear, not a hope for escape, but a block against the agonies. The face of Judas swam forefront in her mind, and for the briefest of hesitations, everything almost faded away.

But her eyes darting to the bloody knife broke the spell.

She gasped, panting, the inhales making her dizzy.

"You surprise me," Mr. Pleasure said.

She blinked, and the solitude she formed in her mind faded away. Her wet clothes clung to her body, but she dared not take her eyes off him.

"Once people start screaming, they don't stop."

He smiled, his eyes darting down to her arm, and she realized that's what he wanted, for her to gaze upon the horror he wrought.

"Look at yourself."

She refused, knowing what would happen if she beheld the revulsions he inflicted. Panic would constrict any sense of agency she might have left, and mania would make her forget the need to get away, to flee.

And, she'd feed him.

He'd grow stronger as she lost her mind. Her emotions, and the control she had over them, only empowered him. This place, him, all of it, thrived on her mind, her fears, and … what it did to her body, only the gods knew.

Looking was giving in, but finding a way to take his power away, his control. Weakening him would strengthen her, but what could she do bound to a chair?

"Look at it!" he shouted.

She refused.

A snarl oozed out of him as he snatched the back of her hair, pushing her face downward, but she closed her eyes.

"Good!" he bellowed. "You don't want to see? You want to close your fucking eyes. Fine! I will cut off your eyelids."

He crossed to the table and picked up something very small, no larger than a fork, with a small blade on the tip before returning and strangling her by the throat.

"Hold still, unless you want me to gouge out your eyes."

Julie struggled at first, moving her head, shying and jerking away, but the cold metal left angry red trails of fire across her skin. She screamed and tried to squint, willing him to stop; anything to keep him from carving her, marring her, but she held still in the end.

Fire danced across her skin, her face burning as hot blood ran rivets down her cheeks. The sharp sting forked through her body like the fingers of lightning, blossoming in the back of her head and shooting down her spine.

Another scream ripped through the air, one so loud it hurt her ears. His hands worked deftly, and by the time he finished, her strength to fight him off had vanished.

"Now look!" he said.

Calloused, rough fingers—hard like stone—snaked through her hair. His grip threatening to rip out locks from her scalp as he forced her to gaze at her arm.

He'd flayed her skin from wrist to elbow. Muscle and blood pooled in recesses, the skin a sickly white and pink, a thin layer of fat clinging to the underside of her peeled flesh. The vivid redness of her muscles burned into her mind. What little resistance remained, the walls she hastily constructed around her mind, crumbled. It all came crashing down after seeing what the monster had done.

A renewed scream crawled up her throat—not one of pain and horror, but of vengeance and reclamation.

"You fat fucking son of a—"

A meaty hand crushed into her temple. Stars filled her sight. Julie's head rocked, her body slumped, and she teetered on the edge of consciousness.

Metal scraped on stone, and vibrations shot through her, starting in her ass and arcing to her head. She had the sense of movement, the chair dragged over the ground. The effect brought her back from the brink, but darkness courted her like a lover.

And then a new sensation, that of heat. Her body protested as his roughness bent her, folding her into an uncomfortable position, and it was the only thing keeping her from passing out.

Sweat poured from her, and her vision fluttered as she dragged herself away, focusing on the luminance before her. It moved, fluid like luminous, and that's when she realized what it was.

From the bed of coals, flames reached up for her, licking the air between.

She jerked her head to the side, trying to see what he'd done. Her arms strained against the bindings, ankles locked to a metal rod—roasting her like a pig on a spit.

A quick, panicked glance caught the bulky man staring at her, his leer widening, eyes twinkling, the white scar catching the glinting flame.

With defiance, she held his gaze.

This monster—no matter what he did to her—she'd deprive him the nourishment of her screams. She'd hold out until she couldn't anymore.

The desire to kill him surged within her, and all at once, her body felt alive, giving her strength to resist a little longer.

But the suffering ascended, her flesh melting, blisters rupturing down her legs and stomach. Even her crotch wasn't safe.

She wanted him dead, and she'd be the one to do it. She fixated on that as the scent of cooking flesh—her flesh—filled the room. His laughter broke her resistance, the torment unbearable, and the last thing she remembered hearing was someone screaming in the distance.

Chapter 27: Mr. Pleasure

The slap came first, dragging her from the blackest depths.

Well, that's different.

Her vision blurred with spots and stinging tears. She tried to focus, blinking away the haze. Heat suffused one side of her face; it felt as if the skin had risen in welts. A prominent underbite, a hateful scowl, and a long, gnarled scar running down the left side of his face greeted her.

"Wake up!"

His other meaty hand stung the opposite side of her face, and she involuntarily yelped. It was painful enough to snatch her breath away. The warm lingering aftereffects tingled long after his hand left her face.

The first one awakened her; the second nearly made her succumb to the darkness again. For a moment, her vision tunneled, and her eyes grew heavy.

Her arms were still bound, and she couldn't see blood, but what else did she expect?

She shook her head, clearing it away, and then the anger flared within her. How many times had this happened? She'd lost count. It was always the same: the slap, the torture, and the suffocating end.

Her chest burned, a fire building within. The warmth of his slap paled by comparison. Fury blazed bright in her eyes.

I'm going to kill this fat son of a bitch, if it's the last thing I do.

And that's when she sensed it. Beneath the budding rage, the helplessness, the ...

Her eyes widened, and she took in a sharp inhale.

In this room, the numerous times she endured the torture, not once had she felt her essence.

But now, she did. It was just there, within reach, pulsing like the hatred throbbing within her. It swelled, feeding on her emotions. No longer was it a silent tomb of lingering wraiths, but a wrathful sky lighting up the heavens, a current so fierce it ripped away logic, morality, or restraint.

"My name is Mr. Pleasure."

He leered down at her, oblivious to the growing swell within her.

"You shall call me by no other name than Mr. Pleasure. Call me anything but my name, I'll carve out your innards and feed them to you."

She sucked her lower lip between her teeth to keep her from lashing out with her tongue. She had to wait. He couldn't see it coming or have time to prepare a defense. She would get only one chance, and it had to be brutal, decisive, and merciless.

Feeling her essence, she pooled it into herself, gathering it like an ember held close to her chest.

He turned and lumbered off to his customary table. Just hearing his voice, the way his steps moved across the stone, his labored breathing, churned the turbulence within her.

A multitude of malevolent images flowed through her, destroying him with magic, cutting into him as he'd done to her, and horrors more sadistic than anything she'd yet to endure.

I'll get fucking inventive.

Shadows stretched in the far corners of the room, deepening like the darkness of her thoughts, mirroring her emotions. She had to act now, or she might lose this precious moment.

Her essence flared to life.

As Mr. Pleasure scoured over his tools, planning his next deplorable acts, dithering over his arsenal, the more her animosity grew.

She grasped it now, definitively, like never before.

The candle in her room back in Dlad City was a laughable attempt, pitiful like she'd been. She couldn't believe the ease in which she called upon her essence now.

And never truly fathomed the depth of her potential.

Judas always claimed she had the ability, and she'd never truly believed.

Every heightened sensation coursed through her. Her tender skin near the elbows where the rope dug into the flesh, the iron manacles around her wrists, the hardness of the wood digging into her ass. But she sensed it now, and more.

She and the sorcery fused together, inseparable, coursing through her veins like the silent blood that kept her alive. The effects were intoxicating, a high of dangerous and potent possibilities.

Her heart fluttered, thundered, demanding revenge. Her skin tingled, the fine hairs on her arms stood on end, awaiting her divine fury. Goosebumps rolled across her taut flesh; the energy demanded release.

Her mind sank deeper in her lust for domination, more effective than any opiate.

And in this moment, she understood Xilor, why he'd fallen to madness, why evil guided his hand. He wanted this control; he thirsted for power and the sensations that came with it.

She empathized with what drove him.

The emotion had been brief and horrifying.

She shut the thoughts out of her mind, not letting it distract her from this pivotal moment. Malevolence took precedence, revenge called for action. She'd unleash a destructive force so volatile, she might kill herself, too.

But at least all of this would end!

A single stray thought almost derailed the entire thing.

Why didn't Judas ever tell me about this side of magic?

She shoved it aside.

This was her moment to lash out against her captor, to free herself from his bonds. The darkness in her promised retribution, an eye for an eye. The scar on the left side of his face came to mind—she'd finish what someone else started, and then she'd take so much more.

She released her restraint on the rage within her, along with the essence coursing through her veins. Something within her took over, not born of conscious thought, but something innate, untaught, and unhindered.

The air before her rippled like a heat shimmer, and a haze of red crept through her vision.

The energy touched everything in the room: the fire, the suits of armor, Mr. Pleasure, even the weapons lying scattered along the walls.

She felt them all—the weapons: a dozen, then two dozen, then dozens more; the exact number became a jumble. They were for her to use. The swords leaning against the walls quivered and rose into the air, their sharp ends pointed at Mr. Pleasure's back. The axes and maces came next, drifting closer to her target. The knives and arrows jumped from their slumbering spots, quivering on invisible strings, hungry with anticipation.

Even the coals from the fire animated. Bows readied arrows, gleaming blades turned, hovering silently in the air, all poised behind the fat man's back. Rocks lumbered up from their resting places on the stone floor; even the bricks from the walls heeded her command, vibrating from their positions, revolving, waiting for the order she longed to give.

The fat man, oblivious to what transpired behind him, began speaking, selecting his preferred tool for the day.

"I have something special planned for you, my sweet."

He paused to admire the gleaming silver blade of a wickedly curved knife.

"I'll even give you a hint—"

The sound of his voice infuriated her, and she couldn't hold it at bay, couldn't hide her yearning for his blood any longer.

The table shook in front of him, cutting off his words.

He took a cautious step back, his head shifting from side to side, trying to piece together what was happening. The metal tools jingled and rattled as the table vibrated, shook, threatened to burst apart.

The fat man whirled around, his sneering gaze melting into abject horror.

Kill the son of a bitch!

If she ever had doubts about her gifts, they deteriorated in this moment.

"By the gods," he whispered.

The weapons, the rocks, the burning logs—all quivered with her hatred.

"They won't fucking save you from me!"

Before she could launch everything at him, he moved impossibly fast. Within a blink he crossed the room, materializing in front of her. Mr. Pleasure lunged forward, driving the curved knife down.

Something cold and hard and impossibly wrong slammed into her skull.

His hand came away, the knife no longer within his grasp.

Her eyes blinked, and her body turned torpid. Something hot and fast ran down her face, pooling in her eyes, coloring the world with crimson.

Oh, gods, that's my blood, isn't it?

Before she was too blinded to see, Mr. Pleasure lowered his head to eye level.

"What in the Shades of the Underworld are you?"

The last sound was the massive clatter of weapons, rocks, and coals hitting the floor—a cacophony so loud, it almost brought her back from the brink.

Almost.

What am I?

What are you, Julie?

Chapter 28: Ms. Pleasure

"Wake up, darling."

Something warm and soft pressed against Judas's lips.

He flinched awake, the sweetness still on his mouth. His eyes opened, focusing on the woman before him. He pulled away, but he found his arms held fast, shackled to a wooden chair.

A weary sigh escaped through his nose, and his gaze flickered up to the woman.

She was beautiful, ageless and ancient, the way he remembered: tall, curvaceous, with lips the color of rose petals and a white cloth barely concealing her breasts or the sanctity between her legs. Behind her shoulders trailed a long tress of hair that rivaled the white of cotton, full of volume and a life of its own.

She leaned forward, bringing her cleavage near his face. She smiled, her breath cloyingly sweet, like vanilla and a touch of sugar.

"Oh, I've waited a long time for you, darling."

Her smile widened, showing her perfect teeth.

"Ms. Pleasure," Judas grumbled, the tone low in his throat.

Her sky-blue eyes sparkled with mischief. They were cold as ice, bright with fire, inhuman, something not mortal.

"You've been gone a long time. The last time I saw you was—?"

"When I broke your hold over me."

He pulled against his bindings.

"What is this? I defeated the Corridor. You hold no sway over me."

She laughed a throaty chuckle.

"Oh, Judas, you mistake your belief with boredom. But I've found a new way for you to experience agony."

He snorted and rolled his eyes.

"Do you remember all the fun we had, darling?"

Her grin widened.

"We can have it all again."

He stilled, his face turning frigid, his eyes hardening.

"Look into my mind."

Confusion touched her face.

"What?"

"Look into my mind."

The air shimmered between them, the pull of his power too strong to resist. Her eyes went wide, and her mouth fell open. The atrocities of war flickered through his mind, a river of visions, visceral and violent. Severed limbs, decapitations, abdomens sickly red like a bowl of pulverized tomatoes and twisted noodles.

Faces flashed between them, every death he recalled, more than most men ever could. Explosions, screams, the slaughter, the lives he'd taken, and the armies sending their might in a clash of iron and steel. The dark lord and their confrontation, the atrocities Judas committed defeating him, and the creature who wouldn't die.

The air shimmered again, and the visions faded.

"Tell me," Judas intoned. "What can you do to me that hasn't already been done? I'm not the same boy who got lost in here."

Ms. Pleasure stood back, her mouth open, face slack.

"You've been busy. It seems you left, but never truly escaped."

The warlock rolled his wrists again, emphasizing the bonds.

"What are we doing here?"

She cleared her throat.

"There was something I didn't see in your vision."

A dark smile touched her features.

"You were never helpless while someone you cared for suffered. Yes, those close to you died, but you never witnessed them break."

"What are you talking about?"

"Your apprentice," she purred, her voice like silk. "Do you ever wonder what it'd be like to see her crack, to lose grip on sanity?"

"Julie won't break."

"Are you so sure? Fragile little thing. How long do you think it'll take for Mr. Pleasure to crack her sanity? When she numbs to the physical torture, and Mr. Pleasure turns to emotional and mental torture, how long before she falls apart? Do you think she'll survive the violation of her body as well as you did?"

Judas scoffed.

"You think bedding a man is torture? I was a boy, then—it was fun."

Her smile faded.

"Keep telling yourself that, darling, but I saw you break when that pretty girl with orange hair came to watch. What was her name again?"

Judas didn't answer. He wasn't listening to her. His thoughts turned to his apprentice. She'd never been tested like this, shouldn't be tested like this. Not yet. These trials were far beyond her abilities, and it'd be a long time before she was prepared. He'd been warned, and still couldn't quite believe it.

"I believe her name was Meristal. Yes, that's right."

Judas swallowed, and he didn't make eye contact. Meristal had been an apparition, nothing more, but yes, it broke him to see her there, to hear her cries, the words of anguish drenching him as he slipped between Ms. Pleasure's legs.

"Do you see your folly? Young or old, you still make the same mistakes, don't you, Judas?"

Judas swallowed. He'd been a fool. He should've never listened to *her*. Not Ms. Pleasure, not Julie or Meristal, but the *Time Warden*. That was the whole reason why they were here to begin with.

That damn woman and her meddling.

Judas eyed the woman before him. It was all playing out just like *she* said it would.

But how did she know?

The Corridor was meant to spark the magic within Julie, but he'd walked right into a trap, opened her up to the horrors he understood well.

Everything else the Time Warden said has come to pass, and the warning about the future is insurmountable. I just never believed...

And he should have. There were things out there more powerful, more knowledgeable than him. He was a spoke in the wheel. She'd come to him in Cape Gythmel, the night Julie recovered, and when he pulled Meristal aside the next morning, he revealed what he could.

Was this whole thing a miscalculation on *her* part? There were stories about children and even some adults walking through unscathed, untouched by the machinations of the narrow strip of land arching over the Abyss.

Ms. Pleasure chuckled, taking his silence as breaking him.

"And now, I have a way to rend you again, my sweet."

She leaned forward, kissing him again. He tried to move, pull away, bite down on her tongue as it entered his mouth, but she rendered him helpless in the moment.

Breaking away, Ms. Pleasure stepped to the side, revealing a massive, oval, silver looking-glass framed by dark-stained oak. Had it always been there, veiled by her small, lithe frame, or conjured by the Corridor at exactly this moment?

The surface glowed green like the Psimond spell as though she called to someone. Julie, strapped to a chair, appeared, the image sharp and clear. A massive bald man loomed into view, oblivious to their voyeurism. His large calloused hand clouted the side of her face, rocking her head backward.

Ms. Pleasure pulled back to the side, stepping out of his line of sight. His focus shifted to the images playing out before him, terrified, sickened, enthralled. He knew what came next, he'd undergone something similar with Ms. Pleasure. From the few stories he heard, only a handful of people ever met the pair. The tales came from those with prominent gifts.

He watched, horrified by the atrocities and knowing he was helpless to stop them. She endured countless beatings, mutilations, and deaths. For every lash she received, his soul and mind suffered, too. Silently, he offered a plea to the good spirits, hoping they hearkened to his anguish and her tormented cries.

And watching all this, what transpired, made him hate *her* all the more. Had she not come to him, not made her wild claims about brimstones and Apocalypse and all the things to come, Julie wouldn't be in this mess.

Gradually, his apprentice broke before his eyes. The first few instances, she passed it off as a recurring nightmare, but the reality burrowed deep not long after. He lost count of the number of times she suffered, recognizing the pain in her eyes, the invisible fractures through her psyche.

"Come on, Julie," he muttered, having witnessed another demise. "It's only in your mind."

But she fared no better the next dozen times. The torture whittled her away, each death costing her something precious. He writhed in his seat. Ms.

Pleasure tortured his soul without raising a hand. He wanted to turn away, to shield his eyes, but the ember of dishonor burned in his stomach.

He'd dishonor Julie by looking away, refusing to partake in her suffering.

The burden of fault was his alone.

Not entirely, but I should've never agreed to this.

The warlock should've foreseen this possibility, of her being unable to break free of Mr. Pleasure. He'd hoped that the Time Warden was right, that this journey would aid Julie, but now he realized how utterly detrimental those notions were. He prayed that she found a way to free herself.

He tried to think back to what the woman had said …

"She must face Mr. Pleasure, and you must not interfere, not until after you've become reacquainted with Ms. Pleasure."

He'd scoffed at the notion then, and now, he was terrified by how right the woman turned out to be.

Something unexpected happened, tearing Judas away from his thoughts.

Julie awoke, a crazed gleam in her eye. Even from here, he sensed the swell of her essence, her rage. It washed over him, potent, searing, and he shivered.

Few times in life had he experienced such a presence, such force: Xilor, and Judas's former master, the gnomling, Fife Doole.

He sat as a silent sentinel—a vigil—as she poured out her magic, controlling the weapons in the room. Everything heeded her command. The table rattled, startling Mr. Pleasure. He spun around, fear coating his face.

Judas swallowed. Julie's control was both beautiful and terrifying. He'd never witnessed such dominance in someone untrained. The awakening he'd hoped for had finally come, and it came with a cost too great and terrible.

Mr. Pleasure lunged, slamming the blade deep in her skull. Her head slumped, and all the objects fell, clattering to the floor.

"What the Shades of the Underworld are you?"

Judas shook his head, amazed, and he found his thoughts echoing his pupil's torturer.

What are you, Julie?

Judas swallowed, sagged against the chair.

What in the Shades of the Underworld did I just witness?

The question tumbled through his mind and only brought more questions. Upon meeting her, he noted the exceptional aptitude, but under Mr. Pleasure's sway … unbridled rage gave her both power and focus. It made the feat no less spectacular for it, highlighting how impossible it was for someone so infantile at magic.

And she conjured without an incantation.

For a moment, he wondered if that's what *she* meant by having Julie come through the Corridor. Not only would his apprentice find out her true potential, but make him realize what a huge mistake he'd made.

Could she be a warlock, too?

He'd assumed she was destined for the Plotus branch.

Is this the reason why her magical skills seem so feeble next to the aura I can feel within her?

Watching all this unfold was the hardest part for him. He remembered his time with Ms. Pleasure, recalled it vividly. This whole thing should've been years off. Julie's raw potential notwithstanding, she lacked the skill and experience.

Why did the Corridor read her so wrong? It's never done that before!

Mr. Pleasure appearing on her first journey troubled him. Only the most powerful ever met the keepers of the Corridor, and many people traveled through their entire lives without stumbling across them. They were the last step—the ultimate challenge.

And she faced it now...

Once someone passed the test of the Pleasures, like Judas had, the Corridor became silent to them. He never endured anything beyond a mild discomfort. It still blocked him from teleporting through, but that happened to everyone.

And Ms. Pleasure had been right, she found a new way of torturing him.

He remembered her shrill voice from long ago, sharp, clear, mocking.

"You'll never escape me."

He blinked, realizing she hadn't spoken for some time, and when he turned his head, she was gone.

And so were the shackles binding him to the chair.

He swallowed, a sinking sensation tightening in his stomach. How long had he sat free, oblivious to his freedom, and done nothing? Just another way for Ms. Pleasure to torture him. It'd eat at him, not knowing the answer. Did she free his restraints the moment she left and only morbid curiosity kept him riveted? Or did she wait until Julie finally displayed some form of power?

The purpose of the Corridor was to test a person—in theory, stretching their limits, rebuilding them stronger. Julie's success rested solely on her failure.

Julie needed him.

He glanced at her in the mirror, still chair-bound. She'd succumb again unless she remembered what he told her.

Right now, she believed everything she saw and felt, and if she didn't cast aside the shroud, she'd lose her mind.

If she isn't already.

Julie could come out of this completely mad, scarred for life.

A tear rolled down his cheek. He'd failed her, and he needed to step in for her sake. The only reason he didn't skip the Corridor altogether was because of the elder fairy, her belief in their prophecy, and the late night visit from the Time Warden.

He rose, the reflection of Julie's suffering burning in his eyes.

In this crucible, she'd failed too many times to continue, and he had to step in and end the madness.

Chapter 29: Meristal

The final interview from the review board concerning Meristal's tour at Mecas River City came to an abrupt yet pointed end.

Their consultation turned into an interrogation concerning the renegade warlock, a brand thanks to the consul and his propaganda machine. Her rising ire never cracked through her calm demeanor, hidden beneath poised elegance, methodical movements, and deliberate speech.

Of course, she disavowed any knowledge of his whereabouts, and when the committee realized they'd get no useful intelligence from her, they slapped her with another tour, this time even further away from home.

With a brittle smile, she gathered her belongings, rejected their offer with decorous finality, informed them of her immediate retirement, and left them slack-jawed.

Turning on her heel, she left them fumbling for words, scrambling to plug a hole in a sinking ship. But that wasn't her problem anymore, and suffering through their grueling inquisition had been worth it just to see their faces.

The chamber was empty save the interviewers, and the grand size juxtaposed with the relative vacancy made her brood as she left. There was a symbology in there, having to do with Ralloc, but she let the thoughts slip away as she exited up the long slope between dark wood benches. The white walls were startlingly bright without occupants to break up the oversaturation.

Though empty, Kayis Dathyr's shadow loomed like a dark phantom over the proceedings. The lack of witnesses revealed his intent to abuse his power in one form or another. In truth, the consul probably didn't care about Judas, just his current location, a place to exert influence over the citizens, encouraging upheaval around the warlock. As an exile, Judas remained a matter of the Republic, not a personal matter for the agents of the city and justice system.

Meristal walked out of the chambers, and for the first time in her life, had no place to be. She inhaled, feeling a burden lift. Two guards in full ceremonial dress stood holding the door ajar, waiting for her to set off. Their gleaming black armor captured the light and reflected the parts it didn't swallow. Narrow, refined silver outlined their breastplates, pauldrons, and greaves. Long polearms with silver blades were gripped in their hands. White ceremonial underrobes peeked through the separation of plates, and silver cloaks hung from their shoulders.

In a segment of the castle off limits to the public, sentinels quickly apprehended those without an escort. Without a word, she started off, and her two shadows moved in concert.

Feels like a prisoner retinue to a cozy cell more than a chaperon.

Small off-white tiles covered the floor in the Hall of Justice, a new segment of side-by-side courtrooms. Those closest to the wing entrance were for the capital, the mid-courts for realm affairs—the surrounding small villages and towns with their presence omitted on maps.

The domain courts came next, those meant to govern all lands extending beyond Ralloc's immediate sovereignty. Their jurisdiction went as far south as the Corridor of Cruelty and to the Golden City in the east.

The last door—the one she exited—belonged to the largest courtroom, the government's Kothlere Court which superseded all others. Only a pardon by the consul or the Kothlere Council overturned this court's decision. Meristal had spent years defending her clients and Judas in there. His multiple appeals had been arraigned and denied within.

There's a lot of history I'm giving up.

But that part of her life was effectively over now. It didn't bother her, to be walking away for the last time. History may be in the past, but her future endeavors mattered now. Still, that life would always be a part of her.

The new Hall of Justice was commissioned three ages ago; the rock was different than the older parts of the palace. The architects tried to color-match the stone, a darker grade than the castle proper—indiscernible during overcast days.

The original exterior, built long before they perfected their craft, was cobbled together from rocks. As the years progressed and expansions were made, the stones changed to brick, like this newest wing.

Molded with exquisite care, inlaid with serpentine stone of black-to-green, it contrasted with the off-white tiles relieving the dark gloom. Numerous torches helped combat the shadows. Darkness encroached this particular passageway; no windows graced this segment, but whether an oversight or intentional, she didn't know.

Do windows signify freedom and solid walls foreshadow guilt and imprisonment?

Intent aside, it didn't matter to her anymore.

Meristal and her troupe moved through the intersection leading to other parts of the castle. Royal Guards stationed at the sides of each double door for the courts snapped to attention as she approached. Royal Guards wore phthalo-blue, while ceremonial sentries guarded the Kothlere Council, the consul's private office, and the Kothlere Court.

Her eyes slid to a door as she walked by. Blooded-ebony adorned the frame, a dense, hardwood, black to the core with stripes of dark red through the heartwood. Small, chiseled squares gilded in gold gave the door texture. The doorknobs themselves were forged with magically enhanced gold, strengthening the soft metal.

Only the best for the Kothlere Order.

She could almost hear Judas's biting comments on the lack of frugality. He'd roll his eyes in disgust and bitch about the waste of resources for vanity's sake.

Still, not as bad as the council's chambers.

Her strides lengthened, the pace brisk, wanting to put distance between her and the decision she made. Behind her, heavy footfalls echoed in the corridor, sharp clinks of metal striking metal accented each foreboding step.

Retirement felt good, at least the first sixty seconds of it. Then, the reality hit her; she was no longer a Grand Wizard of Law, and no one could take the knowledge or achievements away from her. For the first time in ages, she walked the halls of the Kothlus Castle unemployed.

And I don't have to be anywhere!

Not entirely true, but a likable fiction.

Judas needed her, and she'd be there to help.

The floor shifted from serpentine stone to large white tiles checkered with a dark burnt-orange. She took a left, toward the central passages. Without further need, the chaperon halted the escort.

In truth, she'd put retirement off for years; it was the thrill of seeking balance, justice, and the cross-examination, exploiting gaping holes in the prosecution's otherwise robust strategy. And, she'd made a lot of money, too.

There were two types of Rallocan lawyers, government political and government directive. The political side was geared towards being judges, mayors, and politicians, while directive was more for mastery and hired as defendants of the people. The lawyers who prosecuted Judas at his citizenship trial aligned with the political party, while she freelanced for a very specific clientele.

She was almost out of the front doors when someone shouted her name.

Meristal turned to see a messenger bearing down on her. Once he came to a stop a few feet away, heaving, she cut him off.

"I'm retired. Find someone else."

A sense of vitality washed over her upon uttering the words.

Damn, that felt good.

"I can't," he said through gasps. "This person claimed to be part of your clientele. Wouldn't give his name, but he said to tell you, 'I met a horse once who was smarter than his master.' Mean anything to you?"

Meristal nodded.

She'd heard those words before, a long time ago, and only a few people were privy to them. The saying was made up during the Wizard's War, which narrowed down the list of possible people who knew the phrase.

Most were deceased.

She swallowed.

"Take me to him."

The messenger led her back into the castle, weaving through crowded corridors, past guarded doors, and up broad staircases.

Just when I thought I was out...

His pace lacked haste as he caught his breath. After a few flights of stairs and twists and turns, the messenger brought her to a door and stopped.

"He's in there."

Meristal reached out and opened the door, leaving the messenger to return to his duties. Her eyes narrowed in the dim light as she shut the door behind her. She considered reaching for her wand in the event this was a trap, but she wouldn't need it—so long as there weren't any survivors to bear witness.

Judas had his qualms about killing people, despite how efficient he was at it.

She didn't.

Her gaze wandered until she found the sole occupant of the room. He sat on a table on the far side, shrouded in shadow.

He spoke first.

"I met a horse once who was smarter than his master..."

"...but unicorns were never meant to be ridden."

Out of the shadows, he came, a jovial smile illuminating his face.

"Hello, beautiful!"

Meristal rushed across the room, crushing him in an embrace, smiling.

"Daniel! It's been too long! I haven't seen you since the end of the war. What are you doing here? I thought Krey weren't allowed to leave Outpost Dire, even if you are the heir?"

"Eh, I'm not, but who gives two shits what some lawyer says!"

"Hey! I'm a lawyer, remember?"

Well, I was.

"You always acted like a prune, but I see through the ruse! Lawyer? You haven't retired by now?"

"Yes and no. I no longer work for the government, but I'll take cases if I feel up to it."

He laughed.

"Good, got a case for you. What does the legislation say about me coming to Ralloc?"

"You specifically? As what? The Heir of the Krey, or as Daniel the citizen? To be honest, nothing really, why?"

"I'm just trying to make sure I'm not breaking any serious laws by being here without a summon."

His words chilled her, and her mind tried to figure out what she couldn't see, or rather, what he hadn't revealed.

"You came without being summoned?"

He nodded.

Her brows rose at that.

"That could change things. We'd have to look up the texts, which could take hours. Why'd you come if not summoned?"

"Well ... wanted to plan war games with the overpaid jyneruls, what-if scenarios, and whatever else we can think up."

"Hey, if I made their kind of money, I'd never retire, either!"

"At least y'all get paid. I thought you swam in bright eyes as an Advocate?"

"Oh, I did, but the jyneruls make double. Three ingots a month is ludicrous compared to my salary."

Daniel smiled.

"So, how about it? Care to help me out?"

"Gladly, anything for an old friend."

"Anything huh?"

"I didn't offer sex."

"But you said anything…"

She smiled and rolled her eyes, a kiss of blush coming to her face.

"Funny. Still pining for me after all these years?"

"Underworld take me if I'm lying, but yes."

She smiled. She hadn't seen Daniel in ages, and yet, being here with him now, it felt as if no time had passed. And he was still very much the same as she remembered: perverted, crass, funny, but still clueless about women. It was part of his charm; his humor attracted her, his boldness excited her, and his lifestyle without rules had appealing traits. He didn't allow himself to be tied down and riddled with propriety.

"You're still following that warlock around, aren't you?"

The question settled between them, shifting the mood, dragging everything to a halt.

"Come live with me in the mountains, and I'll make you happier than you've been in a long time. We're getting too old to live life with wasted moments."

Her eyes watered.

"Are you done?"

He sighed.

"Yeah, I'm done. I'd do anything to make you happy. I hope you know that."

Finding her voice, she swallowed.

"Let's narrow this down. What exactly do you need help with?"

"Being in Ralloc without being summoned, or for Krey to build defenses for a town."

She inhaled through the nose.

"Shades of the Underworld, you already mobilized them, didn't you?"

He nodded.

"If it's illegal, I need to know loopholes."

"I'm sure I can find some. The council always writes loopholes for themselves—never expecting someone else to use them."

Chapter 30: Raven

The fire crackled, the flames dancing to an inaudible tune. Raven stared into the flames, trying his damnedest not to think about the gnawing in his gut. Dinner simmered in twelve small kettles, and the aromas made their stomachs yearn. He eyed the thick sludge bubbling like brown gravy.

Each of them carried their personal kettles, responsible for cooking their own food. It was easier to manage than an enormous pot for all twelve. Such encumbering equipment made it improbable. Squad mentality only went so far, good for battle, poor for mobility.

The Krey had never force-marched great distances. They were usually magicked in by portal masters. Soldiers of the Grand Royal Army were trained for battle; the Krey of the Hive were bred for war, honed by their skills, defined by their prowess.

Raven's gaze flitted over his squad as he rubbed at the unfamiliar soreness buried deep in his legs from the leagues they'd covered that day. He caught sight of Patch and Two-tons, the only two veterans from the Wizard's War, both older than him by at least an age.

Probably more.

His replacement, should he fall, Xenomene, a virgin, just like the rest of his squad—all bloodless in battle. There was no denying they probably bled in House Eti, smashed lips, broken noses, snapped bones, but that mattered little when it came to the glory of war.

Other than himself, Patch and Xenomene, there was Drumstick, Keg, Bitcher, Mauler, Tiny, and Wrath. Three A'uri accompanied them: the Hand, Heart, and Mind. He didn't know their personal names, and most didn't bother to share, opting for the titles of their roles. Every squad boasted their own A'uri.

Raven leaned closer to the fire, extending his hands out for warmth. The Krey lounged about, all looked lazy, drained, and close to dead on their feet. He couldn't blame them for unburdening themselves, but he noticed that tempers were starting to fray.

"Oi!" Two-tons called to him. "Are you going to tell us what we're doing now?"

"He ain't ever going to tell us, Tubby," Bitcher responded. "That's not the way politics work. You bust your ass for him, and he gives you a promising smile, and you're left with fuck-all."

"That true?" Two-tons asked.

"For once," Tiny said, the largest of all Krey men, "don't live up to your name, Bitcher."

"Do they call you Tiny because you got a small dick," Bitcher sneered, "or a small brain?"

"We bring any ale?" Keg asked. "I haven't had a drink since we left!"

"You don't need any ale, you fucking drunk!" Wrath said.

Shit, here go the tempers.

"Hey Drumstick, are you hoarding all the food over there with Double-Tee?" Mauler asked.

Raven glanced in her direction, surprised she spoke. Mauler was quiet more often than not, but she didn't help make friends, not when she used hearsay, dead-eyed stares, and sharp words to keep most at bay. One rumor that never seemed to die and started when she was young, was that Mauler was a Toshii descendant, a cannibalistic, nomadic tribe from the other side of the Golden Sea—or some such nonsense.

To be honest, geography and history wasn't Raven's strong suit, and it didn't matter. Outpost Dire was his culture, and it didn't matter where people hailed from, they were part of the Krey the moment they walked through the gates with the bloodlust in their eyes.

But the story about Mauler never died, not when tales claimed her tribes ate their enemies alive. But now that he thought about it, she didn't match the tales of near-obsidian skin, but her dusky hues gave credence to the gossip. Raven had never been brave enough to inquire himself, not that he really cared anyway. He couldn't remember where he came from, but he belonged where he was.

Many Krey hailed from around the world, coming to the Hive at all different ages, bringing their cultures and customs with them, but he was pretty sure Mauler was several generations removed from the cannibal tribe—if she was part of one at all. Either way, he didn't lose sleep over it.

The Hive became a caldron of cultural diversity, wiping away one civilization and instilling a new way of life with each entering their community. Raven was pretty sure Mauler hadn't eaten anyone in her life; she was extremely young when the bloodlust manifested in her, but the thought was unnerving regardless.

"Can't help it if I love my food," Drumstick countered. "I guard it like treasure. We bring any wine?"

And they descended into bellyaches, grating on Raven's nerves.

"No, there's no fucking wine."

"No wine?"

"Why isn't there anything to drink?"

"This shit sucks goat ass."

"Why the fuck are we out here?"

"What cock-gobbler thought this was a good idea?"

"I'm about to fuck up your face if you don't shut the fuck up, Bitcher."

"Enough!" Raven snapped, lurching to his feet.

The laughs, whining, and everything in-between stifled in that moment.

"No, there isn't any ale, no wine, not until we get to where we're going. Drumstick, you're on rations just like everyone else. Don't let me catch you stealing; you know the penalty for that. We'll resupply when we can."

Raven shifted his attention to the group's biggest antagonist.

"Bitcher, for once in your life, as Tiny said, don't live up to your fucking name."

"Yeah," someone grumbled.

"And from what Mauler tells me," Raven added, "Tiny's pecker rivals a shovel."

"What?" Mauler said, shock on her face. "I said no such thing!"

Raven couldn't hide his smile, and a few chuckled. He continued. It was better to have them laughing that bitching.

"And I have sympathy for Xenomene…"

He pointed to her with his hand.

"…if she ever finds herself under him."

A cackle rippled through the group.

Xenomene, hearing her name, glanced in their direction with a blank expression, but she was disinclined to comment.

Thought that'd work, like it did with Mauler.

She sat by herself, a healthy distance away from the group as she usually did, gracing the edges of their firelight, over a dozen paces away. Her aversion to intermingling with her comrades wasn't a surprise, but her continued employment of the tactic during their trip was.

Raven had hoped to change that during their journey, and he needed to, especially with the edicts the heir handed down. Returning her attention to her hands, she continued sharpening her dagger, dragging it slowly across the whetstone.

The others must've seen his attention on her, because Bitcher called out.

"Would you care to join us, Miss Brooder?"

"Not really," she countered, her voice soft. Raven barely heard it.

"What's her problem?" Two-tons asked.

"Her tit-strap is cinched too tight," Bitcher answered.

"Come join us anyway," Raven said, hoping Xenomene wouldn't make him order her. Requests were better than demands, at least at this stage.

With a dramatic and sarcastic sigh, she took two steps forward, and dumped herself on the ground, returning to her sharpening. Instead of pressing the matter, Raven let it drop and brought his attention back to everyone. The A'uri, who usually clustered together, hovered at the edges of the fire, listening.

Raven addressed the group.

"To answer your earlier question, yes, I'm going to tell you what we're doing, where we're going, and why. I was under orders not to say until well away from the Hive. If word got out, it'd be bad for everyone."

"Bad?" Bitcher echoed. "Bad as in we have to march all the way back, or bad as in you've got diarrhea while marching back?"

A few sniggers rose around the fire. Tiny sighed noisily, and Raven rolled his eyes.

"As in a declaration of war, shithead," Raven said. "We're to proceed to Cape Gythmel with all haste, traveling by foot across the countryside and avoiding towns, people, or establishments at all costs unless we need to resupply. In the case of supplies, two of the A'uri are to go into town and replenish our provisions. Questions thus far?"

"Oi! I got one."

Bitcher waved his hand in the air.

"Why in the hell are we going to a cesspit like Cape Gythmel? I mean, there ain't nothing there besides pig shit, horse shit, and farmer's shit. Only thing to do there is fuck goats."

"You'd know about that," Tiny said, "wouldn't you?"

"Eat my ass, Tiny."

Raven cleared his throat.

"Thank you for articulating the various reasons why that locale isn't anyone's preferred haven, Bitcher. If asked, we're there to assess the town, its lack of defenses, and effect fortifications to the best of our abilities."

"Like trial and error method?" Wrath asked.

"Defenses?" Mauler interrupted. "Fuck that! We're offensive."

Some of you are, that's for sure.

"Aye," Tiny agreed. "We take the war to the enemy, not sit on our asses like the Grand Royal Army."

"What the hell do any of you know about war?" Raven countered. "The only veterans here besides myself are Patch and Two-tons. None of you have seen war, and most of you have never taken a life."

The words were sharp, stabbing a poignant detail. To be a virgin in the Krey was … frowned upon, to say the least. A silence fell over them, but he could read the unrest in their eyes. They'd grown accustomed to the comfortable life in Outpost Dire: training, drinking, eating, fighting, and fucking—then do it again the next day.

They say you weren't really a true Krey if you didn't do all five each day.

Angst and malaise rippled through those under his command, balking at the simplistic yet mind-numbing task of marching and fortifying a town. He didn't know how long it'd last, or if it'd get better or worse. How many more days until it turned from vexation and dissatisfaction to open sedition?

"Since that's our official story," Xenomene said from the back of the group, "then what are we really doing there?"

Well, that girl's full of surprises.

"Thanks for joining us, Xeno; our real campaign is war. The defenses are a pretense to be onsite."

"War?" Wrath asked.

He nodded.

"Who?" Patch asked.

Raven swallowed, thinking of all the ways his answer was about to land.

"Xilor."

The camp burst into pandemonium as conversations erupted, most of them negative. Shouted interjections and raised voices carried their incoherent words to Raven's ears, noting the reactions of his subordinates. The virgins were up on their feet, gesturing and posturing with aggressive body language.

His veterans sat upon the ground watching the young members, their mouths open, shaking their heads in disbelief.

The generational gap between vets and virgins became apparent by their reactions.

Patch and Two-tons' faces held scorn as they entered the debate from their seated positions.

But not once did a flash of red hair find its way into the standing throng. Raven glanced around, finding Xenomene, the next in line for his rank, still sharpening her dagger, unaffected by the upheaval around her.

At least one person will keep their cool when the battle's upon us.

She rose to her feet, the movement fluid, sheathing her blade. It just reaffirmed everything Raven thought about her, how dangerous she was in a fight. You couldn't train grace like that. It was born to her.

Her sudden motion caught everyone's attention quicker than if she yelled. Contemptuous glares shifted, conversations ceased, forgotten by her soundless disturbance.

"It doesn't matter why we're building defenses," she said.

She glanced at all of them in turn.

"Xilor could bring an army. Dragons could come back in greater numbers. A flock of geese with fiery shit could swoop in to attack…"

She shrugged, shaking her head. She crossed her arms.

"None of it matters or changes the fact that defenses are needed. We've been tasked by the Heir—against standing law, I remind you—and he mobilized us. The Heir's willing to risk all-out war and retaliation from Ralloc, so it must be important."

She reached down, grabbing her sleeping roll where she'd been sitting.

"That's good enough for me, and it should be for you, too. Now, I'm getting some sleep, so keep the noise level down. We're marching tomorrow, and the next day, and the day after that for the next two moon turns, so I suggest you do the same."

"Get fucked," Bitcher mumbled, and though everyone heard it, it wasn't loud.

She didn't bother to acknowledge what he said. Xenomene turned on her heel and went back to her pack.

With reluctance, the Krey dispersed, arguments abandoned, retreating to their areas to claim their respective pots. Some finished their food while others picked at armor and gear.

Raven watched them reverting to their devices and spied Xenomene from a distance, grateful for her interjection. In one stroke, she'd turned them away from fighting each other and told them what they needed to know, not what they wanted to hear.

And it surprised him. She wasn't one for many words, and she was the tiniest Krey in their squad, hell, maybe in the Hive, minus the children, but she commanded their attention when she spoke.

He shook his head in wonder.

Now if we can just work on your people skills, Xeno, you'll do alright with the burden of command.

Raven turned away, returning to his area, freeing his sleeping roll from his pack's lashes. Xenomene would need to learn compassion, or at least fake it well enough to have people follow her into death's embrace.

When the heir asked him to take this mission, Raven assumed he'd die. In fact, he assumed they'd have about an eighty-percent casualty rate. That had been the norm during the war. But with so many virgins in their midst, he gave his survival a fifty percent chance.

He sensed a presence hovering behind him, and he glanced up to see Patch standing there.

Gods, he looks so old. I wonder if I look the same to him.

Raven spoke as he unrolled his blankets.

"Something on your mind?"

"Oh, aye, you could say that."

"Feel free to speak and save me the breath of asking questions."

"It's about when you die," Patch said, his voice grave.

Raven suppressed a grimace. Everyone knew they'd die, hell even planned on it, but it was another thing to talk about it so matter-of-factly. The Krey were born to die, first into battle, the first out, but they habitually failed to return.

"You want to know if you're taking over?" Raven asked.

The other nodded.

Finished unrolling his blankets, Raven sat, leaning against his pack and motioned for the other to do the same. With an audible sigh, Patch sat down.

"Orders from the heir. You won't be taking over."

"What the hell's Daniel thinking?"

"The *Heir* is thinking we're going to die anyway. We're not young anymore. Also, there's talk about resuming the old ways; the strongest will lead, the best with the blade."

Patch grunted, then jerked his head toward Xenomene.

"You think she's strong?"

Raven's eyes went to her, seeing her get ready to bed down, and shrugged.

"She's done nothing to make me think otherwise. The only reason she isn't leading now is that she's a virgin. The heir believes a war will break out, and if it does, that'll be remedied rather quickly, don't you think?"

"She has no experience leading."

"True, but point out one man that wouldn't be willing to follow her, and I'm not talking about the repercussions of disobedience."

"What do you mean?" Patch inquired.

Raven slipped his fingernails into his black hair, scratching his scalp.

"Look at them. Furtive glances, their ability to shut up when she talked. They all want to bed her and give her no cause to disregard them. For that hope alone, they'll follow her."

"Wanting to fuck the bitch doesn't inspire loyalty or faith. Besides, she's

196

not the only female with us. There's Mauler and the Heart."

"Yes, but A'uri are mysterious, aloof, and they're probably too worried that Mauler would eat them."

He chuckled, and so did Patch, then he grew serious.

"You're right, though, wanting to bed her doesn't inspire loyalty or faith. But it instills hope, and with false hope, it'll buy her time for the other two. Given the chance, she'll do well."

"If you say so."

Patch rubbed his chin.

Raven gave him a grim grin.

"Trust me. A little grooming, and she'll make a fine leader, and her sword skills are unparalleled and will only help her rise through the ranks. Who knows, maybe one day, we'll have our first female heir."

Patch scoffed as he got to his feet.

"Yeah, that's about as likely as dragons attacking Outpost Dire, or the Forgotten Isles joining Ralloc's domain. Shit, Apor and Praema are more likely to rise in the south and set in the north. It just ain't gonna happen."

The older man moved away, and Raven called to him.

"Patch? The suns do rise in the south … on the other side of Ermaeyth."

Patch rolled his eyes and sauntered off.

Raven watched him go. He empathized with his old colleague. Times enforced change, an inevitable eventuality. The Wizard's War, both his and Patch's glory days became a figment of the past, glimpsed, discarded, and only relived as tall tales.

The Krey had changed, too. In many ways, advancing more than Ralloc's pretentious, tradition-riveted society, and in other manners, they returned to their old ways.

Giving his squad one last look as they clambered into their sleeping rolls, he nestled into his blankets, too. His eyes tracked over to Xenomene, her diminutive form suffused in her blankets. A small tress of dark red hair escaped beneath the opening.

Sighing, he closed his eyes and tried not to think of the long march that lay ahead and hoped he wasn't on the twisted trail of folly.

Chapter 31: Ralloc Domain

Daniel walked alone, stumbling drunk through Ralloc's dark streets, searching for an establishment one of the jyneruls recommended. As his eyes moved and his feet carried him, his thoughts were never far from Meristal, her jubilance upon seeing him, the past they shared, the words that could never be spoken aloud.

Every time he laid eyes on her, something stirred in his loins, and an overwhelming itch festered in his hand, and the need to slap the shit out of her. Since the war, she hadn't woken up to the realities. She was still stuck on the warlock, Judas Lakayre, and while something happened between them, Daniel didn't know what.

Then again, things happened between Daniel and Meristal, too.

It had to be serious enough to keep Judas and Meristal orbiting each other, even though they were apart.

Why couldn't Meristal see the truth? Daniel loved her, always had since they were young. He could offer more to life than what she settled for. True, Judas had wealth and Daniel didn't, but it'd been over two ages since the war's end, and the warlock still hadn't made an honest woman out of Meristal.

What did she see in Daniel that repulsed her? If it was damaged goods, well ... everyone who survived the war was that.

He shook his head in disgust and spat.

The Heir of Valin rarely made it to Ralloc, but when he did, he made it a point to have a good time. Visiting brought the promise of pleasure, the claws of his vices burrowing deep, the kind that hurt the next morning, his coin purse lighter, the vim of his staff depleted. It was one thing to drink with your brothers of the sword—the Krey—and you could fuck the hell out of your sisters of the blade, but it just wasn't the same.

Daniel had a specific taste in women, and no one quite matched it at House Eti, save one: that young gal, Xenomene. He was easily double her age though, and while he'd till her field and soak her oats, he'd never impose or pursue her. But if she came calling, well that was another matter entirely.

The first time he'd seen her, she did more for his excitement than a stiff breeze. Her taut flesh, the curve of her body ...

He exhaled through his nose, wishing he'd speared her before she left.

She had an innocent aura to her, and Daniel didn't want to be the one to corrupt her, but he'd gladly do it, if given the opportunity.

Finding the establishment, the sign above the door, *The Gentle Touch*, he stumbled in, nearly running into a bearded man clothed in fine silk robes of deep green, brown, and gray.

What the foppish fuck is this? I thought this was a whorehouse!

The man smiled.

"Welcome to Lord Brenton's The Gentle Touch, how may we serve you this evening?"

Bleary-eyed, Daniel blurted, "Redhead."

"We have plenty of red-haired females for you to select from this evening. What's your select specialty?"

Confusion made Daniel's pause, and the spirits weren't helping him think any clearer.

"What the fuck are you talking about, man? Where are the girls?"

"Would you like to view the girls before selecting your specialty?"

"Of course, man!"

Daniel belched, and it almost caused him to sway.

"Follow me, sire."

The host led him up the stairs and through a locked door. Beyond opened into a foyer. Women of all ages and types lounged there, all half-clothed, only covering their breasts and their groin, and they all had red hair.

Daniel's eyes went wide. There were tits everywhere, tits until the Corridor went silent: large, small, those that drooped, and those that defied the laws of physics. One girl, it seemed the damn things stared him back in the face.

The gauze-like fabric gave him a peek of what each girl was working with, some with red pubic hair, others with black, some lacked hair altogether—the latter quite shocking and got his heart racing.

And their eyes, they were like a throne room of gems: green, blue, brown, gray, hazel ... but he didn't see lilac or amethyst.

None like Meristal's.

"Are you satisfied, sire?"

He nodded.

Oh yeah!

"Which specialty would you like?"

"What's this specialty shit you're talking about? Give me a gal who can bob the knob."

The man gave him a small grin, perhaps amusement, or maybe it was contempt. Daniel was pretty sure that if someone like himself showed up in the Hive, he'd kick his own ass.

"Our girls possess fine art skills from all known cultures. However, each girl has a unique talent and are often hired for such devotions."

The host clapped his hands, and the girls moved off into groups.

"These girls," he said, pointing to the left, "will polish your brass quite nicely. The middle girls achieve multiple orgasms with the slightest touch, if being in charge is your sort of thing. These girls over here have superb massaging skills. Those girls to the right are from the Isles, and everyone knows what they say about Islanders. Unfortunately, we don't have the Cornele girl working tonight. We can bring in more girls if you don't find one to your liking."

"How much?"

"Four hundred scepters for a girl of no formal skill, six hundred for a specialized companion or Islander."

"Shades, six hundred scepters? She going to give birth to my brat, too?"

199

He growled out a sigh.

"How long do I get to play?"

"Until dawn. The price is for catering to the elite."

"I'll take three specialized girls."

Daniel handed the host an ingot—an ingot was worth six thousand scepters. The man's eyes went wide.

"I don't care which ones you give me, so long as they have red hair and like to have fun all night."

"Since you are paying for more than two, we'll throw in an extra girl. Let's say a girl from the Isles, if you like, sire."

"Sure, fuck it, why not?"

"Take your pick."

Daniel sauntered closer and the girls made themselves available. After seeing how much money he just gave without batting an eye, they were clambering all over themselves to win his favor. Daniel walked among them, looking for the ones that closest resembled Meristal's face and body type. If he couldn't have Meristal, he'd fornicate with each of these women as if they were.

The Betrayer shook his head, closing his eyes, knowing he courted damnation. The long, cold fingers of decay reached out and brushed against him, or at least, it felt like it.

He shuddered within the Ruins of Sheol, one of the three cursed grounds in Ermaeyth. Here, death lingered in partial metaphysical form. The sheol, creatures of Xilor's machinations, both incorporeal and corporeal planes, remained in a state of animating flux.

He'd made the near-impossible journey to the Ruins in the short timetable. The slave-by-fateful-choices breathed a sigh of relief, but the only reprieve were the moments until he was given another impossible task.

With another shiver, he put the Ruins to his back and faced the small, grotesque horde waiting for him to speak.

Xilor instructed him to incite an uprising, stirring the trolls into action, launching an unprovoked attack against a useless colony, a small town barely registering as a fleck on the map. Xilor rewarded his diligence with an explanation: it'd start another war and mask the presence of outsiders journeying across the foreign soil. The dark lord didn't specify what the outsiders were other than vague hints, wisps of smoke from the Underworld itself.

He'd paled upon hearing such things were possible, and his stomach fluttered when Xilor commanded his return to Gryzlaud with all due haste. A command to return meant Xilor neared the end of his quest, the reemergence of his body.

The Betrayer regarded the assembly; small, squinted eyes, black as flint, stared back at him, and he wondered if they thought of him as a meal or a scion of their dead god. Curving tusks jutted out between engorged lips dripped with saliva. Large, wide nostrils flared with each exhale, their nose hairs dancing like spider legs. A reeking stench slithered through the air; they hardly smelled better than a slop-infested pig pen.

He swallowed, feeling diminished and insignificant standing in the presence of such large beasts. Their towering height cast him in shadow, if there was any light to be had, their shoulders easily one-and-a-half times his own. Like wizardkind, their skin tone diversified, ranging from light green to shades much darker, a sickly gray rivaling granite, and every earthly tone between.

He swallowed, stilling his quavering throat.

As much as he feared them, he feared Xilor more.

With that knowledge, he spoke, orchestrating a weave of words as Xilor commanded. Trolls were not animals as most races pretended, just readily swayed. A charismatic speaker could enthrall them to commit mass suicide—almost.

He clambered onto a boulder, speaking from a respectable height, watching their expressions and their rapidly blinking eyes. Shadows hid his face, his hood obscuring his features.

The trolls listened about the returning dark lord. They'd cast their allegiance to Xilor before, but their loyalty was whimsical. Xilor needed to solidify their resolve and have their unwavering dedication for his plans to work. He needed sacrificial pawns in this game, and he'd leave them to die.

Ralloc would hunt them down after this atrocity against Wizard's Pass. It'd be a slaughter. The capital would shift its attention to them, turning their backs to the amassing army under Xilor's banner to hunt a few rogue elements, if they did at all.

They gathered to hear words of inspiration and promises, swayed by a speech crafted to bolster morale and mystify them. Though the least educated of civilized society, they'd always be captivated by a standard they'd never achieve. The finery of the elyfian, the nobility of wizardkind, the riches of the dwaven, the upper caste of the goblins, all beyond their limited reach.

Education and magic eluded them much like the concept of soap and water. What they didn't understand was that these words spelled their doom, pawns abandoned for Xilor's calculated ambition.

With his spell of influence woven, a great roar rippled through the crowd. Gaping maws opened wide to bellow their adoration. He continued with their master's rebirth, the injustice inflicted upon them, and the promise of prosperity once they crushed Ralloc.

Even barbarians recognize the sting of oppression.

And who would know more than him?

More cheers exploded from the crowd. The echoes reverberated, and the Betrayer sensed the creeping chill of death pour down his spine. A quick glance over his shoulder confirmed his fears; the sheol had congregated behind him, curious at the amassed beings so tantalizingly close.

With another shudder, the Betrayer hurried to conclude their business. He had to get out of here. The promise of rewards gave them focus, and he directed them to their target, a small settlement. The trolls never balked, never questioned the logic. It made sense, and they wanted to please their master.

They dispersed, and the sole wizard wove between them, listening to their conversations, and what little he could understand of their guttural speech confirmed their compliance.

A grim smile pulled at the corners of his mouth, knowing he proved his usefulness again, and that meant living another day, and so would Olga and Miza, the wards in Xilor's care. Wading deeper into the press of large bodies, he distanced himself from the sheol.

Guilt gnawed at his insides. He obeyed his master, and in doing so, sealed the fates of untold citizens residing in Wizard's Pass. Personally, he hoped the trolls failed. Still, he endured the shame from the impending reprehensible act, unsuspecting people and innocent alike would die so that he might live.

A chant raced through the marching crowd, Xilor's name, igniting a frenzy. The chant carried out into the night, swelling in volume. The Betrayer picked his way carefully through the trolls, dodging the massive beings as they jostled each other. Trampled to death wasn't the way he wanted to go.

Disgust rose from his stomach and settled on his face, not from their scent and more to do with being the dark lord's pawn, forever bound to do his will.

But what could he do?

He needed to find a way out the mess. If he did, a much harder task lay before him: learning to forgive himself, if such a thing were possible. He didn't warrant forgiveness, going to his grave filled with remorse and angst, however long that turned out to be.

And in Xilor's service, that could be tomorrow.

With a sigh of relief and trepidation, he set out for Gryzlaud Palace, leaving the trolls far behind.

Chapter 32: Mr. Pleasure

"Wake up!" the gruff voice roared.

She tensed, knowing the slap was coming. The fat man didn't disappoint. Though ready for the strike, it didn't stop stars exploding in her vision, nor the tears that welled up in her eyes.

"My name is Mr. Pleasure."

Her face throbbed, the sting of heat searing the side of her face. The ringing in her ears droned on as a weariness settled in her bones.

How many times had she heard that line? How many times had he slapped her awake? The swallowing darkness was her only absolution, but it came at the expense of immense pain and death, and it was short lived.

Countless times she'd witnessed him introducing himself, but the final tally eluded her. What did it matter? Caring was the least of her worries. In fact, she couldn't remember where she was, or why he was doing this to her. Only a fog lingered; she couldn't recall anything other than him, his words, and his obesity.

He continued their ritual as if it'd been the first day, the first time. Perhaps for him it was the first time every time.

"You shall call me by no other name than Mr. Pleasure. If you do, I'll cut your head off with my knife."

She almost called him a litany of names to skip the misery and go straight to her escape in death; but there was something different today, with him, with the room.

A number of men filled the room. Grotesque brutes, some with missing teeth or limbs, pus congealed from open sores or boils, covered their bodies. These *men* were more like parasites from the farthest depths of a cesspool.

Were they even alive?

Julie hadn't spoken since coming, she had no reason to. The only thing that passed her lips were the screams. But even now, to form the words took a great effort of concentration. She licked her lips, swallowed twice, her mind trying to find the appropriate words.

"Who are they, Mr. Pleasure?"

Her question made the big man's smile widen. Her eyes darted between him, the center of her world, to the newcomers. A flutter of panic threaded her chest, and she felt the galloping thump of her heart against her sternum.

"What are they doing here?"

His slow, gravelly chuckle made her fixate on him.

"Why, they're here to have fun with you. Torture only goes so far, and most minds break, but not you. No, you're different, special. Since it's no longer affecting you, and you aren't breaking like when we first started, you'll learn a new kind of pain: humiliation."

What's he talking about?

She tried to chase the meanings of her words, but the fog around her mind was so thick and opaque, like swimming in sludge. What did she mean?

"Something new?"

Her bloodshot eyes burned and drooped, but as they threatened to close, worry would leech away the drowsiness. She didn't like anything new; she counted on Mr. Pleasure being the same, the one constant in her life. Even so, if she showed her vexation, he'd seize control and never let go.

Her mind, which had been slow to react to him and his words, started to imagine the possibilities as to how this new scenario would end. None of her conclusions brought warm feelings. All would end horribly. She tried to change tactics, hoping to throw him off the scent of her fear.

"I confess you bore me numb with your grotesque overtures."

Mr. Pleasure's head turned toward her, the movement slow.

"I can take anything you give to me."

Now, he faced her fully.

"Aren't you worried that I'll enjoy this new pain, Mr. Pleasure? Aren't you distraught it'll give me a reprieve from your usual? It might not even break me, and then, where will you be?"

The corner of his lips quirked up into a grin, accentuating his underbite.

"What's the worst you can do to me? Are they going to eat me alive? You'll have to do better than that."

He gave a single chuckle.

"Girlie, this isn't about your satisfaction."

His grin split wider, a twinkling coming to his eye.

"No reprieve, no mercy, just your whimpers and begging."

Her brows drew down at his words.

"When these men take from you, when you're tied down and ravaged time and again, that'll be the breech I need. A new horror to rend you anew."

She swallowed.

He chuckled now, taking a step closer.

"They'll do as they please; I won't hinder their sinister impulses. And then, we can go back to just you and me, darling."

Fucking Shades!

He motioned the men forward.

Panic exploded within her, heart fluttering, chest rumbling, breath coming in sharp and hot. In the hysteria, the fog she'd been living in rolled away. Everything snapped into focus, violent and vivid. Her imagination gushed with innumerable sequences, each dismissed, discarded, or improved upon accordingly.

Beyond the men ambling towards her, Julie glimpsed a table with straps behind the gaggle, and she knew where she'd end up. This was her only chance to break out, to free herself from the shackles, the torture, the never-ending cycle; who knew when she'd have another opportunity, or if ever?

The alternative was to let all these men inside her, to let them ravage her and humiliate her.

No!

She recoiled at the thought. She wouldn't let them, would rather face obliteration if she couldn't escape, whether it was a true death or another false postponement.

She opened her mouth to scream, to call him a son of a bitch, but as she did, a gnarled hand clamped over her mouth. They were upon her now. Eager fingers removed the restraints holding her down, and excited hands snatched her up faster than she expected, half dragging, half carrying her to the table.

As they drew near, a few of the men rushed forward, clearing off the surface of the table. Weapons clattered to the floor, flung in haste, before slamming her down. Everything happened so fast, like the flicker of lightning: hands groping, fingers fondling, robes ripping, hands snaking, undergarments tearing, the cold biting into her bared flesh, the warmth as they touched her.

They pressed her stomach-first against the table. Gnarled fingers clamped around her arms as they stretched her towards the leather straps, mere inches away from binding her again. Drool leaked out of toothless, rotting mouths as they stretched her over the unfinished, splintered edge.

She sensed someone taking position behind her, and the sounds of a scuffle broke out, and that was all she needed. The man who pulled her hand closer to the strap stopped, glancing back at them.

Her moment arrived.

Fury, terror, and panic swept through her, and she lashed out with her magic, exploding into action. The blast knocked down all the men; even Mr. Pleasure collapsed to a knee. His head snapped up, finding her, his leering grin widening.

"Well, well, well," he said.

Not caring about her modesty, she left the tattered remains of her clothes behind, her stark bottom visible to anyone who cared to see.

She darted between the fallen men. She didn't have to be fast, just quicker than them. Julie shoved and clawed her way past them, sending a swift kick to the groin of one man who managed to rise to his knees, and an elbow to the face of another.

With strength she didn't expect, she kicked free of a man who latched onto her ankle while she scrambled to the door. The snagging hand slowed her just enough to make her stumble, and she smacked into the door. Grabbing hold of the iron ring, she jerked it open, slamming it shut behind her, buying herself precious seconds.

The resounding thud of the door filled the hallway, and she raced down the stone passage, grabbing suits of armor and ripping them down behind her to impede her pursuers.

Her bare feet slapped the cold, rock floor. A thick coat of grime clung to the soles of her feet. She heaved a door ajar and slammed it with a resounding rattle behind her.

She scanned the new room for any weapons, anything to help her fight for freedom. She spied a stand of swords. Grabbing one, Julie forced it through the handle of the door, wedging it shut. She returned and drew out another.

On the other side of the room stood another door, and she rushed heedlessly through it—only to find herself back in the room she had started in.

The bald man with his bulging skin and broad grin.

"Did you really think you were going to get away?"

He chuckled.

Was there no hope?

But at least all the men were gone. To see them had been horrendous, to feel them inside her …

"I knew I'd hit a nerve in you when you bolted for the door. That's the best response I've received out of you since the first session. I'll have to tuck that away for later use."

He cracked his knuckles, closing the distance between them. He jerked his head to the side, his neck cracking.

"You're going to pay for trying to escape."

He reached for her.

The blade flashed between them.

Hot blood splashed her face as a chilling scream erupted from the obese man.

Without thought, she lashed out again, his arm flying away from his body and landing on the floor. Without caring, without stopping, Julie sidestepped him and dashed through the door in the room, down the same stone hallway she'd retreated down earlier, jumping over the suits she'd thrown, beyond the first door she'd slipped through, and entered through the next.

The door boomed shut.

"Wrong again, bitch!"

She spun around, terrified to hear Mr. Pleasure's booming voice.

He stood before her, both arms attached, unscathed, a malicious grin smearing his sweaty face.

He held up his knife, the same one he'd used to cut out her tongue. He charged her, quicker than expected. She reacted on instinct, stepping, swinging, and her sword went through his leg.

Her strength leeched from her limbs. He toppled to the floor, screaming, holding his stump, blood gushing. She shook her head, fighting the fatigue, the lethargy.

She backed away, exiting through the door, hoping for the hallway.

Luck was with her as she crashed down the passageway, her tilt erratic and uncontrolled, leaping over the armor and dashing past doors. She rounded a corner and darted down another stretch of cool, coarse stonework, seeking as much distance as she could before ducking into another room.

She rushed through the door, and an abrupt and startling malady jolted her body, starting with the ache in her head and the cold suckling her flesh.

Mr. Pleasure loomed before her, his voice washing through her. He jerked his hand back, a blood-coated cleaver in his hand.

"I got you, didn't I?"

His hands wrapped around her throat, and he shoved her against the door, her feet dangling.

His torture room flashed briefly in her vision, but his glinting knife caught her attention as he furrowed her throat. Something hot spilled out of her, running down her breasts and stomach. He was laughing now, as if he'd expected everything and foresaw all the possibilities.

He was mocking her.

Obscurity took her away from the warmth and into an atramentous void.

Chapter 33: Mr. Pleasure

"Wake up!"

Agony and a wash of spots flourished in her vision. She blinked them away, waking up. Her skin stung like the touch of bull-nettle biting into her face.

A ghost of trepidation entered her mind; she knew she should've tensed, but willpower evaded her. She didn't care anymore. The only thing she wanted to do was die.

Slowly, she mustered the strength to raise her head, to breathe; her numb mind pleaded with her to endure. But why should she? She couldn't remember a time before this room, this chair, or Mr. Pleasure.

He was the center of her world, and nothing existed outside of him.

Through the fog of misery, in the undiscovered reaches of her mind, she tried to recall who she was. At the core of her soul, she sensed what he represented, some morbid part of her psyche lashing out in punishment for her weakness, her defective qualities.

Her face stung. She didn't care if he permanently disfigured her with abusive slaps. All sense of self vanished—her identity, her name—figments best not remembered.

The only part that refused to fade was the silent animosity.

She wanted to rail against the abuse, her mind folding, collapsing, then refilling like a bellows for a hearth. Parts of her broke away, rose petals peeled and cast aside, maybe as a way to punish herself, or pieces of her cleaved to save herself. Rarely did his inflictions move her anymore. Only one thought tumbled in her mind—besides the lingering question of why.

Who am I?

In seldom moments of clarity, she recalled a time before, like a fevered dream, the vague impressions repressed. In the flicker of images, she recalled magic and the violent aftermath. She could've sworn she'd done something powerful, something strange, commanded things to rise up with her mind, but perhaps that was only her wishful thinking.

Without the sense of passing time, the burden of recollecting the memories in the correct sequence eluded her, but she noticed that Mr. Pleasure's cruelty rallied after she tried to escape through the door.

How long ago had that been? A hundred times? Two hundred times ago?

A part of her ached to know how she'd fallen into Mr. Pleasure's clutches. When she reached for the elusive memories, they recoiled and skittered away, never answering when she needed them, taunting her when she couldn't bear it any longer.

But the voice knew.

The voice simmered, demanded justice, revenge; each time the voice visited, the well of empowerment washed over her, promising aid to escape. The voice wanted to take over, waiting for permission, urging her to acquiesce;

the eagerness was palpable, poised for the proper moment to strike.

And she was so very close to folding.

Despite the horror of learning what was talking to her—the side of madness she'd become—she kept it caged, locked away, and it seethed with malevolence.

The malignity suffused her, its claws digging deep, ripping, gouging, tearing into her.

This whole thing: the room, her mind, Mr. Pleasure…inescapable.

A man's face loomed in her mind, and a sense of knowing rolled across her, but she couldn't recall his name. The pernicious voice recoiled, searching for shelter in the dark recesses of her mind. Details about the man himself eluded her, but she could examine his face with resolute clarity. His eyes were kind, wise, and azure, soothing during times of greatest angst.

Each visit brought her a measure of peace. Safety and hope washed over her every time she gazed at him. His hair parted down the middle and cascaded down, nearly touching his shoulders. A neatly trimmed goatee hugged his fatherly smile.

"My name is Mr. Pleasure," the droning voice interrupted her thoughts.

She didn't care anymore; couldn't he understand that?

"You shall call me by no other name than Mr. Pleasure."

Death is preferable to this.

In many ways, she was in purgatory, or hell, reliving the same day with only subtle variations to the mechanics.

"If you call me by my name, I'll release you."

She blinked.

A spell of time trickled by as the words gestated, clouding her mind further.

That doesn't make sense. Why would he say that?

Her heart fluttered as the meaning sank in. She desired what he promised, but why would he give it to her?

Freedom?

Something akin to hope but not as strong flourished within her like a rampant contagion.

It must be a trick!

She tried to ferret out what he meant, the ruse she wasn't seeing, the trap waiting to snap shut. Though nothing but weariness and uncertainty plagued her heart, her face, her mind, an inner turmoil roiled within. Desperation gnawed at her insides. Hunger for freedom almost made her leap at the chance, but if he knew, he'd retract the peace offering, the promise…the false hope.

She wanted to give him no cause to detain her further.

She swallowed, gathering her strength, steadying her voice.

"Mr. Pleasure," she said.

Her voice croaked the two words with a slight quaver she hoped to hide from him. The tremor wasn't fear but acrimony, the bringer of silent fury. The voice in her head tensed, stilling like a viper, ready to strike.

He smiled, leering as he lumbered forward. Bending, he untied the straps. "You may go."

His smile never faltered as he took two steps back, waiting for her to rise.

She wanted to bolt for the door, but no, that'd give him cause to come after her. No matter how hard she tried, she couldn't see the trap, and it was undoubtedly one.

Placing her palms on the armrests, she stood, pushing herself to unsteady feet. If he was going to do it, it'd be now.

Her legs shook to hold her upright. Mr. Pleasure made no move to impede her. With halting steps, she turned toward the door, and when she reached it, she glanced back. All the fear, anguish, and mistrust swirling within her. She made herself meet his gaze.

The malicious smile lingered as he folded his arms across his chest.

Somewhere within her, she snapped, and the voice took command.

Abandoning the chance to flee, with renewed strength, she stormed toward him, snatching up a sword from his table as she closed the distance. She swung with all her might, cleaving his right arm at the shoulder.

He didn't fight her. He didn't scream. He stood, unmoved, the smile never fading.

The smile.

The all-knowing grin that held her darkest secrets, the times she broke and cried, when he defiled her, the sanctity of herself—it'd all been his for the taking. He waited until she was a ripe fruit to pluck at his leisure, a sweet nectar for him to consume.

The grin mirrored that of a guilty man who knew he'd walk free, unmolested.

And her rage hated him for it.

She hacked at him, the blade swinging with all her might until there was nothing left of him but pieces on the floor, broken like a porcelain doll, each edge sharp and jagged.

Her chest heaved, her hair a tangled mop around her face. Sweat trickled like tear-streaks. Pausing, she gazed at the remains, but she could still see the smile.

It wasn't enough, not after what he had done to her.

It'll never be enough!

She hacked at the pieces—his arms, legs, and face. Deep gashes appeared in the floor as sparks flew from her relentless swings. There was only the silence and her grunts of exertion until the sword, riddled with nicks, snapped during one of her overhead swings.

She screamed as all the horrors he inflicted returned.

And it plagued her.

Even if she made it out of here, she'd never again be the same, never be whole.

She'd lost something in here, a part of herself, and she'd given more than she imagined. It wasn't just her body, it wasn't just her mind, nor was it the emotions that threatened to rend her apart.

It was all that, and more.

Still, it paled in the wake of his atrocities.

She collapsed to her knees, unable to contain the torment a moment longer. Tears rolled down her face, and her shoulders heaved. Here, at the end of the journey, surrounded by pieces of the man she'd come to loathe, she broke in earnest. The cries made her body shudder, her ribs aching, her face sore from her despair—

A hand fell on her shoulder.

She gasped, her tears stifled. And now, the trap had sprung shut, the thing she couldn't see. It came full circle, and Mr. Pleasure would never let her go.

Resignation coursed through her. She wanted to die; and though he'd never let her, she had to say it. Even if it meant nothing to him, it meant everything to her.

It was a destiny she chose.

"Kill me," she breathed.

Not bothering to look at the hand, she let her sobs surge anew, harder than before. Her lungs burned, her weeping refused to let her breathe. She should've known this was exactly the trick he'd employ, grant her freedom, make her hopes surge, then ensnare her when she failed to flee.

It worked.

She let the other side of her out, the portion controlled by the voice, and missed her opportunity to escape.

But the hand was soft and warm against her shoulder, the rags of her robes allowing for the flesh-on-flesh touch. The gesture was comforting, the antithesis of Mr. Pleasure.

There was kindness in the moment.

She tilted her head and saw the face she vaguely recollected: the man who had made the voice go away. He smiled at her—a sad smile, no doubt, but a smile nonetheless.

"Come, Julie," he said gently.

He reached for her hands, holding them for a moment before pulling her up off the floor.

Julie. That's my name!

Just uttering her name broke whatever spell this place held over her.

"Let's go."

The gentleness of his voice made the seething presence in her mind vanish. The barriers that blocked her mind crumbled, and everything came crashing back.

He held her as she sobbed. After suffering all the vile things she had, she'd never be the same. She shivered in his embrace, crying with relief and joy and sorrow. Her heart fractured beyond reformation.

Her eyes went to the pieces of her tormentor, and among the rubble of flesh, the smile still grinned at her.

She closed her eyes, not wishing to see him anymore.

Memories returned—both real and fanciful—the walls of the room she'd come to know faded away. They stood just under the doorway, the threshold she once entered, and as Judas hugged her, her eyes climbed upward until they fell on the words etched in the bark, the twisted root over the pathway.

Here Madness Dwells.

Chapter 34: The Corridor Of Cruelty

"Do you want to talk about what happened?" Judas asked, his voice gentle.

She sobbed in his arms; the stillness of the Corridor punctuated by her cries. After a time, and still trembling with exhaustion, he carried her away from the doorway, away from Mr. Pleasure and the vile memories. He used his magic on her as he had before, rejuvenating her; though her body strengthened, her mind remained untouched.

Perhaps it would never get better.

She felt like a burden to him and a failure for not breaking free herself. While he carried her, she wept on his shoulder, the mental exhaustion quickly returning. Once he came to a clearing, he called upon his essence, unrolling her sleeping blankets, and placed her gently within the folds.

Julie curled up, her back to him, and he shuffled off. By sound alone, she knew he'd started a fire, and supper. Not long after, the crackle of a fire and the simmering of a pot tickled her ears. The aroma of potatoes, carrots, and beef wafted through the air. His stomach gurgled, and hers mirrored his. The scent filled the evening air, almost driving away the suffocating despair. It still clung to her, a hungry leech not ready to let go.

She remembered the thick sludge she'd eaten on the morning she went through the doorway. It'd been heavenly compared to the stench of her captor's dungeon, and the memory of it didn't turn her stomach, not the way Mr. Pleasure did. Without realizing it, she hadn't eaten anything since she went through the doorway.

How long ago was that?

She tried to ignore the phantoms of her torturer but failed. After everything she endured, her thoughts kept returning to what he'd said the first time she awoke in his dungeon, the one moment of truth in all the chaos. No one would ever know how grateful she was for her life, and she vowed never to be so weak that it could be taken from her.

"Pain connects everything. If you survive, you'll appreciate the pain of other things—the things of the world—and they're nothing compared to what I'm going to do to you. In that, you may find comfort, for your life will be painless compared to this."

A new kind of anguish washed through her, another pain—the agony of realizing how right he was, and that he'd actually spoken the truth. He was a monster, psychotic, but his honesty made him more forthright than Judas had ever been. Judas was supposed to protect her, a solemn vow when he pulled her into this world, and he'd utterly failed.

She swallowed, rolling to her back so she could turn her head and see him out of the corner of her eye.

"How many times?"

Her voice shook as the whisper shattered the brittle silence. She couldn't voice the rest of the sentence. Her eyes moved to him, and she scrutinized him.

And upon his face, she could see that it haunted him, to tell her how many times she died.

Pain connects everything.

"Thirty-eight times," he said.

The fire hissed in the wake of his words. His voice sounded like a man tormented, but by what, she couldn't guess. He hadn't had to live through it.

But he knew how many times, so he'd witnessed it. Why didn't he stop it sooner?

His swallow was audible from across the fire.

"I've never heard of anyone going that many times without succumbing to madness. I died eleven times before I figured it out. But that was a long time ago..."

She didn't know why, but his words made her angry. If anything, they sounded like an excuse.

"You possessed training!" she snapped.

But more than that, the simple truth was that a child commanded more discipline than her; she was just beginning to tap into her abilities. So much lay undiscovered, and Judas wasn't very forthcoming with instruction. Julie saw the guilt dance across his face, his azure eyes full of pity.

"You don't realize how sorry I am. It's my fault for dragging you through the Corridor."

He stopped as if an intrusive thought cut him off, as if he searched for someone else to blame, then he started again.

"We should've circumvented it or, at least, I should've taken the lead. I should've protected you!"

She swallowed, and that hot anger turned cold in her throat.

"Yes, you should've, but you didn't."

Heat spread across her chest as the next words came bubbling out, spoken as if she hadn't summoned them.

"Where the fuck were you when I needed you?"

Ire flashed in his eyes at her cursing, but he let it go.

Wise of him.

She had every right to be angry.

"I was as helpless as you. While you were detained, Ms. Pleasure ensnared me."

Julie's face paled, and her voice grew quiet.

"There are two of them?"

He nodded, and when he spoke, she heard true bitterness dripping on every syllable.

"She made me watch your torture. The hardest thing I've ever done, and I never want to do it again. You have no idea the unfathomable remorse I harbor for not being there. I can never forgive myself."

Disgust roiled through her. Judas had failed her. He'd said before the Corridor remained silent to him, having mastered its cruelties. Had that been a lie? An idle boast?

He's a weak man for letting this happen to you.

Was that her thoughts or someone else's?

Or did he tell the truth, that he was as helpless as her?

With a tender stretch, she called her essence. Her magic responded, and she reached out, sensing Judas's emotions. He spoke the truth; she discerned his guilt, but he'd jeopardized her wellbeing. Beneath his sorrow, almost undetectable, doubt interred.

She couldn't decipher anything more than his indecision, but she found his failure unforgivable.

"Why?"

"Why what?" he asked, unable to look her in the eye.

"Why rescue me at all, or let it go on for so long?"

She shot to her feet.

"Why did he promise to set me free that last time?"

Anger gushed from her, explosive as the dreaded image of Mr. Pleasure filled her vision. A surge of her essence crackled.

"I could've gone insane from what he did to me! Have you no remorse? Have you no heart!"

Her head swam; the magic nearly made her sway. The wrath made her feel unstoppable, as it had that one time in the dungeon.

"You didn't know, did you?" he asked, his voice quiet and brittle. "You couldn't remember what I told you."

His eyes moved to Julie's shaking hands, watching her fight for control.

Her chest heaved.

"What are you talking about?"

He looked her in the eye.

"I told you the Corridor would test you in ways you never thought possible. I warned you, blatantly, and I hoped after a few times, you'd remember."

He shook his head in sorrow, burying his face in his hands.

"I'm so sorry," he whispered.

His subdued elusiveness only made her angrier.

"What the fuck are you talking about? I don't give a shit that you're sorry; sorry doesn't help me! What about the rods jammed into my fingers? The skin flayed from my arms? I'll live with those images for the rest of my life! You warned me? Blatantly? Obviously, it wasn't enough because I didn't get it!"

Her head hurt, a dull ache rising with each heartbeat into a pulsing throb. The pain spread from her temples and came to rest behind her eyes. They itched as if tiny ants were marching across them.

"You asked if there was anything that could destroy you," he said, "and I said, 'No, it can't destroy your body; but if you let it get in your mind, you'll shatter like glass. Magic is in the power of the mind. So is this place.'"

He shook his head as if lost.

"The most important advice I gave you is to believe what your soul tells you, not your eyes. I figured you'd see through the perceived reality."

Did he tell her that? Maybe. She couldn't recall. So much had happened, if that talk took place at all. And once Mr. Pleasure became front and center of her world, everything else faded. She couldn't even recall Judas's name, and his face was but a faint memory.

"That's just asinine," she said.

The itch behind her eyes faded as the mental and physical exhaustion overwhelmed her. Despite her hunger and the rage, her body trembled just to stand, and she needed to sleep.

Though she focused her displeasure on Judas, she did note his honesty, which was a first. He hadn't held anything back. Mr. Pleasure's proverb returned, even though hurt by her master's failure, it was insubstantial to what she'd suffered.

"Pain connects everything."

She lowered herself back down to her blankets.

He should've said pain connects everyone.

Abandoning supper and the argument, she laid down, curling up with her back to him and the fire. With her face away, she let the silent tears come, both of sorrow and relief. Her entire journey shook the fragile faith she placed in Judas, rending whatever bond they tried to establish.

Whatever fondness she had for him, whatever bond she yearned for, to be a part of something and belong, shattered. She'd never get it with him. Meristal, perhaps, but she couldn't assume after a single encounter. Yes, Judas opened the door of possibilities, attempted to guide her, but he hadn't protected, and it proved almost fatal.

A wedge manifested in their relationship. She thought she'd found purpose with him, but now, she realized her flawed belief. She'd placed her faith wrongfully in him. Faith was something sacred, and she'd lobbed it his way without almost a modicum of critical thought. And that, more than anything, made her breaking all the worse. Not only had she suffered needlessly at the hands of Mr. Pleasure, but Judas, the fabled and terrifying warlock who defeated Xilor, couldn't come to her rescue.

I told you he was weak.

Again, she didn't know if that was her thoughts or the voice in her head.

There were still admirable aspects of him, his genteel nature, his gentle, guiding hand. In a way, he filled the role of a father because gods only knew what happened to her real parents.

Is it possible to care for someone and not trust them?

She distinguished the difference between respecting someone and despising what they do. Despite his faults, he was a man attempting to be great, her cornerstone and mentor.

Her master.

But a master's role couldn't be easy, a delicate balance between a guide and a protector against unseen enemies. He failed at what it meant to be one, leaving her defenseless. Julie lacked power and the cognitive faculties to deal with the abhorrent tribulations here. What lay beyond this tiny strip of land straddling the Abyss? What new horror would rise from the darkness?

A stray thought flitted through her head, something Judas had said about the Corridor.

"It's a funnel; like gravity, it draws everyone in, and the only way across is on foot."

She hoped like hell to never come back through here, but the words of drawing everyone in told her that eventually, she might have to.

Fatigue overcame her, and she courted sleep's embrace.

Even in her dreams, she couldn't escape. Judas's inflicted pain didn't compare to Mr. Pleasure, but the wound Judas levied rent her soul. The fault didn't rest with her, and the blame didn't lean solely on Judas's shoulders, but she wanted someone to blame, and he proved the easiest scapegoat.

The voice hiding in the shadows of her mind blamed Judas, and it reverberated in her dreams. The stronger the voice spoke, the more it whittled away her mental barriers. Slowly, she strangled under the crushing weight of doubt, and it was inescapable.

And the voice taunted her with the sleeping truth that no one else could see. She wasn't the one prophesied, and she didn't belong here.

Julie couldn't flee her misgivings or the voice in her dreams. As she slept, the tenebrous voice soothed her with oily words, and Mr. Pleasure's face plagued her mind, his leering smile hovering close.

Sunrise brought relief, liberating her from the growing nightmares. Her head throbbed from dehydration and worse things. The sun burned strangely bright, and the logs turned to fine ashes.

Fresh dew graced the dried earth.

She rubbed the sleep from her eyes. Though clothed in fresh robes, the early morning chill warned her to remain in her blankets. Her breath formed a noticeable wisp.

She shook her head, her hair splaying about her shoulders. She stifled the yawn as she stood. Judas normally had breakfast prepared, his cheerful voice agitating her, but only silence prevailed.

She glanced over at him. He still slumbered, and that wasn't right. Judas always rose before her. She traipsed past the fire pit and nudged him.

"Judas."

He didn't stir.

"Judas!"

This time, she shook him. In the stillness, she eyed him for a moment and realized his chest did not rise.

"JUDAS!"

She rolled him on his back, his azure eyes open and distant, cloudy and veiled. He stared into the world beyond; the Lord of the Underworld, Apocalypse, now held his soul.

Judas's pale skin was cold to the touch. Though she didn't want to admit it, she knew the truth.

All her repressed emotions crashed against her, a tidal wave breaching the shore. She sobbed, and she held a shaking hand to her face, wiping away the tears.

There were so many things to say, so many questions. Yes, she was angry with him, but she didn't want him to die.

Or did she? Had she done something to him at night while she slept? Had her essence responded to unvoiced will?

Knowing that he encroached the autumn years of his life, she hadn't realized his time was so near.

Hot, glistening trails marred her face, cutting rivulets of dirt and dust, droplets splashing her dead master's face. She put her head on his chest, hugging his motionless body. She mourned him as if their lives intertwined the span of her years, domesticated and familial. She didn't want to believe.

How could this happen? He was fine last night. What am I going to do now? I have no guide! I'm not ready.

She wondered if guilt had killed him in his sleep. She stayed there for another minute or an eternity; she couldn't tell which. What did it matter? How long she stayed, she could never recall.

A hand clutched her shoulder, jarring her out of reverie, and for a moment she thought Mr. Pleasure had come for her again, that it was all a test.

In a panic, she spun, flinging the arm off her shoulder, drawing her wand, ready to eviscerate. She pointed her wand at the intruder, only to see … the same man who also lay on the ground.

"Get up, child," his stern, urgent voice commanded.

"Who are … What … How—?"

She glanced back at the lifeless body, then back to the Judas who stood before her.

"I said get up!"

His hands shook her body.

"It's the Corridor, and it's attacking your dreams. Now, get up!"

Her eyes snapped open, and the nightmare faded.

Chapter 35: Out Of The Corridor

Judas curled up in his blankets.

Julie had drifted off to sleep at least an hour ago, but even her dreams didn't let her rest, as she stirred, haunted by anguished memories.

They would plague her for some time to come.

He tried to focus on her, to give her his undivided attention, but more than once, his thoughts returned to Ms. Pleasure's dungeon, the image of her sharp and stabbing, like a dagger through taut cloth.

He swallowed hard.

Julie's anger had been biting, the words scathing, and her gaze vehement. She utterly detested him now, and he couldn't blame her. He wished it wasn't so, but he'd been a fool to listen to Soma.

But what do you do when a god-like creature asks something of you?

His eyes slid out of focus.

You say yes.

Since arriving on Ermaeyth, Julie's life had been in mortal peril more times than he cared to admit, nearly dying minutes after they met. Someone tried to gut her in Dlad City, leaving her for dead. And now, the Corridor tried to claim her sanity which was just as permanent as death.

He wanted to curse at the Time Warden, but who knew if she'd hear him.

Best to keep that creature away from me.

The warlock wanted to comfort Julie, but that'd only drive a wider rift between them. She needed her angst, the only thing she could control, and sometimes it felt good to be out of control. Many times during her rant, Judas had to bite back retorts, further damaging any chance of reconciliation.

His guilt for dragging her through the Corridor burrowed deep, festering in his soul, and he understood her anger. He had his own, and it was pointed at someone who could annihilate him.

He should've rendered more protection and guidance, no matter what the Time Warden said. Julie was an infant in magical terms and couldn't defend herself, and he chastised himself for risking her well-being. If anything happened to her, especially to her mind, he'd never forgive himself.

Setting his role of master aside, Judas tried to empathize as a parent, even if he was one for but a short time. He remembered fond fantasies about watching his child sleep at night, worrying that nothing harrowing befell them, but he never got the chance. He experienced the emotive gut punch as he slipped into those shoes once again, pretending for a brief moment that Julie was his daughter.

The blame and dishonor intensified. No amount of penitence would ever be enough.

He felt sickened by his actions or lack thereof.

Inexcusable. What the hell was Soma thinking?

Judas hoped the mental wounds would heal with time and distance from this place, and though too early to tell, it was never too early to hope. Julie endured Mr. Pleasure's torments, and she might be scarred for the rest of her life.

An ache in his chest formed as slumber finally took him, and when he awoke next, crushing despair sat on his chest. It took him a moment to figure out what caused him to feel this way, and then it hit him as a malevolent glee vibrated through his body.

Xilor…

Xilor's return just got so much closer. Unfortunately, the Corridor distorted time, and Judas sensed either the aftermath of Xilor's achievement or a premonition of imminent fruition.

Either way, it wasn't good.

He bolted upright, flinging his blanket aside. Without the aid of his wand, he called upon his essence; the camp tucking neatly away on its own.

His hurried steps carried him to Julie's side, but he faltered as he neared. His brows knitted as he scrutinized her. She spoke in her visiting nightmare.

Curiosity nagged at him.

Gently, he stretched out, caressing her subconsciousness with his essence, much like he did when she arrived.

What he saw turned his stomach. She faced another trial. The effects went beyond her waking mind and attacked her in her sleep. Judas, unsure how long she experienced the barrage, shook her.

"Get up, child!"

His vision swam, seeing her corporeal form and the phantasm simultaneously. She floundered, wanting to stay in the delusion, enduring the torture.

"I said get up!"

He shook her by the arm.

"It's the Corridor, and it's attacking your dreams. Now, get up!"

Her eyes snapped open, her hands reaching for her forehead. The link between them remained a few heartbeats longer before fading. The pain she suffered echoed through him, a sharp stab through his own forehead. He eased both their anguish away with the aid of his conjury.

"What's going on?" she said, her voice groggy. "You died…"

"Never mind that. We must leave, now!"

"What? Why?"

"The Corridor was affecting you while you slept; it's no longer safe for you to remain. I interrupted whatever it was attempting to do. We must leave now; something's wrong. Time's against us, and we must make one more stop before our destination."

"How do you know something is wrong? How are we getting out of here?"

She rose to her feet as he spoke.

"The place is many things, a testing ground and a focal point. When something of great magnitude happens in the world, it may not be perceived by those that are close by, but here, it reverberates within the Corridor. Though time bends differently for us here than those on the outside, something's happening now, as we speak, or may have already happened, or soon will."

He sighed, catching Julie putting on her boots.

"Whichever the case, it's throwing off the chaotic harmony of the Corridor. The instability isn't tenable. We need to leave."

"I don't understand."

She shook her head. Noting the tiredness in her eyes, he would be surprised if she was retaining anything of what he said.

"The world is a pond, and a pebble causes ripples that go unnoticed by the ducks. Inside the Corridor, they're perceived as massive waves, and they can destroy things in its path, namely us. As far as us getting out, do you remember me telling you that magic is all about the power of the mind?"

She nodded.

"That's how we get out. You're supposed to achieve passage on your own, in your own time, but celerity is required. Do you understand?"

"Yes, I think so."

"Good."

He slung his pack on his back and Julie mirrored him. Judas snatched her arm and began walking away from the camp, closer to the edge of the Corridor.

Once he was far enough away from the epicenter of their camp, his essence surged through both of them. The familiar cold tingle of teleportation washed over them, but they didn't move. The air shimmered like an aura, shaking, fighting against his intent.

The struggle lasted moments, and he broke it with ease. The air around them split, and within two steps, all the oppressive nature of the Corridor vanished, and a foreign landscape greeted the pair.

Julie almost sagged in relief beside him.

"We must hurry."

"Where are we going?"

"To see the saricrocians in the Swamp of Sorrow. After that, to Wizard's Pass."

"Why? What's happening?"

"Something terrible, and we need allies."

Taking her hand, hoping to keep her from asking any more questions, the cool fog of teleportation settled over them. In a blink of an eye, they were moving once again—faster than thought.

Chapter 36: Gryzlaud Palace

The Betrayer watched a nondescript pine box floating in the air. Dirt and grime mired it, stained by its interment. And just behind him, Sidjuous—his normally flowing, golden locks matted with sweat, his arrogant face flushed—marched toward the mirror. The box preceded him like a vanguard.

The Betrayer narrowed his eyes as he watched the foppish lord mutter an incantation, letting the box settle on the floor.

"So, you've returned," Xilor said.

The Betrayer noted the amusement in his voice.

Sidjuous's face faltered, having expected a gush of praise.

With slow steps, the Betrayer backed away from the mirror, sliding out of view, his blue eyes watching Sidjuous with indifference. He didn't dislike the man, but he had no cause to call him friend.

And in a place like this, Sidjuous was the least of his worries.

Sidjuous gave a flourishing bow.

"I dispatched the trolls who toiled, Master."

To this, the mirror said nothing.

The arrival of Xilor's least apprentice in the spacious room made it seem all the more confining. The Betrayer kept quiet, hoping to keep Xilor's scrutiny at bay.

"Open it," Xilor commanded.

Sidjuous stretched out his hand, summoning his essence in silence, in the hopes of calling forth his power without incantation.

The Betrayer rolled his eyes.

Nearly all Xilor's apprentices were adept at Rumigul; only one far exceeded all others: Krurik. Even the Betrayer could manage some small acts without incantation or wand, as rudimentary as they were, but the current task far exceeded his abilities. The same could be said of Sidjuous now.

Upon failure, the blonde lord pulled out his wand and muttered the incantation.

The pine creaked, the nails ripping from their burrowed homes, splintering the wood. With a clatter, the lid fell to the floor. A wispy plume filled the air.

Unconsciously, the Betrayer took a few steps forward to peer inside. Dust littered the interior. A tight grin tugged at the corner of his mouth before he remembered where he was.

Sidjuous knelt, running his fingers through the fine powder.

"Are we sure this is the one?" he asked.

The Betrayer noted the quaking of his voice, the fear coursing through him. It was like a stench that would never wash away, and he knew the scent well, like everyone in Xilor's service.

He worries what Xilor would do with his failure.

Perhaps there was only one who didn't constantly fear the dark lord, and that apprentice wasn't here.

"I'm sure," the mirror confirmed.

The taut atmosphere relaxed upon hearing the words, and the tightness in the Betrayer's chest eased. He even noted the relief on Sidjuous's face. Had he failed, who knew what kind of torments the Betrayer was about to watch, or if they'd be turned on him.

"Soon, I'll be complete again."

"Yes, my lord," Sidjuous said, rising.

His fists were clenched, and the way he spoke, it was like he was giving a speech to a ragtag army living on a thread of hope and stale bread.

"Soon, you'll reign, and no one will stand in your way."

The Betrayer suppressed a sigh.

What a jackass.

"That's not true," Xilor said, his voice quiet.

For a moment, the Betrayer wondered if Xilor's words were in response to his thoughts.

Sidjuous's head cocked to the side as he gazed into the massive mirror.

"What do you mean, my lord?"

"Judas Lakayre still lives, and I sense something … strange. Someone else."

The news prickled the Betrayer's ears. Judas consumed Xilor's thoughts; it was always about revenge for him. The fact that he mentioned another was both odd and disconcerting. It bode both trouble and opportunity.

Who'd be worthy of his notice?

"You shall sweep them both aside."

"By the gods, you're a fool!" Xilor hissed, his voice shrill.

Agony pierced the Betrayer's ears. He winced.

"It's an aura I know not."

Sidjuous fidgeted, waiting for the dark lord to expound. When nothing came, the golden-haired apprentice spoke.

"You'll crush all resistance across Ermaeyth."

The Betrayer released an undetected sigh.

Xilor was quiet for a moment.

"An eternal reign."

"Fitting for one such as you, Master."

Yeah, if he could just figure out the whole mortality thing.

Then again, the fact that Xilor was present even though his body died did lend credence to the possibility.

"And for his wife?" a voice called out.

The Betrayer blinked, shocked at the interruption. Disbelief followed swiftly, recognizing the voice, and panic latched its claws around his spine. He turned his head in the direction of the door.

Olga stood in the doorway, and the Betrayer's face fell as ice formed in the pit of his stomach. Though she was a woman now, a memory of her as a child flashed in his mind. She'd walked into this room so long ago, her wide brown eyes filled with fear and awe. Both of the girls were holding his hands.

It'd been over an era since Olga said a kind word to him.

"Is that what you wish? To be my betrothed?"

Olga strode to the center of the room. Her dark brown hair shimmered. A sheer, dark green robe with a plunging neckline adorned her body. She left little unseen, even from the Betrayer, and that made him uncomfortable.

Dismay washed through him. Olga was one of the young children he sacrificed his future for. She always flaunted his steadfast advice; she now seemed supplicant to Xilor's teachings.

Olga worded her response delicately.

"What worthy gift could I offer my Master as a token of my devotion?"

"Gift?"

"Perhaps a sacrifice? Would that be sufficient for you, my lord?"

The Betrayer swallowed, not liking the direction of this conversation. *She shouldn't even be in here.*

"Yes, a sacrifice would suffice; what would you deem worthy to forgo? To lose your life and be revived as a sign of your trust?"

"A sacrifice of my blood."

Olga knelt with both knees on the floor. Her eyes betrayed her inner turmoil, but to what exactly, the Betrayer could only guess. Perhaps it was the thought of dying and returning that worried her.

"Intriguing. You wish to lose your life-flow and be filled with my blood?"

Olga gave a soft shake of her head, a coy smile curling on her lips.

"No, my lord. I wish to give you my dedication. As a sign of my undying devotion, I'll give you the soul of my sister, Miza."

"No!" the Betrayer barked, startled by what he heard.

He cast aside all pretense of invisibility. His mind flooded with panic. How could Olga be so evil? Hadn't he taught her better than that?

"You object to this, Turncoat?"

The eyes in the mirror slid to the Betrayer as he took urgent steps forward.

"Yes, my lord. Surely there's another way to display her loyalty to you."

"Yes, her loyalties, but since you object, I begin to wonder about yours. Your passions reveal your weakness and duplicity."

The Betrayer knelt on the hard stone in front of the mirror, right beside Olga. This humbling action aroused a snigger behind him from Sidjuous. Olga stood, stepping away, but she stayed in the corner of his eye, no doubt to watch his face, to watch him squirm under Xilor's baleful gaze.

The Betrayer wet his lips, his mind racing for anything to stop this madness.

"My lord, when I entered your service, I did so under the pretense that my servitude, along with your mercy, spared the life of my own."

He swallowed hard, knowing his next words skirted close to outright defiance.

"I've never known you to be without honor or backing from your bond. My only wish is to ensure our agreement—which was first and supersedes all others—is honored."

Curiosity prickled Olga's face as she looked between the Betrayer and the mirror. He worded the statements to be ambiguous. Only he and the dark lord knew what transpired that fateful night, and all attempts to find out by his other apprentices went unanswered. Even when Krurik voiced his desire to kill the Betrayer or those children, Xilor had forbidden him, on pain of torture and death.

"Noted," Xilor said. "I shall decide after my return, when I've won the war."

Relief washed over the Betrayer, but doubt and worry gnawed in its wake. He carefully masked his feelings behind a placid face. Bowing his head, he thanked Xilor and rose to leave.

"Going somewhere?" Xilor asked.

"Yes, master. I wish to change and bathe, and don fresh clothing. The stench of trolls still fills my nostrils."

He bowed his head, waiting for permission.

"You may go. Sidjuous, begin transferring the ash. Only one thing remains and the hour grows near—"

The Betrayer shut the door behind him, cutting off his words. His heart pounded in his chest.

I can't believe Olga would even contemplate such a thing.

He swallowed, stepping away from the door and down the hall.

The lie he spun for Xilor had been a pretense, as it was Miza who he wanted to see.

Another whiff of his robes reminded him that a bath was in order first. Relieved to have postponed a calamity, he set off for his rooms.

Chapter 37: Swamp Of Sorrows

"Why do I see a blue swirl when we teleport?" Julie asked once they emerged.

Judas did a double take.

"You can see that? I'm surprised. Not many can detect the effects of teleportation. However, I'm not trying to mask my abilities, and if I did, you'd never see anything."

He gave her a small smile. She weighed his words, mulling them in silence.

"Come, Julie. A treacherous journey lies ahead."

He turned and climbed a steep incline. She paused for a moment before following.

An ache burned in her legs before she reached the top, and at a glance, Judas had already started down the other side. Did he want to keep his distance, or was the way so perilous that such a lead was necessary?

Maybe he needs alone time?

In truth, she could probably use it, too. Her emotions were still in turmoil about the Corridor and everything that happened to her. Even if it wasn't real, it had *felt* real to her, and that was just as bad.

She let her mind drift as she started the descent. Meristal's face floated before her mind's eye. Julie wondered how her life and training would've turned out under her tutelage. Several times, her thoughts almost caused her to lose her footing, hurrying her steps to keep from stumbling, and gaining ground on the warlock.

Once she was within earshot, he began speaking.

"What are you contemplating?"

"Nothing," she lied.

"Would *nothing* include Meristal?"

Her eyes narrowed, not liking the feeling of invasion. It was too close to Mr. Pleasure, and everything that man did was an invasion.

"You can read my thoughts?"

Judas shook his head.

"No, just glimpses, like a flash of a portrait without words or captions."

I wonder if he's been reading my mind this whole time.

"Yes, I was thinking about Meristal."

"And?"

Uncomfortable with facing the truth she contemplated training under a different master, she switched subjects.

"I thought you said we were entering a swamp?"

The moment she asked, her boot sank a finger's length with a thick sloshing sound.

"Terrific."

Her foot held fast in the muddied ground, making each step arduous. After a dozen encumbering strides, she was ready to quit.

"How far until we reach solid ground?"

"Too far, but we'll make it all right."

"Too far? What if we tire?"

"We'll stop for a rest."

Perturbed, she followed.

I need better answers than flippant responses. Better answers would've helped me in the Corridor!

Knowing she wouldn't receive any, she tried to focus on making slow progress through the sludge, her discontent simmering. With each step, it grew harder, and her mind often returned to Mr. Pleasure, the Corridor as a whole, and the fact that Judas was absent for almost all of it.

Worry whittled her.

The woman she'd been when she entered wasn't the same one that came out. She could feel a change within her, a darkness born. It ate away at the atrocities, acted like a shield in those desperate times, but now that she was free, it hadn't retreated.

It'd just gone quiet.

For now.

She set her foot down, expecting thick mud, but instead, warm stagnant water reeking of rot and decay splashed, drenching her cheek and nearly entering her mouth. She almost hurled then, making a snap judgement that she disliked water of any type other than a bath. Dark, brown slosh churned in the wake of her foot, the mossy green froth riding the ripples before closing the sudden breach.

Judas stopped ahead, and by the time she reached him, sweat soaked her back, and her hair matted the sides of her face.

"Now, we swim."

"Wait, wait, wait. Couldn't we teleport to where we're going?"

"Sure, if we wish to insult them."

"What's the insult?"

"Barging into someone's home unannounced. Well, their yard."

"Whose yard?"

"Saricrocians. That's why I'm taking the lead."

His blue eyes swept over her.

"You're tired. Here."

He withdrew his wand, and a wave of warmth and energy cocooned her, leeching the ache and fatigue from her body.

"Do you remember in Dlad City when you collapsed from magical exhaustion?"

She nodded.

"That's what the rejuvenating spell is for."

Relief suffused her, and she felt strength return to her limbs, but it didn't help with how sweaty she was, nor did it dry her clothes.

Wish there was a spell for that.

"Anyway," he said, "this whole swamp is their home, and saricrocians are touchy with magic."

"They don't like it?"

He grinned.

"No, I mean, they're susceptible to magic, can be controlled with it, and their species has evolved to be quite sensitive to it. Teleporting in might make them go into a frenzy."

Oh, well, I suppose that's a good reason then.

Judas held his hand out, and they continued on together. While this place was heinous in its way, it wasn't the Corridor of Cruelty, and she didn't think anything could go wrong here, not like in Mr. Pleasure's clutches.

"And just when you think nothing can go wrong," Judas cut into her silent musings, "something does, so keep a good lookout. There are dangerous creatures about."

"I wish you'd stop doing that. It's a real pain in the ass when you can't openly think because someone's listening in."

He paused, frowning.

"What are you talking about?"

"You read my mind. Just stop, okay?"

"I don't know what you're talking about, my dear. I haven't read your mind. It's an invasion tantamount to taking advantage of an inebriated woman. I wouldn't do that to you."

He moved forward, and by the way he moved, she could tell she'd hit a nerve with him. It was the most upset she'd ever seen him, but it paled next to her volatile emotions. Still, she was grateful for the space between them.

Water kicked up in his wake as he waded in, sinking deeper and deeper, the water rising past his waist. She followed, reaffirming her hatred of water. By the time she reached where Judas had been, he swam in front of her, a side stroke variant. With her lips pressed into a thin line, she started after him.

This is fucking disgusting.

Judas reached the opposite shore and waited for her to progress through the murky waters. She exited, breathing hard, her boots sloshing on the soft bank. Her robes clung to her, heavy and reeking; sludge marred her hands and neck, and she shuddered at the thought that it permeated through her clothing.

Seeing her safely on land, Judas turned and plunged through thick foliage, missing holes of knee-deep water. Rolling her eyes, Julie traced his steps.

"I can't read your thoughts," he said, " … not like before. Now and then, when you're truly concentrating, I get a vague impression, but to read you like a book?"

He shook his head.

So, does he mean he can't do it anymore, or it's even less now?

"Why?"

"I'm not sure. Perhaps something in the Corridor changed you, changed your mind, made it harder to perceive."

Yeah, no shit.

Then, she remembered what she thought earlier, about having changed, and a coldness swept over her.

He glanced back at her.

"Perhaps Mr. Pleasure's company did more than we both originally thought."

"What do you mean?"

"I'm not sure. Give me time."

She ground her teeth, chafed by the lack of answers.

"When were you going to tell me you could read my thoughts?"

"What do you want me to say?" he asked.

He stopped and faced her.

"That your contemplations screamed at me? There's no simple way to broach the topic. Usually, with time and training, a person will learn to dampen it. Even people with training still let a few slip through the cracks. Often it's but a hum churning in their head, but you?"

He shook his head.

"Nothing. Unless you're focused."

"I had no idea."

"Maybe you attained more control? Ordinarily, this shielding technique is taught, but you're doing it instinctively. Your aura glows more."

"What does that mean?"

He gave a sheepish shrug.

"In layman's terms, it means more powerful. Everyone goes through this type of metamorphosis, their aura is dim until they train. Over time, it brightens to whatever level they'll achieve."

"And mine?"

He smiled.

"Yours glowed brightly since the first day, brighter than most adults. Now, it's even more effulgent. Without even testing you, this can be a way to measure your progress. As you've grown, your mind has closed to me. When you first woke at my house, I could detect a lot if I concentrated. Now? A sliver of a new moon."

He turned and began walking again.

"Let's change the subject. Anything else you want to ask?"

The stench of rot clung to the insides of her nostrils, and she started after him, missed a step, and plunged her boot in knee-deep water. She cursed silently, but in her riled state, propriety be damned.

"Why?"

He stopped ahead, his arm extended, holding half-rotted branch out of the way.

Julie came back up to her feet and closed the gap between them.

"Why what?"

"Why do you want to change the subject? Why?"

A sharp silence settled between them. She was acutely aware of the beads of sweat rolling down the side of her face. She held his gaze, challenging him, not letting him dodge or back down.

"Because this line of conversation can be dangerous," he said in a slow cadence.

She didn't miss the edge in his voice.

Maybe he's finally starting to feel something.

"Dangerous? Like the swamp? The Corridor? Mr. Pleasure? That kind of dangerous are you talking about? How about treat me like an adult and give me a straight answer! I'm not some helpless damn kid."

Judas let go of the branch and faced her. His azure eyes narrowed, and he lowered his head a touch, closer to her level, and it felt like he pinned her there.

"You're angry, probably from the Corridor, Mr. Pleasure, and now this …" he glanced around them, "… lovely swamp, so I'll grant you some leeway. It's dangerous because that conversation would turn to praise."

Her face scrunched, baffled by what he said.

"Praise?"

He gave a single, measured nod.

"I'm exceedingly proud of your progress, even if you can't see it, but with praise comes arrogance, which makes people sloppy, heedless of pitfalls, and tempted to more enticing paths with empty promises."

He straightened, standing taller.

"And my praise must be earned, Julie; I don't give it freely. Now, is your curiosity satisfied?"

She nodded, speechless at his tone and rebuke. Judas turned, continuing down an invisible path, pushing branches aside through the treacherous growth.

In silence, both from shock and timidity, she followed, and several minutes later, he punctured their stillness.

"Solid ground."

Not far behind him, she entered the clearing a few seconds later, thankful for the hard earth. Their way was unhindered by muck, water, twisted roots, or branches for a few yards. Dismay settled over her as she peered through the fog-like atmosphere, noting where their unhampered walk would end.

The marshy bank gurgled at each side of them; the churning, eerie water sloshed in the swamp. For the first time, she noted the quiet, the stillness, expecting more, expecting dangerous things that crawled or slithered.

A chill raced down her spine.

The only sounds she heard came from them, and her laborious breath thundered in her ears. With her wet clothes, aching muscles, and the humidity, her energy waned. She turned to spy the opposite shore from which they came; she could make out the faint line of the cliffs. It seemed much further.

Judas's receding footsteps faded, making her glance back to the front, seeing him continue without relent.

"We should've teleported past the water."

"Magic serves your needs, not your wants. Don't make a crutch out of a gift. And … it'd be rude."

Julie hurried to catch up, not wanting to be left far behind.

He still seemed a touch snippy from before, and though he answered her, it almost sounded like he was winding up for another mini-lecture. She cut him off, delving into something she'd been wanting to ask for a while.

"I've been wondering. You haven't once spoken about your family or children."

It was a loaded statement, she knew, one unearthed. Curiosity slithered past prudence, hoping to delve deeper into the mystery of the warlock.

The question made Judas stop, glancing at her from the corner of his eye. His voice turned a touch hoarse, and weariness laced his tones.

"What makes you wonder about that?"

"You never spoke about it, and I wondered ..." she trailed off.

There was something in his eyes, something she couldn't place, and for a brief moment, she thought he might be getting misty-eyed. She rallied, plunging forward.

"I never saw anyone at your manor besides Staell. The only other people I've met was Todd and Meristal."

He nodded and swallowed before walking away, but this time, the pace much slower, a pace suited for a man of his age.

Unsure whether to pursue the conversation or to let it die, she settled on the latter. When he spoke, it surprised her.

"Yes, I had a family and a child. Both are tragic stories."

Though she couldn't see his face, she heard his pain and withheld tears.

"Which would you like first?"

Shades, if I would've known, I wouldn't have asked.

"Your child—will I ever get to meet this person?"

"No, I'm afraid not. My daughter was born in the wake of the Wizard's War. I placed her in hiding with protectors. Xilor's minions tracked them down and murdered everyone within."

She swallowed.

Good gods, that's horrible.

"I killed their leader, and in turn, they killed what was most precious to me."

An oppressive silence suffocated the gulf between them. Her throat went dry. She wanted to speak, to say something, to console, but the words wouldn't come. What would she say to him anyway? Sorry didn't quite measure up.

What good would it do him, after all this time?

"It was a little over two ages ago," he said. "I met my sweet little girl only once. After what happened, I wish ... No parent should have to mourn their child."

He cast a glance back at her as he continued walking.

"You're slightly older, but she'd be about your age."

"Who were the guardians?"

"Staell arranged the keeping of my child."

"You're still friends?"

"Of course. It took a while to get over my loss—I don't think you ever get over it, but it gets easier to carry the burden—and I held him responsible for a time. In the end, I came to my senses and realized how could it have been his fault?"

Julie subsided, letting him be, mentally kicking the divine hell out of herself for opening an old wound.

"I also had a sibling," Judas said after a time. "An older, twin brother. Our father died before we grew late into our adulthood. During the middle of the war, Xilor took Josiah's life. Our mother died after her sons set off on different paths, but neither parent lived to witness his death or my exile."

"I'm sorry, Master Judas. I had no idea. If I had known …"

"You would've held your tongue? Perhaps, but you didn't know, and you would've found out sooner or later. Better to hear it from me than through hearsay."

"My mother didn't know she carried twins at first, but when she found out, she was ready to name a boy and a girl. When my brother came out, she named him Josiah; and when I came, well, let's just say I would've had a pretty name."

Julie couldn't help but smile, finding humor that Judas's mother expected a girl.

Meristal's face flickered in her mind's eye.

"Does Meristal have any children?"

Judas paused.

"She had a son. The child died shortly after birth. Tragic … a sad day for her."

Shades of the Underworld, what is up with these people and tragedy?

Once again, she wished she hadn't spoken at all. Only death and destruction followed these two, and nothing good came out of their lives, losing family and loved ones but surviving the Wizard's War.

That must be the connection I felt between them. It wasn't love, it was the heartache they shared.

It was heart-rending.

The sky darkened as they waded deeper into the swamp, but it had more to do with how dense the canopy turned, the gray skies blotting out the suns.

"We're about to enter the nest," Judas said.

"Nest?"

"Think of it as our council back at Ralloc, but only three overseers instead of seven."

Mosquitoes and flies buzzed around them as sweat poured from their bodies. By now, Julie could detect her body odor through the dried, fetid clothes. What she wouldn't give for a bath. They sloshed through stagnant water and mud puddles of various depths, tripping over thick tangles of roots and vines.

Guilt still riddled her for asking about his child, and she hoped he didn't think unkindly of her. Their relationship shifted once again, but after the Corridor, everything changed.

The nagging feeling that her destiny fell along a different path wasn't far from her mind. With each hour slipping by, it seemed more evident, but achieving such ends daunted her. The choice to accept Judas as her master wasn't a choice at all, but a decision thrust upon her.

"Okay, we're in the nest. In short order, we'll be in the center."

Sweat poured from her brow, down her neck, wetting her abhorrent robes. How long had they been traveling? She kept plunging one foot in front of the other, the sludge clumping now.

"These saricrocians are old. Their time to die will come soon."

Julie scratched her forehead at the stinging bite of a mosquito.

"How do you know they'll die soon?"

Judas paused long enough to look back at her.

"They're old, wise, and enormous."

"Just what I wanted to hear."

"There's nothing to fear, but be mindful, they can sense it. Fear drives their more predatory instincts; that's how they hunt, sensing the fears of others. Try not to talk or scream; our vocals bring them discomfort."

He took a few more steps and then decided to expound on his instructions.

"Try not to think about anything. These Ancients have powerful abilities to read minds, put my gifts to shame, and I don't know how well they can intuit, so focus on your robes, or the ground, anything but what you want to think about."

He swallowed.

"Above all, don't stare. They're black and red, a distinctive marking of age, very different to the usual earth tones of the younger populace. It'd be taken as an insult to gawk."

He hesitated and gave her a small smile.

"I think I covered everything. Don't talk, don't think, don't stare, don't be afraid. Don't do anything at all."

Why am I even here, then?

"Oh, and if they speak to you, answer them."

"Got it."

All too soon, the clumping mire gave way to soil crowned in golden-brown pine needles that crunched softly underfoot. The trees grew denser with roots twisting and arching above the soft soil, a far more treacherous footing for her and the aging warlock. A deep rustling of breathing echoed through the faint mist, but she didn't glimpse the promised red-and-black beasts.

She kept her head level, searching the ground, expecting things to snap out at her, but nothing did.

Judas led with a steadfast pace, passing over a hill and descending back down into a large bowl-shaped depression. Inside lay three saricrocians, and far, far larger than Julie imagined.

She tried to clamp down on her alarm, a near-impossible feat.

They were like houses—long, wide, and tall, all lying together in a semicircle.

Their various hued eyes glowed faintly and focused on them as they drew near. Julie hastily sized up the glowing orbs. She might be able to match the size of the eye, if she curled up in a fetal position. The weight of their gazes was like a pressure akin to something stepping on her chest.

Curling up didn't seem like such a bad idea.

No fear, no fear.

Judas laid an affectionate hand on her shoulder before he spoke with his mind. Julie didn't comprehend the exact reason. Support or to make her privy to the exchange?

Greetings, Elders. I'm Warlock Lakayre, and this is my apprentice, Julie.

We know you, Warlock. You hold no interest for us and have been among our kind before, the Ancient in the center said. *You bring someone new to the meld?*

She's too young. She hasn't been training long; it might cause more harm than good.

She's of your height, an adult. She should be able to handle the meld, the Ancient to the left spoke.

She's different—special, from the Other Side.

Three gigantic mouths opened, hissing, revealing massive teeth longer than Julie's leg. Their eyes flickered between the wizardkind.

The Other Side? How's that possible? All who cross die. It must've taken you time to get here.

Curious that she hasn't expired.

She's a Wcic, and it's by a miracle that she has survived, Judas thought back to them. *Surely, you don't want to be responsible for potentially harming her?*

Julie glanced at Judas. Did he fib to protect her?

She thinks a lot, the Ancient in the center said. *She's calculating.*

She has many feelings for you, the right one said. *We can hear them, even as she buries them. But there are other feelings lurking beneath. Anger. Fear. Hatred?*

Yes, the left one concurred. *She's strong with passion and desire. There's something odd about her. Can you feel it? It's in her mind, in the scent of her blood. She's different.*

Yes, Judas interjected. *Special like I said.*

No, something ... more, the center one spoke. *Something I haven't sensed in a long time, not since—*

A nephiliam? the Ancient to the right asked.

Yes, the nephiliam, the left one concurred.

Julie glanced at Judas, catching the confusion on his face, the consternation.

Majestic beings, Judas began, *with respect, it's impossible for her to be a nephiliam. They've been extinct for a long time, almost since the beginning of magic. There's no way you could—*

What? the center one challenged.

His head shifted closer to Judas.

You think we've made a mistake? We are never mistaken! Our lives are long, yet our memories are longer, passed down through the generations, like the fairies.

The meld allowed the saricrocians to pass memories to one another, a race with few secrets from each other.

Even if we weren't alive when the nephiliam's light extinguished, we'd know. Any saricrocian would recollect by a mere whiff. The odd thing is how a nephiliam survived. And to be so young...

Hello? Julie interjected, unable to bear it any longer. *I'm still here, and I'd like it if you wouldn't talk like I wasn't!*

The Ancients' mouths opened again, the hiss sharp and much louder than before. All shifted, the ground vibrated beneath her feet. She took an involuntary step back, but Judas's hand clamping around her arm kept her still.

Judas gave her a hard glance before scolding her.

You don't speak unless you are spoken to, Apprentice.

He turned back to the Ancients.

Please, forgive the transgression. She's unfamiliar with your ways and customs.

Exclude her, the creature from the right commanded.

Judas let go of her shoulder and stepped forward, leaving Julie blocked from the rest of the communication.

She glared at the back of Judas's head, fuming, only to realize the Ancients scrutinized her. She smiled weakly, embarrassed that they caught her. They turned back to their silent conversation.

Left to the whims of her mind, Julie thought over the proceedings. Whatever business he conducted, she didn't have any inkling. Judas didn't share secrets.

For a time, she wondered what they spoke about, but the futility of such speculation bored her. Though they'd yet to broach the subject overmuch, she tried to bury the emotional turmoil in the wake of Mr. Pleasure. She probably never would, but the more she focused on it, the angrier she became.

Her essence always came to her in moments of heightened emotions. Judas told her not to rely on feelings alone. Waiting in the humidity and silence, she sat down a dozen paces behind Judas and tried to meditate, search for the elusive magic. She folded her legs under her. Taking a deep breath, she relaxed her posture, the tension melting out of her taut shoulders. Julie visualized the strain fading away, leaving her body in a wispy vapor, seeping from her spine, through her legs and into the earth below.

She felt it.

A small, almost tingling sensation thrummed through her body, rhythmic like a cat's purr. It tickled like a whispered breath on the nape of her neck, envisioning the heat rather than feeling it. She followed the fragile wisps inward, visualizing the journey. When she drew in as far as she could, then, slowly let herself drift out into the earth beneath, the trees around her, and into the air. An out-of-body sensation pervaded her consciousness.

As she let her presence drift, a small but calmly persistent tugging drew her focus, carrying her away from her body.

A fire flickered before her, a radiant flame. Warmth caressed her face. Darkness swaddled the boundary of her vision. A book with strange glyphs settled in her lap; the edges faintly abraded with the passage of time. She'd seen this book before. It belonged to Judas. The symmetry of each stroke gave off an elegant beauty. With the trace of her finger, she marveled at its refinement.

Serpentine whispers of an alien language tickled Julie's ears, resonating all around her, but soft, like a delicate breeze. The hushed tone, neither threatening nor frightening, conveyed warmth, inviting, seductive. The unfamiliar words grew acute, steadfast. Her eyes turned down to the book, realizing the words came from within.

"Your wand, your words can release us … We will tell you everything. You are the Bearer of the Secrets of past, present, and future … Give your name to us. Become one…"

Her wand manifested in her hand, the sensation swelled. The calling was captivating, growing stronger, melting her resolve. She spoke her name.

The book burst open with a burning, pure light, pouring out and carrying her into oblivion.

"The Bearer of Secrets has been found," the book sighed, content.

"Julie!" Judas shouted at her, snapping her out of her trance.

The Ancients hissed in pain. His hands clenched her shoulders tightly, and the booming voice of a saricrocian filled her mind.

What were you thinking, child?

Julie stood and bowed her head, embarrassed. Noting the warlock's hand still on her shoulder, she spoke.

Forgive me for my carelessness. I didn't mean to interject into your minds.

The Ancient on the right spoke up again, *We couldn't hear your thoughts; your mind became opaque, quiet to us.*

What were you thinking? the one in the center asked.

About a book. A book Warlock Lakayre gave me.

I haven't given you a book, Judas interjected.

It was like a memory, yet I know it hasn't happened. It seemed so real…

An audible buzz filled her mind, the saricrocians speaking to each other, too fast and complex for her to make anything out. An ache festered in her head.

Exclude her.

A few moments later, Judas bowed unexpectedly, turned on his heel, grabbed her by the arm, and hurried from the shallow area they'd been standing in. His tight grip twinged with bearable pain, but she kept silent. Something bothered him. Would he tell her?

They left, their pace quick, and when they were far away, he released her. Julie, too timid to violate the silence, perceived her master's agitation and knew it was for her outburst. She waited for her scolding.

When he did speak, the words were unexpected.

"I can't believe the Ancients!" he fumed. "How can they just sit by and do nothing?"

"Why did you meet with them?"

Judas stopped and gawked as if he had forgotten she was there. It took him a second to shake it off and get his bearings back.

"They refused to aid us in the coming war. They said it's not theirs, just like the last one."

"They said that?"

He grimaced and nodded.

"We'll travel a bit farther and camp. I know a clean spring nearby. We can bathe and eat. Tomorrow, we'll reach Wizard's Pass."

"How much further until we get out of the swamp?"

"Not much, but enough."

He smiled.

"I have a friend who would be very interested in meeting you."

Unsure of how to take the comment, she traced his steps, putting distance between them and the Ancients.

Chapter 38: The Abyssians

A dark, dense fog rolled out of the Abyss, invading the world above, a world of shapes and color instead of eternal darkness. The quiet miasma coiled out of a place of nothing and spread like a seeping poison into Ermaeyth.

The murkiness billowed like the dense black smoke of burning oil, rolling over the land with ease. To the east it slithered with deliberate haste, driven by a sentience not its own. From within, the sound of a sinister laugh echoed the closer it drew to Gryzlaud.

This fog carried the will of death.

The miasma's presence, a violation of the world itself, was set to purpose, driven by a twisted and malevolent spirit, one much like its own. The soul—Xilor's fragmented essence—promised the Abyssians, sentients without physical form, the ability to take shape and become masters of their own bodies, never again responding to the pull that kept them within the Abyss.

Languishing without the meaning of time, with no regard to what lay outside their realm, ignorant of the world above waiting to be conquered, they stirred for these words. When the invading anima breached their sanctuary, they became aware. With a newfound knowledge, a bargain was struck, promises made.

They left their home for the first time in the service of a darker entity. They held up their part of the deal; now Xilor would uphold his.

The black cloud rolled over the manse, a palace of malice, passing through walls and doors as if it were air. Inside the walls, the cloud expanded, exploring its destination with curiosity and compulsive intent, like a hound running down a wounded animal. The cloud boiled with frenzy, searching each hall, room, and crevice, always seeking.

Curiosity satisfied, it retreated, plunging toward the mirror in the castle's bowels. Like phantom pains from missing limbs, spirit and consciousness called to each other; a bond growing stronger the closer the miasma drew to the mirror.

With caution, the darkness entered the room, circling the reflective surface. The mirror vibrated, so close to being one again.

"We have come, traveling from the deep," the voice slithered out, an oily hiss, slow and ponderous.

Each word spoken sounded like an inhale, a deliberate pause between every few words.

"Fulfill your promise, High One."

"How can I fulfill my oath if you still hold my soul?" Xilor asked.

"Keep your word, or it'll remain with us."

"Don't taunt me, Vlukus; it would be unfortunate to travel so far only to die. I'll hold up my end of the bargain, but I must become one first. Then, my full powers will be restored."

"You never told us this in the Abyss."

Xilor paused before his anger bested him.

"If you don't give me what I want willingly, I'll take it by force and destroy you afterward. I'm a man of my word, and I reward loyalty. Return my soul, and I'll give you physical form."

He could feel his spirit fighting to be free; the agitation was palpable. Gods, it was so close, and he could almost leave the mirror now and join with it.

The mirror quivered at his next words.

"Bring forth my soul, Vlukus, and let's be done with it."

Chapter 39: The Bearer Of Secrets

The night grew much cooler than Julie expected. As soon as the last of the sunlight washed away, the swamp's temperature plummeted, defusing the heavy humidity. The rotting wood and decaying smells of stagnant water vanished with the fading rays.

Judas started a fire, and Julie caught snippets of his mutterings about stubborn saricrocians. The gruffness he used while tossing wood into the fire —and his curt words—betrayed his emotions. After the fire had taken, he lay down on his pack, keeping to himself.

She swallowed, knowing she bore some responsibility for the change between them, and that was before meeting the Ancients. She'd brought up the subject of Judas's and Meristal's dead children. Since then, Judas remained uncharacteristically quiet and distant.

The fire, the outdoors, the cooking food, seemed familiar. She didn't know when, or how, but the vague stirring wouldn't abate. She'd done this before, somewhere … not here.

"Master Judas? What do you call what we are doing?"

As soon as she asked, the burn of foolishness kindled in her chest.

"It's called enjoying the outdoors. Relaxing, isn't it?"

"No, this whole sitting outside with the fire and the food … I can't remember, but I've done this before, somewhere…."

His head turned her direction, and he regarded her for a long moment.

"It's called camping. Try not to dwell on recalling the life from before; it'll only produce frustration."

"Well, there's nothing to keep my mind off what I can't remember."

"You could always try sleeping."

She almost sighed aloud, but instead, it came out in a noiseless breath.

"I can't remember anything from where I came from, not even the name. Where was that again? A person could go mad not knowing. Teach me something, it'd take my mind off it."

"Hold on."

Judas sat up and turned to his pack. Inside, he retrieved two books, strolled across their site, and handed them to her before resuming his lounging position.

She glanced down at them, rubbing her fingers over the cover, then darted a quick glance at him. He stared intently from his reclined pose, waiting for something to happen. When the moment passed, he closed his eyes and let out a long, deep sigh.

Julie returned her gaze to the books, noting a form of writing she'd never seen before. It arched with strange angles and slants, accented with circles, dots, crossings, and geometric shapes.

She glanced up at him.

"What language is this in?"

"I can read some of every language in the realm, except Angelic, though I recognize it when I see it. This language is an unknown one."

He opened his eyes and glanced up at the stars.

"Which languages do you know?"

"At least a half dozen. Most everyone in this part of Ermaeyth speaks the universal tongue of Myshku."

He sat up.

"We can rule out the beast languages for the saricrocians and gorrillians, Cytuu and Gnilyp respectively. The vampires have Sralucon, the trolls their Taengrenian. The dwaven used to share a language with the trolls, but they've recently invented a new language: Akyhmri. The fairies speak Kaot; and the elyfians have Thymulous."

He pointed to the books.

"None of those languages are that."

"Any other languages?"

"Sure. Far to the south is Isshu, and across the Golden Sea is Brodacci."

"You didn't say goblins."

"An oversight, my apologies. The goblins speak Lythououri and Taengrenian. A long time ago, the dwaven enslaved both trolls and goblins. Since there's a movement within the dwaven nation to distance themselves from the stigma of the past, they created a new language."

"You said everything except for what the unicorns speak."

"It's called Ucoric, but no one knows how to speak it—not even to their kind. Only a few, enlightened elite know their true tongue, and once a generation, the unicorn's maghai changes, and the circle closes again."

Julie frowned at this new complexity as he lay back down, closing his eyes again. A hidden language, maybe forbidden by their ancestors? She lay on her side, staring at the book and twirling her hair in her fingers.

"If you can't read this and few can, then why did you give it to me?"

He yawned, and his voice matched his mood.

"In case you might see something I don't. A fresh pair of eyes usually does the trick."

She turned her attention back to the book. A few moments later, deep breathing stole over the old warlock as he slept. She put the book aside and focused on the second one with an untitled cover. The book creaked a little when she opened it, but Judas didn't wake.

On the first page, a tidy scrawl penned the only blemish.

Property of Judas Lakayre.

She thumbed past the page, noting the conglomeration of handwritten notes, spells, and letters stuck between pages from other people. The first letter catching her attention was a name she recognized: Josiah Lakayre, Judas's twin brother. Untidy, big handwriting littered the page and marked him as young.

The passage was the older brother taunting the younger, spreading the rumors that Judas went mental and ran home.

Julie smiled and wondered if she had a sibling, back wherever she came from. She'd never know. The jealousy from Josiah's words was evident, and she wondered if that altered his path in life, putting them on separate courses. Judas talked about his brother in rare moderation.

She thumbed through a few more pages and saw another letter. This time, a crisp scrawl, angular, and sharp, grabbed her attention. The writer took care in crafting the writing, and she got the impression they held themselves of great importance. Upon reading, she learned that war had engulfed a city, but it remained unnamed. The only landmark she caught was the Emaas River, and she didn't know where that was.

Must not be in the Ralloc domains.

At the closing, Julie couldn't determine who sent it. A military commander? Diplomat? Someone in a position of power and wealth? Whoever wrote the letter took immense lengths imploring Judas to see him or her. She observed the bottom of the page, torn where the signature should be.

Judas hid the identity of the sender. Why? A female friend? The tone didn't imply that.

She thumbed through the book a while longer, but didn't find much of interest. Julie set it aside and picked up the first book with the strange glyphs and marveled at the symmetry, tracing the writing with her finger.

Serpentine whispers of alien words tickled her ears, resonating all around, but soft, like a delicate breeze. The whisper conveyed warmth, invitation. For a moment she feared the seductive call was a saricrocian, but she dismissed it. With Judas present, no creature would try to lure her away.

The unfamiliar words grew acute. She stared at the cover, the strange writing filling her eyes. Then, the lines moved.

She blinked a few times, wondering if she was tired.

She focused, her breath held. The gibberish morphed into something recognizable. The glyphs on the cover contorted into the common tongue of Myshku before disappearing altogether, but not before she glimpsed what it said.

The Bearer of Secrets.

The whispers grew louder in her ears.

"Your wand, your words can release us … We will tell you everything; you are the Bearer of the Secrets of past, present, and future … Give your name to us. Become one…"

Apprehension stabbed her in the chest, and she shook her head.

Too fantastical to be true.

She almost alerted Judas, but something impeded her words. Her fingers ran over the cover of the book in a cautious, exploratory manner.

A book even Judas can't understand, and yet it spoke to me. It'll open for me and no other.

Though doubt lingered, she spoke her name to the book.

"Julie."

Though she said her name, at least she thought she did, it sounded strange to her ears. Was she speaking a different language?

The book cracked open. Radiant light saturated her, a luminosity that would leave her blind had she been anyone else. It rushed into her, over her, filling her, its noise like a giant waterfall.

She closed her eyes, basking in the radiance. And that's when she felt it, a crack, a fissure within her. Something broke, a block inhibiting her from reaching her potential. It gave way, crumbling, obliterated. All at once, the unfathomable well of magic awakened in her, answering her command as easy as breathing, and she felt intricacies she'd never known. It was akin to tasting a new flavor or catching a hidden scent in a flower.

The light faded, and she opened her eyes. Her night vision remained untouched, and Judas still slept, and it made her question whether she was the only one to see it.

"We shall guide you in your greatest times of need. For your instruction to start, you must return to the Place of Origins in the Melodic Mountains. For what is to come, you must give your mind, body, and soul. Don't hold back."

Julie glanced over to Judas, and he still slept, oblivious to what was happening. Seeing him undisturbed, sensing what she did now within herself, she allowed herself to believe what was happening.

She glanced back to the book and began to speak but found the words couldn't come.

"There's no need for words," the book said.

"What must I do?"

"Journey south to the Melodic Mountains, to the Place of Origins."

"What about Judas?"

"It is of no consequence."

"Why do I need to go to the Place of Origins? Judas is a warlock; he can teach me."

"True, but for what comes next, he cannot. Don't delay the inevitable."

"I'm worried about him, what he'll do when he wakes up and I'm not here."

"He's a formidable man of ancient bloodlines. As much as people fear him, they should fear his offspring more."

"He told me his child died—what do you mean?"

Then, she took a moment to realize what she was doing, talking to a strange book and taking orders.

"And how can I trust you?"

"Lies. The offspring of Judas lives as well as does Madam Raviils'. The Time Warden hid the truth to protect them. They have not yet perished and have prominent parts yet to play."

"Who are they? Where are they? How can I find them?"

"It's not a matter of who and where they are, for there was only one birth."

Judas's daughter is alive! Meristal's son is alive! But if there was only one birth, which one was the truth?

"I thought Madam Raviils had a son, and Judas had a daughter. If this is true, then how can they be one?"

"One birth because the offspring of Judas came from the womb of Meristal Raviils. They were told opposing stories to protect the true identity of the offspring—the only true hope of surviving the cataclysm to come. The bloodline must not fail; that's why such

measures were taken to ensure their survival. However, if both should fail, there is another."

"How do you know all this?"

"It was foreseen, glimpsed in the fires from long ago, and recorded here. Everything in this book is factual or foreseen. My creator made me for the Bearer of Secrets."

"Where can I find them? Who's your maker? Why am I the Bearer of Secrets?"

"Enough. I bestow one boon to you. Your mind is chaotic, and your emotions in turmoil. I shall lock your emotions away, but you'll have to face them eventually. The block will remove itself when you arrive at the Place of Origins, when the time is right. You'll know when you search within for the truth. It cannot evade you. Head for the Melodic Mountains. There, you'll study as he studied … and we'll be with you also."

A surge of beautiful light, a cleansing refulgence washed through her. As it did, she glanced around the camp, noting that the light didn't reach the dark places around her.

So, only I can see it.

The anguish she suffered from the Corridor vanished. The memories were there, events, but the book eviscerated the sentiments. But more than that, as the book cleansed her, she caught glimpses, memories, events, and from all across time. The flashes were chaotic and disorderly. And she tasted the faintest traces of Judas's essence in the flood of visions.

The final revelation before the energy stopped was a small creature. Silver hair clung to his pate on the sides of his head. A long, bushy beard cascaded like an iridescent waterfall down to his belt. And she knew with certainty who she saw: Judas's old master, Fife Doole.

Then, the book closed, and Julie found herself staring at the slumbering warlock. She faced a decision, and it didn't take long for her to make it. With all emotion taken out of the equation, logic ruled in its place.

She swallowed and rose to her knees, placing the book into her pack. He'd given it to her, and the book promised to help in times of need. Her weariness burned away, and she stood, revitalized. There were things for her to learn elsewhere, and she couldn't do it with Judas. She gazed down at him, and an odd sensation crawled through her. The once powerful warlock seemed fragile now, not as superior as she once envisioned.

Is it my imagination that he's weak, or is it my impression?

A tree swayed in the distance. She snapped her head around, searching the gloom.

Something called her, out in the swamp, between the dark foliage area, where the ground turned to mush, and the trees grew thick and tall. A sense of waiting, wanting, compulsion. The tug persisted like a gentle call, and curious, she followed the beacon.

The call grew stronger the further she moved from her campsite. A sense of wrongness came over her, mortal peril. Her eyes narrowed, and she warded her mind before she realized what she was doing, and it'd come to her naturally.

A chill ran down her spine.

What in the Underworld?

Was it really that simple? Had removing the block done more to her than she realized, or had it been because she'd tried too hard in the past that it now seemed easy?

Deeper into the darkness, further from the light, she moved, following the persuasive summon. The walls around her mind hardened and repelled the enticement, the sense of wrongness clinging to her, turning her insides cold.

Her boots moved from the soft ground and into ankle-deep water, following the voice.

Yes! That was it. A voice.

With the hem of her robes soaked, she reached the source of the voice and paused. The voice told her to do something she knew would harm her. She surveyed the vast darkness, and once she saw it, terror filled her.

One of the trees approached her, each step slow and silent. A branch swayed. With blinding speed, it reached for her. Impulse took over, and she moved.

She'd experienced it before when Judas teleported her, witnessed the essence, the shift of energy, the surge of movement. Within a blink of the eye, she'd moved thirty meters to the left.

Relief and surprise gushed through her. The tree tracked her movement. Glancing up at the towering thing, her mouth fell open when its yellow eyes opened, glowing within the swaying canopy.

A burst of flame shot out, rushing towards her. She called her mageshield, keeping the flames from burning as they engulfed her. A manic mirth bubbled out of her, her bubble holding strong. Was it always this simple? Had she been trying to do magic with a block that removed ninety percent of her access?

Within the glow of light, she saw a young saricrocian, much smaller than the Ancients, but hungry nonetheless. The flames abruptly died, and it shifted its head to their camp.

Shit, Judas.

The creature lumbered forward, approaching her sleeping master.

Without conscious thought, she reached within and urged her essence forward. Her eyes burned, as they had in the Corridor. An electrical current coursed from her body and through the wand, blasting the back of the large bipedal reptile.

It spun, mouth wide, its hiss a warning. The water churned around her and it charged.

Another blast ripped through scales on its chest, searing flesh, rupturing tissue and muscles. A bone-jarring roar peeled through the night. The arcing blast jumped from its chest to its head, and when his mouth yawned open, stray bolts illuminated his sharp teeth as the current raced down its gullet.

The beast kept coming. A premonition flashed in Julie's mind but too late.

The tail swung for her. Her mageshield took the brunt, but the kinetic energy launched her off her feet. She hurtled through the air. Hardwood and bark rushed up towards her, a bone-shattering death.

Again, something took over her actions. She leaned back, flipping over, her feet to hit first. She concentrated, her life depending on it. Commanding her essence to cushion the blow, she used the tree as a springboard, returning towards her adversary. She accelerated. A stray thought broke her concentration.

Am I flying?

She lost speed; the ground rushed to greet her. Splashing down in brackish water, the impact sent her rolling, her robes drenched and her hair matted. Flecks of dirt and twigs peppered her face. She hurried to her knees, waiting, watching, listening.

The persistent voice filled her head with a buzzing sensation. The walls fortified against the coercion, sensing the mechanical, logical mind from wherever it hid. Judas's words about teleporting, winking, and blinking echoed in her mind.

Oh, shit. He's not even awake! How has he not heard the fight?

Pushing it from her mind, she urged her essence to do her bidding.

Wink.

She disappeared from the physical plane.

Darkness converged on her as she reappeared. Nothing. All remained still.

Wink.

Out of sight, and again she moved, finding nothing. Then, she realized her mistake, searching the ground while it towered like a tree.

Wink.

She reappeared in the topmost branches nearby, peering out. The sound of wind rushing in and out, deafening in the sudden silence.

Breathing!

She surveyed from the left, sweeping fast, hoping to find it before the saricrocian found her. As her head turned to the right, a giant yellow eye popped open three feet from her.

A red energy cascaded from her wand. The limb shook upon impact, sending her plunging. Gaping jaws chased after her, undeterred by the blasts; its intent focused on stopping the pain and filling its belly.

The swamp came rushing up. At the last instant, she blinked away, only to emerge a few meters away at a run. A glimmer caught her eye. The small fire flickered in the distance, much further away than she remembered.

Where is Judas? Why hasn't he helped?

She chanced a glimpse over her shoulder, the saricrocian bearing down, its chest charred but healing. Only a few, faint scorch marks remained where she initially hit it with electricity.

Damn, heals too fast. I won't win a physical battle. But a mental one?

She stopped a few yards shy of the fire. Turning about, she focused her mind on the saricrocian's, melding her thoughts with it.

Leave, leave me in peace, and I won't harm you anymore.

She felt the resistance waver, uncertain. She pressed harder, sinking her mental claws into it, commanding recognition, compliance.

Domination.

Its pace faltered, the foul water splashing in its slowed pace. A flame flickered inside its mouth.

Leave or I'll destroy you!

The saricrocian shuddered, a hiss escaped its mouth before it turned and fled into the murky waters.

"Come," the book called to her.

When she could no longer sense the saricrocian, she returned to camp. The firelight gave off a soft glow. Judas still slumbered without stirring. The book explained, answering her unspoken query.

"I placed him under a sleeping spell, much like he did to you upon your arrival. Nothing short of my destruction would rouse him. Gather your things; it's time to go. Your new life's starting."

"You could've helped me."

"A foreseen victory."

She swallowed, unsure of what to make of that. She cast a glance at Judas.

"What of him? I can't just leave him."

"Can't you? What has he done for you? Other than bring you pain and misery. Haven't you suffered enough? I've watched you since you were first brought into this world, so long ago."

"Long ago? I just got here—"

"Gather your things. We must be out of the swamp before sunrise."

"Will he be okay?"

"He won't die this day."

She took a moment to mull over the choice before her. She could continue with Judas to Wizard's Pass and carry on under his tutelage. Perhaps reconcile the anguish and lack of trust between them. She might, in time, learn to forgive him and let go of her ... animosity.

Once she acknowledged what she felt, it was evident. She hated him for allowing those terrible things to happen to her. She didn't loathe him with utter disgust, but enough resentment settled in her soul that she could no longer follow him. Perhaps with time, they could rebuild the relationship he destroyed.

A mist touched her eyes, and she blinked away the tears, knowing she couldn't learn anymore with him. Not every choice in life was easy, and this was but one.

In haste, she gathered her things. Having collected her pack, the two books, and her meager possessions, she battled with her morals for a few heartbeats. She vaguely realized where she was going, how far it was, and she didn't have any money.

Kneeling next to Judas, she reached for his coin purse and removed it from his belt. Bits of copper, chips of silver, and gold bright-eyes emptied on the ground. A few small gold bars she recognized as ingots peppered the coins. Judas carried more on his person than most made in a year.

Taking ten chips of silver, less than a third of his total, she tucked them away. The rest of his money, she gathered, and placed it back in the coin purse and returned it to his belt.

"You should take more."

"Stealing from him isn't what I wanted to do, but I need money. I'll only take what I need to survive."

The book fell silent as she started away from the camp. She didn't look back until she'd taken a hundred steps, counting each one, weighed down by a chance at freedom and guilt equally. A small lump formed in her throat.

Can I leave him?

Yes.

That answer came from the voice in her head.

Mr. Pleasure flashed through her mind, hardening her resolve.

I'll never be that vulnerable again. I'll never be helpless.

She turned her back on that chapter in her life, plunging deeper into the unknown, heading for her new life and whatever awaited.

Chapter 40: Xilor's Return

The Betrayer cracked open the door, eased into the room, and shut the large oak silently behind him. His mouth fell open. A dark, swirling cloud filled the chamber.

Shades, he's done it.

The compulsion to be far away while Xilor returned to his full might filled him. He could run, but the chances of being found were high. If he wasn't present when Xilor was restored, there'd be no escaping his wrath. The dark lord hunted without remorse, an entertaining spectacle before turning his attention back to his envisioned war.

For Xilor, the war never ended, just halted. He'd resume, and Ralloc would reel in the sudden onslaught.

The Betrayer's eyes flickered, wavering from the dark band of smoke and the mirror. He offered up a silent prayer.

Whatever gods or god may be up there, please let him fail, and I swear, I'll make things right.

Xilor's command cut through his prayer, and his scalp turned cold, the prickling sensations tingling his hairs.

"Bring forth my soul, Vlukus, and let us be done with it."

The Betrayer's breath came in rapid pants, and he found it hard to swallow, his throat suddenly dry.

Please, let him fail; please, let him fail; if there are gods, please, let him fail.

The dense fog rolled across the foyer, surrounding the ornate mirror, expanding, consuming nearly all the light in the vast hall. A cold, impenetrable darkness spread like thick smoke, and while it didn't choke the Betrayer, it stole his breath.

The mirror, Xilor's prison for many years, towered above everyone, wide enough to host three men standing shoulder to shoulder. The frame was made of white-rose, an elyfian tree found only in the Virgin Lands. The wood's name came from the color and texture: white of bone, pink of flesh, red of rose, and deep reddish brown of dried blood. Carvings of gods and animals adorned the frame, each figurine a medley of blood and snow.

Shadow wood hugged the sides, stripped from the Trees of Life and Shadow. Blacker like coal, like vile sin, from bark to core, etched in magical runes and inlaid with gold. Diabolically ornate, beautifully abominable.

Xilor's loud screech filled the gloom.

"Yes!"

The fog spun around the mirror, building speed.

A dark, gruff voice filled the chamber.

"Release me!"

The Betrayer shuddered as if cold. He shook his head in disbelief.

Now, I know the gods are truly dead.

Malevolence permeated the air, clinging to every surface, festering in his lungs, an oily residue of evil's purest form.

A sudden urge to gag stole over him. He felt sick. Why couldn't anyone else feel it?

The fog coalesced into an obsidian sphere, the surface glossy and inky. All sense of movement ceased but the Betrayer knew better. The chamber shook. A gush of wind ripped through, the wall beside the Betrayer groaned from the stress, trembling from the strain.

A vibration started in his chest as a demonic voice screamed again.

"Release me!"

A cold sweat broke over the Betrayer's body. He shivered. Ice poured down his spine, clenching his innards.

That vibration in his chest turned sharp, acute, like his sternum was fracturing from the breathing.

A hum pierced the room, causing his teeth to ache. The floor fractured at his side, cracking, a spiderweb of dust and fragments. He stepped away, hoping not to slip into a dark void of hell.

To his left, Sidjuous fell to his knees, and he glanced at the blond man. Sidjuous lay on the floor, rocking in a fetal position, burying his face with the black cloth in his hands. He didn't know whether to mock him or pity him. Perhaps Sidjuous was more pure than he?

A scream echoed out, not from Sidjuous—a scream not of a man, but omnipresent.

A burst of bright amethyst fire broke through the obsidian sphere, and the silver looking-glass blew out.

In a rush, the darkness retreated to the furthest corner of the room. Shards of silver spewed forth. The silhouette of a man, a ghost or apparition floated forward, too small to be Xilor. The ghostly figure shook violently before submerging into the vessel, Xilor's form-fitted coffin.

Smoke billowed from the casket like rising steam.

A hand breached the sarcophagus, clamping down on the railing, pulling the body out of the confines. The Betrayer gazed in horror as the pale, pink flesh darkened to ashen gray, riddled with blue veins through the length of Xilor's new body. Even as his body filled out, the dark lord's face remained unformed, his eye sockets deepened gray and turned black. The flesh around his lips grew taut, peeling back over his teeth in a vicious sneer.

The Betrayer was so engrossed that he hadn't noticed Sidjuous picking himself up off the floor, only realizing it when the man threw the black cloth around the reforming Xilor. Sidjuous pulled the hood over his still forming face and backed away, his head bowed, eyes averted.

But the Betrayer couldn't look away, and the horror leaking out of him didn't ease his terror. A sick fascination ran through him, wondering what his face looked like when the transformation came to full fruition.

The fiend straightened, standing to his full height, towering far above the others.

A cold panic flooded the Betrayer, and he almost lost control of his bladder. Had it been so long since he'd seen him in the flesh? Had he forgotten what it felt like to stand in his presence?

He swallowed.

There was no mistaking him. This wasn't a trick of light or a sickness in the mind. The deep shadows of his hood turned towards the Betrayer, and he froze, hoping to go unnoticed.

The cowl dipped—barely perceptible.

Was that recognition or just my imagination?

"I told you, Sidjuous," Xilor said. "I told you I'd return, even though you doubted me."

Smoke from the sarcophagus swirled around him.

"My lord."

Sidjuous cowered at his master's feet. Terror filled the blond lord's voice. Sidjuous, unlike the Betrayer, had always doubted. The Betrayer knew that one day, somehow, Xilor would manage it. He survived death once before, a greater trick than escaping his prison.

Damn good thing it's now rather than later.

There was still a small glimmer of hope. Judas Lakayre was still alive. The warlock stopped Xilor once, and he could do so again, but could he stop the dark lord permanently?

"All is forgiven, Sidjuous, but never forgotten."

"Yes, Master."

The groveling lord shuddered on the floor.

Xilor stepped over the broken shards, his long robes trailing across the glass, a slight tinkling sound rustled in his wake.

"Cleverly crafted deceit is lost on you, that's why you remain. I still have uses for you."

The looming shadow walked away from his cowering servant and stepped in front of the Betrayer. A quiver of trepidation ran through him.

"Surprised, Turncoat?"

The Betrayer imagined a sneer curling across his unformed lips.

"Should I be?"

Oh gods, what the fuck did I just say?

"As always, you're never unnerved. I expected as much, unless you count the first time we met."

"I hide my emotions well, my lord."

Shades of the Underworld don't kill me, not yet! We're fucked, we're all so fucked!

"I only detect a trace of anxiety from you, but my apprentice…" he motioned to Sidjuous, "is still affected by me and you aren't. Why?"

"The duties I perform in your name have dulled that edge."

"Accustomed are we? Or does your concern lay elsewhere?"

"Never, but fear kills faster than you do, and you never discard a useful asset."

Xilor's head cocked to the side.

"Well said."

Xilor's head straightened.

"You fear one you perceive more powerful. Would it be Judas Lakayre?"

"No, my lord!"

"We shall see, Turncoat. And you'll learn to dread me again."

The Betrayer dipped his head.

"Not as long as I prove useful."

Xilor turned away, scanning the room.

"Ah, Derms. My faithful goblin servant." The dark lord glided in his direction. "I shall reward you, my pet."

Derms bowed low and spoke reverently.

"An honor it is to serve you, master."

Xilor turned to the next person in line.

"Clan King Niam, did you enjoy the dark moments ago? Deeper than any you have ever encountered."

"Yes, rich with coldness."

The Betrayer hadn't noticed the arrival of the vampire king, but he should've expected it. By Xilor's edict, the vampires attacked Dlad City.

"I commend your raid. Make sure your service never falters. Future endeavors will be measured by your past success."

He turned away from Niam, scanning the room. A hiss of disgust escaped the gloom beneath his hood.

"The Witchen beast-riders of the Grymulohr phyles failed to answer my summons. I won't forgive this transgression. They'll get what's coming to them."

Circling where he stood, he noted others who were absent.

"Where are my xicx?"

Sidjuous rose to his feet.

"Most try not to disturb the Kothlere Order. They're afraid if they're caught—"

"—They have something new to fear!" Xilor said. "Never mind, hearing you speak makes me ill."

Olga giggled from deeper in the room. The Betrayer glanced her way. Just one more person who snuck in without him knowing.

"High One," Vlukus spoke from the fog in the corner.

Xilor held up a finger to him.

"I shall fulfill my promise this night."

"Why not now, Powerful One?"

Silence ensued, a brittle sliver. No one stirred.

Xilor broke the tension.

"I shall walk my halls first."

Perplexity rippled through the room. The Betrayer scrutinized the dark lord as he left the chambers, hushed misgivings furled.

"Find the xicx and bring them to me!"

A shudder ran down his spine when the dark lord glanced his way before exiting. If anything, Xilor wasn't nostalgic. He wouldn't gloat to his underlings.

That'd be a meaningless gesture. No, the dark lord yearned to boast to someone who he held in regard, someone like his old master, Hadius Lacove.

Again, the Betrayer shuddered, knowing what cruel fate the tyrant visited upon his elder. To the world, and the rest in Gryzlaud Palace, Hadius was dead.

Secrets bear a cost, and the tariff for initiation was high; in this case, his life. But Xilor had been gone a long time, and secrets have a way of circumventing their trammels. If the dark lord realized the Betrayer knew Hadius still lived, a swift and terrible retribution overshadowed his near future.

Letting out a breath of relief, the Betrayer sagged against the wall and waited for the coming storm.

Chapter 41: Behold, I Am Death

The towering despot stopped, his hand on the rail before him, looking out at distant horizons, searching for a familiar presence. Xilor stood alone on his terrace, facing the west. The breeze clutched at his robes, the frail gust running invisible fingers through the cloth. Above, the stars twinkled, their delicate light unappreciated and cruelly spurned.

Minor trickles—essence echoes—called out to him, faint traces of auras. He could feel them, but could they sense him? The subtlest aura echoed from the north in the distant capital, too faint to be Judas.

Xilor's exploration guided him away from Ralloc to the southwest, towards the notorious warlock's manor. There, strong tendrils hooked Xilor, drawing him in, siphoning his essence. He smirked at the defenses, wards placed around his residence. Yet, he only sensed an echo of Judas's presence.

His gaze shifted, following the sporadic, faded trail from Dlad City to Cape Gythmel and finally to the Corridor. The trail filled his mind's eye like a striation of light; the longer Judas remained at a location, the brighter the glow became. A quick layover only peppered his vision in a muted shimmer.

It wasn't until he traced him to the Corridor that he felt another presence.

A protegé? Who would the great Judas Lakayre take under his wing?

With keen interest, he followed them to the Swamp of Sorrows where they toiled. It was here that the other presence shone like a beacon in the night. It was effulgent, like a lighthouse in dense fog. Xilor reached out to caress the essence, to taste who or what it was.

Upon first touch, a violent jolt shot through him, causing him to jerk away. The essence arced out, the bolt searing him and charring his mental touch. He reached again with a delicate probe, compensating for the impending surge. A glimmer of smugness overcame him as he wasn't attacked on the second try.

The aura was nothing like he'd ever experienced before: unbridled but untamed. More to the point, he'd sensed power from all walks of life, and there was a common thread among all of them. They all tasted relatively the same, their shape unchanged among the races. But this … was alien.

Has a new race appeared since my imprisonment?

He discarded the notion, striking it down as foolish.

He scrutinized the aura he felt. Once properly trained, the wielder would be a force to reckoned with.

Xilor shook his head in awe.

Not a protegé. A prodigy.

Xilor followed the new essence as long as he could, catching it leaving the swamp only to become obscured from his sight. He searched in vain, almost turning frantic. How could he lose such a prize? He needed to trail it, find it, and bring it to his home. Here, he could twist it to his will.

Disgruntled at finding nothing, his regard shifted to Judas. His essence flickered east and stopped at Wizard's Pass. A smile spread across his face.

You've come so close; you won't slip from my grasp.

Xilor bent his magic to his will and teleported to his throne room.

"Vlukus, I shall fulfill my promise to you!"

"You bring greatness to your name."

"My name is already great," Xilor corrected. "And when I'm done transforming this world, everyone will know it, too."

His irritation at the being shimmered beneath his composure, and he savored it, letting it build, but he wouldn't release it, not yet. He'd let it fester, feeding it, preparing for its release.

"As you've reminded me of our bargain, let me remind you. Your service is required after I give you shape. Serve well and be rewarded, but failure has its consequences, too, Vlukus."

Xilor turned his gaze to the xicx who heeded his edict and returned to his palace. Though their faces were covered with the skulls of dead animals, they animated, displaying the emotions beneath. Terror gripped them now, an initiative for unquestionable obedience.

Xilor lowered himself on his throne, his back rigid and straight. His hands draped across the arms.

"Where were you in my most desperate hour?"

"Master, we—"

"Silence! You incompetent fool. Did I tell you to speak?"

"No, master. I beg your forgiveness."

The xicx flung itself toward the hem of Xilor's robes. Before he could reach him, Xilor moved his feet beyond reach.

"You dare to touch me?"

Xilor rose, a slow and smooth movement.

"You failed me with incompetence, and you flaunted my summons."

He held out his skeletal, ash-colored hand—fingers poised to gouge the xicx like daggers. They hovered, waiting.

He slowly spread his fingers apart; the xicx morphed, stretching. Sickening pops pierced the hush. Xilor's eyes darted to the dark fog as it slowed, watching, which was good. This was a lesson they needed to learn.

Screams bellowed from the xicx—mangled flesh tore, the wet noises drowned out by wails of anguish. Bones ground together, snapping, puncturing its skin—what passed for it, anyway.

"This is the price of failure, Vlukus."

Xilor turned his head, watching the dark fog, then back to the target of his ire.

His right hand reached through the chest of his victim, pulling out the spine and skull. The limp body fell to the floor. His clawed hands squeezed the skull, shattering the blood-covered ivory. Brain matter slid between the cracks of his fingers, clinging to his elongated digits.

Xilor tossed the remains on the steps and turned to face the remains of the gathered xicx. Without prompting, each knelt, heads bowed.

Xilor turned to the hovering fog.

"What you desire is still yours. Shape for service. Faithfulness is rewarded, failure means death. You still wish it?"

The obsidian smoke hesitated.

"Yes."

In a fluid motion, Xilor drew out his grisly wand, sending a blast of energy erupting from the tip. The wand was fashioned out of several black, twisted metal pieces, spiraling around the core and bound in the curved hilt.

The fog segregated, breaking up to form individual clouds, shaping and solidifying into new beings conjured from his endless dark imagination. Shapes emerged carrying the same hue as the oily miasma.

The channeled conjuring ceased abruptly, like halting in the middle of expounding a soliloquy. Fatigue washed over him; he stumbled back, legs trembling. The summoning weakened him—either because the magic was too great, because his body was still new, or because he'd grown weak while imprisoned.

He shuddered, taxed by the power that left him, and the throne broke his fall. He called his rage, bolstering his strength. He couldn't afford to look weak now.

The abyssians, newly embodied, scuttled and thrashed about, growing accustomed to the sudden equilibrium and legs, the concept of gravity that they'd defied since inception. Before him, Xilor saw the corrupt, perverse hybrids—man fused to centaur, spidery and wrong.

Six legs shot out from their flanks and splayed like spindly limbs. A strong, lithe body supported the torso of a man with arms. The hands boasted two large, wide fingers and an opposable thumb. Long, curving nails extended from the fingers, sharp enough to lacerate flesh.

Reptilian scales covered the body to include the face. A long snout protruded from the jaw, lined with serrated teeth; the end of the lower jaw extended beyond the top and curled towards the face, forming a deadly hook.

A crest as hard as stone sprouted from the back of the head, curving downward, flaring out, protecting the back of the neck.

One abyssian gingerly stepped forward.

"High One," he rasped.

"Vlukus."

Xilor rose to his feet.

The abyssian lowered his body to the deck.

"You have our allegiance, Master."

"I'll use you as needed. Until I send you out, you're to remain here at the palace. Am I understood?"

"Completely."

Now was the time to display his superiority.

"Your bodies are extraordinary. Your tongue has healing properties in your saliva. Your legs can carry you at higher speeds than the fastest steed, and they'll help defy gravity. We'll put such wonders to test later. When in war, like gambling, you don't reveal your entire hand at once. But now, I have a task for you."

Vlukus rose and neared Xilor. Bending at the waist, Xilor relayed his instructions.

"It shall be done, High One."

Vlukus turned and retreated from the hall, his abyssians following on his heels. The clacking of their six legs against the stone was the only noise disturbing the somber setting.

Xilor lifted his head to others in the room.

"Leave me."

The xicx, various attendants, and apprentices departed, filing out of the room with haste. When the door shut behind the last minion, Xilor turned to his shattered mirror, his prison for so long. With a wave of his wand, the pieces reformed within the frame.

The mirror's surface flared a sick yellow-green.

"I'm free," Xilor rasped, knowing the whole realm witnessed. "I'll have revenge on every mortal."

He stepped closer to the mirror, forming his words. It wasn't about the truth of his objective, it was about delivering a message they'd understand. His goals were far loftier than the dribble he'd feed them.

"Here's my promise to you. All will die. None will be spared: no man, woman, child, creature, or pet. Genocide and enslavement await you all. Nothing will be left in the wake, except the person or persons that deliver Judas Lakayre to me, alive!"

Chapter 42: Beyond Reach

Judas woke to an empty camp.

A wave of cold panic swept through him. He called to Julie multiple times, and the only answer was the echo of his hoarse voice. He stretched with his essence, sensing nothing but the hidden wildlife around him. Reaching through the bond with her, he learned that she was still alive, and whatever barrier that had kept her from reaching her full potential had shattered.

More troubling was that he couldn't detect her exact location or direction; she'd somehow managed to shroud her presence. She could be in any direction from his current position. Her aura radiated within her, which he could sense, but it was akin to a lantern with a shroud suddenly draped around it, there one minute and gone the next. Whenever he thought he'd found her, he sensed reflections, as if mirrors surrounded her.

No matter which way he looked, the reflected image continued forever.

But he had to try. He closed his eyes, tracing her movements, and reached out.

Julie.

But she didn't receive his telepathy. He might as well be shouting into a bottomless cave.

Julie.

Nothing.

He shook his head, realizing he'd search in vain. Instead of trying to locate her, he focused on the aura within her, her vast essence. Now, an unrelenting current poured into her, a torrent. Only twice had he felt something close to this, and both were dead: his friend, the king, and Xilor.

What he sensed troubled him. Julie fortified her mind in a way she'd never previously achieved, but sporadic bursts bled through. It was controlled yet uncontrolled. She burned brightly in his mind, but fading as more distance stretched between them. He glimpsed her resolve, her fears and worries cast aside.

"You won't find her," a small voice said, scarcely louder than a whisper, but rustled like soft wind chimes.

Judas turned and faced the small floating pixie.

"Is this your doing?"

"No, but it was meant to happen. Even you cannot fight a fate foretold."

"Bah! Fate! I should've never listened to the elder fairy. What did you do to her?"

"Nothing, Warlock Lakayre. What happened was destined to happen regardless."

"Do you think you can keep her from me? She's mine to protect, to train! I told the elder fairy this when she came to her!"

"Train? Like you trained her for the Corridor? You didn't realize that she wasn't a Plotus mage!"

"There were extenuating circumstances—"

"—Like you protected her from the murder attempt?"

"Again, that—"

"—Like you protected her from the likes of Mr. Pleasure and all his horrors? You've lost touch with what it means to be a teacher."

"It wasn't my place to interfere!"

The feeling in his gut confirmed the pixie's truth. The guilt he held for allowing the Corridor to test her beyond her abilities festered like an open sore in his soul, and the words of the Time Warden turned gangrenous.

"It wasn't supposed to happen. How was I supposed to know what it'd do?"

Though the fairy hovered in the air, she crossed her arms.

"You didn't, but you could've stopped it. Where were your morals, then?"

Judas said nothing, and his legs gave out, collapsing to the ground. She fluttered closer, wings sounding like a whistle, and landed in front of him.

"Don't ridicule yourself too much, Warlock; you did as foretold."

"Where? Where did it say that I'd allow her to be tortured?"

"Actions are fluid, not stone, but we prophesied what you allowed to happen, long ago. All events, all planes of possibilities converge on her. It would happen another way, by another means, regardless of your actions."

He shook his head and swallowed.

"Who else would drag her through the Corridor? No one!"

"Who said it'd be the scarrings of the Corridor? Perhaps another wizardkind left the scars? Sheol? What if I told you … had it been anyone else from other possibilities that she'd be physically scarred, deformed? What if, by someone else's hand, she turned into something worse than Xilor and killed everyone who opposed her?"

"I'd be required to kill her."

"Yes, you'd hunt her down. Your blinding quality to see the good in everyone would prevent you from taking decisive action, and in the end, years would've faded before you came to the precipice of choice. By then, she'd be able to destroy you."

"How do you know?"

"I don't. We're talking conjectures, Warlock."

"If we're talking conjecture, if she journeyed with someone else, nothing would've happened."

"Alas, no."

The fairy shifted her weight, taking a step forward.

"You have something that belongs to us. The elder fairy must be returned."

Nodding, Judas called his pack to him, digging out the item she wished for. After a few moments, he pulled out the small crystalline wing and handed it to her. She took the wing in her hands, inspecting the last remains of an elder fairy. With a flutter of her wings, she rose from the ground.

"Heed my warning, Warlock Lakayre. Trials await her. She must be molded and shaped into what she is to become. You'll do more harm than good if you reach out. Stay away! We will be with her now—as it's our duty to our Head of Creatures. She's our prophesied one, meant to become … more. If you search, we'll hide her from your sight. For now, take solace that we grant you the ability to sense her at all. Break our edict, and we'll revoke the blessing!"

"And what is that?" he croaked. "What's she supposed to become?"

"So much more. A balance of darkness and light, a champion of life and a harbinger of death."

She hovered in front of his face before fading into nothing.

Alone in the swamp, his anguished cry echoed out.

Chapter 43: Wizard's Pass

Wizard's Pass wasn't the most legendary of villages, but the cozy reprieve was like a part of home for Judas, despite being so far from a civilized municipality. Many people deemed the small settlement as a retirement haven from the bustling life of the city.

The warlock walked down the small, empty street, closing in on T'son Hans's bar. At the door, he shoved it hard, expecting it to catch on the ground below, as it'd always done in the past.

It didn't.

It slammed against the wall inside, and light filled the doorway, illuminating the owner at the far end behind the bar.

T'son Hans, with a towel in hand, stopped wiping down the wet ale mug, and stared.

"Well, com'n an' shut th' door, will ya?" T'son said.

Judas smiled upon hearing his thick accent; someone not from their village wouldn't understand him, and when excited, it turned indecipherable.

Judas stepped inside, closing the door behind him. T'son blinked a few times and squinted in the darkness.

"Well, if it ain't an archangel, then it's got t'be Judas!"

"Greetings, T'son."

The warlock shuffled forward, his feet heavy, his mood solemn.

"I told you I'd come."

While he buried his roiling emotions under an expressionless mask, his voice betrayed him.

"Y'ur 'prentice, whur' is she?"

"Gone."

T'son laughed.

"Ya still got ya' sense o' humor, I see. Whut can I git for ya'? 'Ow 'bout a good, col' brew? A Bloo'y Vampur?"

"Not today, T'son; I don't feel much like drinking."

The barkeep sobered, his twang disappearing.

"Oh, one of tho' things. Well, glad ta see ya c'me down 'ere an' tries ta su'vive me. Whur's yur 'Prentic?"

Judas let out a weary sigh as he sat on a stool opposite his friend. T'son looked him over, and for the first time, he noticed his less-than-jovial mood.

"Shades! Ya weren't jokin'," T'son exclaimed, dropping his thick accent. "Ya look like shit! Wha's th' matter wit' ya?"

"My apprentice. She's gone."

He swallowed, planting his right hand against his head, fingers buried in his hair.

"I failed her worse than I've ever failed at anything in life."

T'son waved his hand.

"Oi! Don' be so hard on ya'self. It can' be tha' bad."

"You don't understand, T'son; I let terrible things happen to her. I failed her in the Corridor. I should've stepped in and stopped the madness ... and now, she's gone. She left because I abandoned her when she needed me."

T'son shook his head, crossing his arms.

"Oi! Shu' it! I've known ya a long time, Judas, thru' thick 'n' thin, in good 'n' bad, 'n' when th' whole of Ermaeyth was thrown in ta chaos, 'n' never once did ya fail ta see the good in people. Even when they don' deserve it. Ya give the shirt off ya back to clothe someone less fortunate than ya."

T'son uncrossed his arms, and leaned against the bar, his hands planted, holding himself up as he leaned in.

"I don' pretend ta know wha' happened, but I know tha' yur good. Too good for ma likes—but ever'one has ta have some fault—'n' ya moral to ya core, and tha' is somethin' as sure as the risin' suns. Ya made a soun' judgment based on the facts at han'. If she lef', 'n' lef' angry, eventually she'll know ya had the bes' intentions at he'rt. She'll remember in the en'; they all do."

Judas gave a weak smile.

"Was that speech something you had prepared beforehand?"

T'son gave a single nod.

"Always had tha' speech ready fur ya—ages really, ya jus' never needed it till now."

Judas's smile broadened and swiftly fell. "I just can't—"

"Oi! Enuff! No sense dwellin' on the pas'; it's fur the dead. The future is a youn' virgin too far away ta care abou', bu' thur's no time like fuck'n' in the presen'."

"Fucking in the present? That's it? There isn't a line to come after that?"

"No, ya ass, it's a play on wor's. Shades, ya thick."

T'son laughed heartily, pushing away from the bar, and Judas couldn't help but laugh, too.

After T'son coaxed Judas out of his lamenting shell, he served his long-time friend many drinks, drowning the guilt of losing Julie. His mind was filled with regret, and he had no doubt that T'son could discern the shadow in his eyes, the haunted anguish. They'd both seen that look in each other before and long ago.

But the foreigner steered him clear of anything that'd bring up the events of the Corridor or his apprentice. When it was evident that he couldn't accomplish this, T'son asked him how the consul, Kayis Dathyr, was doing, and if they were friends again. That started Judas on an uproar, grandstanding his detest of his old apprentice. With the conversation switching to politics and the lost cause of the Kothlere Order, Judas digressed to the real reason he was here.

"I needed a place to hide and hole up. Someone's either after me or my apprentice. And ... with a war coming, it's an ideal spot to see the opening moves."

T'son frowned.

"Ah, ya talkin' abou' th' broadcas', ain't ya?"

"What broadcast?"

T'son quickly summarized the events of Xilor's realm-wide broadcast. Judas rubbed his temples.

"So, he finally did it. He's out. I warned them that this would happen. Are you prepared? Do you have any men available?"

"'Course. They haven' been doin' nothin' since the war. Thur all slouchin' aroun' 'ere somewhur, gettin' all fat 'n' bored."

"Good, call them here. We need to be prepared just in case, and if Xilor's out, then it may be too late!"

T'son scurried across the wood-planked floorboards of his humble, rickety establishment. It wasn't the nicest place, never attempted to come close, but it was T'son. Compared to the grandeur of Ralloc, this equated to a horse stall, but Judas still felt comfortable here, even with the dark swirl of thoughts shrouding his mood. Worries washed away in the simple life they held here.

More than that, with Xilor returned, it helped him forget about Julie and her journey alone. With him, she'd always be a target, or at the very least, collateral damage, but out there, alone, with no one able to find her? She stood a chance at surviving.

Find some dark hole to hide in Julie. Please stay safe.

T'son reached the front door and flung it open.

"Oi! Drabass! Get yur rott'n, sodd'n bottom up in the pub. Ge' all 'em; Sergyn' of th' Guards, too!"

Judas covered a smile in the palm of his hand. T'son screaming at his underlings brought back fond memories for the warlock, remembering where they met, on the deck of T'son's ship on Judas's maiden voyage. The trading ship was christened *Floating Dreams,* and T'son ferried cargo from port to port, out on the open sea. When times were tough, the former kaptyn smuggled people, weapons, and other rare, off-limits items.

He even recalled T'son's tale about being the only one to ever venture into Lake Feral and make it back out alive.

Years later, Judas learned how T'son made his income. Their main means came from raiding pirates, looting their pillage, consuming the goods, and absorbing the less dangerous crew. The others, the kaptyns, first mates, and the loyal crew, were placed in shackles and returned to the nearest port for the bounties. Occasionally, they'd hire themselves out for private purposes. T'son and his crew were merchants, smugglers, and even mercenaries, but under T'son's banner, they managed to be the good guys, just not lawfully validated.

Judas shook his head, knowing how the story turned out.

T'son would still be sailing had he not lost the two loves of his life. His first mate—who was also his wife—and then his ship, when his cousin, Oslo Hans, won it from him in a card game. Upon winning, Oslo renamed the ship *The Keeling Bitch.* After that, T'son took his earnings from all those years at sea, chose a town, and settled down to make a home.

Judas looked up as T'son returned.

In short but precise order, all the men and women gathered to hear the governor and Judas explain the possible impending war. Many balked until he recounted the vampire's attack on Dlad City. The news of Judas's public branding of renegade and menace by the consul had reached Wizard's Pass, most likely in the hopes that someone would warn Ralloc if he showed up.

"Look," Judas said, "is it so hard to believe that another war is possible? Xilor's out; he made a broadcast, apparently one that I missed."

Judas stood from the stool, facing the small gathering.

"He'll be coming for blood."

Murmurs rippled through the gathering, some agreeing and others not. Whether they did or didn't wouldn't matter once they started dying, and unfortunately, Ralloc took that stance, too.

The group turned to T'son for confirmation, hoping he'd renounce or reaffirm what Judas said.

"Why ya lookin' at me fur? I ain't any po'erful mage, jus' a gov'nor. If Judas says it is, then it is."

"You can stand and fight, or you can run," Judas said. "The victor of the first battle, wherever it may be, will determine the motion of the war. We must do what we can for anyone who wants to travel through the Corridor or make it to a coastal city where they can sail to relative safety. By nightfall, I want decisions on whether people are preparing for fortifications or fleeing."

Chapter 44: Julie

Setting off on her own seemed like a good idea at the time. The book made persuasive and sound arguments. The alluring promise of more knowledge and power intrigued her, considering her unsuccessful tutelage under Judas. With the block removed from her essence and the emotional damage temporarily sealed away, a future without the warlock seemed bright.

Until she started walking.

The suns blazed above; sweat ran in fat rivulets from her brow. Her clumping hair clung to her cheeks. Cramps bit her legs. Her lungs burned as if breathing in fire. Leaving looked less and less like a promising epiphany.

If only I had a horse. Or if I could just teleport there!

But she had neither, and the latter would need to be taught, which was something Judas failed to do time and again. She had little in her repertoire, and she was pretty sure teleporting was an advanced technique. Hadn't Judas said that few people could do it?

So, she was stuck walking. The journey provided plenty of time to look back on her fight with the saricrocian; she'd been lucky not to kill herself with her haphazard winks. It'd been a spur of the moment decision, and with time and distance, she decided not to chance injury until she had a better grasp.

Would she find the answers in this Place of Origins? Whatever the hell that meant.

More than once, the image of a sleeping Judas filled her mind as she replayed kneeling beside him to steal silver chips. She quarreled with her rationale for leaving Judas, but her anger and the images inside Mr. Pleasure's thrall silenced those misgivings.

Is it possible to mistrust someone, and even hate what they've done, but still like that person?

But was that gullibility or optimism peeking through? More than once, that outlook got the better of her. In the silence of her thoughts, those same doubts returned, centered around the book and if it did the same, preying upon her weaknesses. The thought tumbled through her head like a never-ending echo as the leagues dwindled.

She had a vague sense of direction. The book gave her a point to march towards and then retreated within itself, returning to its silent state. Even her mental screams at it failed to rouse an answer. The thought crossed her mind that it was nothing more than a messenger, its only function to find her, reveal itself, and specify the proper path. Would it speak again if she changed course, or strayed too far from the objective? Though an intriguing consideration, she didn't relish the notion of walking in the opposite direction just to test the theory.

Besides, she ached too much.

Another puzzle troubling her was that Judas hadn't caught up with her.

Is he even looking for me? For someone so powerful, it should be a simple task of tracking me down through magic.

When she last laid eyes on the sleeping warlock, he seemed more feeble than she remembered, a thought she attributed to the block that'd melted away.

The book did many things for me—most of all, it opened my eyes.

A new path to discover Ermaeyth lay ahead of her, and she wanted to approach it, like the rest of her life, with eyes open. For the first time that she could remember, she felt excited by the prospect. Since waking up in Judas's home, she'd been pushed down a path she hadn't chosen, trying to make sense of a world forced upon her. Since that day, this was the first choice she'd made on her own.

She trekked many leagues through rolling prairie the first day. With her feet sore from the moderate pace, she slowed to relieve the throbbing pain. By sheer luck, the fortune of the bold, or grand design, she crossed paths with a caravan. When they pulled within hailing range, greetings and a few words were exchanged, a bargain struck, and Julie hitched a ride.

Far Point, the nearest town, was still many leagues off. The journey would take days on horseback. She'd die of dehydration long before she reached her destination.

The caravan master voiced his exorbitant fee of a silver chip for a ride and food. While outrageous, she graciously accepted the theft at knifepoint for a reprieve from certain death. Days trickled by in the tedium of the swaying wagon, interrupted by laughing children or crying babies.

One mother, in particular, had only one volume with her children: too loud. She shouted at them from the time the suns came up until they went down, making Julie reevaluate her decision to join them. By the end of the first day, Julie wanted to drown the woman in the water barrel, and her kids probably would've thanked her.

If I ever have children, please let me be a better mother than that!

Then, she considered another possibility. What was life like for the man that'd married her? Before the children, had the woman turned her disdain upon him? Julie felt sorry for the poor bastard, but she didn't see him, and that meant either he'd left her, was dead, or they were on their way to him now.

Early one evening, they ground to a halt near a river bend. Unable to take the stench of her clothing or body anymore, she decided to bathe. Though she had no soap, she went without, forgoing the gouging prices of the master, who wanted five copper bits for a bar of hard lye. While the families set up pots and children either helped or played, Julie slipped away with her possessions, hoping her departure went unnoticed.

In the bend, the water ran low—more of a weaving stream through a gully than the prominent river it once had been. The shoreline, once part of the riverbed, was littered with large, flat stones, smooth from erosion, and hedged in shrubs and tall, wild grass.

She wove her way down the trail, grateful the hill separated her from the expedition, though it offered little in the way of privacy. The shore, she noted, offered several shallow depressions filled with water, perhaps coming to her knee in the center. The suns ensured warm hollows.

A few paces away, the flowing stream gurgled, and she found it cool to the touch. With the unforgiving heat, her stench, and the multi-day grime, she decided on the latter.

Pack discarded, she shed her robes, debating on trying to wash the filth and stink out of them. Without any soap, it would be a near-useless gesture and wadded them up to discard later. They were too ruined to keep. She'd worn them all through the Corridor—however long she'd been in there—and through the stagnant swamp.

With a cursory glance behind her, she confirmed her solitude. With deft fingers, she pulled the sash of her bosom wrap, letting her undergarments fall to the stony shore.

In haste, she entered the cool water. It was colder than anticipated. The gentle surges rippled around her, and she dipped below the surface, holding her breath. Below, she ran her fingers through her hair, hoping to get out whatever the swamp managed to embed.

Underwater, her hair felt smooth and silky. The itch in her lungs implored her to return to the surface. She broke the surface and gasped sweet air as the wind flickered, snaking through the gully, kissing her flesh.

Goosebumps rippled down her body; everything tightened.

She splashed her face, rubbing the sweat and grime away. Dipping below again, her hands dragged the sandy bed, scooping up silt and rubbing it between her toes, under her arms, and anywhere she could reach. She methodically scoured her flesh as best as she could, requiring many returns topside; each time the sharp, cold wind licked her. Teeth chattering, she'd dive below the surface again.

Before long, the water was too cold to continue, and remembering the shallows, she clambered out of the river. Holding the pack to obscure most of her body, she half-huddled, half-shuffled, to the shallows, sinking in a rush. Because of the lack of depth, she lay on her stomach to cover her entire body. The warm water chased the gooseflesh away from her icy limbs.

She basked in the tepid heat for only a few minutes, worried that someone would discover her. The deeper waters could obscure her body, but not the shallows.

Leaving the shoal, she pulled out a pair of garments from her bag. Though she'd worn them before, they felt heavenly compared with her discarded outfit. As she pulled the undergarment up her legs, a twig snapped behind her. She spun around, catching a young boy of ten or eleven watching her.

Her face went red with embarrassment.

"Get out of here, you little shit!" she screamed.

He turned white, fleeing in terror, stumbling his way up the trail. With darting glances, she dressed in haste. Pack on her back and her swamp robes tucked deep in the brambles, she retreated up the hill, her wet hair hanging in clumps.

When she reached the camp, she spied the boy and thought about scolding him when she saw his mother, the loud woman. The last thing Julie fancied was to listen to more of her. Catching the boy's eye, she narrowed hers before giving him a smirk. The boy was young and curious; she didn't fault him for that, and relatively no harm was done save her embarrassment.

Sporadically, while they traveled, she'd catch the boy glancing her way at various times, a grin on his face, which would bring a fresh surge of warmth to hers. She probably made that boy's life, being a part of his discovery phase. He'd remember her forever, until he had a better memory to replace her with.

After what felt like an eternity of torture—though only six days—the caravan reached Far Point. With the small city in sight, she slipped away and sought the inhabitants of a more civilized and quiet nature. To call it a city was an overstatement. Regardless, she was happy to be there and away from screaming women and young voyeurs.

An hour before dusk, she walked through the gate. The guards surrounded her, keeping their weapons sheathed. With a clattering of chain mail, they settled about her.

"Name?"

"Julie."

She debated using the fake name from Dlad City, Cynthia Fossard, but she didn't want to chance someone catching her in a lie without Judas there to aid her. Further, if Judas came looking for her here, and he also used the alias, they might remember her and divulge her passage.

"What kind of name's Julie?" one sentry asked.

The leader shot him a glance before returning his attention to her.

"Well, Julie," he said, speaking to her as if she was ignorant, "you got a family name? In these parts, when you introduce yourself, it's Julie, daughter of so-and-so, or Julie of House Piss-pot."

The others cackled, and she blushed at forgetting the most basic etiquettes. Agitation flared within her, but she couldn't act on it. That'd only make things worse. Besides, even if she managed to get away, they'd remember her. She decided to fib her way in.

"Julie of the Fossard House, and you had best refrain from calling my house a piss pot. What's your name, soldier? My father will be very interested to hear what you think of his house!"

"Forgive my loose tongue, Lady Fossard. It's been a long day. Please, don't let us keep you."

He gave her a bow of his head and stepped aside. Without wasting any more time, she strolled past, suppressing her smirk. After a dozen paces or so, she heard the start of the guards conversing.

"Nice one, jackass."

"How was I supposed to know she was a minor noble?"

"Fucking nobles, the lot of them—"

The voices trailed off as the sounds of the town drowned them out. A wagon rumbled by, headed for the gate she'd entered. Children raced through the streets playing, and beggars in stained and ripped clothing sat on the porches of closed shops.

At least they don't yell.

Other shopkeepers swept their porches, dirt and mire plumed around her as she passed. Her head swiveled as she walked down the cobblestone road, the town's main street. A thin layer of dirt covered the street; the grit crunched with each of her steps. All other roads were still dirt and rutted from wagons. A few even looked wet in spots, either from a recent rain or horse piss.

In front of her, in the distance, she saw a steeple of red clay shingles of the local cathedral towering far above the other buildings. Most, she noted, were made of a combination of wood and stone, but she spied hovels of wood and mud near the perimeter of town.

As she searched for a place to stay the night, a woman went whizzing by, pulling a boy and a little girl by the ear down the road towards the steeple. Her dark brown hair flashed by, either the wind ripping at it, or her hurried, angry pace.

"...you better pray long and hard to the Father, Mother, and Child for what you've done! You'd best beg for forgiveness and mercy," she said.

At least, she isn't yelling.

Perplexed, Julie made to follow them when a magnificent noise drew her attention: the sounds of laughter and of pewter tankards setting down on wooden tables. A musical instrument played, sustaining the backdrop. The jingle of coin scraping on tabletops was music to her ears.

She adjusted course and followed the sounds and, eventually, the smells to a three-story building made of wood and stone with a sign out in front that stretched the width of the establishment.

"Traveler's Haven," she murmured.

She pushed open one of the two front doors made of oak and glass and entered the establishment. All eyes drifted to her and settled for half a moment before turning their gazes back to what they were doing.

With cautious eyes, she swept the place, noting the filled tables, but they paid her no further heed, attention turning back to the musician. Relaxing, she headed for the bar.

The aroma of pork simmering in a sauce wafted through the air; wheat bread, warm and inviting, followed on its heels. She took a deep breath, and her stomach rumbled.

"Help ya?" the bartender asked, while rubbing down the countertop.

"Something to drink, if you please."

"Well, what do ya want?"

"I don't know. I've never been to a pub before, so I couldn't tell you what I like."

She paused for a moment, eyes lingering on the shelf behind him. A word floated to the forefront of her mind, but for the life of her, she couldn't remember where she'd heard it.

"Got a menu?"

"What's a menu?"

The baffled expression told her such things were a foreign concept to him. Then, he pointed to a big plywood board off to the side of the countertop which listed the drinks and their contents.

"That help?"

He went back to wiping down his tankards and bar top again as Julie rolled her eyes and glanced over the board, making her choice.

"Vampire Dust, if you please."

The bartender set to task and filled her order. Once done, he placed it before her.

"Silver chip."

Her mouth fell open.

"Silver chip, my ass! You're robbing me blind!"

"That's the price here, if you don't pay, I can always call the city watch."

"Gek!" someone shouted. "Get the fuck out from behind ma' bar."

The man who was obviously the bartender, walked around the counter and smacked him on the back of the head.

"Fucking thief, I should call the guards and have ya flogged for taking advantage of a stranger."

He hit him again on the back of the head, his hair flying, and the younger man scampered off. The new man gave a sheepish smile and eyed her cup.

"At least he made ya drink right."

When Julie tried to pay him, he held his hands up.

"On the house."

He jerked his head towards the boy who tried to rob her.

"For Gek's scheming."

"Thank you. I thought a silver chip was outrageous."

She smiled and took a slow, cautious pull of her nip, finding the flavor enjoyable. Her initial sip reminded her of chocolate, but it subtly changed to coconut. The gray and murky liquid alluded to a cross between milk and the stagnant swamp waters.

She turned and faced the room again, glimpsing the instrument that had caught her ear earlier. It stood on the floor like a cello, the musician seated behind. Twelve thick strings splayed out like fingers, and between them another six each—seventy-two in all—stretched taut along its length.

He played in a slow cadence, the bow drawing across the strings; metal fittings at the top lent a faint, chiming resonance.

Beautifully strange, the sound ached with alien tones that pleased her ears.

Turning back to the innkeeper, she found him appraising her, and he pointed to her cup.

"Not to ya liking?"

"No, no. The drink's fine … I think. I don't really know, never had one, but I like it. No, I was curious about that instrument over there. I've never seen one. It's breathtaking. What's the name?"

"Ah." The man nodded and smiled. "A lovely thing, isn't it? It's called a Lylo. Few people can master it, but the ones that can … well, ya can see the turn out tonight, huh? He's a traveling musician, and he'll be making his final stop in Ralloc where he hopes—with the bigger population—that he can establish a shop there. Word has it he's from south of the Melodic Mountains."

"The Melodic Mountains?"

Isn't that where I'm supposed to go?

"Ya, but I don't know if it's true. Ya never really overhear anyone coming over the mountain to get here. Ship maybe. But there are a few who claim to know the way through the caverns and get over here."

Julie's mind raced. Her eyes slid out of focus as she thought about her destination.

"Tell me, what is the Father, Mother, and Child?"

"Ya joking, right?"

"No, I'm not. Not from around here. Tell me about them."

"It's a religion in these parts. The Father, Mother, and Child represent a Trinity. The Father for all that's good in the world, represents protection, provision, and procreation with war and food. He also represents the present. The Mother exemplifies all the evil, death, famine, and sickness. She also embodies the past. The Child is the Child of Innocence, equates to life, love, joy, and the future. But the great thing about the Trinity is that we all came from the Father and Mother, we're the Child, and therefore we're created out of equal proportions of them."

Funny how the woman's the evil one.

"I don't understand how the Father represents good and war."

"Well, war's good, depending on how ya look at it. If ya go to war with a thirst for blood; well, then ya would be doing the Mother's bidding. But if ya go to war because ya King asks, or to protect ya family and land, then ya doing it for the Father."

She cocked an eyebrow.

"And the Child? Is the Child a boy or a girl?"

"Does it matter? That's the beauty of the Trinity, gives no sex a greater advantage over the other. Ya have the male and the female, but the child is just a child. All are created equal under the religion."

"Are you a follower?"

"Somewhat. I'm not a pious man, but when something good or bad happens to me, I renew my standing with the Trinity."

"Are there other religions like this one?"

"Ya," he said pointedly. "I don't like to talk about them."

Julie noted his shift in tone. She might be a traveler, but there was only so much he was willing to tolerate, and questioning his faith wasn't one of them. He turned more brooding, and his shoulders squared with mild indignation.

That killed their conversation. Julie finished her drink and set the tankard on the counter as softly as she could, hoping she wouldn't upset him too much.

"Do you have a room free that I could get for the evening?" she asked, holding her breath, afraid he might explode on her.

"I got a room, ya, but it ain't free. Ya gotta pay. Four bits and ya can have it. And no, ya can't barter me down."

He pointed behind her to the entrance which she came through.

"Four bits! That's twice as much as Ralloc!"

She knew this from the Essence Transference Judas performed on her. One of the books covered the economics of Ralloc, printed in the last year.

"Yeah? Well, this isn't Ralloc. There are dozens of inns within spitting distance in Ralloc; there's only one here. Mine. I'll throw in a dinner and breakfast if it makes you feel better. Take it or do without."

"I'll take it."

She pulled a silver from her pouch and exchanged the chip for a key and twenty-six bits. He gave her directions to the room.

With the common room behind her, she headed upstairs, the last door on the left on the second floor. The tub full of water lured her eye first. Giddy, she bolted the door and tossed her pack on the floor by her bed. Without preamble, she stripped and stepped into the clear, steaming water. Heat suffused her body. The room only came with a lump of soap carrying the vague scent of rose petals, a definite step up from bathing in the creek with silt.

She scrubbed her body until pink and washed her hair twice. Upon exiting, she dressed in a clean set of robes. It felt divine against her skin. Back in the common room, she arranged laundering for her clothes on the following day. Since this was the first time on her own, the excitement of something new slithered through her, and she wanted to explore the town before it got too late.

She left through the front doors and walked down the road under a twilight sky. As she ambled past rows of buildings and small homes, she noted some were one story and others two, rarely did she see a three-story building. Most one-story buildings housed two businesses, which seemed to split the renting and the right to own the place.

As her watchful eye drifted from one building to the other, she observed the names on the signs. Every once in a while, she'd see a general goods store, a bookshop, blacksmith, barber, or a clothing store, but the predominant focus of this town was the magic shops. She saw sign after sign advertising more and more of the same, though they looked more like joke shops, full of tricks and mirrors and smoke rather than the genuine article.

By the time the sun went down and the lamps were lit by the sentries, she'd toured the whole village and chosen three stores she'd return to: the Sleight of Hand Society, the Conjurer's Accord, and the Enchanted Allure Guild. Each caught her eye for various reasons.

By looks, the Sleight of Hand Society seemed more than just magic. The windows had heavy curtains and appeared permanently drawn, as if they didn't want the outside world to know what they taught their students. She had the impression it was more tricks than actual art, but it couldn't hurt to learn a few; she might need them to stay alive.

The Conjurer's Accord was a well-placed establishment near the center of town, and it maintained a prestigious look with clean stone and a pristine sidewalk. Whoever owned the place invested a lot of money into the building.

The doors were high and thick, crafted from the darkest brown wood she'd seen. Curtains tied open with gold lace graced the windows, which were tall and wide, forming an arch at the top. The interior burned brightly from the candles in the gold chandeliers.

From the road, Julie could see winding staircases on either side of the greeting room.

The Enchanted Allure Guild also enticed her eye, but for different reasons. This building was worn and run-down but not dilapidated. This establishment boasted three stories. Perhaps in the past it rivaled all others as the most beautiful building, but not anymore. In the short time Julie watched the building, she noted that the people moved in their nightly routines and skirted the building by a wide margin.

They blatantly avoided it, but the why intrigued her most.

Something must've happened here for all the people to avoid it so much. Something in the building, or to the person who owns it.

Whatever paint graced the building faded away years prior; now, it was gray and splintered from age.

Her mind made up, she advanced to the building and went up its small flight of stairs to the porch. She placed her hand on the doorknob.

From the glass in the door, she could see the interior faintly lit by a few glowing candles. A deep breath steadied her nerves, giving herself a pause, an opportunity to back down and leave.

Something malevolent brushed the back of her mind. It was directed at her. Her head swiveled around, scrutinizing the buildings around her, the guards and people bustling about, all completely oblivious to her or the building.

Nothing out of the ordinary snared her attention.

She narrowed her eyes, turned back to the door, and twisted the knob.

Chapter 45: Harold The Hermit

Julie entered the dim greeting room. The wood creaked underfoot. The air was thick and warm, and a faint scent of vanilla tobacco curled through the air. A red and gold rug covered the center, muffling her footfalls and obscuring the half-rotted wood.

Padding deeper into the building, she worked around the corner to the left and spotted a blazing fireplace. Old furniture graced the sitting room, worn by time and use: a long chair of forest green, and two high-back chairs sheathed in brown and tan. The latter had high backs facing her, and the fabric was ripped and torn.

The room appeared void of occupants. She moved forward and knelt by the fire, warming her hands against the dancing flames.

The sound of a book closing behind her made her jump, her hands struggling into the folds of her robes to grasp her wand. She drew it in haste and almost lost her grip.

An elderly man sat in one of the chairs. Although he sat, Julie surmised his towering height. His head, bald on top, was ringed with shaggy hair that reached his shoulders. The white hair held streaks of its original black and brown shot through it. A potbelly bulged beneath his robes, showing he had weight to him.

His relaxed composure with his wide chin and broad nose gave kindness to his face. Warm, deep-set eyes were inviting, despite their chilly, pale blue-gray. With legs crossed, right heel to left knee, he propped a huge book in the crook as an impromptu desk. His left hand rested on the book's thick, worn cover; in his right, he held the pipe she detected earlier.

A faint, expectant expression graced his face, not quite a smile, and he waited for her to break the silence.

"Sorry," she stammered. "I saw the place outside and the sign, The Enchanted Allure Guild. I was hoping you had something to teach me."

And now that she thought about it, she felt foolish for holding him at wand-point. She lowered it before tucking it away.

He's about Judas's age, perhaps a little older. Maybe six ages?

The man stirred but remained silent.

She swallowed, wondering why he wasn't speaking. Had she offended him? Was he in shock?

Maybe he's mute!

"I'm interested in learning about magic. I have a condition, and I forgot everything … well, everything before I woke up. I only remember my name, and the past few days or weeks. It's kind of a blur, to be honest. There are other things I can remember, but not much."

The old man rose slowly and walked away with a hobble, favoring his left leg.

Perplexed, she followed as he worked his way behind the counter in the main foyer. On the back wall, he opened a door into a huge room with hundreds of books lining the towering shelves. Not an inch was wasted. In fact, she'd be surprised if he could put the book back into the stack.

From the doorway, she watched him gingerly climb a ladder, and it swayed with each movement. She worried it'd topple over.

Quite the fall for an older gentleman.

From the eighth shelf, he tugged on a massive book. Tome in hand, he climbed down the ladder and returned to the dusty counter. Julie retreated to the other side. It was rude to be in his space.

He was probably as strong as a bull in his youth.

His height and broad shoulders lent credence to her suspicions.

The book clattered on the countertop with a loud thud; the weighty tome sat between them. Julie considered the dust-ridden volume with a frayed cover, then looked up to the silent man.

"What's this?"

She fingered the book's binding. It seemed in worse shape than the building, ready to fall apart if the breeze blew too hard.

"I'm not sure I can read it. My condition—"

"You don't have a condition," the man said with a soft, deep voice. "It's normal that you can't remember how to read this language. One of the side effects."

Surprised he finally spoke, yet perplexed at his declaration, Julie took a moment to collect herself.

"What are you talking about?"

"Harold," he said.

"I beg your pardon?"

"Harold," he repeated, extending his large, meaty hand.

Julie blushed, then reached out to grasp his hand.

"Hello, Harold, I'm Julie."

"How is it, Julie, that you remember a greeting, but you can't remember anything else?"

"I don't know. Do you?"

"No. A curious thought, though, isn't it? You say you don't remember anything, yet something as simple as a greeting you remember."

He smiled more to himself than to her.

"This is what you want."

He pointed to the book.

"What is it?"

"Everything you'd want to know about the realm, and probably many things you don't. To be fair, this only covers from Ralloc to the Melodic Mountains, the upper part of the continent Ernrul. But the southern continent, or the three across the Golden Sea aren't within."

"What's over there?"

"The Kran Empire and the Ebbins."

He waved them away.

"You can read up on that stuff at your leisure. This—" he tapped the book for emphasis, "—is for what's right outside the door."

She nodded and thumbed through the book for a few moments before closing it again.

"Wouldn't it be quicker if I just asked you what I want to learn?"

"Now, that's more like it! You aren't lazy, just efficient. Efficiency is severely underrated in my opinion."

He smiled, waved his arm, and limped back to his chair in the sitting room. Julie followed on his heels and seated herself in the chair beside him, with the table holding his pipe and book between them. Snatching up the former, he stuffed tobacco in the bowl, and pulling his wand from the tabletop. A small flame flared, and a curl of smoke rose into the air.

"You can do spells without words, too?" she asked.

"Is that one of your questions about the realm you intended to ask?"

She shook her head.

"No, not really, I was told once by my … this man, that most people can't do spells without the use of words or incantations."

Harold took a long draw from the pipe and exhaled the smoke. It smelled wonderful.

"A valid assessment that's not completely accurate. Some people can do small and simple spells which require no special incantations, but … for the majority of the time, I can't. So, yes, he was right and wrong."

With a nod, she filed that information away for later.

"Who are you?"

"I already told you."

"No, you told me your name, Harold, but not who you are."

"One begets another."

He grinned as if his cheeky answer revealed everything, then grew somber.

"I'm a shut-in, recluse, antisocial, whatever you wish to call me. I've lived here for the four ages. You're the first person I've talked to in three. Quite a long time, eh?"

"Yes."

Thinking about what it'd be like to not talk to someone in such a long time hurt a part of her soul. Then again, having a conversation didn't necessarily mean something productive came from it. Perhaps, in certain circumstances, not seeing people could be a good thing.

"How did you see it?" Harold inquired, his brow arched in interest.

She glanced up at him, blinking, trying to figure out what he meant.

"See what?"

"The building, of course. Did you ever consider why the people skirt past? There's an illusion of a graveyard, but a normal one would bring the curious to investigate. Not mine. This cemetery is for the cursed and the damned. No one dares set foot here, which is how I've lived for several ages."

"Don't you ever go out to the town?"

"Yes, once a month during the full moon."

"You mean the day of the full moon, right?"

"No."

He puffed the tobacco embers back to life.

"At night."

"Why?"

"Let's call it part of the bargain for being here. Now then, I believe you said you wanted to learn something about magic. Anything in particular, or is it the realm you wish to explore?"

Julie was silent for a while, contemplating his cryptic mystery, and to her, they were meant to be solved, and quickly. She gazed at him for a long moment, and he exuded a calm, warm aura. Judas, by contrast, especially in retrospect, always leaned to the colder side, closed off or bound tight. Harold, by contrast, seemed more like the books that surrounded him.

Putting it aside for now, she switched directions.

"Do you know anything about a man named Fife Doole?"

It was a safe question; one that could be passed off from a book, and it wouldn't lead to where she'd been or who sent her.

"Fife Doole, yes, I recognize the name. But he's no man."

"What do you mean?"

"He's dead for starters. Surely you read a history book where you got his name from. He died three ages and an era ago. You just missed him, huh?"

He chuckled, finding humor in it. Julie, at best guess, was about two ages old, missing Fife by an age and a half.

Stumped on the answer, she posed another question.

"What do you know about Xilor?"

Harold stopped in mid-puff, and his voice grew low.

"I don't talk about that monster, not here, not anywhere. He's an abomination and shouldn't exist!"

"Okay, then what can you tell me about the Sleight of Hand Society and the Conjurer's Accord?"

"Both are nonsense."

He waved his right hand, the pipe still cradled in his fingers.

"Sleight of Hand is a Thieves Guild that uses magic to amplify their skills. The Conjurer's Accord is a band of scholarly minds, the childhood weirdos you would've grown up with at school. They think up new illusions, summon elementals, or summon souls to torment. What a waste of their gifts."

Julie leaned forward, pondering Harold's words on Fife, and it hit her.

"You said Fife Doole was no man, which implies that he was something else, regardless if he's dead. Can you elaborate?"

Harold eyed her over his pipe.

"You're a bright one, more than I gave you credit for. You're right; Fife was not a man. Man implies wizardkind when, in fact, he wasn't. He was the son of a halfling, and his mother was a gnome. What would you call that? A half-gnome? Maybe a gnomling?"

He chuckled. His gray-blue eyes flitted back to Julie and saw the joke was lost on her.

She contemplated her next question, one that would elicit a knowledgeable answer, but in many ways, he reminded her of Judas. She wished, more than anything, to have her memories returned, or a more discomforting notion of why she felt a connection to Xilor while Mr. Pleasure tortured her.

And now that she thought it, she didn't want any semblance of a connection between them.

The shocking thought unsettled her. She understood him, and his desire for power. He craved it, just as she did, at least, from what she felt in that dungeon room. Even now, with the block gone ...

She mentally shook her head, chasing the thoughts away.

The most distressing aspect was that she accepted that part of him, even if she detested the rest of him. To accept herself, she had to. She compared their likeness and found what she searched for: a way they were starkly different. Xilor forged his destiny by the blood of others. What was hers?

"What's my destiny?" she blurted.

Harold made an appreciative sound in the back of his throat.

"Mmm. Now, that's a great question. What do you think the meaning is?"

She shrugged.

"Something you were born for."

"No, child, that's fate. Fate is predetermined. Destiny is something you must choose, what you decide. So, what are you going to do?"

Harold reclined in his chair, letting the question hang between them.

It's a damn good question.

She knew the answer almost immediately: Xilor.

To fulfill a prophecy, she must destroy him. She remembered Judas's words as they echoed in her head, 'A powerful mage coming from beyond the realm of magic ... a perfect balance of light and dark.'

Their stillness was only punctured when Harold puffed on his pipe every few seconds. She dwelt on the path before her, but she didn't yearn for it. Besides, who was she? A nobody. She couldn't even perform simple magics in the Corridor. How could she take on the one person that Judas couldn't defeat? At least, not in totality.

If she faced him, she'd die. There was no way around that reality.

"There's something I wish to teach you," Harold said, interrupting Julie's thoughts. "It might serve you well."

"What's that?"

"The ability to perceive events that have either already happened, may happen, would've happened, or are happening."

What kind of nonsense is this?

"To be fair," he continued, "anything you glimpse may not come to pass. The possibility of what you see may change the outcome. One event begets another, and will always, unless affected by an outside source. You must be a shadow when foreseeing these events, present, yet not part of the world which you see."

"That … doesn't make any sense. One event begets another?"

Julie's brow furrowed.

"In other words, what's meant to happen will happen unless you change the outcome by interfering."

"Oh, I get that. Why didn't you just say that?"

He paused, staring at her.

"I did."

"What's it called?"

"Shadowcasting."

"Never heard of it."

He grinned.

"That doesn't surprise me."

Harold lurched from his chair to the floor and crossed his legs with some difficulty. She mirrored him, and when he reached for her hands, she placed them in his. His hands were massive, calloused and warm. She looked into his face, but his eyes were closed, so she followed suit.

"This will require concentration and discipline," Harold said. "When you first begin, your lack of control will only allow you to observe what it wishes. The Shadowcast is the coach driver while you are the passenger. Later, with practice, you'll be able to determine the when, where, and what, at your inclination."

A question formed on her lips, wondering what *it* was, but he continued on.

"It's best to visualize time as a breeze. The present ebbs and flows: a faintest of whispers of the wind, almost unmoving. The future: a gust rushing toward you, the past: the wind moving steadily away. The flow and ebb of time change constantly—though not perceived by the inhabitants of the present. Let your mind empty of thought and stretch out, touch the flow of time."

Julie did as instructed, thinking of the invisible gust, but nothing changed. Their breathing filled her ears. At first, she thought she heard it, but the longer it dwelled, she realized she perceived it instead.

"Further," he whispered.

She stretched her essence beyond them, filling the room and seeping beyond. She detected small life forms, insects hidden in dark recesses of the house as they skittered silently between the walls and under the floor.

"Further."

Pushing beyond, she felt other small life forms, mice and other insects outside the house.

A bead of sweat formed on her forehead from exertion.

Trees brushed the edge of her concentration, the dirt surrounding them, bedding the roots. Water flowed through the expanse of veins, nurturing the large oak. The wind tickled the leaves, slithered through the breaks in the bark.

"Good."

Harold's voice was warm with approval.

"The tree. Notice how it's different from the crickets and termites, the

279

mice and lizards. Can you sense the difference?"

"Yes."

She visualized it in her mind's eye.

"Now … feel how they are the same."

The last statement nearly broke her concentration. She never thought of trees, crickets, and mice having anything in common. Julie searched again for the insects until she found them, then the mice, and lastly the tree.

In her mind, she moved the small lights representing the different life forms. She manipulated them, moving them one over the other, turning and twisting them until she found the faintest trace of resemblance.

"There it is."

She wasn't sure if Harold had said anything, or if she imagined it. When she found the traces of likeness, she followed them. And then, before she could pull away, she was gone in a sudden surge, lost in the tides of Shadowcasting.

Mud clung to the bottom of Judas's boots, and the tenseness between his shoulders wouldn't let up.

Up on the hill, he could see the trolls getting into position. A lone figure at the front waved his arm, and the trolls came, rushing down the hill like a flood waiting to devour an unsuspecting village.

Wizard's Pass didn't stand a chance. It didn't have any walls like Dlad City, or even Ralloc. It was open to the elements, safe only due to its obscurity.

The trolls moved far quieter than Judas would've expected, not while toting clubs, claymores, spears, and knives. As they neared the sleeping town, wizardkind emerged from all over: behind houses, stables, wagons, and old rum barrels. A light show lit up the night as a plethora of spells rent the darkness, splashing indiscriminately against the invaders.

The trolls roared their challenge. It didn't matter now; they'd been seen.

Silhouettes perched on the roofs rained arrows, riddling the monsters as they closed in. They screamed in fury, in pain; if they weren't caught with arrows, they burned, collapsed, or fell to the sword. Once the chaos started, it didn't take long for some trolls to tear into each other.

Judas shook his head as the line rushed into the village. He'd hoped they'd flee, seeing them as not an easy target.

The mass overran the initial line of small resistance. Clubs and dirks caught combatants in the heads or neck, driving them into the ground.

The troll on the hill let out a bellow, and it was like a war horn, guiding his troops, bolstering their morale.

"We can't wait much lon'er, Judas, or th' figh' will be over," T'son said from his position a few bodies down. He and a bunch of others were crouched behind the rise that led to the swamp.

He was right, of course, but if they moved too soon…

The first house caught on fire, causing those hiding within to flee outside. They were butchered in moments. Seeing their success, the trolls set fire to other huts.

"Judas!" T'son prompted.

Judas knew it wasn't easy for T'son to sit here at the swamp, watching the destruction of the hamlet, but patience determined if a flanking maneuver would work or not.

He eyed the men around him, seeing them huddled against the slope, using rock outcroppings, or hiding behind trees to shield their position.

All these years of rebuilding from the Wizard's War. What a waste.

Judas glanced down at his friend, and he could see the disgust on his face. T'son caught Judas looking at him, and the face he made told a story of contempt.

Judas held up a hand.

"Wait. Once the children start running for the river, they'll draw the infantry away, and we can take the commander with ease."

They'd gone over this before, but T'son didn't like that part of the plan. Quite frankly, neither did Judas, but it wasn't his idea. He let the people of the village decide.

Houses burned, screams curled through the night, and the trolls rushed forward like a pestilence. And then they heard it: the first scream of a child.

They've found them.

"Ta th' abyss with this. I'm attackin' now," T'son declared.

Judas's head snapped in his direction.

"Not yet."

T'son stood and yelled, "Charge!"

The men rose up with a shout, rushing from their concealment. Judas followed, knowing more would die if he didn't.

By the time he made it over the embankment, the lead troll had turned to the noise, pointed his sword, and grunted. The remaining trolls rushed to meet them, and monster and man clashed in a chaotic frenzy. Spells flew as clubs and swords rang out, blood weeping on the ground.

Judas ducked underneath an incoming sword and—while crouching—sent a bolt of fire piercing through three charging trolls, melting them from head to foot.

He stood, blasting the nearest troll off its feet, the force of impact shattered its spine.

In silence, he cut a swath through the invaders. Severed arms, missing legs, headless adversaries. He called fire and lightning, churned the earth to devour those above. All the while, he chased after T'son who hurried to the top of the hill.

Another wave of trolls turned in his direction, charging his position. He unleashed a wave of invisible energy, trampling the inbound, mowing them down.

Slowly, the tide of battle turned.

Out-of-body, she soared above a battle, pulled to the ground by an invisible force.

She touched down in their midst; animalistic beings fought wizards and common folk with swords and axes. The battle moved faster than physically possible, the events flashing through her mind.

In horror, she watched bodies fall, littering the ground within blinks of the eye. Children ran screaming, slaughtered by the animals that hunted them. Men were cleaved and flung to the ground.

The screams curled her blood.

Some beasts burned, or were crushed by an unseen force. And still, they moved too fast to be real. It was almost dreamlike as they moved at twice the speed, no three times the speed of a normal person.

And then, when she thought it couldn't get any more chaotic, it slowed, and that's when she saw him.

Within the swell of carnage, the bodies lying on the ground, she saw Judas standing alone.

A man lay at his feet. Her former master wept openly, unashamed tears streaked his face. Seeing him like this shook her to the core, having never seen this range of emotion from him.

She stepped closer, coming to a stop just behind him and to his right.

"He fought courageously. I saw. It was amazing … his strength to carry on," Julie murmured.

It was the truth; she did witness his last courageous act, a spectator to everything that had happened or would happen. And, she'd seen a lot of stuff she wished she hadn't.

Judas sniffed and cleared his throat.

"A magnificent display …" Judas agreed.

He probably can't speak anymore without breaking down again.

She glanced down at the corpse. It was the first time she'd seen a dead person, and it unnerved her. True, with Mr. Pleasure, those people had been monstrous, but they appeared alive. There was something strange about seeing an unmoving man.

And more than that, Judas's emotional state—ruined and weeping over him. Then, she understood. This wasn't some villager or a stranger, they'd been acquaintances at the least, and friends at the best.

"How many years have you known each other?"

"Since before the Wizard's War. Where did all the time go?"

Judas dried his face with the sleeve of his robe.

"I reached him just before he died. He said, 'I see my first mate, my love. I've sailed to you.'"

Silence followed as Judas wept, grieving. Julie remained quiet as he did, and she glanced around at all the bodies. Blood coated the earth like standing water, and dismembered limbs lay like broken logs from a burst dam.

"So much death and violence," she said with a slow shake of her head. "I don't think I can stomach a war!"

"You better get used to seeing it, Julie!"

Judas gasped, spun around, shock on his face. But the moment shifted, dissolving, carrying her away like a current, but not before she heard him speak one last time, more to himself.

"A ghost."

He reached for where she'd been standing, but she was long gone.

Both Harold and Julie exhaled together, and their eyes opened.

The fire had dwindled down to red embers, and cold claimed sovereignty in the sitting room.

Harold stirred, his back, knees, and hips popped audibly as he rose from the floor to his chair. He reached for his pipe and relit the tobacco, drawing quick, deep puffs.

Julie shifted, a slight spasm rolled from the base of her spine to her neck. The pain raced through her, and she, too, moved to a chair, rubbing the stiffness away.

Her voice sounded hoarse when she spoke.

"That was intense."

Harold gave a slow nod as he exhaled a puff of smoke.

"Yes, as it is each time you Shadowcast."

He withdrew the pipe, using the end to point at her.

"But the events you saw will change now."

"What do you mean?"

"You interfered. If the event still happens, an altered outcome will manifest."

"What will change? Will Judas die?"

"Possibly, but for events to change so drastically?"

His head moved to the side and back.

"Usually, it's small things. Small events, words, items. To inflict death, you'd have to interfere a great deal more, or so experience has told me."

"I'll keep that in mind."

"Also, this ability is quite advanced. Not many people are able to do it besides us. To be fair, I'm not acquainted with many people."

He smiled.

"But those who have the talent, as we just proved you do, you'll find the talent runs deep … deeper than you imagine."

She frowned.

"You mean in me?"

He smiled into a puff of smoke.

"In your blood."

She puzzled over this, and before she could absorb it and ask questions, he continued on.

"There are others who can do variations, but to actually Shadowcast—"

"—What variations?"

He was quiet for a moment, and his eyes studied her.

"Warlock Lakayre, your former master, can do something similar."

Alarm spread through her mind, and she tried to connect anything that might've given it away.

"How did you guess he was my master? I never told you."

His smile spread, and his teeth clattered against the end of the pipe before he took another pull. He spoke after the smoke cleared.

"I'm knowledgeable of many things, child, so here's a warning. What we just did is something that archangels do. They live like this, in a perpetual state of casting."

Her eyes narrowed as she digested his words.

"Are you well-versed with archangels?"

He paused, and this time it was quite deliberate.

"I'm knowledgeable of many things, child."

He sighed and stirred in his chair, setting his pipe to the side.

"It's getting late, and a long journey awaits you. Get your rest. You'll find what you're looking for, even if it doesn't manifest in the way you wish."

The grin on his lips sent a shiver down her spine, but not the bad kind. She had the distinct feeling that he knew far more than he let on. Could he see her future's entirety? Did he know what happened to her, what she thought now?

He stood, his back still stiff from earlier. She rose, too.

"Heed my words: you may not like what you find, or you may like it too much. Or you may find that you already found what you sought."

He didn't shake her hand or try to embrace her. Instead, he gestured to the front door with his hand.

She gave a single nod, turning slowly, and leaving the room. As she neared the room's divide that separated it from the foyer, he called to her.

"Don't bother to say goodbye; you'll be back."

She gave him one last look as he returned to his chair, snatching up his book and pipe.

With a slow shake of her head, she silently exited his home.

Chapter 46: Wizard's Pass

Judas waded through the bodies, checking for wounded and lending his meager healing skills.

The citizens of Wizard's Pass fought with a purpose he hadn't seen since the last war, and they'd done so against an overwhelming legion. In the end, they drove off the last remains, the battle turning with the loss of their commander, and it wasn't without a cost.

Nothing ever is.

The citizens took heavy losses, both in casualties and the village itself. Most of it burned to the ground, hardening the resolve of the survivors. And some of the children were trampled underfoot.

Blood soaked the ground and pooled in other places. Bodies and limbs lay strewn; Judas hoped for more survivors after each body he passed.

His friend, T'son, was among them. He had rendered the decisive blow against the troll commander but was decapitated for his efforts.

Judas shook his head.

There was so much he wanted to say to T'son, stories to tell, lives to catch up on, and now, he'd never get the chance. Judas wasn't even with him when he fell, seeing the killing blow from a distance.

All this loss of life for the fall of an out-of-the-way village.

Judas couldn't help but feel somewhat responsible.

Did Xilor track me here?

It was the only explanation that made sense. Wizard's Pass offered no strategic value; the only other alternative intent was to break morale. The mind game had started, with Xilor as the puppet master. By the time he trampled his way over a sea of bodies and reached Ralloc, Judas envisioned them laying down their arms willingly. The defeat here molded a detrimental future.

But he made the same mistake as last time. He couldn't help himself but gloat that he'd returned.

A child started crying, drawing Judas's eyes. It was a young girl being attended to, her arm in a sling made out of sackcloth.

The children had returned from the river as the remaining trolls retreated, and the invaders only left their dead and destruction in their wake.

Anger burned within Judas. All this death, on both sides, sanctioned by a master they'd never see.

Pawns and tyrants, and Xilor's the biggest of them.

Judas stopped suddenly, returning to the corpse of T'son. He hadn't realized he'd come full circle. T'son fought and gave his life for these people. More to the point, he was a foreigner among them, yet their governor.

Judas sensed someone behind him.

"Did he fight courageously?" she asked.

"Yes, he did."

Judas felt the sting of tears threatening to overcome him again.

"Did you know each other long?"

Judas nodded.

"From the Wizard's War. Gods, we got old fast. Where did all the time go?"

Judas realized he was speaking more to himself than the woman. It helped keep him from breaking, but the sorrow trembled within him. Shades, he was close to breaking. He had to say something or do something before it overcame him.

"He didn't get any last words. Most don't. But I've heard my share throughout my life. The places our minds take us when people approach death's door."

He glanced away from his beheaded friend. He couldn't stand to gaze upon him anymore, but everywhere else he looked, more bodies, more limbs, more death.

"It'll only get worse," he said.

"There were so many deaths—and the violence?—how can anyone choose to go to war?"

The words angered him. How could this woman not want to go to war after what happened to her village? There were things worth fighting for, like the right to live, how could she not see it?

"You better get used to it. More's coming—and soon."

He swallowed and knelt beside T'son, closing his eyes. The head moved when he did, another reminder of his brutal end.

"I'm sorry, Judas," she said.

The warlock whirled, glimpsing the fading image of his lost apprentice, and in its place, a woman he knew well appeared.

Meristal rushed forward, wrapping her arms around him.

"I came as quickly as I could, Judas."

Her orange hair tickled his nose, and she smelled of sweet vanilla and flowers. She pulled away, but held onto his arms.

"What happened here?"

"Trolls. The few people you see are the survivors."

She glanced down at his feet.

"By the gods, is that T'son?"

Judas could only bring himself to nod.

"And your apprentice, what of her?"

This, as painful as it was, was something he could talk about.

"She's gone."

Meristal gasped.

"She perished?"

Her hand came to her mouth.

Judas shook his head.

"No, no. During the night, while we were in the swamplands, she took off. She's with the fairies now, or they're with her."

"What can they possibly teach her? They don't have the level of magic that she does. Why didn't you go after her?"

"They're not teaching her magic, at least, that's what I gathered when one visited me. I didn't ask for their planned academics. The fairy warned me that they'd hide her from me if I pursued, so I didn't."

"Why would they waste their time with those trivialities?"

Judas didn't respond. His eyes swept over the carnage. They could remove the bodies, but blood would stain the earth for a time.

"Why?" Meristal pressed.

"Because they believe in their prophecy, and they may be right."

She snorted.

"Since when do you believe in prophecies, fates, and destinies, Judas?"

"The moment I reached out to find her. She's too far away for you to do the same, but what I felt was incredible."

Meristal, thankfully, didn't try to argue with him.

"What about the trolls who attacked? Where did they go?"

"The ones that are left? Retreated. But I fear that another attack is coming soon."

"Here?"

He shook his head in response.

"Then, where?"

"The only probable place, Meristal: Far Point."

"Well, we have to warn them. I can teleport there and—"

"No need, I already tried. A powerful spell's blocking me, and I can't get within two days' walk of the city."

"Well, we could Psimond them, send some kind of warning!"

"I tried that as well. Only Xilor is powerful enough to block me."

She grew silent for a moment, her amethyst eyes squinting.

"But why Far Point? There's nothing of strategic value. It makes no sense."

"Agreed, but it's the largest settlement in the vicinity of the Corridor. As to why, I'm at a loss."

"Sounds like a diversion to get us worked up over nothing. How'd he escape?"

Judas felt his mouth tighten into a line. This was a subject he didn't want to discuss, another reminder of his failures.

"It'd always be a matter of time. Nothing is truly escape-proof. What about you? Who're you delivering the news to?"

"I'm off to meet with the elyves, see if we can get them to join the effort."

"Good luck with that."

She gave a single nod.

"Once I'm finished, I'll go to Ralloc, let them know, but I'd rather be here with you."

He nodded, and though it hurt him to say, he said it anyway.

"Best that you don't stay, at least not at the moment. You have more pressing matters. We're going to need the elyves to join us, but I fear it's going to be a lost cause. Tell the council that the war has started. I'll get refugees moving that way. Better that they have some warning and prepare to receive them."

"If Ralloc even cares."

A grim frown touched his lips. She had a point.

"Okay, Judas, I'll do as you ask, but you know as well as I that they won't listen."

"Make them listen."

She reached out and took his hand.

"Be careful, Judas. Try to stay in one piece for me."

"And you, my dear, *fly* like the wind."

Meristal gave him a quizzical look but held back whatever she thought. The two locked gazes for a moment, speaking with their eyes what their mouths wouldn't, and then Meristal flickered as she teleported away, leaving Judas with his grief and the duty of organizing a mass evacuation.

Chapter 47: Kam And Lily

Upon shutting the door, Julie turned and faced the street, pausing long enough to look for pedestrians at this time of night. It wouldn't do to have her appear out of the illusion around the house.

She didn't see any.

Tugging her clean but tattered robes tighter, she slipped out of the projected enchantment and trudged down the road toward the Traveler's Haven. The same overpowering sense from before smothered her, the malevolent gaze hounding her gait.

With her head moving, she turned, hands reaching for her wand. Her eyes darted through the darkness, but nothing stirred. The still shadows taunted her. Shaking off the dread, she continued, but she clutched her wand in her hand.

A few minutes later, she reached the safety of the inn, and the awareness never relented. If anything, it seemed closer, a stray breath on the nape of her neck. It set her on edge, but there was nothing to lash out against.

The merriment inside the inn broke through her angst and dark thoughts as she opened the front door. The half-filled common room greeted her. A new bartender stood behind the counter, and a couple of girls lilted between tables. Julie couldn't tell if they were servers or whores.

Perhaps both.

After taking a seat at the bar, she ordered her complimentary meal. After a few moments, the bartender dropped a plate of meat and vegetable stew over rice and a slice of wheat bread. Against her better judgment, she ordered another two Vampire Dusts and flicked a copper bit to him.

She took her time eating, recalling the vivid carnage of the battle, but she drank fast.

Gods, it seemed so real. Will it unfold that way?

Before she had finished half her meal, the two drinks were gone. She thought about ordering a third, but decided against it. She only had finite resources.

With a swivel, she faced the room and took in the night crowd. Old, weathered men sat playing games with either cards or pieces of chiseled wood or stone and money. Every once in a while, something elicited a whoop or a cry of dismay from them. Though having never played the game and unable to follow, she reveled in the spectacle.

Others took seats around the room and ate and drank together, talking in low voices while others adored the traveling player bound for greatness in Ralloc. Her gaze swept across the room as she drank, the Vampire Dust making her sluggish, but she savored the experience.

Judas would never let me drink with him.

Her eyes came to rest on a couple sitting alone in a booth in the far corner to her left. The woman straddled the man, and she could almost make herself believe they were just talking, but his hands gripping her ass told the story of a passionate embrace.

Something within Julie tickled. Heat came to her cheeks. Her chest warmed. The familiar tinge of magelust flickered within her as her breath quickened.

The woman, a blonde, turned her head to the side as his lips brushed against her neck, and he gazed across the room at her, making eye contact.

The magelust flared hot and bright, pooling in her core, sending fiery pins across her skin. The alcohol swirled through her head, a tingling fog settling over her.

She'd felt the magelust twice before, once with Todd, and once with the young man at the inn in Dlad City. This was so much more potent, and she couldn't tear her eyes away from him. More to the point, he was watching her, too.

Does it affect him, too?

Compared to her first two experiences, those were mild annoyances to this. Now, she was completely enraptured, her body on fire as she hadn't acted on the impulse gripping her now.

What the hell is wrong with me?

The longer she gazed, the more excited she became.

What am I doing? I shouldn't even be watching them!

But she couldn't tear her eyes away, and neither could he. She yearned, and she could've sworn he did, too. Her gaze flitted to the woman, and Julie wanted to be her now, straddling the man's lap, his hands gliding up on her body.

She closed her eyes, shaking her head. When she opened them, he was still watching her, an unreadable expression on his face. The woman was either kissing his neck or whispering into his ear. The man's hands slid up the woman's back.

Julie could almost feel the man's hands on her; goosebumps riddled her skin, and she thrummed between her legs.

I shouldn't watch them, but I can't look away!

Her gaze returned to the man's face, and the urge almost made her climb off her barstool.

She swallowed.

The blonde woman paused, cocking her head, gazing back at Julie. Then, her eyes went to her partner. She whispered something into his ear, and he nodded.

The woman rose off him, standing, pulling him up by the hand. The man made eye contact with Julie, and she nearly fell off her barstool. That small movement, standing, narrowing the distance between them by a few feet, increased the strength.

Oh, gods.

And they'd have to pass her to get to the stairs. What would she do? Jump on the bar and rip her clothes off?

The blonde led the man by the hand, and as they neared her stool, the woman reached out with her other hand. Julie couldn't stop herself. Like a magnet, she clasped it, sliding off the barstool.

"Come on," the woman said, interlocking fingers with her.

Julie couldn't breathe, couldn't focus or think straight, and that didn't bother her in the slightest.

She didn't remember leaving the common room, nor ascending the stairs, but outside their door, they stopped. Just being in their presence was so overpowering. Her legs shook as if fatigued.

The hallway was dark, cold, and devoid of anyone else. The man fumbled for the key in his pocket. Julie watched, noting his hand placement, how close it was to other, more enticing things.

The woman's fingers brushed her chin, turning Julie's head so they could see each other.

"I'm Lily," she said. "This is my husband, Kam."

Julie swallowed as the words resonated in her head.

Lily leaned forward, her warm lips pressing against Julie's mouth. Julie sensed Kam stilling, no longer worried about trying to shove the key into the lock.

Lily pulled back and grinned.

"Which one of us do you want?"

Heat spread across Julie's lips, but like an object tethered to a string, her head turned toward Kam. As she gazed up into his face, he leaned forward, bending down to her height, and kissed her. It was something hot and fierce and the world fell away. When he pulled back, she was both aroused and mortified to find her hand between his legs.

Lily chuckled.

"Well, I think that answers that. Kam? The door."

The big man lowered his shoulder into the door, and with a quick shove it came open, the key still protruding from the tumbler, unturned. He hurried inside, and Lily pulled Julie in by the hand. Once inside, he barred the door.

Lily guided Julie to the bathtub, stripping her clothes off as she did, letting them fall to the floor. Julie's heart quickened as the woman revealed more of herself. By the time they reached the washroom, she was bare, shaped in a way Julie never would be, curvaceous and ample. She turned on the faucet.

The wife turned to Julie, kissing her again.

"Want to bathe with me?" she said, breathing into her mouth.

Julie felt herself nodding as Lily slipped her hands inside her robes, undressing her, opening her robes and letting them pool to the floor. Her soft fingers peeled down her undergarments, and Lily kissed her hip bone as her hands tickled the back of Julie's thighs.

She hadn't even registered what was happening, but Julie found herself naked, holding hands with Lily, stepping into the tepid water. Lily lathered a rag with something scented like lavender and tea, or maybe it was flowers, and she was touching Julie in places that only fed her hunger.

As Lily knelt in the tub, delicately sponging her, Julie turned, catching Kam watching from the doorway. Julie's breath caught in her throat, and she couldn't breathe. She didn't think he was either. Julie barely noticed the woman washing the soap away with water. Unbidden, she stepped out of the tub, crossing the room. He met her in the middle, the embrace long and hard.

She only stopped when something wrapped around her shoulders. Breaking apart, she saw a towel wrapped around her, with Lily standing behind, smiling.

"Someone's anxious, but he needs to clean up first."

Kam hurried past them, abandoning his clothes in haste, jumping into the tub, splashing water and quickly scrubbing before stumbling out. Lily had barely dried her by the time he was done.

Lily's hand slipped in hers, and she pulled her from the washroom and into their chamber. Like everything that drew her, Julie felt Kam walking behind them, and she glanced back at him as they drew nearer to the bed. Her pulse throbbed in her head, and the world washed in colors she'd never seen before. No, it was so much more. It was like everything vibrated like a taut string, making everything turn unfocused.

Everything but him.

Lily stopped, and Julie faced the front, standing at their bed, every wild, vivid thought coursing through her. And then, someone was kissing her, she didn't know, didn't care. Her eyes closed as something detonated in her head, in her body, and like the rest of the vibrating world, her body thrummed with need and desire.

Something soft touched her back. At some point, her feet had left the floor, and was lying on the bed. Scents filled her nose, cloying and floral, sweet and masculine, sandalwood and leather.

Rough warm lips pressed into her, and she opened her mouth, hungry, searching, devouring. Hands touched her legs, pressing them apart. A tongue laved her soon after, teased her, then consumed her in warmth and pressure, licking and tickling, helping her chase a release she hadn't known to search for.

The room was filled with hot breath and soft pants and the sound of exploring mouths. And she didn't want it to end. The tease between her legs grew in strength and her breath quickened. Julie's lips parted as she panted.

Opening her eyes, she glanced down her body; Lily stared back up at her. The bed shifted, a slight creak as the slat strained under Kam's added weight. He was so close, so very close to her face, and his hard flesh swayed in front of her eyes, a mere whisper from her lips. And before she knew it, she reached out and grabbed hold of his scalding member, drawing him into her mouth as his wife continued her exploration.

Kam gasped, Lily moaned, and Julie could only shiver between them. She felt his warmth in her mouth, tasted his saltiness, and breathed in his scent. He closed his eyes, his head tilted up, his hand following the movements of her head. At some point during the veneration, Lily abandoned her teasing, joining them at the head of the bed. The wife's hand reached out, holding him, and Julie pulled away.

Lily kissed her, leaning over, inching ever closer to her husband.

"He likes it like this," she said.

And she satisfied him with Julie underneath, staring up at them.

Just watching them amplified the lust, but when Kam's hand snaked between Julie's legs while his wife worked him, it was almost too much.

An animality rose within Julie. She coveted to partake. Her eyes glassed over as the woman's head filled her vision, her hand rising and falling in cadence with her head.

Julie quivered, ached for more. A sweat stole over her body.

Kam reached out and stopped Lily, and she pulled away with an audible pop. Saliva dripped from her mouth, glistening his skin as she danced. She pulled back, kissing Julie as Kam settled between her legs.

Julie felt him shifting, but his first thrust had surprised her. All she could see was Lily and her blonde hair. Julie reached out for the nearest thing, and that just happened to be the wife. Her ample breasts pressed into her as Kam slipped deeper into her. Her arousal amplified, burned bright like a falling meteor.

Lily smiled against her lips and pulled away, removing herself from between husband and new lover. Once she vacated, Kam leaned over her, spearing her deeper and faster. He bent her legs, shortening the distance between them, and he buried himself quickly, each stroke seemingly faster than the last. And when he started to grunt, his breath turning heavy, Lily made sure he slipped free of Julie's core, resting before expending himself.

He used her in every way he wanted, and she welcomed each one, barely tracking where one act ended and the next began. But when the time came, he planted his seed deep inside her. It wasn't the last time he'd rushed past the precipice that evening.

And there wasn't a panic in the moment as Julie panted, Kam grunting, their bodies colliding in fervor. The quicker he moved, the darker, more amplified everything became.

Julie shook on all fours, her body trembling, not only from the strain, but Kam's unrelenting thrusts.

And it'd been Lily's suggestion.

"Come in her, Kam."

And that seemed to be all the permission he needed to make it happen. He did seconds later, gushing into her as his wife's lips devoured them both.

The culmination ripped through Julie, Lily on one end, her husband orgasming on the other, and she was stuck between. She responded in kind, gushing as he did, tightening around his length. Warmth spread into her, and her legs quivered.

She savored the near-tangible magic, like being drunk and remembering everything, and never sought the conclusion. The cupidity drove her into a craze, an unreachable itch beneath her skin, saturating her entire body.

The night lasted far longer than there were hours, or so it seemed. It was teeth and lips, tongues and fingers, licking and kissing, tentative touches and amorous massages. The rhythm they found flowed like a harmony in a song, and the only refrain that played its part was when Lily entered into the melody.

If his wife wasn't playing an active part, she guided as she watched, whispering advice to Julie, or words of encouragement to her betrothed. Everything passed in a frenzy: the closeness, the intimacy, fingers snaking through her honeyed tresses, Lily's massaging hands that elicited groans and shudders, or Kam's firmness that explored her body.

At one point, drenched in sweat and breathing hard, Kam and Lily partook of each other; the uniqueness of their exploring, coupled with the closeness, only made Julie ache as the lust didn't abate. As much as she watched Lily, it was always Kam that drew her eyes time and again.

It was his wife who wrangled out his last drop, as if it was a ritual just for the two of them, a way they ended each holy rite. And perhaps they did. Julie couldn't help but feel a little envious as they worked together. She wanted more, even though Kam had taken her plenty. But there was a smoothness to their movements, the way Lily shifted under Kam's control, the precipice they both seemed to race for, a race they'd run many times, always winning no matter who else might've enjoined.

Both their fevered flesh glistened with sweat as they slowed the cadence and he withdrew from her. Just watching them together, coupled with being thrown into the mix, exemplified their panoptic repertoire. They had a deep, unshakable intimacy, and she got the chance to be a part of it. As the heat of their bodies cooled, so did the magelust, slowly settling her down. And despite that, her body yearned for more.

But there were rules about being a guest, and the first was never overstaying your welcome. The candles had burned low by this point, a molten waterfall of wax with more than half of the wick gone. That meant dawn was a few hours off, and taken in that light, exhaustion tugged at Julie.

While she'd partaken, it was his eager wife who attended his eccentric appetites, and Julie was quite sure Lily never felt neglected. Lily moved from her position on all fours, slipping to the edge of the bed, offering a hand to Julie. She took it. As she did, Kam sat at the opposite end, making himself a concoction of herbs and alcohol, creating a chemical reaction that dried into a powder, which he snorted up his nose.

Julie saw something dance in his eyes, wash over his face, and she very much felt that that's how she might've looked to them, present, euphoric, and yearning. She watched his naked body as his eyes rolled up and he laid down on the pillows. She hungered to crawl back up on the bed with him.

As they made it back to the washroom, she glanced back one more time, seeing him unconscious on the bed.

Lily pulled Julie into the tub with her, assuming her earlier duties of cleanliness as she stepped into the warm water.

It should be cold!

She glanced down at the water that was clear of any murkiness. The last time, she'd been too preoccupied to notice runes etched along the edge. She could only guess at their meanings, the art lost to her, but she could intuit their function. Afterward, Julie slipped into her robes as Lily rummaged through her bag. Glass bottles clinked, her hand digging through it. Dressed, Lily came over to her and placed herbs in her hand.

"What's this?" Julie asked.

"One's moonleaf. It'll keep you from getting pregnant this month. If I recall, you and Kam rose to the occasion twice."

Julie nodded.

Lily smiled.

"Kam did a number on you, but I hoped you fancied your time with us."

Julie nodded.

Lily held up the second bottle.

"The second herb is dewgrass, to ease your soreness in the morning."

Julie's brow furrowed.

"Won't you need it more than me? You guys—"

Lily nodded.

"I have more, but it's also something we do regularly. Don't worry."

Lily reached up and kissed Julie.

With the bottles in her hands, it made her question what it truly was, or if it was as the wife had said.

When Lily pulled back, Julie asked, "What's that powder Kam took?"

She glanced in the direction of the bed, even though they were still in the washroom. The urge to mount him as he slept still enticed her.

Lily sighed, shaking her head.

"Something I wish he'd quit using. They call it Oblivion, and because of it, he'll be out until at least tomorrow afternoon. Would you join me in the morning? A late start?"

Julie nodded.

"Sure. Just come wake me up."

Lily was quiet for a moment, a question forming on her face.

"You did well tonight, considering."

"What?"

"You joined us without taking rakette."

"What's rakette?"

"An herbal concoction meant to amplify your sexual desires, lower inhibitions, and make you do things you would've never considered before. If you ever do partake, be careful. Only use it with those you truly trust. I hear it can impede your connection to magic."

Julie nodded, not sure how to answer that. She had no idea what it was before, nor where to get it now. And tonight, she didn't need any herb to strip her bare. Magelust had done that for her. Meristal had said something about regret afterwards and moving on, but Julie didn't have any.

"We'll be here for two more days," Lily said, breaking into her thoughts, "then returning to Ralloc. What about you? Do you live in Ralloc?"

The question caught Julie off guard.

"Yes, sometimes," she lied.

How could she tell her the truth, that she didn't have anywhere to call home?

"But I'm headed south. I planned to leave tomorrow..." she let the sentence trail off.

"I hope you don't. It'd be nice to ... see you again, after breakfast that is."

Lily pecked her cheek and bade her goodnight.

Julie stood outside their door for a few moments after it shut. Exhaustion coaxed her into returning to her room at the end of the hall. A smile lit her face as she tumbled the key into the lock, but the cold presence she felt upon entering quashed the giddiness.

It was still strong and very near.

In three quick strides, she crossed the room, and peered through the window. Not a light flickered in the other houses, trees swayed darkly in the distance. The ominous feeling receded, and she latched the window secure before checking her other window. The presence subsided until she couldn't detect it anymore.

What am I, a child afraid of the dark?

With a pitcher of water resting on the dresser top, she poured it into a bowl to wash her face. She toweled herself dry and poured a cup of water, taking the two herbs Lily had given her, remembering her instructions. One moonleaf, and she couldn't become pregnant for a month.

That'll come in handy with those two here.

But the burden of her task lay before her, and she weighed the pros and cons of staying or going. Julie needed to get to the Melodic Mountains, and she didn't need Kam and Lily. Perhaps her lust-filled head, or something else entirely, coerced her, but she wouldn't make a decision tonight. Besides, it wasn't like they were staying long.

Clothes discarded, the floor boards creaked as she crossed her room and snuffed out the candle on the nightstand. Under the covers of her feather bed, her body ached in forgotten comfort, and drowsiness greeted her like a paramour.

As she drifted off, she idly wondered if Kam and Lily were a figment or real. Since the Corridor, she couldn't be sure. She hoped her imagination didn't run away with her sanity.

Then, the nightmares began.

In her dream, a shadow reeking of death, one that she'd seen before, attacked her. Claws raked through her, twisted fingers lashing out, scratching her face and neck. Its long, skeletal nails dug deep into her skull and plunged horrible thoughts, feelings, and images into her mind.

She woke with a start, gasping for air with her hand around her throat. The dark of her room greeted her. Julie fumbled for the lantern on the night table. The light cast an eerie orange glow about the room.

Panic flooded through her as she noticed many things out of place.

Her clothes were strung about the room, not in the pile she had left them. The water bowl was overturned, but no water splashed the floor.

A cool breeze fell across her face.

With a jerk of her head, she glanced at the opposite side of her room. Her window was open.

Chapter 48: Xilor

Night blanketed Gryzlaud Palace in shadows. The cold lingered, seeping through the stone. Xilor sat sprawled upon his throne. In a previous life, he'd filled his waking eyes with vast amounts of precious treasure. The trappings of his old life clung to him like rotten flesh, but a new obsession curled through him: control—those he commanded, and those he wanted to.

For their own good.

Simplicity ruled his life now; only necessities remained.

Once, there'd been a time when he indulged in rich wines, fine meats, and delectable fruits. The expense cost more than the earnings of five families in a year. Now, he only ate if he needed to conserve his strength; power sustained him and warded off sleep, both a necessity for the weak. Hunger drove his anger and frustration, which fueled the hate of the simpletons who didn't understand and urged his body and potential.

It was a continuous cycle and a key component of his abilities.

The world slept while he planned; destinies were forged and abolished while his slaves slumbered. He searched for weaknesses to exploit and overcome, noting several—their defenses, their strategies—in the very magic they used. Other fragilities existed too, like the spirit, the emotional heart, and the indecisive mind.

While Ralloc deliberated, he moved with purpose, gaining ground where they could've thwarted him.

A long life surrounded by the right people had turned him into a brilliant tactician. He learned by their guidance. Studies prepared him in his youth; tutelage sharpened his skills, and apprenticeship under his former master, Hadius Lacove, turned him into a weapon.

And in the end, Xilor used his acumen to orchestrate Hadius's fall.

Though his former mentor boasted his own brilliance, he failed to use his cunning to exploit the realm. For all his guile, he never envisioned Xilor's betrayal or the possibility of foreseeing his success.

With wisdom comes the forgetfulness of character.

Though the thought troubled him, he didn't want to believe it. He always watched his back around his apprentices. One person gained his trust, Judas, and the morals that shackled him like a fool.

"Judas," Xilor sneered into the quiet cold.

Hatred boiled within him at the mere thought of the man, yet beneath the hate, a grudging respect interred. How could someone younger and less powerful defeat him?

The truth about Judas—one Xilor denied confronting—was that Judas wasn't weak. The warlock chose to hold back instead of unleashing his true potential, and to Xilor's appraisal, this made him weak. In Judas's weakness, he fostered a secret and garnered the advantage when they last met. After all those years trapped in the mirror, the sorcerer was no closer to the answer.

But he'd found others...

While he'd been imprisoned, unable to return to their world, he wasn't in isolation. That was one secret he'd hoard for himself until the time was right to reveal it. Once he did, the truth would deliver a blow to all of Ermaeyth.

Especially to Judas.

Nothing's more satisfactory than reaching into the heart and ripping it out.

The world needed cleansing and strengthening if they were to survive. He promised to raze it unless someone gave him Judas. Even if, by some lucky chance, someone turned Judas over to him, Xilor would still reforge the world. But now, his process deviated from his original intent.

Sacrifices must bow to unavoidable eventualities.

Other reasons helped forge his chosen path. He only glimpsed them around the time Judas defeated him, but in the mirror, confinement had opened his eyes to the truth, to the horror.

A familiar presence brushed his consciousness, one he'd felt many times before, one he created, and it broke through his internal musings. A sole, faithful xicx remained.

Saihk wasn't just a xicx. He was the first.

Xilor chose a mortal he favored, ripped the man's soul free, and forced it into a sheol's half-ghost shell. The fusion created something new: a spirit with mortal memory and will, imprisoned in a sheol's form.

That made Saihk the xicx lord.

Saihk could convert others, binding their spirits to the same twisted state. Those he made were tethered to him, and through him, to Xilor.

"My lord," Saihk rasped, kneeling. "I located this prodigy per your orders."

Xilor allowed himself a small moment to bathe in the glow of success.

"Excellent. And the second part of your mission?"

"With great difficulty."

This troubled him, but he waited for his minion to continue.

"She was aware of my presence while I carried out the task. However, what you asked for is done. Even in her sleep, she fought me, but I succeeded in placing the trace on her."

That was disturbing. Even if she was a prodigy, she was an amateur, so how could she detect Saihk? Moreover, how could she fight him off during her sleep? Would she be able to detect what they did to her? Only time would unfold this mystery. For now, he turned his attention to looming events, satisfied with Saihk's success.

Xilor leaned forward, peering down on his creation.

"You've done exceedingly well. You may go."

Saihk bowed and vanished.

Xilor rose.

Now that he was alone and awaited none, he set out to learn more about this prodigy. With a nudge of intent, he vanished from the throne room and reformed in a small, nearly empty room high in his palace. No one knew of this room, and if they did, he'd kill them for the knowledge.

Here, he held one of his most prized secrets.

The walls mirrored the stone as the rest of the castle; an ever-persistent chill enveloped the room.

"I've returned."

His voice rasped in the emptiness, and it belied the glee he felt budding in his chest. Already, he'd done two impossible things, return to his body and plant the tracker on the prodigy. When the time was right, he'd pull her to him.

"I knew you would," a voice responded.

"Does that frighten you?"

"Why would it?"

There was no one in the room with Xilor, nothing but his sacred cabinet in the empty chamber.

"What has changed in my absence?"

"A great many things."

"And?"

"You'll fall because of it."

Rage surged in his chest, but he restrained himself from destroying the room, destroying the voice. He was unstoppable as he'd mastered death.

Who dares to stand against me now?

"What?"

His hands trembled. He'd already lost so many years from Judas's intervention, and now, he knew truths that changed everything.

"She'll keep you from your destiny, but she may also take your place."

"She? Who is she? The prodigy?"

"A myth, a legend manifested. Where she hails from, I don't know. If you hadn't neglected your lessons of histories and races of the domain, you would understand."

Xilor frowned, caught off guard by something so trivial.

"I know enough, depending on the race."

"Depending on the race?"

Xilor heard the iciness of discontent.

"Surely, I taught you better!"

The room reverberated. Power emanated from the voice, and it rebuffed Xilor. Even now, defeated, strength radiated from him. Perhaps too strong. Doubt whispered in the back of Xilor's mind.

Was it possible for the voice to gain strength since his departure like he had? True, what Xilor had gained was knowledge, which made him more powerful—but had the voice grown in strength?

The voice continued.

"The fairies believe in a legend of a powerful mage who will eventually be brought from beyond Ermaeyth."

Xilor swallowed. This was too close to the truth he'd discovered, and that troubled him greatly.

"This mage will form a perfect balance of light and darkness."

Xilor didn't know how to take that other than literally or metaphorically.

"An elder fairy must give up a wing for the mage, and form a bond between them. This legend is from long ago, almost at the beginning of magic."

This prattling was wasting his time. How did this relate to anything relevant to Xilor now?

"Skip to the part about how I kill this mage or how I can bend this mage to my will."

"You can't bend her will to yours."

"Who is she?"

"I've answered that question."

"Fine. Where is she?"

"Far Point."

So, the prodigy is most assuredly this mage. Good. I can use her to my advantage or recruit her when the time is right.

"What binds you will drive you apart," the voice said.

Xilor snorted.

"Another word of warning about destroying myself?"

There was a breath of silence before he got an answer.

"No."

Xilor rolled his eyes and whirled around, opening the door and departing. His robes billowed with his movements. He could've teleported away, but the walk gave him time to contemplate his next move. Need urged him to watch the mage, observe her, and find a way to bend her to his will.

If she refused, he'd kill her.

Though tempted to devote more time to the conundrum, he had other plans already in motion, and he needed to strike before Ralloc was ready to acknowledge his return.

His feet carried him back to his throne where he sat and decided his next move.

Chapter 49: The Previous Life Of Lily

By the following morning, Julie wasn't sure if she was still dreaming or if last night had been real. She could only describe it as a haze, but when Lily showed up at her door, stirring her from slumber, the fog lifted. And her first words were like splashing her face with cold water.

"Kam wants to see you again," Lily said with a smile. "He's taken quite the liking to you."

Still trying to fully wake up, Julie took a moment to process what she was saying.

"What? Now?"

"Tonight, if that's alright?"

She could say no—of course she could—but after last night, it would feel strange. She also wanted to ask if Lily would be there or if this was just for her husband. And thinking of it that way, it felt quite strange that this woman would encourage their continued relations, especially if the magelust wasn't affecting her.

And with Lily here, I don't feel the magelust at all. So, it must've been Kam.

"If you want to," Lily said, holding up the bag in her hand, "you'll need to prepare for him."

Again, Julie frowned.

"Like what?"

Lily set the small pouch down on the nightstand.

"There's a razor, some oil and lather."

Julie had seen them both naked last night, so it wasn't hard to deduce.

"Why?"

Lily shrugged.

"To be honest, I can't tell you whether it's a Kam thing or an Islander thing, but it's the way he likes it. So, I do it."

Julie nodded.

"Y'all are Islanders? You're far from home."

"He is; I'm Rallocan."

Julie noted Lily's bright blonde hair, and now that she thought about it, Kam had blond hair, too. Was that the distinction for Islanders? She voiced the thought aloud.

Lily laughed.

"Well, yes, that's one way, but I had a pharmacon mage change my hair. Cost a good deal of money, too."

Lily glanced around her room.

"Come on, get dressed. Let's go shopping and get something to eat."

Julie thought about her dwindling pile of money. She didn't want to dampen Lily's spirits, but she had to be frugal. It'd only last so long.

"Lily, I appreciate the offer, but—"

Lily waved the words away.

"I'm buying, so hurry up."

A few moments later, dressed and presentable for the day, the two left her room. Walking down the dark hallway past their door, Julie once again felt the stirring of magelust, but it wasn't as strong as before. Maybe it was because she hadn't laid eyes on him, or maybe now that she'd acted on it, the stirrings subsided. Whatever the case, she asked Lily as they hurried down the stairs.

"Where's Kam?"

The look on the other woman's face told her more than she realized.

"Still asleep. He won't be up for a few more hours."

Julie set her lips in a tight line and decided not to inquire anymore. It was their business, not hers, and if Kam had a problem, she couldn't do anything about it.

They made it outside, and Lily positively glowed in the mid-morning sunlight, as if she came alive in the elements. Perhaps she did. To Julie's reckoning, it was far too bright.

The older woman slipped her arm into Julie's, setting their course, and walking down the road. A lot of questions came bubbling up to the surface as they strolled along, and since Lily wasn't speaking, Julie felt it was best to fill the awkward silence.

"Was last night about you or him?"

Lily turned her head, taken by surprise, but there was a brightness in her eyes.

"Oh, definitely about him."

"But ... you were kissing me and ..."

Lily's grin widened.

"Yes, but your lips weren't the only thing I was kissing, was it?"

Julie blushed, and she averted her gaze.

"So, you like women?"

Lily took a deep inhale, as if she was about to expel her life story in a single breath, but she just gave a little shrug.

"I'm selective."

Puzzled, Julie glanced over at her.

"Meaning?"

"Some women I like, and most I don't. I prefer my husband, though."

So, does that mean I was special or was it something else? Either way, it's a compliment.

Lily gave a little chuckle.

"I can definitely tell which you like."

Heat touched Julie's cheeks.

"Sorry."

"Don't be. You're quite normal."

Julie's brow furrowed, waiting a beat. When the other woman didn't continue, she prompted her.

"And what, you're not?"

Lily's lips tightened as she stopped, waiting for a carriage to roll by. When it did, they continued walking arm in arm.

"It's a long story."

Julie wanted to say they had the whole day, but she didn't feel right pressing her. In fact, she didn't feel right sleeping with her husband either, but the woman had encouraged it. Julie tried to think of something else to get the conversation moving again.

"Why's he so big?"

Lily laughed, covering her mouth.

"I assume you mean his muscles, right?"

Julie couldn't help the cringing expression flashing across her face.

"Yes, that's what I meant."

Lily pulled her arm a little closer, and Julie felt some of her embarrassment ease.

"He's a blacksmith. Works very long hours with his forge and hammer and whatever else he uses. I've only been to the shop once, just to know where it is, what it looks like."

Lily stopped, her head lifting to signs above the doors.

"Ah! Let's go in here."

Lily rushed forward, slipping her arm free, and clambering up across the slatted sidewalk. She opened the door, the bell jingling overhead as she did. Julie hurried to follow.

Inside was cool and darker than outside, which suited her fine, giving her eyes a reprieve. When her eyes adjusted, Julie's spine stiffened.

"What is this place?"

Lily peered back at her, a tease of a grin on her lips.

"Madam Elaine's Garment Shop."

Julie's eyes roved over everything she saw. Yes, there were robes and dresses, but more than half was all undergarments and bosom wraps.

"Lily," she whispered, "should we really be in here?"

"Of course. I plan to spend money."

Embarrassed, she stepped deeper into the shop, out of sight from the street, coming to stand beside her friend.

Julie blinked.

Is she my friend?

If she was, she was her first.

Doesn't last night make us friends?

"Can I help you ladies?" an older woman's voice called out.

Julie turned to see a woman walking towards them. Her silver hair was pulled back in a bun, and her pale blue eyes sparkled in the sunlight.

This must be Madam Elaine.

"Not right now," Lily answered. "Just browsing for now, but I'll let you know when I'm ready to purchase."

The woman dipped her head and retreated.

Once they were alone again, Lily returned to her perusing, leaving Julie to look on with her. It felt strange to browse things she had no intention of buying. And the silence didn't help either. While she wanted to badger the woman with questions, at the same time she felt shame for it, feeling like she was intruding.

Something must've shown on her face, because one of the times Lily looked in her direction, she paused in her rifling.

"What? Want to ask something?"

Julie didn't say anything.

"Don't be shy. Ask me whatever you want."

Lily glanced at Madam Elaine, making sure she was far enough away, and lowered her voice.

"We did share my husband last night, so a few questions won't hurt."

Lily giving that permission felt like a dam breaking within her.

"Last night, at the end, you two ..." she let the words die.

A knowing look crossed the older woman's face.

"Ah, yes, that. Kam's an Islander. It's expected in his culture."

"Really? That type of sex is normal?"

Lily nodded.

"Haven't you ever heard the rumors? The Islander Fashion?"

Julie shook her head. She didn't know anything about them other than that they were from the Forgotten Isles.

"Doesn't what you did last night bother you?"

Lily shook her head.

Julie swallowed, trying to make sense of her words when a new question formed on her tongue.

"Don't you hate me?"

Lily blinked, her face falling.

"Why would I hate you?"

Julie gave her a pointed look. She was about to respond when she remembered Madam Elaine, glanced at her, then back to Lily. She stepped closer, dropping her voice.

"I fucked Kam last night. Doesn't that bother you?"

Lily smiled.

"Not at all, and if I remember correctly, Kam fucked you, not the other way around. I'm quite confident in my marriage."

Lily moved away, eyeing some uncut fabrics. Julie hastened to her side.

"How?"

"The secret to having a great married life is to have a great sex life, and I think I take care of that end of the bargain."

That answer stumped her for a moment, but another question formed, and she had to ask.

"Why are you okay with your husband sleeping with me?"

Lily unfolded a cloth, eyeing the colors and pattern, a dark red and a burnished silver, but her eyes went to Madam Elaine at the far back end of the shop. She started folding the cloth back up. While she did, she spoke, her voice low.

"Kam loves me and always has. He's very good to me."

She stopped, looking Julie fully in the face.

"I'm not so sure you want to hear this. It might change how you feel about me."

Julie shook her head, hoping the woman would continue.

Lily sighed as she finished folding the cloth and putting it back, then moved over to a rack of wizard robes, but these were near sheer and definitely not for wear in public. The first one, a silky pale plum caught Lily's attention, her fingers caressing the smooth fabric.

"I was a prostitute in my youth," she confessed. "A choice done for various reasons I'd rather not get into at the moment. If I could go back, knowing what I know now, I wouldn't have done it. Begging in the streets has more honor. But when I met Kam, he was different. I was different. Long story short, he bought out my contract from the establishment's owner and married me."

Julie's eyes widened.

"Not at first, no. He made me work for it. Kam seems like a quiet, passive kind of man, but he's anything but that. He loved me, always treated me with respect, despite my lowly beginnings, and I adore him for that. But the question was did I love him? So, he made me work to prove that I did."

Lily moved down the rack, pulling out the sleeve of a gauzy black thing—more lace than anything.

"Sometimes, while I was still working, he'd buy me for a night or even a week so I wouldn't work, and he never partook of me unless I offered it. I swear, he's the last gentleman in Ralloc."

She paused in her story, and she turned around, facing Julie. A myriad of expressions flickered across the woman's face: solemn, shame, heartache.

"At times, I feel guilty for my sordid past, what I've done in service to Lord Brenton. Kam has never once complained, even though he has every right to. I try to forget my past, but I still see it every time I look in the mirror. What we do in life, our pasts, it haunts the future. So, I feel shame for allowing myself to become a whore, even for the best of intentions."

She sighed.

"Life deals unfairly, to say the least."

Julie wanted to say that she wasn't judging the woman and her choices, but she couldn't. It was now in the open between them, and it was a factor of her life. While she didn't understand why she'd done it, choosing that road, it at least explained why they were so willing to accept her last night.

Lily moved closer to the window, bending down to look at the different types of boots on display. Julie knelt beside her, sensing the story wasn't over.

"On occasion, when the guilt hits me hard, I find him another woman to enjoy. But he never asks for it, never reminds me of my choices. And he's never run around on me, never does anything to me unless I want it. He provides me a life that I once only dreamed of. That's his purpose, and I have mine."

Lily stood, turning around, facing a display of underrobes. They shifted from black and into the lighter hues of blue, green, and even yellow.

"He worked hard to save up the money to buy my contract, years' worth of savings, and worked even harder to buy me a house and allow me to travel, visiting whatever family will still accept me after my profession."

Lily paused, pulled out a light blue fabric and held it up to her chin. Not liking the color, she returned it to the rack.

"How can I not love a man like that? How can I not try to please him in any way I can? How could I refuse to make him happy?"

Julie felt a question forming within her, but she bit down the impulse to break Lily's cadence. The woman shifted deeper into the shop, coming to shelves with outerrobes.

"Almost every woman I found for him, he turned away, said he'd only join if I was involved. After each one, he told me he never wanted to see the girls again, even the ones we enjoyed together. So each time, the search became harder."

She sighed.

"He's only been with two other women since we married, and each of them only once. You're the first one he's requested to see again. So, I'd say that makes you special."

Julie wanted to ask how. She'd felt like an interloper, and she had to face the truth, everything she did last night was chasing the pleasure. She had no experience, not like Lily and Kam did together.

A question surfaced as her eyes drifted over the clothes.

"So, that's what you're doing in here? Buying something to surprise your husband with tonight?"

The older woman reached out, and held her hand, linking fingers with her.

"I won't be with you tonight."

Julie frowned.

"But, I thought you said—"

Lily gave a dip of her head.

"Yes, always, but tonight, it's just you two."

"Why?"

Lily swallowed.

"Because he asked."

Julie felt her eyes widening, and she shook her head.

"No, I can't. I won't come between you."

Lily smiled.

"You won't. Kam loves me, and I love him. His happiness matters, and if it's important enough to ask, what kind of wife would I be if I said no? Given my past, who am I to deny him a harmless want?"

Julie swallowed.

"This isn't right."

Lily let go of her hand, taking a half step away.

"Yes, it is."

She moved another row closer to the back and Madam Elaine, but they were still half a shop away. Now, they were in the stocking section.

Julie stepped close to her side.

"Are you sure you want this?"

Lily glanced at her, nodding.

"If you feel terrible about it, why don't you come with us to Ralloc? You could stay as long as you like. We have plenty of room."

Julie shook her head, trying to steady herself against the rush of emotions.

"You don't even know me."

Lily nodded, her lower lip protruding.

"That's true. You could be a murderer, or a thief who steals gold from the banks. Are you?"

"No."

The older woman shrugged.

"Then, I think we're okay."

In silence, Lily moved through the racks. Now that she'd divulged some of their past, Julie saw Kam in a new light. He had his faults, his drug addiction, but who didn't have them? She hadn't seen him be vile in the slightest. And if he truly treated his wife the way Lily suggested, then he was near-perfect.

And that gave Julie hope, more for herself than anything. If there was a man like Kam for Lily, maybe one day, there'd be a man for her, even after Mr. Pleasure broke her, after Judas broke her trust. She was damaged, and she hoped someone might one day find a way to heal her. She'd heal Kam of his addiction if she knew how.

Lily glanced at her.

"How many sets of robes do you have?"

"Four. Why?"

Lily shook her head.

"That won't do. Let's find you something."

"No, Lily, wait!"

Lily hurried to Madam Elaine to explain what she wanted to buy. Julie wanted to bolt for the door, but at the same time, she couldn't appear to be ungrateful. Madam Elaine helped them pick out colors, which Julie wasn't a part of, but she was happy they stayed with the darker colors rather than something bright and cheery.

Madam Elaine took the sets in the back after she measured Julie and said she'd tailor them with magic in about ten minutes. As the woman disappeared, Julie caught Lily smirking at her.

"What?"

Lily shook her head.

"Nothing. I've just never seen someone so dead set on not having a gift."

What could she say to that besides the truth?

"It makes me really uncomfortable. I'd rather spend time with someone or talk than be given something."

Lily's head bobbed from side to side.

"That makes sense. Kam's the same way. So, if you don't come to Ralloc with us, what will you do?"

And now that Lily had answered all of Julie's probing questions, she had one of her own. Julie wouldn't lie to her, but she didn't want to tell her the truth either.

Oh, not much, just following this book that spoke to me one time to go on a long trip to a mysterious place that may or may not exist.

"I'm furthering my studies in the magical arts."

"Ah! A genuine mage! Quite refreshing, really. You could be a master wizard or higher in Ralloc!"

She didn't know how to respond to that, so she just shrugged. To be honest, there were still many things she was trying to figure out.

"Is that what you want?" Lily prompted. "To be a master wizard?"

Julie shook her head, moving through the rows of folded clothes and fabrics, much like Lily had done earlier.

"I just don't want anyone to take control of my life."

Lily smiled.

"Hun, I think everyone wants that."

Lily stopped by the section of undergarments, her eyes roving over the selection. Julie came around the other side of the aisle and came to her side. Lily nodded to the fabrics.

"Which do you like?"

Julie felt the blushing heat flower her face, but she didn't respond. Lily picked up a pair of salacious, black silk undergarments.

"Kam likes black. You should wear this for him."

"No," Julie said in a rush, turning redder. "You should wear them for him."

"You forget, it's just going to be you two tonight. Besides, I have so many at home."

Lily sifted through the section, unfolding whichever caught her fancy before putting them back. Madam Elaine returned after a while, bringing the two sets of robes to the counter.

"Right, then, that'll be two sets of linen robes with inner and outer. Total is forty scepters."

Lily gave her an admonishing look.

"Come now, the most people ask is fifteen scepters per robe."

Madam Elaine nodded.

"Oh, aye, but most cannot tailor a set within ten minutes of you picking out which ones you like. Speed, dearie, equates to the extra charge."

Lily nodded and smiled.

"How very true."

"Anything else?"

"Just this," Lily said, tossing up the black silk undergarments.

"No!" Julie protested, reaching for them.

"Hush," Lily insisted, holding her hands away.

"Excellent selection," Elaine commented. "It'll make your husband quite happy."

Lily beamed at her.

"Oh, that's what I'm counting on."

"Silk undergarments are forty-five scepters. Eighty-five scepters total."

Lily doled out three silver chips and received five copper bits in return. Madam Elaine thanked them, and the women left arm in arm, but in truth, Lily had to drag Julie away.

"I wish you didn't do that," Julie commented once they reached the busy street.

Guilt rankled her from lack of having anything to give in return. Having sex with Lily's husband only compounded the issue.

"You need to stop worrying so much," Lily chided. "I'm a giver; giving makes me happy."

She leaned in closer, a slight tease in her voice.

"So, try to be a little excited."

"I'll try. Thank you."

"You're very welcome, my dear. It's my pleasure."

A flicker of darkness clouded Julie's mind upon hearing the words, casting her soul into a tenebrous place.

"Please, don't call me that."

Lily frowned.

"What? What's wrong?"

Julie shook her head.

"Someone I used to know called me that ... my dear. I don't have fond memories of him."

Lily gave a single nod.

"I'm sorry. It won't happen again."

Without another word on the subject, they pulled her by the arm as they walked down the road, finding a small café. They took a seat and ordered a short time afterward. Their conversation remained small, petty, and safe after Julie's reaction, and it was her fault. She'd ruined the mood.

The food came with their coffee, sugary pastries with cream and chocolate. As more time passed between their current conversation and Lily's one slip, she found herself opening up and wanting to speak about things she hadn't dared to with Judas. More than that, a truth started budding in her gut, and she had to say it.

"I want to go to Ralloc with you."

With her fork lowering to her plate, Lily paused mid-bite. She beamed at Julie and finished her mouthful.

"Really? Do you mean that? You'd most certainly be welcomed, I promise."

A pang of sadness hit Julie in the chest, and she had no doubt it showed in her eyes.

"Yes, I want to, but I can't."

"Why not?"

Julie let out a sigh.

"You've told me about your past, but I haven't told you about mine. The trouble is, I can't remember it. For me, this week with you, this will be my past. I woke up not too long ago, but it seems like an eternity. I don't know who I am, where I come from. Do I have a family? Who knows my real name?"

Lily brushed a lock of blonde hair behind her ear, her elbows resting on the table.

"But your name is Julie."

"Is it? When I woke up, that's what he called me. For all I know, my name could be Rebekah."

"Who's he? A lover? Husband? The man you mentioned?"

Julie shook her head and waved the question away.

"I want to come back with you to Ralloc and start my life, a true one, discover who I am, but I can't. You're the closest thing I have to a friend, and I don't have any. I mean, are we even friends, after last night?"

"Of course we are, even if we're not the best of friends. Friendship takes time, like love, and the best thing to do is not rush it."

Julie's eyes misted over.

"Yes, it takes time, time I don't have. So far, you're everything I could want in a friend: you're generous, kind,

"Amazing in bed!"

That caused Julie to smile.

"But there's one thing I can never have with a friendship with you."

"What?"

Julie took a breath, knowing this would be the moment Lily judged her, as she'd judged Lily.

"Power."

The finality of the word rested between them.

Lily leaned back, crossing her legs, her fingers interlaced in her lap.

"What can power bring you? What's it worth? More than me and Kam? More than starting your life you spoke about?"

Julie shook her head, blinking back her welling emotions. "There's so much you don't understand."

"Then, tell me. Help me understand."

Julie took a bite of the cake sitting before her, chewing to acquire time.

"You awoke me to a different side of life, something I hadn't ever experienced."

Lily smiled.

"You're talking about me and Kam?"

Julie shook her head.

"A friend, shopping, sharing stories—where I'm going, I'll never have this. But at the end of my journey, it's what I want. Does that make sense?"

Lily nodded.

"Very much. It was the same feeling when I first met Kam. At the end of my road, I wanted someone like Kam, but I knew along the way, I had to sacrifice immediate wants for the ultimate desire."

Julie set her fork down. She couldn't finish the cake. The next few words made her sick to her stomach.

"Returning to Ralloc with you is my sacrifice."

"Oh," Lily said, deflated. In a rush, she asked, "Is it Kam? Was he rough with you? Did he hurt you?"

"No, no," Julie smiled, shaking the ludicrous questions away. "Nothing like that. Your offer is severely tempting. I nearly wanted to take you up on the offer, but I started something, and I need to finish it."

Worried, Lily inclined forward.

"Are you leaving now? I thought you were leaving tomorrow."

"I don't want to leave, but tomorrow, I have to."

"Kam said that you wouldn't accept my offer."

Julie frowned.

"You talked to him about that?"

"Of course! He's my husband, and it's his house."

Julie nodded.

"I'm sorry."

Lily reclined, crossing her arms, laying them against her stomach.

"Is this goodbye?"

A knot formed under Julie's ribs.

"Do you want it to be?"

"No," came the immediate reply.

"Neither do I."

"Good."

Lily sniffed, sitting up.

"Kam would be mighty displeased if you left without a goodbye."

"You don't think…."

"That he's falling in love with you?"

Lily shrugged.

"Now? No. In time? Maybe."

"Does that worry you?"

Lily smiled again.

"Not at all."

Julie tilted forward.

"The most important question is: if he were, would you want me in your life?"

Lily placed her hand on top of Julie's.

"Without reservation. From what I see, I like. I think you're holding back on details about your life, and while I may not understand the what, the why is evident. If you wish, keep your secrets."

The word secrets sent a chill down Julie's spine, harking back to the book Judas gave her in the swamp. She was the Bearer of Secrets, another affirmation that she made the right choice in leaving. She stood precariously on the edge, tempted to abandon everything and go with Lily to Ralloc, but the seduction of friendship couldn't overcome her vow.

I'll never be weak again. I'll never be helpless.

"Will you see Kam tonight? Just the two of you?"

She blinked.

"Only if it won't cause issues between you."

"It won't."

"I still don't feel right about this... but I'll trust you."

Lily smiled, standing.

"Yes, you do."

She left three bits of copper on the table, more than enough to cover their drinks and pastries. Julie pulled up beside her as they exited the café, Lily snaking her arm into the younger's.

"Are you going to prepare for him?"

The razor flashed through Julie's mind, and she gave a single nod.

"What are you going to do while Kam is preoccupied with me?"

Lily shrugged, a coy smile on her lips.

"Someone's got to start packing, and Kam can't fold clothes worth a damn. I'll come let you know when he wakes, and that'll give you at least an hour to prepare."

"Okay."

Lily pulled her close, whispering in low tones.

"Are you going to try and make him happy?"

Julie nodded.

"Good. Then, be sure you wear the black undergarments I bought you."

Later that night, Kam entered her room. His gray eyes took her in; the black silk hugged her form, and she noted the hunger in his eyes. When he neared her, her tentative touch found him eager and she kissed him, standing on her toes. With slow movements, she undid his sash as the magelust stirred within her.

It was still there, still strong, but now, if she wanted to, she could walk away, but she found herself not wanting to.

"You're leaving tomorrow, and this will be our last time together," she said when they broke apart.

He nodded.

"I watched you and Lily last night."

Her hand parted his robes, then dipped under the cloth, the back of her hand peeling it away from his shoulder.

"Take me like you took your wife."

She kissed his chest, then slid her other hand under his robes, peeling it back from his other shoulder.

He smirked at her.

"You're not Lily, so there's no need to try to be. Plenty of women say they want the Islander Fashion, but not really. So, are you really sure?"

She could only nod, aroused, terrified, ashamed, and exhilarated. He kissed her once more before grabbing her by the arms and guiding her to the bed. There, he bent her over and took his time pulling down her black silk undergarments.

Their time together was a unique experience, quite different than the night before, and yet something similar. There was passion and sweat and moans, coupled with a dozen sharp breath moments as no part of her body went untouched. He'd done as she asked, taking her like his wife, the Islander Fashion, but only once he had his fill of the rest of her.

At some point during their frenzy, the magelust rose once again in her, but something strange happened this time. She could've sworn a trace of her essence slipped free, sparking something magical between them. Or it could've been the orgasm she reached at the same moment. She couldn't tell, and no one had ever told her whether such a thing was even possible.

And as she lay on her stomach, panting and sweaty, Kam retreated from her room, and a soft hand touched Julie, rolling her over to her side.

Lily glanced down at her, her expression questioning.

"Are you okay?" the wife asked.

Julie nodded.

With Kam gone, Lily looked after her, giving her dewgrass for soreness and helping her remake the bed from the tangled mess of the sheets.

Once made, Julie laid down, and Lily joined her. The woman ran her fingers through Julie's hair, and while she thought about approaching the subject of what just happened between herself and Kam, it was something else that came tumbling out of her mouth. She'd never meant to, but once she started, she found that she couldn't stop.

In the unforgiving darkness, Julie bared her soul and spoke of the Corridor of Cruelty and what she experienced, recounting Mr. Pleasure and all the sick, sadistic things he did. Recalling the depravities, how he broke her, how she didn't care anymore was cathartic. The book promised to lock her feelings away, and the bond held true. She spoke with impartial reflection, but inside, a preferred hollowness dwelt.

The desolation made her weary.

Julie spoke in slow whispers, as if afraid to breathe life back into her demons. She relived the nightmare with each halting word. The massive knot in her chest eased, and the words poured out. In a way, talking eased the burden, but she wished to forget altogether.

By the time she ended her tale, tears drenched her as Lily held her tight, weeping with her. The book failed to block the mental trauma or the scars the Corridor left.

Julie fell asleep as Lily held her, and when she awoke the next morning, the woman was gone. Dressing for the day, she knocked on their door, but an older woman with a sour-looking expression answered instead. Julie searched for them in the common room, but they were gone.

Returning to her room, she gathered the last of her possessions to stuff in her pack, but inside, folded parchments caught her eye. In haste, she unfolded it, excited.

Dearest Julie,

314

Our paths crossed but for a fleeting moment. Though your journey pulls you away, you're never far from our minds and hearts. With sadness, I shared the pain of your tale, and with a broken heart, I leave you before you wake. Should you ever come to Ralloc, our door is always open to you in any way you desire.

Yours,

Lily.

Detailed instructions for finding their house came on the second page. Ralloc was a massive metropolis, and without her words to guide her, she'd never see them again. Though sad they left without a goodbye, a part of her was relieved, knowing it'd be so much harder face to face. She couldn't ignore the strong impulse to abandon her quest, and in the end, was glad she didn't put herself in that position.

Her possessions gathered, she left the room without a backward glance. She took her last complimentary meal alone, eating only half before she, too, found no reason to stay. A pang of emptiness rumbled in her chest with Kam and Lily gone.

Pack slung over her shoulder, she left Far Point—and the brief, erotic life she lived—behind.

Chapter 50: Julie

Julie cursed whatever gods listened. She inquired about a horse from the limited stock in Far Point, but the cost of such a noble steed far exceeded the scepters she took from Judas.

Riding would be much better than walking.

A simple riding horse cost two bright eyes and ten chips in Ralloc. In Far Point, the price doubled. The availability was scarce, and people begrudgingly parted with the animals. The stable master had his own answer delivered with a shrug.

"Supply and demand."

What in the Underworld does that mean anyway?

Instead of riding to her destination, she walked in misery. Minutes crept by like hours as she put the city-town behind her.

She thought back to when she decided to leave Judas, listening to the book, but every time she felt remorse, she remembered Mr. Pleasure and that Judas did nothing to stop him.

Back in Far Point, she'd dropped the appropriate amount of silver down on the bar top to pay for her room, but the bartender shook his head and slid it back.

"Your friends paid before they left this morning."

She nodded in appreciation.

An honest man?

Sliding coins across the counter, she left him a sizable tip before following the main road south out of the village. Julie passed the guards as they opened the huge wooden gates. On the opposite side, a line with dozens of people awaited to rush in and buy, sell, or trade their goods. While technically a city, Julie thought it too small, but she could only compare it to Dlad. Perhaps having seen the larger municipality first skewed her perception?

She strolled past the line, giving them little more than a curious glance. After thirty minutes, she passed the last stragglers. The land opened up into rolling hills with sporadic vegetation. Far to the right, barely within sight, lay a forest.

She stared at the ground while she trekked along the dusty road, her thoughts flowing from one thing to the next: Judas, the room she slept in, waking to an open window, and the book she carried. Mostly, she thought about Kam and Lily, more so regarding the hours they shared together on their last day and the conversations they had.

For the first time, she had a friend, this ostensible stranger.

The suns climbed steadily as she trudged on, warming her back from the north. Not stopping for more than a few moments at a time, she kept a slow but steady pace.

The carnage she glimpsed in her Shadowcasting, all for one person's lust for power, weighed on her. The pointless deaths, the bodies littering the battlefield sickened her, turned her stomach. Some suffocated, drowning in their blood; others impaled through their gut or chest. She couldn't shake the images, wanting an end to the pointless butchery. Most of all, she craved to be the one to stop it, but how could she? Her powers were feeble and insignificant.

She couldn't, and that meant it came down to Judas again.

She pushed those thoughts aside. When she did, the memories of the Corridor invaded—a place she never wished to return. Julie doubted she'd ever see Ralloc, not while that horrid place lay between her and the capital. That's how much she dreaded it. And it also made her wonder how it affected Kam and Lily.

Now that they were gone, no longer a distraction, the horrors returned, a pestilence driving her to madness.

But one thing stood out in all that darkness, the euphoric presence of her magic when it surged at her call. She almost destroyed Mr. Pleasure, but she wasn't fast enough. Even now, the memory of the feeling came back to her, as did the empathetic connection to Xilor.

Julie shuddered.

Was she inherently evil like him? She yearned to feel that way again. Only the magelust compared, a close second. Xilor must've felt the pull like she had, and it corrupted him. Would she become corrupt, too?

Judas's power rivaled the dark lord's; why hadn't he fallen under its sway? Perhaps a fundamental flaw within Xilor made him succumb. Maybe there was something wrong with her, too; she was already defective, unable to block the magelust.

But how had she managed to lift all those weapons? A dark whisper fluttered in her mind. The voice made it possible. What remained unclear in those moments was who was in control: her free will, or the lurking voice?

Her ears filled with the sounds of metal striking stone as she hacked that fat bastard to pieces. A savage bloodlust took hold, and she wanted to bathe in his blood, and still she wouldn't have been sated.

But Judas's face, his hand on her shoulder, saved her, chasing the voice away. Why did the voice always flee?

You know why.

She shook her head in denial.

You can't lie to me. I see and feel everything you do, even the things you deny.

Julie frowned as she sent the thought back.

What are you?

Her breath burned in her lungs as she waited.

The part that'll keep you alive.

Julie tensed at the declaration. Judas was the voice's weakness.

Why do you always flee from him?

She sensed a chuckle roll through her, or maybe it was a sneer.

Your shame suppresses me.

She swallowed.

Did the voice speak the truth? Had it always been that way, and Julie just denied it? The voice had awoken while in Mr. Pleasure's thrall—when he broke her.

His words tumbled in her head.

"You'll find that pain and torture can be a pleasure—for me, at least; you'll learn to love it, for it's the only thing that makes you know you're alive. Pain connects everything. If you survive, you'll appreciate the pain of other things—the things of the world—and they're nothing compared to what I'm going to do to you. In that, you may find comfort, for your life will be painless compared to this."

She shuddered, banishing him and whatever truth or lies he spewed.

Midday approached when she finally stopped by a small stream. She worked her way down to the running water and knelt to douse her neck, face, and arms. Cupping her hands, she dipped them into the brook, bringing them to her mouth.

After satisfying her thirst and cooling off, she returned to the road and sat beneath a large oak tree. With her back against the trunk, she drifted off into a light doze.

Voices and the splashing of water awoke her.

Her eyes snapped open, and her head darted around her immediate area for signs of threat.

How long was I asleep?

It was still bright, the suns overhead, so it couldn't have been too long.

Seeing no threats, she climbed to her feet and took a few steps along the path towards the creek. She hunched, staying low. A few feet later, she spied a group huddled around the stream. They were humanoid and more than a handful. She counted nine.

When she adjusted her feet for a better view, loose stones clattered down the gentle slope. With battle-honed reflexes, they jumped in unison, each assuming a unique stance, weapons drawn.

In a panic, she rose from her concealment, backpedaling. Her hands groped through her robes, searching for her wand. She pulled it out, thrusting it forward, but a twirling staff sent it flying towards the stream. She fell back, landing on the ground, sending a sharp pain into her ass and up her spine.

Weaponless, defenseless, the man advanced on her.

The vow tumbled in her mind: *I'll never again be helpless.*

You don't need your wand to destroy him!

The voice urged for blood, and only her fear made her inclined to agree.

A man's voice, further away, barked an order in a strange tongue, halting her attacker.

No, not a man: an elyf.

Now that she could see them clearly, they were all elyves, but unlike any she knew. Skin of pale amethyst, their eyes varying with intense hues: cerulean blue, pale turquoise, strong olive-yellow, smoky-gray, and vivid gamboge-orange to name a few. The man with the staff had red—scarlet more than crimson or rose. Each had vibrant, eccentric hair ranging from taupe to ashen-gray.

A flurry of conversation erupted between them, punctuated by gestures. It sounded fluid to her ears, a merry and smooth poetry. Her eyes darted between them as they spoke. At any given time, one watched her while the other eight ignored her.

A consensus seemingly reached, they gave her their undivided attention. Further down the slope, one male came forward, replacing the elyf nearest her. He knelt in front of her.

"Forgive our transgression," he said.

"You speak Myshku?"

With slow, careful movements, he laid a hand on her shoulder.

"My name is Iddrial."

"Careful," broke in the elyf with staff.

"Peace, Ahn," Iddrial said.

He removed his hand from her shoulder.

"We didn't mean to harm you. We thought you to be someone else."

"Don't tell her our names," Ahn persisted.

Iddrial turned his head to the side, seeing Ahn out of the corner of his eye. Julie's gaze followed, noting their tense defensive postures.

"She doesn't have the faintest idea of who we are, Ahn."

"Not yet," a female elyf muttered.

Iddrial spoke in Thymulous, their native tongue, and the other eight retreated, leaving Julie alone with him. His eyes were vivid gamboge, a shade or two darker and more orange than her own amber eyes. Dark ash-gray hair with thin strips of leather twined through reached his stubbled jawline. By the time Julie took all this in, the eight returned. Iddrial held out his hand, never taking his eyes off Julie, and proffered her property once it reached him.

"I believe this is yours, Wizard."

Once her fingers wrapped around her wand, the eight fled, crossing the stream and fading into the wildlife, disappearing without a sound behind trees, ferns, rocks, and shrubs.

Iddrial rose and took two steps backward before, he too, crossed and vanished.

Out of sight, she hastened to her feet, hurried back to the oak, and collected her pack. She shouldered it and set out at a brisk pace, distancing herself in case they decided to return.

"Do you plan to walk the whole way?" a voice said from beside her.

She spun, brandishing her wand.

Breath quickened as she searched for who called out. At first, she thought the elyves followed her, but she didn't see anyone. Out of her peripheral vision, she perceived movement close to the ground. Eyes and hand redirected, and she stopped herself short.

A small creature stood beside her, a woman, beautiful, toned, and no more than nine inches tall. Julie's hand dipped, lowering her wand. The small woman wasn't a threat. The mage squatted, enthralled by the tiny creature whose hair shone bright like sunlight and spun gold.

"Why do you ask?" Julie asked.

"Most wizards use porting stones. If they can't, they ride a horse. But you're walking, why?"

Her voice sounded like the soft rustle of wind chimes.

Julie's eyebrows furrowed.

"I'm not like other wizards. I can't teleport far distances yet. Can't do it at all, actually."

"At least you can, most can't. And not everyone's fortunate enough to be born with wings."

Julie couldn't tell if she liked the little creature or if she pined for companionship since Kam and Lily left. The tiny creature radiated with an inner light, reminding her of Staell, the unicorn, but they were nowhere the same.

"My name's Julie. What's yours?"

The other gave her a brilliant smile.

"I know your name. You're the mage from beyond, and we share a bond through the wing in your wand."

She paused.

"We talk about you a lot in the community."

Julie frowned at the words, her lower lip protruding.

How does she know so much about me?

Julie gave voice to the thought.

"I'm a fairy."

She twirled around.

"See the wings?"

Julie leaned closer and could just detect her translucent and crystalline wings about half the size of the tiny woman. Light glittered off her as she twirled. A familiarity stole over Julie. She'd seen something very similar, and only briefly.

The core of her wand.

"Where's this community of yours?" Julie asked.

"The Melodic Mountains. That's where almost all fairies live."

Just where I need to go!

And that gave her pause. Was it fortuitous, by design, or was there something larger at work?

Julie stood, shaking out the pins and needles in her feet and shins.

"You never told me your name."

"Ava, daughter of the elder fairy, Fiosana."

"Pleased to meet you, Ava, daughter of Fiosana. Are you traveling, too? Where are you headed?"

"Wherever you are."

Julie squinted her eyes, trying to decipher what she meant.

"I'm to accompany you as your familiar. It's my honor, Head of Creatures."

Ava gave a tiny dip of her head.

Julie's mouth opened slowly, and her words followed at the same pace.

"I didn't expect company."

A faint whistling floated through the air, Ava rising into the air, hovering at eye level.

"You'll want me to accompany you."

"Oh? Why's that?"

"Well, for one, my mother's wing is in your wand, hence our bond, why I was selected. Secondly, unless you want to walk, I can teleport us. Within reason, of course."

Oh, thank the gods. I don't even know how far the mountains are, but I'm sure it's forever.

But Ava's proclamation troubled her. She was the daughter of the fairy who died. Wasn't that … awkward? Then again, her teleport ability outweighed any discomfort.

"You have a bond with me? Why didn't you come sooner?"

Ava glanced left and right, like she would rather be anywhere than here.

"You were … mating."

Julie blushed at the thought of Ava knowing. As she reddened, Ava held up her hands.

"Only I know about it, none of the others do. Don't worry. Where do you wish to go?"

Julie choked down her embarrassment.

"To the Place of Origins."

Ava blanched.

"Why? There's nothing there."

"So, you know it?"

"Yes. There's only one place that isn't for fairies. There has always been only one, and there can only be one. Fife Doole's old hut."

There had only been one?

"Okay, well, that's where I need to go."

"As you wish."

A blue swirl opened before them, and Ava floated towards her, resting on her shoulder. Together, they stepped through the gateway.

Chapter 51: Judas

Judas eyed the remaining people of Wizard's Pass.

"Is this all that is left?" he asked.

A light drizzle soaked him, his graying hair matted to the sides of his face.

The younger man beside him was the newly appointed governor of Wizard's Pass.

"Yes."

He wiped off excess water from his forehead.

The pair walked through the aftermath of the battle. Dead bodies still littered the fields outside, and the charred skeletons of structures still stood upright … their remains anyway.

"Our houses are destroyed, our loved ones are scattered and dead. We're in ruins."

Judas glanced around him. Ruins was an understatement. With the proper materials available, and with some help, he could magically put the village back together in a few days, a week at most, but nothing he did would erase the scars. As he surveyed the area, a woman winked into existence. His heart leapt for a fleeting moment, thinking Julie had returned, but disappointment strangled the hope. She couldn't teleport. At first glimpse, the woman reminded him of Julie, but within a blink, it was gone.

Meristal closed the distance between them; the hood of her outer robe covered her hair. Why did he think Meristal was Julie? A shuddering whisper beckoned him to follow the thoughts, but even as he did, the notion eluded him. Besides, Meristal was shorter, more petite than Julie, but on both accounts, not by much.

The thoughts fled when Meristal spoke.

"Judas. I just came from the Elyfian Enclave. The elyves will march against the vampires. I didn't realize they harbored such ill feelings, but a declaration is miraculous. Perhaps Scodd Yullus's voice is stronger than we realized. An elyfian Portal Master sent an advance guard, but the vampires subdued the forces. They pulled a victory when a legion of goblins flanked the elyves."

She paused, her eyes falling to the carnage before flickering to a cluster of people nearby.

"So, it's begun," Judas said.

He looked off into the distance, northwest, toward the Corridor of Cruelty.

"The board is set, and you had your opening volley. The next one is ours."

"What?"

Judas shook his head.

"Nothing, just that Xilor moved against us, and now it's time for our counter move. Forget about the lower domains of Marcoalyn and Stratu'Geim. He isn't worried about dominating them; he doesn't need to. If he controls Ralloc, he controls the entire realm and possibly Ermaeyth herself."

"What about Far Point and the barrier?"

"A ruse. It holds nothing of value."

"How will he obtain Ralloc?"

"Well," said Judas, pulling out his wand and striking the dirt by his feet. The dirt molded into a hasty replica of the Ralloc and Marcoalyn domains. He pointed to the dirt map.

"The elyves portaled from the northeast Vikal Mountains down to Shadow City in the southwest. Clear across the domain. Goblins marched up through the Corridor," —he pointed to the Goblin Forest that lay in the southwest of the Marcoalyn domain— "and up into Shadow City."

He finished tracing the path through the narrow gap of land and then traced northwest, emphasizing where the elyfian army met them in battle.

"Do you realize what you are suggesting, Judas?"

"Yes. The goblins have an insurrection on their hands. If the Leviathan caste rises against the Palatine caste in Goblin's Terrace, we could be looking at a Goblin Rebellion inside Xilor's new war. Kellis and Lagelm on the council might have more information. They're part of the Palatine caste."

He glanced at her.

"Any word on such things?"

Meristal shook her head.

He nodded.

"That's good. Let's hope we don't entertain a massacre as well as a war."

"I don't understand what the big deal is. If there is infighting, it makes Xilor weak and unfocused."

Judas sighed.

"The Palatine caste is a mere tenth of the population. They hold the magic and the authority, but the Leviathan caste holds the numbers and the brute strength. If they revolt, we're talking population collapse. It's only the fear of Palatine magic that keeps the lower caste in the forest; without it, they'd spill out and run rampant through every settlement they find."

He cleared his throat.

"So, let's assume the Leviathan caste circumvented the seat of power in Goblin's Terrace. They could hit Far Point, Troll City, or Cape Gythmel along the way. Any news in regards to that?"

"Nothing. No sightings, no skirmishes. All is quiet. Any word on Julie?"

The warlock shook his head.

"None."

He hoped she was safe and not lost, injured, or dead. It'd be a great blow to him, as well as to the realm, if the fairy's legend proved true but then she ended up dead. He wasn't disputing the veracity, and he was content to let it play out, if it did at all.

He cleared the phlegm in his throat and continued.

"This is a dangerous time. The strongest fighters, the elyves, were stopped, and goblins are in the Ralloc domain. That's a small foothold, but a foothold all the same. They could be used to flank any of our forces, or attack them at night. Anything to distract us for when Xilor comes in force. But he'll come, and I can tell you where, too."

"Out with it!" Meristal said, her words tart. "I still need to warn the council!"

Judas sighed.

"If they listen."

He gave her a weary smile.

"At the Corridor, Cape Gythmel to be exact. Get back to the Ralloc and gather what forces you can muster, even without the help of the council, if you have to. He'll strike soon while we're still reeling, and this won't be like the last war, something orchestrated and drawn out. Xilor retains the element of surprise, so long as he strikes hard and fast. We'll make defenses at Cape Gythmel. I'll go there myself."

Meristal smiled as the light mist of rain came down harder.

"Then, I have good news in regards to Cape Gythmel."

She hesitated, debating on what to say.

"Daniel came to see me."

Judas didn't respond, making his face impassive, masking his warring feelings within.

"The Heir of Valin."

Judas nodded once and looked away.

"I know who that bastard is."

He never liked the man, and he couldn't stand his crass nature. All of the Krey, really. And Judas still fostered some animosity toward him, as he'd always chased Meristal in their younger years. If he ever was successful in his quest of her, Judas couldn't say, but he could imagine, and that was so much worse.

Judas turned his gaze back to her, and his jealousy bubbled out.

"Let me guess, he wanted to bed you?"

Meristal rolled her eyes.

"He sent a squad of Krey to Cape Gythmel for 'exercises.' They should arrive soon and begin fortifying."

"The Krey," Judas said. Disgust roiled in his gut, his lips frowning. "By the gods, why did it have to be them?"

"You know what?" Meristal snapped.

His head jerked in her direction, hearing the venom in her voice.

"I would've figured an exile like you would be more compassionate to other people who're considered outcasts. Stop being so closed-minded, Judas. You've got more in common with them than you realize."

Then, she was gone.

Judas stared at the ground she'd just vacated, knowing her words rang with a discordant truth.

We may have something in common, but I'm nothing like them.

And in many ways, he was worse. Julie and the Corridor came to mind.

Shoving those aside, he turned back to the town, hoping to find people willing to help him in another town while theirs remained in shambles.

Chapter 52: The City Of Despair

A city of ruins greeted Julie. Once, the stately high walls encompassed the grand municipality, but now lay crumbled, mere rubble cracked with jagged lines surrounding the wasteland. A lone statue of a unicorn stood outside the gate, unblemished upon its pedestal, untouched by time.

"What is this place?" Julie asked. "Where are the mountains?"

With cautious curiosity, she padded closer toward the destroyed remains.

"The City of Despair. Everyone stops here when teleporting. An anomaly similar to the Corridor, sort of."

"Why's that?"

"It was destroyed by some form of potent magic. Perhaps the backwash of such forces drags you out of your teleport. But you have to be traveling fairly close, and we were."

Julie let out a pensive hum, marveling that the statue survived. The cryptic writing at the base ensnared her attention. It seemed familiar, similar to the book.

As she stared, the words moved, bending and rearranging until they made sense.

"No one can read it," Ava said.

Julie ignored her.

"You won't be able to."

"You might be surprised."

She turned her attention back to the pedestal, and the words shifted, unlocking the hidden meaning.

"It says, 'You must understand the lost language, the shield, and the key to entering the City of Despair.'"

She glanced over at the fairy, catching her rolling her eyes.

"I get that you're new to this world, but like I told you, no one can read it."

Julie stepped closer. Focusing on the letters, Julie spoke. "Hello."

Ava zipped closer, her movements fast.

"What did you say?"

"Hello, I think."

As she said that, the statue's head animated.

"Hello."

It returned to its solid state.

"By the One!" Ava muttered, her eyes going wide.

"What happened here?" Julie asked.

The stone shifted again.

"Only the one who did this knows for certain. In one cataclysmic day, the city was destroyed by an unfathomable power."

"What did he say?" Ava asked, her head shifting between Julie and the unicorn.

She relayed what the unicorn said. Ava flew high to peer over the wall.

"There's hardly anything. Just a dead tree to the far north side, and a temple-like building in the center."

She floated back down.

"Ask him how we get in."

"How do we get into the City of Despair?"

"I can take you, but why would you want to?"

What was she supposed to say to that? Everything she saw was something new, and once she got to … wherever she was going, who knew when the next time she'd leave would be.

"Maybe to check out that building."

Julie leaned to the right, peering past the unicorn and through the obliterated gate.

"I shall do as you ask."

She swallowed.

"Yes, please."

"Follow me."

The unicorn's body shifted, the stone falling away, revealing the encased skin beneath. His flesh was not translucent nor full of light but a white coat like a horse. He stepped off his pedestal and trotted toward the opening. The mage hurried to keep up, and Ava fluttered down to sit on her shoulder.

Julie was pretty sure that the unicorn wasn't real, but some form of magic; Staell spoke directly to her mind while this one spoke aloud. She noted the magic, the way the masonry faded, revealing his body. It was a neat trick, one that she'd like to learn.

"What's in the building ahead?" Julie asked as they passed through the broken gate.

"Inside remains unknown to me."

"Can you speculate?" Ava asked.

Julie glanced at her, and they both realized the fairy could understand the unicorn while sitting on Julie's shoulder. To test this theory, Ava took flight.

"The temple was built before the fall of the city, that much we can tell. Most assume Xilor built it."

"A temple for what?"

"Who can tell but the one who built it? It didn't cause the destruction; rather, it was the epicenter."

"What did he say?" Ava asked, settling on Julie's right shoulder.

Julie explained as they waded deeper into the city, drawing closer to the building.

"Doesn't sound like much help," Ava said.

"Agreed. Perhaps we will find more answers once inside."

"You're more likely to find answers here than in the Melodic Mountains," the fairy remarked.

"What do you mean?"

"I've never been to Fife's place, but I'm acquainted with it. Once Fife left, the place vanished, and no one has returned. Probably obliterated by Xilor's

326

army."

"It has to be there," Julie said, more to herself.

"I will, of course, do as you ask and take you."

They reached the structure without further conversation; the guide stopped shy of the stairs leading up to the front door.

"I'll await your return," it said, then dipped its head.

"Thank you."

She made the same gesture before moving past him and up the stairs. Reaching the top, in place of a door, a void of impenetrable shadow veiled the insides. No light or gaze pierced the veil.

"What is this?" Julie asked.

"I don't know."

The mage stepped forward, testing the substance, a light caressing of her fingers. A jarring wave ripped through her, not of power for protection, but an emotional one, an impact of memories and sensations.

What happened here?

"Are you alright?"

Julie instinctively put her hand on her forehead, staggered by the emotional surge.

"Yes, I am fine. I got a sense of what happened here, like all the memories pushed into my mind … I can't describe it."

"Let me try," Ava said, pushing off Julie's shoulders and flying right for the blackness. Before Julie could react, the void swallowed Ava.

"No!"

Almost immediately, the fairy returned. "Mistress, you must come and see this!"

"What's in there?"

"You'll see. Come."

Julie reached back out, letting the jarring images and feelings course through her, but this time, she was ready for it. She stepped into the void.

Her breath rushed out of her in a gasp on the other side. A fleeting cold like ice flickered, evaporating from her skin as she passed the pall. Ava floated in front of her.

A circular room greeted her; in the center, a round podium made of honed granite sat on a tiled floor of creamy, orange clay. She moved to the center of the room, the only object worth inspecting. On the podium were six shapes cut out of the stone and arranged in a circular pattern, each different from the last. The depth of each was minuscule, perhaps a centimeter.

In the center of the ringed carvings, a seventh sat.

Her eyes darted around the room, noting the two other entrances, both the same distance from each other. The room was perfectly symmetrical, a building crafted to mathematical precision.

With cautious steps, she prowled the room before turning back to the dais. She picked up on something she'd missed earlier. The small edge of each carving was colored differently, either paint or chips of stone: garnet, sapphire, pearl, amethyst, umber, black, and topaz surrounded the centerpiece.

Very faint etchings were at the base of each carving.

"That's interesting," she said, bending closer.

"What is?"

Ava fluttered over.

"These markings are nearly identical to the ones in my book. There are slight differences, perhaps for pronunciation?"

"Maybe the same language, just a different dialect."

"What is this place?"

She turned around, wondering what else she might've missed.

"Your guess is as good as mine."

There was something in the fairy's voice, something that sounded like exhaustion. She glanced at the winged creature, and she noted that her wings were moving slower. Ava had a hard time hovering in place.

"You might be right."

A frown formed on Julie's face, trying to figure out why she was acting that way, and then it hit her. It sounded similar to the effects of the Corridor. Ava's voice was empty and hollow in the vast open area, but the slight sound of chimes as she spoke and the distant whistle of her movements were fainter.

The hairs on the back of Julie's neck stood on end and goosebumps raced down her skin. She opened herself to her essence, actively paying attention.

A presence watched her.

Yes, this place felt very similar to the Corridor. A creeping shudder crawled up her back.

We have to get out of here.

Ava moved at the edge of her vision, and Julie turned in time to see the fairy glide toward the floor, ungraceful and haphazard.

"Are you okay?" Julie asked.

"Yes, mistress," she slurred.

The mage knelt to catch her, but the fairy reached the floor, her legs trembling, folding beneath her. Her head touched the floor, and she lay still.

With careful fingers, Julie touched her.

What in the Shades of the Underworld happened? She looks so fragile.

"As do you," a voice called out.

That presence she sensed returned twice as strong. The hairs on her neck quivered. She shot to her feet, reaching within her robes, and pulling out her wand.

"Who are you? What have you done to Ava?"

"I'm a voice from the past, and a guide to the present."

"What did you do to Ava?"

The voice paused.

"I let her rest so I may bequeath what I've learned."

Her brow twitched downward.

"To teach me? Seems like everyone's offering that lately."

Her arm ached from pointing her wand, so she lowered it to her side. She didn't know how much she could do to defend herself, but it was reassuring.

"As should be expected. It's not every day you meet a nephiliam."

She smirked.

"You got the wrong person, then. I'm not a nephiliam. I'm not from here. I'm a Wcic."

The voice laughed, raspy but not cruel.

"That's a lie. You're not Wcic."

"That's what they told me."

"Who? The people who have been closest to you? They'll be the first to deceive."

Her eyes darted around, waiting for someone to show themselves. Was the person invisible? While she sensed something watching her, she couldn't feel the direction.

"Your words have yet to make me doubt them."

Still, what the voice said resonated within her, accompanied by the creeping chill of truth. And Judas often kept things from her.

"Because to be a Wcic, you can't be born on this world, and you were."

Chapter 53: Xilor

Xilor returned to the hidden room.

The voice had goaded him before, foretelling his impending doom. Of all the atrocities he committed for a better future, for the good of Ermaeyth, his doom was to be beaten by some wretch?

The notion was ludicrous.

The brazen thought elicited a laugh from him, but the more he dwelt on it, the more it galled him. If the voice said Judas would destroy him, Xilor would worry. Judas nearly did before.

But a child?

Prodigy or not, she was untrained. Power was nothing without proper guidance.

Xilor closed the door behind him. He crossed over to the room's sole occupant, a cabinet. It'd been a long time since he opened the bureau, but *he* was still inside. The cabinet cracked open, and a cubical mirror-like object sat undisturbed but mired in dust. With a few strokes of his fingers, he wiped the dust motes away.

The object didn't reflect his image. Instead, it reflected the face of his old master. Though he could've killed him, Xilor placed him in this prison.

The irony wasn't lost on him.

The image within faced him.

"What do you want? To gaze upon me as I prattle on about your fate? Or did you come to gloat about your latest accomplishment again, to cheat death?"

Xilor's former master knew how to cut to the quick, robbing him of avenues. Time had sharpened his tongue. His master, Hadius Lacove, looked him full in the face.

"There's no cheating the Lord of the Underworld; eventually, you'll find that out."

"You thought it impossible. What a small mind you possess."

Xilor paused, cocking his head to the side.

"I believe the Lord of the Underworld and I have reached an understanding."

Hadius snorted.

"You haven't cheated death, only escaped its clutches. There won't be a second evasion."

"You might be surprised yet again. Besides, you can't cheat what you are."

Xilor set the cube on the shelf inside the cabinet so he didn't have to hold it.

"That's something you never seem to understand," Hadius said. "You can't change your destiny."

Xilor paused, considering his words. These esoteric musings always befuddled him.

"I'm becoming what I'm supposed to be."

"An abomination?"

Hadius's head shook side to side within the cube.

"All things will be corrected in the end, whether you succeed or not. That is the way of the Time Wardens. Your stupidity will awaken them!"

"Time Wardens? Fool!"

Xilor shook his head.

"If I didn't destroy you when I did, I'd still be a weak servant. You were an incompetent old man then, and your fear motivates you now, coward."

"Fear drives everyone, especially you."

Xilor's lips curled in disgust.

"I fear nothing!"

But was it true? Didn't fear motivate him now, just of a different kind?

Hadius paused, giving him time to let the implication percolate. When he spoke again, his voice was quiet and controlled.

"Those with power can be broken. That's why you sought a solution to mortality."

The words echoed in Xilor's ears. It was a drumming, pounding sensation. Everything seemed to stop.

Could he possibly know?

The thought twisted in Xilor's mind, like a sharp blade cutting deeper, ripping him open.

"How would you know?"

"I've seen it, Apprentice. I told you I saw the future, but I never said I didn't see the past, too. You only inferred what you wish, and I chose to let you remain ignorant."

"Obviously, your gifts failed you, as you didn't see where you'd end up."

"Precision, absolutes, only the Time Wardens have that gift. I only see possibilities."

Xilor felt his hot breath slink out of his nose.

"Possibilities? Again with the Time Wardens. They don't exist. It's a story to make people like us fearful, because we fear nothing."

"And that is our failing, not fearing what we don't understand. When gazing into the future, you can change events just by seeing them. Like a pebble dropped into a pond, the water is still water; nothing changed except the movement. The unfolding of time and events can't dictate free will, an unbeatable pattern."

"I am tired of your riddles."

Xilor rubbed his temples.

"Fine. How's this? Everything you do will be countered."

This ... this was new. Xilor's eyes narrowed.

"Tell me more."

"It's better for destiny to unfold."

"Another riddle? Tell me, or I swear to make your last moments painful and meaningless."

Xilor heard Hadius sigh.

"Knowing what may come, you'll strive to change it or make it happen. What may come is set or denied by your inquiry."

"Out with it!"

"There are five doors before you. The first one is your ultimate destruction. The only opposition is Judas Lakayre, and he'll end your existence."

Xilor mulled over the proclamation. He knew better than to interrupt. Hadius did as he desired, telling him the possibilities, so he understood the odds of his gamble.

"The second door will yield your heart's desire: emperor of Ermaeyth, discovering lost magics from Hagen's time, immortality. Through you, the Lord of the Underworld shall walk in the world of the living."

Xilor swallowed. While much of that sounded like what he envisioned, some of it did not. Was the Lord of the Underworld and lost magics linked? Could he abstain from one to keep the other from happening?

"The third door is shrouded in shadow, but through it, a tapestry of light guarded by a being of time and shadow, a Time Warden, and you will be destroyed. To glimpse her is to glimpse death, but no gaze can pierce the shadowed cowl."

Xilor rolled his eyes. Hadius's prattling on about imaginary creatures ... but if he was doing as Xilor asked, and he truly saw a Time Warden, that didn't bode well for him, even if it was something masquerading as one.

"The fourth door is strange. Nothing like this has ever transpired before or will ever again. There is a magical being; this fallen angel of darkness and light will crush you. This fallen angel will be a protector of Ermaeyth."

This possibility intrigued Xilor more than the others. A fallen angel. He had never seen an archangel and didn't think they existed, very much like the Time Wardens, but if they did, he was sure he could defeat them.

"The fifth and final door reveals the angel and death united. Hand in hand, they conquer realms and worlds in the arms of the cosmos. All bow to your relentless oppression, and civilizations will crumble against the might of the angel."

Xilor swallowed as Hadius took a deep breath.

"What you do with this knowledge is up to you. I suggest, however, that you not force destiny's hand."

Xilor pulled back a touch, taking in the words, the possibilities.

"I'll trust my intuitions."

"Then, be prepared to accept the consequences."

"Who is this fallen angel?"

"What does it matter to you?"

"I've never heard of this angel. If ever confronted, I may offer him a choice and place beside me."

"I never said it was a he. You never grasp the simple fact that not all power lies within man alone. You overlook what you do not understand."

"A woman?"

Contempt gushed through his voice. Yes, they had their uses, but none had ever been masters of the arts. But if this woman was more powerful than Olga, darker and more twisted, she could help beget a lineage potent enough to reshape Ermaeyth.

"She possesses the powers of both her parents' lineage, something that hasn't happened in a long time. The powerful bend or break. She was much like you for a while, unaware of her true potential."

Xilor crossed his arms.

"Then, I'll make sure she finds out what it is. Who are her parents?"

"It's of no consequence; she is a Wcic ..."

A sudden knock came from the door. Xilor whirled around, glaring at it. He shut the cabinet and hurried over to the hatch.

Who the hell found me? No one knows of this room!

He threw it open, finding Vlukus on the other side. The abyssian bowed.

"The army is ready to march, and the xicx await your command, High One."

"How did you find me?"

All his rage was ready to lash out at this creature, intruding upon his solitude, discovering secrets none of his apprentices had.

"We can always feel where you are."

That was a side effect he hadn't foreseen.

Damn!

"Never speak of this room to anyone."

Vlukus bowed his head again.

"Your will be done, High One."

Xilor followed Vlukus through the winding corridors of Gryzlaud to the balcony overlooking the hold's courtyard. While he'd been busy planning, his agents went out and rallied his forces.

A stirring of what Xilor could only call joy flowered within his chest. His army of Leviathan goblins, the small, cruel, and twisted beings of different hues and shades gathered, drawn to his power. He'd conjure darkness for when it came time for battle.

And more would join them, he was sure of it.

But not every creature would come when called. Some he'd have to visit in person.

For a long time, he'd yearned for the thundering sound of conquering footsteps. And now, he'd get it.

The war could start in earnest.

Chapter 54: The Temple

"Have you ever heard of Rumigul?" the voice asked Julie.

Her eyes went to Ava, seeing the creature's chest rise and fall. The voice had male qualities, but it was hard to tell being so disembodied.

"Yes, the ancient magic—one that corrupts."

"Corruption is in the mind of the beholder. True power is the ability to save, to do as you wish. As for being ancient, all magic is, as history clearly states."

"I hear your words, recognize the logic of your argument, see the scaffolding you build, yet I don't see you. You say others have lied to me, yet expect me to believe you with blind faith? Who are you?"

There was a pause in their conversation, as if the voice reassessed her. She wouldn't be its puppet, no more than she'd be Judas's.

"I was once a pupil like you."

Julie detected a smile in his voice.

"Young, foolish, naive, until I learned Rumigul. I discovered its secrets, the true power and nature of magic."

"Sounds like corruption to me. The way you speak of it, glorifying it …"

"To understand the depths, one must view all aspects; not just the arbitrary force-fed axiom through the ages. We've forgotten so much. Magic is old but ever-evolving; therefore, we must evolve with it."

Well, that I can follow.

"Corruption stems from Derengi, a power akin to the Lord of the Underworld."

She rolled her eyes.

"Okay, thanks for the history lesson. If you have something to teach, I'm listening, *but* you speak around the subject. And I still don't know who you are."

The voice withdrew again, and she had the distinct feeling she'd perturbed him. That was fine. He wasn't Judas, and she wouldn't entertain anything until he proved himself.

"Very well," he said, "I'll tell you. My name is Rusem Geim. I was once lord of the lands south of the Melodic Mountains, King of the Stratu'Geim domain."

Not likely.

"What happened?"

"I died."

The voice in her head reared up and screamed at her.

He lies! They all lie. They want you for their end purposes, just like Judas did.

She took that point in stride. Her eyes fell to the fairy.

"What did you do to Ava?"

"I put her to sleep. We can talk without interruptions."

"Is she hurt?"

"That wouldn't foster trust, would it?"

Julie mulled over his words, finding truth in them.

"What's so important that she can't be awake to hear?"

"From my experience, fairies are untrustworthy—conniving pests that only look out for themselves. There's much to teach you, but I'll impart what will serve you best. Consider it a promise of more to come."

"What?"

"The gift to know who is lying to you."

She crossed her arms.

"I find that hard to believe."

"Doubt is healthy, but you can be sure. Let me enlighten you."

Was it wise to learn something from him? He could be trying to harm her. But she'd learned from Harold, hadn't she? She'd gone to Kam and Lily's room without a stitch of worry. Why was she being apprehensive now?

"Fine," she said at last. "Teach me, and if it serves me well, perhaps I'll return."

From the center of the pedestal, a murky, white light arched out of the opening, streaming into her eyes. She could feel the tingling sensation dance throughout her skull, coming in waves. Compared to the book, it barely registered, more like a gentle caress. A warning went off in her mind.

Knowledge shouldn't be easy, but achieved through the process of education and dedication.

But hadn't the book promised something similar?

Mentally she shook her head.

This was too easy. Perhaps she was accustomed to the struggle under Judas's tutelage. Somewhere, in the back of her consciousness, she knew that was wrong, both the struggle and easily acquired knowledge. War raged within her. The enlightenment showed her how to bend circumstances, mold them to her will if she chose.

The voice rose up in her head again.

Dominating someone to do what you want could be a good thing.

It's wrong to possess anyone's mind or soul, no matter how dire the situation is!

Not even to save a life, to preserve it?

No, no life is worth the conquering of a mind.

Not even Judas's? Kam's or Lily's?

She answered with silence. The inner battle shifted, and she slipped from the moral ground. Yes, there were circumstances where she'd bend. The voice sank its claws deep, and she felt it smother her conscience.

She'd wield abilities to end Xilor. Another concession.

She hadn't lost herself, not yet, but she was close. Julie stood on a precipice, not wanting to fall into the breach, but the fortitude to continue her fight abated.

A part of her admired the man who brought her into this magical world; the other half detested him for the Corridor and Mr. Pleasure. That place was a turning point for her, changed her, altered their relationship. She tried to understand his reasoning and couldn't.

And anger budded within her chest. It'd never be quiet, never go away, and it'd keep her warm in this cold, decaying world.

The light stopped abruptly.

A man stood before her. He was older than she expected, his voice more youthful than his appearance.

An aura radiated about him, and his eyes reminded her of Judas, wise beyond his years. Her amber gaze scrutinized him from head to toe. He was a little taller than her, not by much, but a whole head and then some shorter than Kam.

The magelust tickled her insides, stirring her with fire, but not as much as Kam.

She clamped down, willing it to recede. It didn't, but it didn't swell any more.

Am I attracted to him or his aura?

"This," the man said, "is what I looked like before I died."

If he noticed her lust, he didn't give any indication, but he matched her mind's interpretation of what regal would be. Flowing dark locks, a neatly trimmed beard, broad shoulders, flowing robes of silk.

"Pity you're dead," she blurted.

Why'd I say that?

"Yes, but that doesn't mean that you can't come back and see me again."

She swallowed.

Not exactly what I meant.

He stepped closer, the lust growing stronger, and held out his hand. Julie opened hers to receive him. If they touched...

Shades of the Underworld, where's Kam when I need him?

He dropped something into her palm. A ring.

Fuck. What a disappointment.

He retreated two steps.

"This is a teleport ring. It'll bring you straight here to this temple. No need to go through the gatekeeper anymore."

She narrowed her eyes, gaze flitting between the ring and him.

"How do you know?"

He smiled.

"I made it. It fell from my body when I died. Whenever you decide that you're ready, you can return."

Her eyes swam, but as his image faded, so did the magelust.

Ava groaned from the ground. Julie glanced at the stirring creature.

"My apologies, mistress."

"Don't worry about it. It was not your fault."

"How long was I out?"

"No more than ten minutes."

In truth, she had no clue how long they were inside the temple.

"Come, Ava, we're leaving."

Together, they stepped into the void and out the other side.

"Back already?" the unicorn asked.

"What do you mean?" Ava asked.

"You just went in. I swear to you, I have yet to take my eyes off the portal, and you reemerged."

A sense of unease rippled through Julie, and she glanced back with uncertainty, letting her gaze linger for a moment.

"We're done. There wasn't much to see."

The unicorn dipped his head and headed for the gate. They returned in silence, Julie pondering over what transpired and the time that'd passed, or lack thereof.

She fumbled with the Rusem's ring, stuffing it in her pocket. She wanted to test her mind-probing. Perhaps it would serve her needs, one more tool in her arsenal.

And when the time was right, she'd confront Xilor and bring an end to his reign.

By any means necessary.

Chapter 55: Meristal

The Kothlere Council Chambers always had an opulent shine. At least, in Meristal's estimation. But today, the room didn't seem as beautiful. A dark mood rivaling the deep phthalo-blue carpets settled over the coming proceedings.

Each time she came into the chamber, this place represented power, justice, and prestige; to Judas, it represented oppression, vanity, irresponsibility. Since Kayis took office over a half score of years ago, Meristal had to agree with the warlock.

Kayis was spoiled and tactless.

The decor changed with each new consul, signifying their term. Tapestries of the noble Houses adorned the walls. Gossamer curtains, rods of gold and silver, black walnut and cypress wood—all mirrored the attitude of those in power: egotistical luxury. Though charming at times, Kayis's ambition and alacritous rise made him drunk off his success. He wasn't an only child, but might as well be, the youngest with his nearest sibling two ages older.

After being exiled by the council, Kayis publicly shunned his former master. Avarice was a strong incentive in the Dathyr lineage. Kayis rose to prominence while playing on everyone's fears while he campaigned for the highest office. The title warlock made most forget about their disagreement with Judas's expulsion. Many still held him in high regard.

But Kayis, seemingly born without a spine, lost her respect, long ago. Whatever physically attractive qualities he might have had fled with his character.

Kellis, the goblin, leaned forward, speaking to the room.

"Please, be seated."

Meristal sat at the table below the bench, the members looking down at her. A few aides bustled about, helping the scribes with parchment and ink, ready to record the proceedings.

"Greetings, members."

She folded her porcelain-white fingers in front of her.

Lagelm, the other goblin, smiled at her. His needle-sharp teeth peeking through the gap in his lips.

"For one such as you, it's our honor. How may we be of service?"

She paused, considering the collective. About half seemed interested in what she had to say, but others, like Kayis Dathyr and his cronies, Poplu and Capraro, had their minds made up.

Meristal's eyes finally went to Daylynn, and they locked eyes. The woman's face was impassive. The ancient rivalry had yet to cool, but rarely did it when betrayal lay at the heart. Bile rose in Meristal's mouth, but she masked her displeasure.

Meristal leaned forward, addressing the bench at large.

"I'm sure you've heard about the trolls attacking Wizard's Pass. Though repelled, the village is lost and many perished."

"Yes, we've heard," Kayis said, waving a dismissive hand. "Have you come with any fresh news, or have you come to plead the case of your loved one?"

He leaned back in his chair, reclined like a tyrant on a throne, a tight grin spreading on his lips.

"I believe my impeccable record is beyond reproach from the likes of you, Consul, but I thank you for your inquiry, though. And yes, I do come with fresh news, but the more you interrupt me, the longer it will take me to spit it out."

If the mood of the room was dark before, now it flickered with flashes of lightning. She kept her face placid and her voice neutral, as if questioning a witness on the stand. Her eyes held him, but she caught small smiles coming to a few delegates. She wouldn't be cowed.

Kayis bristled and sat up.

Meristal awaited the tantrum, but Lagelm cut in.

"I'm interested in what message she brings. Further outbursts won't be tolerated, Consul."

He threw Kayis a sour look of displeasure.

"Please, Madam Raviils, continue with the news."

Meristal nodded to him, grateful for the vote of confidence.

"The trolls laid siege to Wizard's Pass, and the Elyfian Enclave sent troops to Shadow City. Vampires routed the contingent with the aid of goblins."

"Curious," Dathyr said, leaning forward, "that the elyves marched to war without a declaration. I didn't ask for assistance. I wonder where they got the notion. You? The renegade warlock?"

"I wouldn't know."

"Wouldn't you?"

"I'm here in Ralloc, and Judas is fleeing to only the gods know where."

"Is he?"

"What are you implying, Consul?"

"We're aware of Wizard's Pass, and that goblins slipped through the Corridor and sought shelter in Shadow City. The question is: how are you familiar with those facts?"

"Wait ..."

Meristal stood, leaning on the table before her, this time looking at everyone.

"You knew about enemy movement, about both attacks, and have done nothing? You realize war is starting, and you're unprepared."

She looked to the center, right at Kayis, and spoke her next words.

"How does someone as incompetent as you become elected?"

Kayis's smile stretched, oily and filled with contempt. Meristal wasn't sure where he directed the contempt. Her? Judas? Ralloc in general?

"Careful!" he hissed. "You not only address your consul, but nobility as well, peasant."

Her cheeks flushed red, but her words came halting, fighting for control.

She loathed narrow-minded, pretentious people, and unfortunately, Judas was sometimes in that camp.

"You knew the goblins came through, and the vampires captured the elyves?"

"There is little I'm not privy to. So, the elyves want to play war, let them. What do I care? They're not wizardkind or Rallocan."

Meristal rarely lost her composure. She could see all sides of an argument and value each opinion for its uniqueness, but his attitude disgusted her.

"You're repulsive, cruel, and xenophobic! You have no honor or remorse, and your lack of morals makes you equal to Xilor."

A flurry of murmurs rippled through the room, the aides stilling, the scribes stopping. Even the other council members reacted as if they'd been slapped.

She breathed into the silence, then suddenly, hushed conversations filled the void, all the delegates conversing, acting like they weren't listening.

Kellis broke in before she could continue or the other erupt. He peered down the long bench towards the center.

"Who informed you about the goblins coming through the Corridor of Cruelty? I don't even know about that, and I'm a goblin! The elyves marched?"

"Yes," Dathyr said, almost reluctantly, "we know."

"We do?" Daylynn asked, incredulous. "I'm just now hearing about it."

"When did you hear of this disturbing news?" the other goblin, Lagelm, asked.

"Word reached my ears shortly before the attack. I was pondering on whether to tell the council or not, the outcome inevitable either way, and the elyves' defeat wouldn't sit well here."

"And lying to us would?" Sedrus, the centaur, asked. He stamped his hoof.

"It's not lying—" Dathyr began.

"—No, you just withheld important, time-critical information from us!" Daylynn said in clipped tones.

Meristal noted the color in her cheeks.

At least she has some sensibility left.

Meristal noted that Poplu and Capraro remained mute so far, but they were watching intently.

"Council members—" said Dathyr, holding up placating hands.

"Clearly, you're not doing your job," Kellis interjected.

Meristal wondered how both goblins would react upon hearing their race was involved in open rebellion. Both Kellis and Lagelm were of the Palatine caste and not the Leviathan, the latter having sided with Xilor.

Two castes defined goblins: Palatine elites with magic and vast numbers of Leviathan monstrosities.

"You forget your place, goblin," Dathyr said. "You don't get to question the authority of this office—"

"When you withhold information, it is. It's a blatant contradiction to the vows you swore when you assumed office."

"Don't talk to me about vows! Your race is in open rebellion!"

"Which we could've sent troops to quell," Sedrus said. "There'd be no uprising now."

Lagelm bared his teeth.

"And hampered Xilor's plans."

Dathyr shook his head and rolled his eyes.

"You can't believe he's returned. It was a sham, a hoax by the warlock. For all we know—"

"—We don't know anything!" Daylynn said, rising to her feet.

Lagelm leaned forward, glaring down the bench.

"You're so caught up in schemes and contempt that you can no longer do your job."

Sedrus crossed his arms.

"You betrayed our trust, your office, the people you are sworn to serve."

Dathyr opened his mouth, but Kellis cut him off.

"You tied our hands. You can no longer serve as consul."

"You can't be serious!" Dathyr scoffed.

The goblin shook his head.

"By our own laws, your abandonment of your duty, enforcement of laws, or malfeasant actions forces our hand."

Kayis searched for support among his peers, but Capraro and Poplu wisely remained silent. Even if they wanted to, there was nothing they could do. Kayis had lied or omitted facts, kept information from the assembly, and they held the capability to depose him.

Meristal was sure he had done so in the past, but such acts never reached their ears, let alone become public knowledge. In a closed session, Kayis might be able to slither out of his demise, but aides and members of the public were present. Tomorrow morning, his calamity would be in a special publishing of New Suns Times.

Todd might like this story. Might even get him to stop hounding Judas.

Lagelm spoke up.

"You allowed your hate to cloud your judgement, and your dereliction has caused untold suffering. For what purpose?"

Kayis visibly ground his teeth.

"You don't understand. The warlock must be hunted down—"

"So, you what?" Daylynn asked. "Allowed an invading force to attack a village and move into the Ralloc domain to draw him out?"

"How many people died by your lack of action?" Sedrus asked.

"And for what?" Lagelm asked. "Power? You don't care about the people of this realm."

"Good thing Meristal came…" Daylynn said.

Meristal's eyes widened.

"Otherwise, we'd be blind to your dereliction."

"You can't be—dereliction?" Dathyr said.

"You've brought great dishonor to your position, and the House of

Dathyr," Kellis said.

He looked down the row at the ensemble.

"All those for Consul Kayis Dathyr's deposition, speak now."

"Aye."

"Aye."

"Aye."

Sedrus, Kellis, and Lagelm turned to Daylynn. Meristal watched her dither under the pressure of the tally and the scrutiny of their gaze. Three others remained, and the vote was tied. Piero Capraro and Vamor Poplu would never go against Kayis, tied by politics and House alignments.

The deciding factor came down to Daylynn Reese and her penchant for ambiguity.

Meristal held her breath.

Come on, surely you're tired of fucking him.

"Aye," she concurred.

The other two kept silent.

Four-to-two, and the deposed can't vote. That's official, now.

Lagelm spoke, glancing down at the scribes.

"It is the council's decision that Kayis Dathyr will step down immediately. Record that in the log."

For a moment, none of the scribes moved, then as one, they began scribbling. A deposed consul only happened a few times in their history. The time-honored procedure between the relieving of a consul, whether voluntary or involuntary, was for the consul to bow to the body, showing respect of the office, position, and responsibilities it held. The committee would return the bow. Dathyr, prideful like his cousin, Vamor Poplu, spat on the floor before storming off.

Meristal shook her head.

What a pitiful person.

"Who shall take the mantle?" Sedrus asked.

"I suppose you want it?" Poplu jeered from the other end of the bench. "It'll be a cold day in the Underworld before I let that happen!"

"It *is* cold in the Underworld, sycophant!" Kellis said.

"We have a problem," Lagelm said.

"What?"

"There's no way for us to choose who the consul is and pull the majority to pass if we are voting ourselves. It must be a four to two, minimum, and Poplu and Capraro will veto anyone we nominate within our ranks."

"Damn right," Poplu said. "So, you might as well bring him back."

"What do you suggest?" Daylynn asked.

"We elect in a temporary solution until elections can be held," Lagelm said. "There's a bypass if there's cause, which there is: war."

"I've never heard of such an amendment!" Capraro blurted, joining the conversation.

Lagelm turned his attention to Meristal.

"Advocate? Can you shed some light on the statute I am speaking of?"

Meristal nodded.

"Yes, you're correct, there must be a precedent. With a war, you can select a temporary appointee under the pretense that once the war is over, elections are held."

Daylynn frowned.

"What are the limitations of such an individual?"

Meristal shrugged and shook her head.

"The statute offers no limits and grants full consul authority. A temporary appointee must either step down or stand for election once the crisis ends. Any challenge triggers a special election, same as the usual law."

"What is the length of term they can serve?" Sedrus asked.

"As long as necessary."

"See?" Lagelm said.

"Who do you suggest?" Kellis questioned.

Lagelm went still for a moment, then turned his head to Meristal.

"For now, we let Madam Raviils finish before deciding. Then, with all the facts presented, we can better decide."

"Excellent suggestion," Sedrus agreed, and eyed Meristal. "Please, continue."

His expression gave nothing away. Per Judas's inner circle, they were to treat each other as near-strangers, but Sedrus had abandoned them, and Meristal couldn't guess how he'd react.

Meristal resumed her seat as did the representatives. She took a few moments to collect her thoughts and then launched back into her message.

"Warlock Lakayre suggested Xilor's next move will be against Cape Gythmel. With three attacks to date, and the trolls, goblins, and now vampires siding with him, it's coming soon."

She paused briefly to catch her breath.

"Judas thinks that the lower domain holds no significance at this time, with little strategic value. We believe that if he controls Ralloc, the rest of the realms, and possibly all Ermaeyth, will fall without a fight."

"Is that all you have to report at this time?" Kellis asked.

"Yes."

He nodded.

"I have faith in Warlock Lakayre's wisdom. He's never been wrong before, and I don't think he'd start now."

"I concur," Lagelm added. "We should see if the fairies will lend aid, and the saricrocians. Those are some pretty big 'ifs'."

"Agreed," said Daylynn Reese. "We'll issue orders to deploy some of the army to Cape Gythmel by way of a portal. I think it wise to leave a large contingent here in case the vampires or goblins make a fast attack against Ralloc."

"Sensible," said Sedrus. "The only order left is who will lead the army, and who is the newly appointed consul. We should also nominate a representative to the front lines to assist with communication."

Meristal's lips thinned. She didn't know if she should say anything, but it was better to ask for forgiveness than for permission.

"There's something else," she broke in. "The Heir of Valin sent a squad of the Black Tide out to conduct war game scenarios. This was before knowing about Xilor's return. Since they are already mobile, we should send them a portal master to teleport them to Cape Gythmel."

"The Krey are marching?" Sedrus asked. His voice dripped with suspicion and worry.

"I thought that was against the law!" Daylynn said. "What's to stop them from marching on Ralloc?"

"It isn't against the law," Meristal said. "I checked. The War Council convened and signed off on their expedition. They're not marching to war but for training purposes. As far as I know, they're oblivious. But now that we are at war, we should use them to fortify Cape Gythmel."

"Those are some amazing coincidences," Kellis said slowly. "How did they realize we were at war before we did?"

"As I said, 'war game scenarios.'"

"That you did," Kellis said.

"Even if they did march on Ralloc," Meristal said, "which they aren't, one squad of Krey couldn't take the city. You have nothing to fear."

Lagelm stirred.

"For our representative on the front lines to facilitate communication, we should send Kayis Dathyr. Those in favor?"

Another vote, four to two.

He regarded Dathyr who sat in a pew at the far end of the room.

"You're in charge of the mission and its completion until relieved of duty by one of higher authority or commanding officer of the Grand Royal Army. Should you fail to act in a responsible manner, you'll be exiled, like your former mentor. Your shame will haunt your family's honor and community standing."

"Speaking of your former mentor," Meristal started without being able to stop, "I think it's only fitting that you should answer to him at the Corridor. You're in charge of the army, but you'll ultimately answer to him."

Once she realized what she did, she closed her mouth.

Can't believe I overstepped.

"That … is a great idea," Lagelm said.

"I concur," Kellis said. "It's settled. Now then, the new consul?"

"I would be honored," Sedrus said.

"Yes, you'd be good," Lagelm said with a nod, "but we're at war now, and bloodshed doesn't suit you. Besides, Poplu and Capraro would block your nomination because you cannot vote for yourself. We must think outside the immediate council."

"I agree, but who?" Daylynn asked. "Master Jynerul Tyku?"

"No," Kellis said. "He'd serve best on the battlefield. Madam Meristal? Have you ever considered politics?"

Oh, no, I'm not about to do that.

"Yes, but I was considered too radical for most. I'm an Advocate of Law, and retired now. Perhaps Judas?"

"Under the circumstances," Kellis said, "I'd say you're the best choice. Powerful, wise, an absolute grasp of legislation, and absent an apprentice. Besides, Judas is a warlock and cannot hold any title or office."

Well, just change his damn title, then.

"You have ample time as you are retired," Lagelm said.

Daylynn turned her head, looking at her, and she gave a single nod.

"You're the next best choice."

By the gods, that must've been hard for her to admit.

Meristal could see she struggled with the words, knowing how hard it must have been to admit.

"You're admired by many," Sedrus said. "Peasant and noble alike. And you've served Ralloc and our Republic for many years."

Kellis nodded.

Meristal met their eyes, each of them, and she looked at Daylynn last. She saw the anger there, but something else, too.

I can't believe this is about to happen.

"It's time for a vote," Sedrus called. "All for Meristal as the new consul? I agree to the appointment and place my vote with her."

"Aye."

"Aye."

Daylynn swallowed.

"Aye."

Lagelm rose to his feet, almost disappearing under the bench.

"It's agreed, then! Consul Meristal? What is your first act?"

Meristal drew in a deep breath.

Shit.

Chapter 56: The Place Of Origins

Imposing, fog-covered mountains filled Julie's vision. Her eyes tracked up until the elevation became lost from sight, peaks obscured by white cotton swirls. Climbing the daunting beasts urged her to turn back, and the subtle mystical impulse grew stronger by the moment.

Her mantra of never being weak again persisted, a vigil that spurred her on.

Who commands you? An arcane urge? You're not about to walk away just because someone else wants you to.

But she could not deny the desire with the mountains so close.

"What is this place?"

"The Melodic Mountains," Ava answered. "There's a repelling enchantment upon these lands."

"Who causes this?"

The ability to compel people is a good enough reason to stay, to learn the secret.

"The fairies maintain the enchantment with our presence, but we didn't place it."

"Who else lives here besides the fairies and Fife Doole?"

Julie shot her a sidelong glance.

Ava shook her head, her bottom lip protruding.

"No one; few mortals have set foot here, including Warlock Lakayre. Oh, and Meristal! Perhaps, someday, I'll share the story."

Julie glanced at Ava, not sure she'd heard right.

"Meristal was here before?"

"Yes, long ago."

Again, she regarded the mountains, and already her throat felt dry.

"We won't get any closer just standing here."

With Ava leading, Julie followed her up a rutted path snaking back and forth between towering cypress trees. The incline and treacherous footing compelled Julie to save her breath as her muscles ached, lungs burned, and sweat poured down her spine. Several times, Julie checked her footing, almost falling.

The mountain air smelled of rain and damp decay. A thin humidity clung about them. With a slow pace and mind-numbing exertion, an eternity could've passed. She was surprised and grateful when she reached a plateau.

"Welcome to Fife's, mistress."

Julie swiveled her head, expecting more. Her eyes darted around, noting the empty clearing hedged by trees. A brook bubbled in the distance to the right, and a well-worn path led away, further into the dense trees in the same direction.

"Where is it?"

She felt her composure slipping. The embers of a cold fury kindled within her. Had she wasted her time to come all this way for nothing?

You fool.

Oh, shut the fuck up.

The anger subsided as she waited for a more logical explanation. Perhaps she wasn't seeing something.

"There are many potent enchantments placed here."

Julie's eyes locked on the little creature hovering nearby as her musings turned to what she'd said. The possibility of learning the powerful mysteries lay within her grasp. One additional task. About this time, she realized the book remained silent. Had it all been a ruse? She expected more from the elusive tome.

"Mistress?"

Emotions in check, Julie blinked, coming back to the moment, and regarded her.

"Yes, what is it, Ava?"

"I've done my duty and brought you, as you asked, and kept you from harm. Now that my task is complete, I must return to my home. Should you need me, call my name, and I'll answer."

Julie nodded once. At this point, she needed to be alone. It wasn't that she disliked Ava, but with her irritation, she wouldn't be fit company.

It was all a waste of time!

The only good thing to come from her entire journey happened when she met Kam and Lily. That alone made the trip worth the effort, but she expected more.

Can't forget Harold, too.

But she couldn't have Ava thinking she was ungrateful. The fairy went out of her way to aid her.

"Thank you for helping me, Ava. I'll call upon you again. You have my word."

"Thank you, mistress, most kind of you. It was an honor to serve you."

The fairy vanished, leaving Julie alone, flustered at finding nothing. In fact, she was like an exposed nerve right now. Everything that could've gone wrong did, and in the end, she was worse off for it. Ava wasn't the problem, but she was the easiest target to take out her ire, to blame, and she didn't want that.

Best not to chase her off.

She pulled off her pack and sat down, rubbing her temples. After a few deep breaths, she pulled out the book, her hand rubbing the cover.

"I can't believe I listened to a book."

She tossed it deeper into the clearing. Grabbing her pack, she made it to her feet, and threw her arms through the loops. Then, she started back down the trail.

She retreated a half-dozen steps when whispers tickled her ears. She stopped, glancing back, her eyes falling on the discarded tome. The familiarity stole over her. It was just like in the swamp.

She glanced down the trail, seeing the tiny village far below. She really didn't want to go all the way back down, not when she turned her back now, knowing it'd eat at her. With a sigh, she retraced her steps, picking up the book. In her hands, the whispers became clear, the book calling to her, glowing, light escaping the closed pages.

"Your name, speak it. The Place of Origins opens for the Bearer of Secrets alone."

"Julie."

Nothing happened.

"Your true name isn't the one you recognize, but the name your parents gave you."

How the hell does the book know that?

"How in the Underworld am I supposed to know a name I've never heard?"

"We only impart for guidance. Speak your name, free of emotion, untainted by ambition, and what is locked will open."

The book went silent.

What the fuck?

She shook her head. In her hand, the book trembled, and a soothing peace resonated within her, driving away her agitation and growing despair. More than that, she could feel something touching the edges of her essence. There was power here, waiting to be opened, waiting to be claimed. The book's warning cautioned her zeal. She sealed her feelings away. It would never be hers if she didn't unlock the Place of Origins.

Closing her eyes, Julie cleared her mind and let the aura wash over her, seeping into her essence. The ancient aura suffused her mind. Garbled fragments of voices, disjointed images echoed through her head. It was like she relived the same day over and over again with slight variations.

Those images blurred together. She couldn't distinguish the man clearly, like water had filled her eyes. His face loomed near, young and happy.

"She is beautiful," the man said. "Like her mother."

"What should we call her?" her mother asked, weary but happy. "Hope?"

"No, she's an angel."

"Look at her eyes; they twinkle like stars."

"I'm fond of a name in the druid language: Starriace. It means 'daughter of the sky.'"

"Starriace? I like that name."

The image faded, and darkness smothered her. She sensed someone, a woman, familiar, but not her mother. Her eyes still blurred, but she could detect a chin and lips.

"Hello, little one," the new woman said.

She sounded like thousands of voices speaking in unison, obscuring her true voice. Her words were warm, affectionate, but distant.

"I'm sorry that I am the one to take you from the life you would have, but no one will remember your beginning. It is safer this way, for you to fade from time. I have witnessed, and that is enough, but I can't see your end. No end knows you."

She paused, drawing near. A press of warm lips against Julie's head, the memory so strong she felt it in the present.

"Welcome, Starriace, daughter of the sky."

"Starriace?" she breathed, uncertain.

Her eyes opened, the air shimmering before her, revealing Fife Doole's old cottage. Unscathed, undamaged, untouched for ages, protected by his wards. The front door and windows remained shut, no light illuminating the interior. The small, rickety chimney remained quiet, free of smoke.

Discovering her name, reliving memories, and opening the veiled place fed her hubris.

She'd passed the test and, resolved, she approached the door.

The allure of knowledge hastened her steps. Soon, they'd be in her grasp. Her mind raced, trying to imagine what she'd find, what form the enigmas would take. Texts and scrolls? An amulet? She could almost touch them, read them, consume them.

And I'll never be helpless again.

An aura resonated from within the hut walls. She could feel it from outside. The journey she'd embark on would shape the future. In the presence of the old hut, Rusem and Judas's teachings diminished.

Her time had come.

Opening the door, she stepped through and crept within.

From the cluttered interior to how low the table and shelves sat, Fife Doole was indeed of small stature. Though cramped and overstuffed, the house was meticulously kept, its owner a pretentiously tidy individual and a perfectionist.

Though pure speculation on her part, Fife must've been without a companion at the end of his life. The cozy house lacked the touch of a woman.

With cautious care, she tested the small stool by the workbench, unsure if it would hold her weight. Papers and books covered the desk, and she methodically pored through them, hoping for discovery. A project caught her eye, and she judged it to be from his later years, the writing large, not as cramped or sharp as previous works she leafed through.

Scrolls lay to the side of the desk, a neat stack with all wax seals facing the same direction. A few loitered behind the stack, unsealed. Hesitation rippled through her; a dreaded sense of invasion and violation infected her. Fife was long gone, but his works and artifacts remained. A sense of wrongness at rifling through his possessions made her waver.

The ludicrous moment passed, and she snatched up the first unsealed scroll. She unrolled the parchment carefully, the leaf crinkling as the scrawled title filled the top: Time Displacement.

Julie didn't understand what she read, but pieces stuck out, fragments of words like the false timeline or time reversal. Time, to her, always seemed to be a continuous entity, flowing forward. The possibility of time being false or going in reverse never crossed her mind. Thinking about such things provoked her to return to the book she received in the swamps.

She placed it on the table.

"We have returned with the Bearer. He comes."

A flash of light shot out inside the hut, strong enough to make the walls tremble. She blinked her eyes, chasing the spots away. When she could see again, the halfling stood before her. He wasn't a ghost, but not quite a solid state, almost transparent before solidifying.

Once he became real, it slammed into her like never before.

The magelust.

She crashed to the floor, her back slamming against the ground, driving the air from her lungs. She couldn't breathe. Liquid fire poured through her body, simmering beneath her skin. Her mouth opened, sucking in breath that wouldn't come.

This was so much better and so much worse than she had ever felt with Kam. Then, it'd tickled her, stirred her, compelled her, but now, it trampled her underfoot like the stampede of a horde.

The pain in her head was so strong she thought her skull cleaved in two. Her vision watered, everything sliding out of focus. She trembled as she took her first sweet breath in eternity. It came ragged, shuddering, like a hot knife between the ribs.

Her body contracted, every muscle tense as she drowned in the lust. Agony lanced her from her sex to her throat, a sword slicing through her insides. The restrictive cocoon of her clothes had to go. Her hands flung to her robes, ripping them open, exposing her breasts, trying to shake out as quickly as possible.

"Stop!"

The voice had been deafening, or it was a whisper; either way, a wave of energy slammed into her.

Fife held out his hand, his fingers splayed. All at once, the pain, the pleasure, ceased to exist, and in its place, embarrassment and shame.

Her head hung as she hastily closed her robes.

"What's happening to me?" she cried. Of all the things she'd endured, including Mr. Pleasure, this had been the most terrifying—the absolute inability to be in control.

"That is the magelust; has no one told you how to control it?"

Julie didn't trust herself to speak, so she shook her head.

"Everyone is different; I shall adjust my shield to compensate for your inabilities, yes? In time, you will learn to control your own; it is not something that can be taught, but learned from within, you understand?"

Julie nodded, drying her eyes.

"Introductions are in order, is that not so, Starriace?"

She glanced up at him from her haunches, seeing him for the first time, realizing he knew her birth name, and she didn't know how she felt about that.

He dipped his head in a bow.

"I'm Fife Doole."

The halfling was bald on top with shaggy silver hair circling the sides and back. His bushy mustache grew out the sides of his face and merged with his shaggy beard of the same color, the latter growing past his waistband. Fierce, dark green eyes scrutinized her.

Holding her robes closed, tucking them behind her sash, she found her voice.

"What are you?"

"I'm a halfling, Grand Maghai of the Stratu'Geim domain, and the last survivor of the Great Wizards Council. I lived and taught many prominent wizards throughout time, including your father. And surely Judas spoke of me, is that not so?"

She swallowed back her confusion. It was a lot to take in, his title, Judas, her father, his strange cadence of speaking.

"You knew my father?"

"Oh yes, Starriace."

She shook her head.

"Please, don't call me by that name."

"Why? It's your name, isn't it? Denial is death."

Did she really have to explain it to him? That name, what she was supposed to be, even if real, wasn't her. She was Julie, wasn't she?

"You've traveled a long way, haven't you?"

Fife spoke with an odd rhythm, alien enough to recognize the Myshku language wasn't his primary language. Maybe not even his second or third.

Julie nodded, unsure how to respond.

"They say," Fife began, "the greatest wizards die young, but the wisest live longest, and all are forged in hardship. Traveling here wasn't easy, was it? Hardship tempers the mind. So, what is better, to be great or to be wise?"

The question hung unanswered for a long time. What was she supposed to say?

"Well, Starriace, I've waited long for you to come to me and begin your training. I must say, you are much older than expected. But we have now met, have we not? And you're a lot less educated than I hoped for—a clear failing. But you've come, and that's what matters, yes?"

She didn't know why, but hearing him disregard her wishes irked her. It was like he was trying to erase her, overwrite the person she was. Starriace may have been her when she was born, but Julie was the one who survived.

"My name is Julie, not Starriace, so stop calling me that."

Fife cocked an eyebrow.

"Denial is death, yes? Child, do you know who gave you the name?"

She answered, almost as if compelled.

"A man."

"Yes, your father."

Julie tried to keep tears from her eyes. She didn't know where they were coming from; all that mattered was keeping them from forming in front of him.

"Where are my parents? Are they dead?"

"No, Starriace, they're very much alive. Your place among the inhabitants of the *Other Side* was kept secret for your protection."

An unbidden thought came to her, and she gave it voice.

"You speak of secrets, and it might be foolish to ask, but I must: is Judas's daughter alive?"

Why do you care anymore? After everything he let happen to you?

The tiny man frowned.

"Who told you about her?"

"The book."

It seemed an age ago that Judas had given it to her.

"Really? Interesting ... and cruel."

"Well? Is she?"

"She is ... dead, in a manner of speaking."

"In a manner of speaking ...?"

"Worry not, but yes, she is. However, it is possible to awaken her," he said.

His gaze dropped to his beard again, and he rolled the hair between his fingers.

"Yes, it's possible to bring her back."

"How?"

"Best not to think too far ahead, young one, you will hurt yourself. It's deep magic you're exploring, and foolish for a neophyte."

"But I thought people who are dead can't come back to life?"

To this, Fife Doole said nothing. Her brain reeled from words spoken and those left unvoiced.

Raising the dead is possible?

Hope flared in her chest. She could do this for Judas's daughter, as well as for Meristal's child. But then another realization came to her. She wished Judas's daughter still lived, that she was his daughter, but Fife's revelation dashed those wayward dreams. With the truth out, he quashed her aspiration.

An ache languished in her chest, and the cold voice reminded her of the atrocities she endured, and the man who let it happen. The emotions came back to haunt her, the binding the book placed on her released.

He's not a bad man, just incautious.

"Put away your emotions," Fife said, cutting through her thoughts. "They'll do you no good for what is to come. You are here to train, not cry, is that not so?"

"I want to learn more about my parents. I want to see them."

"No."

Fife frowned for a moment and then softened, as did his voice.

"You'll see them soon enough, child, when the time is right, but whenever is the right time? This time, last time, a time yet discovered?"

He chuckled, then shook his head.

"More important things take precedence over a reunion, or have you forgotten the carnage you saw in your Shadowcasting?"

"How did you—?"

"I know many things, or did you think you and Harold were the only Shadowcasters?"

He chuckled again.

"Would you like to visit your parents?" Fife asked.

She nodded.

"Then study, train in earnest, because the dead have no eyes for the living, yes?"

Crestfallen and slightly perturbed, she watched Fife Doole waddle around the table and help himself to a stool. He pointed to the stool opposite him, and Julie rose from the floor, still holding her robes shut with one hand. Once seated, he took her hands in his and looked into her eyes.

"Clear your mind of everything, Starriace. The only thing that matters now is your acceptance of who you are, what you are, and what you are here to do. Out of the basic skills and arts, you must choose your path. It's the power of the mind. Not many understand. Most place faith in incantations. Fools they are, is that not so? Too easy to use and defend, yes? I'll teach you the hard way, but you'll never understand how hard, because you'll have nothing to compare it to."

He let go of her hands and gave her a small smile.

"Are you willing to try?"

She swallowed. What he proposed sounded horrible, but if it was the path to power, to never be weak again, how could she refuse? She nodded.

"Yes."

Fife gave a single nod.

"Good. Judas started you on the path to unlocking your mind; I shall finish it. But opening your soul? Only you can do that. Tomorrow we start."

Chapter 57: Julie And Fife

Fife showed Julie to her bed and bade her goodnight. There would be time for questions later, and she needed the rest. Dawn came early, and Fife woke Julie with a sharp crack of his staff on her bed, bolting her upright, her head slamming into the low ceiling above.

Fife chuckled heartily.

"I do that to every apprentice on the first day, and it's still funny." He smiled. "You would like breakfast?"

Julie rubbed her head in agitation, a headache blossoming behind her eyes.

"Yes."

"Then, you should rise earlier, should you not? It's much too late, and you're delaying your first lessons. Do you think this is an inn?"

"No."

This early in the morning, with the pain in her head, she was already irritated.

"You never said when I had to get up."

"You should've asked. You will rise before the sun each day. Do you understand?"

He pulled on his beard, his green gaze piercing her, measuring her.

"I understand."

She threw off the sheets, swinging her legs over the side of the bed.

"Master," he supplied.

"What?"

Fife rapped her lightly on the head with his rod.

"Master! You'll address me as master or grand maghai, is that so hard?"

She narrowed her eyes.

"Would you stop doing that?"

He rapped her again.

"Master."

"Ow, fuck, do you know how much that hurts?"

He hit her again, this time harder.

"Master. You'll address me as master or grand maghai."

"Shades of the Underworld, would you stop that ... Master?"

He smiled somewhat.

"Better."

She couldn't trust herself not to say what she really thought, so she only nodded. Her mind darted back to Rusem's ring. She had but to put it on, and she could leave.

"Get dressed, Starriace, and meet me outside."

When she didn't respond promptly, he raised his staff in warning.

"Yes, Master."

The ring's sounding better by the second.

But she hadn't even trained yet. Surely there was something to learn, even if his methods were eccentric. Hadn't Judas trained under him?

He probably got the same treatment.

And if he could do it, so could she. She'd endure pretty much any hardship as long as it meant she wouldn't be weak.

Her mood didn't improve when she stubbed her toe on a chest in her room, or when she sprained her wrist as her fist smashed into the low ceiling while slipping into the robes. Twice she smacked her head on the low ceiling as she headed to the door, darkening her surly temperament.

By the time she exited the small hut, she cursed like a storm, and her presence roiled like a cyclone. The blinding, early morning light of the suns did little to improve her disposition. Fife had his back to her as she entered the clearing to the side of his hut.

Strike him down, the voice urged. *You'll feel better.*

While sorely tempted, she knew she wouldn't live long after that. She'd felt the magelust manifest in his presence, and if the strength responded by magical prowess, she'd be inconsequential to him.

"I can see giving up power is difficult for you."

Fife faced her as she closed the distance.

"Do you not like feeling helpless, Starriace?"

"My name's Julie."

An invisible wave smacked her on the side of the head, right where her headache blossomed. She bit back curses and the thoughts of retaliation.

"My name's Julie, Master."

He nodded and paced, his short legs making his movements almost a waddle. Now that Julie stood fully erect—which wasn't tall—she noticed Fife only came up to the top of her thigh.

"Your name's Starriace. Should I not call you by your true name?"

With Fife speaking Myshku as a foreign language, and the ache erupting in her head, she didn't bother arguing with him.

Call me whatever you want, little man. My name's Julie, and you can't change that!

"You're my Master, and you may call me what you wish."

Fife's eyes flickered for a moment, doubting her honesty.

"Shall we begin?"

He sat with legs crossed and waited. When she didn't mirror him, his eyes narrowed.

"Sit."

Julie complied.

I don't have to call you Master when I don't respond.

"Master humility, Starriace. Submission and obedience inherently create a sense of discipline and respect."

He closed his eyes, and Julie warily followed suit.

"I wake all my apprentices the same way, causing headaches to teach them their first lesson; but you're a slow learner, so you'll receive several lessons today, is that not so? Rumigul is about the power of the mind, and yours is hurting, is it not? Before magic turns outward, you must turn inward."

He took a breath.

"Clear your mind except my voice and your pain. Sense where it ends, how far it stretches, where your brain ends and your skull begins. Follow the pulse, the throb, can you do that, Starriace?"

Julie followed Fife's instruction while ignoring the name, tracing the edges of her misery. The throbbing reached her eyes, an ache similar to lack of sleep. At last, she traced the entire area of her headache.

"Yes, I can."

"Now, visualize it."

"How, Master?"

"As anything you wish. You possess an imagination, do you not?"

Julie repressed a sigh and imagined her pain as a ball of bright, white light, which hurt her eyes.

"I have done so."

"What do you envision?"

"A ball of white light."

"Ah, white light, very good. Most people think of it as a light, but white is good, isn't it? Blinding and painful, just like the suns. Darken it."

"How?"

"Imagine your light like that of the sky, darkening as the sun sets. Darken it and your torment will recede."

So, Julie darkened the white light, changing from blinding white to a darker shade of gray. Immediately, she noted a reduction of discomfort, but it still lingered.

She heard Fife inhale.

"Now darkened, picture a cloud of steam from boiling water. As it rises, it disappears. Separate your malady as steam."

She did as instructed, imagining the now gray light as mist, watching it dissipate the further it went from the source. Again, the ache yielded. The smog dissipated within the bubble where the light had been, only a slight twinge remained.

"Now, make your bubble small."

Julie shrank the bubble, collapsing it until the last of her headache was gone. She opened her eyes.

"Is it that simple?"

The invisible force rapped her on the head.

"Ow—is it that simple, Master?"

"For headaches, yes. Rumigul is the power of the mind. I foresee you having many more headaches while here, Starriace."

Julie's lips twisted, but otherwise remained silent.

"Defend yourself!"

Fife leaped to his feet, far more spry than she'd thought possible for such a small, old being. He twirled his staff as it caught aflame, slamming the end into the ground. A wall of fire raced toward her.

She let out a yelp, scrambled to her feet, and dove to the side. The fire went past as she rolled up to her feet, fumbling for her wand. Once free, her limited repertoire of spells flew across the distance. Fife batted them away with the flick of his hand.

"Do better, child! Use your mind!"

An invisible fist hit Julie in the chest, lifting her up off her feet. She landed hard on her tailbone and rolled up backward.

Her hair splayed in a mess as she hurriedly brushed it out of her eyes. A ball of ice formed in the gnomling's hand, and he launched it. The icy sphere smashed her in the chest, driving the wind from her lungs. In a terrifying moment, she felt more than heard the detectable crack, her ribs breaking from the impact.

A deep cold raced down her body.

"You're half-trained and poorly educated, Starriace."

She sucked in breath, barely hearing his words. Flame rose from his palm like a flickering inferno, launching pebble-sized balls of fire. Still gasping, Julie ran sideways, trying to outrun the searing volley. She dove behind a willow to catch her breath.

"Do you think a tree will stop an attack?"

A loud crack resonated at Julie's back; splinters furrowed along her spine, her scalp blazed with fire from shrapnel. The wood groaned. Fife had blasted the tree, shattering the trunk. Another groan and it started to topple, falling toward her.

She dove, the trunk missing her by inches. A sharp ache punctured her ribs as she rolled up to her feet, her left hand going there.

Fife, over ten meters away, swept his stick in front of him, knocking her legs out from under her, and she toppled backward, her head bouncing off the ground.

Head pounding, she rolled over, facing Fife. With a sneer, she muttered a curse, hoping to catch him off guard. Again, Fife motioned with his hand. Instead of batting it away, he sent it back at her, the curse rebounding off Julie's chest. Red fell over her gaze, her body burning in distress. Blood seeped from her scalp, running into her eyes, courtesy of the splinters of the exploding tree.

"Are you so weak that you can't defend yourself, Starriace?"

His words sounded like mockery.

I hate you!

She didn't know if that was the pain speaking, resentment, or embarrassment. Deep within, a beast wanting to claw its way out of her throat.

She struggled to her feet, dodging an additional wave of energy, more from stumbling than skill. Rage rose as blood trickled from her nose. It came to her naturally, the anger, like the harder her heart beat, the more she felt.

Without conscious thought, she lashed out, and maybe that's what he wanted. The spell erupted from her wand, intent on annihilating the gnomling. The ground ripped, churned in the invisible wake. Fife waved his hands down into the ground, the energy subsiding, killing her attack.

"Better. But you're relying on hate, are you not?"

He motioned with his hand, and Julie felt a sudden jolt shoot up her left arm. A small rock the size of her fist struck the ground at her feet.

"Hate is a good motivator, Starriace, but fear is even greater. You don't properly understand your abilities. You don't fear."

His hand moved again, but this time, in an upward motion, lifting Julie into the air. The wand slipped from her fingers, her feet two meters from the ground. Hands struggled for her neck; the air constricted as he held her.

"You should be very afraid, Starriace. Fear begets respect."

Whether from a lack of air or the sound of Fife's voice, panic shot through her. The pulse of her heart thundered in her ears, her lungs raw and scorched. Still, he held her as she felt veins spiderweb across her forehead and along her face.

He's going to kill me!

Undeniable terror reached her eyes.

Fife stirred.

"There's the fear I speak of."

He smiled at her, and it only seemed cruel to her.

"Your enemies will kill you without hesitation. They lack nobility. Remember that."

With an overhand motion of his rod, Julie plummeted to the ground.

Julie gasped for breath, her eyes snapping open. She was still seated as before, her legs still crossed. Her hands flew to her face and came away clean, no trace of blood. Even her hair, which should be unkempt from the fight, remained neat and tidy.

Though no physical injuries manifested, the soreness throbbed as if real. Across from her, Fife opened his eyes and stood, using his staff for support.

"We didn't fight?" she asked.

A quick rap across her skull reminded her of protocol.

"No, we didn't, Starriace. Would you have preferred that? Destroying my yard in a scuffle is not the best method to teach you, yes?"

"I hurt all over."

"Another lesson, yes? Learn how to ease your pain."

He waddled back to his hut when he stopped and turned to her.

"You did well when you quit muttering incantations like a fool. Rumigul uses the mind, not the mouth."

Julie winced as she repositioned.

"Tend to your wounds," he said, leaving her to apply the earlier lessons to her body.

The next morning, Fife Doole stood outside his house, his stick twirling lazily in his hands, waiting for her arrival. She emerged from the hut at a slow pace, exhaustion oozing from her. All night she healed the 'wounds' inflicted by their battle of minds, forgoing sleep. She had yet to eat, dressing slowly with her sore muscles screaming in protest.

Fife didn't speak when she stopped in front of him. She shifted her weight, hiding her discomfort. His unorthodox methods, his relentless demand for deference, and Myshku not being his primary language, annoyed her to no end. The words he spoke were curt, brash, but his tone denied such prejudice. In the sole day she'd spent with him, he taught her many things, primarily awe and dread.

He could have killed me with ease.

That was the most intimidating part. When Julie accompanied Judas, she'd known he was powerful, yet he never displayed or flaunted his brilliance. In fact, he went out of his way to refrain from doing magic. But Fife humiliated her with an ease that belied his skill.

No, he just kicked my ass.

And maybe she needed it, to motivate her to do better, to never be weak and helpless again.

His skill and prowess on blatant display pulled the wool from her eyes. Another epiphany arose from her devastating defeat: the awareness of being on the losing end, a place she never wanted to be again. And Fife was right, if she lost, her enemies wouldn't be noble.

Her pride was just as bruised as her body. Despite her helplessness against Mr. Pleasure, he merely dominated her; Fife confronted her with her wand at the ready, alert and observant, which made her defeat all the more terrifying. She noted the difference between the two: being helpless and attempting, or just finding yourself helpless.

With reflection, she reconciled the difference in lessons, magical versus without. In a minor aspect, she learned to heal. Removing aches, swelling of muscle, and bruised bones took time and energy. He had shown her the door, as Judas always said, but Julie twisted the knob, and Fife kicked her through. She struggled with the lesson, but the benefit outweighed her efforts.

Perhaps there's something to these teachings.

Fife raised an eyebrow.

She needed to attain mastery, but she didn't have to like him. Rusem's ring crept back into her mind.

I could just leave…

"Good morning, Master."

"A morning of goodness to you as well."

He pulled on his shaggy beard.

"Today, we study a new lesson: respect. What do you think that means, Starriace?"

I have so many answers for you, little man.

Julie remained silent until she found a satisfactory answer.

"Submission to an elder, letting the elder have the right of way or letting them speak and not interrupting."

"Wrong!" Fife Doole said in a stern voice. "… and correct. But I'm not talking about reverence for people but of things."

"Calling people by their correct names, Master?"

"No, a name is the wrong type of thing. Try again with less attitude."

Julie took a deep breath, pondering what the gnomling wished to hear. His instructional method differed from all she experienced thus far, a practical application compared to Judas's by-the-tome-while-on-the-run approach, and Rusem's freely given knowledge. The latter appealed to her more than she cared to admit, but she had scruples about effortless attainment. *If it's easy, it probably wasn't worth it.*

The warlock's method would be better suited for a classroom environment. Still, she took an immediate disliking to Fife.

If I never submit, I'll never get anything out of his training.

Thinking back over her journey, a brief flash of the innkeeper in Far Point came to mind.

"Someone's religion. You never know if theirs is the correct one or not. Also, showing disrespect to the religion can create a great deal of enemies."

Fife's lower lip protruded in thought, his brows rippling.

"True. Though not having consideration for a religion can't kill you, unless, of course, you offend the zealots."

He adjusted the rod in his hand.

"I'm talking about respect for magic, Starriace. Was it so difficult? It'll kill you faster than all else, either by an adversary or improper use. Always appreciate what you can do with it and what it can do to you, yes?"

She nodded, and that seemed to satisfy him.

"Magic allows you to use, direct, and channel, but never dominate. Absolute dominion isn't impossible, but not plausible. Not unless ... " he trailed off and looked at her. "You'd dedicate more years than you have to obtain that level. Now, child, how powerful does your essence allow you to be?"

"Are you saying I'll never gain control, Grand Maghai? Then, why waste my time?"

"I didn't say you won't possess an element of control. Clean out your ears, Starriace!"

She listened as Fife repeated his first question again.

"How powerful does your essence allow you to be?"

"As powerful as it lets you, I suppose, Master."

"No, no. Not the bottomless well; the abilities already within you. What you are born with."

"I don't know, Master."

She hated to admit it, but him speaking of endless potential intrigued her.

"Before you can tap into the well, you must find your limits and expand beyond. You feel your essence, but you don't hold sway. It requires a constant struggle, do you understand? There's no quick, easy way, but every day you must stretch beyond, for the rest of your life."

"How would I expand what I am?"

"First, you must recognize how much you truly are."

Fife touched her hand, showing Julie her essence, the one born to her. The process was slow with meanings lost in translation, but eventually, Julie figured out what the grand maghai tried to accomplish. Everyone was born with an inherent ability, much like a soul. Unseen but acknowledged.

Julie's task was to find hers.

Fife once again began the period of instruction and then wandered off. Yesterday, he'd fiddled with the experiments, and today was no different. Under the rising and falling suns, Julie spent hours sitting, sweating, searching in vain. Dusk set, and Julie failed to find her aura without his guidance.

Fife returned, lugging a large wooden bucket.

"The last sunset, I shall sleep now. You won't, nor shall you have food until you complete your task. It's very important you don't sleep."

She wanted to ask why, but exhaustion and stubbornness kept her from saying anything.

He placed a bucket down beside her filled with water.

"Drink as much as you like, but do not eat, understand? Keep searching for your essence."

Julie, still sitting with her eyes closed, only nodded in affirmation to his words. Fife returned to his cottage. His snores fractured her concentration not long after.

The last sliver of light had disappeared beyond the horizons, the sky turning dark as stars glittered against the black velvet.

Julie swallowed.

Her tongue swelled from lack of water and sitting outside all day in the sun. For a moment, she gave up the search, reached for the ladle, and spooned herself a cool drink. It was refreshing, and nothing tasted better at that moment. She greedily ladled a second spoon, followed swiftly by a third and fourth.

By the fifth ladle, Julie felt the sensation.

She experienced something similar to this before, once with the alcoholic drink, Vampire Dust, and the second in passionate ecstasy with Lily and Kam. By the time the truth registered, she was too far gone.

That little bastard drugged me!

She breathed deep, and the world tilted.

Her hand braced her from falling. The movement made her aware of effects she didn't notice before. When her hand stirred, she saw an echo of her movement or a phantom hand moving slower than her physical hand.

The world tilted again, and she carefully lay down on her back, holding her hands up against the backdrop of stars. She shifted them, watching the phantom hands move in a slower blur and then reunite with her skin. For what could have been seconds or hours, Julie focused on the phantom limbs, detecting something...

It finally flashed through her where she experienced it before: while detained by Mr. Pleasure. The moment she had opened herself up, lifting all his weapons and tools into the air, her element of manipulation absolute. In her rage, she had reached inside of her, latching on to her aura, the core of her power.

Fife was right; anger could serve its purpose.

The phantom limbs were her essence.

"Shades," she whispered, a small smile caressing her lips.

I finally found my essence! Maybe I really am learning something here.

Giddy with excitement, she lurched to her feet and headed for the cottage, her steps staggering, halting.

"Hey, you stubby bastard. I can see—"

She tripped and fell.

The world spun.

And she hurled, expelling the drugged water before passing out in her bile.

Chapter 58: Julie And Fife

Julie couldn't find her magical essence the next day, nor the day after. Without rage or strong emotions, her affinity diminished.

The cycles of day and night blurred as her stomach screamed for sustenance. Today, only a single sun rose, and the hours whittled away until the lonely sunset. At night, the three celestial bodies loomed bright; when all three full moons aligned every three months, citizens of Ermaeyth marked the passing of another season.

Tonight, Auqyn, Nykron, and Faellon formed a lopsided triangle.

Fife presented the bucket, which she drank from greedily; the phantom limbs appeared shortly after. Like the previous excursion, the laced water brought her to a stupor. She managed to hold her stomach when she passed out.

The following day she woke with the sun creeping into the sky, Fife hovering over her, leaning on his staff. She wiped her mouth and sat up, not bothering to ask for breakfast or to change her clothes.

And so she sat.

That night recycled the repetitive pattern—ladle, water, phantom limbs. This time, she didn't drink as much. She traced the magical essence over her body. The difficulty lay in detecting herself, distinguishing her aura from the magic flooding the Melodic Mountains. The mountains themselves hummed with a strange resonance that she couldn't attribute to herself or Fife. Both of them felt distinctly different, and yet Fife wasn't the same as her, either.

His hut, the books with runes—she felt each distinct essence, but not her own, and not without Fife's special water.

On the third night, she reached an epiphany, correlating the distinct quality of other magical objects or people to subtle scents, then adding a scent to her own essence. From that moment on, she could detect it like a second skin.

After many days of fasting and becoming delirious from dehydration, Julie was allowed her two days of rest. On the third day, she woke early enough for breakfast, shocking her as much as the grand maghai.

After they had eaten a hearty breakfast of fruits, eggs, bacon, a grain-based porridge, and chilled goat's milk to wash it down, Julie found herself scrubbing pots and plates while Fife tinkered with his latest invention. Her irritation made her shoot him scathing looks, though she couldn't help but smile as he worked.

His passion for inventing seems more important than my training.

Fife's lessons were grueling and hard to master, but she learned quickly, and she begrudgingly admitted the little creature knew his craft.

His lessons were like his first, many bundled into one. Each lesson manifested in steps, each tethered to another through a series, until she learned them all. Judas never delved this deep, relying more on a *let-me-show-you-this,* and *try-to-remember-that* mentality. That would've worked, but she lacked any ground work or understanding. She knew almost nothing, and Fife approached her that way.

By punctual routine, Julie found herself outside, sitting in a crossed leg fashion for Fife's theoretical instruction. Later would come the practical application, and it'd be grueling, regardless of how it manifested.

"What keeps you alive, Starriace?"

The grand maghai planted the end of his rod in the ground.

"Magic, Master."

Fife smacked her on the head with his magic.

"That was for guessing. Try again, and this time, think before you speak, Starriace."

Not Starriace. Never Starriace!

Julie quietly contemplated. She'd forgotten the initial reason. Her face pinched up, concentrating, coming up with a guess.

"Your heart."

"True."

Fife grinned, then frowned.

"And false. For your heart to beat, what must you have?"

"Blood?"

"What is in the blood, Starriace?"

"Water?"

"Homugons, Starriace!"

Fife cursed as he threw up his arms.

"Do you just go through life stumbling and guessing? Do you ever pause for an educated answer? It's air."

Julie slumped. Each admonition, she noticed, was short, scything, and pointed; he never expounded and dwelt on her failures despite being quick to point them out. Would Rusem treat her the same way? Her thoughts danced back to the ring in her pack.

"The air you breathe is invisible like your soul, is that not so? How do we know there is air? Our lungs breathe, don't they? Air serves your purpose, just like water and fire. Fire warms you, cooks your food; water washes you, nourishes, does it not? Air keeps you alive, but it can also hide, obscure, and even deflect."

His thick thumb and finger combed through his long, bushy beard.

"If I throw a rock into a strong gale, would the stone not return to me?"

Fife began pacing as he usually did when lecturing.

"Air is made up of the same thing as water and fire. Do you think me crazy?"

Julie shook her head, her mouth parting, trying to find the words.

"Master, I'm not sure what to think, or see how it correlates."

A quick rap of his rod reminded her of her stupidity.

"If my lessons mean nothing to you, then why waste my time?"

He stormed off to his cottage while Julie remained motionless, unsure of what to do. She felt terrible for blurting the truth.

What the hell's wrong with me?

Nothing. You told the truth. He deserved it for all those times he hit you.

The voice had a point; perhaps he did deserve it. Before she could muster an apology, Fife exited his hut carrying a small, white ceramic plate. He placed it on the ground, cupped a handful of soil, and dropped the granules on the plate.

"Count," he instructed.

"How, Master?"

"That's your exercise. Use your essence: feel, search, know. With magic, it matters not how large or small, it only matters."

Shades of the Underworld.

Fife took a step and halted.

"And no happy-water for you either!"

She let out a groan.

Get fucked by a sheol.

With every waking second, the gnomling agitated her.

No, we surpassed agitation on the second day.

Demanding, insensitive, boorish, impatient, he set her nerves alight.

His improper usage of Myshku is driving me madder than Mr. Pleasure.

She sighed and rolled her eyes. Eventually, she'd learn what she needed and then leave.

Not soon enough.

Apor, the largest of the two suns, bathed the mountain with its pale cerulean hue and all but drowned out the pale, brilliant amaranth of Praema, the smaller sun. With the seasons rotating into winter, the world tilted, creating magnificent cascades of colors with each dawn and dusk.

The typical blues, purples, and reds prevailed throughout the year, but in the colder months, vivid oranges, greens, and yellows came into focus. Other breathtaking colors emerged during these months: lime, cyan, emerald, aquamarine, with golds, ambers, magenta, and the ever-rare silver streak, hence their saying, the silver lining.

Counting the sand particles turned out harder than she first imagined. His pinch held thousands of fine motes—some so small that counting seemed impossible. She stretched out with her essence, coming easier now with Fife's tutelage and her constant use. She enveloped the plate with her essence. With slow, methodical care, she sifted through each granule. Three times she lost tally when an unexpected gust of wind scattered the piles.

The setback helped her understand Fife's original assignment and his allocution on air. She fortified the air around the ceramic; in her mind's eye, she created a thicker bubble of air around the platter.

Apor and Praema retreated and the three moons, Auqyn, Nykron, and Faellon, ascended. Praema climbed the next morning, its brilliant amaranth casting a soft, eerie fire over the land. A Praema-only sunrise was infrequent, and Apor lumbered not far behind.

The rarest celestial movement occurred with Praema rose as sole occupant, eclipsing Apor throughout the day, a happening that occurred perhaps twice in an age.

But Julie took no notice. She continued counting, flicking tiny, infinitely-fine grains across from one side to the other. Her thirst was a distant tickling of her throat, her faint hunger an obscure pang. The multiple days fasting made the overnight undertaking effortless.

She submerged herself, delving into acute and profound depths, working at a finite level. Sweat beaded Julie's brow as she continued with her computation. Apor reached its apex before Julie completed her task.

Fife stood beside her as she finished. Her lower back ached, spasms shooting up her cramping spine. Hastily, she recalled Fife's first lesson and soothed the pain away. Able to move without grimacing, she handed him the plate.

"There are six hundred and seventy-three thou—"

She stopped as Fife dumped the soil on the ground. She lurched to her feet.

"What the fuck! Do you know how many hours I spent trying to count that for you? What in the Underworld is your problem?"

Fife's bushy eyebrows rose as he watched her, and she felt the quiet pooling of his power. Perhaps he anticipated an attack, or maybe he did it to remind her, either way, it was like a slithering snake waiting to strike.

She fell quiet.

"The assignment wasn't if you would complete it, but if you could count at all. You've proven my point by your tally, yes?"

He planted the end of his stick in the ground and leaned forward.

"Now, using the analogy of sand, the grains of the air will be much more finite. Think of air as dirt you are unable to see, it is still dirt, and it is still there, is it not? Now, we must find the grains of air."

She sighed, knowing how grueling that would be.

"But that can wait until the morrow; you've earned rest, have you not?"

He held his hand out towards the cottage.

What kind of asshole just throws away my efforts like it's trash?

Without saying a word, she stormed off.

Over the next dozen sunsets, Julie struggled to find the motes of air, or as Fife liked to put it, the invisible dirt. Fife had her begin with the pores on her arms. At one point, he scraped her skin roughly with the blade of a knife and had her search the dead skin on the end of the knife.

Once she had a better understanding of her skin and pores, Fife lectured from inside the house for a change, using a slab of slate and a small white calcite stone for writing. He began with pictures and diagrams on the board, drawing circles and dots, orbits, and something about charges ... honestly, it was all lost on her. By the time he finished, Julie swore she'd be cross-eyed for life and that her mind had regressed.

"I just don't get it," she said, for what felt like the tenth time.

"What's not to get? I showed you, yes?"

Fife turned to his drawing again.

"This barrier, this outer limit, is the end of the home. This center part, this core, is a fireplace, yes? Now, these circling motes, think of them as old people or babies. They need to keep warm, do they not? So they move around the fireplace very close. The other motes don't need to keep warm as much, so they stay further away from the fire, do you understand?"

"Look!" Julie rubbed her eyes. "I get what you're saying, your analogies at least, but what does this have to do with anything?"

"Us, Starriace, us."

His eyes twinkled.

"We are made up of these small granules."

"So, we're made up of sand?"

"True, and false. The sand and our bodies are the same yet different. You can lick your skin, do you taste of mud? I think not. You can stomp the ground, but if you get stomped, you'll bleed, yes? But internally, farther than you can see with your eyes, things begin to look the same."

"How do you know, Master?"

"I have seen it, Starriace."

"But you just said—"

Fife picked up the knife again, scraping her skin like he did before, then shuffled towards his table of tinkering trinkets. He rubbed the knife on a sheet of stainless glass and gathered materials from the tables and adjoining shelves. His invention was comprised of four parts.

He placed the metal base on the table, connected a swiveling mirror, and removed a cylindrical tube with glass at both ends from the shelf, elongating it like a spyglass. Clamping the spyglass to the top of the base, he made fine adjustments. He slid the glass with her skin between the tube and mirror below.

Lastly, he attached a small ball of wire which jutted out at a forty-five-degree angle. With a rub of his fingers, a ball of yellow-white light erupted inside the wire mesh, the metal caging the flame.

Fife cleared his throat with everything in place.

"This is one of my inventions."

Julie noted the pride in his voice.

"This will help you understand. The light will help us see your skin better. But it can't be seen directly. Thus the mirror, do you see? The light is reflected, and you can see your skin through here."

He pointed to the top of the small metal tube.

Julie peered through and finally understood what Fife had been teaching this whole time. She spent the next two days looking through the contraption, focusing on skin cells, hair follicles, eyelashes, mire, grass, and other plant life, ash, and more. While enjoyable and unique, the theory became lost with each peer through the spyglass. With his instruction, the invention, and the diagrams, Fife's teachings completed a circle she would've otherwise missed.

"What do they each have in common, Starriace?"

By now, Julie understood and used Fife's terminology.

"Each is made up of many houses; each house has a hearth…"

"Very good, now we must look smaller, beyond the abilities of the eye or my invention. We must find the granules of air."

"How small are they?"

"Compared to what?"

She shrugged.

Fife glanced up, taking in his cottage. He held up a finger, thinking through his words.

"If this house is one home made of your skin, then the air is one grain of sand."

She swallowed.

By the fucking gods!

Despite learning the depths of magic and biology, or realizing how daunting her task was, Julie couldn't help her growing irritation. Thus far, Fife hadn't taught her anything of value as she measured it. She wanted to know how to defend herself, to fight back, to lash out at her enemies, the power to defeat Xilor. But as the days melted to weeks, she resigned to studies and futile searching.

Daily, she applied what she had learned from Fife's invention as she searched for the granules of air. Every sunset she came up empty, and he would smile, encouraging her to search smaller on the morrow.

And so the cycle continued.

Apor rose and fell repetitiously; even Auqyn went through its full cycle of sky dominance—three weeks out of four—before she fathomed even the slightest inclination of an air granule. With the long-awaited reward, her work truly began.

Now that she'd found what she sought, Fife taught her how to manipulate it. What she discovered is that she'd already manipulated it before, almost at a subconscious level when he instructed her to count the grains of soil. She had, in her mind's eye, imagined the air around her plate as thicker than the air without. Once she established this connection, everything else took form with ease, and she made leaps with her progress.

The glow of satisfaction warmed her at doing the impossible. She returned to the grass outside his hut for her next lesson. Deep in concentration, she focused her thoughts and aura to her will, to bend and mold to what she wanted. Ten stones, ranging from twice the size of her head to a thumbnail, floated around her head in orbit.

That turned out to be the easy part of his multi-faceted lesson.

When her efforts revealed the air granules, she set to task manipulating them to levitate small objects. The key component for success involved fortifying the air beneath the object, displacing its weight coupled with using air to move it where she willed.

Thrill and exhilaration rolled off her in waves. New possibilities unlocked with this novel ability, but when she tried to lift a boulder near the outskirts of Fife's clearing, her hopes were quashed.

Shades! I still have a long way to go for mastery.

But for now, she grew content with her smaller stones.

The next part of the lesson focused on influencing the temperature of the stones. She noted the rise in temperature compelled the air motes to move faster. Some rocks sizzled, burning bright as steam streamed off the surface. The reverse held true. After completing the first portion of her exercise, she cooled the cores, plummeting them into freezing temperatures. Once completed, she opened her eyes and waited.

"Good," Fife said.

She wilted from his lack of praise.

"Now I want you to change all the stones to different temperatures. No two can be the same, understand?"

She exhaled her sigh through her nose.

"Yes, Master."

She rolled her eyes just before closing them. Eyes clamped shut in concentration, the rocks shifted to various temperatures. The first three pebbles changed with little effort, but with the fourth, the assignment taxed her. Frowning in concentration, her inner control remained, but the power she drew from outside her 'shell'—as Fife put it—became erratic.

The orbiting stones slowed, vibrating violently before shattering.

The grand maghai raised a hand, and his shield flared up, blocking the rocketing debris.

"You still need much, much more work, Starriace."

Julie ground her teeth as he said the name.

"Again."

Closing her eyes, she started again. The thought of slipping the ring on her finger persisted, tantalizing, persuasive, and every day it grew harder to find excuses to stay.

Chapter 59: Julie And Fife

Julie sat hunched over the table inside Fife's humble hovel, though generously enriched with junk, trinkets, and inventions rather than decor. Concepts and contraptions cluttered his cupboards, artwork hung gracefully on the walls, and books overflowed his shelves, all cramped and cluttered without any commonality. A thief wouldn't take anything, confounded by the lack of apparent value, but there was more here than what Julie's eyes distinguished.

She could *feel* it.

Fife hobbled over to where Julie sat and took up a chair opposite.

"Tell me, what importance is history?"

"An ambiguous question answered several ways."

She'd learned to hedge her answers to see if he'd reveal anything more. She hated getting anything wrong, and he was never gracious in her defeat. Plus, Fife never revealed everything on the first exchange.

He nodded and brought his left hand up to stroke his beard thoughtfully.

"Take liberty to explain your answer, and I won't interrupt until you finish."

"History is learning from past mistakes, but for future generations, it'll show the mistakes of our time. However, the past also tells us who prevailed as right or wrong regarding philosophy and principle, but not necessarily who was right at the moment."

She stopped and took a deep breath, seeing him nod before she trudged on.

"It's both accurate and false, depending on the observer, how the observer relates what happened in words, and their feelings. More than anything, history is determined by the victor. Had Xilor won before, how wrong would Ralloc have been in a book written by him?"

"So, it is important, yes?"

"Yes and no. Yes, so we don't make the same mistakes. No, because someone biased may have written the book, or someone who chose to leave certain views, ideals, beliefs, or events out."

Fife grew pensive, absentmindedly stroking his beard, his eyes went distant. He spoke after a long pause.

"Good answer."

Hopping down from his stool, he waddled over to the bookshelf nearest to his desk. His tiny fingers rustled over the bindings of the books, much like a spider would crawl over its web. When his hand swept across the book he sought, he tucked it under his arm and returned to the table.

"History is fickle. I have found that the best way to record events is to put your very own memories to paper."

She frowned, her brows furrowing.

"I don't understand."

Fife looked at her coolly before continuing.

"Most people don't. In fact, none except the exceptional few of us."

He flipped through pages in the book and muttered to himself. Julie regarded him as he sifted before she noticed something troublesome: the pages were blank. Not a few, but all of them. Whatever Fife sought, Julie presumed he'd never find it. She almost pointed this out when he spoke.

"Ah, here we are."

He laid the book flat on the table between them, his eyes boring into hers.

"Would you like to see history in the making?"

Uncertainty clouded her mind, unsure what game Fife played.

Cautious curiosity tickled her brain, but she was wary of falling for another one of his teaching schemes.

"Who is it about?"

"You'll find this particular person to be of great interest. You know this person, but this happened before your birth."

"Show me."

Fife reached across the table and held out his left hand. Julie reached out and grasped it. Fife then took his right palm and laid it flat on the page.

To Julie, it felt like her soul was sucked out of her seat and into the book, but her body had stayed in the present, sitting in the chair, while her consciousness drew into the blank page. As she neared the parchment, she could see images, flashes of light and memory as she hurtled over treetops, up the steep slopes of mountains she recognized.

The Melodic Mountains.

Before she could fully grasp all the images that whirled by, she landed outside Fife Doole's hut. The door creaked open, and Fife waddled out but without the help of his staff. He worked his way to the edge, looking down at the forest below.

Julie followed his lead. In the distance, flashes of light peppered the night like lightning bugs. The flashes lasted a few moments, and then a faint scream drifted up the mountain.

Julie turned to ask Fife what was happening, but she remembered that this was a recollection of something he witnessed. The gnomling shifted on his feet and waited for a few heartbeats. The sounds of stomping, scraping brush, and clattering of falling rocks from the trail reached their ears.

Who is he waiting for?

The footfalls were heavy, the person treading up the path most likely a male, the steps uncertain and erratic, varying from hurried to ponderously slow. A face appeared, then the torso and legs as the figure came over the rise, climbing the trail. The person, still too far for Julie to discern, halted.

Fife Doole straightened a bit more, drawing himself up taller. The stranger halted still within the grasp of the shadows.

"I told you not to seek me out till you were ready," Fife said. "You're still too young, but there's a profound threat hanging over you. I can sense this in your thoughts. If you're indeed who you should be, what did I tell you to remember?"

"Above all else," the young voice said, "people will fear what they don't understand."

Julie's mind raced. She had heard that before, from someone, long ago, but the recognition evaded her.

"Come inside, then."

Fife returned to his hut while Julie waited to see the newcomer. A young Judas Lakayre stepped out of the shadows, approximately her age, maybe a little older. He looked boyish and helpless, but still carried an aura of authority about him.

Julie felt the pulling sensation as Judas passed, and her mind and consciousness were being sucked back from the memory, returning to her body.

A weighted silence filled the cabin and Fife's face was impassive.

"He started the same as you," Fife said.

She thought about that, and while there were similarities, on the whole, it was wrong. She shook her head, a slow movement so he wouldn't think she was being contrary for the sake of it.

"Not precisely. Judas had prior training before coming here; I didn't."

Julie was surprised by the bitterness oozing out of her voice, but not the fact that she was bitter. Every day that went by, Fife annoyed, antagonized, and irritated her, and her memories of Judas brief tutelage turned darker and virulent. And what's more, while she was learning things she would've never found on her own, she still wasn't learning what she desired.

She saw progress, but not the kind she hungered for. If attacked right now, and Fife wasn't there, what would she do? Heat them up? Cool them down? Turn the air heavy between them?

"Yes, but the essence is the same. You both came here, Starriace."

Julie clenched her teeth; the ring called, taunting her. Her tutelage had turned wearisome, but it was his blatant disregard for her wishes that really annoyed her.

He tapped on the desk, pointing to her paper. With a sigh, she picked up the quill and returned to her writing exercises.

As the days progressed, he found new ways to bruise her ego. His newest method came from pointing out the gaps in Julie's education.

"Massive gaps, is that not so?" he would say.

Though able to speak Myshku, she couldn't read very well, and couldn't write at all. She knew some history of Ermaeyth but not all. Once, Fife told Julie to recite the chronicles of Na Laa Lusen, and the rise and fall of Borus the Evil. The tale started easily enough, but soon, words failed her, revealing one of many gaps in her knowledge.

Fife only sucked his teeth in response.

When her lack of knowledge became apparent, Fife changed his instructional periods, alternating between magical lessons and rudiments of language and grammar skills, arithmetic, and history. Teachings from books became more prominent than her mystical ones, and she chafed. Yes, she saw the reasoning, even acknowledged it, but she hated that everything halted for the sake of lines on paper.

When she made leaps and bounds with her Rumigul, her arithmetic suffered. With massive jumps in mathematical skills, her Rumigul staggered. She constantly shuffled her mystic and cognitive feet in a vicious and monotonous dance.

Julie started to hate life here in the mountains. Each passing day, the ring grew vivid in her mind, but she clearly recognized that Fife held a fount of knowledge yet revealed. Determination to never be weak again, to not show weakness by quitting, and not loyalty, kept her there.

But escape was never far from her mind.

Fife worked her from first light to the last sliver of sun, each day ending with her mind fogged, like clay molded too many times by an obsessive sculptor striving for perfection. When she wasn't exhausted from her studies, he mentally taxed her with Rumigul lessons, and if neither applied, physical weariness took its unique toll.

The weather turned, the days cool and the nights a brittle cold. At dusk, Julie would walk outside and lean against her favorite tree, the willow tree that almost crushed her in the mind battle with Fife. Fogged breath plumed from her mouth as she surveyed the rainbow of colors setting against the cosmos.

Here, she'd awaited her favored color of turquoise, a bleeding effect from the lime green and cobalt blue, until she saw the infamous 'silver lining.' From then on, silver became her favorite color. She rummaged through what little possessions she had accumulated to see if she had anything in silver.

She didn't.

Whenever I leave, I'm going to buy me a robe of silver.

It seemed like a suitable celebratory gift.

The weeks slipped into months. Every night, Julie watched as all three moons went through their individual phases, full, waxing, waning, and crescent. Eventually, all three aligned again, marking the start of another season.

From there, the days turned colder, the nights haunted by the howling wind, and Julie saw her first snow. Followed by her second. By the tenth time, the magical white powder lost its magnificence, and she prayed for a swift return to warmer weather. Fife assured her that winters were mild here.

Though Fife's cottage resided on the mountainside, in truth, she climbed less than an eighth of the mountains' full height. She tried to imagine climbing the daunting beasts and was grateful she didn't have to.

Another sign of the shifting seasons: Praema and Apor no longer rose from the same place in the sky. What began last season was now undeniable: Apor climbed north to south, while Praema arced from the northwest to the southeast. No matter their paths or phases, each day brought Julie more knowledge and more grief, though she couldn't tell which weighed heavier.

Fife, satisfied she had made enough progress in her studies, returned to grueling instructions on Rumigul. Her first lesson was an answer to what she sought. Why hadn't she been able to lift the boulder at the edge of the clearing?

"Small things rise smoothly enough, is that not so? Small objects we can displace with enough channeled power and granules of air, but there's another factor that fights your ability to lift."

Fife picked up a small stone and dropped it.

"Why did it drop, Starriace?"

Julie ground her teeth before answering.

"Gravity, Master."

"True! We must fight against gravity as well as displace the air beneath it, yes? To fight gravity is hard. To displace the air is hard. Together, the Rumigul is difficult to master, but in the end, the feat is simple. It requires less energy to do both together than apart. Do you understand?"

Julie nodded.

"Displace the air while negating the effects of gravity. Pulling weight away from the ground is difficult on an object of great mass, and lifting the same mass with displaced air is even more difficult. Channeling both of the spells requires a degree of mastery I haven't attained, both abilities working in tangent to produce an effect is easier than each by itself."

"I see the studying of vocabulary has paid off, is that not so?"

She smiled briefly at his praise; she just wished he'd do more of it. Without it, she felt like an uneducated burden.

Both types of lessons took up much of their time, and the grand maghai combined Rumigul exercises with assignments of text.

"Incorrect!" Fife growled.

The towel in his hand whipped out, the end cracking smartly against the back of Julie's writing hand. The giant boulder above them dipped a half foot due to Julie's instant lack of concentration.

"That isn't the correct symbol. You speak this language, but you can't write it. What will you do when you try Thymulous?"

"I try, Master," she said, her chest burning against his ridicule.

"Try harder!"

He knew he was a demanding teacher, especially to her. He had to. She'd learned her powers, but she couldn't perform rudimentary skills of reading and writing that a novice half her age could with their eyes closed. Fife did credit her with the progress she made.

Old habits and muscle memory deteriorated, the figments of her previous life—what she could glean—and the mild curiosity faded to silent echoes. Julie didn't know if that was a good thing or something tragic. Only time would tell.

"You lack patience and concentration. They'll be your undoing. Without mastery, we waste both of our time, is that not so, Starriace?"

She ground her teeth at the name. Fife spoke with a serious and firm voice as Julie sat with crossed legs. He paced around her.

"Your objective today, and every day until mastery, is to sense the aura in all things. Feel it, touch it, draw it into you and channel it back into them."

"Them, master?"

"Yes, them. Are you deaf, Starriace? Must I repeat everything?"

She waited for him to elaborate, but when he didn't, she spoke again.

"What, exactly, is them?"

"Everything. I thought that would be obvious by now."

He shook his head as he padded around her, leaning on his staff for support.

"Everything has magical properties; everything can feed you. To draw upon it in dire need is acceptable. Having spent yourself and death is moments away, the magic around you will grant life. But to take from another being of sentience is unforgivable."

He muttered something under his breath and walked further around her, shaking his head and mumbling things. Julie couldn't catch everything, but she swore she could hear another voice talking to Fife Doole, almost too quiet to hear.

"... you shouldn't have told her that."

"It matters not. Cannot change what hasn't happened and what may not come."

For a moment, Julie thought she was going insane, hearing another voice talking to her master, but since Fife answered back ... he might be cracked.

She vowed to pay closer attention to him.

What if the problem wasn't her? What if he was insane? That could explain so much, why he mocked and ridiculed her, why she felt so agitated all the time. If his mind was fractured, it might explain why he treated her this way.

Acting like she hadn't heard the other voice, she inquired about his instructions.

"How will I know—and how will you know—when I achieve what you want?"

When he answered, it seemed like he didn't address her but someone else.

"I'll know because I'm shifting through the changing currents of time and events. You'll know because you'll detect the change and"—he paused and stopped in front of her—"I'll tell you."

Julie took this into consideration as she pondered the outcome of her next question. She'd yet to bring it up, and perhaps the fault lay with her. Seeing as he wasn't one for open debate and encouraging her with questions, how would he react to a request?

And what if her request made him angry like before? She still remembered the day when she shouted at him, felt his power coil within him. And that was to say nothing of the day she'd felt the magelust rise within her, how just his mere presence overpowered her, stripped her bare, and set her body on fire.

She swallowed.

"Master? When will you teach me true magic?"

He stopped walking around her, his dark green eyes locking on to her, a quizzical expression on his face.

"True magic?"

She nodded. She'd already voiced it, so now it was a matter of following through.

"Will you teach me to fight? You've taught me so many things that I can use to turn inward. You've taught me basics of healing, of protection, even to test the air for poisons, but you never once showed me how to attack."

His right eyebrow cocked up.

"Why would you need to attack, Starriace?"

She ignored the name he called her. She was so close to an answer.

"To defend myself against those who would make me suffer. To protect others against people like Xilor."

Fife's head tilted back, and he gave a slow nod.

"Ah, I see. Who said Xilor was a person?"

He waved the question away, shuffling towards his cottage.

"You can defend yourself and others when you master defense, not before."

I'm learning defense? How is any of this defense?

But there was a ray of hope. He'd acknowledge it, and he'd inadvertently set a goal for her. So, if mastery of defense was required, that's what she'd do.

Still, it irked her that he was so dismissive. Through her conflict of emotions, her curiosity outclassed her.

How did Judas survive with him?

That thought brought her back to the time when Fife shared the memory.

She spun, glancing at the retreating figure.

"When can I learn more of Judas?"

"Master the task before you and worry not about Judas," he said, without looking back.

Then, he stopped.

"And when you find yourself."

What in the Underworld is that supposed to mean?

He left her sitting, facing away from him and his house.

"Don't come in until you've done both."

She twisted around.

"Where am I supposed to eat and sleep?"

"Not my problem."

A sharp and resounding crack from the door punctuated his sentence.

Put the fucking ring on! Leave! How many times must you be shunned and pushed aside before you act?

She nearly rose to do as the voice bid, but at the last instant, she resisted.

Not yet. But soon.

Chapter 60: Julie And Fife

"We're low on necessities, and the winter is not yet over," Fife informed Julie one morning. "Today, I'll teach you the basic properties of metal. When you finish your lesson, you'll take the ingot into town and buy supplies."

"What ingot, Master?"

Julie possessed over half of what she took from Judas, just over six silver chips of the total ten. Never once had Julie seen money in Fife's residence.

"The one you'll create."

He padded over to a small wooden box at the foot of his bed and retrieved a small bar made from some form of metal. Which one Julie had no clue. He placed the bar in her hands.

"Looks like an ingot, does it not, Starriace?"

Julie pressed her teeth together and focused on the object rather than his words.

Decimate him!

No—the time wasn't right despite the implied gratification. Not yet, anyway. And there was still value in learning what she could.

"Yes," she answered, "except for the lack of gold."

Fife waved his hand and shook his head.

"Ever the bright one. This will guide you. You shall shape the gold to match this precisely, do you understand?"

Her brow furrowed.

"How do I forge one? With a smelting chamber?"

She glanced around the cottage.

"Do you have one hiding in here beneath all this crap?"

Fife's bushy beard quivered, and he sighed through his nose.

"Have you not paid attention the last season? Three months, and you still ask me questions! I taught you all that's needed to accomplish a simple task, and you balk?"

Fife spat on the floor.

"I endure your contempt, Starriace. I endure your attitude and disrespect. I even endure the part of you screaming for my blood."

The gnomling's eyes narrowed. She couldn't be sure, but she could've sworn his dark green eyes blackened.

"And you snivel when I grant you a task!"

Julie sprang to her feet, her eyes flashing with hate and resentment she'd been harboring. The voice in her head screamed with glee.

Yes, finally! Destroy him!

Before she could reach for a wand, let alone contemplate her move, an overbearing power slammed her back down into her seat. The chair buckled under the pressure. She found herself on the floor, the wood creaking beneath her weight and the force the grand maghai applied.

Fight him!

I can't. He's so strong, and I was disrespectful.
Pitiful coward.
She didn't respond.
By the gods, you're so weak.
The one who shows the most restraint is the victor.
Just admit it; you're helpless!
Those three words wounded her more than Mr. Pleasure ever did.

The anger flared, and her fear burned radiant, hot, like a nova. Her skin itched with fire while she fought against Fife's oppression. She reached for his pressure and punched a hole through, like a blast of liquid fire through a slab of ice. In a sudden and jarring instant, Fife's hold broke, and she surged up to her knees before his hold took her again.

On her knees, she beheld Fife's fury.

She should've never doubted that Fife would kill her in their first mental battle. And now, she was truly terrified. Perhaps a god or demon possessed him, augmenting his already unfathomable abilities. His face blazed, molded into an iron grimace.

When he spoke, his voice thundered with near-divine power, though he didn't shout.

"You shall never raise a hand to me again!"

She tried to look away, but his power ensnared her head, too, forcing her to look straight.

"You lack a proper fear of what can kill you. Either by my hand or your own."

She reached out, trying to punch through his essence again, but the same trick wouldn't work twice. In fact, she could've sworn he was blocking her ability to reach for it.

See? I've learned something new again.

"You will lock away whatever demons lurk within you, Starriace, or you'll be gone."

She couldn't discern if he intended to make her leave or kill her outright.

His eyes still blazed with that fury she'd kindled, but when he blinked, it was gone, receding like a dying flame. His aura faded, the overwhelming force against her retreating, though it was still there.

"You can't fight who you are forever. You must accept your birthright. By denying yourself, you are closed to your potential, helpless, pitiful, do you understand, Julie?"

Shock rolled through her, and she had no doubt that it showed on her face. That was the first time he used her name, the one she knew.

And then, his presence was gone, the power receding. She gasped, not from a held breath, but from the control he had over her body. He could've done anything with her: stripped her naked, flayed her skin, or just pulled her apart, and she would've been helpless through it all.

And now I know why he's called Grand Maghai.

His voice softened, as did his face, and for a moment, she had to wonder if it had happened at all. But even though he acted like nothing happened, she could feel the ghost of his power still wrapped around her. If she so much as stepped out of line again, he'd have her within the span of a thought.

"We still need supplies, and you need your lesson, do you not?"

He traipsed outside, and Julie came to heel, following in his wake like a meek dog.

The grand maghai continued into the woods; the juniper fragrance filled the air, while dead twigs and bark crunched underfoot. She realized something in the silence. Fife, though always quick to judge and harsh with his words, rarely fixated. Even now, certain of her imminent death, the gnomling shrugged it off.

The transgression had passed, the lesson learned.

In the distance, a stream bubbled, racing through serpentine twists down the mountain. A bird chirped in the limbs above her head. Julie never realized before now, but all these sounds were never present while in the vicinity of Fife's cabin. Months had slithered by since she heard a bird. Did he have a deadening spell of some sort around his cottage? A shield?

The singsong of birds lifted her spirits in a way she couldn't fathom or describe, having gone without such simple pleasures. Five minutes later, Fife stopped just inside a cave's opening. With a flick of his fingers, the torches lit in their iron sconces. The walls glittered orange and wet in the light.

"Tell me, apprentice, what's the difference between an ingot and a bright eye?"

The question threw her off, but she adjusted quickly, expecting a magical lesson instead of economics.

"A bright eye is the term for a large, round, heavy gold coin. Metal is mixed with the gold, diluting the purity, dropping the worth. An ingot is a small bar of pure gold three inches long by a half-inch wide by a half-inch tall, rectangular in design, and magically enhanced to keep its shape and firmness without dilution."

"How much is each worth?"

"A bright eye is six hundred scepters, and an ingot is six thousand scepters."

"Very good. And how many people make an ingot's worth of money in a month?"

She took a moment to recall the information. It was there, buried in her memory.

"The professions are rare. In nongovernmental jobs, this includes farmers and blacksmiths, but they pay out so much for the upkeep of their lands, tools, and livestock that they don't make the most money. Government-related jobs include positions of the noble houses: consuls, mayors, and governors in addition to the three highest ranks of the military: meyjour, kernoyl, and jynerul."

Fife held up a hand.

"That's enough. You'll make one ingot from the gold of this mine, following the example back at the house. When you extract enough from the rock, return home and craft it."

Fife left her, and for once, Julie didn't ask how she was to accomplish her task.

Julie sat in front of the wall like she would outside Fife's hut, the flickering torches dancing across the slick walls. Julie's robes soaked up the moist, cool air. With her essence, she brushed the wall, tracing along the cracks and crevices, feeling the strengths and weaknesses. Then, she pushed, not invasive but passive, her aura like a mist passing through the rock.

She closed her eyes, searching for a rich vein. For several minutes, she'd passed right over one, but once she caught the scent of it, much like her essence, it became apparent. With slow care, she manipulated the soft metal on a molecular level, siphoning through the rock until she extracted a small ball the size of a tangerine in her palm. It hardened in her hand as the last of it coalesced.

Julie returned to Fife's cottage, sitting at the table, slowly comparing her work against the guide he provided. Hours trickled away before she completed the replica.

Fife gave her a coin purse, and she deposited the ingot inside. He gave her a list and an additional bag of small stones.

"When you finish filling the list, place a stone in each crate. The stone will teleport the crate here. Keep the coins you receive in return. This is work, and you must be paid for it. We can make another if needed, is that not so?"

Julie nodded and set out for the small village at the foot of the mountains.

Korlin's Cove was a small settlement established by distant relatives of the Korlins. Korlinville remained the seat of the minor noble family. Korlin's Cove, however, lay outside castle walls, the majority of the buildings snuggled against the mountains. The Cove matched Cape Gythmel in size—near nonexistent.

The castle walls, small in stature, lay in a great state of disrepair. Deep wagon tracks rutted the compact dirt streets. Cobbled buildings of half-rotted wood littered the sides of the main road. A town this small had but one establishment for each need: a general store, a mill, a blacksmith, barber, bank, stable, and a flock of geese. The prevalent aroma of pig excrement hit Julie's nostrils before she entered from the south gate. No guards patrolled the streets, but everyone recognized her as a stranger.

The sole rock building, hedged in manicured greenery, caught her eye. The Arctic blue wood paneling around gleaming, spotless windows seemed fresh, a sharp contrast to the shambles clustered around it. The sign overhead with gilded lettering read: Royal Treasury.

The building stood as opulence amongst the grime of swine; a sense of regality percolated the air around it.

She entered.

Inside, only one man was present, engrossed in his ledger. A look of shock came over his face when Julie cleared her throat, breaking his attention.

"Madam," he said, clambering up from his chair. "How may I be of service?"

"I need to exchange some rather large currency, and I don't think the general store will be able to break it."

The man flourished a smile.

"You've come to the right place."

I came to the only fucking place.

"We deal in all currency from Ralloc to Stratu'Geim: goblin, troll, scepters —"

The thump of the desk when Julie laid the ingot before him shut him up. He rocked back on his heels and reevaluated her, his eyes gleaming with greed.

In a breathy voice, he said, "We can break that."

He's probably never seen this much money in one lump sum.

Julie handed him her coin purse.

"Then, please do. Give me half in bright eyes. The remaining I would like divided with fourteen hundred in chips and one hundred in bits, or something close."

The clerk licked his dry lips.

"Right away. It'll take some time, however."

"Fine; I have a shopping list to check off. I'll be over at the store filling the order. How long will you need?"

"Half an hour tops, Madam."

Julie gave him a dip of her head and took a step back, but lurched forward, leaning over the desk, the movement fluid. The dark voice emerged, dominating her.

"If you run with my money, there's nowhere you can hide that I won't find you."

The clerk's eyes widened, and his slack mouth hung open, an expression of disbelief on his face. He gaped at her like she discovered some dark, dirty secret, terrified she'd tell the whole town.

Julie smiled as she straightened.

"Good day to you, Arysto."

Julie exited the bank, noting the clerk's mad scramble to fulfill his promise in the allotted time. She worked her way down the street to the general store. The building, though big for Korlin's Cove, seemed no bigger than the tailor shop in Far Point, but easily four times the size of Fife's cottage.

After she surrendered the list to the owner, he filled her order in twenty large, wooden crates and placed them on the front porch. By the time the last crate arrived, the banker had stumbled out of his door and sprinted towards her as if beasts chased her. He skittered to a stop in front of her. His breath ragged, he handed her the purse she left with him, ponderously heavy compared to before.

"As requested."

He sucked in his breath as he dabbed his perspiring forehead with a handkerchief.

"Five bright eyes equaling three thousand, ninety-five silver chips equaling two thousand eight hundred and fifty, and one hundred and fifty scepters remaining in bits. Here's your receipt, Madam."

Julie halted the retreating man.

"Wait!" she commanded.

She handed him ten bits.

"Thank you for your haste."

She turned, retreating inside, the banker all but forgotten. The manager finished tallying her total, double and triple checking.

"Is there some noble's feast no one told us about?" an old man on the front porch asked, laughing as he eyed Julie's items.

"That's gotta cost mo' than a feast," another chortled.

"Four hundred and fifty scepters, Madam," the manager said, finishing his third tally.

Damn, it does cost more than a noble's feast.

These supplies would last her and Fife a year, perhaps longer. Julie withdrew fifteen silver from her coin purse and settled the bill. She pulled another silver out of her bag and flipped it to the manager.

Tucking her money away, she reached for the other bag holding the small stones. Dusk approached as she placed a stone in each of the crates while the town folk gathered and heckled her with jokes only the elderly found funny. When the boxes began to disappear, abrupt silence fell. It scared one old man so bad that he shat himself—or at least sounded like it—as the first box vanished. Julie palmed a stone for her, and she, too, vanished.

With her late return, Fife took care of the stock while she scarfed down her measly dinner of beans and bread. The journey was a happy necessity, given what she had to eat, and it gave her a reprieve from the normal rigors of tutelage.

Again, grudgingly, she had to admit, Fife knew how to train her despite his eccentric approach.

After her meager meal and a quick bath, she fell asleep, her stomach tumbling, anticipating the next lesson in the morning.

She awoke to voices in the main cottage room. A quick glance at the window told her it was still dark. Though groggy, she lay still, quiet, until she could discern the voices. At first, she thought the gnomling talked to himself again, but two distinct voices twined, one belonging to Fife, the other to a female.

"...the end draws nigh," the female spoke.

"Impossible, she hasn't learned enough yet! Have I not kept her from learning magic she could use in aggression?"

So, the little bastard is keeping things from me.

"She stands upon the precipice."

"I don't believe it. A darkness sways her, true, but I don't believe she's inherently evil. This, I know!"

"She'll submit to other masters, just as she had a master before you. The seed of madness is within her, and it'll rise. There's nothing you can do to expunge the darkness."

"The girl is defiant, true! Confused, uneducated, disrespectful, and every other negative trait she could possess, but are there not other good traits she retains?"

It took her a moment to escape the fog of sleep. Did she hear this right? Did Fife defend her?

"Besides," Fife said, "whose fault is it that she's gone mad, Soma? I've seen her defiance, stubbornness, felt her hostility with mistrusting eyes, but are those not good qualities, too?"

"To a degree, Grand Maghai, to a degree. You're not the only one who watches her. She's ambitious beyond measure. Too ambitious. She'll break sacred vows and laws in her determination, and she's intolerant of anyone that defies her or tells her she's wrong. Do those sound like good qualities?"

Julie could hear Fife's resigned sigh.

"Is she not to break the cataclysm to come?"

They were silent for a few heartbeats when Soma spoke again.

"She is but what you make her. When the seasons change, you'll know. I've seen it."

Then, the voices died, and silence ensued. Julie tried to go back to sleep but couldn't; the solemn warning kept her awake.

When the seasons change, you'll know? What did that mean?

Fife queried the woman one last time but received no reply.

"Do I not already know? Are you so different than that which you chastise?"

Julie's eyes darted to the pack where the ring lay unattended. She swore it pleaded with her to slip it on, or was it a figment of her overzealous imagination? Moreover, who was the woman, this Soma, and what did she mean to Fife?

Julie wondered who was more powerful, and who answered to whom. Or were they equals? From the sound of it, it seemed as if they both knew more about her life than she did, at least, what was to come. And that didn't make sense at all.

She chased those thoughts in circles until sleep stole over her, but the morning didn't bring solace, nor the days after. Julie still burned with embarrassed resentment over Fife utterly defeating her. While she could acknowledge that she had been wrong in wanting to lash out, he could've stopped her attack by other means, but he hadn't.

He shamed you.

Her pride wounded, she felt like a small child, humiliated in front of the masses. Bitterness festered, compounding what had already been growing since the beginning. With each passing day, she found more reasons to be irritated with him, and since the morning he shamed her, holding her down on the floor, he neither called her Julie nor Starriace, always referring to her as apprentice or child.

He humiliated her further with menial chores around the cottage, a duty not previously given. He explained his reasoning, passing it off as a custom, saying: "You have been part of my house for over a season and no longer considered a guest, you're a member of the household until you leave."

It wasn't the chores that galled her, but his condescending voice. It was always so now.

Or is that just in my head?

He despises you. When will you see it? What will it take?

When the seasons change, you will know.

Those words flared white-hot in her mind. What did Soma mean by that? Was that even her name? It'd been several days ago, and Julie couldn't be sure if she remembered it right.

What little free time she had, she spent as far away from Fife as she could without being blatant. After lessons, she returned to the willow tree near the edge of Fife's clearing and meditated the way Harold taught her. She reached out, touching the life within the humming insects, the chirping birds, the tree itself, connecting the links between the different life forces, tracing them, finding the similarities. The process, which once took an odious amount of time without Harold's guidance, eased each day as the effort lessened and the process quickened.

The first attempt took hours to reach completion, then minutes, now it was near instantaneous.

Each time she entered the Shadowcasting, seeing a dark future, one where she relived her death at Fife's hand, it ended the same way. He stood over her body, his face dark with fury.

The first time shocked her, jarring her out of the Shadowcast; she had been unaware of the ability or possibility to see one's future. With trepidation and sick curiosity, she returned to her meditation. The events started out nearly the same; she'd say or do something that displeased him. He rebuked her, then a magical battle ensued.

Each time manifested differently; the location changed; the pretext to their fight evolved. Sometimes, Fife destroyed her; other times, she nearly won. He'd always call her *empress* right before he destroyed her. The end never changed, which fueled her anger and resentment, knowing he kept things from her.

It's like Judas all over again!

Fife's caveat from the Shadowcast haunted her dreams and plagued her while awake: "Empress, I shall die before I suffer your vileness upon Ermaeyth."

What did he mean by that?

He means to kill you.

The changing of the seasons wasn't far off, and on that day, she'd have been with Fife for half a year.

And when he calls me empress, that's when I know he means to kill me.

Thoughts tethered with doubt hearkened back to Rusem's ring. She had a way out. Right now, she could leave before Fife had the chance to kill her. Rusem promised to teach her if she returned.

But Harold's warning also echoed in her head, that the possibility of what she saw might alter the outcome.

And it was true.

Each time she saw, events and circumstances always changed, except Fife's warning and her demise.

The moons lurched through their cycles at an alacritous pace; perhaps they seemed to do so, with Julie being acutely aware of her imminent death.

When the seasons change, you'll know.

Caliginous shadows relinquished the faces of the celestial bodies. Soon, all three full moons would fall into alignment, marking the new season.

With the omen clear, the fated rivalry was only days away.

Chapter 61: Julie And Fife

Fife placed a small bag in Julie's hand. Perplexed, she opened it, spying several smooth stones of different shades and colors.

"What is this, Master?"

"Today, you shall learn by feel. Can you do this, apprentice? You will find porting stones within, which will teleport you to random destinations."

He reached within the bag and held up a bright red stone.

"This one shall bring you back here when you're finished. Are you ready to learn, apprentice?"

She nodded, wary this was some kind of trick, or just waiting until the verbal lambasting began.

"This is no fool's quest, don't be so suspicious, child. Each will take you to a place."

He held up another empty bag.

"The used ones shall go into the empty bag, yes?"

Julie nodded.

"Good, now off with you."

"What am I feeling for, Master?"

"For the magic, for the effects. When the teleport happens, open yourself not only to the granules of the air, but the granules of magic. Observe how they move and shape and change to achieve the port. Do you understand?"

"Yes, Master. Granules … again."

Fife nodded and grunted. He left her standing outside, closing the door to his cottage. Julie stood there for a moment, not sure what to think, then her strides took her to the sloping trail, leading down to Korlin's Cove. Adjusting her belt, she ran both bag loops through her belt and stuffed the red one in her pocket. Now, she could pluck from one and discard in the other, one at each hip.

She reached within and took out the first stone, pale pink and flecked with blue, rolling it in her fingers. Cool to the touch with a faint inner light, the polished rock was otherwise ordinary except the color. She curled her fingers around it, her knuckles turning white. The magic swirled around her hand, then her body.

Air granules and magic melded together, and something else. A power, the same one that thrummed within the mountains, fed into the magic as the teleport started. Her surroundings stretched before her in a blur, her body moving forward at unfathomable speeds, yet her feet never moved. Stretched scenery swirled, creating a cyclone as she hurtled down the eye of the storm, the light shifting colors. Before she could take a breath, she emerged at her destination.

A dark, sunless gloom settled over her on the first stop, cooled by canopied shade high overhead. Moss grew thick, a heavy earth and mulch odor hanging stagnant in the fetid air. The atmosphere was damp, with a reeking humidity clinging to her hair and robes. But the world also had a muted quality to it, much like the sunlight.

At first impulse, Julie feared that she reached the Corridor of Cruelty, thinking Fife betrayed her, but quickly realized her mistake by the time she drew her wand. The swamplands came next, but the trees that pressed in around her were too thick for the swamp, and she wasn't standing in water.

No, this was someplace new.

Stray and queer sounds reached her ears, her eyes searching the cloister of trees. Shadows stretched like wisps of smoke, curling, coiling like a serpent. A rustling drew her eyes further into the deep, damp forested area. Another rustling to her left startled her; she pivoted, her breath erratic as she searched.

Grunts, haggard respiration, and a burst of noise like the crunching of dead leaves descended upon her from behind. She turned as a grotesque creature of a green-gray hue rushed her like a gorilla on all fours. It had two legs and four arms, two protruding from its back. The face, marred with gouges, protruding teeth, and three eyes, promised her a grueling death.

But something in it sent a flash of recognition through her. No, she'd seen something like this before. Yes, it'd been in Dlad City. The creature had been small, tried to get her to buy something.

A goblin!

Now that the image came to her, she couldn't mistake what few similarities there were. The ears, the way the limbs bent and moved. But this one ... this one was going to eat her, to crush her. And in the time it took her to identify it, it'd closed the distance and leapt.

Without deliberate thought, her wand rose, and she displaced the creature, launching it backward. It howled as it came crashing back down, with tree limbs snapping, and leaves rustling.

Julie didn't care to watch where it landed, to see if it came back, she only wanted to leave. With haste, she dropped the used stone into the empty bag and pulled another stone from the other one. She heard the rustling again, but this time from a multitude. Four more creatures of similar build bore down on her. One leaped, but the scenery stretched, swirled, and changed, ripping her from the heart of the Goblin Forest.

Her feet hit a fine powder. The impact sent a plume into the air, softer than snowflakes falling lazily from the sky. In many ways, it reminded her of dust motes caught in sunlight streaming in through Fife's cottage window, and these were different. Some continued up, disappearing into the air.

At first glimpse, she thought she was in a desert, but without the unforgiving heat, that hunch seemed unlikely. Though the new location lacked the deep cold like driven snow, a fierce ache gnawed at her bones. It felt wrong, vile, like it was slowly killing her, leaching the marrow from her bones.

The experience was unlike anything she'd witnessed before, even the Corridor, and she could only describe it as a void; her breath lacked sound though her lungs filled with air. No, it was more like the absence of sound. She supposed she was just so used to hearing her breathing that her mind filtered it out, and now that she was paying attention, it unnerved her.

The air remained still, unmoved by breath or the wind. The prior location scared her with the sudden arrival of the grotesque goblin, but this place creeped her out. Her breath came quick, her eyes wide, darting around, trying to find a way out of this … void.

In the distance, much further than she cared to walk, she saw the edge. She could reach it on foot in a dozen minutes or so, but that was too long. Her hand darted down into the pouch, fumbling for a new stone that would take her far, far away.

When she cleared her newest teleport, a black ground, darker than charcoal, greeted her. The grit crunched beneath her heel, flaking and crumbling away. The clouds above were bulbous and billowy, a heavy gray as if laden with rain, and it blotted out the suns, their rays diminished through the aerial veil.

Monolith stones and epitaphs littered the way before her, and wisps of an inky blackness twined about like oily smoke. In the distance, she noted statues eroded by time. She pulled her wand again; the tip illuminated at her thought. She pointed it at the closest stone, peering at the epitaph:

HERE LIES TARQUIN KOTHLUS
LOVING FATHER, BRAVE WARRIOR
BELOVED BROTHER TO THE KING
Kothlus? That's similar to the Council in Ralloc. I wonder if there's any relation?

She moved slowly within the graveyard, peering at more monuments and engravings; names flashed across each stone face she passed: Kothlere, Kothlus, Poplu, Tyku, Lakayre, and too many others to remember. Other than the Kothlere and Kothlus names, she couldn't tell whether they were all from noble houses. She did, however, see ancestors of Judas within the maze of names.

In fact, once she saw one, she saw several. They were clustered together, like she stood within a family plot. She turned taking in all the tombstones with the name Lakayre. Perhaps she was standing in an extended family plot. The names were strange, bizarre, ancient in the way they sounded when she spoke them aloud.

"Mezakaius. Kanezar. Shaetolimae. Boltoph. Jaeken. Rundelton. Hostalund. Boulerton …"

The list went on and on. She didn't notice any female names, but for all she knew, some of them were, and since the name was so archaic, she hadn't a clue if it was or wasn't a woman. Shaetolimae sounded a touch feminine.

A shadow slinked in the distance, and when she glanced up, it skittered toward her. A soft shriek it emitted grated her nerves like the grinding of teeth from a sleeping child. The scarcely discernible noise of gurgling breath sounded from the deep. The sound echoed, impossible for her to catch when the sound began and where it ended.

"What comes?" a deep, rattling voice called slowly.

Julie bolted up from the sojourn among the epitaphs. Her fingers fumbled for a new pebble as the shadow snaked towards her. Through the cloud's obscurity and light-diminishing properties of her surroundings, Julie recognized the entity. She'd seen one before, somewhere.

A cold sweat prickled her spine, the returning memory felt like a dream. Judas had fought with one from—somewhere?

Gods, where was that? Was it a dream or did it happen?

She remembered stone crumbling above her, monsters breaking out of the statues high overhead. Red eyes. The cloud of black smoke billowed in and out as it neared. She scrambled backward as her fingers finally found purchase. The stone's power rushed up and enveloped her, taking her far from the monoliths and the approaching shadow.

Her eyes were blinded for a few moments as the suns blazed hot and naked in the cloudless sky. A burnt smell reached her nostrils while she noticed charred wood, crushed rocks, and shattered remains of a town. It was a small village, far smaller than Far Point, an insignificant speck on a map next to the grandiose scale of Ralloc or even Dlad City.

Her beating heart slowed, knowing she was far away from the creature, and that's when she remembered what it was: a sheol. A demon of living-death.

She swallowed, trying to cast it far from her mind, but her eyes found a new horror to witness. She'd found the aftermath of devastation. Bones jutted out amongst the remains. Someone attempted to clean up the carnage, but abandoned the operation. Peering closer, the charred remains, broken bodies, and corpses in various states of decomposition filled her eyes. She'd seen this place before, too. She was sure of it. Though destroyed, it was still recognizable.

This is Wizard's Pass, where the trolls first attacked. I saw this in my Shadowcasting.

And the memory came back, all the death and blood and destruction. Even the exchange she had with Judas returned.

Seeing it firsthand … it was madness.

Is this the lesson for today, Fife? To show me war? The scariest places in Ermaeyth? What Xilor's reign will look like?

But she didn't need further prompting to hate the dark lord. Anger blossomed in her bosom, her skin itched with ire, tingling and quivering with malice channeled toward the being responsible for the massacre. As Judas had said, and with Fife concurring, her strong emotions augmented her abilities, and now, her sensitivities. The faintest touch of a presence communed with her, strong and radiant, warm and caring. The touch like a memory, faint but familiar.

Judas.

He'd felt her from … wherever he was. And now, he knew she was alive, still whole.

She noted his concern, knowing he recognized her wrath and pain, and she allowed him that brief touch—the communion to know she was alive—but then she clamped down on her aura, her essence, and withdrew into herself.

She turned her attention back to the scene before her. Seething at the injustice and plotting revenge for the fallen, she couldn't help but wonder if this was Fife's true lesson today. Every place she ventured to seemed, in some way, tied to the tyrant; this last stop affirmed the suspicion. Perhaps Fife's intent was to motivate her to choose her fate or fulfill the destiny orchestrated by the fairies.

She hardened herself from the flood of emotions the massacre invoked. For strength, she repeated her vow, her mantra, but with an amendment.

I'll never be weak again. I'll never be helpless. And if the fairies believe me to be the mage from beyond, I'll fulfill their prophecy by killing this fucking son of a bitch or die trying!

Chapter 62: Xenomene

Six months ago…

The night pressed in on Xenomene as she stood vigil over the sleeping Krey. It was her turn for the Hour of Challenging, a segment of time set aside for someone to stay awake during the night, mindful of silent enemies slipping among them.

Out in the elements with no clouds overhead, the night turned chilly, but not enough to make her breath mist in front of her. A wolf howled in the distance. She twirled her sword lazily in her right hand.

Scrotum of gods, when is my hour up?

She yearned to return to her blankets, to strip off her clothes and sleep, but she couldn't, not while out on the trail. Xenomene wore clothing out of necessity. Had they been in tents, or in the privacy of her own room, it'd be a different story. The only difference between here with her squad and back in the Hive was that now, every once in a while, one of them saw her flesh. She was surprised no one hounded her or made advances. She'd expected Tiny to. It wouldn't have shocked her in the least had any of them come forward.

But they could also be fearful of her.

The last person she battled in earnest was Mauler, and Xenomene damn near killed her. So far, none had bothered her, except Bitcher, but that bastard irritated everyone in one way or another. The only privacy she had was her blankets, but it wasn't like none of them had seen someone naked before. She yearned for her room in the Hive, where she could bolt the door and parade around her room as she saw fit.

Or just sleep in peace without hearing everyone else snoring.

She sighed. When would she ever return to her room? Or if war really did come, would she return at all? She glanced among the sleeping Krey. Some of them definitely wouldn't make it back, the way it was meant to be.

She turned away from them.

War was what they were born for, and they'd die for it, too. When the impending battle was expected to be a grueling press with high casualties, the Krey were the first in.

She lifted her head. The stars twinkled above, and Auqyn glittered with its pearl luminescence; Faellon had already departed the sky. Dawn was still a few hours off, and she'd be able to get some sleep. When she first heard they'd be walking to Cape Gythmel, she hadn't expected it to be so exhausting, or so damn far. Hell, they probably weren't even a quarter of the way there.

A movement behind her set her hairs on end, and she pivoted, raising her arm, bringing her sword point just shy of Bitcher's throat.

She narrowed her eyes at him.

"It's unwise to sneak up on me," she warned.

"I ain't sneaking, bitch, I was walking quietly so as not to wake the others."

His gloved finger pushed the point away.

"I've gotta piss, and it's my watch next."

Xeno nodded but didn't say anything. He moved away, standing a good twenty paces away and next to a tree. It was far enough that they probably wouldn't smell it, even if the breeze shifted.

He stopped, glancing back, then proceeded. She turned away when he removed his manhood from his pants, a pretense for privacy she desperately sought for herself, but she did cast a glance over her shoulder. He let out a quiet moan as he sprayed his stream to and fro, drawing crooked lines on the ground. Xeno rolled her eyes and sighed, turning her head away, wishing to be away from him and the rest of her squad.

It wasn't that she disliked her fellow Krey, but she'd never had to endure them for so long without a break. It would've been better to move in pairs. She could've handled that. But just by numbers alone, she would've been paired with a man instead of one of the few females of the squad. If coupled with Mauler, they'd kill each other inside of a few hours on the first day. If paired with Bitcher … besides him driving her mad with his incessant discontent, she'd be fucking him inside of a few days, if not because she found him attractive, then to get him to shut up.

And Tiny … she shook her head, not wanting to start on that whole ordeal.

The arrangement they had would have to do. While futile to indulge in thoughts of being back at the Hive, at least she had her tent to look forward to whenever they arrived in Cape Gythmel.

If we ever get there.

Bitcher returned to her side a few moments later, coming up beside her. His hand reached out and squeezed her ass before letting go.

It was the first touch like that in … forever. Had they been in the Hive, she might've pulled him into a room and rode him until his dick ripped off.

But they weren't. They were out here in the open, and it's not like any other members of the squad were having sex.

She narrowed her emerald eyes, turning her head towards him.

"Can I help you?"

"If you want."

He gave her a toothy grin.

"Haven't had my cock sucked since we left over a moon turn ago."

You should try years of celibacy then.

True, some of that was chosen, but also because no one dared to solicit her.

She glanced at him out of the corner of her eye.

"Is that why you are up early? In the hopes I would suck you off before you assumed watch?"

Had he not grabbed her ass, if he wasn't such an irritating cunt, and some semblance of privacy …

Internally, she shook her head, letting the thought die.

He shrugged.

"Well, it'd be a starting point. You know how we Forgotten Islanders are."

He smiled, teasing her.

No, I don't, and it's only rumor. It's not like I asked one.

His offer, no matter how brazen, might've been taken up in the Hive, but in the dead of night, she just wanted to sleep.

She lowered her voice, almost to a whisper.

"Oh, so you want to fuck?"

Bitcher cast her a sideways glance, but said nothing. In many regards, he froze, just like a virgin recruit did the first time they picked up a sword.

"It has been a long time for me. Do you want to fuck?"

Her eyes twinkled, but like prey sensing a trap, he hadn't moved.

"How do you want to do it?" she continued. "Lie on the ground while I straddle you, or am I just going to bend over? Do I suck your dick before or after you fucked me?"

She knew what she was doing, using the provocative talk to swell his manhood. She'd be justified leaving him here with engorged loins.

He turned to her, finally taking initiative after her encouragement, but he stopped short when she pressed the blade of her long knife against his favorite body part.

"If you value your friend as much as I think you do, never grab my ass again unless we're fucking. At least have the decency to wait until we're at the Hive, or I have my own tent. Understand?"

"Yeah," he breathed, nodding vigorously. "Yeah, no problem."

"Besides, everyone knows you got genital warts or some other type of fungus growing on your shit."

Xeno returned the knife to her sheath.

Bitcher playfully shoved her, his ego bruised.

"That's what you meant by how you Islanders are, right?"

He shook his head.

She let out a huff of air.

"You're taking the rest of my hour for grabbing my ass. Consider it payment. Hope it was worth it."

He chuckled.

"You've got a great ass, so it definitely was."

The words made her smile.

"Thanks."

She patted him on the shoulder and turned to go when a blue light burst into existence outside their encampment. She spun toward it, brandishing her sword. Blue … like the army, like Ralloc. In a wink, the brilliance was gone. Five wizards stood where the light faded; their dark robes made the Kothlere sigil on their chests stand out.

Fuck! They found us!

With sinking dread, she knew what this would mean: a traitor's death.

"To me!" she screamed, rousing the Krey. They had to kill them and quickly. If word got back to Ralloc…

She let the bloodlust consume her, a fire kindling to life in her limbs, and she leaped for the nearest one. The gulf between them spanned ten meters. With the bloodlust, her fighting style, and her dragon-plate emboldened with runes, the distance wasn't a problem.

The blade whistled through the air and would have split the mage in half without his barrier enveloping him. The frenzy took her over, and all she saw was red and people who needed to die.

As she hacked at his barrier, the meld latched onto her mind, pressing in on her temples, then expanding out beyond her skull. She felt the others waking, rising, feeling the bloodlust pump through them. Their rage joined with hers; swords screamed free of their sheaths. In moments, they'd overwhelm the mages, but not before one could escape.

Indistinct shouts cried out in the night. The mages formed a tight circle, backing away.

Fan out, to the sides—Attack as one!—How did they find us?—Get them before they flee.

STOP!

The mental voice screamed through the meld, echoing through the heads of all the Krey. She recognized the voice, it belonged to the Mind, the A'uri who controlled the meld. Her bloodlust howled for the mage's blood, to bathe her steel with their insides, but the power of compulsion from the Mind's command kept her sword at bay.

Slowly, and with no small amount of disappointment, the red veil drained from her, dissipated by the power of the Mind. Her limbs trembled, the adrenaline vanishing.

It was then that she could hear the mages shouting.

"We mean you no harm!" a mage yelled.

"We were sent by the consul," another called out.

Damn it.

While the bloodlust had cooled, the meld hadn't fully dissipated yet. She sensed weapons returning to their sheaths, but she kept hers out.

"That cunt," Bitcher shouted. "That castrated fool is a gutless worm."

The mages glanced at each other, their expressions mixed with shock and confusion.

One brave mage—or a fool—stepped closer.

"I wouldn't call her that to her face."

"Her?" Xenomene echoed.

"Aye," the first mage said. "Many things have changed since you left the Hive. There's a new consul."

"Daylynn Reese?" Raven said, coming to stand beside her.

"Oi, that's just fucking perfect," Bitcher said. "Instead of that witless cock of a consul, we have his lapdog, a cock-sucking piece of ass for our commander."

"Bitcher, stop being a cunt!" Xeno said. "Let the mage fucking speak!"

"Who are you calling a cunt, bitch?"

"She's calling you a cunt," Raven snapped, "so shut the fuck up."

"I don't—"

"Xeno's my second in command, and you'll answer to her as you would me!"

Raven turned back to the mages, and Xenomene caught the apologetic smile on his face.

"Forgive my ... associate, Arystos; he wasn't schooled in propriety. Please, tell us of your news."

"Apology accepted."

The mage glanced around the Krey, and judging from the way he looked at them, he'd never seen them before. It was something of a marvel for him.

"Please, forgive our abrupt appearance; we didn't mean to teleport so closely. That was an error of judgment on my part. I am John of the Gyles House."

Xenomene frowned.

What's a minor noble lord doing all the way out here?

When it came to houses and nobility, the distinction was in the way they introduced themselves. Every Krey was taught such etiquette in case any dignitaries visited from Ralloc, which was more often than anyone admitted. John was of a minor noble family, hence his proclamation John of the Gyles House. Had he been of a noble family, he would have introduced himself as John of House Gyles.

"Lord Gyles," Raven said with a bow of his head.

"I'm not here in that capacity, but as John Gyles, Grand Master Wizard of portals."

Xenomene glanced behind her, watching the A'uri, the mages of their group. They were unsure of how to react, and that meant she would reserve judgement. She faced the front.

I swear by the gods, if he goes on some long rant, I don't have the patience for that shit.

"I've been charged by Consul Meristal Raviils, Lady of the Kothlere Council, Lord of Ralloc Domain, Commander—"

"Get to the fucking point," Bitcher said.

Thank you for that, Bitcher. I might have to suck your dick after all.

John stopped, flummoxed for a moment. He exhaled through his nose.

"We're here to portal you to Cape Gythmel."

Silence filled the gathering. It was so quiet, they could've heard a serpent slithering on the ground.

John took their silence as a sign of mistrust.

"I assure you, my intentions are pure. A lot has changed."

Xenomene broke the brittle silence.

"Shades of the Underworld, what the fuck has happened in Ralloc?"

Chapter 63: Meristal

"Why is it every time I wake up and come in here," Meristal asked the council with as much decorum as she could muster, "there's another big pile of shit that I have to clean up?"

She noticed Poplu's and Capraro's venomous stares, but what else was new? Besides, it's not like they added anything to the meetings with their words. They spoke little and agreed on even less. She also caught the other glances from the council members, embarrassment, shame, and apprehension.

"What else do I need to know about?"

She held up her hands, entreating them.

"Let's get it all out today, because I swear by the gods, if I come in here tomorrow and I find more stuff to clean up, political heads are going to roll."

Poplu smirked.

"Which gods?"

"Does it matter?" she retorted, losing her calm composure for a brief flash. "Dwaven, troll, vampire, wizard, whichever gods are listening. By all of them, I don't care!"

She sighed with frustration.

"Who's in charge of our treasury?"

Kellis spoke, "Many offices are charged with our finances, but no single one has ownership. There's the Office of Legal Tender, the Office of Tax, the Office—"

She held up a hand to stop him.

"This is going to get tedious. Let's drop the 'office of' and keep the core names."

He gave a dip of his head.

"Imports and Exports, Expenditure, Acquisitions, Foreign Currency and Trade—"

"—Never mind, you've made your point."

Meristal massaged her temples, and she caught Poplu and Capraro smirking at each other.

Yes, it's not as easy as I assumed, but at least I didn't cock it up and make it worse.

She lifted her head.

"Let's do this the easy way. Bring me the person in charge of each office."

"Now?" Lagelm inquired.

"Yes, now. I don't care what they're doing. If they're in meetings, interrupt them, if they're enjoying a day off, send a herald with an escort of guards. In fact, send each with a team of guards, so they know I mean business. The only exceptions I'll make is if they're sick, their wife is giving birth, or if they're dead."

The heralds below the council's dais stared at her for a moment, unsure if she was serious or not. The scribes even paused and attended expectantly.

She pounded on the desk twice.

"Go!"

Pandemonium erupted as each herald hurried to their assigned tasks. When the bluster faded, Meristal eyed each council member.

"What else needs to be brought to my attention?"

Sedrus harrumphed.

"The channel being dug from the Golden City to Ralloc. Construction by the Golden City is well underway."

"Is it too late to stop it?" she asked.

"Yes, construction began a score of years ago."

"And how much does it cost us?"

"The amount's unknown; the Office of Labor holds the details to that."

Meristal lifted her head up and scanned below for a messenger. Finding none, she glanced down the council's bench at Capraro, one of the former consul's supporters.

"Bring me the person in charge of the Office of Labor."

He balked.

"You can't be serious?"

Meristal just let her amethyst gaze pierce him until he felt the urge to flee her scrutiny. She moved on once he vacated the chambers.

"Next?"

"There's the increase in costs for warhorses for officers in the Grand Royal Army," Daylynn said.

When Meristal first took this job, she loathed each day because she'd have to see Daylynn; however, she quickly found her to be one of her strongest advocates. It was a welcomed shock, and while Meristal was silently grateful, she still despised the woman. The feud between the two would continue unto the grave, and perhaps even after.

"What cost increase? Do the horses talk now? Make dinner?"

"An epoch ago, we agreed to order less as a means to save money and bolster the cost for the sellers. But with a war starting, our need has increased again, but the warhorse breeders demand time and a half for their stock."

"Correct me if I am wrong," Meristal said, "but aren't the warhorses rather expensive?"

"Yes, the average cost is ten thousand scepters. Currently, the breeders are asking for fifteen."

Meristal snorted.

"Not a chance in the Underworld. I'll give them two ingots, twelve thousand scepters, but no more. At which point, it was already ridiculous before, and now it is more so. Shades, most people don't even make that much in a year!"

"The Army's upper echelon of officers do," Kellis noted.

"Thank you for reminding me. What else?"

"You intend to swell our Army ranks by an additional one hundred thousand," Sedrus said. "The money we've allotted for this year's tax collection is already spent. We're broke."

"Broke? Last time I checked, our treasury is full of gold. Are you telling me if I go down to the vaults right now that it's all gone?"

"No," Lagelm spoke up. "That's our reserve. The reserve is untouched— the operating treasury for this year is empty."

"Reserve? Jackal and Shades! We could go without collecting tax for an age and barely put a dent into it."

"Perhaps," Sedrus agreed, "but I think you exaggerate, Consul."

"Sounds like we have a surplus. Okay, spit it out all at once. What else do we need to work on?"

Sedrus took a deep breath.

"Increase in mining, product yield for harvest, taxes, money for more ships to be built, and the felled timber for its construction, lumberjacks, ship builders, haulers…"

Kellis picked up where he stopped.

"There are the demands for increased wages, better living accommodations, better food and cost of living expenses, and the relocation allocation for all the canal workers either in the Golden City or en route."

Lagelm leaned forward.

"It's the cost of the war: increased productions, the need for armor and weapons, leather, gear, clothing, and wagons to haul supplies and goods to Cape Gythmel."

"And that's without touching the woes of Ralloc," Daylynn added.

"How?" Meristal queried, letting her forehead rest against the palm of her hand.

"How what?" Poplu asked.

"How could you let it get this bad? Were you not paying attention at all, or was Kayis hiding all this from you?"

Kellis coughed.

"Public opinion and image mattered more to him. He did make the masses happy, and they loved him, regardless of what he failed to do as the consul."

Meristal was afraid of what she might learn, but she had to ask.

"Does the general populace not know about these problems?"

"Oh, they knew," Daylynn admitted, "they just blamed all the offices for dragging their feet. It was never Kayis' fault. He was good about letting others take the fall, as long as he didn't go down with them."

The sounds of approaching footsteps interrupted Meristal's next question, and by the sound of it, a lot of people were moving down the hall outside. The doors to the chambers opened a few seconds later, and they began filing into the room. Numerous guards ushered in the heads of offices she'd requested. Dirty sandals, muddy boots, disheveled robes, expressions of fear … it was good they worried, because a lot of things were about to change.

The metal clinked as guards traipsed over the phthalo-blue carpet, leaving stains of murky water, mud, and other untold specimens. Meristal watched as they filed into the room. Forty men and women stood below the dais, and probably double the number of guards behind them. This close to so many guards in mail or plate, she could smell the oil they used on their armor.

"Is this all?" she asked.

A man sitting at one of the tables below the dais stood, glancing at those who were gathered before addressing her.

"These are for the offices you asked for."

Her brows rose.

"Are you telling me there are others involved with our treasury?"

Kellis's nod drew her attention.

"Yes; many more."

She leaned back in her chair, crossing her arms.

"Bring them; I'll wait."

Chapter 64: Cape Gythmel

Just as Grand Master Wizard John Gyles promised, the Krey and A'uri arrived at Cape Gythmel unmolested.

Xenomene, with the Black Tide squad at her back, emerged from the portal and walked right into a dilapidated village. Thick chunks of mud and manure served as the main road; potholes overflowing with vile, stagnant water filled the air with the scent of mold and decay. Half-collapsed structures remained standing—or rather leaning—in their current state of disrepair.

Outpost Dire and House Eti were heavenly by comparison, and Xenomene had a lot to complain about with both.

Loose farm animals milled about, defecating on the road, on the sidewalks of stores, or wherever else they felt like releasing their bowels. The outer wall, what little of it remained, lay in crumbled ruin.

A breeze kicked up, bringing those wonderful scents their way. It almost covered up her own unique odor. She didn't know how long it'd been since her last proper bath with a bar of soap, but she was pretty sure she could smell her own cunt.

She shook her head, not wanting to contemplate how the men smelled.

"This place is even shittier than I imagined!" Bitcher said.

I think I have to agree with him.

"Shut it," Raven said.

To the north end of town, the side closest to them, she spotted a structure that appeared to be the start of a castle, abandoned around chest height. She wondered what caused them to quit before it was completed. Money? A curse? They got bored? Either way, it was a poor excuse for defense or scenery.

"I hope they have food," Drumstick said. "I'm hungry."

Xenomene looked off to the left, the east side of town, and she saw farmers tilling the fields and planting crops, but they'd stopped to watch the Krey procession. It's not every day that nine Krey and three A'uri just appear in your village.

Someone in the back of the group spoke up.

"They better have ale or wine or rum, whatever passes for alcohol in these parts!"

That must be Keg. Of course, leave it to him to want to drink.

"We're not here to eat and drink, but to work," Raven said.

I hope no one realizes that's not what he said when we were marching, otherwise there's gonna be a revolt.

Raven came up to stand beside her. He glanced around, taking in the few scant buildings that seemed operational and assessed the land. He glanced to the west, and she did, too.

Out there was a densely wooded area. Where they stood to the north and to the east was farmland. Toward the southeast quadrant lay a rock quarry.

Raven pointed to the right.

"We'll make camp to the west, but not directly in front of the woods; we'll need that clear for when we fell them."

Raven turned around, calling for the largest member of the squad.

"Tiny, take charge of setting up camp while I'm gone. Mark out our area for tents. Make sure it is well away from the village, but not too far to where we can't respond if something arises. Patch, help him. Mind, you're coming with me."

Raven glanced down at Xenomene standing beside him.

"You, too."

Tiny trudged away, and the rest of the squad fell into step. Raven, Xeno, and the Mind turned towards the town, entering the perimeter of buildings. A tumbleweed blew across the street, and the Mind laughed.

"What's so funny?" Xenomene asked, missing the humor.

"I always thought tumbleweeds were a jape. I never knew they were real."

"Yeah," Xenomene replied drily, "it was a first for me, too. Was it good for you?"

"Quiet," Raven chided them.

They reached the general goods store without incident except a stray gust of wind, though once the townsfolk saw them in their midst, most came out to watch, or in this case, stare at them. Was it because they were Krey, or because they were strangers?

At the threshold, Raven spoke, "Mind. I want you to take the lead in there."

The man dipped his head.

"Any particular reason why?"

Raven smiled.

"You're much better at speaking to people than I am."

The Mind nodded, turned to the door, twisted the knob, and pushed inside.

When they breached the threshold, the hiss of a sword clearing its scabbard greeted them, and it wasn't one of their own weapons. Their hands went instinctively for their steel, but the Mind's meld was already in control, cooling their stirred bloodlust. Raven let go of his hilt first, letting it hang at his waist.

Xeno's knuckles grew white before she, too, released her sword, pulling her hand away. Her eyes darted around, trying to find out who or what drew on them. And then she saw him as he came into view from behind a shelf, the naked steel in his old, frail hand.

"I know who you are! You're that cursed Black Tide! I know the laws. It's illegal for you to be here!"

"Indeed, sire, you're correct," the Mind said, "however, we're on orders from Ralloc and no law has been broken."

Xenomene let her gaze fall from the old man. Yes, he was tall, heavier than her, but his age ... she wouldn't need the bloodlust to overcome him. She glanced down at her chest, seeing the flat-black plate.

We probably should've left our armor with the others so we didn't scare people.

The Mind continued.

"If you'll allow me, I'll reach into my pack and pull out our Royal Edict, still sealed, and available for your perusal. You'll find everything in order, I assure you."

Xenomene glanced over at the Mind, seeing his calm smile. His calm demeanor, soothing tones, and vocabulary were quite impressive, but then again, he was from nobility. She couldn't remember if he was noble or a minor noble. Didn't really matter anymore, not since he became an A'uri and one of them.

Still, she'd never fucked a noble before, and she might have to, just for the novelty.

If he's not too scared of me.

The old man shifted, drawing her attention back to the front.

"Nothing crafty, now," he said.

With care, he slid back behind the counter and into the light. Xenomene hadn't been wrong about his age, but in the light, he looked even more ancient. His back was stooped by ages of hard work. Dirty spectacles rested on his nose, and sweat poured freely from his sallow skin. His head was devoid of hair, and a bushy mustache rested on his upper lip.

As the Mind approached him, Xenomene and Raven held their hands away from their swords and backed toward the door near the front. Even with a slight hunch, the man was startlingly tall.

Might almost be as tall as Tiny.

The Mind produced the Royal Edict for the elder. Once in the old man's hands, he retreated from the counter, giving him time to look it over without feeling threatened.

The old man laid the sword on the countertop, cracked the seal, and unrolled the scroll, taking a few moments to inspect it.

Xeno caught the Mind's eye, giving him a silent prod, her eyebrow quivering up ever so slightly. He nodded and swallowed, then glanced back at the old man. They waited in silence as the man, transfixed by the seals inside the vellum with ribbons accompanied by the offices of the executive order, looked up.

The Mind spoke.

"Would you like for me to read it to you, sire?"

The old man scowled, and he laid the scroll down.

"No," he said. "I may not be able to read well, but I do know the consul's seal. What does it say, exactly?"

The Mind took three steps forward, about half the distance to the counter.

"I'm paraphrasing, because this is what the mages told me. It states that you, or anyone we show the edict to, is to help us with all materials we require. In compensation, you'll be substantially rewarded with monetary gain from the treasury."

The old man moved his lips, sounding out his cultured words.

Scrotum of the gods, this is taking too long.

"What he means," Xeno said, "you give us supplies, determine a fair and honest price, and Ralloc will pay it."

Recognition dawned in his eyes.

"Aye, I can do that. What do you need?"

"A fucking tent," she said.

Both the Mind and Raven turned their heads and glared at her.

"What? I want a tent. Oh, and some soap."

Raven shook his head as the Mind handed him their list. The old man looked it over, grunting every once in a while.

"I can fill this, but I'll have to put in a requisition for resupply—it'll be a while before it gets here. Comes from Dlad City."

"That won't be an issue, good sire," the Mind said. "We'll be here for some time and routinely place orders with you. Perhaps we could start a tally of all the goods we procure, and the Royal Treasury will reimburse you."

"A tab, eh? I'll need a down payment."

By the gods, is he serious? He knows we're Krey; it's not like we've got money.

The Mind laid an ingot on the counter, the royal seal pressed into the gold, promising authenticity, and that quickly shut her up.

Where the fuck did he get that?

The only logical explanation was John Gyles.

All ingots were stamped from the bank they originated from, but an ingot from the Treasury retained the Kothlere sigil.

The old man's eyes widened, a smile creeping across his face.

"I think we can do business."

"Good," Raven spoke up for the first time, "I'm Raven, the do-don of my squad. This lovely lady is my second in command, Xenomene. This mage is called Mind. I assure you, sire, we will be the only three to place orders or come into your shop. I'll keep the rest of my group away, but I have a request to make, if you'll permit me."

"Sure, speak."

"When we come, please don't draw a weapon. To do so could cause … a dire situation."

The old man nodded his understanding.

"I can do that. I'll inform my grandsons as well."

Raven stepped forward and shook the man's hand.

"A pleasure doing business with you …?"

"Lem," the old man supplied. "Lem of House Yeates."

Raven pulled back, shocked. Even Xenomene caught it, the name, the body language, the tension, but what specifically, she didn't know.

Xenomene's eyes narrowed in confusion.

"Arysto?"

"Lord," Raven corrected.

"Lord Yeates," the Mind breathed. "The Lord Yeates? A veteran of the Wizard's War?"

"All are correct, but please, Lem will do."

"But …" Xenomene stuttered. " … if you're a lord, then you know how to read. Why did you need a summary?"

Lem chuckled.

"Oh, aye, I can read. My calligraphy skills are a bit rusty, but I can read fine just the same."

"It was a test," the Mind said, and Xenomene caught the approval in his tone.

Lem's eyes twinkled with amusement.

"Don't tell the others of your squad."

That wouldn't be too hard, as they promised to keep them out of the establishment, but Xenomene didn't feel like pointing that back out.

Lem swore to fill their order in a few hours with the help of his grandsons and indicated that he'd deliver it to their camp instead of the Krey making several trips. Still, Xenomene didn't leave the shop without a tent and a bar of soap in hand.

I'm going to bathe, and I'm going to take these fucking clothes off, and I'm going to finally get a good night's sleep.

As they stepped outside, the Mind shook his head.

"Can you believe it? Lord Yeates."

"Who's Lord Yeates?" she asked.

"Xeno," the Mind sighed, placing a hand on her shoulder. "You just met a living legend. One of the last. It's a hell of a story."

"Later," Raven said. "Let's get back to the camp before Bitcher finds some way to fuck that up, too."

And Xenomene had to admit, the man had a point.

Chapter 65: The War Council

Meristal didn't feel much like her titles today. Instead, she felt like a housemaid. In truth, when she ascended to the highest office, she became Lady of the Kothlere Council, Consul of the Ralloc domain, Commander of the Grand Royal Army. Today, however, it was closer to Mass Murderer of the Kothlere Council's dreams.

The War Council required her attention this morning, and if they had it their way, she'd be with them for a week. With her practiced lawyer's face, she schooled her aristocratic features, took a deep breath, and entered the chambers.

"Madam Consul," Master Jynerul Tyku greeted her.

All the jyneruls lurched to their feet as Meristal swept into the room with three other individuals in tow. Her dark purple robes with gold embroidery swirled about her. The five highest officers remained standing as she took her chair. Her small entourage spied chairs and seated themselves with haste at the far end of the table.

"Be seated, good sires," Meristal said.

The swelling of their ranks and the needs of the war machine were the two main topics up for discussion. War costs money and men, and the jyneruls expected both. Of all the offices pawing the Treasury, she created three billets filled by three individuals, and then cut off everyone else. An unpopular decision, but popularity wouldn't win a war.

Her first appointment came from the offices of imports and exports, selecting the person best suited, which didn't engender her further. She named Master Wizard Roxie of the Vernetti House, which caused backlash among the council.

Most objected to her age, low rank, and her minor nobility status. With politicians divided, some insisting on a noble house, she elevated Roxie regardless. While not unheard of, the level of conferment had been unmatched.

Thus, Roxie became the Master of Commerce.

The jyneruls took their seats, glancing nervously at her and the trio that followed her, setting up at the far end like they intended to stay a while.

Meristal's second appointment could, theoretically, combine into the previous, but she split the duties, removing an internal struggle. One to spend, the other to save. For taxes and income, she chose an obtrusive and extremely frugal man: Grand Wizard Wes of House Bevyl, her Lord of Coffers.

Master Jynerul Reginald Tyku fidgeted in his chair, his walrus mustache rippling across his upper lip. All the men in the room were jyneruls; the highest position within the army rested solely on Tyku's shoulders. At the War Council, all opinions were considered equal regardless of rank. Meristal's entourage removed parchment, ink, and quills to take notes. Meristal quickly made introductions and then started the meeting.

For the third and final position, the Steward of Disbursement, she selected someone to spend the saved money: Grand Master Wizard Maryssa of the Joel House. Chosen for her qualifications, and against Poplu's and Capraro's vocal protests of minor nobility, she'd achieved the rank of Grand Master Wizard—near-unprecedented.

The last appointment was ten ages ago, and rumors circulated that Maryssa was slotted for the rank of Maghai, joining the Circle of Five.

Wherever work beckoned Meristal, the other three followed, as they did now. By beautiful happenstance, the trio disliked each other, making it easier for them to focus and keep each other in check.

Meristal interlocked her fingers and leaned forward on the desk.

"Where do we stand, gentlemen?"

Tyku led the discussion.

"Consul, our current count puts the standing Army at fifty thousand strong."

"So little?" Meristal blurted.

"No, Madam Consul, that's standard. Those are the men employed as a career. We have an additional one hundred and fifty thousand scabs in our service."

"Scabs?" Maryssa asked from the other end of the table.

Tyku cleared his throat.

"Forgive me; scabs is a slang term. Conscripts is what I meant. Our standing count is two hundred thousand strong, with over eighty-five percent housed within Ralloc or the surrounding area. Very few are deployed afar, except the ten percent taking barracks in the Golden City."

"Why's there ten percent in Golden City?" Meristal asked.

Jynerul Vikal leaned forward to answer.

"Per orders of Kayis Dathyr, a standing portion is sent to the Golden City as a workforce for the canal."

"You mean to tell me that we are using our army as common labor?" Wes gasped. "That's a waste of manpower."

"We don't disagree," Vikal said, "but when we receive orders—"

Meristal nodded.

"Well, that's rescinded as of now. Recall them, effective immediately. Tell them to pack up and be ready to mobilize within seventy-two hours."

"At once, Madam Consul," Tyku said, a tight smile quirking on his lips.

He looked down at a herald, snapped his fingers and pointed to the door. The messenger leaped from his seat and left hastily in what Meristal could only describe as terror.

"Where would you like them to march, Consul?"

"March? They aren't marching anywhere. Portal Masters are going to take them straight to Cape Gythmel."

At the other end of the table, Wes cringed. He leaned forward.

"That would be expensive."

"How so?"

"Portals cost money to use, a tenth of the army is twenty thousand men, the costs—"

He sifted through the parchment in front of him

"—is two thousand scepters per use for up to ten people. With twenty thousand soldiers …."

He went silent to do the math in his head.

"Son," Tyku intoned, "you need to calm down before you die of seizing heart. That was ten percent of our standing numbers, not including the sca—er, conscripts. So, it's only five thousand personnel."

"Still!" Wes shrieked.

"Still nothing," Meristal said. "The cost is what we say it is. The cost of two thousand scepters is for families and businesses. The portal masters are employed by the government; we supply the materials needed, and we pay ridiculous amounts of money to create them. Last I heard, our stock of portal stones flows in overabundance. I think it is time to break open the storeroom and use a few."

Tyku smiled.

"But the materials for the stones aren't free," Wes interjected.

Maryssa leaned forward, her long wavy hair framing her face.

"Then, I'll gladly pay it from the vault," she said.

Wes said nothing, and he leaned back in his chair, crossing his arms, and sweating. Meristal imagined him counting the dwindling money he saved.

"That could work," Meristal said, nodding in agreement. "We'll reimburse the cost of the materials so they can create more. Otherwise, they'll use their services for the Grand Royal Army. How long until we're mobile in Ralloc?"

Tyku cleared his throat.

"To mobilize all personnel will take time, but the smaller units can move quicker. Also, I don't recommend mobilizing everyone; that would leave Ralloc defenseless."

"Agreed."

Jynerul Mecas leaned forward, speaking up for the first time.

"If I may be bold without being impudent, I recommend a sizable force to Dlad City to begin bolstering its defenses."

Vikal shook his head.

"That isn't a certain attack vector."

"But it's along the way, isn't it?" Meristal inquired.

Vikal nodded.

"Then, we must be prepared," Mecas said, "even if unlikely."

"That would waste time and supplies—"

"You've said your peace. It's for the consul to decide."

Tyku turned to her.

"What is your wish?"

She sent him a warm smile.

"I like you already, Master Jynerul. Half of our forces will stay here. We will send battlemages from the Aegis Caste to help the soldiers rush to complete the wall. I'd like to send a quarter of our forces to Dlad City, and the ones in Golden City to Cape Gythmel to help fortify the defenses there."

Tyku gave a single nod.

"It'll be as you say."

"Unless, of course, you have objections or suggestions?"

She scanned the jyneruls. Most shifted uncomfortably in their seats and remained quiet. Her lower lip protruded. It was clear to her they had thoughts, but had Kayis beaten them down so bad that they feared to speak up?

"I'm sure you're aware, I'm not Kayis Dathyr," she said. "I'm quite comfortable in my abilities, and I'm not threatened by ideas that are not my own. I must confess a small secret: I don't know everything, and I prefer the experts to give voice to their thoughts. I promise, you won't hurt my feelings."

And still, they sat there, as tightlipped as before.

What would Daniel do if he were sitting there with his Krey?

The answer came to her easier than expected, but instead of using his delivery method, she chose to use her own personal touch.

"But here's what I do know: I'm very good at finding the right people for the job, and if I have officers who can't be assertive in their area of expertise, then I'll have a new War Council by tomorrow."

Her words loosened tongues.

They talked strategy and the strategic importance of Cape Gythmel, and most of them thought they were wasting time, energy, and men on a useless outpost that had no real value. They wanted to pull everyone back to Dlad City, over halfway between the Corridor of Cruelty and Ralloc. By then, Xilor's entire horde, however large that turned out to be, would have an undeniable foothold, and there'd be a lot less land between him and Ralloc's walls. Plus, at Cape Gythmel, it served as a natural choke point.

When she explained Judas's reasoning for wanting it fortified, they begrudgingly agreed to a proper assessment of the town. They might not agree with her had she voiced the idea as her own, but when she framed it as Judas's, even if he was a warlock, that got them to sit up straighter. Judas was, after all, a hero of the first war. They might lose faith in her for trying to impose her ideas for tactics, but not him. Most of the men in the room had fought in the war alongside him, so they fostered a quiet respect.

A few hours later, the jyneruls left their meeting feeling much more jovial than their last with Kayis, and Meristal smiled, knowing that she'd empowered them to do their jobs, which reduced her stress.

But Wes Bevyl, the Lord of Coffers, looked pale and sickly as he crawled out of the room.

Chapter 66: Cape Gythmel

Xenomene wiped the sweat from her brow with her forearm.

From early morning to late at night, their axes cleaved wood, hammers drove nails, pickaxes smote stone, and felled trees echoed through Cape Gythmel. The weather didn't cooperate either. Through sun, rain, and the occasional bizarre snow flurries lasting mere heartbeats, the Krey and A'uri labored to ready the defenses. They dragged logs from the woods, stripped them, and cut to build structures, those above ground and below.

Xenomene's favorite involved honing sharp spears that they buried the blunt end into the ground. A charging horde would impale themselves and do half the work for them. They even arranged pits where the enemy would trample over wood, causing a cave-in. The death toll would be catastrophic and horrific.

But they were Krey, and war was the one thing they longed for. Xenomene was actually glad to be on the frontlines. She couldn't imagine training her whole life for one purpose and never getting to fulfill that end. It'd be like a whore training for sex only to never have a customer.

Her zeal didn't go unnoticed by the squad around her, and Drumstick asked her why. Her reply that blood was pretty made him shuffle off with a nervous titter, and he steered clear of her for more than a week.

Now, if only others steered clear.

The one great thing about being in the Cape, even if she performed hard labor all day, was the tent and a bar of soap. Who knew that such small things taken for granted would be a soothing balm. And now that they had privacy, she entertained thoughts of Bitcher and the Mind, but at the end of the day, she was so damn tired that she let the notions die.

Lord Yeates visited every day, sometimes to bring supplies, other times just to chat, but always he gave advice when asked. From overhearing him talk with Raven and the Mind, Xenomene deduced elements of his story. He was a retired kernoyl of the Grand Royal Army, a veteran of the Wizard's War, and a feared tactician proficient in hand combat. During his last campaign, he had been hit so many times with arrows and blades that his clothing fell off in tattered chunks, but not one blade lacerated his flesh, nor an arrow pierced his armor.

With an idle chuckle, Lord Yeates confirmed he still had his cloak from the engagement, framed in his house with rips and all. Some whispered his story, claiming he was touched by the gods. Xeno's typical response would be to smirk, but the fact he wasn't injured gave her pause, considering the possibility.

What if the gods are real?

And if they were, which one?

Lem supplied tent canvas for everyone, oats, flour, beans, salted meats, and fresh vegetables. He also provided their tools: hammers, nails, rope, shovels, saws, chisels, and more. Each day, the Black Tide slaved away, repairing old establishments within the town and creating new defenses and structures.

After a week of working, one balmy day, a portal opened at the north end of town. All fell quiet within the Krey's working party. Hammers stopped driving nails. Saws ceased in mid-stroke. Their eyes, in search of an enemy, honed in on the invading force exiting the blue mass. A sea of soldiers spilled out of the opening.

Xenomene glanced around at her fellow brethren, noting how their tools dropped, their hands itching to draw steel. She knew, but she'd done the same. Usually when magic was involved, it meant one of two things: their own A'uri, or Ralloc.

The Grand Royal Army soldiers poured out in droves, more bodies than the Krey were accustomed to seeing at once—minus their own numbers in the Hive. The problem was that when you grew up in a small community, it didn't seem all that large. Witnessing them pour out of portals was a different story.

Behind the initial dozen, more opened in the distance, further away from the small town. Xenomene had to admit, even though she marched in her armor for weeks on end and detested it, she felt decisively naked without it. It'd become a second skin, and it did her little good sitting in her tent. But she wasn't without means. None of the Krey went without their sword. Their mantra: 'live and die by the sword,' was their way of life.

And death.

A feeling of claustrophobia crawled up her spine, and she sensed the others in the Black Tide felt the same way as the Mind's meld control slipped over them like a familiar sock. She could hear their collective breathing through the meld, the tenseness of their postures, and though some stood more than one hundred meters apart, their breathing synchronized and slowed.

Calm washed through the meld.

She narrowed her eyes against the suns' glare as horses with officers riding atop emerged. Wagons rolled through shortly after them, and the clanging of plate and mail ringing into the once peaceful settlement disrupted their solitude.

To the left, another three opened as more bodies, horses, and wagons crawled through the blue, circular opening.

Shades of the fucking Underworld, how many assholes are they going to squeeze in down here?

Had it been just the first dozen portals, the Krey could've decimated them if it turned to violence, but now, with almost a dozen open and more streaming through, they'd lose the fight. True, they'd slaughter a hell of a lot of them, but they couldn't overwhelm those numbers.

What once started as a cacophony of jangling discord quickly turned thunderous as the soldiers multiplied, doubling every few moments. When the last had come through, the portals closed, the bright blue luminance dying away, leaving the Krey tense and searching for one bad sign to unleash hell.

The officer in charge, or so she assumed with his garish metals on his collar, rigid spine, stern countenance, and the rod rammed up his ass, came forward. Another officer, clearly the junior due to his youthful appearance and deference, trailed behind.

Xenomene shifted closer to Raven as the Mind came up on the other side of him.

"Just like in the town," Raven muttered.

"Of course," the Mind responded.

The first officer came to a stop two horse lengths away, not crowding them, but not so far that he had to shout. Xeno glanced up to his black slits for eyes. He had a pointy mustache flecked with gray and equally pointy beard. The sides of his face remained shaved.

If any man embodies all the shit people dislike about nobles, he fits the bill.

The officer lifted his right hand to show he held no weapons.

"Greetings, I'm Kernoyl Runsel of House Korlin, this is my second, Kaptyn Dillon of House Tyku."

The kernoyl gave a weak smile, unsure of how to proceed with the Krey. Chances were, he never fought in the Wizard's War, so dealing with Krey was a novelty. After a moment of hesitation, he snapped his fingers and held his hand towards his subordinate who produced a scroll with the Royal seal.

"These are my orders as well as yours. I'm taking charge of the fortifications of Cape Gythmel."

Xenomene noticed he raised his voice a little, probably so the other Krey further away could hear him. His eyes surveyed the less-than-a-week's progress the Krey had made.

He chuckled.

"You haven't done much, have you?"

The Mind spoke.

"There are only twelve of us."

The kernoyl sighed.

"Very well, we'll fix that. I'm also here to take charge of your squad."

Those words were like a slap in the face to Xenomene.

"Like hell, you will!" she said.

The kernoyl leaned forward in his saddle, looking down at her. His lip curled, half in humor, half in disdain.

"Are you refusing orders from your superior officer? You might've forgotten who you answer to up in the mountains, but I assure you Ralloc has not. A pretty face and a warm gash won't wash away your insolence. And your...*malady* won't stir my sympathies."

Xenomene crossed her arms and shifted her weight.

"I'm not diseased, cretin. And the Krey don't follow the weak, only the strong, and you're clearly not."

Korlin gave her that placating smirk and lifted his hand, a lazy, bored gesture. Behind him, archers drew back on their longbows, arrows knocked. She heard the creaking of their wood. He glared down at her.

"I have but to drop my hand and a volley of arrows would make you into a sewing cushion. Perhaps that'll wisen up the next squad of Krey to be more respectful."

His toothy smile seemed more like a leer, so cocksure they'd do nothing, but assholes like him never respected what could kill them just as quickly.

She smiled back up at him.

"You'd lose your hand before it fell."

Raven shifted on his feet, and she knew he was ready to spring into action.

"Your head as well," Raven added.

The Mind's arms fell to his side, readying himself to loose his magic.

"And the arrows would never reach us."

A bead of sweat trickled from the kernoyl's brow, but whether from heat in his armor or predicament, she couldn't be sure. His eyes darted between all three of them.

"You won't survive," he growled at last.

Raven nodded.

"True, but how many men did you bring with you, Kernoyl Korlin?"

"Five thousand strong from the Golden City."

"You know what I see?" Xeno asked. "I see five thousand dead bodies, and just as many widows."

A gust of wind blew Xenomene's dark red hair in her eyes, and she brushed it away.

The kernoyl's eyes darted between them again and he sighed, waving the archers to stand down.

"Have it your way," he said.

He glanced beyond them, to the squad, then to their tents.

"You'll need to move your camp further out. I don't want you mixing with my soldiers, they're wary enough of you. To have you in their midst would make them … jittery.

Yeah, it'd be a real shame if we went into the bloodlust and killed your men before the war starts.

The Mind dipped his head.

"A wise choice, Kernoyl. We'll move at once."

She didn't like it that the A'uri just took it, but Raven made him the spokesperson, and his educated tongue was better than Xenomene's. Hell, she almost started a bloodbath in a few sentences.

The kernoyl turned his horse and retreated; the kaptyn waited a moment, smiling an apology at them, and he, too, turned and left.

Once out of range, Raven rounded on the Mind.

"What in the Underworld do you think you are doing, allowing him to dictate to us? You forget your place, Mind!"

"I'm doing our mandate. Whether we like it or not, we do fall under the command of the Grand Royal Army, even if they're pompous. It's Xenomene who forgets our place. He was by far in the right when he told us to fall under his command. We're too far removed from Ralloc for too long to remember our oaths, whom we serve, and those who command us. Since you lack the ability to think before speaking—a trait she has in common with Bitcher—I

412

seized the opportunity to smooth tensions between our factions."

Raven scowled, and he turned to Xenomene.

"And you. What the fuck were you thinking?"

Her brows furrowed, irritated by everything that just unfolded.

"I wasn't about to lay there and take it like a paid whore. If that guy wants to fuck us, he better damn well woo us or have a massive cock, and five thousand? We could make him suffer."

Raven ground his teeth.

"Not without our armor. Use your head, girl."

She leaned forward.

"He doesn't know that. All they know is what they've been told. Rule number one: you don't fuck with the Krey."

Raven sighed in frustration, shaking his head. He turned to the squad behind them.

"You heard the man."

The do-don glanced back at her.

"Move our camp back."

"Me?" she scoffed.

"Yes, for your lack of thinking before speaking."

In her ire, Xenomene had the camp torn down and moved back an additional two hundred meters within a half hour. She was grueling in her vindictiveness, but by the time the tents were back up, she'd cooled. Within that half hour, the army had fanned out and set up their tents.

When it became obvious their encampments would entwine just from sheer numbers, she gave the order to pull up stakes, but by then, Lord Yeates had arrived and offered them the use of his land to the east of town.

I'll abide two relocations, but if they ask for a third, I'm going to start thinning the herd.

"Are you sure, my lord?" the Mind asked.

"Oh yes, it's a field for planting crops, but I didn't this year. I was too tired and getting up there in years, not as young as I once was."

"As you say," the Mind said with a smile.

Scrotum of gods, would these people make up their fucking minds?

Xenomene gave the order to move again. This time, they skirted to the north, and set up camp in the Lord Yeates' field. As Praema began to set, the junior officer, the kaptyn, returned on his horse.

"Forgive the intrusion," he said by way of greeting. "I was ordered to inform you that your help with fortifications is no longer required."

"It was expected," Raven said.

"Also, unofficially, I'd like to apologize for our less than courteous arrival. The kernoyl has never been one with manners."

"Don't make excuses for him," Bitcher called out. "It's not your fault that cunt has a broadsword so far down his throat he shits steel."

Raven turned to Bitcher and stared at him before turning back to the kaptyn, cocking his head to his side. He pointed to the saddle.

"Are you using your riding crop, Kaptyn?"

The officer frowned and glanced down, as if checking if he had one.

"It is decoration, I've never used it."

"But it works?"

"Yes."

"May I use it?" Raven asked.

Kaptyn Tyku gave him a doubtful expression but shrugged, tossing it to him. Raven turned it over in his hands before he handed it to Xeno.

A deliciously malicious smile spread on her lips.

"Bitcher?" she asked.

Raven nodded.

"Bitcher. But first, we must wait until our honored guest leaves. It'd be uncivil to ensure good order and discipline in his presence."

Raven glanced back up at Kaptyn Tyku.

"I must apologize for the rudeness of my man. We'll ensure it never happens again."

Tyku nodded.

"Don't mean he wasn't right."

Tyku smiled, eyeing the riding crop in Xenomene's hand.

"Gods and homugons, I miss the old days."

With that he turned and left, and once far enough away for politeness, Xenomene descended on Bitcher in a storm, the riding crop lashing out like an unrelenting tidal wave.

She made him scream until the suns slinked past the horizon.

Chapter 67: Judas

The morning Judas arrived at Cape Gythmel, he was immediately surrounded by swords as soldiers shouted in shock at his sudden appearance. Even as the last of the cacophony died away, one voice rang out loud and clear.

"Get on the fucking ground, bitch!"

Judas arched an eyebrow in that man's general direction. Shaking his head, he strolled forward, attempting to move deeper into the camp. The soldiers shifted in front of him, readying to strike, but he pushed their weapons and them out of his way with a simple thought. As they parted and fell back in shock, most of them realized who he was.

And he didn't miss the unmistakable fear in their eyes.

Even though they didn't try to stop him again, they followed him to the commanding officer's tent. The guard standing outside announced his arrival. When the warlock entered, the commander stood, accompanied by his second, and much to Judas's surprise, Kayis Dathyr.

Didn't really think Meristal would send him to the front lines.

A quick glance at the man's uniform told Judas his rank.

The kernoyl eyed Kayis out of the corner of his eye.

"Snap to it, then," he barked at Kayis.

The former consul fled from the tent, his face flushed. Judas watched him leave, turning as he retreated.

"Warlock Lakayre," the officer said, his voice polite and neutral, "what brings you to these parts?"

"The war, Kernoyl…?"

"Korlin."

The officer cocked his head to the side.

"I was informed you'd be showing up, but not the purpose of your arrival."

Judas let his gaze dart around the tent, searching for small details, but he found none in the meticulous space devoid of personal touches.

Judas nodded.

"To make sure the fortifications and defenses of Cape Gythmel are up to the task of fending off thousands of goblins and whatever else Xilor throws at us. You're prepared to fight off thousands, right?"

"We'll be ready enough."

The kernoyl proffered a hand toward the only other individual in the tent.

"This is my second, Kaptyn Dillon Tyku. He'll be your escort throughout the camp."

The tone didn't imply a request.

"I have no need for an escort; I've been in plenty of army camps before."

"I insist. The royal edict says to follow your instruction, but the men need to see their officers taking orders seriously and not to undermine our authority. With the kaptyn present, it'll reinforce those ideals."

Judas granted the commander's logic, but a warlock in charge undermined his authority. With at least a kaptyn present, he could keep watch from afar.

It didn't matter to Judas. It wasn't a wand measuring contest, not yet, anyway.

"Very well, I'd like to tour the camp and the preparations."

"As you wish, Warlock. Kaptyn?"

The kaptyn clicked his heels and waved Judas to the tent entrance.

"By your leave, sire."

Chapter 68: Xenomene

The Krey, relieved of their duties and with idle hands, spent time repairing or crafting anything Lord Yeates required. It was the least they could do, not only for his overt kindness, but for letting them set up in their field. He never asked for their services, but when Patch discovered the broken water pump at the well, he asked to fix it. With granted permission, the Krey took it to heart, going out of their way to find things to fix.

While it kept them occupied, it didn't relieve the pressure building around the town. Xenomene could feel it, and it was something entirely unexplainable. It wasn't one thing but several: the way the horses fidgeted, the dead stare some of the army folks got when gazing out in the distance, the quiet dread pulling them under.

Even Lord Yeates was affected. Sometimes when he was walking among them, he'd pause mid-step, glance around, watching something unseen. Whenever the ancient lord came out, Xenomene spent a great deal of time shadowing him, hoping to learn more about his past or him. She picked up on his subtle shifts in temperament.

In this gods-forsaken shit hole, he was by far the most interesting person. When a story started, she noted his effective leadership, inspiring subordinates to follow him into the maw of hell and back.

How the hell did he manage that? It's not like those soldiers were Krey.

But she supposed courage took root in every man, not just the rage-induced ones.

Little information was forthcoming about his past, but that didn't deter her from following him around. She didn't know what she expected to learn or soak up in his presence, but he'd survived the worst war in generations. Surely there was something she could glean.

One day as she walked with him among the fields, he stopped and stared off in the direction of the town.

"Who are those people?" he asked.

Xenomene glanced that way, not sure who he was referring to. She didn't see anyone except the army personnel. Did he mean them?

"It's the Grand Royal Army, remember?"

With a slow shake of his head, he seemed to leave himself, reliving memories from long ago. After a few moments, he blinked and looked down at her.

"He'll come through the Corridor, a horde of expendable infantry. Probably goblins. And he'll have a secret weapon."

"Who? What secret weapon?"

"Xilor. And if I had to guess, dragons."

Xenomene repressed her smirk.

Dragons, right.

And then, the ancient officer said nothing more, and continued on to his house. The sudden reversal in him left her off balance, and while he might be old, he had experience that shouldn't be dismissed, so she kept the dragon part to herself.

Before long, the Krey ran out of things to fix and spent their time attending their gear, armor, and honing their fighting skills. Each time they took up arms, they made sure the army or any stragglers were well away from their area. Xenomene made doubly sure Lord Yeates wasn't present.

Fighting, even if within the confines of keeping their skills sharp, alleviated the growing tension within their camp, but not the army's. They'd often watch from afar, jeer, or shout insults at them. The soldiers didn't like their presence; the threat of a war loomed in front of them, and the Krey were idle. What else were they to do? She was sure the other Krey felt the angst, too. If she didn't hit something soon, she might snap.

Or fuck somebody.

With boredom setting in since they were relieved of work details, Xenomene spent time with her gear and lodgings, the canvas that offered her privacy. She hoped to find ways to enhance it or at least make it more personalized, but there was little she could do. Instead, she took liberties with her clothing.

Since they no longer had to dig in the mud or topple trees, she took half of her pants and cut the legs, making shorts. She did the same to a tunic, removing the sleeves so she could be cool during the rare hot days. The fabric irritated her skin, and the less that was touching her, the better.

Unfortunately, in public, clothing came as a requirement, so she worked around it. Her alterations elicited chuckles, whistles, and glances from both Krey and soldiers. She promptly replied with universal sign language or by telling them which body part she'd dismember.

Even the Mind took notice of her; she caught him staring more than once, but she couldn't tell if it was something of a lustful hunger, or if it was him noticing her for the first time.

Nice to know former nobility has the same urges as the plebs.

The only thing tolerable was her armor, and that had more to do with how many years she'd been wearing it, but once the Krey donned their armor, she could feel the tension rise in the camp.

One day, Keg returned from Lord Yeates's store with a bottle of rum in his hand and a crate filled with eleven more, one for each Krey and A'uri. He came back with strange tidings that *the* warlock had entered the camp earlier that morning. Her squad laughed and scoffed at the preposterous notion and drank the day away, but she didn't forget the haunted look in his eye. Even if the warlock hadn't arrived, Keg believed it.

More than a week had slipped by since the arrival of the army's first incursion into Cape Gythmel. More arrived each day, their ranks swelling. By then, the camp found its rhythm, and each day seemed no different than the last; the Krey would fight and tinker with their armor and slouch in the sun while the men of the army broke their backs, muttering curses at them and giving sour looks.

It wasn't their fault. They'd be digging in, too, if they could.

On the third day after Keg returned with rum and his tales of the warlock, Judas Lakayre walked into their camp.

That old man is the infamous warlock?

He didn't seem as…mythic as the tales made him out to be, but the longer she stared at him, the more unnerved she became. There was indeed something about him. She noted it in his eyes, in his stance, the way he comported himself: still, reserved, methodical. And she finally knew what it was. Those were her mannerisms as well.

So, he's a predator.

Xenomene sheathed her sword smoothly and rose, walking over to Raven and the Mind. She studied the warlock, having never seen him before. If truth be told, he looked no different than any other magic caster. Middle aged, the gray of his hair foretelling his autumn years, but sharp blue eyes, intense and calculating, a clear contrast to his warm voice. He wasn't old, but old enough to be her father.

She stopped beside Raven, and the warlock noted her arrival.

"Hello, madam."

The warlock dipped his head.

"I'm no madam, my lord, that's for sure."

"No more than I'm a lord. I'm Judas Lakayre, and you are…?"

"Trouble," Raven muttered.

She rolled her eyes.

"A bored individual with no war to fight. Who's in charge? You or the kernoyl? If we had something to do—"

Raven cleared his throat.

"Forgive her, sire; we've yet to housebreak her with manners. She's Xenomene, my second."

"Really? One so young?"

"Within the Krey, the only thing that matters is how you handle your sword," she said.

She noted the way the warlock stood, his tense shoulders. Did he expect a fight? Was he readying his magics to protect himself? Or was he one of those individuals who looked down on them? Those people usually fell into one of two camps: either thinking them diseased with the bloodlust malady or frowning upon their lifestyle.

Let's find out which he is.

She lifted an eyebrow at him, and the faintest traces of a smile blossomed on her face.

"Do you know how to handle a sword, Warlock?"

The older man's brow twitched downward.

"Well, I've—"

"How good is your thrust?"

The Mind, who'd been standing to the side of Raven and Judas Lakayre, bit his lower lip. Raven sucked in a sharp breath. For a moment, the warlock just stared at her, and then he blinked a few times as recognition spread across his face.

"If I require any instruction, I'll know who to find."

Pity. No sense of humor.

"Xeno," Raven said. "See to Lord Yeates, and make sure he has no wants."

The dismissal was curt for Raven, but she recognized that if she didn't leave, she'd most likely say something so sarcastic that no one could dig her out of the hole. More than that, she heard the tone in his voice, and it was something close to fear.

She'd already courted trouble with her innuendo, and if it was enough to rattle Raven, she'd be wise to notice.

"As you wish."

She turned and eyed Judas one more time.

"Warlock."

He dipped his head again.

Turning on her heel, she left, making sure the warlock got a good look at her shorts.

If he looks at all. Might be too much of a prude.

To be fair, she thought about changing before going to Lord Yeates's house, in the event his younger grandsons were there, but she dismissed the notion.

When she reached his front steps, she ascended to the porch and rapped sharply on the door. Instead of a grandson, worker, or the old man himself, an old woman answered the door. Where the lord towered, she was tiny, even shorter than Xenomene, the shortest and most petite of the Krey. Most adolescents were taller than her.

"Who calls?" the woman asked.

"Xenomene, second of the Krey. I'm here to see to the needs of Lord Yeates. Where might I find him?"

"He's taking his nap, child. Do come in."

The elder, crowned with short, curly silver hair, stepped back, permitting Xenomene to enter. It marked the first time she entered the house. Even though it was hot outside, Xenomene immediately detected the stone hearth and the crackling fire. Two oversized chairs stuffed with cotton sat near each other with a small, round wood table between.

The base of the table was a stand housing small knickknacks with elaborately decorated and detailed dolls inside the glass. Xenomene couldn't tell where the dolls came from, but all were unlike any she had ever seen.

Probably some culture so far off that I have never heard of or ever get to see.

She sighed.

I wonder if they have any good fighters there?

"Please, sit, my lady," the wife offered.

Xeno abstained from correcting her, deciding it would be better to hold her tongue.

"My husband should be rising soon; he never sleeps for more than an hour."

Xenomene took a moment to let her eyes wander the room. Though spacious, it was crammed full of trinkets, litter from all cultures of their world, from the vaguely familiar to the bizarre. She noted the silence, then posed a question to fill the quiet.

"How did you meet your husband, Lady Yeates?"

"Call me Ene."

She picked up her knitting needles and yarn and went back to her work.

"It's short for Earlene, but I'm sure you knew that. Bless me, where are my manners? Would you like something to drink?"

Ene began to rise, but Xenomene quickly stopped her.

"No need, Lady—er, Ene; I won't be intruding long."

"Okay, let me know if you need anything."

The older woman settled back in. The silence ensued as she went back to her knitting. Xenomene cast her eyes about the sitting room; she'd never seen so much wood in a house, except, of course, House Eti. The manor's floors, walls, ceiling, and stairs were made of a wood boasting a golden tone with hints of dark reddish brown throughout. The floor carried a high gloss sheen. A dark stain coated the stairs.

"I met him before the war," Ene spoke up suddenly.

Xenomene whipped her head around.

"He looked so smart in his conscript uniform, which is nothing compared to the uniforms they give you when you become a career military man, but I was smitten. I saw him when I visited my sister in Ralloc."

She chuckled.

"That must have been before they started the outer wall. It didn't seem like a war was going on in Ralloc, but there was. They appeared so calm and unbothered, but it was only borrowed time."

Xenomene didn't know how to respond to that, so she posed another question.

"How long have you been married?"

"In two seasons it'll be half a legend. Doesn't seem that long when looking back."

Half a legend? Shades, five ages! I don't think I could stand the same face for five seasons, let alone five thousand years.

Ene pointed to the table with the cabinet of dolls on the bottom.

"I noticed you admiring my dolls."

"Yes. Far better than the one that I received in my youth."

"Just one?"

"Yes, my sister bought it for me, but when the Krey came and took me away, I had to leave it behind. It was a cheap doll, nothing like these you have here."

"The one in the red dress, I bought that one in the southern continent Sonkol, a city called Elysys. The twin dolls with purple and pink dresses were a

421

gift from Lem when he came back from the Kran Empire."

The Kran Empire? He got to go there?

"From all the way across the Eastern Sea?"

Ene gave a noncommittal grunt.

Xenomene shook her head, trying to imagine how far away that was. It'd seemed impossibly long just to get to Cape Gythmel.

"The Kran Empire is the furthest south continent, right?" Xenomene asked. "I can't remember the name."

"Vesole," Ene said. "But Kran's Empire spans two continents—well, they claim it anyway—the southernmost and the smaller one just north of Vesole, Cronele. But the doll came from the capital, Kran's Prime."

Xenomene's eyes roamed over the dolls. One, in particular, stood out among the others, crafted with fine leather and painted.

"What's this leather one?"

"That doll came from the continent Groyntahl, the furthest north continent on the Kran Empire's side. I purchased it in Merlul, Cronele. Wouldn't dare travel in Groyntahl."

"Why not?"

"There are beast riders there, warring clans; I can't remember the name of them."

"Ebbins?"

"Yes, Ebbins. A savage wilderness. Lem says even Ralloc wouldn't dare invade even if they had cause to."

That prickled Xenomene's curiosity.

"They're mighty warriors?"

She wouldn't mind traveling there to find out. No one matched the Krey in battle except the elyves. Who better to boast of their abilities than the Krey themselves? Still, she always wondered if other nations retained people or organizations like them, warriors and expert fighters. Many years passed since anyone in the Hive proved a challenge for her. She yearned to test her abilities.

Which was why she was glad to be here on the front lines. At least now she'd truly be living their mantra of live and die by the sword. She'd been besting other fighters before the Age of Maturity, and she'd humiliated many older Krey and teachers after that.

With the Krey mobilized and the arrival of the Grand Royal Army and Warlock Lakayre, war seemed inevitable, even if she saw no signs of the impending conflict. Soon, she'd test her merit in earnest, but it'd be within the confines of fighting with her squad, and that hindered her more than helped. In battle formations, she downplayed her skill to compensate for others in her squad. It was a group effort, and if she fought to her full potential, she'd leave them behind, making all vulnerable.

Another doll caught her eye; the eyes painted in such detail they seemed real, moist.

Xenomene turned to ask another question but discovered Lady Yeates had fallen asleep, her knitting lying in her lap, her head listing.

Quietly, Xenomene extracted herself from the chair and left the older woman in peaceful dreams, but even as she exited the house, all that unease she'd been feeling never went away. The breeze was absent, the birds were quiet, and the dread she'd been feeling in her chest ticked tighter like a coiled spring.

Something was coming.

Chapter 69: Judas

As the army hurried to ready defenses, Judas helped where he could, often enlisting the Krey's Hand and Heart. He never pulled the Mind away; to do so would likely cause a bloodbath at the slightest provocation. Judas and the two battlemages used their magic to fortify the hastily constructed walls.

In the quarry, Judas would often blast rock, saving time and effort for the scabs and the men-at-arms pouring in through portals every day. Levitating heavy objects eased the conscript's burden; each load required fastening winches in place, a lengthy process. With magic, he chopped down trees or helped with repairs, or in this case, building roads through the town, turning muddy wagon-rutted trails into proper paths.

Though he tried to keep his distance from the Krey, he helped with their half-crazed scheme courtesy of Xenomene, blasting huge holes into the ground, making a pit lined with spears. Once finished, large sheets of thin wood covered the openings. The Krey then put a meager layer of earth over the wood, concealing the pits.

Judas worked diligently for three weeks, his mind focusing on the task of hurrying defenses. He toured the camp every day, making different rounds, conducting spot inspections. Twice a week, he met with leaders of working parties for progress reports on repairs and plans on future endeavors.

Alone in his tent, a stray thought crossed his mind, an obvious detail he missed. He hadn't seen Kayis since he arrived. Wherever he was, it couldn't be good. The warlock stormed into Kernoyl Korlin's tent without waiting to be announced.

"Where's Kayis Dathyr?"

The kernoyl looked over his shoulder but continued to pour his coffee.

"He's busy at the moment, Warlock; why do you require him?"

"Busy doing what?"

"An important task, I assure you."

Korlin seated himself and took a sip of his hot brew.

"I'll be the judge of that. Where is he?"

"Again, I ask, why's it so important? I've vouched for him, is that not good enough?"

"No."

He stepped closer, barely contained the ire simmering through him. He hoped it shined in his eyes.

"Where?"

The kernoyl set his cup down.

"He's in the stables."

Judas bolted from the pavilion and descended upon the stables like a storming gale. The smell of hay, horses, and manure assaulted his nostrils as he checked each nook and cranny. Judas finally found Kayis halfway down the stalls, a manure shovel in his hands.

He stopped and turned as Judas approached.

"I thought you forgot about me. Come to gloat?"

A sackcloth stained with food, grain, and feces replaced Kayis's once resplendent robes. His immaculately trimmed facial hair transformed into a burly bush of twisted knots and fleas; his hair, disheveled and matted, shone with oil and dirt. Even as he spoke, Judas could see his yellow-stained teeth.

"What happened, Kayis?"

The sight was revolting, and he couldn't hide the empathy in his voice.

"You should know, you put me here!"

"What are you talking about?"

"The kernoyl said it was your order to put me here. If you don't mind, I have work to do, *Master!*"

"I just found out today, and I assure you that I didn't place you here."

A repugnant scent reached Judas's nostrils.

"When's the last time you bathed?"

"That was also a civility you denied me, you and your kernoyl! By your leave, my lord."

Kayis tried to pass Judas, but the warlock didn't budge.

"Come with me."

Kayis's eyes locked with him, and Judas thought the bastard would argue. Instead, he followed as they made their way across the camp.

The guards standing post at the kernoyl's tent announced his imminent arrival, but by the time Judas got there, the canvas was gone. Gathering his magic, Judas blew the pavilion away, the cloth somersaulting through the air, leaving the kernoyl sitting at his desk without his canvas.

Judas leaned down and placed his arms on the desk.

"Is this your doing?"

The kernoyl's head jerked around, noting where his tent landed before snapping back around to Judas, his eyes wide with surprise, but he quickly schooled himself.

"You're out of line, Warlock!"

"Is this your doing?" Judas shouted.

Kaptyn Dillon Tyku came running up, but slowed and watched from a respectful distance.

"Why? For what purpose?" Judas asked.

When the senior officer said nothing, Judas straightened.

"I hereby relieve you of command."

The kernoyl scoffed.

"You can't do that; you don't have the authority!"

"Watch me."

He had to tread carefully. Some might think he was authoritarian. Judas turned to the kaptyn. It was then that he saw how many soldiers were watching, slack-jawed and silent.

"You're promoted to the duties and responsibilities of your senior officer. Do you think you can handle that?"

The kaptyn clicked his heels.

"With ease, sire."

"Wait just a fucking minute—"

Judas held up a finger to shut Korlin up.

"You do realize I'm friends with the consul?"

Korlin's face went white.

"You wouldn't dare play that card with me, you treacherous bastard."

"I think it's time you've had a chat with her."

Judas gripped Korlin's shoulder, and they disappeared.

A few heartbeats later, Judas reappeared minus the officer. The warlock glanced at Kayis then to the kaptyn.

"Clean him up. Give him a bath, food, rest, clothing, and quarters fitting of his stature."

"At once, sire," the kaptyn bowed.

Judas turned and strolled off, but he wasn't too far away to hear Kayis's faint thank you.

Chapter 70: The Krey

Xenomene eyed the Krey as they ate supper, noting their physical attributes, tall, short, fat, bald, skinny, scarred. She measured herself against Mauler, the only other female Krey in the squad. Where Xeno was porcelain, Mauler was dark, with tattoos across her body. Mauler was ferocious, a descendant of the Toshii, a warring tribe from Groyntahl, or so Xenomene assumed.

Xenomene and Mauler had their share of turbulent times when pitted against each other in the Pit. Mauler drew first blood, but Xeno nearly ended her life. Absentmindedly, Xenomene's fingers went to the faint scar that traced from the right corner of her mouth to mid-cheek.

Bitch! You fucked up my face.

But Mauler didn't leave the match unscathed. When Xeno touched her face and saw the blood, she drove her sword through Mauler's shoulder blades, the end coming out of her chest at her right breast. Mauler would've died without fast-acting A'uri healers. Xeno chose stitches instead of magic, a reminder of how close she'd come to losing her life and to never underestimate her opponent again. The heir forbade any further fights between them.

Xeno's attention wandered the Krey until she found the Mind. He was pleasant to look at, high cheekbones with tanned skin. His dark blue-gray eyes and military-cut brown hair articulated his comely looks, especially when he smiled. He was fairly tall, too, but then again, everyone to Xenomene was tall. His height actually played a mark against him and didn't factor in when Xenomene considered potential mates.

Disregarding a man on height alone seemed trivial, self-centered, and depthless.

He had decent shoulders and tapered down to a narrow waist. The Mind lacked the typical Krey build, molded from manual labor, fighting, or constant conditioning. He was gangly and thin. In a scuffle, he'd have reach, but she'd break him in half. The Mind was talking to another A'uri, the Heart—the only female A'uri with them.

The Heart was beautiful in a way that Xenomene never would be. In comparison, Xenomene felt plain next to the brunette with bright eyes, a wide, white smile, ample bosom, and an unmarred face. Whenever she heard Heart's merry laugh roll across the distance that separated them, Xeno rolled her eyes.

Bitcher's complaints ensnared her attention, her eyes flickering to him. He came closer to Xenomene's preferences, despite his namesake. Attractive with pale gray eyes, blond-white hair, and tanned skin, the latter fading due to his time in the mountains. His personality turned her off, at least the public bravado, and she idly wondered if he was the same without such confines.

Rumors circulated about Bitcher and others like him, the Forgotten Islanders. While listening to his moaning, Xeno stood and moved to scrape the remains of her plate in the waste bucket.

"… so I told that fuck, I said, 'you try that on me, boy, and I'll stick that shovel up your ass and have your friend fuck you with it!'"

Bitcher laughed, and the others joined in.

"So, what do you think of the men-at-arms?" Keg asked.

"They're like a bunch of cackling hens, women in dresses. When the war starts, they'll be getting fucked!"

Xenomene scraped her plate clean, sticking the spoon in her mouth as she poured water from the skin to clean it.

"No, but really," Drumstick said, "what do you think of their prowess in battle?"

"What fucking prowess? They're like children with sticks, swing, swing, you can't hurt me, I'm an Aegis mage!"

That elicited more laughter. The japes, to Xeno, lacked the dry, dark, and sarcastic sense of humor that catered to her tastes. Then again, she wasn't drunk. If she was, she might be laughing, or fucking him.

Xenomene poured water from her waterskin over her spoon and scrubbed it clean.

"Oi! Check this out!"

Two-Tons stood and bent, his ass near the fire, letting out a blast of air, and the flames rose higher.

"That's what I think of them army boys!" Bitcher said. "Fucking fart stain in my breeches."

With her shirt, Xeno wiped her spoon dry before turning away from the table, wading through the Krey.

"Those little cunts, I tell you, they're worse than a prostitute with no teeth!"

"Yeah, but they can't hold a sword to save their lives," Keg said.

"Tell 'em it's like a woman holding their cock; you never want her to let go!"

"Careful, they might surprise you," Tiny cautioned.

"They're like a little girl with a dress with those swords."

"Bitcher, some of those little girls can best you," the big man said.

"Not bloody likely. Those bitches ain't got shit on me. I haven't ever met a woman who could put me down on the ground. You find a female who can put me down, and I'll eat shit for a day."

Xenomene, passing Bitcher, pivoted suddenly, her boot slamming into his chest and knocking him from the log to his back.

"Fuck me, that hurt. What the fuck are you going on about, Xeno?"

Xeno tossed her spoon, the silver utensil landing on his chest. Picking it up, a puzzled expression clouded his features.

"What the fuck's this, love?"

"You just found a female who put you down. I was going to say you could eat my ass now, but that seems like a reward."

He smiled.

"We could make it a punishment. Didn't know you were freaky like that."

I just might let you.

She shook her head.

"You can use my spoon to feast from between Two-Tons's cheeks."

Xeno kicked him in the ribs, more insult than injury, but a grunt escaped him anyway.

The other boys started hooting and howling with laughter, throwing sand on Bitcher and punching him while he was down. Even Mauler, who sat alone and never laughed, smiled.

Xeno left the ruckus of the campfire far behind and worked her way to her tent. She spied the Mind watching her, a small smile on his face.

Careful, A'uri, one night I might find your tent.

In the privacy of her tent, she stripped naked and crawled beneath her covers. It'd be hours yet before the rest went to sleep, and she'd wake many times from their drunken merriment. Rolling to her side, she pulled the covers up higher, covering exposed skin before falling asleep.

Chapter 71: Judas

In the late afternoon, the noises of bustling soldiers radiated through the camp as shift change took place. The first night shift assumed their duties. Each shift consisted of six hours: a shift of fortifications, a second spent for training and drilling and preparing for the next day, and two for sleep. This way, each soldier worked and honed their battle skills.

Judas sat in his tent, a small wood table held his books, parchment, and ink. A mug of coffee sat idle and steaming. An expensive and recent import from the Forgotten Isles, it became a new favorite. Other locations might grow beans, but none as near as the Isles.

He took the warm mug in his hand, leeching the chill from his fingers. The change of season was a few days away, marking six months since he'd last seen his apprentice. The warlock heeded the fairy's edict and did his best to stay away, to not pursue her. Some days, the command seemed easy to follow, preoccupied with fortifications. Other days he obsessed over his mistakes.

It was hard not to wonder where she went, if she remained healthy and happy. He raised the mug to his lips and sipped, feeling the hot coffee cascade down his throat.

In quiet moments like these, he thought of Julie the most.

A faint whisper of an aura called out to him, strange and distinct, but vaguely familiar.

His brow furrowed.

Did I just feel that, or is it my longing?

He sensed it again, faint, as if a great distance separated him from Julie, but unmistakable. He set the mug down. Something or someone startled her.

Scared?

Judas reached out to where he perceived the sensation, but couldn't find her.

Goblin Forest?

He shook his head.

Impossible, what would she be doing there? I must have imagined the whole thing.

The aura brushed him again, briefly. She seemed skittish, startled. When he honed in on her location, she disappeared.

What the Underworld's going on?

Almost immediately he noticed her again, this time, much closer.

Jackal and Shades! She's teleporting! Where'd she learn that?

Her essence gleamed, effulgent, a light drowning out the shadows.

He smiled.

Thank the gods you're alive.

Relief washed over him as he appreciated her from afar. He didn't reach out to her, but his presence hovered near hers, basking in her radiance. As sudden as snuffing out a candle, she became terrified. He sensed the frantic nature of her emotions and just as he reached out to assure her, she vanished, moved.

She reappeared a moment later, clear on the other side of the realm and even closer to his relative position. With a gentle touch, he caressed her aura, her essence blossoming like a supernova. The anger rolled off her, white and searing, but not directed at him.

She blazed like an ardent beacon.

This time, he reached out to her to console her, a brief, delicate touch to let her know he thought of her. At first, she didn't seem to notice, but a subtle shift made her aware of him. She neither accepted his gentle caress nor shied away; she let it be, like meeting the eyes of a friend-turned-stranger, unsure of how to react.

Then, she withdrew, her essence shrinking and diminishing to where Judas had trouble detecting her. But he searched and found her, aglitter, though well-dampened.

Julie teleported again and came out in the Melodic Mountains.

What are you doing there? Is that where the fairies are keeping you, or is it something else?

He couldn't deny her power or her level of mastery. She was leagues ahead of where she'd been, but she still lacked control of her emotions, which would hinder her abilities.

When Julie left him, she was torn, broken, and their estrangement never resolved. The gods only knew the full reality of the horrors she faced. Where had she been? How did she gain such attainment? He realized the fairies could teach her some magic, but it didn't seem quite right.

What have you done? What unlocked your mastery?

A stray thought entered his mind, and he brushed the idea off as ludicrous, but the speculation festered. He shook his head in doubt, yet the persistence remained.

Have you found Fife's old home, Julie? Is that where you went? What secrets hide among his ruins? What did you learn? Are Fife's teachings helping you, as if he is teaching you from the grave?

He didn't know, but he wanted to find out. The next chance he got to slip away, he planned to make the journey, regardless of the fairies' warning.

Chapter 72: Cape Gythmel

Judas glanced up at the aligned moons.

The changing of the seasons went unnoticed by everyone.

The gathering of wizards and men-at-arms shifted from eager to bored, then restless. Each day, they turned aggression into fortifications. The walls climbed steadily higher and thicker. Painted, sculpted, or chiseled runes embellished raised stone. Trebuchets were modified—smaller versions erected atop the new wall while larger, modern structures lay within the grounds of the castle walls.

Battlements boasted slits for archers, narrow gaps from which they could fire upon the hordes below. Massive enclosed towers anchored the corners while several smaller towers littered the space between, each open to the elements, sparing materials for other defenses.

The original decorative wall now towered forty feet high, and the spires of towers built along the curtain wall achieved greater heights. When Judas deemed the walls high enough, they started adding width on the insides. With each new layer, he, along with other battlemages, placed runes and spells upon the rock, fortifying against the onslaught of arrows, fire, and impacts of inevitable siege engines.

The moons slid through their rotations in a seamless fashion, at what felt like a breakneck pace.

The colder months are on us now.

Because of the uniqueness of the twin suns and their courses through the heavens, Ermaeyth lacked polar icecaps. While it grew colder to the further east or west one traveled, and lands abroad were laden with snow, the shifting sun deterred any major icecaps from forming.

During the colder months, nowhere escaped the winter, though some areas suffered more than others.

Though grateful for Xilor's delayed entrance, Judas was troubled by the lack of visible force. Thus far, all their preparations seemed to go unnoticed, though he couldn't say that with certainty. With a massive army, Xilor had to come through the Corridor.

Doubt clawed the warlock's insides, wondering what kept the malevolent tyrant at bay. Nearly half a year went by since the attack of Wizard's Pass and the capture of the elyves in Shadow City, yet their enemy did not stir. It unnerved Judas that so far, Xilor remained unpredictable.

For a brief moment, and not for the first time, he worried that Xilor went the long way around the abyss and sailed up the east coast to take Golden City before marching west to Ralloc. He dismissed this idea.

What in the Shades of the Underworld is he doing?

His reverie shattered as a distant rumble reached his ears, not that of thunder from far-flung clouds, but of thousands of marching feet. He glanced around at the soldiers near him, and they stopped to listen, all eyes on the

Corridor.

Good, it's not just me then.

The sound carried the forewarning long before he spied them pouring out of the Corridor of Cruelty.

He used magic to project his voice throughout the city.

"STAND TO!"

Pandemonium broke as the guards on the wall clattered in their mail and boiled leather, peering through the quickening darkness. In the camp, sleeping soldiers scrambled from their tents half-dressed. Shouts and orders pealed across the ranks of enlisted men as master serjynts overlooked formations led by serjynts—the backbone of the Grand Royal Army. Men-at-arms and scabs alike threw mail over their boiled leather, cinching boots, and strapping on their specified weapons of swords, bows, axes, and long spears.

The last of the failing light bled from the south. In the creeping night, trolls and goblins marched under a cloud of darkness.

"No matter how many of them or how few," Judas shouted, "don't engage them in hand-to-hand combat. Though undoubtedly you are all well-trained with the sword and spear, use your magic as best as you can, for as long as you can. They can't repel a magical assault."

"How did it come to this?" a frightened voice asked at Judas's shoulder.

The warlock jerked his head, observing a dumbfounded Kayis Dathyr. Judas hadn't noticed the former consul clambering up the stairs.

"It happened while you were too busy slandering me and running Ralloc into the ground."

Kayis's face showed how much his words stung the heart. He shut his eyes, trying to hide his guilt.

"I'm sorry I doubted you...*Master.*"

Judas hid his surprise. The elder reached out with his magical essence and brushed up against Kayis's, noting his sincerity and something stronger.

Shame.

Judas changed the subject so Kayis wouldn't feel embarrassed.

"Don't be sorry yet. Xilor still hasn't shown himself. Probably preoccupied, or he wants to get our hopes up."

As if on cue, the advancing legion came to a halt. Thunder bellowed, and lightning flickered from the sky above, fracturing the quiet. An arching bolt came crashing down between the goblins and the wall. Smoke curled from the obliterated earth, and Xilor emerged.

Shades, I spoke too soon.

Terror swept through the ranks, gasps of shock, awe, and horror turned into murmurs and panicked conversation. Judas turned to them to rally their courage.

"Look at me," he called, hoping they'd forget their fear. "I stand here unafraid. I said all along that he'd return. You've seen him with your own eyes, and I'm still here, standing with you. He was defeated before and will be again. Even with his dark magic, he can't stand against this army; he isn't powerful enough, and never will be. Your fear and despair only feed him, making him more powerful. Stand and fight; don't sway in the darkness before you."

"You have a way of saying what is needed, Master Lakayre," Dathyr said quietly, still shell-shocked.

His eyes were glazed, like ghosts haunting his vision.

"Well, hopefully, it worked. Master? Now, that's a title I haven't heard from you in a long time."

"I was wrong..." Dathyr started, his voice was soft. "My father and grandsire..."

"All's forgiven, pupil. Never think that I was angry with the decision you faced; it wasn't an easy one," Judas encouraged.

He turned his attention back to Xilor's army.

"Yes, but that doesn't make it right."

"No, it doesn't, but if it's right in your heart, and you're truly sorry for things you have said and done, then all is forgiven."

Judas brushed Dathyr's essence again, the sincerity evident.

Xilor's amplified voice carried on the mystic wind.

"Surrender now or the souls the Underworld claims tonight are on you."

Judas opened his mouth to counter, but earsplitting roars ripped through the sky. The sound of giant swooping wings filled the air. The soldiers searched the sky, shifting, quaking in fear. Dragons filled the air, rushing through the cloud of darkness hovering over Xilor's numbers.

Upon their backs, the xicx rode them.

So, that's why he took so long! He went to parlay with the dragons!

They swooped down on cowering prey, smiting them with fire, razing them with teeth. Men, burning alive, ran screaming. The Grand Royal Army abandoned their formations, fleeing for their lives.

It seemed to Judas that now, as he was taking cover from the creatures of the air, no one would be able to stand against the onslaught. Xilor had brought in an element that none could stand against, and they were woefully unprepared. No wall was high enough; no building was safe. He had to think of a way to repel the beasts.

He only hoped he could do it in time to save the men below.

Chapter 73: Xenomene's Quest

Xenomene slipped soundlessly into the tent like an assassin. She stood still for a moment, letting her eyes adjust to the darkness, waiting to distinguish his form. The Mind slept on his makeshift bed. Standing in his presence, the longing came over her again.

Many a night she dreamed of him, each fantasy different from the last. Some dreams he was dying; in others, she fell in battle. In a rare few, he abandoned them, and she hunted him down; alternative fantasies portrayed a more favorable picture as he rode her into delirium.

And there were the nightmares—everyone dead, the Heart favored, or Mauler slit his throat, robbing her of her quest.

She'd dreamed of Bitcher, too—erotic, carnal, deliciously perverted—but if he died in her dreams, she probably wouldn't shed a tear.

But just as the Krey took kills on the field, so too, they took quests—a body count—to their beds. The Krey, unlike their prudish Ralloc neighbors, lived life naked, raw, and unfiltered—more to the liking of those who resided south of the Melodic Mountains. By the Black Tide's standard, Xenomene was one of the most prudish within the Hive.

But tonight, she was on a quest. She would mount the Mind, ride him through a foray of flesh, and then discard him like a corpse on the battlefield.

Xenomene dropped her robe, revealing her stark skin beneath. She hadn't bothered with undergarments—not when she came for sex. Her hand found his leg beneath the blanket, her fingers lightly running up to his groin.

He stirred but didn't awaken.

Xenomene knelt beside his bed, pulled the covers aside, and took him into her mouth. He awoke with a start as he grew firm, and she continued her rise and fall in the darkness.

"Oh, gods. What—?"

She clamped a hand over his mouth, withdrew him from her mouth, and shifted her body to straddle him. Her warm flesh rubbed against his, her small, smooth breasts against the coarse hair of his chest. She kissed him quietly, hungrily, but without a mote of love.

"A quest," she breathed into his mouth. "Shut the fuck up."

She slid backward, maneuvering herself over his member, and slowly sank as he breached her. An exhale escaped her as she wiggled down on him. He filled her, and even though slick, it was snug.

It'd been too long, too many years since her last time.

His warm hands clutched her buttocks, and she felt his mind reach out to meld with hers.

"No. Stay out of my head."

His mental caress died away but not before she could feel his disappointment, or how soon he'd finish. Tonight wouldn't last long.

He sat up, hugging her petite frame to his. She rocked back and forth, then up and back, and the thrusts turned smoother as she grew slick. This close in the darkness, she saw his eyes widen, and he stifled his moans into her chest.

He kissed her neck, holding her tight. Xenomene let out a groan, not love, but animalistic desire. She slowed her up and down movement to draw out the moments they had together, wiggling back and forth, rubbing her bud against his groin. She closed her eyes, focusing on the growing sensations within—

A clear, loud call rang out in the night.

"STAND TO!"

Xenomene stopped abruptly, her eyes snapping open, pushing him away, head snapping around in the direction of the voice. His back hit the bed, and a gasp of irritation escaped him.

"Just a little more," he said. "I'm almost there."

But the voice, the magical voice, she knew what that meant.

War had finally come.

She rose off him, his hardened length slipping free, forgetting him as if he'd never existed. Creeping toward the opening of canvas, she sought out the origin of the voice, but it was too far away, to the southwest.

"We can still finish!" the Mind said behind her. "We haven't even started!"

She felt her head shaking as if in a trance. Xenomene squared her shoulders, her spine straight. The quivering ecstasy in her body from earlier changed as realization moved through her. Now, something else quickened within her. Her body thrummed with purpose, anticipation, with excitement.

Behind her, she heard the Mind grunt, and she glanced back at him, seeing him finish what they started, using her backside as a visual, her warm slick still clinging to his skin. He swung his legs off the bed, reaching for a cloth to clean himself.

"What's wrong with you?" he asked.

She bent and scooped up her discarded robe.

"War," she said, her voice breathless.

"Yeah? So? We expected it."

"You're about to watch a fucking artist work."

She shouldered her robe on, not bothering to close it.

"There will be blood, and I'm going to bathe the ground in it."

Gods, why did she feel so drunk at the thought?

Before she realized what she was doing, she bolted from the tent, hurrying to her own.

She raced past tents and rousing squad members, rushing to don her armor. Her robe rippled behind her in her mad dash, and she felt the cold kiss of night air against her ass.

Someone hooted at her, and if she had to guess, it was Bitcher. Who cared? They didn't know what she was doing. For all they knew, she was rushing from the privy instead of a sexual rendezvous.

Inside, she shrugged into her cloth tunic and breeches before the boiled leather. With the dragon-plate armor quickly strapped into place, she emerged with her helmet tucked under her left arm, and her sword hanging from her left hip.

Raven sidled up beside her, and he started to say something but stopped, his eyes going distant as he focused on a sound. She heard it too, the sound of massive wings before a roar that split the night.

She turned her gaze up as dragons descended.

Chapter 74: Cape Gythmel

Within an eyeblink, the battle had changed. Judas watched as huge talons ripped through the wizards and shredded the armor of soldiers; all men were defenseless against the dragons. Everyone ran for cover, cowering at the nearest refuge, but that wouldn't save them. Liquid fire seared flesh in a bright flash.

Amid the screams and roars, a haughty, sinister laugh echoed as the dragons lay siege to the helpless army.

"Is this all you can muster, Judas?"

Judas wanted to go down there, but he couldn't. It wouldn't be a fair fight. Once Xilor saw him, he'd either teleport away or he'd have his minions fight on his behalf.

"Is there no one who dares to challenge me?"

Kayis climbed out from under what cover he could find, coming up to Judas's side. Through it all, Judas stood untouched. Was that by Xilor's orders, or did the dragons think him insignificant?

Kayis stepped to the edge of the wall.

"Someone needs to stand against him, and I will if you won't."

Judas grabbed him by the arm, pulling him back.

"No, you can't face him," Judas urged, attempting logic and reason.

"Someone has to. I don't fear him!"

"You don't fear what you do not understand. Listen to me; you can't defeat him. This is what he wants, to demoralize us."

Kayis spun, anger in his eyes.

"You have no faith in my abilities, Master. You never have."

"It's not a question of—"

"You're trying to hold me back, as you did so long ago. I won't cower."

Kayis glanced out at the tall, billowy figure clad in black and shadows.

"I'm ready to right all the wrong I have done."

"At the expense of your life?"

Kayis swallowed, and Judas heard it.

"If that's the price."

Judas let go of his arm, knowing he'd be unable to dissuade the youth.

"Then, I won't stand in your way."

Judas couldn't hide the sorrow in his voice, but he doubted Kayis heard it.

"May my teachings quicken your heart and nimble your mind."

Kayis nodded, then plunged over the edge of the wall between battlements, his fall slowed with displacement. Judas watched as the younger man landed safely and stalked forward.

Judas enhanced his hearing to catch anything that might pass between the two before their personal battle ensued. Xilor spotted him quickly, and he flung his arms wide in anticipation.

"He's mine!" Xilor bellowed.

Kayis closed in at a trot. Fiery breath illuminated the night. Goblins and trolls stormed the wall with ladders and ropes with grapnel hooks. A battering ram lumbered forward, heaved by a sea of bodies.

Kayis pulled his wand and broke into a sprint, closing the last thirty meters. Xilor braced himself. As Kayis ran, he flicked his wand out to the side and heaved a large rock at Xilor, his incantation said under his breath, drowned in the sounds of battle.

The rock hurled through the air until green luminance spewed out and shattered it. Xilor made a shoving motion, sending the fragments back at the oncoming attacker. Kayis threw up a shield in time to block most of it, then hurled a shockwave through the earth as he closed the last ten meters. With an outstretched hand, Xilor absorbed the blast, and Judas saw that it'd surprised Kayis, throwing his stride off.

Kayis screamed an incantation, and a swirling pillar of fire erupted from the tip of his wand; the vibrant yellow spun with life and heat, a magical sword ready to cut through anything that stood before him.

He charged, sprinting, a growl simmering in his throat. Judas wanted to warn him, to cry out about overextending, but it was too late.

In the last instant, Xilor mirrored the wizard's conjury, a vortex of green light spewing from the tip of his wand.

Kayis lunged, stabbing.

The magical yellow blade was caught in Xilor's skeletal hand, wrapping around and absorbing the energy. Xilor glanced at the energy, then turned back to his opponent. With a jerk, the dark lord wrenched the blade aside and pierced him in the gut before dragging the blade up, disemboweling Kayis in one stroke.

As Kayis's body fell, Judas closed his eyes, turning away. He should've stopped him, kept him from going down there, but who was he to determine one's life or death?

Xilor's magically amplified sneer snaked through Judas's ears, a taunt to goad him into coming down.

"Pathetic."

Judas glanced back. Xilor stepped on the fallen body as he closed in on the wall, his hordes rushing behind him.

Chapter 75: Judas

Judas watched as the next dragon swooped down, spewing fire as it dove. In minutes, the battle would be over—unless he stopped them, but that meant killing them. He didn't want to; he had enough killing from the first war, but these people, these soldiers and Krey, didn't deserve to die because he did nothing.

The dragons would turn all of Cape Gythmel's defenses to slag in heartbeats.

Judas reached out for his essence, that deep resonance from the core of the planet, feeling how magic encompassed him and everything around him, from the dragons above to the hordes below. He drew from the well, siphoned from his enemies; their lives and energy would feed the protective spell.

Like jerking his hand away from a fire, his movement drew from them, and in a mighty blast, he shot the magic upward, forming a protective barrier around Cape Gythmel. In an instant, many goblins perished, and the fiery breath reflected upon the airborne predators, incinerated by their flames. The apex creatures were impervious to almost everything except surgical, magical attacks, the claws of another dragon, or their inferno breath.

Shrieks escaped the dying beasts as they plunged to the ground. As they fell, Judas launched each of the dying carcasses towards the invading army, obliterating hundreds beneath the crushing weight of the colossal creatures. The carcasses rolled through the ranks.

Try as he might, Judas couldn't deflect them all. Two beasts plunged within the defenses, and the tail of the second cleaved a massive gap in the wall.

The trolls hastily capitalized on the opening.

Above, what dragons remained circled, then retreated. Judas glanced down at the inner yard as the master serjynts formed their troops in ranks, spears in front, swords and shields behind. Archers offset behind them, arrows nocked and ready for the approaching storm.

Before the dust cleared, the rushing horde broke through the gap, clambering over the lifeless bodies, armored in boiled leather at most. Even if they killed all of them today, it wouldn't dent Xilor's numbers. The goblin populace outnumbered wizardkind seven-to-one.

The first wave crashed against the spears and fell by the dozens; guts, blood, and bone spewed from deep gouges and hacks, but the throng didn't slow, only stepped on the deceased and continued on. The only saving grace came when the trolls stopped to feast on the dead, dropping the attack velocity.

Goblins swarmed through the opening, overwhelming the soldiers. Bodies fell upon spears, rebuffed with shields; swords whistled through the air cutting into whatever fell into their paths. Limbs flew, heads dropped, bodies fell, and still the soldiers gave precious ground.

Many soldiers were lost: torn with claws, ripped with teeth, gutted by blade, or crushed underfoot. The dirt ground turned slick with blood.

Judas could only watch as he held the protective shield in place, consuming his focus and strength. When the barrier went up, over half of the dragons died in moments. But for now, the soldiers were on their own.

The first rank of conscripts fell, as did the second, and the third.

Then, a massive wall of fire cut Xilor's legions off from the Grand Royal Army. It kindled bright and hot, then rushed forward, sweeping over the goblins and trolls.

Judas jerked his head away from the battlefield, wondering who was doing it. A black wave of plate flew over the army personnel, landing in front, a hardened wedge of shields and gleaming swords. And behind them, orchestrating the chaos, stood two of the three Krey battlemages; the third rushed up the rampart, nearing Judas's position, overlooking the battle from high ground.

With fluid grace, the Krey advanced through the wall's breach and fell upon the multitudes. Their irises gleamed scarlet with bloodlust, and they saw nothing but enemies that needed to die.

In short order, their gleaming swords glittered red and black, filth drenching their steel. When one Krey attacked, another stepped forward on each side to defend the vulnerable member. The Krey fell upon their enemies in a frenzy, granting no quarter, showing neither mercy nor pity. They undulated with precision Judas had forgotten, moving as one, like an expanding set of lungs, all driven by one mission, one purpose.

Their wounds didn't bleed, the bloodlust keeping their muscles taut and barely registering the pain. An A'uri standing in the center of the formation reached out with her hand, a yellow-white light flowing into a Krey's back she'd touched. The wound healed, a faint, narrow white scar rose where the cut mended.

From the left, a mass rushed the Krey. The wedge pivoted in unison, the center person changing to another member. Judas looked away, focusing on the barrier as soldiers below rushed forward to shore up the massive hole in the wall. He glanced at the sky, noticing the retreating aerial threat. Of the few dozen that had attacked, only seven withdrew.

Judas dropped the shield and searched for a flat, reflective surface. A sparkle gleamed at him in response; a small, glass shard lay just a few feet away, most likely blown up there from an earlier explosion.

He snatched it up, not caring if he cut his hands, and waved a hand over the surface. A green-yellow fog swirled over the shard. A familiar face with hair the color of flame, amethyst eyes, and porcelain-white skin appeared on the other end.

"Meristal," he shouted. "Xilor brought dragons! It took us by surprise. The wall has fallen. We need help. Send reinforcements! The Krey have taken the fight to the enemy, and I don't know how long they can hold them. Send us whatever you can and quickly!"

Chapter 76: The Black Tide

Move.

Is everyone here?

Of course, can't you tell?

Yes, unfortunately.

Bitcher, hurry up, you're lagging behind.

Shut your fucking mouth.

The dragons are burning! I can see them falling...

How's that possible?

The warlock took care of the aerial threat for now, the Mind said. *Defend the Army!*

Twelve hearts beat in unison as each foot fell in harmony, echoing across the ground. The thundering of attuned breathing echoed through each ear.

I reached the ramparts, the Mind called out. Whatever he saw, he could send to them, if he chose to.

And he did.

A sea of bodies stretched out before him, all marching to the wall. Thousands, as far as his eyes could see.

The first rank of the army has fallen, Mind said.

Move faster! Raven commanded.

They put on a burst of speed. The ground flew beneath their feet, and the earth churned in their wake.

I ate too much.

Shut it, Two-Tons, you fat fuck.

Up yours, Bitcher.

Shut the fuck up, Bitcher!

Up your ass, you redhead cunt, and a fine ass it is, too. I'd bury my face in it! Might shove my cock in it, too!

Bitcher sent an image of Xenomene's bare ass through the meld, and she burned with shame, though she had to admit, he was right about one thing: she did have a great ass. She should've known it was him making those noises at her. All twelve got to watch her in agonizing slow detail, and it fueled Xenomene's bloodlust, which in turn, amplified the others.

Even the A'uri could be pulled in.

The second rank has fallen. Weapons...

Drawn, they harmonized.

Hands, I need you to send a—

—wall of fire. Incoming.

Third rank is down.

Leap!

Nine Krey leapt through the air, leaping into the buffer created by the wall of fire that the Hand had cast moments before.

Wedge formation, I'll take the lead! Raven called.

They fell in step, an impenetrable wall of black dragon-plate and gleaming blades.

Position yourselves in the gap and stand fast there. Choke them in the gap.

They moved collectively. Each Krey controlled their body, but they noted each footfall, breath, thought, or feeling like their own. The Mind, who controlled the hive-like state, could block out people from the meld if they were dying, as the event would affect all in the squad, witnessing and feeling the death as it happened, compounding the agony.

And then the horde was upon them.

Here come the bodies—I count fifty-plus in the first wave—blood for my sword, it'll be so pretty—I fucking hate these cunts already—I love blood, especially theirs—stand ready— brace—strike—step back—Xeno pivot, I'll take the opening—done, block that incoming blade—shit that stung!—I think they cut me—you were—Hands, heal Mauler—already doing, summoning—that's warm, that light—I feel it, too—I severed his head, did you see the blood spurting?—clamp it down, Xeno—it's still tingling, your healing—it will for a time, just block it out—side, step, wave forming up to the left, hundreds—shift in three, two, one, shifting—I have the center, to me—moving—Hands!—working on it, takes time, casting—sweet gods that's pretty—yeah, so are the burnt crispy bodies—shut it, cunt—I hope you die, Bitcher—threat cleared, shift center in three, two, one, shift—I have the lead again—hell no, bitch, I'm going to survive just so I can fuck you up the ass—block the incoming attack—ready, step—sword down, reaching—block for him—weapon retrieved— oh sweet gods the blood...

Xenomene struck hard with an overhand strike, her teeth clenched, her steel cleaving the goblin's head in half. Its blood splashed against her face, its brains splattered her helmet.

Another weapon whirled before her as Raven took the chin, jaw, and nose off another one with a vicious swipe. One troll swung at Raven, but Xeno's blade was there as Raven coiled back after his strike. Her sword whistled through the troll's mallet, shattering the wood and carving through his skull.

As she pulled back, Tiny, on her left, reached out and struck a foe down. Raven swung low, amputating two goblins at once while Xeno went high, cleaving at the neck.

Waves of bodies crashed upon them, and the Black Tide crushed, trampled, repelled, cut, or routed each. Brains and blood were the least of what fell that day. Arms, legs, guts...Xenomene was pretty sure she lopped off testicles, too. And the screams...they all sounded the same, and it didn't matter the race, they were all shrill and high and keening with agony.

Before long, the bodies littered so high that the Krey started fighting upward, the lifeless husks stacking like a berm around them. More than that, they were falling behind them too, cutting off their retreat back through the wall that the army was no doubt fixing.

That pile of corpses in a sea of enemies became a mound, then a hill. Each steel stroke added to the mass as it turned into a mountain of limbs, legs, and heads. Xenomene screamed as she lunged forward, and the black blood coated her tongue. Together, the Krey lunged and pivoted and climbed up as a cohesive unit.

In short order, the gap was swallowed up by corpses, and still the goblins and trolls rushed them. The wedge formed into a circle, all swords facing out, shifting on the stack of bodies. Higher and higher they rose, fighting down the multitudes. The departed crumbled, their bodies lifeless, tumbling down, crushing those beneath them, adding to the mountain of corpses.

Every descending body took out two climbing up, creating a domino effect. The rhythm of battle slowed as fewer managed to ascend. Most of the casualties now occurred from falling bodies.

One troll managed to reach the summit, sneaking beyond the sight of the Krey. He reared his ugly head, his war hammer gripped in two hands, coming down to crush Xenomene's skull.

Raven leapt forward to divert the blow, deflecting it, leaving his side wide open. A javelin tore through his side, erupting from his chest. Bright red blood gurgled from his throat. Pain and fear radiated through the Krey as they relived his death. The Mind cut Raven out of the meld so the Krey could continue to move as a unit.

Seven blades flickered out like lightning, and the troll fell down the mountain in just as many pieces. With his death, Xenomene ascended.

Your orders, Xenomene?

Fucking kill them all!

The warlock is shouting at us.

What's he saying?

Not sure, but I'm pretty sure he's telling us to jump to the ramparts.

Are we really up that high?

Close enough.

Bloodlust still pooling through them, they gathered their strength to leap. From below, arrows shot up toward them, and one unlucky one caught Two-Tons through his eye.

His body turned limp, and he fell, crashing into climbing goblins, adding to the bones, blood, and guts below.

For the briefest of moments, Xenomene saw someone standing before her, someone she needed to kill, to hack at, but the bloodlust retreated, and she recognized the warlock. She gazed up into his cold blue eyes as he swept over what remained of her squad.

The Heart moved behind them, touching those who needed healing, making sure they didn't bleed out as the bloodlust cooled, allowing their muscles to relax. Without immediate healing, they'd bleed out, all wounds weeping.

"Where is Raven?" Judas asked.

"He fell."

Xenomene met his eye.

"I'm in command now."

He took a step back, as if the words wounded him.

"I'm sorry," he said.

"He died a warrior, with a sword in hand, next to his brothers and sisters of House Eti. As he would have wanted, as it should be."

She swallowed.

"As it was."

The warlock's eyes narrowed as he mulled over what she said, and he seemed to search for how to respond.

"Right. You all fought magnificently. Rest; you've earned it. You saved the Army from death; without your timely intervention, we would have been routed. I thank you for your service."

Xenomene glared at him, and a haunted anger filled her eyes.

"Didn't they tell you, Warlock?"

He shook his head.

"Tell me what?"

"You don't thank slaves."

"You're not—"

"—We're fodder, what we are born to be."

She turned away and left the old man sputtering to himself, and in silence, in honor of the fallen, they followed.

Lightning flashed, the sky rumbled, and the heavens opened as if to weep for Raven.

Chapter 77: Xenomene

The battle was over, both sides retreating to an unspoken respite. Other than the few lines Xenomene had said to the warlock, she remained silent. It was hitting her all at once: the do-don responsibilities, caring for those under her, Raven's death, the gore of battle, the fog of war.

She felt numb, and she'd give anything to feel something again. It was almost as if this wasn't her life, and she was living a dream. Her movements mere motions, her thoughts little more than scattered leaves on the wind.

At Tiny's suggestion, she transferred her scant possessions from her small, one-man tent to the do-don's spacious pavilion.

Raven's.

She felt like an invader as a few squad members wordlessly helped her remove Raven's possessions. They carried on as if nothing monumental had happened, but that was their way. They lived and trained for this day, and muscle memory was the only thing keeping her going.

Once Raven's things were gone, and still covered in sweat, grime, and blood splatter from her enemies, she sat at the makeshift desk and wrote to the Heir, requesting two additional Krey to fill the gap. She folded the letter and sealed it with wax and the do-don's seal.

Pulling the heavy flaps aside, she stood in the doorway. Tiny spied her and hurried over. The man had to be part troll for the way he towered over her. With Raven and Two-Tons dead, he became her second.

He took the letter, glancing at the wax seal.

"The A'uri will deliver it," he said. "You should have your answer by night's end."

She nodded and turned to go, but the big man stopped her.

"I know, Xeno. It's hard to kill someone, especially the first, and we just survived where most people can't."

She left him standing there, reentering her pavilion, but the big man followed her in. She stopped with her back to him.

"I know what you're feeling," he continued, speaking to her back. "Survivor's guilt, the chaos still coursing through you. I remember my first kill, and it'll always be with you."

He sighed, and she heard him scratching, either his face or his head.

"You expected glorious battle but received the cold reality of war. You've trained since what? Five? Well, you surpassed everyone, and now you've tested yourself in battle, but no amount of training prepares you for the aftermath."

He paused a moment.

"We each manage it in our way. If silence is the way to distance yourself from the action, then keep your silence, and I'll speak for you, for as long as you wish. I'm your second, I'll follow you until I die, or until you fall. I'll have the camp hands boil you water so you can bathe."

She heard him take a step forward, but thankfully, he didn't touch her.

"And if you don't want to be alone tonight, I can do that, too."

The mention of a bath lifted her spirits. He turned and left, and she took a moment to take in the details of her pavilion. Raven had a tub, and the bastard hadn't shared. Well, it was hers now. Another bonus of being the do-don.

The shock of losing Raven and Two-Tons weighed on her, a crippling fog as she went through the motions of removing her armor. Perhaps a bath and solitude would clear her head?

She let her armor clatter to the floor as her vacant gaze drifted throughout the dimly-lit palace of canvas, furs, and sparse furniture. By the time she'd stripped off her boiled leather, the camp hands delivered her water and filled her tub. When they left, she stripped, laid her armor in an orderly fashion, and moved toward the steaming tub.

Her reflection in Raven's mirror caused her to pause. Her emerald eyes stared back, dull and lifeless. Had a part of her died on the battlefield?

She continued on to the steaming tub and sank beneath the surface. She soaked in the heat, the tautness releasing, but not enough to relax her. After the water turned tepid, she washed her hair, scrubbed her face, and lathered her body.

Upon exiting, she dried off with a coarse cloth, and brushed her hair a hundred strokes on each side. Since she had the privacy of her new tent, she treated it like her room back at the Hive and went without clothing.

On the trail, she'd slept with covers, but now with the seclusion of canvas, and that no one would just barge in, she attained a level of seclusion. She crawled atop the large pallet and lay on her stomach. Every night, she'd slept on the ground; now she had a bed with wood slats and covered with a thin mattress of cotton.

At some point, sleep ensnared her without intention, but the sound of her canvas flap opening brought her awake. She expected the Mind or perhaps Tiny, but Bitcher stood in the doorway. He let the canvas close behind him, and she noted that he was bathed the same as her, but dressed in clothing suited for camp.

His eyes fixated on her nakedness. A small bag clutched in his hand, all but forgotten. When he didn't stir, Xeno broke her silence.

"Have you come to 'bury your face in it?'"

When he found his voice, he nodded.

"That, among other things."

She narrowed her eyes, not sure what he meant, or if he was just being his usual crass self.

"Then do it, if you want to chance the consequences, or get the fuck out of my tent. Your choice."

In truth, she wouldn't mind company, but was Bitcher a suitable choice? She certainly didn't want Tiny here.

Lying her head back down, she wasn't surprised when the pallet creaked, signaling Bitcher's presence. His hand traced her back, and she froze, not in fear or trepidation, but to see what he'd do, to make a choice. She hated that she held still for him, letting him choose the next move. More than that, she waited for him to declare his quest, and he had grounds to. She'd embarrassed him in front of the others, and if he was here for the quest, he acknowledged her dominance.

But a single thought tickled her brain as his roaming hand touched her. Like everyone else, she'd heard stories about Forgotten Islanders, but were they true or just malicious rumors?

She'd taken few lovers over the years, discarding each as they didn't provide what she sought. Trouble was, she didn't know what she desired and longed for, only that her partners hadn't provided it. Even the short-lived excursion to the Mind's tent hadn't fulfilled her.

Bitcher as a lover wouldn't be as terrible as it sounded. Fit and pleasing to the eye only went so far; his personality gave her pause. He could serve her carnal needs, but more?

She didn't want to encourage the thought.

The saying about Islanders twirled in her head as she turned her head to face him, watching him disrobe. If she was going to stop him, it was now, but seeing him naked stirred a neglected desire. Her stillness was her body's consent, and that infuriated her mind.

From a bag, he pulled out a bottle and tossed it on the bed. His hands caressed her buttocks before his arms snaked between her legs, spreading them, raising her hips and stomach off the bed, and burying his face in her.

His smooth tongue tickled her insides, the exploring depth between her cheeks. She gasped at the odd but pleasant sensation. At first, she vowed to be indifferent to his touch, but her body defied her mind.

She wet her lips, and before she realized what she was doing, she pressed back against his delicate invasion. His warm hands groped, his silky tongue charmed, and she closed her eyes, enjoying the scandalous novelty. Sometimes, he was slow and methodical, and other times, he commanded her with fierce attention and speed.

Eventually, she forgot about the tension in her muscles, the burden of command, and the deaths of her Krey. The moment he started, she gave all that up, and there was only the moment. But when his pace slowed, she tasted the disappointment in her mouth, swallowing back her vocalization of it.

She yearned for more, but she wouldn't tell him. In many ways, she just wished he'd continue without her having to tell him. Now that he was here, had stoked the flames, she'd be willing to let him explore.

He sat up, his hands still caressing her. He leaned over her, his mouth close to her ear, his hot breath tickling her.

"Roll on your side, so I can fuck your ass."

A touch of heat and iron had entered his voice, and it was a tone she hadn't heard from him before. She turned her head just enough to catch him out of the corner of her eye.

He gave her a pointed look.

"Your body already said yes, and we both know it. Do what I said."

She caught a twitch of a smile on his lips, a smirk of knowing that he was right. Before her mind caught up, her body answered his commands, and she found herself facing the canvas on the opposite side of the bed.

What the fuck just happened?

The shame wasn't that he commanded—it was how fast she wanted to obey.

His body shifted, laying down beside her. The sound of cork popping free of the bottle filled her ears as warm liquid dripped over her skin and between her crevice. His hand returned, massaging the oil into her, slickening her flesh. Hot breath tickled her ear as he spooned her, his teeth pulling lightly on her lobe.

Bitcher massaged her opening with amorous fingers, soft and teasing, and like she'd obeyed his instructions, her body responded, warring against her mind. His finger probed her, slick, smooth, and slow. It wasn't rough, but she sensed his coiled tension and knew that later it would be.

She breathed in deep through her nose. A heady sensation washed over her, an immediate euphoria. She shivered. Her legs tightened, knees curling into her chest. What was it? The first-time act? Him? Something else? Letting him have that much control?

His chuckle tickled her ear.

"Do you like that, whore?"

His soft breath tickled her ear. Before she could stop herself, she nodded.

"Shut up," she said in a breathy voice.

Stars swam in her vision, pupils dilating.

"Breathe deep," he whispered.

She did as commanded, and everything within her sizzled, a simmering fire. A haze of bliss coursed through her. She floated as if drunk, vision swimming.

All that tightness in her shoulders faded into vapor.

"Again."

She inhaled through her mouth, a fiery heat raced through her lithe body, the skin on the small of her back prickled, sweating. His finger slipped further into her. Fire burned within her, a dark gratification, and she was tired of waiting.

Her hand reached for him, pulled his face closer, tongue snaking into his mouth, pouring into him what ran through her body. She jerked away, gasping, a sickly-sweet dizziness washing over her.

What the fuck did he do to me?

It didn't matter; she felt too good to care. She just hoped the buildup didn't turn into disappointment.

His finger slipped free, and she felt the tip of his shaft against her tight opening, his hand cupping her cheek, lifting, spreading her for entry.

I guess what they say is true about the Islanders. The vagina is for procreation, the ass is for recreation.

But she could stop it now. They hadn't done anything yet, nothing to get worked up over. This could just be—

He slid into her, and her mouth opened in a silent gasp. Something in her unclenched—not her body, but something deeper that no one had ever touched until now.

With that deep breath, all those sensations she'd been feeling rushed back to the forefront, stronger than before. The buzz, the stars, how he filled her, the smoothness of the movement. His hand wrapped around her, cupping her small breast, and he squeezed. It was pain, it was fire, and it distracted from her desire for just a moment as he thrust again, pressing into her.

A pant escaped her as his hand dragged down her belly, his fingers tickling between her legs, another tease as he worked within her. She rode a cusp of something indescribable. And there, he worked her until he noticed something she hadn't, a response of her body. With his hands in control of her body, he rolled her onto her stomach, then up to her hands and knees.

Why did she like this? Why did she let him? But she knew why, at least her body did when her mind didn't.

The tension all but disappeared, her body floating. Shivers of pleasure ricocheted through her flushed skin. It'd been a long time since she took a man to bed, and the Mind prior to battle didn't count. They never truly started. He'd barely been inside her, and nothing like the way Bitcher took her now.

Still buried in her, he grabbed her hips, and he thrust again. His oil-slickened length felt like warm satin, making his cadence smooth and steady.

And she couldn't deny the rumors anymore.

Definitely true what they say about the Islanders.

As his tempo increased, so did the warmth of their friction, the oil, and the stronger the sensations rose. She gulped with her mouth open, and that only made everything stronger. It was like each breath made the wave ride higher, as did his length sliding into her, coming faster now, eliciting a moan.

She clamped her lips shut.

Can't let him know I'm enjoying it. He'll never shut up about it.

But even those thoughts died away as the intensity kindled anew.

His gentleness fell away, perhaps spurred by her moan, and his fingers snaked between her legs again, stirring her core. His speed increased, as did the depth of his exploration. Her altered mind rode the currents of swelling tides. A rush of lechery shot through her, sudden, unexpected, soaking his fingers that tickled her sex.

Unable to control her body, she clenched around him. With a shaking breath, her legs trembled, and she moaned.

He knows now.

She hadn't expected it. It came out of nowhere. Just the sensation, then the breach like a hole punched through a wall.

Her arms trembled to stay upright, her legs shook at the sensations, and her body rocked with each of his thrusts. Those sensations she'd been feeling, she'd never experienced them before, even while drunk. Beneath her rising desires, a buried question seared, knowing he did something to her, yet it was fleeting, and she caved, coveting more of his control, his debauchery.

Bitcher persisted without reprieve, the last tinges of her bliss rolling into a new building sensation. His hands latched around her petite waist and pulled her into him as he plunged into her. There was a zeal to his caged savagery, and she didn't know if it was the position, the act, or being able to watch while he did it.

The soft moan from earlier was only the first, which turned to her grunts. Writhing beneath him, she forgot about the promise to not let him know—she didn't care anymore. She twisted and turned and tried to angle him just right to keep the passion soaring, the sensations building. And just as she found it, another abrupt release came.

Her body trembled as if cold, but she was anything but.

"Shades!" she breathed. "Fuck me."

Her breath caught in her throat.

Scrotum of the gods.

"What?"

She could hear the smile in his voice.

Let him smile.

"Fuck me harder!"

She hated how needy her voice sounded, but hated that she needed him to hear it more.

Mouth open, she heaved, breath coming in pants with his relentless tempo. His hands pulled on her shoulders, drawing her back against his chest, bringing their bodies closer together. He cupped her breasts briefly, then one hand went around her throat, and the other snaked fingers through her hair.

Pinning her against him, she was at his mercy; he had none, and she found that was the way she liked it. Fucking her ass aside, she'd never been with a man like Bitcher, pulling her hair, making it harder to breathe, and it all played into her arousal.

A loud, long moan escaped her, and he pushed her face into the covers, stifling the noise. The canvas flapped in the sudden gust, disguising her groans.

"Pull harder," she moaned, and he did.

Her body rocked under his unrelenting onslaught, bringing her to the precipice she longed for. Her skin prickled, nipples hardened, and the wet sounds from sweat and oil filled the tent. She wondered if her squad heard them. Would they investigate? The thought of being watched while Bitcher dominated her was erotic, kinky, dark, salacious.

Part of her wished they would.

She climbed dangerously close to another summit, and she had an inkling of what caused it. It wasn't the sex itself, but the oil he'd used. Squeezing her legs together, she focused on the energy rumbling deep within her. Lightning arced through her, trailing fire in her veins, pooling in her core.

Fuck! Isn't he done yet?

The start of tonight was but a faint memory, and somewhere deep inside, Xenomene was turned on by the Forgotten Islander. Was it the sex, the way he commanded, or something else?

His hands reached up around her throat, and he squeezed.

"Harder," she begged, her hands touching his. "Harder."

She melted beneath him as stars filled her vision. Laying on her stomach, she gave him the unrestrained freedom to thrust as deep as he wanted. His breath quickened, and he let out a grunt.

Fuck, he's almost spent!

"Don't even think about stopping."

And that must've been too much for him. He quickened, his flesh slapping against hers, and a warm gush flooded into her. His breath hitched, his body jerked as he slowed.

Fuck.

He lay atop her, his body contoured to hers, still buried deep within her.

"You're not done, are you?"

He kissed her temple, and shook his head.

"No, we've got more in the bottle."

Her brow twitched down, trying to decipher his words.

"What?"

"The oil. Makes me stay hard, increases your sensations for more satisfaction, alters your mind."

His length withdrew, and he stood, pulling her by the arm. Once standing in front of the mirror, he posed them as they had been, one hand around her throat, the other fisted in her hair. He pulled her body against his, still feeling his hardness.

"Look," he said. "Your pupils are dilated. The oil makes you crave, itch, want more. We Islanders have made this into an art."

She wanted to ask why, but the first question that came to her mind started at the beginning.

"Why'd you have me lay on my side?"

He kissed her cheek.

"Makes it easier for a virgin ass."

She caught her surprise in the reflection, and he chuckled. She hadn't expected that answer, something so straightforward, and that he'd known.

"Now, be a good girl—bend over and grab your ankles."

Like before, she found herself complying before her thoughts settled.

Xenomene experienced 'the art' until both were sated. Her covers lay twisted, drenched in sweat, semen, and the oil. They lay tangled at the end of the bed. The tent's stifling air hung thick with the scent of their transgressions.

She thought back over their encounter, his words, how she'd complied.

Fuck! I practically begged for it!

Something cold slithered through her. By his own admission, the oil had changed her, interdicted her reservations, but how much, she couldn't say. Where did she lose herself? When did it stop being a choice and become compulsion?

She let him eat her ass, even if she hadn't explicitly said yes. She let it happen, so that wasn't it. He told her to turn on her side, knowing what he planned to do. Those were choices, but—

He poured the oil on her, coated his fingers and hardness with it. That's when it had shifted, becoming a tangled mess like her twisted sheets.

What the fuck is in that bottle? I can't believe I just did that!

She lay on her pallet, watching him dress, not bothering to cover herself. He'd already been inside her the way no man had. His tunic in place, he bent for his trousers, and her eyes glanced down at his still-swollen member.

That oil's dangerous.

She would've done anything under the influence. Giving up that much power terrified and thrilled her. He commanded, and she obeyed. The scariest part? She wanted to do it again.

She never said yes or no.

She didn't encourage him, didn't stop him.

And no quest was declared, a common occurrence among them, and that was an important distinction.

Quests were answers to complete dominance or embarrassment of a person, initiated by the victim, subjugating the other as retaliation, but declared from the start. The act was an admittance of being bested. Xenomene had embarrassed Bitcher when she kicked him off his seat, but was it enough to warrant a quest?

Prolonged eye contact, a dominance display, was the far more subtle sign of the other means of initiating a quest, and each instance was a one-time occurrence per grievance, or until the next time they deployed.

Any more than that, it was considered rape and not tolerated.

So, what was this experience she had with Bitcher? A question burned within her, and she had to confront it before it grew too wild to tame: did he rape her?

That answer was an unequivocal no.

Rape was a violent, sexual act. While they were rough, she wanted it, craved it, asked for it, most importantly, obeyed his commands.

So, not a quest, not a rape, but an occurrence.

That seemed right.

But that fucking cunt drugged me! I didn't agree to that.

So, he'd need to be punished, reminded that he crossed a line. Next time, she'd give her consent, to all of it.

Dressed, Bitcher leaned down and kissed her, but she didn't return the gesture this time.

Your dick is out of me and so is your drug! It doesn't work anymore, asshole.

Before he slipped out into the night, she started plotting an appropriate response to his transgression.

Chapter 78: Cape Gythmel

After Dathyr's fall and the initial resistance led by the Krey, Judas ordered all troops to fall back and hold the perimeter. He and the battlemages hastily rebuilt the wall from the inside while the Krey continued to fight outside, covered by archers.

Meristal committed over one hundred battlemages from all three castes: aegis, barrage, and pharmacon. When they arrived, they assisted with the wall, ripping up stone beneath the roads or below the pile of corpses.

With all their forces pulled back, they settled in for the siege, conducting war counts, what the army referred to as the ABCs of War: Arrows, Bread, Corpses, Disabled, and the Enemy. Between Judas and the battlemages, they placed several additional enhancements on the walls, including wards against dragons. The work devoured the remainder of the day. Xilor didn't press the attack, instead waiting for his hordes to clear the Corridor.

That night, Judas arranged the posts and orchestrated construction on more weapons and armor to replace the lost or destroyed. Even with magical aid, it'd be days before the first shoddy piece was available. Smithery took time, more than they had. A sword could take months to forge, and armor even longer. The aegis and pharmacon imbued the smith's tools and metal with enhancements, but not enough to deplete them.

Smithies labored over scorching coals, forging swords, axes, daggers, and war hammers. After it was tested for quality, a mage took the product for enchanting, then a smith apprentice for sharpening. The blades were ugly, hastily scraped together, but as long as they cut, that's what mattered. Most enchantments were feeble at best, but if it helped them survive another day, it was worth the effort.

Once production commenced, Judas gathered the unskilled women and children he could find and organized them into a mess hall crew. Bread was the easiest to make in large quantities, but they also prepared rice, vegetables, potatoes, and boiled grain for porridge. Two of the younger women, who weren't as adept at making meals, tended the cleaning.

A hungry army or a defenseless one would lose quickly. Placing a few belated enchantments on the defenses, he gathered the women and children into a central area in the town.

"These defenses won't hold for long," he said as he gazed upon their frightened faces. "Thank you for the assistance, but now, we must go and prepare another place for them—north to Dlad City, to help the garrisoned personnel there."

He gathered the strongest battlemages, those who could teleport—few as there were, and the slow exodus of women and children began.

"Give me ten," he called to the crowd.

Dozens surged forward, trying to grasp for him. After many assurances that he'd be back for more, the pushing and shoving subsided, and he and his first ten vanished.

It was late into the night before he finished shuttling the women and children to Dlad City. He took groups while the other mages only took one at a time. Once everything was in place with the officer in charge, Judas returned to Cape Gythmel.

He regretted not attending the wounded earlier, but he was relieved to find the pharmacon mages still working. He helped them where he could, lent power, but he only slowed them down.

Dawn was still a few hours away.

Judas retired to his tent, finding Dillon Tyku waiting.

"Kaptyn."

Tyku dipped his head.

"Warlock. I'm here for the debriefing."

Judas motioned toward his tent, and the other followed him inside. The kaptyn wasted no time.

"Some elements I don't know, such as the rebuilt wall details. That's for masters of magic. The women and children who augmented my mess-hall personnel were greatly appreciated. They managed to cook enough food that we'll be feasting on leftovers on the morrow and perhaps the day after. All told, I lost three hundred and twenty-seven men. The wounded number one hundred and fifty-three. Additional losses include eight modified trebuchets, two unmodified trebuchets, one armory full of arrows, bows, swords, and uncounted armor. We estimate losses at roughly ten to twelve percent. Your help with the smiths negated the effects."

Tyku paused.

"Other losses include three stables with grain and feed for the horses, sheep, pigs, and goats, due to dragon breath. We lost half as many animals as we did men."

"What of the Krey?"

"From the reports I gathered, they lost two members, their superior and another. The red-haired girl assumed command. Earlier, she dispatched a letter, no doubt to her superior, requesting more personnel. If I may be frank, Warlock, while they held off Xilor's minions and gave us a chance to regroup, I question whether it's wise having them among us. With the war underway, what if the Heir should send more squads? I must consider the safety of my men."

Judas nodded.

"If the Heir should dispatch more squads, it'll be because Ralloc ordered it. We'll be extra careful to give no provocation. I commend your thoughtfulness, a duty befitting your rank. Most noblemen are bored and jaded. I'm sure the Krey will keep their own in line, and we'll do likewise. The first skirmish is over, but the battle has just begun. Seek your bed, Kaptyn Dillon. The morrow isn't very far away."

The kaptyn left and Judas heeded his own advice and slept the few hours away till dawn. He rose and washed his face with the cold water in his basin. Patting it dry, Judas exited his tent, greeted by bright morning light.

Soldiers scurried attending their duties, their bustling making their armor ring. Judas blinked a dozen times until his eyes adjusted to the harsh glow. Grunts and shouts carried from further distances. The churned mud reeked of animal urine, the air stank with blood and body odor.

Judas pulled a small mirror from his robes.

"Meristal," he said as her face materialized.

"Judas. Where are you? I have reports placing you in Dlad City. Are you okay?"

Worry filled her voice.

"Cape Gythmel still. Xilor nearly routed us. I sent a few men along with the women and children to Dlad City. We have fortified our position here, but it's not meant to last."

"So, where do you want reinforcements directed?"

It was a good question. He needed some here, but even more in Dlad City.

"Send all the wizards you can to Dlad City, but direct a battalion of men here while the rest go to Dlad City. Let the jyneruls advise you on the finer aspects."

"Won't you need more battlemages to help you?"

"No. I only have to contend with Xilor. I can hold off his xicx; with the hundred you sent me, minus the few in Dlad City, we should be fine. No sense in wasting time and men here when we'll eventually be routed. Think you can pull it off?"

A devious smile crossed her face.

"I can work something out, yeah."

"Good. Thank you."

He ended the transmission.

"Don't let me down," he breathed to himself.

As Judas tucked the mirror away, Tyku found him. He was rubbing the sleep from his eyes.

"Any word?"

"Yes. We'll receive an additional battalion of soldiers shortly. After that, I plan to make do and hold Xilor as long as possible. We need to collect our dead, but with Xilor's army breathing down our necks …" he trailed off.

Another thought crossed his mind.

"What rank commands a battalion?"

"A kaptyn. Once you receive Meyjour, you're removed to a higher position."

The kaptyn's brow furrowed.

"Why?"

"I like you, Kaptyn. You've done a fine job in the absence of a superior officer, and I don't want someone else coming here and stirring trouble. It's usually customary for a member of the Grand Royal Army to issue in-the-field promotions, but since I'm acting under orders from the consul, I hereby elevate you to the rank of kernoyl. That should keep people from interrupting our smooth operation, eh?"

Dillon stood dumbfounded for a moment, and a smile blossomed on his face. Judas just knocked off over an age of service to ascend to the rank.

"Thank you, Warlock."

"Now," Judas said, "let's send a mage off to Ralloc to get you proper insignia befitting your new rank. And then, let's get some breakfast."

Chapter 79: Xilor

Xilor stood in front of his followers, a black pillar among his legions, staring at the destruction his army had created.

The chaos of battle, and by extension, life, was a beauty unrealized. The weak succumbed, the strong survived, as it should be.

As it *needed* to be.

Even in death, the bodies would make him stronger, siphoning the trapped energy. Instead of letting life take its time to dissipate the energies, Xilor took them for his own. He'd need it, not only for the war, but for what came after.

This skill, if others discovered it, would be considered a dark magic. Judas would never use it, but Xilor held no qualms about taking the free energy that was useless to the deceased. Why shouldn't he? Why shouldn't he be the strongest? There were threats that nobody realized, not even the high and mighty Lakayre. To protect required him to be the strongest. His rule would be absolute once Judas fell.

Xilor wasn't sure if he'd just kill Judas outright, or if he'd let him live, drawing power from him every day, making himself strong and leaving Judas helpless and weak. There were drawbacks to leaving Judas alive; he could eventually escape or be freed from his grasp, and it robbed Xilor of a potential totem to draw upon. If he escaped, Judas would come for him again. Not that it mattered; by then, Xilor would possess immeasurable power and would easily destroy him.

If Judas ever figured out how Xilor drew power from him, if he escaped, he could do the same to all Rallocan wizards. Within a few hours or days, Judas would be as strong as he, if the warlock made it back to Ralloc.

A movement ahead pulled his attention from his dark musings. Judas appeared before him, standing fifty meters away.

"He's mine!" Xilor bellowed.

His startled army fidgeted, wanting to engage, but fear of their master stayed their action. He took a step toward him.

"So, you have finally come?"

"I haven't come to fight you," Judas said, his voice carried on wind and magic.

"Why are you here?"

Judas walked forward, keeping a slow pace.

"I've come to make a magical pact, an accord between us—our army and yours."

Xilor noted Judas's eyes darting to the sky, the army, Xilor himself, the ground, and the carnage. What was he searching for?

"Let us hear your pleas."

Judas was up to something; he didn't come to make an agreement—or maybe he did, but something else spurred him into action. Xilor had to figure out what that something was before Judas turned that to his advantage.

"If you're so bent on destruction, perhaps you should try to win over those you wish to oppress."

Beneath the cowl, Xilor's lips twisted in disgust. What game was he playing? What was the goal?

Judas sidestepped fallen bodies.

"If you win, those you oppress will rebel."

Then, I'll have more enemies to drain.

Xilor paused a beat, letting Judas think he was mulling over his words. Instead, he was trying to ferret out why his nemesis had come, and what the end goal was.

"What do you mean?"

Judas paused in his approach, glanced around, then stepped around the bodies. Once he found a path, he continued on and spoke.

"After each battle, you allow us to collect the fallen, unhindered, so that we may return the soldiers to their loved ones."

Judas stopped after his sentence. He squatted down next to a body and touched the soldier before rising and continuing forward. The distance between Xilor and Judas closed to thirty meters.

"If you manage to come into power, they'll have that to say about you. Despite oppression, you were honorable."

What's the point? What's he after?

But it was better to prune this, turn it on its head before Judas could spring whatever trap he was setting.

"On one condition: only after I say. I'll send a messenger two days after each battle, and then, you can collect your fallen."

That stopped Judas's movements. His head lifted to stare at him.

"Two days?"

Judas sounded disgusted, and that pleased Xilor.

"Why two days? The dead will start decomposing. How are their families supposed to give them their rituals?"

"I don't care! Two days is what you'll receive, or nothing!"

Xilor noted how his face gave away his internal battle, his mind working, trying to ascertain why he wanted two days.

"Two days, then," Judas relented.

Kneeling by another body, Judas placed a caring hand on the soldier. Xilor swore Judas's eyes misted over; frail emotions exposed a fatal weakness in him. As Xilor peered closer at the body, he tried to discover why it'd bring out those feelings. Who would be so important to Judas to make him almost weep?

Xilor's eyes danced between the two, the warlock and the fallen. He took two quick steps forward, trying to discern the lifeless husk, and that's when he realized the details. The man didn't wear armor but robes. Judas hadn't come for the body of a soldier, but that of his student: Kayis Dathyr.

Why does Judas care for this one?

That answer came quickly: he was the previous consul. Judas intended to take the body to Ralloc, so he could be buried for all the citizens to see, spread a tale of Dathyr facing down the Dark Lord, and become a rallying point, a figure of bravery for their men. Their resolve would harden behind their martyr.

Xilor couldn't allow that to happen.

"Get him!" Xilor screamed.

But it was too late.

Judas winked out of existence, taking the body with him. He seethed in rage, vowing Judas would pay. His first thought turned to attack, to exact a toll for his duplicity, but the magical accord stayed his hand. If he attacked now, he couldn't freely siphon the dead's energy after the next engagement.

Simmering, Xilor turned on his heel, his black robes billowing behind him. It was time to destroy Judas from within.

Chapter 80: Ralloc Domain

Judas had never seen so many people in one place, all standing still and quiet, a solemn vigil.

Ralloc's cobblestone streets were filled with citizens of all births: noble, minor noble, commoners, bastards, prostitutes, and servants. The casket, made from white-rose wood from the elyfian lands, passed down the main road. Gilding graced the crystal-adorned coffin.

House Dathyr spared no expense. Miniature busts decorated the corners, symbols of the archaic religion House Dathyr kept.

The casket progressed slowly, carried on the shoulders of six Royal Guards; their full ceremonial dress gleamed, catching the light from the suns. The refined silver outlining their breastplates, pauldrons, and greaves shone like mirrors. Their white ceremonial underrobes were drawn tight, their silver cloaks like floating gossamer.

Though he failed as a governmental steward, the people loved Kayis Dathyr, never realizing his true nature. Kayis made the lives of his citizens better while breaking the back of the Kothlere Council and depleting the stores they'd accumulated. He spent for adoration, buying love, while burning down the institutions to cinders.

Meristal now attested to the fact.

Within the packed streets, a lone figure wove through the forest of people, and Judas spotted him long before he came close. The warlock could see the man's whispered apologies for jostling people, interrupting their time of mourning. His black hair, probably once brushed, was now disheveled.

The man pushed people without an ounce of grace when they didn't move, but usually a soft hand on the shoulder would alert them to his passing, and they let him squeeze by. Sobs filled the air as the coffin traversed passed incalculable rows of mourners paying their last respects.

But this young man didn't weep, and Judas had a suspicion he knew why. The boy knew the truth, as any decent reporter would. His vibrant blue eyes found Judas, and he surged through the last of the onlookers blocking his path.

"Warlock Lakayre," he breathed into Judas's ear.

Judas eyed him.

"Todd."

"I was just wondering—"

"Now's not the time. This is a funeral. You're here asking to continue the interview, aren't you? It smacks of disrespect, and I expected more out of you."

Todd's features flushed crimson, and his eyes hardened, but he said no more as he watched the casket in silence.

Meristal stirred beside Judas, casting a glance at the reporter. Her face was expressionless, masked, placid, but she probably had a dozen things to say, but couldn't decide on which was best.

Kayis, dying at less than four ages—and at the hands of the savage monster—made him a martyr for the younger generation. Many feared that his death would lull the raging war spirit, but many joined the cause. The War Council reported a surge in scabs joining their swelling ranks of the indentured servitude. Those with magical skills filled the ranks of the battlemages. Blacksmiths, farmers, horse breeders, and the like felt compelled to lower the prices all in the name of patriotic duty.

The wood and crystal sarcophagus made its way with slow military procession to its final resting place among his forefathers. Many people came forward with words of kindness, fond memories, compassion, and other accounts of the man.

Since the battle, Xilor had made no moves—odd, but not unexpected. He'd always been a creature of honor, even if twisted.

The weeping and mourning carried on as the burial song rang out, drifting on the wisps of the wind. The family of the fallen walked behind the coffin, and Kayis's sire and grand-sire stood vigil as the mourners paid their respects.

The heir sat at his desk in House Eti and read the tiny scrawl that belonged to Xenomene.

The cute redhead. Nearly the same color as Meristal's, but darker in shade.

He read the news with a heavy heart, but he didn't show it on his face. He was the heir, and he had to be strong, even when he didn't want to be.

Raven was a good man, young for a do-don, but a veteran, loyal, and he ran a tight squad. Daniel hoped she'd prove worthy of stepping up in his place.

He looked up at the Hand of Xenomene's squad.

"I will give you two new Krey to replace the ones lost. You can take them tonight."

After the funeral, Judas returned to Cape Gythmel.

The forty-five hundred men—nearly a regiment—were ragged and tired. The arrival of another battalion of soldiers—an additional one thousand swords—helped revitalize their fledgling spirits. A short-lived reprieve rippled through the camp. Soon, the new bodies fell into the grind of life, filling roles and billets the force needed to continue fighting.

Judas and the promoted Kernoyl Dillon Tyku, and the new battalion kaptyn and his five leftenants, worked out a rotating shift for all duties: watch commander of the walls, mess hall workers, weaponry and armor maintenance, and general cleaning crews. The plan: hold Cape Gythmel as long as possible, stall Xilor, and retreat.

An all-hands withdraw required wisdom and timing; Judas hoped he possessed both.

Judas spent many early years studying tactics, strategy, and war from an ancient scroll documenting a dying nation from long ago, around the time of Hagen: the nephiliam. The race dwindled until their numbers scarcely made up a tribe. Conquerors when provoked, they used magic except in battle, attacking their enemies with flawless tactics and simple weapons, defeating all who opposed. Fights rarely exceeded a few hours, resulting in bringing their enemy to the brink of extinction.

Then, mysteriously, the nephiliam vanished without a trace, like they'd been wiped out overnight.

No other scroll, book, record, or account the warlock ever found spoke of them again. The mystical scroll and the lack of corroborative information piqued his fascination.

Even now, some speculated whether they existed at all.

On the third night of the accord, the battlefront remained quiet, though Xilor's army swelled larger by the day. Judas made several quick trips to Dlad City to oversee defenses. Other than those short jaunts, he waited with Kernoyl Dillon and the men of Cape Gythmel.

Sitting on a makeshift wooden bench, watching the dancing flames, Dillon sat opposite him, bringing Judas out of his reverie.

"Cold night," Dillon said.

"Reminds me of so many other nights."

The kernoyl paused.

"One cold night reminds you of them all?"

"No. Just a select few."

Judas's gaze flitted up to the man, and he sensed the kernoyl's frustration and emotions, tired and worn, saddened by the loss of friends two days prior. The emotions rolled off him like an odor, and it burned to breathe in his presence.

Judas took a deep breath, glancing up at the stars.

"The first cold night of any significance that I can remember was the first night I snuck out of my dormitory at school and broke into the library after hours."

The kernoyl withdrew a pipe from the folds of his tunic and lit the end. He puffed, offering to share.

Judas waved it away.

"I find when I smoke the elyfian leaf, I tend to conjure for amusement. Now wouldn't be the time or place."

"Amusing conjury, huh?"

A curl of smoke escaped from the corners of Tyku's curling lips.

"Yeah, making a cat chase a mouse, and when it corners the mouse, I manipulate the rodent's presence and make him three times bigger. Then, the mouse chases a frightened cat, corners it, and I take away the magic."

He threw up his hands in a helpless gesture.

"That's pretty humorous. What else do you do?"

"I conjure a giant worm, and my chickens chase it all over the yard, but they never catch it."

The kernoyl gave a small chuckle, and Judas supposed that was the appropriate response. It's only funny when smoking the elyfian leaf. Judas plucked up his wand, twirling it in his fingers.

"I read about you, you know?"

Judas cocked an eyebrow, then began doodling in the dirt.

"What did you find?"

"Not much, though I didn't search for anything in particular. It was a project in school. Modern marvels or some such, so, I did my research on you."

Tyku took a swig from the jug sitting beside his left boot.

"When I presented it to the class, the teacher was furious with me and with the school library. She told me to be quiet and to take my seat. After the class, she gave me a high passing grade, but forbade me from researching you again."

He took another swig.

"Why did she tell you not to research me?"

"A few years before, you'd been declared a warlock. The library staff hadn't taken all references to you off their shelves."

Another huge gulp went down his throat, and a few droplets dribbled down his scruffy chin.

"And why did you consider me a modern marvel?"

"You left the school at the age of nine, which only happened one other time, a feat yet to be repeated. It'll never happen again. The Wizard's War ended because of you: one man."

He shrugged.

"Seemed like a marvel to me."

Judas's lips thinned.

The officer took a deep breath.

"How powerful are you?"

Judas felt his brows nettle.

"I beg your pardon?"

"How powerful are you? You must be exceptionally gifted to leave school so early. I bet your parents and your brother were proud. That was before anyone knew you were a warlock. Probably before even you!"

Judas shook his head.

"Pride isn't what I'd call it. I'm sure my mother, in her way, rejoiced, but my father? He attended me with disdain."

"Why?"

"I'm not the first born."

Judas stood, taking his leave. The conversation killed his mood. The night ended uneventfully and dragged into the next day. With each dawn, the only movement detected was the amassing of Xilor's army. Hours stretched into days, which bled into weeks, but not every day passed without incident.

Xilor probed the defenses with small parties, usually under the cover of darkness. A few times, a couple hundred would attempt an assault, repelled with minimal effort, the runes on the walls holding firm, or the Krey responding with alacrity. By the third week, the fortifications of Cape Gythmel ran at peak efficiency despite such small numbers.

Soon, Xilor would grow bored of the lull and order an all-out assault, forcing them to retreat. He couldn't afford another repulsion. It had to be a decisive victory, or his followers might abandon him.

Between Dlad City and Ralloc lay Crossroads, a small village half the size of Dlad City. Crossroads already evacuated the population to Ralloc, and they left a booby-trapped ghost town in their wake. There was only one direction Xilor wished to go: north to Ralloc. He already controlled the vampires to the west, and to the east, lay Vikal Village and the Elyfian Enclave.

As long as he didn't tarry with the elyves, his path remained clear to Ralloc.

Either his age or his first experience with commanding men had been unique, Judas discovered controlling fifty-five hundred men with only seven officers was difficult. Tyku promoted more men: serjynt Leon to master serjynt, and a few men-at-arms to serjynts.

From the night they met around the fire, it became their nightly ritual, sharing stories, talking philosophy, or passing the time with idle conversation.

"My grandfather's proud, but my father's going to be pissed when he finds out!" Dillon said.

He took another deep pull from the jug he always brought with him.

"What do you mean?" Judas asked.

"My father will be furious. You see, I've been in the army for an age and an era."

"Yes?"

"Well, my father's been in for three ages longer, and he just made meyjour about a score of years ago."

The kernoyl laughed, chugging his ale.

"He's got to take orders from his son!"

"Who's your father?"

"Meyjour Dillon Tyku Jr."

Judas's head snapped up from his gaze into the sputtering flames.

"Tyku? Jr.?"

"Yeah, why?"

"Any relation to the teacher? Scholar Tyku?"

"Yeah, he's my grandfather," the kernoyl said, then gave a drunken laugh.

The sudden revelation brought back a vivid memory for Judas.

"Well then, it's evident the boy cheated," the Overseer said, his eyes darting between Scholar Tyku and Judas. As a boy, Judas remembered sitting at the Overseer's desk, his teacher hovering behind him. His hands held more interest than the conversation, waiting for his chance to speak.

"I thought so, too, at first, but there's no way the boy could cheat. He's the brightest in his class, by far. How he managed to do all the work inside his head is beyond me. Even you and I would have to write it down."

"Is the exam that hard?" the administrator intoned.

"Yes. I made it that way, on purpose."

"I see. So how are students supposed to pass a test they can't even fully understand or answer?"

"I grade what's completed, not on whether the exam is complete."

The Overseer scrutinized him.

"Test him again. This time, alone, and under both of our supervision."

Led into another room and given the same assessment, he completed the exam before a half hour elapsed. As Judas was permitted to leave, the Overseer called out to him.

"Wait. What's your name son?"

"Judas Lakayre."

"Did you meet him?"

The kernoyl's voice broke into Judas's memories, and he blinked a few times, seeing Tyku smile at him from across the fire.

"Who?"

"My grandfather? Scholar Tyku?"

Judas nodded, but didn't elaborate. Instead, he switched the topic from grandfather to father.

"Where's your old man?"

"Part of the reserve unit that stayed behind at Ralloc. I'm rather glad about that, too."

With another sip of ale, he shook his head.

"He likes to be in the midst of things, doing it himself, instead of letting other people do their jobs. A micro-manager and a pain in the ass. You should have seen my childhood. He would've been right there leading the charge down to Xilor, right along with Consul Dathyr."

Judas smiled. If Kayis Dathyr becoming a symbol of courage, it was one to be remembered.

So long as it doesn't get overshadowed in the history books.

Still, it pained him that the rallying symbol came at the cost of life.

He found it odd no one admired him for his courage in telling the truth, for defying a corrupt government, but his branded title ensured a stigma followed him like a stench. Which begged the question: why was the kernoyl trying to befriend him? What was in it for him? Back among his superiors, Tyku would drop him like a sack of stones.

Judas cleared his throat.

"Tell me about yourself."

The kernoyl glanced up at him, a puzzled look on his face, suspicion and other emotions lacing his voice.

"What do you want to know?"

The warlock's brow frowned, and he conjured a sheet of paper, inscribed a message, and waved his wand over the parchment which vanished in a bright, quick flame.

"Anything. We've talked about your sire and grand sire, but not you."

Over the next half hour, it became increasingly clear to Judas that Kernoyl Dillon Tyku hid something so significant that the man jumped across subject matter seemingly at random. Several times the kernoyl tried to excuse himself, and each time Judas politely insisted he stay and continue his story.

"Warlock Lakayre, I don't think it's appropriate for me to be seen in your company for too long by the men. They might get anxious."

"Nonsense! It's good for morale. They need to see their leaders working together."

There was a clattering of metal and mail as footsteps approached their fire. The warlock regarded the two newer leftenants walking up, one holding a crumpled parchment in his hand. The first stopped short, looked pointedly at Judas, and gave a slight shake of his head.

With a small nod, he spoke, "Continue on, leftenants."

Judas returned his attention to Tyku, and he noted the man saw the parchment. Confusion and a myriad of emotions danced across his face. His eyes quickly shifted back to Judas.

"So, tell me, Kernoyl, what do you know about me?"

Tyku's eyes darted around. Judas's lips pressed into a thin line as his wand doodled in the dirt.

"Well ... I, er, that is to say ... can, uh ..."

"What's the matter, Kernoyl? Are you alright?"

The man only nodded.

"Perhaps you're sick? Here, lie down and let me examine you. Perhaps it's food poisoning?"

"Food poisoning?" Dillon exclaimed. "Do you think someone would do that to their senior officer? Perhaps I should visit a pharmacon mage."

"Yes, there's a motive for such a thing. Perhaps someone is jealous of your excellent achievements?"

Judas let the sentence hang there for a moment.

"No, I'm sure I'm fine. Don't worry about me."

He waved off the help.

"Are you sure? You seem like you are barely...holding it together."

Running footsteps thundered behind them, the two leftenants pulling up short. One spoke.

"We have him."

In a flash, Judas teleported across the fire, his hand clutching the kernoyl by the throat.

"You," he growled. "I'll ask you again, what do you know about me?"

In a fraction of a second, he went from an old man to a battle-hardened warrior. He felt the vigor returned to his hands, the fire in his gut, the pulse of battle reigniting in his limbs.

The madness of war.

"That you're going to die," the kernoyl croaked.

Gritting his teeth, Judas shoved him, pointed his wand, and a blaze of light erupted from the tip. A scream pierced the night, an inhuman shriek as the... thing dissolved into black mist.

One of Xilor's sheol: a xicx.

"STAND TO!" the warlock shouted, amplifying his voice with magic.

In a jumble of motion and sound, bodies arrived at their posts, and within minutes, all were settled into position, armored, and awaiting orders.

Hell awaited them, and each of them knew the plan, spoken like a mantra: resist, destroy, and evade.

In the absolute stillness of the dying outpost, they heard.

The first footfalls of the advancing doom.

Judas spun around, toward the interior.

"Flight one, go!"

Twenty-five battlemages teleported away, ripping through the night in a blind race against time and death.

He just hoped they'd get back in time.

Chapter 81: Cape Gythmel

Xilor sent in a decimating legion of twenty thousand goblins and trolls. Anything less would spur Judas to stay in defiance; cutting off his options, Judas would be left with two choices: flee or die.

The Corridor wasn't Xilor's objective; his final destination and ambition rested in Ralloc, but if he had to choose between the two, he'd sacrifice eighty percent of his forces to ensure he took Ralloc. The question remained: how much had Judas figured out, if anything? Caution seemed prudent while the rest remained a mystery. He hoped Judas believed that Ralloc was the objective, that if he controlled Ralloc, he controlled the realm.

Logical but fallible.

All domains followed Ralloc—conquer Ralloc, and all would fall.

To the south lay the Geim domain, beyond Marcoalyn and the Melodic Mountains. Geim meant nothing to Xilor. He cared little for its inhabitants. Perhaps, once he controlled the realms, he'd return one last time to the cursed place and destroy it. Burn it. Raze it to the ground.

The thought gave him pleasure, but he hesitated, noting the significance and the history, a stepping-stone to his power from so long ago. Still, he mustn't become distracted.

What he desired remained in Ralloc, not the city itself, neither the government nor its dignitaries, not the buildings, or the treasure within, nor the vast stores of knowledge lining the shelves of the Great Library. He coveted something far more simplistic in design, and yet far more dangerous than anyone could imagine. And he'd destroy it.

The Mirror of Imaesion.

Once in his hands, he'd bring back the descendants of those who followed him, and once through, destroy the gateway. Those descendants would fulfill the blood oaths their ancestors swore. With their obedience, his quest would be finished, and he'd begin in earnest: preparing for the greater threats.

Judas never realized the folly of his actions in creating the Mirror of Imaesion. In many ways, it was the twin to the Mirror of Razen, Xilor's prison. His war would save Ermaeyth and cull the weak. If ever faced with an invasion, any adversary would find them formidable opponents, even by those whom none of Ermaeyth could fathom.

Totalitarian rule, a by-product of his aims, didn't spur his action.

His musings came to a halt, and he turned, regarding the nine that stood before him.

These elyves intrigued Xilor. Skillful, professional, and untraceable, it'd taken much of his strength, resources, and time to find them. His absence of attack was due to the search for them, and the fallen angel; the woman Hadius spoke about eluded his grasp. He couldn't even detect her, which was strange.

Now that he had the nine, he'd focus all his efforts on what he could control, but the elyves evaded him for nearly three weeks and obtaining their services proved burdensome. Only overt threats spurred their cooperation.

Xilor might be considered ruthless, cutthroat, and driven, but never a fool. He threatened for compliance. When diplomacy failed, he turned to dark promises and harsh realities, but once he issued a threat, it was damn-near useless to use again.

He had, however, no intentions of keeping his word; he never did. Iddrial and his followers erred by assumption and underestimated his desire for revenge for defying him. He could torture them, but physical pain lasted moments, emotional and psychological scarring lasted forever. To destroy their dreams and hopes, shatter any chance of redemption…it would have to wait.

The weight of their gazes fell on him.

"I'm grateful you changed your minds," Xilor said. "Your part was a success, but the mission, my xicx, failed me. I'm a man of my word; you're free to go."

Iddrial, the leader, glanced at those in his charge before turning away.

"One more thing," Xilor called out.

Iddrial stopped, turning back.

"How is it that you roam undetected, obscured from sight? Better yet, how did nine elyfian smuggle in a xicx, and the warlock was none the wiser?"

"Our agreement was to smuggle in one of your followers, and you would leave the Elyfian Enclave and us alone. Revealing our secrets was never a part of our arrangement. I thought you were a man of your word?"

Xilor dipped his head. He didn't trust himself to speak at the moment, so he waved them away with a languid motion. The elyves turned their backs, walking away, but Iddrial walked backward, not taking his eyes off Xilor.

Perhaps he isn't such a fool, after all.

Xilor watched them go, amused by their audacity, but he trembled with anger. The strange elyves with pale amethyst skin defied him again. One of his xicx failed to kill the warlock as he slept.

The pale horizon to the north reminded him that a new day roused. A faint, lone figure caught his attention against the glowing skyline, someone on horseback beyond Cape Gythmel. The horse stood motionless, facing the town below and Xilor's army. A cold chill crept down his spine, a warning.

He reached out with his mind, probing the rider, finding his essence, but he wasn't Judas. Satisfied, he withdrew and continued watching his army pour through the walls.

They just breached the walls when the world erupted in fire and death.

Kernoyl Dillon Tyku sat on his horse, gazing over the ragged outpost, his personal asylum and home for the past few months. A tinge of bittersweet lanced him, knowing what awaited. He would miss the Cape, but was glad to see the town used to turn the momentum away from Xilor. He would've liked to do the honors of blowing the place to the Underworld, but he lacked the magical discipline. Instead, he opted for a spectacular view, even if it meant he'd be the bait.

For all the men who'd fallen to the blade of the goblin, axe of the troll, or the breath of dragons, Kernoyl Tyku hoped they killed twice as many with their final act. He chuckled when countless bodies fell into the Krey pits filled with wooden spears. Even after the first few waves discovered the holes, others blindly followed. When the pits filled up, the advancing horde used their bodies as a bridge.

Should've dug the pits deeper.

"They're breaking through the wall on the south end," Tyku commented.

"A little longer I should think," Judas answered.

The warlock sat on the far side of the hill, not ten meters away from Dillon, with his back facing Cape Gythmel.

"We'll wait until they break the inner walls and storm the courtyard."

"Are you sure this is going to work?"

Tyku almost turned to Judas but caught himself when he remembered the warlock's words.

"For this to work, you cannot, under any circumstances, look at me or in my direction. You must remain forward-facing, or this will all be for nothing."

"Yes, I'm sure it will. I know Xilor; he's smart but never thorough. He'll probe you, but when he does, he'll probe only you and not the area around you. Once he's satisfied you aren't me, he won't consider you a threat."

"Will I sense the probe?"

"Depends. Maybe, if you're sensitive enough. There's the possibility that Xilor may be careless or sloppy and perform a forceful probe. He would only do that if he were certain I was up here because he'd immediately strike afterward."

"So," Dillon spoke again, slower, taking in everything the other offered, "will I feel anything?"

"It should be informative if and when it happens."

Dillon heard strained patience in Judas's voice, but sometimes talking to the old man was just as irritating as talking to a woman. Then again, he didn't have much experience in that regard as he was still a bachelor.

Tyku basked in the rising heat of the mighty blue sun, Apor, his back soaking in the comfortable warmth. A gentle breeze brushed over his skin, a soothing caress, easing his trepidation. The moment was serene, nearly perfect, warm for a chilly time of the year, and it was a damn shame such moments couldn't last forever.

A sudden bolt of cold punched his gut, spreading through his body like a raging fire over dried tinder.

"Whew," he exclaimed, shuddering. "That was cold!"

"Cold?"

"Yeah, really fucking cold! Why do you ask?"

"That was it!" Judas said. Tyku heard him crawling forward near the crest of the hill.

Probably wants to watch the end.

The warlock sucked in a breath.

"Why didn't you tell me they were already in the courtyard? Damn it!"

"They weren't the last time I looked. They were just past the outer gate, and then the cold happened. Next thing I know, you come crawling up."

"Damn," Judas groaned. "His probe must've lasted longer than you realized."

Dillon cast a glance at the warlock; an almost-sinister grin flickered across his face.

"Unleash the fires of the Underworld upon them!" the kernoyl ordered.

In the early morning gloom, the distant town lit up brighter than the sun.

Chapter 82: Starriace

Months had passed since Julie left Judas in the swamplands. In the Melodic Mountains, she was cut off from the world. Judas's fate remained a mystery to her. At this point, she didn't care; the events were too far removed. She had her personal war to wage, either with Judas, Fife, or Xilor.

Julie hated the six months she spent with Fife, but her capabilities grew exponentially. The grand maghai even attested to her strength, noting her command had improved thrice since she arrived. The long and daunting way filled with mastering concentration and discipline to perceive the energy around her frayed her patience, which deteriorated her focus.

When the seasons change, you'll know.

She neared a self-appointed mastery, and her final traces of uncertainty fell away. While wary, and always would be, she no longer doubted her place in Ermaeyth. The day Fife told her to find herself, she let go of her need for control. Once she did, she felt alive.

Julie didn't care if he called her Starriace, but he never did. Anything was better than nothing. By self-evaluation, she found herself fighting perceived destiny, but once she acknowledged that she'd never control everything, a burden lifted from her shoulders. Though she didn't 'find' herself as commanded, she did discover revelations about herself.

Gradually, she reconciled with her true identity, her real name: Starriace. Perhaps when she acknowledged who and what she was, she'd attain mastery? Other decisions weighed on her mind, costing her precious time and energy.

I should've put the ring on long ago.

Even now, she carried the ring in her pocket.

Many questions remained unanswered, and many answers begged questions she never asked.

First: her power.

On rare occasions of emotional levity, an occasion very uncharacteristic for Fife Doole, he tittered about how much progress she'd made. His exact words were, "breathtakingly powerful." After hearing his conversation with the woman, Soma, whoever she might be, Julie no longer trusted him.

Every day she honed her abilities, stretching beyond the limits, straining to become better, stronger, faster. Progress granted independence, freedom from a master's shackles who kept things from her. Every test Fife set before her, she failed. Not barely, but miserably, never achieving a proximity to his capability.

Not since the day in his hut, when I broke free of his hold.

If her power tripled since arriving, when would she reach her limit? Fife's limit? Judas's?

Second: her true self.

Her name and her heritage. She accepted that she may never know, but greatly desired to. What importance did her name possess? Who were her parents? Why did her mother and father leave her on the *Other Side*? What could have been so horrible, so terrible, that they abandoned her to some archaic existence? The atrocity incited resentment, and she hated her parents for their grievance.

Third: magic.

Simplistic in its construction, almost like basic math skills: one plus one equals two. Beyond the basic structure, magic became more complicated, theoretical numbers to calculate the heavens.

Fourth: the *Other Side*.

She couldn't remember her previous life, didn't want to, but she couldn't forget she lived there at one point. The thought festered, always lurking in her mind, an obstacle like glass, transparent yet still there. Perhaps something would come of not forgetting, or maybe it'd fade altogether.

She snapped out of her reverie, eyeing the gnomling.

Today was crucial; it would decide and shape her training. Today she faced a test. Fife measured her progress through dueling, a way to scrutinize her ability. Would she ever be ready for more lessons?

Today also marked the change of the season.

They stood ten meters apart, too close for the apprentice's comfort, aware of Fife's lightning-fast reflexes.

Even for an old man, he's fast.

They circled on opposite sides, always in motion, only their sides exposed, presenting the smallest possible target. Without warning, Fife launched a fireball at her. She responded with ease, casting a mist of ice. The fireball passed through, the spells canceling each other. During her time with Fife, much to her resentment, he only instructed her to defend and evade.

Without learning how to attack, how would she overcome an opponent? She grew weary of having her questions and motives blocked by the elder. Each week passed with her becoming more aggressive, taking the fight to him. It wasn't so bad, was it? Showing initiative on her part?

Maybe he'd take note and quit sidestepping her inquiries and training.

Another flare of energy flew at her, more quickly than she realized. Unable to counter, she avoided by rolling to her left. From a kneeling position, she sent a ball of ice toward her mentor.

The staff moved in a flash, almost too fast for her eyes. Light flared as his rod made contact, but no sound escaped. He repelled her attack, redirecting the energy back at her.

The incoming ball of ice picked up momentum, but she countered the conjury with an invisible wall of heat, melting the ball instantly and leaving the ground unscathed.

"Impressive," Fife said, "the first time you tried that one, you nearly burnt my house down."

"I try," she answered.

Her thoughts raced with what he might throw next, but in the back of her mind, a voice screamed, wanted to be heard, acknowledged.

Enough! Take the fight to him. Attack! He isn't expecting it, and it's time you learned. If he still doesn't teach you, you can go elsewhere.

Rusem's ring filled her mind over the past few months.

"Keep your mind on the here and now, in the present," he warned.

He emitted another spell, and a small, silver-white wall rushed her. With no time for precise measurements, Julie decided to make a jump for it.

She bounded off the ground, but as she went up, the light followed, lurching upward to catch her. Willing herself higher, displacing herself, she broke gravity's hold and rose higher, long after the effects of her jump. She floated over the rising energy. Her right palm snapped out toward Fife as she came down.

A red glow enveloped her hand, and the same radiance encompassed Fife, siphoning across the expanse between them. The voice compelled her action.

If you're unwilling to go to fight, then I will. Let me show you what you're capable of.

Landing on the ground, palm still outstretched, her eyes widened.

She couldn't tell what was happening; she felt possessed, a helpless witness to the event.

Fife's face paled from the evident strain. He fought for control, whatever he suffered had a secondary effect. The longer the spell lasted, the more aware Julie became, infinite in her limited body.

The channeling grew in potency and the power swelled, exploding upward, filling her. Her vision dimmed, and her thoughts darkened with sinister satisfaction. The effect was akin to the book in the swamplands, but this time, she took rather than received.

In what seemed like a frantic effort, the gnomling swiped the staff between them. The contact broke, flinging both parties away from each other.

She landed in a heap; her breath was knocked from her lungs.

"What was that?" Fife bellowed.

When she sat up, she saw his smoldering fury, his eyes ablaze. Whether from fear, caution, or the physical toll of impact, she rose to her feet more slowly.

"I don't know, it just happened."

"Where did you learn that?"

"Nowhere! Like I said, it just happened."

She tried not to show her own rising ire. If he detected animosity, he might retaliate as he had before, bringing her premonitions into reality.

"I'll ask one more time, child, where did you learn to do that?"

Julie shrugged her shoulders, exasperated, but kept her silence. How could she say it came from within? How could she claim it, let alone tell him where the unexplainable ability came from? Did he not recognize the truth, her sincerity?

"I see," Fife intoned, calmer, but still angry. "What you did is forbidden, dark and terrible. No decent wizard would attempt such vile practices. You performed a life drain, do you understand? A power of the Underworld, the brimstone of the void. It drains the life and regenerates you. You siphoned life and knowledge from me, is that not so? It's no different than using your abilities for killing. It is the same for those people who mutter silly words."

Fife uttered that last part with contempt, the idea of using incantations.

It seems I'm not the only intolerable one in the realm.

"If you would teach me offensive spells, what to do and what not to do—"

"No! You're not ready. You missed blocking a spell, let it fly past you, making you partly responsible for killing innocent bystanders. Until you learn defense and recognize spells without incantation, you're not fit for offensive tactics. You've failed this test!"

Is this the part where he kills me? He hasn't said the warning. Perhaps the female's voice was wrong? Perhaps her Shadowcasting was wrong!

Her resentment boiled as she detested his scathing personality. She loathed his belittlement. Perhaps forgivable, but after six months, it grated her nerves. The second-guessing and ridicule agitated her. Walking precariously around him was exhausting. Fife never took her feelings into account, and she became jaded from his lies and omissions.

Just like Judas.

She hated him for it.

"So," she muttered, crossing her arms, "that's your final word?"

"Yes."

He stamped his staff on the ground like a judge dropping a hammer on the verdict.

"I feel…," she began, but faltered, choked on the words she contemplated.

It didn't matter how she felt, she had six months of proof to back her up. That wall in her mind finally gave way, and the voice took over.

"There's nothing more I can learn from you."

Malice swaddled the words like a second skin.

Fife gave a slow nod.

"I sensed this would come. What has brought this change in you?"

She rolled her eyes and swept into the cottage and gathered her pack and her books. Enmity scalded her insides with each passing moment, every hammering beat of her heart. By the time she returned outside, she was beyond furious, in a borderline psychotic rage.

"Starriace! If you leave now, no one can help you."

There it was, the name he always called her, the name he stopped calling her.

I don't want your help, fool! I've been asking, and you denied me!

She glared at him, seeing him shake his head.

"Not even me. Your journey leads to darkness, can you not sense it? Everyone travels the dark road within themselves, but you won't fully return. Not until it's too late."

She considered his words, but just the sound of his voice disgusted her and fueled the hatred. Julie basked in her rage, like a brewing storm at sea, contained by the resolve of her delicate will.

She swallowed, and she failed to keep the malice from her voice.

"I should've known learning from you would be a mistake, a waste of time."

"You shouldn't be angry at me, but at yourself. Your impatience drives you to resentment, like a child throwing a tantrum, is that not so? Decisions made in haste will have grave consequences, for all involved and for all who aren't."

She rounded on him.

"You shouldn't have held me back!"

Manic glee filled her heart, like when she hacked away at Mr. Pleasure with the sword.

Fife exhaled from his nose.

"The only thing held back was your true self. Try as I might, I could only slow the inevitable. You can't handle offensive spells. Your attitude has driven you mad, is that not evident? Your lust for power is already showing signs, yes? You must not go. Only darkness will be awaiting you out there."

She shook her head.

"I don't see any way around it. If you won't help me, I know someone who will. Someone who'll teach me all that I yearn for."

For a brief moment, she contemplated pulling out the ring from her pocket, where it slumbered, waiting to be slipped on, but brandishing it in front of the gnomling might not be wise. He'd probably try to take it, stop her.

Rage simmered in her blood the longer she dithered.

"Everything that has transpired is part of a path," he said.

Was it just her, or did his voice sound remorseful and ashamed? The thought ripped away too fast before she realized the implications. The other voice took over her mind, filling her head.

Are you going to fall for his tricks again?

"What do you know...of anything?" she snapped. "I don't have time for this. I'm going. Don't try to stand in my way!"

Fife gave her a slight bow and, as his head came up, she caught a tear running down the side of his face. His appearance almost stopped her cold, her anger flooding out of her like a broken dam.

But the other part of her wouldn't give up so easily, the dam repaired, her hate restored.

"I won't suffer your evilness upon Ermaeyth, Julie! If it must fall to me, then I'll destroy that which I create."

And at last, Fife's warning fell. He didn't say it the same way, and he used her name, the identity she'd always clung to, but what good had it ever done her? Julie's life had been a lie, a sham, hatched by a warlock who failed her. Julie and all the name implied was a husk to be shrugged off, a serpent slithering from dead skin.

Fife hefted his staff, his fingers rippling, bettering his grip.

"You shall not leave here, Empress."

Empress.

The pieces of her Shadowcasting materialized, though out of sequence. It mattered not, she wouldn't be staying, regardless of what he said. She wanted nothing more than to get out of his sight, away from his presence. Fife's essence flared at the edge of her senses.

She rounded on the gnomling. Hate, contempt, and malice filled her voice.

"My name is Starriace, and I won't suffer you!"

Starriace returned to a feat she once did six months ago in the swamplands. Gathering acrimony, determination, and command of her essence, she concentrated before bounding for the sky, taking flight down the mountainside, leaving the grand maghai and his half-gathered energy, far behind.

Fife let his power dwindle.

"Neat trick," he muttered. "She obviously got the talent from her mother, yes?"

"Is there wisdom in letting her go after what we've done?" said the voice that sounded like a thousand voices in unison.

"You should've thought about that before you asked me to anger her."

Fife glanced to his side as the Time Warden materialized, the shadows bending to her, obscuring her features.

"The darkness is coming," she said. "Perhaps we're not as wise as I thought."

"Soma, what is wise? What does your divination tell you about her future?"

He glanced in the direction Starriace had left, but she'd long ago vanished from sight. He took a deep breath.

"She'll find her way, her path, her peace, or she won't. True peace only comes from within, is that not so?"

Soma dipped her head.

"Let us hope you're right. Everyone makes choices; nothing is set, and that's the damnable part of it all. I've said it many times, but this woman is really pissing me off. Even my whispers are driving her mad, but I feel somewhat justified as she's the cause of it all going wrong. It'd help if her end wasn't blocked from my sight."

Fife shrugged.

"It's the way of things, to not have all the answers. What comes is both devastating and magnificent."

He felt more than saw the woman nod.

"Things are becoming clear, even now."

Fife went quiet for a time, wondering if they'd done the right thing.

"Her anger will kill her," Soma said after a time.

Fife smirked.

"Rage is part of the nephiliam, is that not so? In the blood. That's not to change. At least her eyes aren't glowing yet. Did you see her face when I called her Empress?"

"Yes. It was like she knew you were going to do it."

Fife smiled.

"Because she did. Shadowcasting is a powerful tool, but also a weapon to foil others. I'm glad she learned it. It made manipulating the events easier."

Soma floated in front of him, rounding on him and looking down.

"It's good that you called her Empress instead of using the old tongue. It'd only confuse her. I take it you know the original word?"

Fife gave a single nod.

"Rohgla. Empress…or a female god."

He paused and stroked his beard for a few moments. When he spoke again, his words were hushed whispers.

"The path remains unblemished, but what if we're mistaken? What if we just caused what we wanted to avoid? The wrong time for me to meet her would explain much."

Soma smirked.

"Always a possibility, but we both know you're never mistaken."

Fife sighed.

"So, who is her mother?"

"Ah, so something can elude the Grand Maghai?" Soma teased. "Can you not puzzle it out?"

"I like surprises, even the ones I bestow, but knowing everything breaks choice."

"And sometimes it's best to remove choice altogether."

Fife shook his head.

"What did you do?"

Soma gave him a bittersweet smile.

"I buried those particular events deep."

Fife inhaled through his nose and let it out.

"What. Did. You. Do?"

"What needed to be done, Grand Maghai. I blocked the memories from both mother and father, altered them, and they're none the wiser. But her mother is an archangel, hence the flight."

"Impressive, is it not? She didn't even have wings, and she—," he used his arm to show a flying action, making sounds with his mouth, "—down the mountain."

"Expected, though her mother left immortality behind for a man, perhaps her powers carried over to the offspring. When she chose him, she gave up her gift of immortality, but not her abilities, which could destroy your star pupil, Judas Lakayre."

"Her mother walks among us still?"

"Us? We aren't them, and they're not us."

He waved away the colloquial term, and Soma continued.

"Yes, she walks among them still."

Soma shifted, floating to his side, and both gazed down the mountainside.

"Are you going to tell Judas his daughter still lives?" she asked.

Fife snorted.

"Which one?"

Soma gestured in front of them.

"This one."

"He thinks I'm dead, won't know to look for me."

Soma grew pensive, and they both took a quiet moment to gaze out over the beautiful panorama. Like many of Fife's apprentices before, Soma knew this view quite well.

"I've always liked it here," she confessed.

He noted the melancholy in her voice.

"Of her father: are you going to reveal that Starriace is here now, among us, alive and well?"

Fife glanced up at her, his eyebrow cocked.

"As you said, we aren't them, and they're not us."

"You know what I mean."

"Do I? Don't forget that while we might not be them, the gulf between you and me is unfathomable."

Soma dipped her head in quiet acknowledgement.

"But yes," he said, "I think it's time to tell Judas his daughter lives. Perhaps in a dream?"

Soma grew quiet as she turned her head to the side as if listening or seeing something he couldn't.

"Yes," she said, "I need you to. It's the only way forward."

Fife dipped his head once.

"Then, I will."

"And now," Soma said, taking a deep breath, "we wait, and watch."

Chapter 83: Starriace

Unable to control her emotions, Starriace's concentration broke, forcing her to land at the foot of the mountains.

Astonished and perplexed by the feat, the revelation disturbed her. She'd done it once before for a brief moment, but as she gazed back up the towering mountains, the reality of it hit her.

I could've died at any moment!

What if her concentration broke during midflight?

She swallowed. She needed to discover how to tap into her hidden talent. Did the power manifest from the strength of her aura? Emotions? Thoughts? Passion made sense—her anger towards Fife still burned bright and hot.

With her feet under her, she felt weak, her legs shook as if fatigued.

She recalled her battle with the saricrocian in the swamp, when she'd first done it. Flying required a level of concentration akin to her training under Fife. Uncertainty shifted into resolve; the power was within her. Now, it was about finding the trigger and control of the ability.

Could others fly, or was she the only one?

She glanced up the mountain, seeing that she wasn't followed. She'd survived Judas's lack of training, survived the Corridor and Mr. Pleasure, survived Fife, and it brought her mantra to mind again.

I'll never be weak again. I'll never be helpless.

Her eyes drooped as hunger pangs gnawed her insides. The flight, magical exertion, and the emotions drained her. Cold rippled through her body. With shaking hands, she pulled the ring from her pocket.

A cold, raspy voice spoke from behind her.

"I found you, young one!"

She whirled around. A shadowy wraith moved toward her. Her hand slipped the ring back into her pocket as a sense of déjà vu swept over her.

I saw this at the graveyard! The creature Judas fought when he saved me. It found me!

She swallowed.

"Leave me in peace."

"I've come on behalf of my master."

She backed away from the sheol.

"I don't want anything to do with you. Leave me."

The wraith floated closer.

"How did you obscure yourself from him?"

I don't need this. I'm too tired. Why did the flight drain me?

"My master wishes your presence. If you don't come, I'm to destroy you."

"Why? What have I done? I'm no threat."

"Xilor doesn't believe so."

The mention of his name ignited her rage. The bodies of Wizard's Pass flashed through her mind, reminding her of all his destruction. Her wand twitched, jerking up, but the creature was faster.

The wraith materialized before her, its hand gripped her throat. Its icy touch sent shivers through her body. Her essence fled. Her hands clamped around his, trying to free herself. Through the fog of panic, the creature's cold laugh washed over her.

I'm going to die here!

Its cold, skeletal hands tightened. Her panic turned into hysteria, her face tightening, lungs burning, eyes watering. This was her end, dying on the obscured slopes of the mountain. But more than that, she felt her body growing weak, as if her powers were being siphoned as the life fled her dying body.

Her forgotten fury rekindled.

The sheol had given her the answer to her dilemma. It drew her life-force, and she could do that, too. Hadn't she just done it with Fife?

Fear motivated her actions, regardless of Fife's earlier warning. She'd die without it. The fire in her soul burned, consuming all she'd once denied.

The fairies' prophecy.

She didn't find a balance of darkness and light but scarlet.

The heat rushed through her, sweeping from her stomach, ripping through her throat, and rupturing behind her eyes. The creature awakened something deep and terrible within her.

"Xilor will reward me with your death."

She released everything she'd been holding in since she'd awakened that fateful day so long ago. A blood-curdling scream poured out of her mouth, a shrill cry ascending with her pain.

Her eyes hurt, itched, and burned with pain and power.

Red and purple bolts flowed from her, tendrils arcing through the wraith. Its grip fell away as it was thrown back by the blast. It crumbled to the ground, writhing under the flowing light and energy. It thrashed, convulsed, and shrieked.

I have to stop.

It wanted your life, wouldn't stop. It never will. If free, it'll try again, on you or someone else.

And there wasn't a counter to that, not one that she could find in the moment.

Kill it!

And she screamed, jettisoning all the malice in her heart, the rage that burned within her. The monster would butcher her, and her naive folly almost made her pay the ultimate price.

Because you were weak!

No, never again.

"Fucking die!"

The itch behind her eyes festered, smoldered like the sharp, hot pain of immersing a hand in scalding water. The power wrenched free of her control, carrying her away, the agony rising to an unattainable crescendo. She sensed a pop buried beneath the pain, unnatural lightning, and screaming.

The energy gushed from her eyes, blinding her. Her vision fell away, and the last thing she saw was red while the current circulated through the dying sheol.

Her body hitched, the last of her energy depleted, and the power faded in a sudden paroxysm. Where the heat once coursed through her, a hollow throb clung, her bones aching. Without sanction, her knees buckled, and she tumbled to the ground next to the charred husk she'd killed.

Death was but a few breaths away. Only now, at the end, did she understand why Fife thought she wasn't ready.

It drains you completely. I should've listened to you, Master.

HE'S NOT YOUR MASTER ANYMORE!

She lay there panting, blind and frail.

Movement pricked her ears—the creature stirred.

It'd be a race to see who'd recover first.

The memory of Fife fighting off the life drain flashed in her mind. Should she? Sheol were predators, subservient to none but one, and it wouldn't hesitate to destroy her, and she was dying.

Only the strong survive, and you're not strong.

The sheol neared death, too. Pointless for both to perish.

Do it!

With a shaking arm, she stretched her palm toward the being, and a red glow swelled over her hand. The siphon enveloped the wraith. The last of the creature's life-force leeched away and returned a trickle of vitality to Starriace. A handful of heartbeats later, the monster no longer stirred.

Emptiness filled her, sensing the creature's end, but she buried the despair deep, not wanting to acknowledge what transpired, what she allowed herself to become.

There was no choice.

At least you finally proved that you're not weak anymore.

With the declaration, her split consciousness was no more. Only one remained.

The part that helped her survive.

With the last of her energy fading, she slipped on the ring and hurtled toward the temple in the City of Despair.

Chapter 84: Starriace

Starriace whimpered in the chilling darkness. The hard stone floor embraced her with a cold, damp greeting. Lying on the unforgiving surface, her face grew numb, but she knew it was fatigue more than anything.

A fine dust stirred with each painful exhale; a cold ache filled her nostrils. Anemic from her brush with death and fighting for her life, she found the flight's exacted toll was more than she expected.

It'd almost killed her.

She lay motionless. Through the nebulous pain filling her head, fragments of memory trickled in. The last thing she remembered was teleporting with Rusem's ring.

Stirring, she sat up, opening her eyes, but the darkness lingered.

A sharp pain lanced through her head, festering behind her eyes. In her mind, flashes of red and purple light permeated, the screaming sheol, the distinctive pop, the heat pouring out of her eyes.

Even now, they burned.

Tentatively, she reached up to rub the irritation away.

"Don't touch them," Rusem said.

His presence brushed the edge of her essence, his aura distinct, calculating, methodical, and aloof.

Shouldn't he be dead? Why do I feel a presence?

"Why? What's wrong with them?" she asked, her voice hoarse.

Her throat ached like a flared infection; even swallowing hurt. Disorientation waltzed away with her senses; the unforgiving darkness revealed nothing.

"You tapped into an ability too strong for you."

His words were smooth, but his tone turned thoughtful.

"It should've killed you. I'm surprised by your resilience. Strange."

He paused, and she felt his essence brush against hers.

He shouldn't have an aura!

"By attempting the ability, which appears innate in you, you lacked the control required for such conjury. The power drew from the only available source, your life, and it cost you dearly, I'm afraid."

"What do you mean?"

"It taxed your body, and you'll be affected for the rest of your life."

"What will?"

"Your eyes."

The finality of his words was like a stab in the heart; the breath left her lungs.

"You're very lucky."

"Lucky? How does it affect my eyes? What's wrong with my eyes? Why can't I see?"

"Permanent disfiguration."

She swallowed at the words, and the world tilted around her.

"Am…am I ugly?"

She was horrified at what the answer would be.

Will Kam still want me if I'm disfigured?

Deep down, she knew the answer that she didn't want to acknowledge.

Rusem's deep chuckle rumbled with patronizing tones.

"Do I detect a modicum of vanity? You wouldn't happen to be royalty, would you? No. You have nothing to fear; you look the same, with the exception of your sclera, the whites of your eyes glow scarlet, or is it crimson? I can never tell."

A faint gasp slipped out of her, a precursor to a quick sob before she wrangled her emotions.

Kam and Lily will never look at me without being disgusted.

"Contain your sentiments," Rusem said.

It sounded like all the other times Judas had said the same, and she was pretty sure Fife mentioned it while training under him. Maybe she was broken, and they all were trying to help her.

"They'll give you energy, but will leave you weak and vulnerable. Besides, during heightened emotions, well, let's just say that most regret their actions. Be the antithesis of passion, become placid, a sponge; let nothing escape from your face, voice, or mannerisms. Only at the end of a battle, when you're ready to finish off your opponent, should you release the hell that storms inside you."

His words put a new twist on everything she'd been hearing since day one, and gave her a new path over well-trodden ground.

"I understand."

She was anything but—her passions remained untethered, unbound, and the more she tried to confine them, the more they rebuffed her.

"I think now's a perfect time for you to train."

Her body trembled at the thought.

"I'm tired."

"Learn while you are exhausted and vulnerable, and the lessons will guide your actions in times of strength."

"I still can't see."

"A momentary setback. Like I said, luck played a part. In a few days, your sight will return. Now, let's begin."

Three days passed before her sight returned, and Rusem used the time to teach her how to fight blind, guided by her aura. Through Rusem's teachings, the loss of her sight, and Fife's grueling discipline instilled in her, she grew to trust its guidance. The loss of one of her senses heightened the others, and her mastery of air granules helped her detect incoming attacks from distorted air movements.

Rusem, like the others in her life, answered questions with deliberate pauses. She heard the hesitations, the half-truths, and the calculated lies.

It was poison in her veins.

He withheld, like Fife, like Judas. Too weak to leave, she suffered his patronizing attitude. The loss of her vision emboldened his manipulation, but she would leave recovered and indemnified.

Disgust formed in her stomach for the ghost, but her former master, Fife, took the brunt of her scorn, despite realizing the truth behind his words. Now, she believed it was never a question of her being ready, but that the grand maghai had been terrified by what he might unlock.

Killing the sheol, using the power on Fife, that had been what he feared. But a more important question: how did she do it, and what power was it?

Fife said it was a power of the brimstone, whatever the hell that was, and it was a magic of the void and the Underworld. Was that the truth or another lie?

Rusem taught her the rejuvenation spell Judas used during her short-lived apprenticeship with him. With the ability, she worked day and night, every hour, to hone her skills. Eating and sleeping became a luxury; she did both as little as possible, making up for wasted time with Fife Doole.

Perhaps she would return later on and extract revenge.

Being with Rusem helped sideline the thoughts that ruled her emotions. Judas, Meristal, Staell, Ava, Fife, even Xilor, persisted as faint impressions best left forgotten.

She was better on her own, and she could see that clearly now. Yes, there were benefits to being drawn in their orbits, but it had to remain short. Her strength came from within.

On the fourth day, Rusem introduced a dim light to the dark room. The dimness didn't hurt, but a bright light would, so he gradually increased the luminance in the temple. After almost four days of darkness, the dim light seemed like Apor and Praema high in the sky.

Over the scant time they spent together, the spirit opened up about his previous life, divulging the tale of how this place came to be.

"When I was younger, I took control of a domain. At the age of twelve, I was the Lord of the Valley of Stones domain, which lies south of the Melodic Mountains. I was surrounded by wizards and elyves more powerful—well, more accurate—but all obeyed my commands. When I became older, nearing the Age of Maturity, I rode out with my marshal, the commander of my vast army."

"Why do wizards use armies instead of magic?"

"Not everyone is as powerful as you or me…not everyone is meant to be great."

He hesitated, then continued.

"We were at constant war with a neighboring city, Chissu'Nanuci, no more than a week's ride for a swift steed. They set up an encampment about a two-day journey from my home, along the river that runs to the Valley of Stones in the east. We went to destroy the encampment with the help of the stone giants.

"When the dust settled, one of my scouts reported an opening in the ground with stairs that led into a huge cavern. There, I encountered what I can only describe as an echo of a thousand deceased wizards, a collective called the

Genah. Over the course of several years, after proving my dedication, they instructed me to build seven focal temples, the eighth one in this city as the focal point."

Sounds like—

"If you haven't noticed, there are seven engravings in the pedestal in the center of this room. Each for a stone. Once all seven temples were in place, I took on the quest to find seven unique stones for the engravings, but someone else was on the quest, too. A dark creature of heart and mind called Xilor. He already possessed six, and I held the seventh. Placing the six in the circle, he overcame me, taking the seventh…"

Rusem wavered, a blank expression came over his face.

"With the seventh in place, the whole world went white. I can't tell you what happened next; I don't remember, but I've been here ever since, pondering what exactly happened."

"You didn't try to leave?"

"I can't."

She took his admission in stride, and he continued speaking.

"Some people say that when cursed with a vile evil, or when someone murders you, your spirit is scarred for eternity, becoming a corporeal ghost. I don't believe that's true. I believe that when you are given too much, beyond the capacity of your body, you become what I am. If you had an alternative source to draw from when you performed your attack against the sheol, the same would've happened to you."

Starriace sat, entranced by his warning. What were the eight temples and seven unknown stones for? Why had Xilor searched for them, claiming six for his own? Did he still have them? He was still alive, so she had to assume so.

What happened when the world went white? Did it make Rusem a ghost? Why hasn't anyone else ever talked about the world going white? Judas never mentioned it, neither did Fife.

That night, she surrendered to sleep for the first time in four days, but the temples and stones flooded her dreams. In her slumbering fantasy, it was she who exposed the cave, built the seven temples, claimed the mystic stones, and placed them on the pedestal. The bright light engulfed her and faded.

The quest repeated several times through the night. Starriace took the dream as silent confirmation of her next task. In a way, it seemed almost natural, as if she were meant to fulfill the quest Rusem spoke about.

But her nighttime vision didn't come unaccompanied—another vagary wove between, more like reliving a memory. A shadow attacked her, claws swinging for her face, catching her flesh, ripping through her cheeks. Long skeletal nails dug deep into her arms as it tried to drag her away. Without success, the sheol reverted to sinking its claws into her skull, leaving a trace of itself in her. Death, carnage, and obliteration filled her, the remnants of events done in service of a master.

She bolted awake, gasping for breath. While the temples faded, her journey remained clear and concise. The hallucination with the shadow happened before, in Far Point, the night she met Harold, Kam, and Lily.

The thought chilled her.

How could she have forgotten? What was its significance? She pushed the thought away, trying to recollect the temples. A cold certainty fell over her. Xilor placed the seven stones on the pedestal and destroyed the city, turning it into the City of Despair. Conflicting thoughts reemerged.

She once empathized with Xilor, seeing the parallels between the two of them.

Starriace understood him, his addiction to unchecked potential, but he was inherently evil and driven insane. No matter the choices she made, Starriace was not him, not like him.

He needed to die before he hurt anyone else again.

But how could she defeat such an entity? She damaged the sheol with the life drain lightning, but the attempt nearly killed her. Dim hope flickered in her chest, having arrived at a possible course of action, but could she repeat the feat?

Doubt gnawed her insides.

With torpid eyes, she cast about for the spirit, rubbing the sleep away. She didn't find him; he always left when she meditated or slept. Running the notion by him seemed like a good idea, not trusting herself with such an important decision, but perhaps it was too trusting. Passion ruled her life, but she lacked age-old wisdom.

An internal deliberation ensued, but she put the debate on hold when a small chitter snared her attention, loud in the vast quiet. Movement caught her eye, a little mouse padding cautiously towards her.

I thought everything here died. How did it survive?

The curious thought fell away to reason, hypothesizing mice and other animals were not affected. Xilor's blast from combining the stones most likely wiped out all life in a brief, intense flash. Since then, all sentient beings kept away from the city, but animals? Perhaps it didn't affect them the same.

She shifted, leaning towards the mouse, a perfect candidate for her experiment, manifesting her thoughts into action. But did she have enough control? Could she start and stop the life drain as she wished? The results of flirting with such dangerous sorcery could prove grave or miraculous.

Best to start small before trying it on Xilor.

As the rodent approached her, she stretched out her hand. The mouse paused, its little nose rolling around, the whiskers quivering.

Starriace closed her eyes, frowning in concentration. She reached out like Harold taught her, distinguishing the mouse's life force; it barely clung to its existence, starved and emaciated. A few more hours, a day at the most, and it would keel over.

Relieving the rodent of a miserable few hours of pain seemed merciful.

She tugged, drew the last wisps of life out of the animal. The small creature didn't offer up much, but Starriace detected a subtle change in her essence. As the last of life sapped from the being, it rolled to its side, stiff and unmoving. Careful not to absorb the life into her essence, she waited for a few heartbeats before releasing the energy, filling the diminutive form.

The mouse stirred and twitched.

A smile flashed across her face, her eyes wild. The smile fell as the rodent struggled to its feet. She reached out with her essence, encompassing the vermin, detecting the change. What her essence knew, her eyes confirmed.

The mouse's hair promptly turned from brown to ash gray, sickly and withered. To her startling discovery, the little mammal didn't even breathe; it stood motionless, black lifeless eyes staring at her.

She sent small nudges of psychic power to it, suggesting it perform what she wished.

It did.

Unexpectedly, it keeled over, dying a second time. As it stilled, a red-black element escaped the body and floated away, dissolving, fading.

She laid the small creature down and grew thoughtful. Perhaps it was too small, too close to death already. Could she perform a life drain on a ghost? Naturally, it wouldn't technically be called the same, but the concept remained. Rusem took physical form before when Ava accompanied her, or whenever he wished, often doing so when they conversed.

Would it be enough?

Her time in the temple reached culmination, her sight restored, and a task fueled by a story, begging for completion. She'd have to act quickly, take Rusem by surprise, unsure if he had the ability to fight off the attack. He'd lied and manipulated her, prodding her towards a hidden agenda of his own.

Did he think to possess her? Was it possible?

I'll never be weak again. I'll never be helpless.

"Rusem?"

"Yes?"

He materialized with a smile on his face, his eyes glittering.

She waited until he formed fully. He took a step towards her, a hand extended.

Her hand jerked out, moving before she could talk herself out of it. She called upon the life drain. Her hand reached out, palm up, her fingers mimicking curling spires, like palming a small ball.

Rusem glowed red; the force leeched from him. The luster traversed the expanse between them, entering her outstretched hand.

His face spasmed in a jerk of strain, his face paling. Dark satisfaction flared in her chest, a smile coming to her lips.

"I sense your terror. Not of me, but of what I can do to you. You lied to me, Rusem, tried to use me, manipulate me. You are no different than the rest of them!"

"You dare?" he strained. "I taught you while others abandoned you!"

His words invoked her need for retaliation, pulling harder on the siphon, strengthening her command. A howl of rage ripped through the room, and for a brief moment, Starriace thought he'd break her grasp.

"How can this be?" he screamed.

He strained against her hold, fighting, clamping down. He tried to diminish himself, returning to the place where he wasn't fully present. Her grip slipped, and in a panicked attempt, she attacked him with her psyche.

She imagined his determination like a hand clamping around a gushing wound, and she mentally pried the fingers away, weakening his resolve. The weaker his grasp became, the more his panic flooded him, enveloping both combatants, but where he drew fear, Starriace drew strength.

His mind raced for a solution, knowing he was losing. As quick as he thought of one, Starriace countered.

The red energy rippled between them like tight-spinning lightning tendrils. The air crackled and thrummed. The more of his essence she consumed, the more corporeal he became.

A stray, bleak thought flashed through his mind, and she snatched it away, making it her own.

"You fear that I'll bring you back repeatedly?" she asked.

She couldn't tell him the truth, that the siphon taxed her as well. Sweat prickled her brow, and she altered his thought, ingenuity taking root.

"No, Rusem," she said. "I'll only bring you back once; you'll be the first of many. Imagine what an army could do!"

She basked in his brimming terror, gorging herself, and it gave her strength —just like Judas had always warned, but now, she used Rusem's emotions instead of her own.

The last link of the chain broke his defiance, and his mind lay exposed.

The secrets he kept belonged to her now, even if she had to pluck them out one at a time. He crumbled to the floor, his knees jarring into the stone, and the funneling stopped for a brief moment.

Finish what must be done.

With her palm stretched out, the red glow arched out of the body on the floor.

"This won't hurt. At least, not anymore."

A sick, oily laugh rose in her throat, curling like smoke. Color faded from Rusem's flesh, the light from his eyes dimmed, and the red siphon dissipated. Holding the essence, contained yet apart, she channeled it back into the corpse. The luminosity flowed back into Rusem, giving him life once again. She tapered off the ability as the body twitched and rose to his feet.

He glared at her, unmoving like a statue passing judgement in silence.

"You'll be the first of many," she promised.

Yes, that seemed right. Imagine what she could do with an army of risen creatures! She could fight Xilor, and no one would have to suffer.

A dark, manic glimmer sparkled in her eye. The problem she faced now was finding deceased beings and an energy source. She could use her aura, but it would require her raising them one at a time.

She needed an army.

"You'll be a lord over our marshals like you were long ago."

An army of one risen wouldn't get her far, and she wasn't about to kill people to get what she wanted.

She wasn't Xilor.

And Rusem was already dead, technically.

She took a cautious step forward to examine him when she felt a sudden jerk pull her from behind. At first, it was a tug, like someone grabbing a fistful of her robes before she slipped free. Then, it came back, stronger than before.

Fighting the grip encircling her waist, she almost succeeded in breaking the hold. Someone or something attempted to rip her away from the temple. The moment passed in a heartbeat where her exerted force canceled the other out. Then, it was gone, and she was jerked off her feet, hurtling backward.

Blackness chased her for a few moments before she landed hard, sprawled on the floor.

A towering shadow loomed over her, and he bent down to look her in the face.

And without a doubt, she knew she'd come face to face with Xilor.

"Welcome, Fallen Angel."

Chapter 85: Gryzlaud Palace

Mouth agape, her arms holding herself upright, Starriace stared up at the impossibly tall creature.

From the floor, he seemed even taller. She expected fear to take her, to hold her close, but was surprised that she was only startled, wrenched unexpectedly from the City of Despair.

A slow blink let her know it wasn't a hallucination, and that's when the terror sank its claws deep.

How did he find me?

Yes, she hated Xilor—everything he stood for—wanted to kill him, but she wasn't ready. Hating to admit it, she was woefully inept.

Starriace half-scooted, half-skittered back, putting distance between them. Her eyes never strayed from him as she rose to her feet. Without thought, her hand inched closer to the wand in her robes.

"How did you find me?"

Xilor didn't come closer, but he squared up to her, either because he didn't think she was a threat or because of something she couldn't see. Either way, he didn't show that he was ready to duel.

"I've been tracking you for some time."

"How long?"

"Over two seasons."

"How?"

Tension tightened between her shoulder blades, and Xilor chuckled.

"One of my xicx tracked you to Far Point. He placed a trace on you, though with some difficulty."

Her breath quickened.

The night she found her window opened, the water bowl on the floor flashed through her mind.

The night I was with Kam.

The dream of the sheol clawing her face was a memory, attempting to get inside her mind.

And now, it all made sense, especially how it found her so quickly at the bottom of the Melodic Mountains.

"But I lost track of you," he continued. "You disappeared from my sight when you went into the Melodic Mountains. How and why?"

Her lungs burned as if she held her breath.

She sidestepped the question. If Xilor didn't know about the fairies in the mountains, or Fife, he wasn't going to learn it from her.

"Are you going to kill me?"

Xilor's cowled head cocked to the side. Being unable to pierce his shadowed face unnerved her.

"It's not my first choice, but if left with no other recourse, then, yes, you'll die."

492

"What do you want?"

Cold fear, coiled in anger, surged in her tight chest—more of the former than the latter. Though she fantasized of this meeting, the moment of destroying him, cleansing Ermaeyth of his vile oppression, now was too soon. Though hard to swallow, she wasn't ready to face him.

"To offer you an option," Xilor answered.

"What option?"

"Walk with me."

For a moment, she considered refusing. The command tasted like bile, her inner defiance rising. In many ways, what he said mirrored her time with Fife, words that expected obedience, but stronger reasoning outweighed her discomforting compliance.

He said killing me isn't the first choice, but if I refuse, he may do just that.

She swallowed.

With cautious steps, she padded beside him, though well outside the reach of his arm.

Xilor set a slow pace.

Starriace's eyes danced about, looking for possible weapons or avenues of escape. Her steps carried her over a smooth stone floor, near the color of beach sand. She expected something darker, more sinister.

The only decoration in the floor came with large segments cut in squares, each square easily five of Starriace's feet end-to-end, both in length and width. Recesses, both dark and shallow, separated each square.

Eight massive pillars lined the room, four on each side. A high, arched ceiling towered overhead, and the walls were chiseled ornately like balconies for homes.

The decor seemed too simplistic, a recreated cityscape, all standing in stark contrast to her assumptions about him.

This place is a mausoleum and a museum.

Two other striking objects drew her attention. The first, a throne at the far end of the room, a high-back chair of unyielding granite. The stone chair seemed an odd choice, and even more bizarre was the design, the arms tall and wide, giving the seat a bucket appearance.

The other object was a tall, wide mirror unlike any she'd ever seen, and was made of a white and red wood. Some parts were white as milk and shifted to crimson with a blend of the two throughout.

Xilor noted where she looked.

"It's fitting that your eye should catch the Mirror of Razen. That's where we must go."

"What is it?"

"My prison for nigh three ages."

Something cold touched her gut at the words. Did he mean to trap her there? She spoke the question aloud, and he chuckled.

"No. I don't know how to do that, only Judas Lakayre."

His words soothed away the extra anxiety, but she remained vigilant.

The closer they drew to the mirror, the more detail she could discern. It boasted elaborate carvings of gods and animals. Each carving portrayed a bust of a being, or an animal ranging in color; each figure shifted in pigmentation from cloud-white to rose-red and all blending in between.

An oily, black wood framed the sides, dark as ink. Engraved runes gilded in gold adorned the timber. Four legs made of a precious metal she couldn't identify formed the base.

Remembering what he said earlier, she probed him again.

"What option?"

They stopped in front of the silver glass. Starriace noted her reflection, her glowing red eyes. Unnerving? Absolutely. Hideous? No. In fact, it was almost unnoticeable.

"To rule beside me. To conquer all and have them bowing at your feet."

"That doesn't appeal to me."

That has never been me.

She glanced him over.

If anything, I'd be the puppet master behind you.

But in the space of a few heartbeats, the thought grew on her. Her idea varied from Xilor's, primarily, him being uninvolved. If given the chance and capable, why shouldn't she rule? With her as a protector, Ermaeyth would be safer, better. A society of bliss without fear and carnage.

"Then what does appeal to you, child?"

His skeletal, metallic-black hand reached out and caressed her honeyed hair around her left ear, then her face, his fingers resting near her glowing eyes.

His touch feels like ice, like death.

His question loomed in her mind. The first thought was of riches. Wealth had its appeal, but while a pleasantry, it failed to motivate her. Gold did offer her something that nothing else could: freedom.

The next thought was of a home and land. She recalled Judas's manor clearly though she had been there a few scant moments, but property was for the future, not the now.

Knowledge and the power it brought rushed at the heels of her previous thought. She yearned for both, but neither would serve her in death.

The last inkling flickered imperceptibly through her mind, buried beneath her emotions and ambitions.

Family.

She coveted the feeling of belonging, a part of a whole, more than herself, love and acceptance, peace of spirit and mind. People who wouldn't stir up strife or lie to her.

"Peace."

She turned to look up at him.

Xilor let out a hiss, and she took it as a laugh.

"What do you think I'm doing?" he mocked.

"Destroying lives," she snapped.

Her face flushed, emotions bubbled, and her glowing eyes started to itch.

He waved her comment away like it was frivolous.

"Chaos promotes change. You view me as malevolent and malicious. A distorted perspective. You can't judge what you don't understand."

"What's there to understand? You wish to stand on a pedestal of dead bodies, giving those less than you two choices: enslavement or death. And for what? Personal satisfaction? Revenge? Domination?"

"For peace," he whispered back.

His calm demeanor chilled her, but his mockery infuriated her. The entire conversation riled her. Xilor arrogantly assumed he knew what was best for everyone, had the audacity to ask her to join his delusional spectacle.

"I don't understand."

He chuckled again.

"Of course not. Once before, I started a purge, removing all thorns from society, and once again, I pick up the task but for different reasons."

The manner in which he carelessly talked about countless deaths vexed her, like a gardener conversing about a tree needing pruning.

"You call my campaign domination, I call it restructure."

"That screams of needless slaughter."

"Needless?" he chuckled, shaking his head. "I've taken away the weak, leaving survivors capable of resisting the purge. When I'm finished, there'll be no weak to prey upon. I envision powerful wizards, living without fear, able to protect. I'm far from finished, and the ones left will equal me. Who'll be left to oppose? When it's done, I'll cleanse Ermaeyth of the infestations I created."

"Infestations?"

"The sheol, the xicx, and the abyssians. Rid the realm and Ermaeyth of them. Nothing can remain, or it would undo what I'm trying to achieve."

"Sounds like you're breeding an army."

What's next? Kill all the unicorns, dwaven, and elyves?

"Perhaps, in a way, you're correct. All subservient races must be purged."

Starriace fought to control her face, not letting her horror show. Xilor spoke of a deep-rooted hatred for anything that didn't fit his design and plans for wizards. Extermination of all races.

Genocide on a massive scale.

"Breeding's such an animalistic term. Think of it as encouraging an army."

"Why? For what purpose? What's the point? Why destroy everything and everybody for this army that you 'encourage' to be subservient to you?"

"In my...imprisonment, stranded beyond this life and the next, I discovered doorways."

He paused, glancing at the mirror, touching it with reverence.

"There are other worlds out there, other Ermaeyths. Places with beings who have no drive, ambition, or structure."

"And you feel it's your duty to 'restructure' these beings?"

Bile rose in her mouth.

"To have structure, you must have a ruler. My dominion here is nothing more than readying the realm for what lies out there, beyond."

He used his hand for emphasis, gesturing to the great unknown.

"As many planets that have beings with no ambition, there are some with powers rivaling our own, even superseding. It is because of them and their threat that I do what I must to ensure that Ermaeyth survives."

He waved to the mirror.

"See for yourself."

His fingers danced over the surface. Starriace fidgeted, shifting closer. The mirror flashed with creatures and beings Starriace had never laid eyes on before. Whole worlds with people living simple lives and others with dizzying, towering heights. The flashes were fast, too quick to count them all, but she guessed the number over several dozen.

One such place seemed vaguely familiar, a sense of déjà vu crawling over her. She saw a single pearl moon in the sky. And then it was gone.

"Do you see, child? Do you see what lies out there?"

She didn't miss the hope in his voice.

"Yes, I do. You want to extend your oppression to these unsuspecting, innocent people. For what? To bend and control them as you see fit, like you do for all your henchmen, like you're trying to do to me now?"

He shook his head.

"No one's truly innocent."

He nodded to the mirror.

"How do you know they aren't planning the same thing this very instant? My aims are far simpler than suppression of other worlds. I don't care about them; I care about this one: ours. They may not know we exist at all, or they might and are trying to find a way to reach us. Together, our goal should be to ready ourselves against possible incursion. I have plans in motion to do just that."

"What plans?"

"Come with me, let me guide you. Who knows what achievements you could reach? Together we can demonstrate what order should be. With you at my side, the fighting will cease, and we can topple anything that rallied against us."

"Through domination?"

"No!" he hissed. "Ruling Ermaeyth is but a small portion of the grand scheme. A byproduct, a necessity. We'll bring order to the aimless, end conflict and war, tame the beast riders of Groyntahl, subdue the country Cronele, and topple the Kran Empire of Vesole. Can't you see the logic? Unification. One world."

She felt her pulse pound in her ears—a steady thrumming rhythm.

"And all you want in return is for me to kneel to you?"

"Align with me. Today, you would stand beside me. Tomorrow, you'd be my equal. In the future, my successor."

He shifted on his feet, facing her, blocking out half the mirror.

"I would kill every single one of my apprentices right now to have us unified."

She swallowed, not knowing what to say. Was it all an act? A ruse? Get her to drop her guard so he could stab her in the back? Did he know of the power she just stumbled across? Did he fear her?

"Stand beside you?" Starriace asked. "Not kneel at your feet?"

"It's not necessary unless you need to learn your place—" Xilor mused aloud.

"I bow to no one!"

"Don't be a fool! You don't know what we can accomplish together!"

"All that I know is to hate you!"

She waved her hand behind her.

"I've seen your restructuring firsthand. I watched the trolls butcher the people of Wizard's Pass, seen the aftermath, the devastation."

Recounting the bodies, both in the Shadowcast and when she walked the ruins of Wizard's Pass, made her throat constrict, burn with righteous wrath. Her hands trembled with rage and the repulsiveness he elicited. Her eyes burned like they were tearing up, but her face remained without showing her weakness.

How could I have ever empathized with him?

"So, you won't join me?"

She shook her head.

"How could you ever—?"

His hand moved with an alacrity that belied his size.

She jerked toward her wand, but an invisible force clamped around her. His commanding presence was overbearing, more than anything she felt or recalled. Judas never called this much power so quickly, so effortlessly. Maybe Fife, but she'd been terrified then. Either Xilor attained far more power than they both realized, or both her former mentors never brought the full might against her.

"You don't understand who you're dealing with."

He turned his back on her, gazing into the flashing scenery in the Mirror of Razen, but the hold never wavered. While she fought to break free, a part of her couldn't help but admire his totalitarian control, an important lesson to learn.

"I can see into your mind, and you think you're powerful, but you've only been lucky. You're a misguided fool. The Corridor of Cruelty broke your mind beyond repair, and warped your perception. I feel the warring within you, hear the echoes of the whispers."

Panic rushed through her. How could she, with a mere two seasons of training, overcome Xilor? She knew where it'd all gone wrong, but the fault wasn't hers.

It was my masters'.

They failed her, blundered her teachings, and proved ineffectual at keeping her safe. They lied to her, outright or by omission, dithering in remembrance of a time long gone, rekindled with her arrival.

She was a fool for not seeing it sooner.

Enmity rallied against Xilor's would-be truths. She'd die here unless she freed herself. No one was coming to save her, they never would.

Focusing her intent, she willed herself to move, to be free of his grasp. Neck corded, a vein throbbed in her temple, her lips thinned as she concentrated. With relief, she felt her finger wiggle.

A fleeting thought manifested.

In the past, no matter the strength of power levied against her, she always managed to answer it.

By the time Xilor quit sputtering about idle dreams and turned around, Starriace had freed herself. In an instant, she drew her wand, sending a blast of energy.

Xilor dodged to the side, reaching for his own.

Glad to know I'm not the only one who ducks or dodges.

Again, she lashed out, lightning quick, fire racing, bearing down on the dark creature. The rolling flames stopped in mid-air, turned to ice, and shattered, the shards flying out in all directions.

"Amateur," Xilor mocked.

Starriace let an invisible wall of heat rise between her and the incoming ice. The air shimmered, frozen particles turning to mist.

Not giving him a chance to recover, she displaced him, and shoved with all her might, sending him hurtling away. Before he made it more than half a dozen meters, his momentum stopped, his feet touching the ground.

The tip of his wand flared to life, and a spiraling green pillar spat menacingly. He disappeared, vanished. Starriace lunged a moment later, almost too late. The towering shadow winked into existence behind her, stabbing with the spiraling energy, the edge faintly scoring her left arm at the shoulder.

Pain lanced through her as she rolled away.

He lunged a quick step to impale her chest. Without thought, she splayed her fingers, lightning arching from her tips. The red-purple energy encompassed the dark figure, and the swirling green energy from his wand dissipated.

His knees buckled, and he staggered, but didn't collapse to the floor. A groan, more in irritation than pain, gurgled from his throat. The arcing lightning shot out from his form as he stood to his full, towering height.

Her eyes burned, itched, festered, watering her vision. Holding his hand up, the lightning danced from his body to the palm of his hand, congregating there before it sputtered and died altogether.

Shock lanced her, realizing Xilor choked off the ability.

How's that possible?

Maybe she didn't do it right, or maybe—

In a swift movement, he jerked his palm towards her, launching Starriace off her feet. The hard stone floor greeted her as she landed in a heap five meters away. Stars peppered her vision, and her lungs burned as she gasped for air.

Through the bright spots, she spied Xilor closing in, his black robes smoking, tears and holes littering the cloth. His slow pace gave her hope, noticing his body wincing with every step.

So, he can *be hurt! He's not invincible.*

Xilor's sudden disappearance moments earlier awakened her awareness of other abilities at her disposal. Rising to her feet, she charged. The unexpected advance caught him off guard, stopping short. His stance shifted, bracing, and she leaped.

Winking, she reappeared behind him with all her momentum, her foot striking a solid blow to his back. The impact bowed him the wrong way, sending him reeling, landing on the floor in a pile of tangled robes and limbs.

Capitalizing on her advantage, she charged again. With a speed she didn't think possible, he jerked to his knees, his arm swinging in her direction as if to backhand her despite the distance separating them.

A burst of kinetic energy caught her in the chest, propelling her in the opposite direction. The floor rushed up to embrace her, and she winked out of existence, coming out behind him, her body colliding with his.

She sprawled across him, and she rose enough to drive a knee into his face.

A roar of fury bellowed from within the shadowed hood; another kinetic blast launched her away. Breath deserted her, and her mouth stood agape, trying to suck in air.

"You're a foolish girl. Young, weak, naive, the powers you possess are only the beginning of your potential, but they are no match."

I'll never be weak again. I'll never be helpless.

"You should've stayed in the Melodic Mountains where you could hide and be safe."

In a final attempt, Starriace lashed out, unrestrained. If her end neared, she'd face it doing as much damage as possible, making him pay for taking her life.

The life drain ripped from him, the red glow blindingly bright, making her want to look away.

But she didn't dare.

The siphon lurched across the expanse between them, a torrent of swirling energy.

Frantic pleas filled her head.

By the fucking gods, if you let me kill him, I'll help rebuild Wizard's Pass. I fucking swear! Please! Shades, I'll go back to Judas and apologize for leaving and continue training under him. Please, if you're fucking listening, I swear I'll do anything you ask. Just let me kill him! Let me survive!

Xilor collapsed, his knees striking the hard floor. Vitality saturated her, strength returning, and she poured it back into the channeling, redoubling the siphon.

Her eyes burned, her vision turned red, alight with liquid fire. Manic frenzy permeated her, the bloodlust falling over her vision.

Red.

All she saw was red.

Her pulse pounded in her ears, and she dared to hope that whatever gods did exist were listening. Blood trickled from her nose, running over her lips, dripping from her chin.

Xilor hitched, collapsing to all-fours.

In a violent jerk, he swung both arms up and out like shooing away a swarm of insects. The world tilted in an explosion of pain, the blue-white force flinging her across the room like a cannonball.

Her skull cracked against the floor as her body bounced nearly half a dozen times before she skidded to a stop. She lay in a tangled mess. In the tumbling, Starriace felt a sharp crack, her left arm breaking.

Pain riddled her body; a fog of disorientation suffocated her. A blurry, dark figure ascended in the distance. The last ripple of red energy flickered out. Violent convulsions wracked her body, the infliction more than she could bear. Darkness encroached, offering a comforting finale.

Another volley struck and she twitched, her body seizing out of her control.

A shadow loomed over her, a muffled voice coming from far off. Heat radiated through her body, cooking her from the inside. An acrid smell of burnt hair and flesh filled her nostrils. A spiderwebbed floor cradled her broken body.

The last words he said came through clear.

"Give the Lord of the Underworld my regards."

The tip of his wand flared again, a familiar swirling green. The acidic energy blade ascended for the coup de grâce, but he paused. A backwash of white light illuminated around him.

His shadowed cowl turned towards the light, and he screeched in agony, his hand hiding his face. He fled, away from the light, away from the pain, shrieking in agony.

Something or someone lifted her body from the floor; a soothing presence and being blinded were the last things she recalled before she faded.

Chapter 86: Ralloc

Nykron started to slide from its apex, and Meristal sat curling her hair around her finger.

Contrary to appearance, she focused on every uttered detail, every person present, every breath taken. Now that she was consul, she, Judas, and the others of their group no longer had to meet in the Desert of the Forsaken or some other godawful place. The dungeons provided the perfect balance between secrecy and seclusion.

The known but mysterious problem of prying eyes and unwelcome ears had fallen away about the time of Kayis Dathyr's death. Many of the group believed the former consul was the leak, the traitor, but it didn't add up.

The biggest hole in the theory that most overlooked was that he was never a part of their group.

The theory flourished when someone posed that the actual traitor in the group reported to the late consul and Kayis passed on what he learned to Xilor or whomever. Many urged this, but Meristal riddled the notion full of holes when she pointed out that Dathyr adamantly refused to believe Xilor had returned.

Staell, the Clydesdale-size unicorn, countered that Dathyr's actions most likely covered his true intentions.

Plausible deniability.

Meristal still didn't believe the conspiracy. It was too tidy.

Racing minds put the theory down when someone pointed out the obvious: Xilor killed Dathyr. Speculation ensued that Xilor killed him for failing to murder Judas, or because Xilor had no more use for him without his lofty position.

Meristal's eyes rolled over the speaker opposite her who sat with a military posture. He was the newest member of the group, Scodd Yullus, Supreme War Commander and coordinator for the elyves of the Enclave.

Like most elyfian, he kept to himself. He achieved his position with intelligence and cunning scarcely matched by his kin despite being a half-breed. The recommendation from the previous Supreme War Commander didn't hurt, either. Meristal hoped he'd prove useful in the war against Xilor.

But one question remained: would his elyfian side win out, or his wizardkind side?

That was all the rest of the world knew, but not Meristal, thanks to Judas. Being his companion had advantages. Judas relayed some little facts about Scodd, and it helped her not see him as a complete stranger.

Yullus was half-elyf and half-wizardkind, a unique oddity in his own right. Scodd was the sole survivor of his bloodline with no siblings or parents. All perished in the Wizard's War.

Some considered him the perfect specimen of two races while others thought of him as the absolute abomination. Regardless, he made an apt ambassador between two untrusting races.

Aware of his unique breeding, Meristal could discern the subtle differences in his features, things that probably screamed at the elyfian.

His ears were wider and shorter than a typical elyfian, less sharp at the tip. His eyes, though still elegant, seemed less angular than the rest of his chosen race. Where elyves had slender, tall faces with prominent bone structure, his was wider, rounder, and far softer.

Lastly, Scodd looked like a tanned farmer next to Mella. Elyves were never attractive to Meristal, but she would suspend her tastes if the mood struck her.

It wasn't the only reason Meristal watched him carefully.

Judas believed the spy still resided in their midst, biding their time, waiting for the right moment to become active again. How he knew, she hadn't the faintest, but she trusted his judgment.

Meristal scrutinized everyone with due diligence despite her muddled feelings over the whole traitor aspect. Still, she tried her best to ferret out the dual-identity individual.

Sedrus returned to their fold with his ever-brooding and hypercritical attitude.

Atz and Lurx were always present whenever Judas was present.

Judas himself was there, as well as Mella, the rare combat mage of the elyves who had accompanied Scodd Yullus as a personal assistant, diplomat, and bodyguard.

Beside her, Scodd Yullus sat, followed by Staell, and Zmora.

Newcomers Lagelm and Kellis joined their ranks, invited before their race joined Xilor's horde. Now, they were the object of ridicule, but not here. Initially, they wanted to bow out of the secret council in shame, but Judas wouldn't have it.

When Meristal pressed him, Judas informed her that keeping the goblins close opened up political arenas which might preclude further support for Xilor. Though the goblins were of the Palatine caste and only a small fraction of the entire race, each faction affected the other.

Judas never voiced his suspicions on who the conspirator was and never gave reasons as to why he did certain things, but everyone trusted his judgment. He proved right in Xilor's return, and his gallant efforts at Cape Gythmel kept Xilor's forces at bay, creating time for fortifications and evacuations.

All present considered the traitor dealt with except Judas, and he hatched a plan with Meristal.

"Whoever the informer is, they're intelligent. Stopping their espionage activities around the time of Dathyr's death places blame on him and shifts attention from themselves, but the spy also blundered the timing. They stopped their activities around the time of his death, not the day of, or even the hour. The traitor, or traitors, is still here. By holding the meetings in Ralloc, it lets the informer think we've taken the bait, that Dathyr's the spy. Now, they'll be emboldened, and this time, we'll be watching and waiting."

Meristal shook her head, chasing the memory away.

"I understand your point," Meristal agreed, after Scodd Yullus finished his battle presentation. "What I don't follow is why the elyves want to pitch in now and help with the fight?"

"We did fight," Scodd reminded her coolly.

"No, you didn't," she countered. "A few of you did, yes, that's true. But as a whole, you didn't fight. Had I been consul when those few elyves decided to attack Shadow City, I would've refused to sanction the act unless you—as a race—decided to join our war efforts."

"Your point is noted, but you weren't part of the decision process, were you?"

Mella, Meristal noted, put a hand on Scodd's arm, reminding him where he was and whom he addressed.

Scodd paused and composed himself.

"Forgive my outburst. I'm not accustomed to anyone challenging my words, especially in matters of war. We can't change the past; only the present can affect the future. The elyves will march to war, with or without Ralloc's approval."

"War Commander," Meristal soothed. "It's not my intention to upset you, but it's an odd reversal of decisions on the elyves' part. It's strange that as we send you refugees, you wish to become part of the war effort."

"I don't speak for all elyves, but as for the Enclave, we haven't put forth the effort or suffered our share of hardships in this new war."

"Then your motion to join us is most welcomed. Of course, tomorrow, we'll make everything formal. There should be no problems allowing you to honor the old allegiance. However, I won't accept your proposal for your forces to attack Shadow City—or at least, not yet."

Murmurs rippled through the small antechamber at the announcement of her decision.

"Why may I ask?"

"Timing and diplomacy. I'm aware and sympathize with your readiness to avenge the fallen and imprisoned, but before we tromp in and destroy the vampires, diplomacy must be tried first, if only as a courtesy."

Scodd sat still, unblinking as others around him nodded at her words.

Meristal looked pointedly at Judas, to have him jump in and say something, but what she saw troubled her.

He sat with his eyebrows knitted in concentration, a bead of sweat clinging to his temple, and his white lips quivered. It'd all go unnoticed with a quick glance.

He reached up and rubbed his forehead, massaging some unseen knot of stress away. His eyes snapped open, and his head jerked towards Meristal.

"I can't find her."

"Find who?" Meristal and Sedrus spoke at the same moment.

"Julie. I can't find her anywhere. She was somewhere dark and in terrible pain. Dying. I could sense fear and anger, and a rage that wasn't hers. I felt him."

"Him, who?" Mella asked.

"Xilor."

Staell was the first to speak.

Judas, you aren't infallible. It could be that nothing happened.

Sedrus shifted on his feet.

"If he can't sense her …"

He left the rest of the sentence unsaid.

"…then Xilor killed her," Judas finished. "She's dead."

"No," Zmora, the fairy, spoke up for the first time. "She isn't dead. I'd know instantly. She's still alive, but where, I'm uncertain."

Chapter 87: Starriace

Luminance enveloped Starriace, pure, warm, and majestic—a cocoon of healing power.

But the light didn't only surround her; it illuminated from within, highlighting her flaws, revealing her stained soul, showing her fractured mind.

But now, in this moment, her body felt young, whole, vibrant. Even her eyes no longer burned. She blinked, letting her eyes adjust.

The room had white walls with crystalline strips at the corners and around the doorframe. She called on her essence, like Fife had taught her to heal headaches, and it answered her call, effortless. Noting her treated injuries, she pushed off the bed.

The air had a buoyancy to it, and she couldn't discern the reason. Absent a door, the same white of the walls filled the doorframe. Hesitantly, she tested her hand, pushing through as if nothing was there.

Confident, she walked through.

As she entered the greeting room, several angelic beings turned to regard her. Their secretive conversations paused as she approached. She could scarcely believe her eyes, thinking she dreamed, a mortal among gods.

Or was she dead and this was the afterlife?

Large white wings loomed behind them, not supple and leathery like a bat, not feathered like a bird, but made of light and the softest rabbit fur.

Blank faces with high cheekbones and sharp features regarded her in stillness. Too still. And their eyes…there was a soft glow to them. After what seemed an eternity, a woman came forward and spoke.

"It's good you're up and about."

Starriace kept her silence but managed a nod, allowing the woman to carry the conversation. A stranger or guest, she didn't know what would offend, so she chose the safest option.

"Would you like to go for a walk? Stretch your legs?"

By the gods, the woman was beautiful, making Starriace feel paltry and grotesque by comparison.

"Yes, please."

The archangel nodded.

"Good. You must yearn for answers to questions you have yet to ask."

"Only if the questions bring truthful and productive answers."

The woman smiled.

"Only truth and peace will I speak."

A man spoke up from behind them; Starriace didn't notice his presence until now.

"Perhaps," he said, "you should take her to him."

The woman smiled knowingly and nodded.

"Yes, he'd like to see her, I imagine. This is a first, is it not?"

"Spoken of truth and peace," the man replied, bowing his head to the two women.

The brief exchange showed Starriace a flash of insight into their culture—one of honor, tradition, discipline, and respect. Gracious and elegant, flowing with impossible benevolence and tranquility, Starriace felt restless, disquieted, akin to Xilor coming to an open hall meeting in the heart of Ralloc.

"Who am I going to meet?" Starriace inquired.

The archangel smiled.

"Your grandfather."

Epilogue: Judas

After their meeting in Ralloc, Judas teleported to Dlad City. The survivors of Cape Gythmel joined the Grand Royal Army there. The battlemages Judas sent when Xilor started his second attack returned in time with the portal masters. They evacuated everyone, and Kernoyl Tyku and Judas were the last to leave.

Xilor suffered a decimating loss, and it'd be a while before he mobilized again.

Judas raised the flap to his tent and entered, taking a seat on the edge of his pallet. His heavy heart and mind lingered on Julie. While he believed Zmora, the fairy, she could be mistaken.

After kicking off his boots, his pillow greeted him. He had but few precious hours before the start of another day.

He drifted off and entered a lucid dream of a familiar mountainside, a place he hadn't been to since his youth, not since the fateful day tragedy befell his master.

Reaching Fife's hut, he noticed the old circular arena where he and his master held many lessons. Nostalgia took him, his feet carrying him to the ring.

"You won't find her here," an old voice lilted from the right.

Judas turned, finding his former master, Fife Doole.

At first, he only stared; even dreams had a way of catching him off guard. He drew closer, peering carefully down at him.

"BOO!" the vision said, lurching forward, making him jump in surprise.

Despite the dream, the emotions seemed real, and as he did so long ago, Judas bowed his head in reverence.

"Master."

He searched for words to follow up with, but they never came.

"Hard to take in, is it not?" Fife asked. "Well, things will become stranger, old friend. The young woman you seek is no longer here; she just left—took off. Just poof and there she went."

"What do you mean took off?"

"She bounded off the ground and flew away, this I know!"

"How's that possible? Where did she learn to fly? How can she? Better yet, how are we talking about the same person?"

Fife chuckled.

"Yes, yes. She rivals you, is that not so? And all without wings. A gift inherited."

"Inherited?"

Fife shrugged playfully at Judas's question.

"Impossible! I can't fly, which means she'd inherit the ability from her mother. Magical genes pass from the father, not the mother, that's why they still arrange marriages—to breed powerful descendants and House alliances."

"True, but her innate genes come from her mother and her father—you."

Judas shook his head, disbelieving. Anger welled up within him.

What kind of cruel dream is this?

"My child died!" he shouted.

"This is a dream, that's true. But I'm also real."

Judas shook his head, not hearing his master. His thoughts were on his lost apprentice.

"I have to find Julie."

"She no longer goes by her former name. Nor will you find her. She holds no tethers of her past life and accepted her true identity. She knows not of her parents."

"What's her name, then?"

"Starriace."

Judas felt weak and lightheaded. Ermaeyth spun, and he sat down hard on the grass. Fife waddled closer.

"My Starriace?" Judas whispered.

The truth of Fife's words echoed within his chest. He no longer thought of Julie the helpless girl, but of Starriace, the daughter he lost. More than that, Fife was long dead before Starriace was ever born, so he wouldn't know the name.

Then again, it could all be a trick in his head.

Fife nodded.

"She's your daughter, but she's not herself."

"What do you mean?"

"She left, out of rage and impatience. She is angry with me because I would not teach her offensive Rumigul."

"Rumigul? You mean she accomplished Rumigul?"

"Yes. She's magnificent, unstable, powerful, and impatient. Seems she inherited things from you as well, is that not so?"

Fife chuckled.

Judas shook his head.

"I have to find her, tell her."

"No! Don't be foolish! Above all, you mustn't tell her you're her father. At least, not now."

"Why? Won't she be happy?"

"No, it'll break her mind, and her heart. According to her, it's you who didn't rescue her in the Corridor of Cruelty. In moments of clarity, she realizes it's not your fault. If her psyche breaks, too much stress, cataclysmic events await."

The gnomling paused, letting his words sink in.

"Can you be careful? I remember a bumbling pupil before. When you confront her, if at all, remember, she's changed, passed beyond the young woman she once was. Search in your heart, and you won't find her either. She's lost now, passed from luminosity and into obscurity. Until she's ready to be found again."

"Starriace isn't capable of—"

"False! You knew what her heart once was, true. Not anymore! Violence and death are her companions."

"I don't believe it. I can't!"

"You've always had your faith. It's strong, yes? You'll believe when you see it with your own eyes. Rest not on such thoughts now. More important is the future she may yet embark on to bring an end to Xilor."

"Have you seen it?"

"Her hate will drive her. Maybe not now, but eventually, she'll see that he stands in her way. If she takes him, in his place we'll have an empress. Only you and her mother could rid the realm of her."

"So…" Judas hesitated. "She's a renegade?"

"Like father, like daughter? No. To her, what she does is right, for the right reasons, though the method is wrong."

"Oh, gods, her mother—" Judas murmured.

Fife barked a laugh.

"Unadvisable. A mother's pull to her offspring is even stronger than a father's. Her mother would tear the realm apart looking for her, and only be devastated and heartbroken. Besides, you had trouble in that area, did you not? Even now, you're guessing who the mother is, is that not so?"

Fife smiled, tapping his temple knowingly.

"I must find out. Meristal never actually forgave me…"

"Again, unwise. Does stupidity riddle your bones with old age? You should wait. When Ermaeyth finds out about Starriace, the mother will present herself. Hopefully, there aren't too many possibilities, yes?"

Then, under his breath, Fife continued.

"Though there's not much hope of that."

"What?"

Fife sighed.

"Did you not take the conquest of women a bit diligently in your youth?"

Judas could feel his face flush with the shade of shame. Unfortunately, there were too many possibilities of who the mother was, and the most prominent was Meristal, but they both knew her boy died. There was Daylynn, too…and if that turned out to be the case, the animosity would never die between Meristal and Daylynn.

"Soma agrees with using caution," Fife said.

Hatred flared bright within Judas.

"I don't ever want to hear that woman's name again—don't want to see her. It's because of the Time Warden all of this happened."

"Worry not, I doubt you'll ever cross paths again."

Judas bolted upright from his pallet, waking from the dream.

No, a vision.

A voice called to him from outside his tent. He bade them to enter, and the redhead do-don of the Krey, Xenomene, entered.

She crossed her arms, a quirk of a grin on her lips.

"I have a favor to ask."

Epilogue: Xenomene

Xeno stood alone in the vast wastes of the Desert of the Forsaken, west of Dlad City. She shivered from the cold, but the chair in front of her remained unmoved by the gusty, cold clime.

She frowned.

The desert was always cold at night, but with the changing of the seasons, it was much more so now.

The moments ticked by, waiting for the warlock to come through with his promise. One other would be present tonight, the Heart. Typically, she'd only ask the Heart to participate with her scheme, but she lacked the power to do as Xenomene desired. Also, the do-don didn't want the Mind or the Hand involved.

It was none of their business.

The night she'd spent on her quest in the Mind's tent was left unfinished. He attempted to reignite the occurrence once they fled Cape Gythmel to Dlad City, but she wasn't inclined. She'd finish what she started, most likely—she always did, no matter what.

For now, she had other issues to settle.

As if in answer to her diligence, an unconscious person appeared before her. With a hell of a lot of effort, she moved the unresponsive form into the chair and bound him with rope before looping a coil through his teeth, effectively gagging him.

With cautious care, Xenomene ran her tiny fingers through the fine, satiny hair of the unconscious form.

"I'm sorry for what I'm about to do," she murmured.

Stepping back, she swung her arm, the flat of her palm striking his face. Fire flared in her hand followed by a tingling numbness. The man hollered in muffled shock, snatching his head up and looking frantically about before his eyes fell on Xenomene.

He yelled something through the gag.

Xenomene replied with dead eyes staring back, centering herself, separating emotion from the deed. While awaiting the Heart's arrival, she could tell Bitcher why he faced disciplinary action.

"Good evening," she began formally. "You're probably wondering why you're here. I asked a certain warlock to send you to the fucking freezing ass-end of nowhere so I can render punishment without interference or being overheard. Reasonably, you're wondering 'what justice?' In short, you violated me."

She held up a hand to forestall any muffled screams.

"I'm not saying you raped me. The truth is: I let you take me. You told me what you were going to do, and I rolled on my side and let you. But it's the other thing you did without my leave. You drugged me. You didn't tell me that your oil would alter my mind until after you came the first time. I thought you were just being a nice guy and lubing up."

She took a deep breath through her nose and exhaled.

"I believe I warned you about consequences. Tonight's the manifestation of said consequences."

She wholeheartedly agreed that the punishment should equal the transgression, and a part of her paused. Her first plans revolved around castrating him and be done with it. However, she felt differently once she cooled off, recalling the experience. She didn't care that he sodomized the hell out of her, she'd already acquiesced, but she did care about him stealing her agency. Besides, leaving him castrated made her feel guilty, having enjoyed the experience, so she struck a compromise with herself.

Upon asking the warlock to help, he'd refused outright. When she gave him assurances that he wouldn't be disfigured or killed, and when Xenomene said her life would be forfeit otherwise, the warlock agreed.

And so here they were, in the desert, the last piece of the puzzle having yet arrived.

A small flash of light announced the arrival of the Heart, and she came up behind her.

"What kept you?" Xenomene grunted.

"Warlock Lakayre. He intended to make sure you understood the arrangement."

Xenomene shrugged.

"Fuck the warlock. He's not Krey."

The Heart almost said something in response, but instead, she inquired, "Are you sure about this?"

"Are you sure you can do it?" Xenomene countered.

"Yes."

"Then, I'm sure as well."

Xeno faced Bitcher. She pulled her knife free of its sheath and advanced on him.

Bitcher's gray eyes went wide in terror as he shouted at her.

"Shh," she said.

She leaned down to caress his face, then kissed his forehead.

"You're lucky that you were a good fuck, otherwise, this would end badly for you."

She slid the knife carefully into his trousers, cutting them free of his body, careful to avoid lacerating his skin, and did the same to his tunic. Naked, Bitcher's nipples hardened, and his manhood shriveled.

"Bit nippy out," Xeno commented.

It brought a grin to her lips.

She knelt in front of him, her left hand fondling him, warming him, encouraging arousal, to untuck his taut skin.

"I was going to castrate you and let you bleed, but I have a soft spot for you now. The next time we fuck, I'll know what the oil is, and it'll be my choice."

She nodded as Bitcher shook his head.

"I'd do it again, among other things. The Islander's fashion isn't the only way. Had it not been for you, I would've never tried it, but I'm sure you'll like my pussy, too."

She looked down at his flaccid state.

"Am I going to have to take you with my mouth to get what I want?"

His pale gray eyes widened but still held panic and uncertainty.

"You know," she whispered, leaning in close, "I always wondered about you Forgotten Islanders, and now I know. What's your saying?"

He mumbled something through the rope, but she couldn't make it out. She regarded his manhood again, still passive. She leaned close again.

"Don't make me suck your dick in front of the Heart because I will, if need be. I'm sure she's seen stranger things. But while we wait, I want you to know I enjoyed it. Did you? Did you enjoy—what did you say?—virgin ass? I liked it when you pulled my hair, choked me. I loved the drug, whatever it was. I would've done anything you asked, and I think you know that."

She pulled back a little to look in his eyes.

"Anything," she repeated. "How many times did you cum in my ass? Three times?"

Glancing down, she found what she wanted, his skin loosening from his body.

"I'm glad to have experienced your culture..." her voice hardened, "... now experience mine!"

The knife flashed between his legs as she severed his left testicle. He screamed through the rope, his body shaking, convulsing, veins spiderwebbing through his temples and forehead, screaming between each gasp.

"'Did you like that, whore?'" Xeno recited his words back to him.

He wailed so loud the gag was almost worthless. She was glad they were in the Desert of the Forsaken. She stayed kneeling, watching him scream and shake violently.

A few moments later, he passed out.

Blood flowed freely, pooling on the seat, trickling down the legs of the chair to the cold ground beneath. She stood and wiped her blade on his now tattered clothes.

She motioned the Heart forward.

"Is this a first for you?"

The mage only nodded.

"Didn't know if you were going to fuck or punish him."

Xenomene shrugged.

"At least now you can practice this type of healing. I left you one testicle, in case you can't figure out how to reattach his other."

She backed away, fascinated as the Heart worked putting Bitcher back together.

Justice is being served. One down, two more to go. One for every time he came in me.

Epilogue: Starriace

Two weeks had passed since Starriace left the archangels and the fateful confrontation with Xilor behind.

The man who claimed to be her grandsire didn't impart knowledge she yearned for. Instead, he removed the trace Xilor's minion placed on her. His words were sparse and unrevealing, yet his presence seemed familiar, like she'd encountered it before, but only fleetingly.

She'd crossed paths with someone before, as the presence was eerily similar, but who was it?

He seemed genuinely happy to see her, but he imparted that no archangel would ever come to her rescue again. A once-and-done for her, a mere mortal, though he promised they'd meet again, just not under the same circumstances.

Though grateful, she couldn't help her growing despair knowing she'd never visit them again, nor the swelling anger for unanswered questions. With nothing left to gain, she asked to be returned to where she belonged.

Not knowing where to go or who to turn to, Starriace traveled waywardly at first.

She couldn't go back to Judas, wouldn't return to Fife. Both tried and failed to train her, to protect her. She trusted them, a mistake, and only she could assume the responsibility.

With youth and innocence stripped away, only an aching heart remained filled with resentment and cruel indignity.

Her priorities had changed. Her resentment toward parents she never knew shifted, and she let go. While curiosity still prevailed, other matters took precedence, and a reunion would have to wait.

Acknowledging that she barely survived her encounter with Xilor, she still had hope. She'd injured him.

He was beatable.

Without making the same mistakes again and redoubling her efforts to learn and gather more abilities, she set her mind to figuring out a way to topple him.

A silent craving slithered through her.

I'll never be weak again. I'll never be helpless.

Her future was up to her now. She would never lean on another to show her the way. Starriace would forge ahead, complete her training on her own, but where would she start?

It looks like the fairies get what they want.

One thing she considered, and would rely on, were teachers from ancient times.

At least their methods are proven; a solid history, their theories and hypotheses are no longer considered myths or philosophies, and they now have become common doctrines for the realm.

She remembered a saying from a long time ago from some forgotten place:

listen to, learn from, and respect your elders.

Where the thought came from, she hadn't a clue. It wasn't significant, but its truth was.

The matter of Rusem and his tale of seven stones, while a mystery, needled her. Whatever secrets he had, they'd be hers. Though several places for where to start came to mind, she needed to research first. Multiple possibilities manifested, but none provided her with everything she needed; the foremost was anonymity and safety.

But if she could hide where no one saw her, where Judas didn't know about…the perfect place came to mind. She'd go and trace her steps toward the stones and power.

And in a few days, she'd be there.

Harold, the hermit, would soon be getting another visit.

About the Author

Kyle Belote is a prior active-duty Marine, writer, musician, and painter. He's lived in Texas, Hawaii, and Okinawa, Japan, and has traveled the globe. When not writing, he enjoys sketching, researching companies and investing, and reading and listening to audiobooks. Kyle enjoys a diverse collection of films, books, and shows—just not the abomination called Disney Star Wars.

For more information, visit the author's Substack: https:// www.outpostdire.com

Back Jacket

A young woman named Julie, crippled by amnesia and a unique past, is thrust into Warlock Lakayre's life. Sinister forces hunt them both, and together they seek refuge in the distant settlement of Wizard's Pass, but the journey is long and fraught with dangers.

Their path leads them through the Corridor of Cruelty, and Julie faces perils that shake her faith and fractures her sanity. Her greatest challenge lies on the other side: a great evil is rising from the ashes of defeat and has taken an interest in the new prodigy, hoping to twist her to his will. Perhaps she's someone—or something—no one can control or predict.

The Bearer of Secrets is the first volume in Dark Legacy Series.

www.ingramcontent.com/pod-product-compliance
Lightning Source LLC
Chambersburg PA
CBHW051934020726
47501CB00001B/116